angel of death

book one of
the chosen chronicles

karen dales

Dark Dragon Publishing
Toronto, Ontario, Canada

This book is a work of fiction. The characters, incidents, and dialogue are drawn from the author's imagination and are not to be construed as real. Any resemblance to actual events or persons, living or dead, is entirely coincidental.

Angel Of Death:
Book One of the Chosen Chronicles

Copyright © 2009 by Karen Dales

ISBN: 978-0-9867633-1-1
eISBN: 978-0-9867633-5-9
AISN: B004XJ6VY3

Cover Art, Design and Author Photo
© 2010 by Evan Dales
WAV Design Studios
www.wavstudios.ca

Dark Dragon Publishing
313 Mutual Street
Toronto, Ontario
M4Y 1X6
CANADA

www.darkdragonpublishing.com

For more information on the Author,
Karen Dales and The Chosen Chronicles
www.karendales.com
www.thechosenchronicles.com

In Praise of The Chosen Chronicles

"A dark and gripping tale by a true mistress of supernatural fiction. Karen Dales brings fresh blood to the vampire genre."
- **Michelle Rowen, National Bestselling Author**

"For readers who adore textured layers in their literary tapestries, rich in colorful emotions, Karen Dales is one writer of vampire fiction they'll want to read." - **Nancy Kilpatrick, Author:** *The Power of the Blood,* **Editor:** *Evolve: Vampire Stories of the New Undead*

"A fresh and intriguing new look at the vampire mythos."
- **Violet Malan, author of** *The Novels of Dhulyn and Parno*

"...is a must-read for any fans of Twilight *or other books in the popular Vampire genre."* - **Oakville Today.**

"This is a mature book...that makes it easy to enjoy...a story that has multiple layers and depth to it...the book reads fast because Karen never lets it slow down." - **Ruth Ann Nordin, Author.**

"...one of the best stories by a new and upcoming writer that I have read...This tale was wonderfully written. Every character has a complete and utterly unique personality...The Angel of Death will make you smile, and it will cause your heart to break. Very few stories are the equal to this tale. When you read this story, have a box of tissues handy. Ms. Dales I am trying to await the next instalment patiently and it is not working out so well." - **Siren Book Reviews (5 out of 5)**

"...a poignant and epic tale... a brilliant example of good overcoming and prevailing against evil and prejudice... an emotional ride of literary genius, both heart-warming and heartbreaking at the same time..."
- **Bitten By Books (5 out of 5)**

"a grand tale of eternal life and its many challenges... I greatly enjoyed Angel of Death by Karen Dales and ... recommend it..."
- **Two Lips Reviews (5 out of 5)**

"I would definitely recommend this book to vampire fans.. a good solid read for both Changeling and Angel of Death... I'm definitely looking forward to where Dales goes with this in the future."
- **Once Upon A Bookshelf**

"I was hooked...a good book to read on a cold and stormy day."
- **Night Owl Reviews (4 out of 5)**

Also by Karen Dales

THE CHOSEN CHRONICLES

Changeling
Angel of Death
Shadow of Death
Thanatos (forthcoming)

acknowledgements

Never in my life have I been so blessed to have so many supportive people in my life. As always, the love and support, as well as the patience to sit and listen as I read my drafts, or natter excitedly about my characters and plots—my husband, you are always cherished.

Michael, Stephanie, Derek and Danielle, your support and help, encouragement and love, has always made me work to my highest ideal.

Adam, thank you for your expertise in French and being such a wonderful guy. I'll make you dinner whenever you want.

And an extra special thank you to Michael and Angela, Rick and Jean-Guy who have been so supportive to me to make these dreams come true.

I

he sound of his heels clicked against the cobbles, reverberating in the cool hours before dawn. He enjoyed the quiet walk back to the flat they rented from Mrs. Heathrope. She was a nice retiring widow of eighty years. Nearly blind, she enjoyed having a polite scholarly man of the cloth and his unusually tall assistant living on the main floor of her home, while she resided in comfort and solitude upstairs. She was off on her six month vacation to the south of France, where she would escape the ravages an English winter played upon her. She left her home in the care of these two young folk never knowing that they had each outlived her by more times than she could count.

Walking through Trafalgar Square, he could make out a few homeless or passed out individuals curled up on benches. The gaslight made the night bright to his preternatural sight, allowing for the dingy grey and brown colours to fall to the background of the occasional punctuation of colour. It also made it easier for him to see the degenerates littering the square with their prostrate forms.

The sooner he made it down to the Embankment the better. There he could gaze at the Thames and the south side of London. It gave the momentary illusion of being out of an over populated city where the smells and sounds assaulted his senses. This was not the first time he and Notus had come to London, and most likely it would not be the last. Oh how he disliked, nay hated, this city. Every time they came it gave him good reason.

Turning west onto the Embankment the reduction of gaslight around him allowed for more starlight to float down, but only a little more. The dark waters, quiet in the still night, reflected not only the old waning moon, but also the many lamps that lined the bridges and walkways. True night never came to this city, and he missed it.

He did not know why Notus decided to come back to London after being away for nearly two centuries. Notus had explained it was because he was offered the once in a lifetime job of restoring ancient manuscripts and illuminations at the National Museum and Library. What the monk did not need to say was that he had had many of these types of experiences, but for the first time he was getting a chance to see how some of his own work had withstood the ravages of time.

To Notus, the illuminations and book copying were his passion and he would spend hours upon hours working on intricate patterns and artwork before even contemplating how the words would be calligraphed. Sometimes he would become so engrossed that he would forget to satiate his hunger. Now, with the opportunity of a nearly two thousand year old lifetime, Notus was getting a chance to play in one of the largest playgrounds outside of the Vatican.

Notus' Chosen shook his head in disbelief, his white hair swaying. It was always the same. If Notus got even the slightest whiff of a manuscript, no matter how far away they were, they would up and leave so that Notus would satisfy his thirst for beauty and knowledge intricately intertwined. It usually left him either choosing to come along or to go off in another direction for a period of time. Always, in the end, he would go with Notus. He just wished that this time it was not London. Nothing ever good came from coming to this place.

He sighed, remembering the last time. They had been here for only short while, arriving mere months before the worst outbreak of the Black Death. That had been in 1665 and they had lived pretty close to where they currently were residing at Mrs. Heathrope's, off of Fleet Street near Fetters Lane. The neighbourhood had boasted some of the best bakeries and specialty shops in London. Even though the shops closed on Sundays they did a thriving business for the parishioners of St. Paul's, until the plague came. Doors were marked with crosses one by one until it seemed that no where could one go without seeing the results of disease and death.

Foul smokes competed with the stench of rotting corpses left waiting to be taken for burial. Many of them waited too long because those attending the dead soon fell to the malady crushing the city.

The nights were worse. Cries of pain and despair came on the breezes to fill the sensitive ears of the two Chosen who bravely feasted upon the poor souls craving death and release from pain. Notus had insisted while the other Chosen turned their backs. Notus would walk amongst the barely living, giving succour and deliverance to those who asked for it and expected his Chosen to do the same. He did so begrudgingly, never speaking to the diseased people, but giving them some sense of comfort before he transformed their infected blood into life giving energy his own body craved. It took more to feed off of them, than to feed off of a healthy person, but Notus insisted that it would help those who would otherwise die in excruciating pain. They had done this sort of thing in the past, but never in such a situation as that.

As knowledge of their help spread, so too did the name they bestowed upon him. An old name – the Angel, the Priest's Angel – and he did not need to ask which angel they believed him to be. He had been called the Angel before. He could see it in their eyes. He was the final thing they saw in this life. No matter that they were dying anyway, relief and then fear would illuminate diseased dulled eyes before giving way to the darkness of death. Even those of the New Religion allowed him to come to them, when they refused his Chooser. He had hated it.

They existed on death and disease for over a year and relished the reprise winter brought, but it was the Great Fire that proved yet again that London was not a place where he wanted to be – ever.

It was near dawn and they were in their small flat, readying themselves for a peaceful days sleep, when the sounds of rising chaos and the smell of cinders took them out of doors to see the night ablaze. Worse of all it was getting closer, too close. Grabbing what they could of their belongings they ran to the Cathedral. He only managed to take Geraint's now ancient sword.

Into St. Paul's they fled, following Notus down into the sepulchre. Cooler air relieved their lungs, but not for long as they became disastrously aware that the fire was upon them. With nowhere to run, they did what they could and individually hid in the sarcophagi of wealthy individuals long dead.

It was brutal lying there in a stone box too short for him, curled up against a rotting corpse, hugging his sword in terror that their long lives might be snuffed out any moment. Then the excruciating heat came, taking his breath and his consciousness away. When he finally awoke, there was no heat and he tentatively lifted the lid only to have it completely yanked free by Notus.

Climbing out of the coffin, he could see the devastation all around them. He did not know how long they had hidden, but the sarcophagus was blackened. Both haggard, they carefully made their silent way to ground level and stood in horror at the devastation around them. Nothing was left except blistered and burnt wood smoking in the light drizzle. St. Paul's lead roof was gone, exposing a clouded sky.

Stepping out of the ruins of the great church, they stood in stunned silence at the destruction of the city. The horrific proportions of the fire's appetite sent their minds reeling as they walked numbly into the streets that used to be called London, their ravenous hunger forgotten.

Their flat and all their possessions were gone. Notus wept for all the books and scrolls he could not save.

Clutching his sword to his breast, he said a silent thanks to the old Gods that gave him the wherewithal to save it.

Many of the Chosen who had remained in London had fled to the

Courthouse, which was home to the Lord of the Chosen. It too was gone and so were those that had hidden in it, having to either choose between the blazing fire or the burning sun.

In the months that followed, many had beseeched Notus to become Lord and Master. Having no stomach for the politics nor for how the Chosen were changing over the centuries, they enthusiastically packed up their meagre belongings and left, only to return half a dozen years ago.

He turned to cut through The Temple to get to Fleet Street. He enjoyed this area, as finally there was something of nature here in the Temple Gardens. Even the ancient buildings, now housing lawyers, did not take away from some greenery of grass and flowers. It still did not replace his desire for the sense of home he felt in thickly forested areas, but at least it was something.

He walked up Inner Temple Lane that would take him onto Fleet. He was getting close to home, and none too soon as the feel of dawn tickled along his skin even though the sky was still dark.

Home.

It was a strange word for the place they lived in. Most nights he would go out, feed, and then find some place to take in some entertainment where he would not be noticed. Darkened theatres and concerts he enjoyed. Sometimes he would join Notus in going to the Museum and then drift off to the Library where he would sit and read until it was time to go home. Once a week he would meet Yong Zheng Ru on the rooftop patio of the apothecary he and his daughter ran in Chinatown. It was from there that he was returning.

A lone solitary figure flashed in the corner of his eye. Recognizing the individual as one of his own kind, he shook his head in annoyance. He made it a point never to have anything to do with the Vampires, as the Chosen liked to call themselves now. Notus was right about the changes and he too did not like the way the younger ones, and some of the older ones too, modeled themselves off of the silly stories mortals wrote to try and explain a brief encounter with a Chosen. They both knew they were thought of as strange by refusing to have any dealings with these new fangled Vampires. Once, a long time ago, Notus had respected and honoured the Chosen hierarchy, but now he refused outright to play their Vampire games and ignored the Mistress' calls to court. It was a choice both he and his Chooser had consciously made over great discussion, and neither had regretted it.

He glanced up at the paling sky as he turned onto Fleet. The sky now a dark blue heralded the rising sun. He knew beyond any doubt that Notus would be adding to the groove in the Persian rug, worrying himself and complaining to his Good God about his temerarious son. He smiled in spite of himself at the image of the monk imploring to his God, arms gesticulating heavenwards, only to stop at his entrance and begin again the long rant about how dangerous it was to be out so late. He did not know why he did this to Notus. Maybe it was to provide some perverse pleasure at seeing the monk distraught and fuming rather than fixated upon his books. Maybe it was just to see that the man still cared for him even after all these centuries. No matter the reason, it was also to ensure that when he returned Jeanie would not be there.

Jeanie.

He could not fathom why Notus had decided to keep her around, let alone hire her as their maid. Never before had Notus hired a woman. Always a young man in need of some extra help would be taken off the streets and given responsibilities that could only be met during the day. Jeanie had those responsibilities now, as well as the cleaning. Jeanie also made him extremely uncomfortable to be in his own home. He did not know what it was and thought best to leave shortly after she would arrive from the room at the Inn Notus paid for. She, like all the others who came before her, never knew their true natures. Notus was very careful of that, easily explaining about his Oaths never to see the sun until God's son came to mankind again. Explaining his pale Chosen took a bit of creativity mixed with some truth that seemed to work to keep curiosity away.

Notus had brought the fourteen year old girl home on Christmas Eve no more than five years ago to become their housekeeper and helper. In that time they watched her blossom from a young maid to a fiery young woman of nineteen. A vision of her sparkling green eyes the colour of spring, her long curling burnished copper hair, and sensuous curvaceous form sent a shudder through him. Like it or not he found her one of the most beautiful women he had ever laid eyes upon.

But if one thing his centuries of long life had taught him is that the women he had been with wanted only one thing from him – to say that they had been with him. He was a curiosity, even amongst the Chosen, and after Notus had made it clear what was going on, he had stopped the fleeting one or two night experiences. He did not like being used.

It was not hard to imagine that she had the same intentions towards him. She always had a brilliant smile for him, which always made his breath catch. She scared him.

No. That is not right. He shook his head and realized what she evoked in him was confusion and made him feel the way he did when he was first Chosen. She made him uncomfortable.

He barely understood Notus' desire to have her over almost every night for several hours. After cleaning and setting things in order from her daytime errands, Notus would practice his new culinary hobby and fix her dinner before she would go home.

Most times Notus would stay behind, handing over the chore of walking her home to his Chosen if he had not fled soon enough. They would walk in silence with him hidden deeply under his cloak wanting only to be done with it so that he could go on with the rest of his evening. He suspected his Chooser was exploiting a perverse sense of sadism, secretly enjoying his Chosen's discomfort around Jeanie.

It had not always been like this. In the beginning she shied away from him. Maybe it had to do with how they initially met. He grimaced, remembering coming home just before dawn on Christmas, going to his room, undressing for bed and then the God awful scream that made him jump out of his skin. His ears had stopped ringing by the time Notus burst in to take stock of the scene before him and go to calm the young girl in his bed, apologizing for forgetting to mention the girl upon his arrival. That day he discovered how uncomfortably short the sofa was. Now she always had a smile for him and would find reasons to brush past him, cleaning wherever he went, even if she had already cleaned that spot.

Turning off of Fleet and onto the side streets, he followed them down and around until he saw Mrs. Heathrope's house. It was perfect timing, too, as the sky was shifting to a paler shade of blue, calling to the rising of the sun mere moments away. Notus was sure to be fuming.

Snuggling deeper into his black cloak, he took the handful of stairs up to the door that led to the portion of the building that housed him and Notus. He pulled out his key and halted.

Pale yellow gaslight spilled across his black shoes from a door that stood slightly ajar. Something was wrong. Notus never left the door open like this, unlocked on the occasion, but never open to the street. Maybe he had gone to sleep and left it open in case keys were forgotten, but he knew that never happened.

Closing his eyes, he took a deep steadying breath, and Sent to him, trying to sense if Notus was asleep. Nothing. The absence of any perception of the monk filled him with apprehension. Not even a sense of his connection to Notus was available. It had been centuries since the first and only time that happened and that was because they were separated for almost three decades. This was more complete – shocking.

Placing a shaking hand on the brass doorknob, he pushed the door open.

Ruby eyes widened at the sight of his ransacked home. The living room, usually so neat and tidy, was a travesty of orderliness. Papers and books splayed randomly over the floor and overturned furniture. Notus' favourite chair sat crumpled on itself, wooden legs ending in ragged spikes. Inks and paints pooled on the monk's large writing desk, permanently staining in colours that should not exist in wood.

Ducking his head under the lintel, he took a tentative step into his devastated home, his foot meeting the floor with the crunching of broken glass. Numbly gazing down, the remnants of a crystal vase and its red and yellow flowers lay under his feet. Taking in the full extent of the devastation, he could not comprehend how or even why his home would be ransacked this way. Worse yet was why Notus was not there. If it had been thieves, Notus would have easily dealt with them. Something more must have happened.

Again he sent out a silent plea for Notus and was rewarded with nothing, not even a sense of his Chooser. In a dreamlike state he moved about the room, searching for Notus even knowing he would not find him here. He had to do something. Shock faded into panic as each righted piece of furniture or lifted paper refused to relinquish the man who cared for him over the centuries. His hopes of finding the monk dissolved into nothingness when he slammed open Notus' empty bedroom.

Without the connection with the man who had come to mean more to him than anyone else in the world, he walked numbly into the center of the room and sat down on the couch, elbows on knees and hands rubbing his face as if to wash the sight and reality from his mind. He did not know what to do. He could not do anything. The sun was already up. He groaned at the unbidden thought that came to mind. He could not allow himself to believe Notus was dead.

A soft moan lighted his senses and he stared at the closed door to the kitchen. Hope leapt and he stood. Of course! He had not checked the kitchen. It was possible Notus was there. Swearing himself for a fool, he ran into the dark room.

The door swung closed with a bang and his feet crunched on a floor strewn with broken glass and crockery. He did not need to call out for Notus. He was not there. The source of the cry came from Jeanie's sprawled form in front of the stove. Whoever had attacked his home had met heavy opposition.

Ignoring the broken shards, he knelt down beside Jeanie's unconscious form. Even in the pitch blackness of the kitchen, he could see her pale fine skin framed with a mass of long curling copper coloured hair. A long thin gash over her right perfect eyebrow slowly oozed. The smell of her blood impacted him, forcing him to take a steadying breath. Her large emerald coloured eyes remained closed. Knowing that she needed some help, he lifted her into his arms and walked to the living room, where the brocaded chesterfield had already been righted.

Gently placing her on the soft padded seating, he went into the untouched washroom and brought back a dampened cloth. Taking off his cloak, he went to blanket her, and halted. Pinned to her yellow flower patterned blouse was an envelope. Ornately penned, it stated simply;

The Angel

Frowning at the note, he carefully removed the message before draping Jeanie's unconscious form in his cloak. He stood back and tore open the red wax seal, dismissing the large *'V'* embossed into it and pulled out the yellowed vellum. Hands shaking in growing anger he opened the folded paper, and read the same flourished writing,

Her Majesty,
Lady of Vampires,
Mistress of London,
Ruler of the British,
Demands the audience of the Vampire called
The Angel,
To be held on the eighteenth of October,
In the year eighteen hundred and ninety-eight,
At ten thirty.
Failure to be in attendance will result in the immediate dispatch of
Father Paul Notus' Immortal life.

Valraven
Advisor to the Lady.

He could not believe what he read and read it again and again until the truth of the words shook him in rage. Crushing the expensive vellum in his white palm, the words disintegrated into a small ball of dead sheep's skin before he let it fall to the ground. It did not make any sense. Notus was the one who always dealt with the Court, and even though Notus shied away from their new ways, if the demand had come, he would have reluctantly obliged. Now they had his Chooser and they wanted him. They did not have to do this. They did not have to threaten Notus' life. They could have just asked.

With nothing to be done in the light of day, he resigned himself that tomorrow – the eighteenth – he would go to the despised audience and get Notus back.

A soft moan escaping from Jeanie's lips instantly reminded him of why he was holding, in his other hand, a soggy cloth. Kneeling beside the girl who so disarmed him, he gently cleaned away the sweet smelling blood to reveal a small scratch. He had forgotten how bad head wounds could be and watched in rapt attention as her brows creased into a frown, her full red lips pouting as she slowly shook her head in an attempt to fend off a bad dream.

Quite suddenly she sat up, her breath short and fast, her heart fluttering in panic as malachite eyes flickered about the room. Her unexpected arousal surprised him and he dropped the cloth, watching in alarm as her eyes gradually focused on him.

"Where is he?" she demanded, her Highland accent still strong after all these years.

Rising to his feet, he grabbed the blood stained cloth and placed it on the tea table. He could not tell her, and he did not want to lie to her. Instead he chose the only route open to him. His voice low, he asked, "What happened?"

She looked up at the tall pale man with beautiful red eyes and sighed, relief flooding her features that he was with her. Tentatively she touched her forehead, finding the source of the pain, and removed her slightly stained fingers. Her head throbbed in time with her pounding heart. She swung her legs around to sit up properly, noticing for the first time his cloak wrapped around her. Without gazing up at its owner, she sighed.

"I'm no' too sure. One minute I'm cleaning, the Good Father's at 'is work, then the next the door's burst open and three men come flying in. The Good Father tried t' defend himself. I even tried, but they took him. I thought I was dead when one came after me, but I guess they dinna want me."

Gazing at the mass destruction still evident from the battle's remnants her eyes widened. "Och, what a mess!" She groaned as the loudness of her own voice pounded through her ears.

He could see the headache in her eyes and relaxed his harsh tones. "Did they say who they were or why they were here?"

"Nay." She frowned in concentration, not willing to attempt shaking her head. "Wait. Aye. One of them mentioned something about neglecting the court for too long and that 'twas time to pay up."

He sighed and hung his head. It made a sick sort of sense, but he could not fathom their reason for abducting his Chooser.

"Do ye ken where the Good Father was taken?" she asked.

He gazed down at her, soaking in her beautiful green eyes and sadly nodded.

Some positive news at last, she bolted to her feet. "Well, then, let's go fatch 'im back."

It was the wrong thing to do at the wrong time. A wave of nausea knocked her back to the couch. The cloak fell to the richly decorated Oriental rug.

Seeing her sway and heavily sit back down, he found that he wanted to help her, but stayed rooted to his spot, towering over her, afraid that if he did so he would lose his composure.

"No," he responded, unwilling to provide any explanation.

"Aye. I think ye're right." She placed a shaking hand to her head and pulled it away at the painful touch. "I'll be going nowhere right now. That bugger mus' have got me good after I flung that dish at him." She mustered a little laugh and gazed up into worried exotic eyes.

Uncomfortable with the weight of her gaze, he glanced away. "I have to get some rest."

"What about the Good Father?" she implored.

"I will get him back tonight," he stated firmly and then softened his voice. "You can stay until you feel better." He did not know why he said it. She had never stayed the day, nor the night for that matter, but he knew he could not send her back to the inn while the effects of her attack were still on her. If he did and Notus found out, the monk would make him wish he had never been Chosen.

Walking over to the door to his bedroom, he stopped before turning the crystal and brass knob on the mahogany door. "You can rest in Notus' room, if you like."

"That's righ' kind of ye, but what am I t' wear? All my kit is at my room." Copper curls flowed down over her shoulder as she cocked her head.

His brows creased in confusion and then smoothed. What does a young lady wear to sleep in this age? Entering into his large bedroom, he walked over to his dresser and pulled out one of his handcrafted tailored white shirts. All his clothes were handmade. Figuring that this would most likely do the job, he hoped, he walked back into the living room and Jeanie.

"You can wear this, if you like." He handed her the freshly laundered shirt, refusing to look into her eyes, and vaguely heard her mention her appreciation before he went back into his room, closing the door behind him.

He leaned his head against the dark wood frame, his white hair spilling forward, and breathed a sigh of relief. Never before had he so much contact with her. He always left her alone, even when he walked her home on occasion. Whenever she tried to initiate conversation he would quickly end it. It was not that he did not like her. It was the fact that she evoked feelings he had long since buried and wished not to exhume.

Cufflinks of jet set in silver released at his fumbling. He could not seem to get his shaking under control. Whether it was from the rage of Notus' abduction or Jeanie's presence, he could not begin to decipher. Placing the cufflinks down on the silver plate on the mahogany dresser, he sat down on his four-poster, wood canopied bed and unbuttoned his white shirt and black vest. Kicking off his shoes, he stripped out of his clothes and collapsed on the bed made to take into account his unusual height.

Yong Zheng Ru's lessons and the shock of Notus' violent removal of their home exhausted him more than he thought. He so wanted to go to Notus' rescue and the thought of his impotence to do so during the day was frustrating. Every fibre in his being cried out to throw caution to the wind and storm over, but he could not. At least, not yet. Pulling the linen sheets up over his shoulders, he rolled to face the door.

Jeanie was on the other side. The thought kept his eyes open. The image of her wearing his shirt and nothing else made his mouth go dry and he thought about locking his door and realized there was no lock on it. Jeanie had nothing to fear from him and there was nothing she could do to make him fear her.

Rolling onto his back, he dismissed her from his thoughts, bringing them grimly back to the summons. He could not even recall who sat on the throne. It did not matter. They had taken his Chooser. He would go and get Notus back, whether they liked it or not.

II

eanie stared in astonishment as she watched the Angel's quick retreat into his room. The sound of the door clicking shut made her jump. When she had opened her eyes to see him resplendent in his black trousers, finely made white shirt and black vest, her heart had skipped a beat before realizing why she had been unconscious in the first place. It was the hurt and concern in his ruby eyes that worried her. She had never seen him like that. He was always schooling his features so she could never figure out what he was thinking, but this time, to see such blatant emotion flicker through his mask made her fear that the situation was graver than he led on. If that was the case, she could not understand why he would opt for sleep rather than go and get the Good Father back.

She knew that Father Paul had sworn an oath not to go out in the light of day until His return. He had told her as much in explanation for the strange hours she would work, and after how he found her, she was more than willing to accept his strange ways. What she had difficulty accepting why the Good Father had such a strange person such as the Angel with him.

The Angel, she sighed.

She had never seen anyone such as he. She knew his name, or at least the one that Father Paul rarely used when trying to get the Angel's attention. She would never use it. It would be too much of an imposition, and for some strange reason she did not feel that she had the right to call him by name. To her the Angel was something out of the fairy stories her mam used to tell her when she was a little lass. Even the softness of his voice when he spoke ran shivers up her spine.

Bringing his white shirt to her face, she breathed deep of his scent and remembered how he was with her and frowned.

Och, why dinna ye notice me?

She gently placed the shirt beside her and slowly stood up.

A wave of nausea passed over. Placing a hand on her forehead, she noticed the bruise on the inside of her wrist. Lowering her arm, she studied the blackened spot and for a moment she thought she saw two tiny holes. Dismissing the notion, she surveyed the dishevelled room. She did not want to sleep just yet. She was too riled up from what had happened and decided to do some straightening. Picking up his cloak, she carefully folded it, hugging it to her breast before placing it on the couch to begin the arduous process of cleaning up.

The train station had been crowded as she left its platform for the unknown streets of London. People crushed around her, pushing and shoving to get to unknown destinations. She pushed too, making her way out of the station with the surprise that she still held her meagre belongings.

Christmas Eve was a poor time to travel, but what else was she to do? It was the last day she could use her one-way ticket her father had given her.

She did miss her sire, but not his drunken rages, especially on this night traditionally held for family and good cheer. To her these were fantasies from her distant childhood when her mother was still alive. Jeanie was not surprised to have the ticket thrust into her hand by her strangely sober father. At fourteen she was out on her own to seek her fortune in London. It was that or marry pimply faced, gap toothed, Angus MacGregor. She chose London.

The cobblestones were slick with snow and ice, causing her ill made shoes to squish and slip beneath her. The street lamps illuminated large snowflakes gradually descending from a blackened sky. She shivered beneath her wrap, searching for a room to spend the night. Tomorrow she would begin her search for a job. Maybe Christmas would soften someone's heart to take on an inexperienced fourteen year old girl from the Highlands.

She walked down streets emptying to the late hour. Her wood handled brocade bag became increasingly heavy in her hands. Each no vacancy was a notch to her increasing worry that she may have to spend the night on the streets. She laughed in spite of her situation.

I bet 'tis what Mary felt like. Jeanie looked around. *'Tis too bad that there be no manger 'round here.*

Cold, wet and tired, Jeanie lugged herself into a crowded pub. The heat from the bodies and the fire in the corner hearth melted away the cold as she trudged up to the bar, dropping her heavy bag with relief. Carefully, she uncurled her stiff and frozen fingers until they were straight enough to rub together and was rewarded with a tingling rush. When the substantial barkeep loomed over her from the other side she meekly ordered a hot tea. She was famished, having eaten nothing since that morning, but she could only afford the beverage, the rest was for a bed.

AɊGEL OF DEATH

The plunk of the white and blue chipped teacup brought her mind back to the situation. Wrapping cold hands around the porcelain, she watched the lazy steam drift roof ward, and luxuriated in its warmth. The sounds of the other patrons dwindled into the background at the hot taste. Her whole reality focused on the steaming brown liquid, even to the exclusion of the smiling man who sat down beside her.

"Tea's nice to warm up with, but I've got somethin' that will take the edge off."

Placing the teacup onto its equally chipped saucer, Jeanie turned to face the man with the Cockney accent. He was plainly dressed and appeared quite average, even to his unwashed brown hair and missing bottom tooth. She figured that he might have been good looking once, had it not been for the bad setting of a broken nose from long ago.

"And what migh' that be?" she replied. The tea was hot, but it was not warming her as she had hoped.

The man grinned and turned to the bartender. "Oy, Jack, 'ow 'bout a bottle of your best whiskey."

Jack wiped his meaty hands on his apron, adding to the continuation of discolouration, and leaned over the bar. "You know, Joe, I can't do that. You haven't paid up last month's tab."

Joe frowned and noticed Jeanie avidly watching the exchange. "Awright. 'Ow 'bout if I pay for the bottle and not put it on the tab?"

Jack smiled and nodded. "That I can do." He took Joe's money and disappeared into the back only to return a moment later with a bottle of golden brown liquid and two shot glasses. He plunked down the glassware on the counter and walked away to serve another customer at the other end of the bar.

"So wot ye doin' in London, luv?" asked Joe. The cork came out with his expert administrations and he poured her the first glass. "Ye don't sound like you're from 'round 'ere."

Taking the glass, Jeanie sipped at the pungent familiar liquid, before downing the whole shot. "Thank ye," she wheezed, enjoying the radiating warmth the alcohol produced. Whiskey was her father's preferred drink so the smell was of home and made her feel more relaxed. "I've come t' find work."

"Do you 'ave a place t' stay?" Smiling, he poured another shot.

Jeanie shook her head, red curls floating everywhere. "I dinna ken where there's a place. The one's I've checked are all full. Do ye ken where I can find a bed?" She downed a second and then a third, luxuriating in the whisky's fire as it obliterated her hunger.

The man smiled and poured yet another round. "I do. If you finish up, I'll take y' there."

"Oh thank ye."

Did she slur? She was not sure but was beginning to regret drinking on an empty stomach. Downing her fifth – or was that sixth – shot, she stood wobbling back and forth on unsteady feet. She laughed at her own clumsiness as she took an uneasy step and grabbed Joe's proffered arm.

He rose and took her bag, threading her arm through his and guided her into the cold night.

It was so nice to find someone to help her, she thought as she watched in fascination as clouds of breath floated in front of their faces. She was feeling better about the whole idea of London. She grew up with the stories of what the English did to her people, but this man was kind and willing to help her.

Together, arm in arm, they walked down the now quiet streets, laughing at each slip. After a while she asked where he was taking her and laughed when he said to his place.

Jeanie's mirth was cut short by his angry expression.

"You think I'm funny, eh?" He grabbed her by the shoulders, giving her a furious shake that made her cry out. "You think that after the liquor I gave you, you don't owe me somethin'?" He pushed her into a straw strewn short alley, obviously inflamed by her growing fear. "You owe me and you're gonna pay. No one laughs at Joe Rumble." He grabbed her around the neck and kissed her hard, bruising her lips.

Terror cleared away the last vestiges of the whiskey's effects and she kneed him hard in the groin. Doubling over, he caught her as she tried to run. Falling to the cold ground, Jeanie let out a cry. She tried to kick, scratch, and bite her way free to no avail. He was quickly on top of her, his weight pinning her to the cold wet ground.

"So y' like it rough, eh?" he grinned, maliciously. "I like rough." He kissed her again, this time forcing her mouth open and thrust in his tongue.

At the hideous feeling, she flailed her legs, her scream cut short by the fist across her face.

Reality faded out momentarily and she fought to remain conscious despite the black flickering dots in her eyes. It was enough time for the man to yank down his trousers and quickly lift her heavy skirts.

She felt his hard member press against her and she tried to squirm away, screaming for someone to rescue her. Forcing her legs apart with his knee he cut off her scream with another kiss while his free hand painfully pinched her nipple through the fabric of her ripped dress.

Lifting his scratched face from hers, he purred, "You know, my dear, pain is so close to pleasure."

She screamed as he impaled her, violently breaking past her barrier. She could not believe this was happening to her. Tears rolled down the sides of her face, her screaming urged him on as he painfully entered her over and over. Groaning his pleasure, his fetid breath came faster, and then quite suddenly, miraculously, he was no longer on top of her.

The last image she saw before she allowed the darkness to overwhelm her was another man embracing her rapist.

She awoke some time later in the warm comfort of a large soft bed;

more comfortable than any she had ever been in. Lit candles on the bedside tables and dresser softly illuminated the richly decorated room filled with expensive mahogany furniture. Her eyes widened at the broadsword mounted on the wall to the right of the bed.

The sound of the door clicking open snapped her attention to the realization that she did not know where she was. Achingly, she sat up wearing nothing but a man's large white shirt, the sleeves neatly rolled up. Frightened and curious she watched the short dark haired man in a brown monk's robe shuffle in with a tray of hot food.

"Ah, my child," he smiled warmly, placing the tray on the bedside table and moved the candlestick to its mate on the dresser. "I am so pleased to see you awake."

"Wh—where am I?" she asked, hesitantly.

"Why, my dear, you are in the safety of my home." He sat down on the edge of the bed, his hazel eyes absorbing her. "I think you should eat before your dinner grows cold."

She gazed down at the steaming plate and gasped at the food. On fine china lay a perfect Christmas dinner of goose, pudding, potatoes and even cranberries. Where he could have even found fresh greens astounded her. With his help, the tray was set firmly on her lap and she picked up the sterling silver fork. Ripping off a chunk of the white flesh, she melted at the delicious taste.

Remembering her manners, she offered a piece to the monk.

"Oh, no thank you, my dear. I have already eaten." He grinned.

She gobbled down the best tasting food until all there was left to do was to lick her fingers. Allowing the monk to place the empty tray on the dresser after downing the glass of cool water, she muttered her thanks.

"You are most welcome, my dear. And now that you have put some food into your belly, please allow me to introduce myself." He sat down at the end of the bed, the mattress dipping under his weight. "I am Father Paul Notus, and, as I said, you are a guest in my home."

"I'm Jeanie Stuart," she replied, starting to like this unusual monk. "How did I get here?"

Father Notus sighed. "I was walking home from services when I heard your cries and relieved you of your distressing situation. I carried you home after you fell unconscious. Would you like to tell me about it?"

Memories of the night's earlier events crashed into her, forcing a sob from her throat. She nodded, not knowing what it was that made her feel so safe and secure to bestow upon this kind man the horror of what happened. The words spilled out of her until all that was left was to cry out her frustration and guilt as he held and gently rocked her.

When she regained control, Father Paul lifted her head, forcing her to gaze into his gentle hazel eyes. "It's not your fault," he stated. "You trusted and that man took advantage of that trust. In the Lords sight you are blameless and no harm has come to you. You are washed of the sins forced upon you. Do you understand?"

His words flowed over her, relaxing her, reverberating in her mind until all that was left was a refreshing sense of peace.

"Good," he smiled. Standing up, he went to blow out the candles. "Now get some sleep, for tomorrow you start work."

Surprised, she exclaimed, "What?"

He held open the door, allowing yellow light to streak the room. "I have need of a housekeeper. You have need of a job. I think this will work out well for both of us, do you not agree?" He opened the door further, his smile reflecting her shocked expression. "Do you think two pounds a day is reasonable?"

He closed the door behind him, leaving her in total darkness and staring slack jawed at the door.

Two pounds a day! She never imagined such wealth and it was visions of what she would do with all that money that guided her to her dreams.

Sometime later, the sound of the doorknob turning roused her from sleep. Groggily, she watched as a very tall slim figure slipped into the dark room illuminated by one guttering candle. The long hair confused her into thinking it was a woman, but she quickly dismissed the notion. She blinked the sleep from her eyes at the sound of shoes being kicked off and buttons being undone. It was then that she realized that this man was undressing. Fear gripped her and she let out an earth shattering scream. She did not need to see in the dark to realize she had frightened the man.

The door banged open to allow Father Paul to enter, lit candle in hand, asking what was wrong. The single candle illuminated the room and when she saw the surprised man by the dresser her jaw dropped. Never before had she seen anyone with his colouring. His long white hair and shocking red eyes filled her with trembling awe, and strangely enough she found him to be the most beautiful man she had ever laid eyes upon.

"Gwyn, go out. I will deal with this," declared Father Paul.

His name sounded exotic to her ears and she watched in fascination as he turned to the priest.

"What is going on? Who is she and why is she in my bed?" His voice was tight with anger, yet soft in its obvious Welsh accent.

"I will tell you later," replied the Father. "Now if you will, please leave."

With the grace of a cat, he left after giving her another glance.

Once he was gone, Father Notus came over to her bedside. "I am so sorry, my dear. I did not know he had come home."

"Who is he?" she asked timidly.

"He is called by many The Angel. He is my ward and my warder. You have nothing to fear from him."

Father Notus glanced back at the door, and then leaning over to her, he whispered with a wicked grin, "Frankly, my dear, I believe you frightened him more than he did you." He gave a little laugh. "Now, try and get some sleep. You have had a very trying night."

Watching him leave, Jeanie snuggled down, knowing that her life had finally changed for the better.

Jeanie fluffed the pillow and sat down on Notus' lumpy bed, smiling in amusement with the memory of her first meeting with the Angel. He seemed to accept her as an integral part to the workings of the home, but he always shied away from her.

She did find it odd that she, as their housekeeper, lived at a nearby inn and worked only at the night except for the occasional errand that had to be done during the day. The Good Father's explanation made some sort of sense. The Angel, he explained, had no choice in the matter. His skin was far too fair for the sun.

The Angel, she thought, running her hands along his shirt she now wore, the shirttails tickling her knees.

She did not understand why he avoided her. Yet, when he was home, she felt his eyes on her as she worked, only to look away when she caught him staring. He even shied away from her touch. Oh, how she longed for him. Even from the first night so far in the distant past.

She lay down on the lumpy mattress, wondering how in heavens name Father Paul could sleep on it. Unable to get comfortable she sat up and sighed. Her neighbour who rented the room next to hers had tried to give her advice on matters to do with men. Nervously, Jeanie decided that the opportunity finally presented itself to follow her friend's advice. Worrying her lower lip, she stood and with trembling steps left the Good Father's room.

iii

ights flitted past at remarkable speeds, creating blurring streaks of yellow in the brightly lit night. A gibbous moon shone high above adding blue to the mixture, outshining the immediate stars.

Somewhere far below, he felt, rather than heard, the breaks grip steel

as the train glided into the station, its dark structure blocking out all light. Cut off from the view he turned his attention to the cabin. Sitting back into the plush velvet seat he was riveted onto eyes the colour of spring.

She smiled, flashing perfect white teeth that sent his heart hammering in his ears. Long wavy copper hair was pulled up into a beautiful arrangement that was held in place with a small straw hat and pin. The forest green dress dignified her voluptuous body.

Shocked to hear her speak, asking his destination, he tried to reply but found he could not utter a single word. He did not know where he was going but he wanted to go with her. Gracefully, she stood and sat again beside him, bringing her slender arms up to release fiery hair to spill down over her shoulders and to land on the tops of her breasts.

Somewhere between the seat across to the one beside him, her clothing changed into a simple brown wool robe. Turning her face away from his to laugh, brown seeped into her hair turning it first to chestnut and then to a dark golden brown. He caught his breath at the recognition of the young woman next to him, now wearing a gown of white and blue.

Tilting her face to gaze up at him, her smile intact, she exposed her perfect white neck.

He clenched his teeth, forcing back the flickering hunger and his desire as she slowly undid the top two buttons of the blouse she now wore. Fiery hair curled and tickled the sides of her neck. Her pulse jumped and throbbed in time to the sound of her quickening heartbeat until it was all that he could hear, all that he could see.

Soft ambrosial lips encased his own and he responded equally. Quickly undoing the laces of the bodice of her gown, he slipped his hand in and cradled a full heavy breast. Gently caressing the nipple, she gasped, urging him on. Ravenously he sucked and nibbled, working his way down to the tantalizing throbbing vessel, his own body hard with need. She moaned and then cried out as his sharp teeth pierced her tender flesh...

He woke with a start, her heartbeat thundering in his ears. His eyes adjusted to the darkness and the dream fog over his mind lifted enough to realize that the heartbeat continued.

Bolting too fast out of bed, he cracked his head against the lip of the wood canopy and landed hard on the bed with his head in his hands. Long hair spilled around his face. Lifting a hand away from his forehead he stared at the streak of blood in a star filled background. He pressed his hand back on the quickly healing wound and groaned.

Gradually the flecks of starlight dissipated until he was aware of movement on the bed. The sound, smell and light of the match being struck brought him back to why he had recklessly leapt out of bed.

"Blow it out," he ordered. The sound of her gasp confirmed it and he repeated his demand through clenched teeth, anger filling his voice.

It was the sight of the wide parallel silver scars on his back that caught her off guard. Jeanie had never seen anything so gruesome and to see them bisecting his muscular back shocked her. It took the second issue of the order before she realized that he had spoken and hastily blew on the wick, cancelling all light in the room.

She made a move towards where he ought to be, concerned about his wellbeing, but found him gone. She had heard him hit his head and then fall back to the bed. Worried that she was the cause of his suffering and injury, she spoke into the darkness. "Are ye all right?"

"What are you doing here?" he demanded angrily, rising from the bed. He found his pants where he left them on the floor and hastily pulled them on. He could see her sitting on his bed clad only in his white shirt, frowning into the darkness. He was furious, both at himself and at her.

I could have killed her! The thought made him tremble as he slipped on a shirt, leaving it unbuttoned.

"I couldna sleep," she spoke blindly. She could hear him moving easily about, but she could not see an inch in front of her face. "The Good Father's bed has lumps and...and..." She broke off, almost afraid to admit the truth, that she wanted to be near him.

"And you had to come in here?" He picked up the box of matches on the side table and lit the candle.

Surprised at his sudden proximity, Jeanie jumped and gave a squeak.

He sighed at her reaction, his anger dissipating. "If you wanted my bed so much you could have woken me. I would have left it for you." *And painfully endured that couch.*

Jeanie frowned. She had been afraid, but she had also wanted something more. Absently, she left the bed, pulling his shirt down so that it covered the top half of her thighs. His gaze descending to her legs did not go unnoticed by her and she tried not to smile. "I'm sorry, but ye were sleeping so soundly that I dinna want to wake ye. I guess I could have taken the sofa."

Gods she looked beautiful wearing nothing but his shirt. Tearing his gaze off her well shaped legs, he felt the fool at her admission. Any embers of anger were doused.

"No," he sighed. "It's alright. It's just that you caught me off guard."

"I do that a lot, don't I?" she asked meekly, hearing his admission. This was the first real conversation they ever had and she wanted it to go on. In fact, tonight was the most he had ever talked with her and she wanted to know why. She did not think she was that horrid to be around otherwise Father Notus would not have hired her in the first place.

Quickly closing his slacked jaw, he wondered how she was able to catch so easily off guard and be so bloody accurate. Recovering himself, he simply stated, "I'll go so that you can get dressed."

"That's no necessary."

He released the doorknob and turned around, suddenly afraid to see her smiling eyes.

"My clothes are in the other room," she added, picking up the candle. "Ye dinna mind if I take this, d'ye?"

He shook his head. He did not need it. Opening the door, he stepped out of her way and was surprised when she stopped before him.

"You're head, how is it?" she inquired. She had heard the crash and his groan, but he seemed perfectly fine now, not a scratch could be seen.

"It's fine." He watched her frown as she left his room. Once past, he quickly closed the door knowing that at some point very soon he would have to acquire a lock.

Leaning his head against the wood, inhaling the scent of cleaner and varnish, he breathed a sigh of relief. After all these centuries, he preferred the anonymity and impersonality of a bloodied battlefield to the personal one on one contact with others, especially women, and especially after Notus told him how he was being used by them early on in his life. He had not wanted to believe it, and he turned a blind eye to it, but in the end he conceded the truth. What he was looking for he would not find. What the women he was with wanted they got – the Angel as their prize. He thought that having Jeanie around would help him overcome his reluctance. At least that was Notus' reasoning, but after this, she made him even more uncomfortable and confused.

The thought of his Chooser brought his attention back to the summons from the Court. Guessing he had short time to prepare, he figured that he had best dress appropriately. He slipped out of his hastily thrown on clothing and picked out a fresh black suit and shirt, all the while continuously glancing to his unlocked door, unnerved by the idea that Jeanie might come in again. It took him a while to dress. His mind kept playing out different scenarios he might have to deal with.

Snapping on the jet cufflinks, his eyes fell on his sword – Geraint's sword – hanging on the wall. Oh how he wanted to don it like he used to, when wearing a sword was commonplace. Today men duelled with pistols. The smell, sounds and distance was such an impersonal way to hunt and kill. Resigned that it would be deemed improper at the least and at the most it could cost him not only his life but Notus' life as well, he thought better of wearing the weaponry.

Jeanie did not know whether to smile or to frown as the door closed behind her. She was not sure how to take his reaction to her presence. She understood why he was angry at finding her there in his bed, but it did not seem to be completely the full reason either. Maybe he did care for her more than she knew, after all he did stare at her legs and seemed awkward when the candle was relit. A smile touched her lips. Maybe showing up in his bed had not been the disaster it could have turned out to be.

Walking around the living room, Jeanie lit the gas lamps. Satisfied with the nice bright yellow glow and the sight of the tidied place, she went into the cluttered room of the Good Father and shook her head at the mess. Her folded clothing on the stool was the only thing that was neat and organized. Deciding that she would break Father Paul's rule never to clean his room, she quickly dressed, made the bed and began to tidy up. She wanted the Good Father to come home to a nice neat place once she and The Angel brought him back.

It was the sound of a door clicking shut that brought her attention from settling some loose papers into a stack on one of the dusty shelves. She would have to dust later. Leaving the small closet-like room, she found the Angel searching around the living room, his black suit jacket over one arm. She smiled at the sight of him strikingly dressed in black vest and pants, his long white hair disappearing into the background of a pristine white linen shirt. She knew she was staring but could not bring herself to break off the gaze.

Glancing up from the end table to find Jeanie staring at him, he dismissed the intrusion and suppressed a flicker of irritation. She had done this before and he still found he had to get used to it. Then again, sometimes Jeanie would catch him staring at her, only to have him turn away embarrassed.

"Have you seen my pocket watch?" he asked.

She nodded, sending untamed curls bouncing, and walked over to the tea table placed under a painting of a sunrise. Opening the engraved antique wooden box, she lifted it out. "I kenned this would be a safe place for it."

"Thank you," he said, their fingers slightly brushing. Flipping open the casing, he read the time and snapped it shut with a frown. There was not enough time to feed and get to the Court. Shoving the silver watch into a pocket, he took notice for the first time that the evidence of last night's assault was gone.

"When did you do this?" He turned to Jeanie, a brilliant smile blossomed on her face.

"I cleaned after ye went t' bed." She was so happy that he noticed.

"I did not think..." He blinked back his surprise. She had been wounded, and when he left her she was the worse for wear. He never expected her to do this.

"That's what I get paid for." Her smile widened.

He nodded at her logic and then after glancing around the room once again he asked, "Where did you put my cloak?"

"I hung it in the closet."

He found it exactly where she said it would be and draped the heavy black fabric over his shoulders after putting on the black suit jacket. Out of a pocket he pulled out a very old cloak clasp and secured the cloak on his shoulders.

Grabbing her coat and huddling into it, Jeanie gazed up at the Angel in his resplendence. He turned away from her gaze and went to the front door.

"I will walk you to your inn," he stated. "I don't know if Notus will need you tomorrow night. If he does, he will send someone."

He opened the door onto a new night.

"I'm no going home," said Jeanie, a little nervously.

He turned on his heel and gazed curiously down at her. "Then where are you going? If it is not out of my way…"

"I'm going with ye." She locked onto his ruby eyes and a shudder of fear ran through her as she saw his eyes flash in anger.

Her admission surprised and irritated him into silence.

"I'm going with ye to help the Good Father," replied Jeanie, at bit more firmly. Her heart pounded in her ears, but she knew what she had to do, and this time she would not be dissuaded.

"No you are not," he stated, controlling the anger that threatened to seethe through. He could not allow her to come with him. It was too dangerous for a mortal. It was too dangerous for her to find out about their true nature.

"Aye, I am." Her green eyes darkened over.

"I said 'no'," matching her glare.

The vehemence in his voice was something she had never heard before, but it was the words that made her angry.

"I'm goin' with ye and that's that."

She opened the door and was shocked to have it forcibly slammed shut before it was even half opened. Spinning around she looked up into furious eyes. She pressed her back against the door in an unconscious attempt to move away from him.

"Listen to me very closely." He was not going to use the Push on her. He learned long ago that for some strange reason he could not make it work on her. Notus had no difficulties, but he could not. But despite that, he had to knock some sense into her. "Where I am going is very dangerous. And so are these people. I am the only one that can help Notus."

"No, ye are not," she spat. Jeanie did not like the way he was treating her as if she could not take care of herself. Nor did she like that he was trying to tell her what she could or could not do. He was not her employer, the Good Father was. "I'm capable and hae gotten myself outta worse messes. I can help and I *will* help. It's the least I can do for all the good he's done for me."

He shook his head and let out a breath allowing his own frustration to dissipate enough to get his thoughts under control. She just did not get it. "It's not a matter of capability, it's a matter—"

"So ye dinna think I'm capable?" she stormed.

"I didn't say that," he spat back. Why was it that she was so able to keep him completely turned around? "It's just that—"

"What? Because I'm a girl?" she shouted. "You're no much older than me!"

"No, just let me finish!" He put up his hand to halt her reply. He could see her chest heaving. He never met anyone so infuriating. He could not fathom how Notus could have even considered bringing Jeanie into their lives. "It's just that I'm the one who takes care of him and he takes care of me."

"And what am I? Dog spittle?" she retorted. Jeanie resented his remark after all it was she who took care of the place and spent the most time with the monk who had become a better father to her than her own. She was the one who was there when the Good Father was taken. She did her best to fight against their assailants while the Angel was wherever the Angel happened to be. He was not there when the Good Father needed him. The Angel was either always out or in the process of leaving.

He opened his mouth to reply and then thought better of it. He could not remember the last time he was so furious. Through a clenched jaw he replied coldly, "You are the housekeeper, nothing more." And knew that she was much more than that.

She glared up at him. "So, that's all I am, am I? A servant to yer every whim?" She took a step forward, making him take a retreating step back. She could not believe what she was hearing. It was not the truth that she wanted to hear and wanted to hurt him as much as he was hurting her.

"You're twisting my words." He glanced up at the ceiling in hopes to reform his position before the next attack came. Fighting with hands, swords and knives he could easily do. It was combat with words that he was perilously ill equip to handle.

Jeanie took another step forward, pressing her advantage, "But I'm no' yer servant. I work for the Good Father. No' ye! I dinna take orders from ye!"

Quietly, he forced the words out, "You are not coming with me."

"How dare ye! After all the good the Good Father has done for me, and now ye tell me that I canna help?" She matched his venom.

"That's correct."

She wanted to scream at him, and then thought better of it. Any thoughts of wanting him were dashed. "What right do ye hae to tell me what I can or canna do? That God fearin' man has done more for me than he you. Yer never around. Ye fly outta here as if somethin' is gonna bite ye. I'm the one who helps the Father. What have ye done? Ye weren't even here to help fight against those who took the Good Father. I hae more right to be helpin' him than ye!"

Whatever Jeanie was expecting from the Angel was not what she received. Hurt flashed over his features to be replaced by a cold clear anger she had never seen in him before. She instantly regretted her words. She knew nothing about the strange relationship between the monk and the tall pale man, and she realized that she just crossed over an invisible line.

"I'm—I'm sorry."

The force and truth of her words staggered him, forcing his guilt to the surface. She could not know how much Notus had done for him. It has always been Notus who made the money so they could live, except for the years he worked as an assassin. Those days were long past, but the reasons were tied up with the truth of their nature. Whatever he had started to feel for her evaporated, her apology did not erase the sting of her words. Reaching into his inner jacket pocket he pulled out some money.

"Take it. Get something to eat and go home." He pressed the bills into her hand and left, lifting his hood over his head, before she could reinitiate the argument.

Jeanie held the sterling notes and watched him go, a dark winged figure in the black of night. She knew she had hurt him, but he had hurt her too. She needed to help Father Paul. If there was ever a time to pay him back for all the caring generosity and help he provided her, it was now. She would not abandon him no matter what the Angel demanded of her. Resolved in her determination to help the Good Father Jeanie stuffed the money into her coat pocket and left the flat to follow at a discrete distance.

Keeping him in sight was difficult. Had he been of average height Jeanie would have quickly lost him, but she managed. The constant sounds of shoes clicking against cobblestones and the monotony of the chase gave her mind time to wander to when she awoke this evening. Angrily, she brushed away tears threatening to spill over.

Oh how could I hae been so wrong about his feelings towards me?

After she helped to get the Good Father back she would resign her housekeeping position. She could not work in a place where she was unwelcome.

Ignoring the burning of Jeanie's hatred on his back, he focused only on traversing the streets to get to the Theatre that was now the central hub of the Chosen in the United Kingdom. People passed him by, leaving him alone in the crowd. Only on the occasion did someone notice him due to his unusual height. These he ignored knowing that the night and the cloak obscured how different he truly was.

This night it was easier for him to ignore the strangers and their looks as his mind shifted from the argument he left to the confrontation he was heading towards.

Tumultuous emotions roiled within him, blocking out the undercurrents of his rising hunger. He understood Jeanie's desire to help Notus. She was right that his Chooser had done much to help so many people. Notus deserved and received the love and respect of those he helped – even Jeanie's love. She was also right that he did not help Notus, especially when he needed it the most.

The Good Father. That was what everyone called Notus. A prodigious title for a simple man of God who was nearly as ancient as the Christ himself, who earned money through his illuminations and scribe work, only to give it to those in need.

And me, he sighed. *I am the Angel – the one who takes.* A disturbing accuracy even Jeanie easily figured out.

Crossing the street, he absently shook his head. He knew that he had, again, become too dependent upon his Chooser, but Notus never seemed to mind. They had a strange symbiotic relationship that was formed in an age of violence. Now it was no longer necessary. People no longer came out of the wood to accost them. No longer were there villages fighting villages and clan feuds that resulted in bloodshed. It was in those brutal days where his warrior skills were needed by the monk, and honed by centuries of practice.

Now, in these days of peace, the warder had once again become the ward and had neglected his responsibility of protecting his Chooser.

Because of my lassitude Notus is gone. He prayed that he could remember how to be the protector and not just the Angel. He had to get Notus back.

He needed and missed the monk more than anyone in his life. Not discounting the rare few that Notus had introduced him to, who, accepting his strangeness, had become friendly and even a fewer still became teachers. Nor could he ever forget Auntie and Geraint.

A special few knew their secret and accepted them still, marking them more precious in their immortal hearts. Only Father Colwyn knew in this time and place. Not even Jeanie could find out. Too many times they were forced to flee because someone either figured out their secret or broke their trust in exchange for money from the Witch Finders.

Sure, the girl was trusted with everything pertaining to their home. Her loyalty in trying to defend Notus and her insistence on helping to get him back was proof, but she also was very young and liked to gossip with her friends at the Inn. It had gotten so bad at one point that one night, when he walked Jeanie home, he was accosted by one of her girlfriends, forcing him to make a hasty retreat from Jeanie's company.

He rounded another corner. The old Theatre that now served as the Court was only a few blocks away, down through some back streets. He could not fathom the reason why they would abduct Notus, nor why they wished that he attended the Mistress. It was well known within the Community that he and Notus preferred to be left alone. He agreed with Notus that the changes overcoming the Chosen were vile, threatening to expose them to the mortals they had remained hidden from for centuries.

The new Chosen, the Vampires as they liked to be called, were sadistic, living only for the next rush the blood gave them. They killed indiscriminately and revelled in a new hedonistic lifestyle. None of the older Chosen, who tried to distance themselves from their younger's, could understand or fathom the reason for this gradual decline of such a noble race to one of degenerates.

Notus had prophesied this decline during the Plague. Somehow his

Chooser had seen it, but it still did not ease the pain of having Notus ripped from him. Nor did it justify the abduction. Then again nothing could justify such an act. Never before had he heard of any Mistress or Master, of any country, kidnapping one of their own to get the attention of another. Had respect and common decency between them been tossed out? It appeared so.

ío

He halted at the base of a short set of concrete stairs. At the top large black double doors served as the entrance to the new Court in the disused old theatre. On either side of the massive doors two huddled forms sat wrapped in torn and threadbare blankets. At first glance one would take them for nothing more than two unfortunates forced to live on the street. They did not move. If not for the slight rise and fall of their chests and the occasional blink they would have easily been passed over as statues. He knew otherwise. They were two mortals kept under the power of the Mistress to do her bidding. They were nothing more than automatons. It was another piece of evidence of how far the Chosen had fallen.

With nothing left to lose and so much more to gain, he took a deep steadying breath and ascended the stairs two at a time.

The man crouched to the right of the doors, stood at his approach. No longer the grubby street urchin, he stood tall and broad. Clearly he had been picked for his strength and not for his mind. Vacant hazel eyes focused on him and in a monotone spoke, "Who goes there?"

"I have been summoned by the Mistress," he replied, searching for any sign of intelligent free will.

"Who goes there?" repeated the servant. Obviously the answer was not the appropriate one.

A click and a snap drew his attention to the other servant now standing, making bookends of the doorframe, but holding a loaded pistol cocked and aimed.

If it was to be that way, then he would play the little games so long as it served his purpose. Catching the vacant eyes with his own, he spoke softly, intently, and in rhythm with the guard's beating heart and Pushed. "*Let me in.*"

The guard nodded as the order plucked an unknown string in his soul. Placing a thick muscled hand on the large brass door handle, the door opened with a click and a scrape.

The reception hall was dimly lit to take into account the sensitive eyes of the Chosen. Small lamps illuminated fine art interspersed along walls papered in red velvet patterned into blossoming roses. A large silver candelabrum hung in the middle, alight with more than a dozen fine beeswax candles. If he did not know any better he would have thought he was in the middle of an art gallery.

The doors closed behind him, shutting out all sound from the outside world and he glanced around the audacious room. Even the large heavy oak doors leading to the theatre were lavish in their workmanship. It was more ostentatious than the last, but then again the last Court hall was devastated by the Fire and he had never set foot in it until it was nothing more than a charred ruin holding the bones and ashes of the Chosen who had hid there.

His eyes widened in realization of which Court hall he was comparing it to. Had it been that long? He ran his hand through his long thick white hair, pushing back the hood of his cloak. An involuntary shudder ran through him as he remembered the Roman built manse Master Antonius and his Lady Julia used. Visions of mosaic floors crowded by people in togas and the more common dress of the era made him cringe. There had been too many people, too close together.

He shook himself out of the past and realized he was gratefully alone.

Along the wall, near the front entrance, a grandfather clock, standing taller than he, indicated that he was five minutes early. Deciding to look around while he waited, he went from painting to painting, revolted by the gruesomeness of the dark images. It was the large oiled canvass of a demon with burning red eyes subduing and forcing the submission of a fair haired angel with his wings hideously ripped off, that caught and held his attention.

Master Antonius stood on the dais wearing the finery of a Roman Primus Pilus. The Master gazed angrily at him while Lady Julia, seated in a throne made of gold and draped in a fine white toga laced with gold, covered her horror with the back of her hand.

"Kill it!" The order issued from the Master of Britain.

He started at the touch on his arm and gazed down at a waif of a man.

"It is time, sir."

The sound of the servant's fearful heartbeat rang in his ears. Smoothing his features into a mask of non-expression, he nodded once, steadying himself to enter into the lion's den.

The little man turned around, keeping his eyes on the Chosen as long as possible and led the way to the heavy double doors at the end of the hall.

Notus begged for his life on bended knee, pleading for forgiveness. Seeing his Chooser humiliate himself, he stepped forward only to be surrounded by finely forged steel blades. They did not know what such a weapon could do to him. They could never know. It had taken almost two years to come here, more than a year and a half in Ynis Witrin healing and learning to use his arm again.

The order that he be stripped came from Lady Julia. He needed to run. Even among the Chosen he was too different.

"They are ready for you, sir. Can I take your cloak for you?"

He shook his head, trying to clear his mind of the unwanted memories. Abasement on the servant's drawn and tired face made him realize he gave the wrong answer. Unhooking the cloak, he folded it and handed it to the man, keeping the clasp to be pocketed. "I'm sorry. I was thinking."

"Yes, sir." He hung the cloak over a thin arm. "You are to go in immediately, sir." He bowed his bald head and backed away.

Turning the cool polished brass knob, he entered into the realm of the Court. No seats lined the sloping floor that ended at the stage. A single high backed chair, ornately engraved and upholstered, stood before large drawn red velvet curtains. Those Chosen who had decided to come and pay their respects, or more likely, to watch the show, stood along the walls. Seated in the throne sat the Mistress, flanked by her select few. She did not notice his arrival; her attention was on the dark haired man in lavish attire standing before the stage.

"*Sua puta fodida!* You cannot do this to me!" hollered the man. His dark shoulder length hair whipped around in a wavy mass. The accent was unpredictable – Portuguese.

"Ah, but I have, my dear," purred the Mistress, her chin resting in her delicately boned hand. Dark long curls framed her pale painted face. "I can do whatever I wish. I can even take all your possessions."

"You wouldn't dare!" roared the man.

"Dare?" Her musical voice turned sour. "I've done!" She snapped red painted fingers and the man beside her with short black greasy hair produced a folder. She grabbed it out of his hands without so much as a thank you and opened it, showing the contents to the one before her. "Your deeds. Your leases. Your signature!"

The man made a move to leap up onto the stage, halting as the hiss of metal issued from the sides of the theatre. "If you have everything of mine what do you need me for," he spat.

"All in good time. All in good time." A victorious smile curled her red lips and the Mistress languidly sat back in her throne.

Ice blue eyes flickered up the carpet to the figure at the back of the theatre. The Mistress bolted upright in surprise.

His presence acknowledged he stepped down the sloping floor, ignoring the murmurs of shock and surprise. Another throne and another Mistress threatened to superimpose themselves upon this time and he clenched his jaw, trying to force back the memories.

Clothes ripped from his body. The sound of Notus' begging in the background. He was forced to his knees. The cold tiles reflected the torchlight as he was made to bend over. His arms yanked up behind his back. The searing touch of sharpened steel on the back of his neck immobilized him.

"I am so glad you came," purred the Mistress.

Forcibly repressing the rising terror he knew was reflected in his eyes, he slipped his cold mask into place, but even as he did so, he felt it slipping. The thin scar at the back of his neck tingled.

"You did not leave me any choice." He kept his eyes locked onto the Mistress. Distinctly aware of all the eyes upon him, he was more aware of the measuring gaze of the Portuguese Chosen. *Let them stare,* he thought.

Her eyes darkened despite the chiselled smile. "Our kind always has a choice."

Your kind. Of course he would not say it. He chose to say nothing.

Realizing that she was not going to get a response from this near mythological Chosen, the Mistress absently dismissed her irritation with a wave of her hand. She was used to power unquestioned, civilities enacted. Steepling her painted fingers, she relaxed into her throne. "It has been a long time since you have been to Court. In fact you have refused to attend your Mistress on several occasions."

"I am here now." The theatre now consisted only of him and the Mistress. The others he ignored.

"Yes. Yes, you are. I had to go to great lengths to set up this audience with the Angel."

Now we get to it. He set his jaw and lifted his chin. "Where is Notus?"

"Here." She saw the flicker of hope in his ruby eyes. "You will see him soon enough."

"I want to see him now."

The Mistress sighed in exasperation. "I will permit it if you agree to listen to me."

He felt the trap ready to spring. There was only one way out and that was through. He nodded once.

Pleased with the answer, the Mistress turned to the man on her right, the one with the lanky black hair who had handed her the portfolio.

"Valraven, please be a dear and open the curtains," she ordered.

"My Lady Katherine, I must protest. What if the rumours about him are true?"

"Then I will deal with it. Now open the curtains."

Valraven bowed and left the stage.

He watched in silence as the heavy drapes gradually parted. The mask shattered at the sight of his Chooser brutally chained and crucified in the middle of the stage, his brown homespun robe torn and bloodied from wounds that had already healed. Automatically, he reached out to find Notus unconscious and unresponsive, his blood nearly drained.

In two strides he leapt up onto the stage, his only thought was to free Notus from the mockery of the Mistress' grasp. He heard his outcry of defiance mingled with the one Notus had yelled as the axe came crashing down oh so long ago. This time it hit. Instead of the axe slamming down in front of him, the blow from a staff hit him squarely across his back, sending him reeling. He landed heavily, face down on the stage. Reality blinked out.

The Mistress' obvious dismissal of his presence infuriated him. Somehow that bitch had changed the deeds and papers so that all his accumulated wealth was transferred to her. As to her reason, he had no clue. *All in good time. All in good time.* In time she would deeply regret her intrusion and her usurpation of his life and property. He never did like Katherine Dumonte. Now he despised her. Mistress or no, she had no right to mess with Fernando de Sagres.

He turned around to see who caused the Court to buzz. His dark brown eyes snapped wide at the sight of the tall pale vampire steadily walking towards the stage.

Merda do Sando Deus. It's the Angel. It has to be! There was no other that matched the rumoured descriptions. When Bridget and others murmured their fables, he believed them to be such; fables — lies conjured to explain the unknowable. But now he watched the myth walk towards him, and the Mistress.

I wonder if the other parts of the story are true?

He stepped out of the tall man's path. The Angel stood a good head and shoulders taller. Was that fear that lighted the crimson eyes for the briefest of moments? Fernando knew himself to be a fair reader of men. He touched a brawny finger to his lips, trying to read the man before him. It was not easy. The mask slipped into place and he could discern no more. He could not fathom the reason why the Angel would fear the Mistress and her lot.

Fernando watched the interplay between the Mistress and the Angel. At the mention of Notus' name Fernando perked up, his attention grabbed. Notus—the Angel's sire. She had him. The two were legendary.

Completely unlike others of their kind, sire and fledgling were still together. Who would have imagined? He had left Bridget long ago.

The sound of rusty pulleys brought his attention away from the pale vampire to the stage. His eyes darkened at the sight of the crucified vampire on the large T-bar. The sound of the Angel's cry brought him back to the erupting chaos and he involuntarily winced at the crack resounding off the staff as it crashed across the Angel's back.

He felt hands pull him roughly to his knees, his arms drawn up behind his stinging back. The stars quickly cleared from his vision to see the Mistress lording before him. It was like before.

No, not quite. He would never allow Mistress, Master, or anyone for that matter, to drink from him again. He did not care if she saw the burning hatred in his eyes.

"That was a very stupid move." Her hand gently caressed his smooth face, revelling in the surge of control regained. "Of course I can forgive your tiny indiscretion, having never been in *my* Court, but any more inappropriate behaviour and I may have to do something to your pretty face."

Ignoring her threat, he watched as she turned to face her Court. His eyes bored into her back.

Lady Julia floated down the dais to stand before him. Her finely decorated hand, every finger covered with at least one jewelled ring, cupped his chin, wet with tears of fright, and lifted him to his knees. Cold brown eyes met his and then turned to Antonius. "He is not but a child. A sweet innocent child."

She returned her frosty gaze. "Is that what you are?"

Too frightened, he said nothing.

The Mistress painfully grasped his chin, forcing their eyes to meet. "I command you. Answer me!"

"I don't know?" he nervously blurted.

Lady Julia released her grip. "Are you not one of the Chosen? Do you call Father Notus a liar?"

Before he could even think to form a reply, Notus spoke up. "He is Chosen, my Lady. By accident."

Her blond brow lifted. "Is that so. But is his blood pure?" Her finger followed the scar on his arm from shoulder to as far as his pinned arms would allow.

He did not hear if his Chooser made any response before Lady Julia bit deep into his neck.

*   *   *

"You do not have the authority to hold Father Notus," he stated flatly. The sting across his face was expected.

Mistress Katherine's face was tight with fury. "I am the Mistress. I hold all authority over every Vampire in the United Kingdom. You will do my bidding as I see fit. If not, then he dies!" She swung her arm to point at the tormented priest. "Is that what you want?"

He set his jaw, tasting blood. "No."

"Then what do you want?" she glared at him. Even on his knees he was of a height with her.

The two holding his arms behind his back gave a sharp tug that threatened to pull his arms from their sockets. He refused to allow the pain to override his response. "I want Notus back."

This time her slap was unpredicted. At least she had balanced out the stinging sensation in his face.

"Wrong. What you want is to serve me. For if you do not he will die. Make certain of it. Now what do you want?"

He bit his tongue. He had no choice if he had any chance to free Notus. With venom he spat, "I want to serve you."

Her mood brightened immediately as if some switch was turned. She waved off the men holding him. "That's much better."

Slowly he regained his feet, rubbing back the feeling into his shoulders. Following her motion to get off the stage, he jumped down to stand beside the richly dressed man. He ignored the appraising gaze, keeping his attention on the Mistress.

"Now that I have your attention." She went to stand before her throne. "I will tell you both why I went to such great lengths to force your attendance." She snapped her fingers and continued. "We British Vampires have a problem. Somehow we are being poisoned to death. Or more to the point, our food source is becoming tainted."

Two others he had not seen before dragged a thin, ragged man out of stage left. The man, weeping with his head down, did not struggle; his scuffed and worn shoes scraped the wooden stage. Following behind, a woman carried a double edged dagger in one hand and a large ornately decorated gold chalice in the other.

"To illustrate my point I had this street urchin delivered so that you will see that I do not lie." The Mistress took the proffered blade from the woman who then curtsied to her Mistress and moved off to the side.

The mortal was made to stand before the Mistress and she grabbed a handful of dirty mousy brown hair, lifting the weeping man to face the Court.

A flicker of recognition passed on the Angel's face. *Peter!*

The look on the man's face turned into one of hope. "Angel, please save me from these crazed pe—" His pleading was cut short by a hand at his throat.

Standing rigid, he controlled himself as the Mistress grabbed Peter's arm and cut deep lengthwise along the long blue vein at the wrist to the sound of his thin scream.

The smell of hot pungent blood swept into the air even before the first rushes of scarlet liquid were caught up in the chalice. He could do nothing to save the man that had called to him for help. All he could do was watch impotently as Peter's life filled, and then spilled over the chalice.

The Mistress released her grip on the now flaccid arm and allowed the men to release their hold on the corpse. It hit the stage with a loud splat as it landed in its own cooling blood. Lifting the chalice, it ran red with blood at her movement.

"Angel? Strange that it would pray to an angel in such a manner. Unless it was expecting that *you* would save it," she taunted.

Carefully, she kept the chalice at arm's length so as not to soil her fine attire. "Somehow I cannot imagine Fernando saving anyone, not even a puppy. But you I can imagine doing such a thing. Now why is it that you are called the Angel? I can see you being called a demon, a devil, yes. Tell me so that my curiosity is satiated. Speak!"

He loosened his jaw to answer. "It is a name. Nothing more."

"Is that all?" she probed.

He refused to say anymore.

Dismissing the subject with a shrug, the Mistress said absentmindedly, "Now where was I?"

"You were about to illustrate your point, my Lady," offered Valraven who came to stand beside her.

"Yes. Now I remember." She startled as if waking from a dream. "Valraven, would you be a dear and take this to Fernando and the Angel?"

The Mistress' assistant took the heavily filled chalice, ignoring the wash of blood streaming over his hand, bowed and moved off into the wing only to re-emerge onto the spectators' level only a moment later. He offered it first to Fernando, who eyed Valraven and the chalice with extreme prejudice.

"Take a sip," ordered the Mistress, seeing his reluctance.

Fernando flashed an angry glare. Unaccustomed to receiving orders he stiffly pulled out a finely tailored white handkerchief bordered with lace from an inner pocket of his tailed jacket. Flicked out to full size, Fernando used it as a barrier to keep his hands clean as he took the chalice, careful not to spill any blood. Mocking a salute by slightly raising the cup, he did as ordered and gave it back to Valraven, soiled rag and all.

The Mistress' assistant ignored the handkerchief and hesitantly went to stand before the tall pale vampire. Valraven did not look up to meet the angry red glare and instead chose to stare at the black lapelled suit jacket that fit perfectly across the muscular chest.

Carefully, taking the cup from Valraven, he soiled his hands as the blood soaked through the kerchief. This was all that remained of Peter, a homeless nobody who never did anyone harm, one of the countless many who received what little help they could from a priest wise in the world of suffering. He did not salute the Mistress. He just took a slight sip and passed back the chalice. At first he could not bring himself to swallow, but hunger won out, but not before he noticed the subtle, almost nonexistent, sickly sweet taste.

"There is nothing wrong with this blo—" Fernando halted in mid-sentence, his anger rapidly dissipated to a look first of surprise and then illness.

Trying to blink away the blurriness, the Angel ran a pale hand across his face. He followed Fernando's collapse to his knees, all sensation in his extremities suddenly replaced by paralysing numbness.

"You bitch!" croaked Fernando, "You poisoned me!"

"Not quite, my dear," purred the Mistress, enjoying the submission of her subjects. "Give it a moment. It will pass."

She was true to her word. Feeling rapidly returned to arms and legs. Blurred eyesight cleared. Steadily they rose to their feet. Glancing quickly at the other out of a habit of concern, Fernando seemed fine and yet somehow familiar. He did not match the other's enraged expression. He finally believed the threat the Mistress mentioned.

"You see that I do not lie." She sat down on her throne, absently smoothing out the wrinkles in her black dress.

"Lie? You sit there after you poison—"

"If this is what you wished to show me, you need not abduct Notus," his soft spoken words cut short Fernando's rant.

Brown eyes flickered from the Angel to the Mistress. "Nor steal my holdings," remarked Fernando, jumping on the bandwagon.

"Ah, but I had to." The Mistress smiled and raised her hand to halt the words ready to explode from Fernando's lips. The Angel stood silently still, waiting for her to make her point. "Taking the Father and the possessions were not only to get your attention, but to hold your attention until such time as I decide you are worthy for me to release them. Think of them as my hostages."

"What?" he balked. This was impossible, unheard of. To hold another Chosen hostage was an anathema to the honour he was taught that the Chosen should hold. His cool façade slipped into horror.

"O grande puta! Como e que tu podes fazer isso? Eu vou te cortar em pedacos. Meu Deu que quero—" Fernando absently slipped into the language of his birth, his fury forcing him to forget English.

"Quiet!" roared Valraven. His voice reverberated throughout the theatre until there was nothing but silence.

Satisfied that Fernando's seething would not burst forth into another non-intelligible rant, Valraven nodded to his Mistress and placed the chalice on the edge of the stage. A red ring connected gold and wood.

"Thank you, my dear," said the Mistress, sweetly. Reclining into the soft cushions of her throne, she crossed one slender leg over the other, exposing a finely shaped pale calf.

Suppressing his shudder of rage, her nonchalant attitude infuriating him to the point he could not hide it, he stated through clenched teeth, "What do you what?"

"How wonderful that you should ask such a question. It is too bad that you didn't phrase it correctly, but no matter." The Mistress leaned forward, hands folded on her knee. "I cannot expect too much from you too soon."

"Get on with it, Katherine," spat Fernando, his patience at an end.

She glowered at the Portuguese vampire, angered at the use of her name. After all, she was the Mistress and not some common vampire to have her name bandied about. "Fine, Fernando," her small mouth warping his name, "what would you do to get back your holdings?"

Sensing a trap, Fernando slowly said, "Depends on what I'm requested to do."

"And the Angel," she pivoted in her seat. "What would you to do get back your sire?"

"Anything," he said without hesitation, ignoring the surprise on Fernando's face.

"Is that so? Hmmmm." She placed a graceful finger against her lips, red against red. "Such devotion of a fledgling for his sire is rare. Notus must be a remarkable vampire."

His gaze moved beyond the throne to the T-bar that held the unconscious form of the man who cared for him through the centuries. "Chosen," he absently corrected.

Confusion momentarily blackened the Mistress' features only to have the darkness replaced with the brightness of mirth. "Chosen, yes, most definitely. Now where was I?"

"You were about to tell them—" reminded Valraven.

"Ah yes." Her face became sombre and she leaned forward in her throne, hands placed on the padded armrests. "Fernando and the Angel, to get back what I hold hostage you are to discover who is behind this poisoning and put an end to it before we are all dead. You found what one sip could do to you. Draining a mortal will kill you. I have seen it done to others of our kind. Find the reason. Squash it. Only then will I give you back what I have taken. But take heed. I have sent others out before and they have been found dead or not found at all. If you fail, what is yours becomes mine."

She leaned back in her chair, a pallor overcoming her features. "Go now. I am weary of you."

Fernando opened his mouth to protest but stopped as Valraven stepped before him. "You will leave now. My Lady needs her rest."

Furious at the dismissal, Fernando turned on his heel and strode out of the theatre.

Watching the Portuguese Chosen stomp up the slope to the doors, he turned to look down at the assistant to the Mistress. "What will the Mistress do with Notus?" concern lighting his tone.

Startled at being addressed by the enigmatic vampire, Valraven quickly glanced up at the fearful face and then back down. "Anything she wishes," he stated plainly.

Taking a heart wrenching last look at his Chooser, he closed his eyes and silently vowed he would see Notus safe and out of her clutches, and frowned at the lack of response. Slowly, he walked up the slope and cleaning off Peter's blood with a handkerchief, left Notus in the care of an insane woman.

eanie halted and watched from behind the protection of a lamppost as the Angel ascended the steps to the old abandoned theatre. It was when he paused at the top that she noticed the two burly men standing guard.

This must be the place. She poked her head closer, squinting to see into the shadows. What she did see was the Angel entering the theatre.

Turning her back to the building she leaned heavily against the lamppost. She needed to find out if the Good Father was in there and why. The Angel would be angry with her, she knew this, but swallowing the fear of his disapproval she turned to walk up the steps.

"Who goes there?" demanded one of the guards as he lifted to his feet, discarding the tattered blanket.

She paused before taking the last step, her heart thumping loudly in her chest. These men could easily break her in half. She coughed her nervousness.

"My name is Jeanie and I'm here with the Angel."

A large hand, snaked with ropy muscle, unhooked the holster and pulled out a gun.

"Who goes there?" he repeated, his eyes focusing on nothing.

Her eyes widened as the barrel levelled onto her position. She did not need to be asked a third time.

"Sorry. Wrong address," she blurted before fleeing down the stairs.

Halting at the lamppost, Jeanie breathed a sigh of relief and blotted her forehead with the cuff of her coat. She turned to look back up the theatre stairs to find the two guards huddled under ratty blankets. Heart still hammering in her chest she realized that this was more serious than she first realized. Staring at the large double doors, she decided that if she could not get in she would keep watch on the place.

After what seemed to be an indeterminably long time Jeanie sat down on the ground under the lamp, ignoring the damp permeating through her skirt. Her feet had grown sore from standing so long, waiting for the Angel to re-emerge from the theatre, and with no other option, she made do with the walkway, leaning her back against the base of the lamppost, her skirt tucked warmly around her legs. She could not imagine what could be taking so long. All he had to do was go in, get the Good Father and leave. Or so she had originally assumed. Waiting was not one of her strong points and once again she had to force down her rising irritation.

A loud rumble arose from the depths of her stomach bringing her attention to how famished she was. She had not eaten in over twelve long hours and images of steaming meat pies and mashed potatoes and peas made her mouth water and her stomach roar louder.

With a sigh, she placed her hands into her coat pockets to warm them, knowing food would have to wait. A crunching piece of paper rubbed against her hand and she pulled out the note the Angel had forced upon her. The sight of the five-pound note staggered her to her feet. Not believing her eyes, she turned it this way and that under the yellow glow of lamplight.

I could buy a hundred meat pies! she thought. That would surely fill her up, and at the most, make her explode.

The sound of shoes rapidly clicking against stone brought her attention away from the small fortune to face the bobby walking towards her. A little too hastily she jammed the note back into her pocked as he walked past, taking no mind of her except a polite nod.

Not three steps past he turned around, the echo of his shoes swallowed up by the night, and frowned down at her. Jeanie's eyes widened at his approach into the sphere of luminescence, his brass buttons and badge reflecting brightly.

"What's a nice looking girl like you doing out here all by yourself?" His voice was deep, issuing forth from lips veiled under a thick brown moustache.

"I'm waitin' for my friend," she stammered. She could see in his brown eyes that he did not believe her. "No, really, I am," she hastily added.

"Now, luv, waiting for a friend is fine, but in the middle of the night I have to be questioning the manner of that friendship." His tone was condescending as he gave her another thorough look over.

Biting her lip, Jeanie tried to decide whether to tell the police officer about the abduction and the retrieval of the Good Father. Then again, there was no need. The Angel would be out with the priest, and hopefully very soon. The glowering brown eyes told her that she was taking too long in answering, so she decided to bend the truth. "My friend is the son of my employer and—"

"Meeting for some extracurricular employment, wot?" The bobby's eyes alighted.

The implication of the officer's words instantly darkened her mood. "How dare ye!" she fumed. Relentlessly, she ploughed on, not caring even it was the Queen Herself before her. "I'm no whore and I resent bein' thought so."

His eyes went wide at her unexpected explosion.

Heedless of his attempts to calm her to rationality, Jeanie continued, "I'm just mindin' my own business, which is innocent enough, and 'cause I'm standin', waitin' for a friend, I'm accused of prostitution!"

"Listen missy," agitation rang in the officer's voice once he had an opportunity to get a word in. Jeanie crossed her arms over her chest, angrily waiting for him to continue. "I did not accuse you of anything. It is my job to keep things right on the streets. Since you have stated—quite fervently— that you are not a prostitute, then it becomes my job to see if you're safe."

"I am safe."

"I can see that." He turned around to continue his beat. "No one in their right mind would bother you," she heard him mumble as he walked away, clicking heels fading into the distance.

Jeanie glared at his retreating figure. She could not believe the audacity of the bobby. *Thinkin' I'm a whore,* she exhaled explosively, leaving a faint cloud to dissipated. *I'm no even dressed like one!* She shoved her cold hands under her armpits. She was not even in the right district. At least the confrontation diverted her from the rumblings of her stomach.

The large heavy wooden door clicked shut, leaving behind the hope for Notus' emancipation. He did not want to let go of the brass knob. Every instinct screamed that he should storm back in and save Notus, but he knew that they would both be dead before he even reached his Chooser. The staff across the back was just a warning.

Cold steel lined the walls with the Chosen. He had heard it hiss when the other tried to reach the Mistress. It could have been possible if he had brought his sword, his age and training most likely outmatched everyone in the theatre, but at what cost? Releasing his grip, he hit the door, palm open, causing the wood to cave and crack. The door was reinforced.

Damn! he raged. He was as trapped as Notus.

"Putting a crack in the door isn't nearly as satisfying as the idea of putting one in Katherine's skull, not to mention her lackey as well."

He spun around to find a wry smile edging the corners of the Portuguese Chosen's full lips. *Fernando. That is what she called him.* A spark of recognition flared again. It seemed that Fernando should be wearing something from an earlier time, instead of the dark charcoal suit and the cravat studded with a ruby pin.

A half smile pulled at Fernando's face and he took a step towards the infamous Angel. Despite what Katherine had tangled him into, he had a chance to do something no other Chosen before him had even attempted—to find out more about the Angel from the Angel himself. Bridget would be thrilled and would do almost anything for any sort of tidbit Fernando could glean. He could not pass up that opportunity for the world.

"Since Katherine was so rude as not to introduce us, I imagine we have to do it ourselves." He stuck out a dark, strong hand, one that had never known toil or hardship. "I am the Noble Fernando de Sargres, the last heir to the title, Fidalgo de Sagres."

He let his hand fall to his side when the Angel did not take it. His brows rose in mild amusement as the Angel suspiciously watched him. "And you are, of course, the Angel."

They turned at the scratching sound of the little bald man shuffling out with black cloaks draped over each arm. The distraction was perfect. There was something slightly disturbing about Fernando de Sagres, something the Angel could not put a finger upon. He lifted his cloak from the servant and draped it over his slim, muscular frame, and pulled out the ancient clasp from his pocket. The little man bowed his head and went next to the Noble.

Fernando acquiesced to the interruption with a scowl. Loathing the perceived impertinence, he yanked his cloak, causing two daggers to hit the carpeted floor with a loud thunk. Silence reigned momentarily as all three stared at the curving blades. The panicked mortal heartbeat was audible to immortal ears.

The scowl deepened on the Noble's face, forcing fear to widen the servant's features. His cry was strangled off as Fernando's hand whipped out to grip the mortal's throat.

"Why you infinitesimal slug. I'll teach you to be respectful of your betters, and their possessions," hissed the Noble.

The servant's squeaked his fear at the tightening clasp.

The whole display seemed surreal and completely unwarranted. The Angel could not understand Fernando's anger. It was an accident. Not worthy of such an outburst. But one thing he did understand was that if he stood by and did nothing, the man would be dead very shortly. "Let him go," he ordered, his voice barely audible.

Fernando turned to look up at the Angel, scowl intact. "I think not. This dog needs to learn some manners." He pulled the servant closer. The man's eyes bulged with the lack of oxygen.

"I said, let him go." He placed a bone white hand on Fernando's finely tailored arm.

"Or what?" spat Fernando. He glared into determined crimson eyes expecting to stare down the Angel but found himself backing down as the pale hand squeezed painfully. With a growl, Fernando released his grasp, allowing the servant to fall to his knees, gasping in great quantities of air.

Kneeling down beside the man, ignoring the Noble's burning glare, he asked, "Are you alright?"

"Yes, sir," wheezed the man, hand rubbing his bruising throat. He allowed the Angel to gently lift him to his feet. "Thank you, sir."

"Go home. It is not safe here." He glared over the servant's head to Fernando. He was met with a look of disgust, but did not care. He was disgusted himself. The servant nodded and fled the room without so much as a glance to the Noble.

"I see that rumour proves itself true," spat Fernando. With a flourish, his silver embroidered black cloak landed on broad muscular shoulders. "I'm starting to wonder if the other parts are true as well," he sniffed.

Glowering at the Noble, he bent down, retrieving the two daggers by their hilts. "I believe these are yours," he stated impassively. Standing, he offered them, hilts first, careful not to touch the blades. He had to snatch his hands back lest they be cut as Fernando grabbed them, making them disappear beneath his cloak. Situation resolved, he turned and walked to the double doors. He had more important things to deal with than a Chosen with an oversized sense of himself.

"Wait," he heard the Noble call.

"What do you want?" he replied without turning around. Any delay was time away from Notus and their freedom.

"It seems that we are in a similar situation."

Slowly turning, he waited for the inevitable continuation. He did not like Fernando. He crossed his arms, face impassive as de Sagres continued unabated.

Fernando smiled. He could forgive the Angel for denying his pleasure. It had proved one point. The Angel was soft hearted for the mortals. Unfortunately, it did not explain why. That would have to come later if he could convince the Angel to work together. He loathed the idea, but it offered too many opportunities, and a greater chance of success.

"We both want what Katherine took from us, and to do that we have to do this chore for her. Personally, I do not like having to be made to do anything, but she's got us by the jugular and I would like my things back. As I'm sure you would like your sire back. I do not like the idea of requiring assistance to get the job done, but I am neither a fool nor an idiot. This venture would have a greater chance for success if we teamed up. I do not wish to risk my possessions, nor my life for that matter. What do you say?"

He measured the Noble's words and the man before him. He did not trust this one. He was too much the Vampire, relishing in pain and fear. Any semblances to what a Chosen should be were not found in de Sagres. He must be one of the younger ones. Recognizing the merit of the words, if not the motive, he replied, "Are you proposing a partnership with me?"

"Yes, damn it. Didn't I just say that?" This was not the response

Fernando was expecting. In one simple question the Angel had manoeuvred dominance of the conversation into his corner and Fernando did not like that one bit.

"Why?" the Angel asked, dubious when it came to others wishing contact with him.

Fernando's face puckered in anger. "I told you why. If you do not wish to work together to get Katherine for what she's done to you that's fine. I'd probably do better on my own than with one such as you." He strode forcefully towards the door and abruptly halted when the Angel did not move. The Noble glared up into red eyes that momentarily flashed with pain before settling into burning anger. This time Fernando did not back down from the flaming eyes.

"I did not say I would not work with you." The Angel's voice was cold, hiding his anger.

"Get to the point." Somewhere inside, Fernando smiled at his victorious return of control.

"If it will free Notus faster than it would be prudent to work together."

"Are you now asking for my help?" This time Fernando did smile a sadistic lopsided grin.

"No," he stated flatly.

"Ahh, I thought not, but no matter. The point is made. You and I will work together." Fernando's smile disappeared to be replaced with a look of great concentration and he walked to stand in the middle of the room. Turning abruptly to face his new, yet strange partner, he tapped a jewelled finger to his chin. "I don't suppose you have any idea where to start?"

Realizing that he too had no clue where to begin, he frowned. He had nearly stumbled into the night almost expecting the answers to present themselves in a neat little package, and silently cursed himself for a fool.

Dark brown brows rose in wonderment. Fernando let his arm drop to his side. "Well?" Accustomed as he was to having a one-sided conversation, the Noble did not like it when answers to his questions when unspoken, and the Angel's lack of communication was starting to become irritating.

He sighed; the condescension in the Noble's voice did not go unnoticed and he returned it. "I do not suppose that you have any ideas."

Loud boisterous laughter rang through the room, surprising him. He could not imagine what was so funny. Fernando confused him. In a short span of time he had witnessed his newest unwanted companion run a gambit of emotions that he, himself, never dreamed of displaying so openly.

"Don't look so surprised, my pale friend." Fernando wiped a tear from his eye, his laughter coming to a jittery halt. "I guess we both don't have a clue. Shall we be like Holmes and Watson and search London for the man with the limp?" Boisterous laughter exploded again and was quickly suppressed at the incredulous look on the Angel's face. "No, I didn't think so."

Fernando sobered, frowned and flung wide his arms, his cloak billowed behind. "This situation is ridiculous! Preposterous! Totally insane!" With a snap of cloth the cloak wrapped around Fernando and he strode towards the Angel and the door.

Completely bewildered, he stepped back away from the Noble.

Slamming open the door, Fernando stated icily, "She will not get away with this," and glanced up at him. "Let's go. We have some planning to attend to."

In stunned silence, he followed de Sagres outdoors to stand between the guards. He kept his eyes on the Portuguese Chosen and felt as if he were on a chain, being jerked this way and that, and resented it. His frown deepened at the flicker of amusement that sparked Fernando's brown eyes. Following the gaze, he discovered the reason for the shift in Fernando's malleable façade, and clenched his jaw in rising anger.

Turning his head over his shoulder to look up at the Angel, Fernando smiled. "Something to wash away the bad taste of this evening?"

Before he could restrain his newly made partner Fernando raced down the steps with preternatural speed towards the girl under the lamppost.

Muttering a curse that Notus would have been furious to hear, he quickly followed, hoping to catch up before Fernando caught Jeanie. He pulled up behind the Noble in time to hear him say; "Now here's a tasty morsel if I've ever seen one."

He closed the large oaken doors to the theatre behind him with a click, noticing with a frown the large depression and cracks in the wood and turned to face the lobby. The paintings flickered alive in the dancing candlelight. Gruesome images looked ready to spring from framed canvas, and indeed one seemed to jump right at him. It startled him and he leapt to correct its angle. His hand paused momentarily as he stared into the demons red eyes, and wished he could cross himself for protection from his very real imagination, but the painting hung no threat to his rational mind.

Turning from the painting, he noticed the doors to the outside had been left open. He would have to deal with those two simpletons most appropriately. Excellent guards they were, they still would not open or close the doors.

Maybe I will have to requisition a doorman, he sighed and walked to close the doors.

Absently, he gazed up from the brass knob, his eyes falling upon the two Chosen standing across the street with the girl.

This would not do. Not do at all.

He watched the trio a moment longer and then slowly closed the doors.

ʊí

eanie spun around, startled at the sudden sound of the unknown voice, to face a swarthy man who stood only a little taller than she. She had not heard his approach, nor the Angel's who stood beside this stranger.

Angry crimson eyes momentarily flashed from beneath his cowl and Jeanie felt an emptiness in her stomach that made her ill.

There was no choice in the matter; Fernando had to be dealt with. The Angel could not allow the Noble to let the secret he and Notus had hidden from Jeanie all these years to slip out. Then again how was Fernando to know that this girl was something more than prey?

The look on Jeanie's face also did not pass his notice as he took it all in with cool anger. Granted, he was slightly impressed that she was able to follow him for there was no other explanation for her presence, but it proved that he had to be more careful. It was too easy to become lax on survival skills learned long ago.

Before Fernando could make good on his threat, he stated coolly, "What are you doing here, Jeanie?"

"You know this whore?" asked Fernando, gazing up at the tall Chosen in surprise.

"I'm no' a whore!" answered Jeanie, infuriated that she was accused of such twice in one night. Any feelings of dread flew from her to be replaced with the familiar Scots temper. She gazed harshly at the stranger, wishing she could burn him with her eyes. Instead he rocked slowly on his heels, his brown eyes rose in mild amusement. The Angel was, as usual, unreadable.

"Yes, I know Jeanie," he answered, "She's the housekeeper."

"Keeping her for a nice light snack?" Fernando replied, impressed with the Angel and with Notus for keeping such a beauty and then recoiled at the intensity of their combined glares. "What? I'm just sorry that I didn't think of it first. A nice tasty morsel like her would quench any Va—"

His final word was abruptly cut off as he was slammed into the brick wall of the building next to the lamppost. The fine cloth of his cloak pressed against rough stone promised to tear. He had not seen the Angel move. He did not know one of their own could move *that* fast. Fernando had the supernatural speed of their kind, but what the Angel seemed to possess went beyond.

Recovering his shock, Fernando gazed into burning eyes as the Angel held him firmly in place by the lapels. Somewhere behind, the Noble heard the girl's astonished cry. Bearing his sharpened teeth, Fernando smiled and tried unsuccessfully to grab his daggers sheathed at the small of his back. This indignation would not go unremembered.

Ignoring Jeanie's cries, the Angel leaned close to the Noble's face. The flash of amusement did not go unnoticed and nor did Fernando's attempts to reach the hidden blades. He had no choice; de Sagres had forced his hand. Making sure that Jeanie would not hear, he whispered, "Do not ever state or imply, in front of her, that we are Chosen, Vampires or whatever you call yourself. She knows nothing. She is not to find out." With that he let go.

Fernando stumbled at the sudden release and caught himself. Swearing under his breath, he hastily righted his attire, smoothing out the wrinkles from the Angel's white grip. The girl had stopped her ravings to stare at the newcomer in astonishment. Fernando took this all in, even noticing how pretty the girl truly was and matched the Angel's glare with one of his own.

"Who the hell do you think you are dictating the rules to me?" the Noble stated icily. "I am the one who makes the rules. I am the last heir to the Fidalgo de Sagres. What are you? An anomaly of nature!"

Opening his mouth to reply, the Angel heard Jeanie pipe up, her ire up. Surprised, he let her continue knowing that once started no one, not even Notus, could quiet her. A smile twitched and was gone.

"How dare ye? D'ye even ken who ye are talkin' to? Who do ye ken ye are? No wait. Ye're the last 'ear to the Feedalgo dee Sargase." Her Scottish accent, thick with anger, warped the Portuguese title.

"That's Sagres." Fernando glared at her impudence.

"Sagres. Sargase. What's the difference?" She thrust out her chin defiantly.

"The difference is in the pronunciation," he stated coldly. Fernando looked over at the Angel, scowling at the hint of amusement on the pale face. "She's your housekeeper. Keep her out of my way, because if you do not control her, I will."

"She is not my housekeeper," he replied, amusement gone. "She does as she wills and I cannot, nor will not, force her to anything." He gazed down into her wide green eyes. "She has already proved this," he sighed.

Jeanie's face brightened into a smile, making him uncomfortably warm.

Reluctantly, he pulled his eyes off her beautiful face and back to Fernando's scowling features.

The Angel did not like the threatening expression on de Sagres' face. "And you will not do anything to her either."

Fernando's scowl deepened, his eyes flickered with anger. No one told him what he could or could not do, and he resented the Angel for trying, but he would wait, bide his time, an immortals lifetime if necessary. Gathering his cloak around his broad muscled body, he strode up to his new partner without sparing the girl as much as a glance. "Never tell me what to do and I will spare this low born gutter swipe—" he flicked his eyes in Jeanie's direction "—from my charms."

Ignoring the fuming girl, the Noble swung around and stalked down the lane, his heels clicking loudly on stone. "Are you coming or are you not?" he called without turning or halting.

"Don't." The Angel laid his hand on Jeanie's shoulder to still her from bolting after the Noble. He could feel the anger shuddering through her, and somehow sensed her need to go and tear a strip off of Fernando. He understood the feeling and released the tight fist of his other hand. There were reasons why he stayed away from the other Chosen, and Fernando proved part of the rule.

Shrugging off his touch, Jeanie spun around. "Were those only words ye spoke just a minute ago? Or are ye now a liar?"

Suddenly weary of all the confrontations, he closed his eyes and shook his head. He wanted this fiasco to be over with. He wanted Notus back safe and to be left alone to do as he wished, but the strings kept tugging him. Now he had to keep Jeanie safe from all this madness. "Do as you will, but I *will* see to it that you are kept safe."

The anger guttered out of Jeanie's eyes and she allowed him to guide her down the lane and back onto the street. She hardly needed protection, living over a pub had its own hazards, but she felt oddly comforted that he wanted to do this for her. No one had before. She glanced up to notice that beneath his hood he looked down trodden, that something was wrong, and then it hit her; the reason for tonight.

"Where's the Good Father?" she blurted. "Ye were supposed t' have gotten him back."

He looked away.

"Where is he?" she forced them to a halt.

Images of Notus' beaten and drained body suspended in a cruel mockery of Christ's crucifixion flashed into his mind along with the Mistress' victorious smile, making him wince.

"I could not get him back," he whispered. *I failed him,* but he could not say this.

"Then we must go to the Bobbies." Her voice rose in panic.

"No." He shook his head. Bringing the police would not only endanger Notus, but most likely set a war of mortal against immortal – something that must never happen.

"Then how d'ye propose to get the Good Father back? Oh God, he isna dead?" Her hand flew to her face, covering her mouth. "Ye're no' saying he's dead? Oh God, I—"

"He is not dead," he blurted more in denial of the possibility. Her panic was beginning to affect him. Her exquisite face was full of fear. "He is being held hostage," he stated. Trying to regain control of emotions threatening to break free, he guided them to resume their pace. "I have to do something to get him back."

"Then I'll help."

He shook his head, sparking a flicker of anger in Jeanie.

"Ye said—"

"I know what I said," he cut her off. He was in no mood for any more arguments. "There is a chance that if I fail not only will I be dead, but so will Notus. I also said I will keep you safe and that means I will drop you off at your place and you will stay there."

She opened her mouth to protest, but he quickly interrupted her. "I cannot afford to be distracted by the possibility of you getting hurt," he said, softly.

"It's that bad?" asked Jeanie, gazing down at the stones she stepped on. The fire was squashed before it took full light. Now that the reality of the situation seemed to present itself, danger or no, she wanted – needed – to help. "I dinna care. I want t' help. Ye said that ye would no stop me from doin' what I will. Well, I will help ye whether ye will it or no. I dinna want another fight. I just want t'help. The Good Father has done so much for me. I just want to do something to repay him. Please?"

They walked in silence, Jeanie's plea hung heavily between them. Her desire to assist could not be dismissed as she waited for his answer. He frowned. Her need was so much like his own that he glanced at her as she watched the cobblestones. Her hair bounced and flew around her face, creating a fiery halo, and he knew in that instant that he wanted her near him, no matter the cost, and that frightened him.

Gazing into the gas lit illuminated night, he whispered, "Alright." Jeanie jerked her head up, green eyes wide with surprise and quickly closed her mouth. He continued on without looking at her. "I do not know how you can help, but you have to listen to me, to do as I say and not argue." Jeanie opened her mouth and quickly shut it. "It is for your own safety."

"Tell me what's goin' on," she asked, bringing her gaze to Fernando's fluttering cloak far ahead of them. She knew in the way he spoke, the Angel's impassive mask was back in place, and cursed it.

"I cannot. I have told you everything I can. To tell you more will put you in greater danger and I will not allow that. All you need to know is that Notus is being held hostage until Fernando and I ..." he trailed off with a sigh. "You are just going to have to trust me. I cannot answer all your questions."

A frown formed on Jeanie's face as they walked in silence. The only sounds were their footfalls and the occasional horse drawn carriage clattering down the street so late in the night.

"Can ye tell me one thing?" she whispered, breaking the silence. "If ye do, I'll agree to yer terms."

He tilted his head expectantly.

"How is it," she cautiously continued, "that ye would be so strangely paired with a Priest? I've never heard of a Priest living with and being so close with someone not of the cloth. Ye two are as different as night is to day, and yet, are close like father and son."

The query caught him off guard. He had not expected it and glanced away from her searching eyes.

"He saved me once, a very long time ago," he whispered.

Silence crashed between them, isolating them to their own private thoughts. Jeanie wished to alleviate the tension by pressing the issue. She had discovered more about the Angel this night than in the years of being the housekeeper. Now she yearned to know more. Her next question died on her lips before a word could be uttered as a wild carriage hurtled thunderously down the street towards Fernando, and at them.

Fernando leapt out of the way, barely missing the burlap bag that flew at him and landing on the cobbles with a wet smack.

Not as neatly as the Noble, he shoved Jeanie out of the foaming horse's path. Jeanie landed painfully on her rear with a cry to watch the Angel leap, roll and come quickly to his feet in a blur of motion, safe, and out of the way. He stood absolutely still, poised for another attempt. When the carriage did not return he realized that his hood had slipped, revealing his pale white features, and hastily flipped up the concealing fabric.

Reams of unintelligible cursing spewed forth from the Noble, and in one hand a blade flashed menacingly. The dark stained burlap bag lay ignored at his feet. Words finally spent, Fernando gazed down at what had almost hit him and frowned.

"Are you unharmed?" The Angel held out his hand to Jeanie. Even rumpled from the fall she still captivated him as her warm hand slipped into his.

"Aye." She noted the cool softness of his fingers as he gently lifted her to her feet.

He's always so cold, she silently remarked. "Thank ye."

Jeanie glanced up at his hidden eyes and realized they were but a breath apart. The light from the lamp shadowed all but his perfectly full pale lips. Heat rose, flushing her cheeks as she wondered what it would be like to kiss those lips. Instead she backed away, allowing her hand to slip from his. Head and shoulders taller than herself, she let her eyes fall on his cloaked chest and turned away.

He drank in her yearning eyes and followed the heart shaped curve of her jaw to the quickening vessel on her neck, tantalizing him with each pulse and was relieved when she pulled away and turned her back. He did not know what to make of what he saw in her face. He had not seen that look directed at him in such a very, very long time.

Frowning at her back, he turned his attention to the Noble now crouched down using his blade to pick at the bag. The strong scent of blood filled his nostrils, drawing him forward. Jeanie hesitantly followed on shaky legs, the object of curiosity catching her. They both stood over Fernando who paid them no mind.

"If you are so damned interested, why don't you just ask?" spat Fernando, still fuming from the near miss. Frustrated, he dropped the knife to lay, blade leaning, on the crumpled burlap bag and stood, his hands coming to rest on his hips, causing his cloak to spread out like black wings.

"If you expect me to do all the work, you have another thing coming," he sneered. "I usually demand servitude." His eyes flashed momentarily on the girl. "And since fate has tossed us together, may I suggest that you understand that."

With a growl Fernando bent his knees to crouch down once more before the bag, a half smile curled his lips when the Angel joined him on the cobbles. Only the girl remained standing.

The rest of Fernando's smile flourished as he took up his blade and resumed the examination. "What do you think? A clue? A warning? An accident? One thing is certain this is not the blood of an animal. Shall we open the wrapping and see what the present is?" A glint of mischievousness flashed in his smile.

Manoeuvring his cloak over his shoulders to free his hands, he and the Noble worked together at the gruesome task, carefully pushing and pulling to finally reveal the treasure from the blood soaked burlap. He ignored Jeanie's strangled cry and pursed his own colourless lips at the sight. Only Fernando seemed unaffected by the severed arm, the hand in a fist set tight in death.

Careful not to allow the gore to ruin his clothing, Fernando lifted the limb to study the only ornamentation beside the blood. The ring gleamed gold and blood, and with an expletive the Noble tossed the arm back onto the burlap, splattering crimson droplets around it. He spun away from the sight.

"Shit!" he exploded over and over as he paced. Abruptly, he turned and resumed his place by the severed limb and said, "Do you know who this is …was?"

Mystified, the Angel shook his head.

Taking up the dismembered arm, Fernando gazed at the ring. "Sebastian," he said vehemently. "Sebastian von Hausen. The most sadistic individual among the—you know." His tone softened somewhat. "Half of Bridget's whores are branded with this signet. He would have gotten the rest of the mortal ones, but Bridget put an end to it when she found out."

Ignoring the slight slip, he suppressed his disgust. "You sound as if you envied him."

"Envy? No. Never that." Fernando gave the Angel a sidelong gaze. "Admire, yes. He always had more imagination than I."

Revolted by the Noble's admission, the Angel stood and wrapped his cloak tightly around him and noticed Jeanie leaning heavily against the lamp, beads of sweat dotting her brow. Her heartbeat rapidly pulsed in his ears. Glancing down at the Noble, who as now trying to figure out how to get the ring off, he wiped his soiled hands on his cloak, turned and strode over to her.

Her eyes fluttered open to see his cloaked figure standing before her. "I guess it was a good thing I dinna have any dinner." She gave a half-hearted laugh and then swallowed thickly, wiping her forehead with the back of her arm.

"You don't look well," he said softly, unable to keep the worry from filtering through his veneer. "I am going to take you back to your room." Jeanie opened her mouth to protest but quickly shut it as he raised a bone white finger. "If you are still intent on joining us," he continued, "you can meet me at my home after sunset tomorrow. Is that agreeable?"

Recognizing defeat, she nodded. "Aye. It is."

Leaning the back of her head against the lamppost she shut her eyes. "I believed myself to be able to deal with anything, ye ken? After that first night here, so long ago, I could withstand anything, but this...ye said it would be bad, did ye ken it would be this bad?"

He glanced quickly at Fernando who had managed to open the hand and was now pondering a small phial between his thumb and forefinger. Warning or clue, the wild carriage and the bag with Sebastian's arm was no accident, and whoever had done this to one of the Chosen meant serious business. Looking back at Jeanie, he realized he could not tell her it was worse than he first expected.

Opening her eyes, Jeanie stood without support of the post. "What is that smell?" She inhaled deeply. "It's delicious."

Astounded at her complete change of demeanour, he blinked in confusion and inhaled. The ever so slight scent that Jeanie so easily picked up made him gag. It was the worst thing he had ever smelled. Taking another whiff, he realized the direction the scent came, from Fernando and the now open phial. Following their noses, he and Jeanie walked towards the Noble. The sight of the dismembered arm no longer adversely affected Jeanie. For some strange reason Fernando seemed unaffected.

"Do you have any idea what this is?" Fernando stood. Sebastian's signet decorated his outstretched hand, open phial raised.

The source of the smell, so close, forced him to jerk his head away and take a retreating step.

"Oh come now," exasperated Fernando.

"You smell it," he interrupted, his voice muffled with the edge of his cloak.

"Ye're acting as if it'll bite ye," piped Jeanie. She moved to take the little bottle from Fernando, but he pulled it away from her grasp. Jeanie cocked her head and pursed her lips. "Ye dinna hae t'do that. We can share it. Whatever it is."

Screwing up his face, Fernando said, "I do not think so," and deeply inhaled the aroma from the lip of the bottle.

It was all that Jeanie could do to catch the phial before it fell as Fernando's mouth once more issued forth unintelligible expletives.

His hand covering his mouth and nose did not dissuade the smell, now imbedded in his nostrils. "*Meu Deus*! That is the most disgusting—Ugh! I can't even get it out of my nose!" Whipping out a finely embroidered hand-kerchief, Fernando blew his nose and looked at Jeanie who was now inhaling the contents with great sighs. "Do you mind if I cap that?" he asked, sarcastically.

Jeanie's dilated eyes opened and clutched the bottle to her breast protectively. "Aye!"

"Give it to me," said the Angel. He figured that the less he spoke the less he would have to breathe that sickening smell. It was strange that Jeanie had picked up the scent before their preternatural senses could.

Blinking rapidly, Jeanie hesitantly handed it to him.

The phial was standard medical issue, yet the label glued lopsidedly on it had only a series of numbers that did not make any sense. Tipping the mouth over his white palm, he tapped a small portion of the brownish-green powder and was instantly glad that he too had not had any dinner that evening. Whatever consisted within the powder was vile.

Spilling the contents onto the ground, he rubbed his hand against his cloak, praying that the scent would wash off. He did not want to go through the hassle of having another cloak tailored.

"Seal it," he stated, handing it back to Fernando who was more than willing to be compliant to the order.

"Why did ye do that?" implored Jeanie.

"What do you mean?" he replied.

"Why did ye waste it?"

"I did not waste anything. I had to see what was in it."

"Better you than me," butted in Fernando, slipping the sealed bottle into a vest pocket.

He frowned at the Noble and turned his attention back to Jeanie. "What would you have me do? Put it back? And since your appetite has returned, I am returning you to the inn."

"But— " stammered Jeanie.

"It looks like it'll be the boys night out," mocked Fernando. "Unless you wish to be dinner."

He shot the Noble a pointed glare and grabbed Jeanie's arm, careful not to squeeze too hard, and walked her down the street.

Ignoring her protests, he let go when it was clear she was going to keep pace. Fernando walked at his side, a smirk on his dark features. He welcomed the silence and the relief to Jeanie's constant arguments and Fernando's—well, Fernando's attitude was almost expected. *Now why is that?* He strained to remember but only flashes of finely dressed people from another time floated in his mind.

Somewhere in the distance a bell rang the hour and, as if on some predetermined plan, a light misting rain began. Jeanie sighed and pulled the neck of her coat tighter while Fernando grumbled, shrouding his head with his hood. Hunkered in the depths of his cloak, the Angel was not affected by the rain.

It did not take long for the streets to become slick with water, reflecting gaslight back up into the darkness above, making the night seem brighter. Even the sounds of sleepy horse's hooves hitting cobbles seemed louder and clearer. No other wild rides threatened them. Everything felt lazy and he was momentarily surprised to hear Jeanie break the silence.

"We left that…um…arm back there. Should we do somethin' about it?" She wiped the beads of water from her brow. Her fiery hair was alight with clear pearls.

"The police will find it," lied Fernando. Both Chosen knew that once the daylight touched the arm and the blood soaked bag, all that would remain would be ashes. "Let them do their job."

Jeanie glanced quickly at the Noble and without another word silence over took them again.

It was not long before they came upon *The Rose and Thorn*. The rain teetered the sign out front. An old inn, the Angel remembered it being there before the Great Fire. Totally destroyed, it was rebuilt by the surviving family and handed down from father to son or son-in-law. Each generation left their mark upon the place with subtle modernizations. Now Tom ran the inn with his wife Alice, who issued orders with her large wooden spoon.

"Go," he said to Jeanie.

She gazed up at him, her eyes wide with the realization that the Angel meant exactly what he said.

"Come tomorrow night, half seven, and we will see how you can help," he stated before she could reply. His voice softened, "Tonight get some food and rest."

He watched Jeanie turn and hesitate with her hand on the door before pushing it open, allowing warm yellow light to spill momentarily onto the street before disappearing, taking Jeanie with it.

"That was nicely done," commented the Noble, a smile on his face. "To keep a mortal girl—and a beauty at that—around. I think I like her quiet and demure. Her tongue takes away her lusciousness."

He spun around. He did not like Fernando's implications.

"Oh come now," irritation perked Fernando's speech. "You must have noticed. She is a delicious sight. Another time perhaps? We have some work to do, I believe." He walked back the way they had come.

Allowing his eyes to linger for one last moment on the doors of *The Rose and Thorn*, he turned to catch up with the Nobel.

I have noticed, he sighed.

He hoped she would be safe. The more he could keep her out of it the better. He could not afford to have his attention divided.

ᘎíí

Being around that girl has sparked my hunger," stated Fernando after a time. "And I do not feel in the mood for—ahhh perfect."

Watching Fernando approach the two prostitutes regaining their positions on the street corner, the Angel's hunger flared. He did not need to feed as often as a newly made Chosen. At his age the hunger depended on how much he exerted his abilities, and in this day and age that was not often nor excessive, leaving him to feed once every week or so. It had been that long since the last time he hunted London's streets with Notus.

By the time he reached the girls, Fernando already had his arm around one of them, leading her off into a nearby alley. He loathed the idea of feeding off of someone not causing anyone harm, but the hunger flared within at the scent of the young woman's blood, demanding its due. He would satiate it, but this was not the hunt he relished.

Pulling the hood low over his brow so as to shadow his unique features, the short, dark haired woman looked up at his approach. Closing her mouth, obviously astonished at the short wait for a new customer, she checked herself, patting and smoothing out the wrinkles in her stained brown skirt.

He stopped, the hood shading eyes and hair, and asked, "Are you for hire?" He had done this a thousand times, if not more, over the ages, yet he still did not like the need for it.

"Yea, 'ow much ye willin' t' spend?" she replied, gazing up with a false sultry smile.

"That depends on how much you charge," he whispered. No, he did not like what his need for blood could drive him to do. He wished for the forest hunts or the battlefield where everything seemed fair.

"Two pounds fo' quarter of an 'our. Five fo' 'alf an 'our." She placed a short wide hand on her hip.

He raised a snow coloured brow at the increased prices. "Quarter of an hour will be sufficient," he replied.

"Quick like a rabbit, wot?" she smiled, offering her hand and was unaware of the cold touch as he brought it to his lips.

Bending to kiss her warm hand so filled with life, his hood slipped to reveal the whiteness of his hair and the unnatural colour of his eyes. Her gasp and attempt to flee were cut short as he locked her eyes to his.

Whispering, he Pushed, *"You will not remember any part of this night. You will not remember me. You will feel no pain."*

Mumbling his words back at him, proving his glamour over her to be complete, he gently bit into her wrist in a mockery of the first kiss. The flesh gave way to his sharp teeth. Her heart carried the sweet blood to his mouth as he fought the urge to suck—an urge that would surely kill such a weak creature as she—until her heart slowed to a plodding rhythm.

Pulling out, satiated, he left her alive, but drained. Carefully, he assisted her to sit at the curb and placed a five-pound note in her hand. He folded the flaccid fingers shut, securing the bill in her possession as he kissed the crown of her filthy head. She sat there, blinking and sighing as if she had run a great distance.

He heard Fernando clear his throat and turned around to find the Nobel looking quite confused.

"You kissed her on the head?"

"Yes," he answered, walking to the Noble, suddenly uncomfortable that a Chosen other than Notus had seen him feed.

"You paid her?" Fernando kept pace with the Angel as they left the street corner.

He nodded.

"And you let her live?"

Again he nodded with a sigh.

"I'm not going to ask. I don't want to know." Fernando shook his head in disbelief. Turning down the lane, he declared, "Let's go. We don't have all night."

This time Fernando had to wait for the Angel to follow. Biting his lip, the Noble absently led the way. More and more aspects of the Angel bothered him, got under his skin, to a point he had never thought possible. Even the Angel's pale appearance and blood coloured eyes sent unconscious shivers up his spine. Fernando appreciated beauty in women and in men; his preference was always for the ladies, but the Angel's features were more androgynous, lending to a strange beauty that unnerved him. *What the hell is he?*

"You killed her." Despite its hard edge, the Angel's voice was soft and sensuous.

Fernando glanced sideways. The Angel still faced straight ahead. "She is…was…nothing more than a titillating treat." He ignored the angry glare. "Oh come now, mortals are rabbits to us wolves. They have no value except for the blood they contain and the service they provide."

He brought his stare away from the Noble. He had heard this many times and it still bothered him. "Did you believe this when you were mortal?"

Brown eyes became menacing. "Do not trifle with me," sneered the Noble. "There is too much at stake."

"To be trifled with is a small matter compared with how you view mortals." The Angel's voice reflected the impassivity of his well-devised mask.

Deciding to turn the tables, Fernando stated, "They have value to you. Why?" His eyes widened with insight. "That's why that whore…that housekeeper, what's-her-name?"

"Jeanie."

"Whatever," dismissed Fernando with a wave of his hand. "But the best way to see something's value is to have it taken away." He glanced up at the Angel. "Yet we both know this, do we not? Katherine is exploiting this even now. Do you not miss the day? The sun at high noon with its heat pressing down, lighting up everything in its brilliance? You value their mortality, the ability to walk in the sunlight, to live a mortal life. I refuse to regret anything, thus giving no value to them."

Praying that the Noble could not see how his words stung him, he could not stop himself from saying, "I never had the day," and stared into the black rain curtained sky.

Fernando blinked at the unexpected reply, a snippet of conversation with Bridget floated into his consciousness. One phrase lingered: *He was born a vampire.* Knowing this piece of gossip to be ludicrous left Fernando wondering. There were no others like the Angel, at least to his knowledge.

Peering up at his strange partner, he asked, "What are you?"

The question caught the Angel completely off guard, shattering his carefully constructed façade. Spinning around to face the Noble, he halted their progress. Slowly the horror in his face became hidden as pieces of the mask slowly knit together leaving only sadness in his crimson eyes. "You are the second Chosen in nearly fourteen hundred years to ask me that."

Fernando could only gape as the Angel turned to continue their journey. *Fourteen hundred!* His mind boggled at the antiquity of this vampire. If the Angel was that ancient, how old was his sire? His eyes widened further realizing that Katherine captured probably one of the oldest and strongest of their kind. His mouth still open in shock, Fernando shut it with a click and followed, taking the lead once again.

ANGEL OF DEATH

They walked in silence. The time crawled by. Row housing dark with sleeping occupants gave way to others where lights still flickered, and syncopating rowdy laughter joined boisterous music. Parties where money was as disposable as the champagne they drank. Defoliating trees reached skeletally to a velvet black embrace, searching for the moon that danced behind thick speeding clouds destined to unknown places. Cabs for private use lined the lanes. Sleepy drivers longing for their comfortable beds slept in their cabs or chatted congenially with each other, while others chose the comforting company of their horses.

The two Chosen walked unnoticed, watching everything around them.

Turning down yet another lane, he found his patience dwindling. How long have they been walking? Pulling out his pocket watch, he flipped the engraved golden lid. *Half past two!* He snapped it shut and put it back in his pocket. This was going on too long. Wherever Fernando was leading them, they could do it at a much faster pace and he decided to ask where they were going, a question he immediately kicked himself for not asking earlier.

"I have to deliver the bad news to someone who can possibly give us an explanation for Sebastian's current state." Fernando patted the pocket where the phial was securely tucked away. A grin painted itself across the Noble's face into something maniacal. "I think you are going to really like it there."

"Is it safe?" he asked, not knowing the answer, whether positive or not, would ease the sudden anxiety Fernando's tone evoked.

"Well," mused the Noble, "mostly safe. Don't worry. Would I let anything happen to you?" Turning another corner, he led them down into a cul-de-sac lined with three story detached homes.

He could only stare at the Noble, rejecting the statement immediately, yet allowed him to be led away by a most anxious and surprisingly, happy, Chosen. This in itself seemed to be a paradox, considering the news Fernando had conveyed. Shaking his head in disbelief, he came to stand beside the Noble now halted before the flagstone path to a very large home with most of its lights still on.

Preening off any dirt from the journey, Fernando motioned to his partner to follow him to the door. "Come on, we don't have all night."

He fell in behind as the Noble lifted the large brass knocker and let it fall with a resounding bang.

Nothing happened and then a loud clunk of a lock being thrown back replied, followed by the squeak of the hinges as the door opened to reveal the head of a brunette girl of about twelve.

"I'm sorry, sir, but we're closed." Her voice was small and nervous and her hazel eyes darted anxiously back and forth between the two strange men.

Fernando frowned, unused to this type of treatment. "Look dearie, it is obvious that you are new here, but I am an old close personal friend so take your pretty little ass and get her, now!"

The girl gasped in astonishment as the dark haired stranger easily forced the door open and strode in, the hooded man following close behind. She did not need to be told twice and darted towards the back of the large parlour, her sheer lingerie fluttering open to reveal soft pink curvaceous flesh.

"Madam!" she yelled in near hysterics. "There's two strange—"

"Do not fret, Juliet." A petite young woman, in the blossom of youth, dressed as if to receive an expected lover, walked from the kitchen. Her long blonde hair fell in waves that framed her china doll face. Ice blue eyes sparkled with satiated pleasure. "I know this dashing young man." Her voice was lascivious, made even more so by her thick French accent. "But I do not remember if he ever had such a tall friend."

Staring into the comforting darkness of his hood, the Angel wondered why he had considered trusting this rogue. To be brought to this whorehouse made him very uncomfortable, evoking memories he wished never to remember. Memories of being used and using others to fulfill a need he denied until Notus put a stop to it.

Fernando's smile returned at the opening of the familiar game. "And I do not remember you ever checking up on me or my associates."

Shocked at the reference to himself, he shot Fernando a look of surprise.

Fernando ignored the glance and gazed at the three nubile young women lounging on the plush deep furniture cascading the modern Victorian décor, recognizing them instantly as Chosen working the house. Judith, Anna and Beth each returned his smile.

"Someone has to keep an eye on you," stated the Madam, her sheer white shift slipped off one shoulder as she slinked over to the Noble, revealing soft pale perfect skin.

Fernando's eyes lingered momentarily on her alabaster neck before being drawn to her shapely breasts outlined in white silk.

"I see that you are keeping an eye on me as well," she laughed, a sound like morning birds.

"Ahh, but my dear," replied the Noble, huskily. "You are so much better to keep an eye on." He ran his hand from her neck down her chest to cup one of her perfect breasts, her nipple hardening under the soft fabric.

His unease growing, the Angel turned his gaze from the sight of Fernando and the Madam, feeling suddenly the intruder.

The Madam allowed Fernando's hand to linger and returned his smile. "Yes, that is true."

"And where is that infamous female hospitality you girls are supposed to offer?" Fernando asked, removing his hand.

"Please forgive me," she mocked, undoing the elaborate cloth hook on his cloak. The heavy material fell into the awaiting small arms of Juliet now standing behind him. Awkwardly, she folded it and laid it on the red velvet chair beside the door.

Leaning down, Fernando brushed the Madam's blonde tresses away from her ear and whispered, "I brought you a little surprise."

Confused, she frowned. A sight that did not take away from her delicate beauty, only enhanced it.

"And don't forget my friend here," added Fernando, speaking openly.

With a smile and a nod, she walked over to the tall stranger standing in the middle of the room, her professional smile back in place. "You must forgive me, *monsieur*. Fernando has again left me to introduce myself." She shot an annoyed glance at the Noble.

Fernando stared back, unimpressed.

He took a hasty retreating step as the Madam raised her silky hands to unfasten the ancient clasp of his cloak, his heart pounding at the idea of being exposed.

"Let me be the proper hostess, *s'il vous plait?*"

Trap sprung, he tilted his head and held his breath, reluctantly allowing her to try to undo the clasp. Her frown increased as her balance on her toes made her fumble on the Celtic styled broach. Not being able to let her embarrass herself, he took over; his hands brushing hers caused her to smile for real.

He did not want to take off the cloak—to reveal himself. He felt safe and secure in the draping that hid his unusual colouring, but he also knew that it would be rude to stay undercover. Notus had taught him that much.

Hesitantly, he turned the broach as the woman stated, "My name is Bridget, and this is my home, and you are?"

The clasp released its hold on the material, allowing the cloak to fall from his shoulders into Juliet's waiting arms, revealing his long white hair and ruby eyes. He swallowed nervously, waiting for the reaction that always went with this revelation.

"Oh my!" exclaimed Bridget, her smile widening to reveal her lengthened incisors and canine teeth.

The others gasped and stood up at the sight of the legend standing in their midst, giving credence to the rumours they had heard. Juliet backed into the door with a thud, her mouth gaping open and her eyes wide with fear, his cloak forgotten on the ground.

"Bridget," introduced Fernando, a mischievous smile curled his lips, "meet the Angel."

"I–I am so very pleased to finally meet you," she stammered, offering her hand. "I have heard so much about you."

He peered into Bridget's eyes that now seemed to sparkle without the help of candlelight. Movement caught his attention and he glanced to see Anna, Judith and Beth slowly moving towards him. The sight of their near nakedness made the pit of his stomach bottom out. Glancing back to the snickering Noble, he brought his attention back to Bridget, noticing her hand for the first time. He was trapped in a den of hungry lions.

Noticing the panic in his eyes, Bridget's smile softened and she lowered her hand. "Do not fret," she soothed. "You are safe here."

Clearing his throat, he willed his voice to work. What came out was controlled by the nervousness he felt. "Fernando said that…that you may have…um…some information."

The three girls circled closer, like vultures waiting for him to die.

Bridget glanced over to the Noble, her brows furrowed in wondering. "What information, *mon petit chou*?"

It was obvious that she was disappointed, but why? He did not even want to hazard a guess.

The smile left Fernando's face at the mention of the pet name, to be replaced by a scowl. He crossed his arms over his chest. "*O Grande Puta*, we need your infinite wisdom," he implored sarcastically.

Blue eyes smouldered and she barked, "*Vas t'en!*"

At first the Angel thought she meant he and Fernando, but the girls jumped at her order and quickly vacated the parlour, their bare feet whispering up the stairs. Little Juliet needed no further encouragement to sprint after them, her feet thumping loudly.

"I've told you before, don't ever call me that!" shouted Bridget, spinning around to face the Noble. Her silk shift swirled around her body as she turned towards the couches and sat down.

"Fine," stated Fernando. "As long as you drop that phoney accent. We're not customers, Bridget." He landed heavily in a plush burgundy chair set across from her, leaving the Angel standing.

Shifting in her seat, Bridget spoke to him, her accent gone. "You must excuse my fledgling." Fernando scowled. "Please sit." She patted the brocade beside her.

Bridget was Fernando's Chooser? He blinked at the revelation. It seemed they did not even like each other. Shaking his head to clear it, he moved to sit nervously beside the nearly naked Chosen. The pale curve of her breast plainly evident under the plunging neckline made it difficult for him to tear his gaze away.

Despite his hesitancy, Bridget smiled at the way he moved, like a predator, lean with sinewy strength. She laid her small delicate hand on his. "Now, tell me why the Angel has deigned to appear at my humble abode. And it is not because Fernando thought you would like to sample my wares. Though how you and he know one another still eludes me." Her eyes locked onto his large expressive crimson eyes and smiled. No one had ever told her that the Angel was beautiful.

Disgusted at the spectacle, Fernando stood up. "That's enough!" he stomped up before her like a petulant child.

Languidly, she turned her head to stare up at him.

"You want to know why we're here? Here!" Fernando fumbled with the ring on his finger and dropped it into her lap.

The ring was heavy yet Bridget twirled it around a slim finger. The recognition of the signet made her gasp.

"Where did you get this?" she exclaimed, standing up. Even though she was shorter than the Noble she was still able to stare him down.

"We found it." His dark brown eyes shadowed over. "Or more to the point, it found us."

"Where? Sebastian would never take this ring off." Her voice rose in volume and power.

"He didn't," taunted Fernando, obviously enjoying his Chooser's growing anxiety.

"What are you talking about, Fernando?"

He just smiled, his eyes alighting with something more sinister.

"Stop playing with me," ordered Bridget.

"I took it off his finger after his dismembered arm was dumped at my feet." Fernando ignored the accusatory glare. "Such genius is now lost, the likes of which we'll never see again."

"He...he's dead?" Her eyes widened in disbelief.

Fernando hitched a shoulder.

Staring down at the ring hanging heavily around her finger, she murmured, "He would never take this ring off. He said he would rather die first." She shot her head up to glare at the Noble. "You're lying. This is all some elaborate hoax. Some disgusting trick to—"

"No, it is not." The Angel's voice was soft, yet penetrated the tension. He recognized the fear in Bridget's eyes as she shifted to face him, and understood it. Anger mixed with fear and sadness. Loss. He could not allow Fernando to play with her any longer. "Fernando does not lie." He stood, towering over both of them. "It is as he stated. Only you know for certain if Sebastian is dead."

She stared up into strangely sympathetic eyes; her own shimmered with unshed tears. She had heard of the Angel and shared in whispering the stories, but none had revealed what she saw in his eyes.

With a nod she closed her eyes and opened herself to connect with her Chooser. It had been so long since they were intimate this way, but the connection had always been there for her to follow the threads back to him if necessary. This time there was nothing. No hint of his presence. No sense of his feelings. No words of his thoughts. There was nothing. He no longer existed.

Gasping at the disconnection, Bridget opened her eyes. Ignoring Fernando's bemused expression she hastily wiped her eyes with a trembling hand. "I guess I should have expected as much," she murmured. "I never thought I'd feel this way about him. Will you feel this way when I'm gone, Fernando? I think not. Oh, don't look so hurt. Remember, I know how you feel about our relationship."

"And you never let me forget it," snorted the Noble. He began to pace, uncomfortable with her reminder.

"How did Sebastian die?" she asked, refusing to be diverted into Fernando's semantic games and brought her attention to the Angel who stood strangely still.

"I thought you might know," snapped Fernando. "After all, you're Sebastian's whelp."

Her eyes froze over. "Just because he is…was… my Chooser, does not mean I know everything about him, and just because I'm yours does not mean you know everything about me. Now, if this was the reason why you came, you can leave."

"No, we're not done. I want to know what Sebastian was into that got him killed."

"What do you care, Fernando?" exploded Bridget. "You only care about yourself."

"True," smiled the Noble. "And it is for that reason that you are going to answer my question. What was Sebastian up to?"

"Alright," she sighed. "You might as well sit. I don't want to get a kink in my neck."

"I knew you cared about me," gloated Fernando as he retook the chair, leaving a surprised and confused Angel to sit on the couch with Bridget.

Shooting a scowl at her Chosen, Bridget began, "Several months ago Sebastian came over. I thought it extremely strange that he didn't want to go with one of the girls and instead wanted to sit and talk with me, something he had never done. He seemed edgy, very worried, definitely not himself. I would have thought him scared to death if I hadn't known him better. Can you imagine it, Fernando? Sebastian afraid?" The Noble shook his head. "So I opened myself up to him—something I do not like to do— and found a terrifying fear. I asked what was wrong. He wouldn't say because he didn't want to endanger my life. My life. I was astounded. He actually displayed genuine affection, something I had never experienced from him. All he said was that if others came after him I should dissuade them. Then he left, saying he had to go. When I asked him where, he mumbled sadly, 'I miss fish,' and left." She glanced from Fernando to the Angel. "Do you know what he meant?"

The Angel shook his head, frowning at her words.

"Did Katherine summon Sebastian to her?" asked Fernando.

Staring at the ring held in her lap, Bridget pouted in thought. After a moment she lifted her head. "Why yes, come to think of it, he was summoned."

"When?" pressed the Noble.

"I believe it was about a week or two before he last came to me. Why?"

Staring at the rug, refusing to meet Bridget or Fernando's eyes, the Angel sighed. *Because if he was summoned for the same reasons as us, then she was telling the truth and someone is killing the Chosen, and we are probably their next targets.*

Dismissing her question with a wave of his hand, Fernando continued. "Did Sebastian tell you Katherine's reasons?"

Bridget shook her head, confused as to where this was leading.

Taking the phial out of his vest pocket, Fernando tossed it to his sire.

"Do you have any idea what this is?"

Bridget frowned at the little glass bottle and its askew label and opened it, taking a whiff before the Angel could stop her. The smell exploded into the room, causing Bridget to swoon.

Trying not to breathe, the Angel quickly stoppered the bottle.

Bridget came to with a choked gasp. "What is that stuff?" she coughed.

"I had hoped you would have been able to tell us," said Fernando, unconcerned with his sire's collapse.

"I've never smelled anything so horrible. Why do you ask?" She waved a hand at the phial now in the Angel's possession.

"It was in Sebastian's grip."

Bridget shook her head in dismay. "He must have gotten it after he left me. Why would anyone do this to Sebastian? Oh, don't tell me. I know how he could be. But to kill a vampire of his age? What is going on Fernando?"

With closed eyes, the Noble sighed and told her about the poisoning of the blood supply and how he and the Angel were forced into finding out the culprits of the caper.

When he finished there was a long moment of silence, broken only with Bridget's soft whisper, "Fernando, would you stay the day? I don't want to be alone right now."

A gentle smile softened the Noble's features and he nodded.

Realizing that the end of the night was approaching, the Angel stood. "I should be going."

"You don't have to," offered Bridget. "You could stay here."

The offer and her generosity took him off guard and he glanced from Chosen to Chooser. "No. I should go home." He walked towards the door, found his cloak and put it on.

"In that case," she followed, "please let me call you a cab. I'll have my personal driver take you home."

Bridget pulled on the bell-pull next to the front door and turned to face the Angel. "You are most welcome here anytime."

He made to leave, but her hand caught his and he noticed her sad smile. "Take care of yourself, and take care of your Chooser. What the two of you have is rare among our kind."

He returned her smile with a nod and opened the door. As he exited he heard Fernando call out, "Half seven. Your place."

VIII

The door closed behind Jeanie, cutting her off from the strangeness of the nights events, and the Angel. The other—Fernando—she was pleased to be rid of. He was what her father would have called an arse, and rightly so. She could not believe the way he acted, as if he were superior to the Angel. He had some nerve.

Standing before the door, she felt safe taking in the quiet of the inn. This late in the evening, only a handful of patrons sat in chairs and benches in groups numbering no more than two or three. In the huge hearth along the west wall a fire blazed, warming the large open room with its gloaming heat. Quiet conversation drifted incoherently, punctuated with the occasional boisterous laugh.

Pounce, the mouser, was, as usual, passed out in front of the fire, purring contently, ignoring the goings on in his home. The large orange cat always knew the best places to be. Smiling at the curled form, Jeanie found an empty table beside Pounce as Tom came out of the kitchen.

"Been worried about you," stated the innkeeper with a smile. "Alice was edgy all day and night—your bed not even slept in. I'll have something brought over."

"Aye, that'd be wonderful," beamed Jeanie. Exhaustion and starvation vied for attention as she sat down on the chair and watched the plump balding man nod and turn back to the kitchen. Staring at her folded hands, she sighed, secretly glad that the Angel had insisted she come back here.

Tomorrow night she would meet up with him—*too bad Fernando will probably be there*—and she would help in...in what? She frowned. To get the Good Father back? That was surely part of it, but it did not explain the severed arm. God, that was horrible. Nor did it explain what was in that phial that turned her disgust into ravenous hunger. Her frown deepened. *Why did it revolt the Angel, yet the arm dinna?* She shook her head. There were so many questions and no answers to satisfy her. The Angel made it clear he would reveal nothing.

The smell of hot beef stew drew Jeanie away from her ponderings to find Alice carrying a tray with a large steaming bowl, bread and a mug, walking towards her. Placing the food down before Jeanie, she settled her round form onto the chair across from the girl. The chair groaned under Alice's weight and Jeanie feared, as she always did, that the chair would collapse. It did not. The angry frown on the cooks face increased Jeanie's apprehension.

"Well, you might as well go on and eat. I didn't keep it hot so you could watch it freeze under your nose." Alice pushed the loaf of bread towards Jeanie.

Breaking off a thick chunk of the hard-crusted white bread, Jeanie quickly dunked it into the stew and popped it into her mouth. A big mistake. The heat was more than she expected and after quickly swallowing, she grabbed the mug, cooling her burnt mouth with dark ale.

"I told you it was hot," reiterated Alice, the side of her mouth curled into a half smile.

"Aye, but ye dinna say it was that hot." Jeanie took a last cooling gulp and put the pewter mug down. This time she ate with more caution, blowing on the soaked chunks of bread until the steam stopped rising and watched Alice with each bite. The woman's features never changed, and this worried the girl to the point where she could no longer taste the food.

Ever since the Good Father had brought her here to live, Alice instantly took it upon herself to properly mother Jeanie since all her girls were out, married and with children of their own. At first Jeanie found the woman's constant worrying quite annoying, but after a few months Alice felt like the mother she remembered from childhood. Seeing Alice glowering, Jeanie worried and secretly wished that the cook would come out and say what was on her mind. She knew it would not take long. Alice was not one for patience when it came to the people she cared about.

"You did it, didn't you?" stated Alice, crossing her fleshy arms on the table and leaning forward, her motherly diatribe beginning.

Jeanie popped in a cooled mouthful. "What are ye talking about?" she asked, hesitantly.

"Oh don't you give me that, li'l miss." Jeanie's eyes widened; this was serious. "Violet told me what you planned. I'm shocked that you would listen to that trollop. If it weren't for the fact that she's out all night, sleeps all day and pays her rent on time, that streetwalker would be living on the streets! But to actually take that whore's suggestion is beyond me, girl. I supposed that is the reason why you didn't come home last night and only now show up?"

Jeanie's appetite vanished. She knew. Alice knew! Alice glared at her, waiting for a response. Deciding to tread cautiously, Jeanie asked, "What did Violet tell ye?"

The cooks grey brows shot up. "Don't try that with me, li'l miss. I've raised four daughters and three sons. You know very well what Violet told me—you trying to seduce the Angel."

Jeanie gagged on a chunk of meat. It was not really a plan. It was a dream and an unlikely one at that. Even being so bold as to slip into his bed had taken nerve she did not believe she could muster again, especially given how he was towards her after that.

"Everyone knows that he's the Good Father's sworn protector," continued Alice. "And even if he be no priest, the Angel might as well be as untouchable as one. What were you thinking of, girl? Just because you have the honour of being their housekeeper doesn't mean that little stunts like this."

"Nothing happened," piped in Jeanie, a little too loudly. Some of the other patrons had turned in their chairs to listen.

More than a little embarrassed, Jeanie lowered her voice, "I swear nothing happened." *By God, I wish it had.* She pushed the half empty bowl away not looking at Alice's surprised pudgy face, and sighed. The fullness in her belly made her feel weighted down, sleepy.

"I'm quitting." She took another swig of ale hoping it would dull her feelings and ignored Alice' astonished gasp. "I'm gonna move on. I've been there, what, five years? 'Tis time."

She did not realize she wanted to do so until she said the words, but only after the Good Father was home safe and sound. That she could not admit. Too many people relied on his work with the poor and if they found out about his abduction it would not help the situation. It was the idea of leaving the Angel she could not bear.

The drooping double chins wobbled side to side as Alice shook her head in dismay. "You do have it bad for the Angel, don't you? I can see it in your face. Oh, don't cry." She took a cloth from her apron and passed it to Jeanie.

Fatigue and shock of the night's events had stripped away her defences and Jeanie found her eyes blurring with tears. "Oh Alice, I dinna ken what to do. I believed with all her experience Violet would hae some good advice." She wiped away the wetness on her cheeks.

"That girl knows nothing of love, my dear. You do love him, don't you?" Alice's harsh tones were replaced with the motherly affection that Jeanie had come to love.

New tears spilled down her face as Jeanie nodded.

"Oh dear," sighed Alice. "Does the Angel know how you feel?"

"I dinna ken," sniffed Jeanie. "I've never told him. I guess he must have some idea. I just don't know. Sometimes when I'm cleanin' and he's home, I can feel him watchin' me, but when I turn to look at him, he turns away. And when I try to get close, he either backs away or leaves. I fear he hates me."

"Now that's just plain silly talk. He doesn't hate you." The sternness returned, but only slightly. "When he walks you home, I see him stand outside and wait until you've turned off your light and gone to sleep. Someone who doesn't care about another doesn't wait around to see if she's safely tucked in." Her fleshy hand patted Jeanie's.

"I guess so," muttered Jeanie, managing a weak smile.

"Don't give your resignation just yet, my dear. Give it some more time. Maybe things will change. After all, the Angel is not a priest. He's a man just like any other man, isn't he?" Alice did not sound too sure.

"He's the most beautiful man I've ever met," she said breathlessly, and looked away, suddenly embarrassed, red filling out her cheeks.

Alice's smile widened. "I wouldn't know, my dear. You and the Good Father are the only ones who have ever seen his face."

Slowly, Alice came to her feet with a groan of effort. "Though, I must admit he does have a lovely voice, when, on the rare occasion, I've heard him speak.

"Now get off to bed, my girl. I've got cleaning to do and you've taken up too much of my time already." Placing the bowl and mug on the tray, she turned towards the kitchen.

Matching the cook's smile, Jeanie rose, the creek of the chair bolted Pounce awake. "Thank ye, Alice."

"Don't thank me, girl. I'm doing this for selfish reasons. I don't want to lose my best tenant." Alice flashed another toothy grin and disappeared into the kitchen.

Jeanie stood for a moment and sighed. She felt better, as she always did after talking with Alice. Images of the Angel waiting outside her window, making sure she was safe, warmed her. Turning, she hiked up her skirts and went up the stairs.

Fernando languidly stretched under the shimmering red silk sheets. Its cool caress did not match the sheer pleasure he felt. Bridget's sun yellow curls covered his chest as she slept content and safe, her head resting on him. Brushing some of her locks away from his face, he felt her tighten the hug, cool naked bodies pressed against one another, and he returned her embrace.

The puncture marks on their necks were no longer visible, but the memory of their lustful undertakings made him smile. He kissed the crown of her head and gazed up at the black canopy. If this was going to be his last day on earth, Fernando was well pleased. Nothing could top what they had done to each other. Well, maybe not. He hoped for another try.

If I'm still alive tomorrow night, he sighed.

The single candle on the bedside table guttered, leaving him in darkness wondering about his new partner and the wisdom of that connection.

Bridget did not have to say anything. It was obvious she was disappointed that the Angel chose to leave.

Fernando, on the other hand, was pleased to see the tall pale vampire go. Was it jealousy? Fernando dismissed that notion, but he did not like they way she had stared into those red eyes. He shuddered. It was more than the Angel's unnatural height and colouring that bothered the Noble. There was something about the Angel that terrified him.

More rumours drifted to mind. One in particular jumped to the surface. One that originated with the mortals and had made it to the Vampires, something that had never happened before in his long life. *The Saint's Angel, that's what they call him.*

Fernando chewed on his lower lip. Who the Saint was obvious—Notus, that strange member of the Chosen who continuously chose to actively participate in the lives of mortals as if he were a real priest. But which angel? Fernando knew of no real saints ever having angels to rule over. Then again, he never did well in catechism. His eyes widened as he realized that he did not even know the Angel's name.

The sudden movement of Bridget turning over, releasing her clutch, brought his attention back to his sire. Rolling onto his side he gazed at her back so beautifully pale, yet lined with silver marks. He petted her hair, feeling the soft silkiness of the waves. A nobleman's disinherited daughter sold into prostitution because he had too many daughters. Secretly Fernando was glad that her father had given her up.

The caress on her shoulders stirred her from sleep and rolling onto her back she gazed groggily into Fernando's brown eyes. "Are you alright?"

He smiled back. She looked so lovely. "I'm fine. Just thinking. Go back to sleep."

"I don't want to sleep any longer." Her smile widened and lowered her Chosen's face to hers.

They kissed; savouring each other as his hand gently caressed a perfect breast. It seemed he would not have to wait until tomorrow, and his hand slipped lower. Katherine would never take this from him. Bridget would be his forever. Tonight he would see to it, but for now they were together.

A perfect fit. He smiled and sank his teeth into her awaiting neck.

íx

He exited the steam filled bathroom, drying his long, thick hair with the white towel before wrapping it around his slender waist. Drops of water trickled down his front and back. He had hoped that a bath would have helped to ease his mind after returning to an empty home. He found the only difference was that he felt cleaner.

The smell of the powder residue had easily washed off. The phial now on the tea table beneath the painting of a sunrise, his watch and keys surrounded the little bottle as if to guard it from theft. He would not forget it there tonight, nor would he forget its occult numbering: "*211233124.*" For the umpteenth time he wondered at its meaning.

Standing outside the bathroom, he stared into the emptiness that was his home and sighed. Notus should be seated at his large writing desk working on one of his numerous projects; either illumination or calligraphy, until he would come up to tell his Chooser that it was time for bed. Sometimes Notus would grudgingly give up his work for the day or interrupt himself long enough to let his Chosen know he would be working late, or that he wanted to work on a culinary experiment for Jeanie to try. Today the chair sat empty and broken, the books untouched.

Entering into his darkened home had felt eerie, everything in the flat missed the monk, or that he was feeling the loss more than he could ever have imagined. He had never really been separated from his Chooser since that time so long ago, so far away. He took a deep steadying breath. This is not then, he reminded himself. Notus will be back.

He did not want to step into the lonely room where only the gas lamps and blazing fire in the hearth signified life, but he did anyways.

Visions of his Chooser being held by the Mistress weakened his knees and he collapsed to the ground feeling battered and drained. He knew that he was feeling his Chooser. Notus was alive and in pain. The pain diminished enough for an instant to allow a single focused thought through.

I'm so sorry, my son. I must do this. My pain will only bring your downfall and I would die before that was to happen.

As suddenly as the feelings appeared, they vanished, leaving him gasping on the hard wood of the floor. The severed connection left a vacuum of desolation. Notus had closed himself off. Chooser and Chosen were now separate for the first time in centuries. He was now alone.

On shaking limbs he came to his feet wiping away the dampness on his cheeks he first thought was water, and stared at Notus' desk, desolate and shaken. He understood why Notus had cut himself off. The feelings had come with the words. Feelings of desperation, concern, pain and above all the soul shattering fear for his only Chosen son.

He would not accept it. He could not and resolved to remain open to whatever he could feel of his Chooser. Even pain was better than the absolute loneliness left to him. He could not bear that again. It was too much like being back in that cave so very long ago.

His eyes fell onto the large leather bound tome standing prominently on the top shelf of the writing desk. It was old and it was Notus' private journal. It called to him, drawing him to open the cover and discover its secrets; the secrets of Notus' life. He had never broken into Notus' book and was loath to even attempt it, but he had to do something to alleviate the loneliness. He could not sit there alone in their home disconnected. He needed Notus desperately. The monk had become more to him than any other in the world. Even more so than Auntie or Geraint, he admitted reluctantly. Decision made, he silently prayed that his Chooser would understand.

The leather book felt heavy in his hand as he lifted it off the shelf and went to sit cross-legged before the roaring fireplace. Its flickering luminescence added to the warmth of the gas lamps. Placing the journal on the floor before him, he took off the protective grill of the hearth and carefully added a few more logs, watching as the heat instantly dried the water droplets off his arms.

He left off the screen, watching the undulating flames as he slowly unravelled the knots in his hair until it lay gleaming and dry down his back. He wanted to make sure he was dry before he would dare to open the book, lest he ruin it with water. Notus would never forgive him that. Even though he felt no cold, the fire warmed him.

Laying a hand on the book, its dark leather strongly contrasted his colouring, and again he wondered if he should open it. Never before had he invaded Notus' privacy like he was about to do, but it was the only way he could feel close to his Chooser; to drive back the sense of despair.

I will get you back, no matter the cost, he swore.

He lifted the book to his lap, the towel now dry and hesitantly turned back the cover. Unbidden the thought of Jeanie and his acquiescence to let her help came to mind and he groaned. He would have to protect her as well, not only from those poisoning the Chosen, but also from finding out about the Chosen. Burying his face in his hands, he tried to push back the rising anxiety. The cost would be very high now that she was part of the equation. He knew he did not have the reserves within him if he had to pay.

He raked his hair back out of his face to stare at the fire.

And what about Fernando? The Noble seemed to relish in his discomfort and even tried to provoke it. The curiosity was invasive, rude. But there was no choice, Fernando was right; to solve this situation as quick as possible they had to work together no matter how each detested the notion.

He gazed down at the first page, an illuminated panel that surpassed most of the monk's works. It was an illustration of him and Notus seated outside a grey and black shadowed cave framed by two large conifers. The night time image was alive through the use of silver leaf for stars and to outline the blackness. He stared at the remarkable likenesses. Even the image of Notus was precise, down to the silver streaked dark hair. Somehow the monk's preternaturally steady hand captured his red eyes. A trembling pale finger lingered momentarily on his ghostly image before quickly turning the time darkened parchment. Flipping magnificently scribed work, searching for what, he did not know.

"G'nigh', err, I guess 'mornin', Violet," Jeanie yawned through her smile and closed the door behind her. She had not expected Violet to be back at the inn before her and was more surprised by the prostitute's insistence that Jeanie join her for a nightcap.

Well, it was more than insistence. Violet nearly dragged Jeanie into her room and Jeanie had let her. She was too tired to resist. Too tired to be angry with the woman and the idea of relaxing with a bottle of twelve year old Scotch enticed her.

Despite Alice's regard for Violet and Jeanie's own opinion of the girl's chosen profession, Jeanie enjoyed having someone about the same age to talk to. After a few drinks she had angrily recounted the disaster that Violet's suggestion had resulted in. Violet frowned and immediately came up with new ideas, most of them shocking, and before the crudity descended further Jeanie quickly put an end to the scheming.

With a shrug Violet shifted the conversation by asking for extremely specific details of what happened, making Jeanie repeat the story, searching for any juicy morsel she could find. These Jeanie tried to avoid, and did so somewhat successfully without becoming too angry with the prostitute. She did not want to think about the horrendous mistake, and turned the conversation around to Violet and her men. A topic Violet was always pleased to discuss. Before long they were on the floor sore from laughter.

Karen Dales

Now Jeanie stood outside Violet's door and gazed wearily down the hall to her room, her soft bed calling. Over the years Alice had seen to her comfort, providing a down bed with matching pillows and furniture she would have expected to see only in a Laird's manor. Jeanie suspected it was the Good Father's doing, but allowed Tom and Alice to take the credit. Now Jeanie had the best room at the inn. Wearily she pushed herself away from Violet's door and made her way down the corridor.

The wooden door opened at the turn of the key and into the dark room illuminated by the large picture window. The bed called her even more strongly, its coverlet folded down invitingly. Smiling at Alice's considerations, Jeanie stepped into her room, unbuttoning her blouse. Stars exploded in her eyes an instant before the world turned black in a mire of pain.

The parchment lay wordless. The painted illumination took up the whole sheet within the journal. At first glance it seemed out of place in a book filled with radiant colours. This panel was all grey and silver and black. In fact it looked quite ominous. If it were not for the fact that he recognized the figure draped in black armour as him he would have snapped the book shut.

Whatever had possessed Notus to draw him like that? He had not needed to dress in that manner in centuries. The only real colour in the panel was, again, the redness of his eyes. The ancient sword Eira had given him was drawn tip down and his black gauntleted hands rested on the pommel. It was a disturbingly menacing portrait, even to him.

It took an effort to move his hand from his image. Had he looked so horrific? He had not meant it to be so, but the black leathers and armour had given him the protection he needed not only from the iron weapons he met so often in battle, but also from searching eyes. The only thing that was inconsistent was the black helmet that had a thin black fabric over the eyeholes so that he could see during the day, when he was expected to fight at that fearful time. No one on the battlefield ever saw what he looked like, especially his eyes.

Hesitantly, afraid to find what other examples of Notus' visions of him held, he turned the page, breaking the trance the picture held on him. The lack of artistry and the disarray of the penmanship shocked him and he read the first few lines at the top of the page. The High Latin came easily to him as if he had been born to it.

Oh, my dear God. I have sinned most terribly in Your sight with my arrogance, stubbornness and vanity. I do not ask You for forgiveness for I will never forgive myself. Only within these pages do I confess to You, Redeemer of all

ANGEL OF DEATH

Men, my sin against my son.

The book slid off his lap to lay on the floor, the page with all its words clearly legible in the firelight. If the illuminated panel had surprised him, this revelation floored him. Closing his mouth with a swallow, he stared at the writing with fearful wondering. He knew of no sin or injustice imposed against him by Notus. This was ludicrous. Notus generally had his best interest in heart, no matter the situation and the circumstances.

Returning the journal back to his lap, he continued to read, curiosity driving him through each painfully written word.

I do not know where to begin. I want to tell everything, yet the rush of words fills my head, confusing me more and more. I must start at the beginning, as all stories must, and pray that I make sense.

The year it happened was in the year of our Lord 1191. We had returned to London so that I could pay respects to the new Master on behalf of my son and me, after spending nearly a century in Wales. It was here I learned that horrendous barbarians called Saracens overran the Holy Land, the place of our Lords birth and sacrifice. It was unbelievable that something like this could have happened. War raged on sacred soil, and England's King, stirred up the fever to free Jerusalem.

I am ashamed to admit that this fervour swept me into its insane embrace. I, a Chosen, caught in the hysteria of mortal men, but as a servant of our Lord, I knew what I had to do. Disregarding my son's protests and fears, I hired a wagon that was a wooden box on wheels that would protect us from the searing sun and prying eyes.

I horribly know now that I should have listened to him. We could hide the fact that we are Chosen – I have done so hundreds of times through the ages – but I could do nothing to hide my son. Even the name would draw attention. The Welsh are not well accepted by the English. So intent on witnessing Jerusalem freed, I overrode his arguments with ones I believed logical at the time. I had the black leathers and armour made for him. Knowing how adamant I was and that I would have indeed left him terribly alone in England, my son begrudgingly agreed to join me. Once again he took up the task of my warder, slipping it on like a well-worn shirt.

We were accepted by the army and were allowed to join

them in their travels, travelling with the baggage train and the camp followers, far behind the Nobles, the Knights and, of course, King Richard.

During the day we slept in the safety of the wagon while David drove. David, a most wonderful and dedicated mortal, bound by words and Chosen powers never to reveal us and to defend us. David, a young man with no other prospects and abilities to serve the Crusade, but serve he desired. He was loyal and good and true and I paid him well.

At night we camped within the boundaries of the army, sharing space with the armourers, blacksmiths and the many others who are never documented but are necessary for any army to go to war.

To the footsore soldiers, it seemed, drew faith and strength at my presence and I revelled in it, ignoring my son who stayed in the confines of the wagon except to feed. In all the time it took us to reach the Holy Land my son spoke naught a word. I had grown accustomed to his lengthy silences in the centuries, but this was more. He was angry and deeply uncomfortable. He had turned inward.

Again, in my folly and exuberance of being of help to the mortals, I ignored him. It was only when one of the soldiers asked who the cloaked figure I traveled with was did my attention briefly turn back to my son and explained that he was for my protection.

Thus we travelled on, hiding the fact we are Chosen by time-tested methods. I told one Captain that I swore an oath not to see the sun until the return of the Lord. It seemed that reason was as good as any. All the time my son spoke to none and hid his features under his black cloak. I revelled in the attention from the soldiers.

It did not take long before we saw battle once in the Holy Land. My son had taken to wearing the leathers, armour and sword under his cloak after being accosted one night by two drunken soldiers after a small victory over the barbarians. He had rendered them unconscious very quickly, but they had seen his face. No one believed them, but it did not matter to my son.

The following night, just before dawn, the Saracens attacked us. It was quickly over in our part of the encampment. My son had jumped unarmoured into the thick of it when one ululating heathen took up a torch and tried to incinerate our wagon, in which I was hiding. I saw my son in his deadly dance. His sword sprayed Godless blood over the thirsty ground and coated him as he slew mercilessly and silently. It was quick, and it was, in a perverse way, beautiful to behold.

Once the remaining attackers fled, there was a pile of corpses littered around my boy. His sword gleamed and dripped red in the firelight. Exposed, his white hair mottled red with drying blood, he quickly covered his head with the hood of his cloak. It was too late; too many surviving soldiers stared in dumb shock. Whether at his colouring or at his massacre I do not know. Probably both.

Centuries had made my son a very efficient killer, but the soul within despised it, and it showed. Bending down, he wiped the blood off his blade and strode into the solitude of the wagon, pushing me from the door.

I was surprised by his actions, not about what he did to the attackers, but how he basically ran me over with no thought or recognition of my presence. And that was when he rounded on me, his voice husky from disuse and filled with raw anger.

"Don't. Do not say one word," he commanded, and violently sheathed his sword.

I stood there, my mouth ready to praise him, and stared in shock. Never before had I heard my son speak like this, with such venom and self-loathing. I was just as unprepared for the rest of it.

"Do not praise me for murdering those men. Killing to feed or in defence of life is one thing, but this...this was senseless slaughter by people defending their land, not ours!"

"Those were not men," I hotly replied, caught up by his anger and fuelled by my disjointed beliefs; the old arguments rushing to fill my hurt. "They are Saracens – barbarians. They took the Holy Land away from God!"

I know now that I should have said nothing. I was as fanatical as the King himself. I was out of my reason. Even the horrified expression on my son's face should have brought me to my senses. Instead I came down even harder. "They must be driven out at any cost."

I shudder to think that I actually spoke these baleful words, words that would haunt me to this day and cause my son so much hardship and pain.

Anger flashed in my son's eyes, suddenly making me fearful. "If God wants Jerusalem then He can take it. He does not need us," he said slowly in measured tones.

My own anger flared, or was it his that I felt, I will

never know, but before I could retaliate with words of my own a new din took up outside. The King had come to our portion of the encampment! Cries from the soldiers, hailing the Lion, swung my attention from my son. My anger dissipated into excitement. The King was here!

I left the wagon to stand in the precarious twilight of dawn, hoping to see this great man I had only heard of. I was oblivious that my son followed me, the anger still smouldering within him.

"Where's the fight?" hollered the Coer de Leon, in his resplendent plate armour, flanked by his banner men, guard and collected nobles. His voice was commanding, authority driven and charismatic. Everything about the man, even to the way he sat his horse, demanded and expected obedience.

The soldiers cried their garbled replies of how they drove off the Saracens. Richard looked impressed, it was obvious the fight had gone harder elsewhere, and nodded knowingly. Again his voice boomed over his men. "The desecrators flee!" A roar resounded from the crowd, my voice added to the cacophony. "They retreat, screaming that Shai'tan fights for us."

All sound stopped. Only that of distant continued fighting and dying screams of fleeing Saracens filled the predawn. It was then that many of the soldiers now gawked openly at my son standing silently cloaked and hooded behind me. Richard followed their gazes and turned his horse towards us, his face set in stone.

I ignored my son's rising panic. I was too caught up in the attention of the King. He nodded at me and joy filled my soul, and then he did the undreamable, he spoke to me.

"Father, is this the one those dogs are running from?"

Too stunned to reply, the soldiers around us filled my silence.

"—killed a dozen before they knew it—"

"—moved faster than the eye—"

"—swoosh an 'e took off 'is ead—"

"—saved me from bein' chopped in two—"

"All those o'er there are his, Your Highness."

"Is this true, sirra?" Richard tried to get a glance under my son's cowl, wanting to see whom the enemy was calling the devil, and who his troops declared as saviour.

Silence fell between us. I could feel the rage and the fear in my son and knew he had fallen silent again. He would not speak to the man he perceived to be the cause of my madness.

"It is true, Your Highness," I piped in. The look on that rock hard face forced me to continue. I did. I was elated. I, Father Paul Notus, was talking to the King! "Please forgive my intrusion. I am Father Notus—"

"Does he have a name?"

I could hear the word "no" form in my son's mind and interrupted before he could speak. "Gwyn, Your Majesty. His name is Gwyn and he is my Warder."

The King studied me up and down, and then he did the same to my son. I was excited. Reining his nervous brown horse to stand still, he ordered, "Pack your things and move them next to my palisade. You now serve me." With that he turned his horse and rode back to his camp, his nobles following.

I bade David to pack our things and hitch the horses. We were in service to the King. So elated, I once again ignored my son and completely forgot our fight – our first and only fight.

In the weeks that followed I became more involved with the people who surrounded Richard, and at times spoke with him. Other nights I enjoyed the songs and tales with which Blondel, Richard's minstrel, entertained us. But more often than naught I spent the nights with the wounded, nursing those who would heal and giving the dying to God.

Once I asked my son why he would not join me with the wounded as he had at other battles in other times. I did not expect an answer and was surprised to hear him state, "Here I am the Devil, not Death," before he stalked away from me.

My son now worked for King Richard and he seemed resigned to the fact. He did not speak, nor did he allow the King to see what he truly looked like. His Highness seemed content with that so long as my son followed orders successfully.

In the weeks that followed it became my son's duty to go out and hunt down bands of Saracens. If the group was small enough, my son was to slaughter them all. If they were too large he would come back and write down where the allied forces could find them. When he came back from a slaughter he always brought a strand of ears as proof for the King and a wineskin filled with blood for me. Praise he ignored, thanks he scorned, and he withdrew further into himself, doing what others wanted him to do so that I could get what I foolishly thought I wanted—to see Jerusalem freed.

I did not see his sacrifice until it was almost too late.

It was two months before Acre, and in retaliation for a failed assassination attempt on the King's person, King Richard sent my son to assassinate Salah al Din ben Yusif, better known amongst the ranks as Saladin. I know now how self absorbed and obsessed with his own ego the King truly was, but at the time I believed that a great honour had been bestowed upon my son. Oh how wrong I was!

Clad only in black leathers, his cloak and a band of braided black leather circling his head to keep his long white hair out of his face, my son left on the black charger the King had given him. His cloak merged two dark figures into one.

Saladin's army was several leagues away and it was up to my son to sneak into the encampment filled with thousands of soldiers so as to fulfill the King's quest to kill his rival. It was suicidal, but he went anyways, leaving as the new moon slowly dipped westward. I watched his lonely solitary figure shrink and disappear in the distance. Having no comprehension how large an army Saladin actually possessed, I assumed it would be an easy task and that my son would return triumphant and Richard would reward our presence. I went about my nightly routine spurred by excitement.

I did not realize my son was overdue until the texture of the night shifted to predawn and the Lion came out of his tent roaring to start the day. It was then that I truly began to worry. If my son did not return, and return quickly, the sun would kill him. My focus had finally been brought back to my son, and I frantically paced the departure point, waiting and reaching out through our connection to find nothing.

The sky shifted from indigo to a paler shade of blue. It was going to be a gloriously clear day. I put my hood up to give some protection. I would have to retire to my wagon soon and mourn my loss – a thought that terrified me.

I waited as long as I could when I saw two horses ride over the dune, kicking up sand that obscured my sight, but not before I could make out my son's horse. Panic strangled me. I could not see my boy!

With what seemed hours but were only moments, the two horses reined in by me. The scent of horse blood mingled with other blood. The soldier on the other horse, who I discovered was on perimeter patrol, screamed for the surgeon. I was numb with shock. I could not move. My son, still astride his saddle by some miracle of God's, lay on his panting black horse. His cloak covered him, but not so much that one could dismiss the spear head with the broken shaft protruding from his left thigh, his blood on his breeches glimmered in the approaching light.

Time was of the essence, and berating myself, I acted. Slowly, gently, ever so carefully, we lowered my son's unconscious form to the ground, careful not to touch the haft. I knew what they would find and was too late before the surgeon declared my son to be dead. Kneeling down beside my boy, I willed him to breathe and slapped his face. The show was convincing enough. The surgeon was wrong; my boy was still alive, but barely. We carried him under the canopy covering that curtained the door to the wagon. With David's help, the surgeon and I got my boy inside.

All this time I had managed to hide my son's distinct appearance. Only David knew the truth, not even the King knew, but now the surgeon was going to find out. Swearing the confused man to silence, we took off the bloodied clothing. The astonishment was expected, even the fear, but he was bound to help. Cutting the breeches revealed the damage. The spear point was fully embedded in mangled and bleeding flesh, it had to come out.

The surgeon studied the wound, probing and pulling, gazed up at me, and sadly shook his head. "'Tis barbed. Pullin' will rip the flesh. Through is the only way."

I nodded and held down my son's hot—hot!— shoulders. It was impossible to believe, but my boy was burning up with fever. The spear point was made of iron! On the count of three the surgeon pushed, my son screamed and my heart shattered. The spear point would not come out. The frown on the surgeons face deepened.

"What is it?" I demanded in near hysteria. The iron was slowly poisoning my boy.

"The long bone is shattered and the spear is lodged in it. Pushin' it through won't work," he explained. "There's only two ways, and at best he loses the leg."

"What do you mean?" My worry exploded. To live an immortal life with only one leg! He would be put to death by other Chosen if he were found out; only the perfect were Chosen.

"One way is to cut it off—"

"No!" That I would not allow. "What is the other?"

"Pull it out." He did not sound sure.

"You said it would tear."

The surgeon nodded remorsefully, "But he may have a chance to walk again, if he lives."

It made sense, anything to help my boy. Reluctantly, I agreed. There was no other choice. It took three tries before the vicious weapon came free in a horrific ripping sound. Flesh should not make that sound. Pleased with himself, the surgeon did not notice at first that the wound was cauterized. Baffled, he followed my orders to sew up the wound and set the leg. Using the Power of the Chosen I bound him never to speak of what went on and he left.

I sat alone beside my pale beautiful boy, praying and trying to keep his fever down by bathing him with wet cloths. I tried feeding him my blood, believing it would help him heal faster, but he brought it back up. I sat listening to his fever induced dreams and prayed for his health under my tears.

Thus I stayed all day and the next. I covered him in blankets when he shivered uncontrollably, and uncovered him and bathed him in water when he burned the hottest. I placed his damaged clothing and his sword away. I would have to go out soon to feed and bring some for my son, if he could manage it. I was preparing myself when King Richard opened the door and came in.

My madness for the cause was gone and I finally viewed Richard as just another mortal, no more, no less, until I realized his countenance was filled with horror and disgust directed at my son, laying palely on the cushions. The blanket covered my son up to his waist and his long white hair splayed on the pillows around his head. Slowly the look of horror was replaced by a look I had seen Richard give to a more than willing Blondel. It was a look of desire and wantonness.

Remembering my presence he asked, "How is he?"

I told him and he shook his mane. Crouching down beside my son, he asked if my boy had said anything about the mission. It was my turn to shake my head. "He has not awakened." My lack of the honorific made him scowl and he stood as my son's eyes fluttered open.

I rushed to his side. Whether it was the pain or something else, tears filled his ruby eyes. Taken aback by the colour, the King remained standing yet looked ready to bolt. My worry increased.

"Did you kill Saladin?" asked Richard, gruffly hiding his nervousness.

ANGEL OF DEATH

Closing his eyes, my son softly whispered, "I'm sorry."
Richard set his jaw at the answer and left.

I knew the apology was for me. I could not believe it then and I cannot believe it now, but my son was apologizing to me! With those two simple words came the unhindered emotions and thoughts of how he failed to help me realize my dream of a freed Jerusalem. I was moved to tears. It should be I who apologized! Before I could say a word my boy fell into a fever filled sleep, muttering something in a language I had never heard before.

I sit here now, in a cave above a monastery far to the east in the lands of Chin. It took us months to travel here, and in all that time my boy lay in fever, wasting away in pain as his leg refused to heal. I had to keep my boy away from the possibility of the Chosen finding him in this state. It was here that I heard of their monk's goodness and healing abilities, anything to help my son.

Here they believe and worship differently, and have not heard of Christ or God, but worship a deity named Buddha and practice arts of defence. It is their healers that took my son into their care, opened his leg and took out the pieces of iron left behind, poisoning him. It was their healers that broke and reset his badly healing bone. It was their healers that will teach him to stand, to walk, to run and to be whole again. All the while I sit and be the coward, afraid to confront my son with my sins, afraid to see the pain I have inflicted upon him, afraid to see his desolation. I cannot bear it. I am not strong enough.

There is a lesson learned at a most horrible expense. I know my son will never forgive me. I will never forgive myself. I do not expect God to either.

Here ends the confession of Father Paul Notus.

Closing the book, he stared at its ancient cover in disbelief. The ragged scar running from left hip to knee burned hot in the memory. It had taken him two years to relearn to walk and another decade before the deep burning pain was gone. In all that time and the thirty years afterwards in the monastery, he had desperately missed his Chooser, until Notus' return. But he found contentment and a sense of peace he had never before felt. They accepted him, they treasured him, and they taught him their skills and their ways until he held mastery in them and made them part of who he was. They never judged him knowing what he was and cared for him anyway.

He caressed the old leather that protected the pages, unsure whether to continue reading, afraid of what else he may find hidden. Tears spilled down his face.

Notus was wrong. He did not blame his sire. In fact, he believed it was his fault and his clumsiness that caused him nearly a decade and a half of pain. Then again he could have refused Richard, and Notus would not have had any chance to realize his dream. He shook his head.

Now was what mattered, but the dreams of that time still haunted him in half remembered flashes. How he was in the void with the white-faced demons pushing and pulling him to come with them, taunting and abusive, and cackling at his fear. Of how the void dissolved, taking with it the demons screaming in rage, turning into what looked like a thickly foggy day. And of how three beautifully ageless women, one blonde, one red headed, and one with raven black hair, came to him, imploring that he go with them. He did not remember their words, but the feelings of need were explicit.

Twisting his body around so that he lay on his stomach before the fire, he opened the journal and began reading at a brightly illuminated page — its calligraphy perfect.

X

he banging grew louder in the darkness; forcing the demons from his past to flee in a rage, back into the void. Slowly, he lifted out of sleep to stare bleary eyed at the cold, dead hearth. Not even the ashes stirred. Swallowing the dryness from his mouth he frowned. He could not remember the dream, except for its ending, but what worried him was the memories of those white faced demons were popping up again. Thankfully they were not back.

Again the banging resounded through his flat, clearing his mind from sleep enough to realize that he was not in bed. In fact he lay on his stomach

ANGEL OF DEATH

before the deceased fireplace with Notus' journal as a pillow. Sitting up, he closed the book and placed it on the couch. Sometime during the day he had fallen asleep reading. What exactly, he could not remember. The journal entries were all a blur, except for the unbelievable confession.

The lamps softly illuminated the dark room and the banging came again. Someone was at the door. Sweeping his long hair out of his face, he groggily got to his feet, securing the towel around his slender hips and nearly stumbled into the couch. He must have stayed up well past noon and whatever the time was now his awareness told him night had fallen a short while ago.

Exhausted, he walked to the door, not caring at this moment who saw him. Another round of knocking exploded into the silence, this time accompanied by muffled Portuguese expletives. With a sigh he opened the door, cutting off the string of profanity that issued forth from the Noble.

Fernando stared openly and lowered his fist, closing his mouth to resume his natural superior stance. "I've been met by many a beautiful woman wearing not much more than you, but..." he trailed off with a gesture at the Angel's attire.

His sigh was filled with annoyance and fatigue, but from the look on the Noble's face it was taken as something else. Standing back, he let Fernando enter.

"May I suggest that you put some clothes on," sniffed Fernando. "I've been pounding on that bloody door for the last ten minutes. I was starting to think that Bridget's driver remembered the wrong address."

Fernando yanked off his white gloves and turned around, his cloak fluttering about his finely trousered calves, and studied the apartment as his host closed and locked the door.

"A quaint place you have here," he strolled around. "A bit drab, but usable." He halted at the tea table to stare at the painting above it. "What is this? A sunrise or a sunset?" and instantly dismissed it in a huff of incredulity. "And no mirrors?" He turned to face his nearly naked host. "I guess I can understand why." Fernando paused at the narrowing of the Angel's eyes, and then smiled. "Vanity is a sin, if I remember correctly."

Turning, the Angel walked to the door of his room and he shook his head, he was too tired for this. He was distinctly aware of the Noble's measuring gaze. He did not want to provoke Fernando, yet it seemed that his presence was enough to get the Noble started.

"A warrior even before the Choosing, eh?" probed Fernando, unexpectedly.

"After," he absently replied, instantly realizing his mistake at being taking off guard so easily. He was much too tired for this.

Turning around, the expression on Fernando's face was one of surprised wonder. It was blatantly obvious that the sight of the scar on his arm triggered the comment, and his accidental reply now triggered dangerous speculation within the Noble. No one, except Notus, knew of his reaction to iron. Any deviation in the belief in the purity of the Blood meant death for a Chosen.

Quickly mastering his fear, he left Fernando for the safety of his room. It was possible that Fernando would never understand, and better it be so.

He closed the bedroom door, leaving it open a fraction to keep an eye on the on goings in the rest of his home.

"I guess I'll make myself at home." Fernando broke the silence and began to wander around, picking up things that interested him so as to get a better look.

With a sigh, the Angel stripped off the towel, thankful that it hid the scar on his leg, and that his hair covered the claw marks raked across his back. Fernando was too intrusive. Rummaging through the dark stained mahogany wardrobe, he searched for appropriate attire. In earlier times breeches and a shirt would have been fine for...for what?

Slipping on fine black wool trousers, he searched for a white linen shirt and put that on as well, buttoning the ivory buttons except for the top two. He did not like feeling constricted. Tonight would be the beginning of finding the key to the release of his Chooser and he hoped the phial to be a clue.

He sat on the bed to put on his black socks and shoes and stared at the sword mounted on the wall. The new leather scabbard reflected none of the soft yellow light that spilled into the room. Plain, except for the intricate stitching, the only colour was of the hilt that shone in a silver glow.

Without thought, he stood and walked to the ancient blade and removed it from the studs in the wall. It felt so right in his hands. He caressed the leather and fingered where it would go into baldric or belt. It had been so long since he last wore it. Nobody wore swords nowadays, preferring the explosive means of a pistol, but the touch of his sword drew the urge to wear it.

Grasping the grip of the hand and a half sword, he pulled nearly five feet of ancient steel from its sheath, making the metal ring. As old as he, it showed as much physical wear as its master. The dragons were hardly visible and the edges thinly sharpened. It was still dangerous, possibly more so. Sheathing the blade, he held it on his palms. He would not wear it tonight. Hanging it back up, he turned and went into the other room.

Fernando sat uncharacteristically quiet on the couch, his back to his host, deeply absorbed with something on his lap. He was not aware of his host's reappearance, or the incredulous look on the pale face.

Silently standing, watching the Noble, he wondered what had the man's rapt attention, and then it came to him. *Oh dear Gods!* His ruby eyes widened in horror and he all but ran to yank Notus' journal from prying eyes. He could not believe his own stupidity, leaving his Choosers private thoughts where Fernando, let along anyone for that matter, might pick it up and read it. Snapping the book shut, he hugged it, returning Fernando's shocked expression with a livid glare.

Recovering his surprise, Fernando smiled and stood. "A beautiful book, it's too bad I couldn't finish it. Maybe I can borrow it?"

"No!" he barked. He shook with fury. How dare Fernando invade his life in such a manner! Too many secrets lay buried between those pages. To be exhumed twice in one day, and once by a stranger, it was all too much.

"You don't have to get so hot under the collar," said Fernando, nonchalantly. Fernando smiled knowing his shot hit its mark as his pale partner turned stiffly to place the journal back in the shelving. "After all, what secrets can it hide? We are all vampires here."

"Chosen." He swung around to stare down at the smug man.

"Chosen...Vampire...what difference does it make? We are the same by any other name and would still feed so sweetly. No secret to that fact." Fernando waved his gloves, shooing the point away.

"What do you want?" Anger tight under control threatened to break free.

Brown eyes narrowed. "Why, the same as you, of course."

"I do not think you want my Chooser back." Ice flowed through his words.

The corners of Fernando's mouth twitched into a smile, his brown eyes alighted mischievously. "But of course I do. I'd love to meet the Chosen" – he inclined his head – "who can create such beauty and write so exquisitely so as to bring alive a dead girl as delicious as her name. Tarian, I believe?"

"Get out." The implicit threat of promised violence rang in the two words, his body tense and shaking for its release.

"Now, now, that isn't any way to treat a guest," chastised Fernando, enjoying how easily it seemed to get under the Angel's skin tonight and sat down on the couch. "I was simply praising your sires creative abilities. I guess I cannot expect much from one who came from such an uncultured background." Fernando sniffed. "And an accident no less. One would think that in all these centuries someone would have trained you in proper social etiquette."

Frustrated beyond belief, he stood and glared down at the Noble studying his nails, and then turned on his heel to walk to the front closet. He halted with his hand on the knob and swung around. It was fine if Fernando knew about his Choosing. It was fine if Fernando knew about Tarian. It was fine if Fernando knew about the other one, the one he had to give up, Tarian's granddaughter. To even think of her name would be unbearable, but the thought of her took the fight right out of him.

"What do you want of me?" His voice was strained, tired.

Fernando lifted his head and stood a victorious smile awash over his face as he turned to face his reluctant host. "Why nothing less than to know you, and nothing more than to get my possessions back from Katherine."

The realization stunned him, and he stared at the Noble across the room. No one had ever wanted this from him. All that anyone had wanted from him was to be left alone or permission to approach Notus. Suspiciously he eyed the Noble. "Why?"

"Curiosity," shrugged Fernando. "What reason need I have?"

"No. That is not it." He did not believe this man.

"I want to know if the rumours about you are true," smiled Fernando, triumphantly. He had not expected to get this far with the Angel so soon. Something had unbalanced the Angel to reveal this vulnerability and he was reaping the rewards.

Closing his eyes, he sighed. The rumours. The gossip. The fiction others made up to explain his existence. He had lived with them since before he was Chosen. They would always follow him. "No, they are not true. No, I was not born a Chosen."

"And what of the rumour that you were never human," pushed Fernando.

Never been human? He opened his eyes. Yes, this one floated down the centuries, popping up occasionally among the mortals to explain the Angel. He had never heard such talk from the Chosen. Fernando could have gotten this impression from what little he read in the journal, but even still, this speculation was dangerous.

He could not lie. He was a horrible liar and Fernando was sure to pick it up. Notus would be able to dissuade such prying. His Chooser was a master at bending the truth and diverting attention from dangerous topics. The look on Fernando's face expected an answer. Precarious speculation was better than to have the Fernando think the opposite of a lie.

"What do you think?" he stated coolly.

Fernando stood stunned, confusion written on his dark features. This was not the answer he was expecting. "What do you mean 'What do I think?'"

"Can you not leave it at that?" he asked the Noble. The inquisition had gone on far too long. If Notus had been here none of this would have occurred.

A dark brow lifted in interest. Fernando was not about to leave it at this, not when the conversation was just getting interesting. If he was going to work with this strange, tall young man, he damned well wanted to know everything he could so as to keep his own rear out of the sun. Not to mention the prestige he would receive in disclosing the enigma to the rest of the community. Even Bridget's adoration at the new information would be well worth it.

"Can you really expect anyone in my position to leave it at that?" he stated, approaching the Angel. "No. I didn't think so, therefore I'll ask you again. What do you mean, 'what do I think?'"

Intense brown eyes bore deep into his, searching for an answer, but what he met with was a wall so strong that Fernando was forced back a step, almost believing the blood red eyes flashed with their own inner light.

Straightening to his full height, he continued to glare at the Noble and coldly stated, "Do I look like I was ever human?"

The sound of a nervous cough was the only reply. What was Fernando to say? Every instinct in him pointed to the fact that the person before him was something more—or is that less?—than a Chosen. An image of angry ruby eyes flashed forward from some distant memory. No, not human. Not Chosen, but what? He shook his head, clearing the speculations. Now was not the time. Later. There would be time later to uncover the truth and evidence of the fact.

Momentarily glancing up at the Angel, Fernando turned and paced a few steps. "Any thoughts of where to begin?" He hoped the change of conversation would relax the atmosphere that had turned hostile. There would be more time to find out the truth.

"I thought that you might," he replied, relaxing his stance to comfortably observe the Noble. He was glad that Fernando had not answered his question, but the Noble's brown eyes could not hide the uncertainty that he also felt.

Fernando shook his head and puckered his lips. "You're the one that took that hideous little bottle. Let's start with that."

With a weary nod, he walked to the table under the rising sun and lifted the phial from the midst of his other items. The tension permeating the room slowly dissipated with the focus shifted away from him and back to why fate had flung he and the Noble together.

"I managed to wash it off," he explained, handing it to Fernando. "I would rather that you not open it here. I do not wish to be run out of my home because of the smell."

The cork, half out, was slammed tightly back in. Fernando contemplated opening it again, but held the little bottle between thumb and forefinger, eyeing the brownish green contents. "What do you think?"

"I do not know." Finding an unbroken chair, he turned it around and sat backwards on it, arms resting on the back, watching the Noble turn the bottle this way and that.

Returning the conversation to the task at hand did not dissuade the suspicion or the mistrust he felt for the Noble. He was not about to let the intrusion into his personal life go from his mind. "I would imagine that it is some type of herbal combination," he suggested, trying to keep the anger from his voice.

"That would explain it," nodded Fernando, studying the numbers. The Angel's tone did not go unnoticed, and he allowed himself a small grin of victory. "And it would explain what is poisoning the humans to us, but how do they get it into the mortals, and what the bloody hell do these numbers represent?"

A frown formed on his pale lips and he shrugged a shoulder. "I do not know what the numbers mean. It could be anything. As to the powders function, if it is poisoning the humans to us then it would have to be ingested either as some type of medicine or as a seasoning of some type that they place in their food. By our reaction to the smell I would count on it being the cause. Jeanie's reaction, I think, would confirm the food theory."

The thought of Notus' housekeeper bolted him upright. Turning to glance at the clock on Notus' desk confirmed his concern. It was well past the time Jeanie should be here to help get his Chooser back, and he could not imagine that she would back out now. She was too intent on pushing herself into the cause. A flicker of worry flashed in his mind. Rising from his seat, he strode past a puzzled Fernando, to take his black cloak from the closet.

"What is it?" demanded Fernando, trying to put indignation into his confused tones as he stood. One moment his host was making perfect sense and the next...Fernando shook his head at how much more he had to learn about his partner.

"Jeanie should have been here by now," he replied, draping his cloak over his shoulders and clasping it in place with the ancient broach. The feeling that something was wrong tugged harder. Grabbing keys and pocket watch, he stuffed them into his trousers pocket and headed to the door. Fernando did not follow; a disbelieving look on his face.

"Let's go," he stated, maybe a little too anxiously.

Fernando's brows shot up and he inclined his head momentarily before walking ever so slowly towards the now opened door and his tall pale companion. "I've met many a trollop and all could fend for themselves very well. I will not allow this investigation to be deterred for an incompetent whore."

For a brief time they had been civil to each other, now his jaw tightened again in anger. "She is no whore," he stated coldly, "and I do not wish to delay getting my Chooser back, but something is wrong. I mean to see that she is safe if she has decided not to help. We can continue the discussion about the powder along the way. If that is alright with you."

"It is," sniffed the Noble, and walked out of his host's home, his nose slightly up in the air and very aware of the Angel's glare.

The door shut with a thunk and locked with a jingle of keys that were silenced by being stuffed back into a pocket. A quick glance at the street reported that no one witnessed the exit or his hurried movements to cowl himself under the black cloak. Following the Noble, he fell in beside, walking at a casual pace to Fernando's hurried steps.

"You do look quite ominous like that," remarked Fernando, nonchalantly, eyes intent on their immediate surroundings as a hunter in a forest of stone. This time he was hunting his partner as well as his property. He was in a unique position and he knew it. No other vampire had managed to get this close to the Angel, and reading the first few pages of that diary and the Angel's reactions only fuelled Fernando's curiosity. If he lost all his possessions to find the Angel's secrets it would be a small price, but not a price he necessarily wanted to pay. A smile flickered momentarily across his lips. Despite the barriers, the Angel could possibly be tricked into revealing his sacred secrets and Fernando was determined to try.

"It is better this way," replied the Angel, his mask back in place, firmly this time. He resolved that he would not let de Sagres get the better of him again. The extent of their relationship would be as partners to resolve the mystery, nothing more.

To make this clear, more so to himself than to the Noble, he directed the conversation. He did not need to be told how foreboding he appeared. He already knew.

"Tell me about Sebastian," he asked.

"What do you want to know?" The change of subject was not a surprise to Fernando, he was almost expecting it, but the subject itself caused him to raise a brow. "You already know everything," he lied. "Sebastian is ... was Bridget's sire and died on the same search we are now on, if I hit my mark, which I usually do."

"Then does it not bother you how we came upon the bottle and its contents?" he asked coolly.

Noticing where the Angel was possibly leading the conversation, Fernando worried the inside of his cheek. He had not realized it before, but having the instance placed before him as speculation, bothered him. "What are you implying?"

"Who left us with this clue, if it is a clue?" he replied and shook his head. "Something about this does not seem congruous. Think about it. Not even a few hours of being sent on this mad hunt we are tossed Sebastian's dismembered arm with the possible culprit to the poisoning clutched in his dead fingers. It seems too easy. Much too easy."

"What are you saying? That this is a set up?" He did not like the possibility at all. "Katherine may be a bitch and the Mistress of London, but she is one of us. Sebastian hated any type of responsibility, and I don't think you're the type to have people bow and scrape for you."

He shot Fernando a glance and nodded. No, he would never want to be Master of London. There would be too many prying eyes, especially when one pair was more than enough. "I do not know," he said.

They needed more, thought Fernando. "It is possible that those who threw Sebastian's arm did not know that we are on the case but threw it at me because they know who Sebastian associated with."

"If you're correct," he countered, "then how did they know where to find you?"

"Damn it, I wish I knew who *they* are," exploded the Noble, realizing the Angel was right.

Surprised at the Noble's outburst, the Angel glanced down. He too wanted to know who *they* were, for it was very possible that *they* were the ones poisoning the humans. The other issue he chose not to mention was who could have found out about the Chosen to issue such an attack? Other Chosen would not do such a thing. A group of humans might if they had found out about the Chosen, and with all the publications about vampires lately that made this seem most likely.

"We will find out," he said. Fernando glanced up wonderingly. "I will have Notus back."

"If that is the case, why then are we going to check on your housekeeper? We should be trying to follow this lead."

"And how do we do that? All we have is the powder and the numbers on the bottle." The worry he felt over Jeanie's absence bothered him more than it should.

"We also have Sebastian," added Fernando, very aware of the Angel's evasion of the Jeanie question.

"What about him?"

"That whoever was able to do that to an eight hundred year old vampire means to see us and every other vampire dead. And *they* will," explained the Noble. "As to the powder, we need to get it analyzed. Maybe then we will find out whether our theory is correct. The numbers themselves are going to be a problem."

The Angel nodded. "But where do we take it? Most places close when we wake. And I do not know of any scientists. Then again maybe we do not need to get it analyzed. If we run on the assumption that the powder is the source, then we can follow that line back."

"Which line," eyed Fernando, suspiciously.

"Where would one get herbs to make this powder?" His question was more statement than query. "Or more to the point, where do they come from?"

A smile formed on the Noble's face, brightening a dower look. "An apothecary," he stated victoriously. The Angel nodded, encouraging Fernando to continue. "They are usually open later and could tell us about the powder itself. The problem is that unless you know of one that remains open after dark we'll have a hard time finding one."

"I know of one. The one where Notus buys his herbs. Their stock is quite complete."

"What would a vampire need with herbs?" inquired Fernando.

Ignoring the Noble's gaze, he stated, "He helps those who cannot afford a physician."

Blinking at the shocking revelation, Fernando tried to contemplate the motives of a vampire to help heal lowly mortals. He gave up, shaking his head in disgusted disbelief. "Why?"

A quick glance reported what he expected; Fernando could not understand. Then again all Chosen seemed to either misunderstand the motives or gave up speculation because no reason could be reasonable enough. He had to try anyway. "Because they are..."

The words died on his pale lips as he turned the last corner and halted. Fernando came to a stop beside him.

The *Rose and Thorn* was engulfed in manic orange flames that flickered and licked, its clawing tendrils reaching out to consume the shops to either side, hunting for more to devour.

People lined the street, watching in obscene fascination as the remains of the roof collapsed, forcing the charred timber frames of the front wall to come crashing down into the street, dashing dangerously glowing sparks into the cool night air. Shocked and fearful screams from the onlookers melded into the cacophony of destruction that was accentuated by the alarm bells of approaching fire trucks. It was too late for the Inn and maybe for the buildings on either side.

Only one clustered group of people did not watch the spectacle as a source of entertainment. Huddled together in their blackened clothing they stared in dumb shock as their home and livelihood slowly disintegrated before their eyes. He barely recognized the plump proprietress for all the soot. Quickly scanning the small group, he recognized them all as employees and guests. Nowhere amongst them could he sight Jeanie. Worry turned to dread that tightened the knot in his gut and with a quick glance back at the blaze he rushed over to the group, Fernando hurrying to keep up.

"Mistress Reiley?" He could not keep the worried tones out of his voice as he reached the group.

All eyes turned upward, away from the fire, and some widened in surprise as others gasped their shock. Only Mistress Reiley reacted by breaking into more tears, staining her already wet chubby cheeks. One of the serving girls he could not name had to support the larger woman.

"What happened?" he implored. "Where's Miss Stuart?" Orange light cast an ominous glow on the group and he pulled his hood lower to shade his eyes.

At the mention of Jeanie's name the once strong Alice Reiley collapsed into a sobbing mass on the paving stone. The woman whose name he could not recall remained standing beside the older woman. Unshed tears threatened to spill yet her voice remained rock steady. He then remembered the woman to be Lily, Tom and Alice's daughter.

"Some men I've never seen before came to talk business with my father just after dusk," explained Lily in a hardened voice, anger accentuating her words. "I only heard parts of the conversation, but I heard them threaten that if we did not agree to use their special spice in our food they would shut us down. My father, being a man not to cave into threats or pressure, ordered them to leave. They did not take the demand well and left, but not before crashing a couple of bottles onto the floor and starting the fire. It spread so fast. My son tried to get the guests out, even with the smoke so thick, until it overwhelmed him. My father had to take him to the hospital."

"What about Jeanie?" he demanded, staring into Lily's hazel eyes that now overflowed. *Oh Gods, no.* The realization took his breath away. This was not happening. It could not.

"I'm so sorry," he heard through his rising panic and found he could not get a breath to reply. He spun around to face the fire, its glow painfully bright in his eyes. Lily's words floated to disbelieving ears. "Tommy could not reach her door before the smoke and heat consumed him. He was only able to get Mr. Wilkes and the Abernathy's out. He could not alert Mr. Simmons or Miss Flowers, either. I'm so sorry."

His mind raced. It was not possible. Jeanie must be alive. She could not be dead. She could not.

Firefighters rushed with hoses and pumps, pouring gallons and   gallons of water on a fire that seemed to feed on the cold liquid. The two buildings to either side were now fully ablaze and more bells signified the advance of reinforcements in the war against the blaze.

A high pitched wail, coming from within the wreckage of the Inn, crescendoed. To his ears, and to those around him, it sounded like a woman screaming, but to his mind he heard Jeanie. She was still in there, somehow alive, and he had to get her out.

Fernando watched the whole spectacle with a wry grin. The blaze was quite beautiful, and the mention of the housekeeper's death in the blaze sparked his imagination. He could imagine how the fire would slowly, like a lovers caress, work its destructive powers upon such a beautiful girl. He had seen others burn to death, even his own kind that fell into inquisitors' hands. In the eye of the fire, immortals and humans were equal, so it was a bit of a surprise to find the Angel approaching the screaming blaze.

Recovering himself, Fernando rushed up to the pale man and grabbed the cloak to stop him as the scream reached its pinnacle with a deafening blast that nearly knocked them both off their feet.

Clothes slightly singed, Fernando whirled to face his partner. "What the bloody hell do you think you were doing?" he raged, ignoring the pained defeated look in the Angel's eyes.

Refusing to meet the Noble's baleful glare, he continued to stare at the blaze. All he could think of was that somewhere amongst the flames was Jeanie, and that thought left a hollowness he never imagined could be there. He had known and witnessed the deaths of people in his very long life. Some were gruesome and horrible to bear, others were by his hands, but never before, in his life as a Chosen, did he feel the desolate hole that Jeanie's death rendered in him and it terrified him. *Jeanie's death.* He still did not want to believe it, but no one could survive such a disaster.

Closing his eyes, shutting out the horror, he only opened them after turning to face Fernando. He had heard the Noble say something and from the furious expression on the man's dark face, he knew that Fernando was expecting an answer. But what could he say? With a sigh and a shake of his head, he looked back at the survivors of the *Rose and Thorn* to find them gawking.

"Your hood," muttered the Noble, anger still tightened his speech. He did not like the answer, or more to the point, the non-answer. Nor did he appreciate the Angel's lack of recognition that it was he who pulled him from foolishly throwing himself into the fire.

Hood down around his shoulders from the impact of the blast, he raised his hand to pull it back up, only to let it drop instead. It was too late; they could see him. Shock mixed with either fear or horror filled their faces, all except Mistress Reiley who did not lift her head to gaze up at him and her destroyed life.

Unable to feel anything of Notus, he still knew what needed to be done. Straightening himself to his full height, he walked over to the group, aware of Fernando's inquisitive stare and the increasing wariness of the group. A couple of them even took retreating steps. He could not blame them. He had come to expect such reactions and the hurt he felt at it. He even admired Lily's protective stance beside her mother. Alice and Tom had raised a strong daughter.

With a quick saddened glance at the young woman, he knelt on one knee before the owner of the Inn. "Mistress Reiley," he ventured and watched as she lifted her heavy head.

She no longer cried, but defeat played its mask across her features. At first she gazed through unseeing eyes. Slowly, recognition alighted. "You are an angel," muttered Alice through soot-covered fingers. "She was right. She was right."

A frown tugged at his pale lips. He knew who *she* was but did not understand what Jeanie was right about, he so wanted to know, yet did not know why. Bringing his gaze back to the suddenly old woman, he spoke, "I am so sorry, Mistress Reiley. I wish I could have…" He trailed off. What could he say?

Rising to his feet, he addressed Lily who now stood more at ease in his presence. "Take your mother to St. Benet's Welsh Church and ask for Reverend Iefan Davies. Tell them that the angel of the south wind sent you and that they should help you as much as they can. Reverend Davies will know what to do." He glanced down on Mistress Reiley and then to Lily. "Tell them to give you anything, even if they have to break into our coffers."

He turned to leave, Fernando gazing speculatively at him, and he felt a hand on his arm. Turning back he faced Lily.

"Why are you doing this?" she asked, taking back her hand as if she had been burnt.

"For Jeanie," he replied, and left with Fernando walking silently beside him. Feeling their eyes sting his back, he cowled himself.

Even after he and the Noble rounded a corner, blocking out the holocaust of the Reiley's lives, he could still feel them — feel their remorse and desolation. He knew what it was like to have your home and your life burned by those who wished nothing but harm. The ancient hurts from lifetimes so long ago pricked at his consciousness, but this time it held Jeanie.

It was only when they were a few blocks away and the light of the fire could not be seen over the buildings that he allowed himself to steady his weakened legs by leaning against the brick of a wall, and slid down to sit, his eyes closed. At this moment he did not care that Fernando would use this as another excuse to pick and pry.

"What the hell is the matter with you?" demanded Fernando, silent for so long in simmering rage. "I stop you before you throw yourself into that inferno and I don't even get a thank you for it. And then you help – actually help! – those pitiful mortals. Who cares if one puny, annoying one dies? We have more important things to worry about!"

I care, he thought, refusing to look up at the fuming Noble. Raking his bone white hands through his thick white hair, he pushed the hood back and gazed up at the Noble.

"Thank you," he said sternly. He hoped this would placate the storming man.

It did not. In response, Fernando blew up. "Thank you?" roared the Noble, glaring down at the Angel, his hands balled into tight fists, wishing he could pummel that pretty face into a pulp. "Is that all you have to say? Are you crazy? You have said time and time again that you will have your sire back and then you do this! Vampires do not sacrifice themselves for dead—dead!—mortals! You had a mortal housekeeper—correction, your sire did. You don't kill when you feed—which reminds me I'm famished. And your sire plays doctor to our prey. Pray tell me that this is just a dream, a very bad dream, or am I crazy to be around one such as you?"

He matched Fernando's gaze and slowly lifted himself to his feet, not breaking eye contact. "Chosen have forgotten their humanity. Most on the night of their Making, and I am not talking about their mortality." His voice was filled with wintery contempt. "We take from them. We take their future, their dreams, *their* immortality, and give nothing back, not even to each other. Our lives are less than theirs because we chose to give up what we take away in others—humanity. And yes, I would gladly give my life so that a human may live. I have done so in the past and will most probably do so in the future. And if I choose to grieve for one I could not help, then I am closer to finding what I never had."

Realizing that this was the longest speech the Angel had ever spoken, Fernando simply raised a brow and clenched his jaw. No one had ever talked to him in this manner since his Making. It was too esoteric for him, yet the argument whirled around in his mind, replaying itself over and over as if it held merit. Stifling a shudder, he realized that he did not want to see the truth of the Angel's words.

Unable to find a snappy retort, Fernando chalked one up to his partner and decided to change the subject. There would be time enough later to deal with his whirling thoughts. "Do you remember what that scrumptious morsel said about how the fire started?" he asked carefully lest he release the anger he felt.

Crimson eyes narrowed suspiciously and he nodded. He remembered that Lily mentioned that two men had started the fire after a sale was refused, but what did that have to do with anything? Enough people witnessed the arsonists and could describe them to the Bobbies.

"Then you remember that the fire was started because the innkeeper wouldn't buy their *special spice*?" asked Fernando, suspiciously. After the Angel's irrational display, Fernando was none too sure about him and from the look on his pale partner's face he knew that the Angel had missed this important fact. With an exasperated sigh, he continued, "It is possible that that *special spice* is the same as this." He fished out the phial out of his vest pocket and held it up.

"There is nothing to give credence to that theory."

"And there is no proof that this is what is poisoning us," retorted the Noble, "yet we made our own conclusions about it. The fact is, is that we have no facts. Everything we have is circumstantial."

"Then what is your theory?" If there were a connection between the poisoners and the fire that killed Jeanie, he would have his revenge.

A half smile flickered across Fernando's face. "I propose that this is indeed a sample of that special spice. That it is the cause of the poisoning. And the way to infect as many mortals as possible is to coerce innkeepers, taverns, soup kitchens and maybe the ware mongers, to buy it and then sell it in their food."

The Angel frowned. It all seemed plausible, yet there was one thought that nagged at him. "How does such a spice work? Nothing has ever affected the Chosen, not plague, not pox, not cholera, and not mortal drugs. Stay out of the sun, don't drink dead blood, and you will live forever."

"You forgot fire," stabbed Fernando. He was not going to let the Angel forget that.

"And fire," he scowled. "So tell me, if that is the cause, how can it be so?"

"Hell if I know. What do you think I am? A herbalist? I thought that was the reason for checking out that apothecary you mentioned. It's probably closed now..." Fernando trailed off, his attention drawn to a solitary figure standing at the entrance of the blackened alleyway.

Turning to see what had silenced the Noble, his long, fine fingers tried to grasp at a sword hilt that was not there. The woman, for it was clearly a woman, stood silently in what appeared to be a sheer shift. A finely knitted white shawl was held tight about her shoulders and over her head, pulling so that it covered her features, leaving only a strand of blue-black hair to float in front of her piercing blue eyes. He relaxed his fist but not his stance. Something was strange about this woman wearing almost nothing on a cool October night.

"Ahh, a tasty little morsel here," grinned Fernando, and took a step towards the girl who looked no more that nineteen.

She took a step back, her eyes flickering nervously from the Noble to the Angel.

Everything about her cried out that she wanted to say something and it made him think he had seen her before. He shook off that possibility.

"You're—you're the Angel?" Her voice was soft and sultry despite her obvious trepidation.

He nodded as Fernando glowered, "You're sure popular around here."

Ignoring the Noble's remark, he addressed the young woman. "I am sometimes called that." She nervously shifted her shawl, staring at his exposed white features. Expecting to find his hood in place, he only met his hair. "What is it that you want of me?"

Wide ice blue eyes cast their gaze onto the slick paving stones as if searching for the answers there. She lifted her eyes back onto the Angel, worry creasing her brow. "Jeanie Stuart works for you?"

The mention of Notus' housekeeper caused him a momentary flash of pain before he set himself against it. "I did know Jeanie. She is dead," he stated it more bluntly than intended. "What do you want?"

Surprised, the young woman's eyes widened. "No. That can't be. She was alive when I saw them take her."

"What?" He took a step towards the young woman. It was his turn to be surprised.

"I—I—I saw two men," she stammered at the intense crimson gaze.

"Where?" he ordered, his mind reeling at the glimmer of hope.

"*The Rose and Thorn.*"

"When?"

"This evening."

"Before the fire?"

"Fire?" She glanced in confusion from the Angel to the man with him.

"The Inn's been arsoned, my dear," explained Fernando. "Now why don't you tell the *Angel* what you saw, and you," he turned his attention to his partner, "stop interrupting and let this pretty young thing continue."

Both the girl and the Angel blinked at Fernando as if he had popped out of thin air. Returning his attention to the young woman, the Angel apologized.

Casting her eyes down, she bobbed her head, releasing another thick black curl. "At about seven, or half past seven, I saw two men, one carrying Jeanie like a sack of flour. I thought she was dead, but I saw her move. I don't know what they wanted from her so I followed them."

"You followed them?" admired Fernando the same time the Angel blurted, "Where?"

Momentarily rattled by the bombardment of questions, the young woman stammered, "Bankside, near Southwark Bridge. I tried to go unnoticed."

Frustrated at her incomplete answer, the Angel pressed, "Where on Bankside?"

"There's—there's a soup kitchen just west of the bridge. That's where I saw them take Jeanie."

He straightened with a sigh, hope filling him for the first time this evening.

Fernando, on the other hand, continued to scrutinize the girl. "Now, my dear, why should we believe anything you say? You haven't even given your name."

The young woman flickered her gaze up at the Angel, obviously confused. "No one ever need tell the Good Father or the Angel their name if they wish it," she answered, more as a question rather than a statement. At the Angel's nod, she continued, "I know Jeanie. I'm one of her friends. I work as a maid at the Alexander residence."

"A maid?" echoed Fernando, hopefully, as he took a step closer to the girl. "I haven't had a maid in—"

"Leave her be, Fernando," ordered the Angel, noticing were the Noble was heading.

Taken aback at the ferocity of his partner's words, Fernando backed away and raised a brow. "What? Another one under your protection?"

"You might say that." Returning his attention to the young woman, he continued, cutting off any remark the Noble may slip from his lips. "Thank you for your information."

Turning on his heel, he did not wait for a reply before leaving to wind his way to Bankside, yanking up his hood as he walked. The sound of racing clicks told him that Fernando was hard pressed to keep up, but he did not care. His whole focus was to find Jeanie alive and see her safe.

The young woman stood in the alley mouth watching as the black clad figures strode off into the night, and quietly chuckled to herself. Shifting her shawl down to her shoulders, she released the tight grip on the material. Long black hair fell in luxuriant waves, making her violet eyes glimmer more brightly.

She had not expected to see the Angel uncovered and knew that what she had been told was a pale rendering of his beauty. A beauty she desperately desired to acquire for her own pleasures, despite what she had been ordered to do. Maybe there would be time for both. She smiled at the fantasy. *Truths mingled with lies are almost the best intoxication.*

Inhaling the scent on her wrist that was her namesake, Violet Flowers turned down the alley. Her job was done for tonight.

XI

he single candle that spilt its white wax onto the barrel dimly illuminated the small cell that took up the back third of some type of storage cellar. Its futile light reflected in the iron barred, grime covered window. Not much stirred in the place, only the sounds of footsteps, voices and clanging that permeated through the floorboards above.

Outside the rods that formed the cage, barrels of unknown contents littered the floor. Inside, sitting on a bundle of straw, Jeanie sat contemplating the tray of tantalizing smelling food that her captor had sent. She was famished from a long day behind bars, but her stubbornness about her situation refused her even the luxury of contemplating the food. It did look good, piles of meat with peas and potatoes steamed in the cool air. It was a much better sight than what hung on the southern wall.

She did not remember much of the night before, nor how or why she was brought to this place. One moment she was hopeful for a good night sleep in her own bed and the next she woke with a headache worse than any hangover. Dirty straw had clung to her face and stuck out of her disarrayed locks so that she had to spit, brush and yank the itching plant matter from bothering her any further.

The bright light from the autumn sun had made her eyes water in pain, and yet let her see clearly her unknown whereabouts. At the sight of the dismembered arm and two legs still chained to the wall she let out a shrill scream that even threatened to burst her own oversensitive ears. Nowhere was there to be found the torso or the head of the corpse. Judging by what was left of the clothing, he must have been some nobleman.

Her screams had not brought anyone to her aid so she had shouted her throat raw and rattled her cage door, demanding to be let out. When that failed, she yelled to her nonexistent captor to at least show himself until the strip of sunlight turned orange and lengthened, casting the remains of the last tenant into dark shadow. Jeanie finally resolved herself to the fact that she was left forgotten and sat in a heap of straw, waiting.

It did not take long for the dungeon to be cast into the pitch black of early night. Crying in frustration, she thought back to the Angel. Soon he would be expecting her at his home, but she would not be there. Would he care? She doubted it. He would probably be pleased, one less person to get in his way. Still she wished that he would come and rescue her from wherever she was. But if she did not know, how was he to? It seemed unlikely that he could come, being so focused on getting the Good Father back.

Alice is wrong, she thought sullenly, *he dinna care.*

At the sound of footfalls above, Jeanie had gotten to her feet and yelled for someone, anyone, to get her out, or at least bring her something to drink. She was actually surprised to hear a door open and see a nervous young girl bring the tray of food and a wineskin. Jeanie had tried to get the girl of about eight to tell her where she was, if she could not let her out. The girl ignored Jeanie's attempts at conversation as she slid the tray under the barred door, but she did leave the candle as Jeanie requested.

The water in the leather skin tasted strange, and despite her great thirst she spat out the mouthful and refused to drink, or to eat. She would not give her captors the pleasure of her co-operation.

Resolved to the fact that she was most probably here for quite a while, Jeanie sat and waited, watching the food cool and the candle melt shorter and shorter.

Thoughts of the Angel rose in her mind and no matter what she did to try and think of something else, his beautiful face returned to haunt her. To her mind she was unnoticeable to the strangely coloured young man the Good Father called son. Forgotten and ignored, she cursed herself a fool for the stunt of the day before. Showing up in his bed uninvited! Her face burned hotly.

Why could he not see she cared for him? Brushing her cheeks, she was surprised that they were wet. She so desperately wanted to know what was wrong with her that the Angel would want nothing to do with her.

A sound of clinking keys made her look up. Someone was coming down the steps. It was a solitary man with short dark hair and a fierce expression that forced Jeanie to her feet and back against the stone of the far wall. He looked ready to kill. Absently, she felt along the rough brick hoping to find one loose enough to use as a weapon.

"I see that our food was not to your liking," he remarked after a quick glance at the tray. "That snivelling girl will be punished for that." His dark brown eyes bored into Jeanie.

Terror and disgust filled her. That shy little girl was to be punished for her not eating. "Why?"

A malicious smile formed on the man's face, but did not touch his eyes. "Why what, my dear?"

"Why are ye gonna punish her?" she stammered.

"Oh that. I thought you would have asked a more poignant question." He hitched a broad shoulder. "Because it will be fun." He ignored her gasp and began to pace before the gaol cell. "I am here to answer some of the questions I am sure you have, but first I will answer the standard questions all my captives ask. It will save time.

"You are in the basement of a soup kitchen in the south of London. There is no point telling you where exactly, just know that it does not matter. You are here for my amusement and to keep you from ruining our plans. My name is inconsequential, though I know yours, Jean Anne Stuart, daughter of Heather and Charles Stuart – a poor joke on your father's parents in naming him that. Do not look so surprised. I have my sources."

"Ye're the one's who kidnapped the Good Father," blurted Jeanie. She glanced at the remains even though she knew them not to be him.

Her reply was a deep chuckle. "I would never be so bold as that. I am not at all fond of holy men nor their trinkets."

"Then why are ye holdin' me captive? I've ne'er been a threat t' anyone." She felt her courage returning so long as he remained outside the cage.

He halted before the door and peered into Jeanie's eyes, into her soul. "No, you are not a threat. In fact you are inconsequential, and that is why you are here." With that he turned around to walk back up the stairs.

"Wait!" she called out, and he halted halfway up. "If I'm so inconsequential why kill me?"

Pivoting on the stair, Jeanie's captor grinned manically. "Because it too will be fun."

Jeanie watched in dumb horror as he disappeared up the steps, and only when she heard the door close with a click and a tumble of a lock did she collapse onto the straw, crying her fear and desperation.

Their heels clicked loudly against the stone walk as they wove their way around and through groups of people out for the evening. Most of the passers-by did not notice the two who hurried down the streets. Those that did saw two men, one unusually tall, and his features obscured under a black hood, and the other, short yet stocky and of obvious foreign origin. The shorter of the two looked angry and it was his expression that forced many from their path.

They walked in silence for the last several blocks. The number of mortals in their midst roused Fernando's hunger and his anger. He could not believe the Angel to be so naïve as to believe that beautiful stranger. Who cared whether or not Jeanie was alive? Fernando surely did not, and even

ANGEL OF DEATH

after the Angel's short sermon, it seemed ridiculous to sidetrack their quest for one simple mortal girl.

There were more important things than she – even the Angel more or less stated so by declaring over and over that he would have his sire back. But actions spoke louder than words, and the Angel acted as if she were important. How important and in what way, Fernando wanted to know, especially since she had become a liability if she was indeed alive.

Winding their way closer to Southwark Bridge, they left the company of mortals for a more quiet, deserted lane, one in which not too many would risk taking without being accosted by some of London's lowlifes. The Angel walked in silence, vaguely aware of the Noble's presence. Hope carried his steps. Hope that Jeanie was alive even if she were in some type of trouble. He prayed that the girl in the shawl was telling him the truth. She knew him to be the Angel, yet he vaguely remembered her, from where he could not recall. His reverie was broken when Fernando cleared his throat.

"Tell me again why we are doing this," remarked Fernando, without looking up.

"I did not say," he replied after a moment of silence. He did not want another confrontation with the Noble.

"They why don't you?" Fernando huffed in exasperation. "If I'm going to risk my neck for a mortal girl, I damn well want to know why. And I remind you—*if*. It may well be that that so-called maid was lying. After all, I don't know about you but I don't know many women, maids or whores, who would walk about at night in only a shift and a shawl."

"I know." It did not seem right, or more to the point everything seemed too easy.

"You know what?" fumed Fernando. "That she was lying? Or do you know what the hell is going on, because if you do pray tell."

"It was obvious that she was not who she said she was," he explained, keeping his attention on where they were heading.

"I know that," spat Fernando. "Then why believe what she said?"

"Because I would rather believe in a half truth than a lie."

"Huh?" Now he was confused.

"She said two men took Jeanie to a soup kitchen. Lily said two men started the fire because a sale of *special spices* did not go through. We have a bottle of some strange powder that was left at your feet by two men, one driving the carriage and one in the cabin. We are very carefully being led into a trap."

"*Santo Cristo Foda do Deus!*" exclaimed the Noble. "Then why the bloody hell are we going?"

He stared intently into the night. "Because the only way to find out who laid the trap is to spring it."

"That's the most ludicrous thing I've ever heard! We should turn around and—"

"And what?" he inquired. Cold blood red eyes narrowed at the Noble.

"Leave the possibility that Jeanie may indeed be alive and a captive? Leave the possibility of quickly solving this case and being quit of each other?" He came to an abrupt halt, black cloak fluttering against his calves, and stared down at Fernando. "I do not like having my life turned upside down. I want this over, all of it."

"I'm hurt," feigned Fernando. "And after all that we've been through. I was beginning to like you," he mocked and his brown eyes narrowed in anger. "I want this over as well, but, as I told you, I am not going to risk my neck for some mortal girl that you so obviously care about."

Taken aback at the Noble's accusation, he just blinked, allowing the other to continue.

"Oh don't give me that. I've seen the way you look at her and she, you, and the way you worry over her." Fernando turned to continue walking, but not before saying in a disgusted tone under his breath, "A vampire in love with a mortal, *rai esta parte da minha vida!*"

It took him a moment to register Fernando's words before he followed. *Love?* He could not believe it and he shook his head in denial. Fernando was just being Fernando—an antagonist trying to rile him up again. Catching up to the Noble, he walked at the slower pace with eyes focused on the path ahead and frowned.

It had been so long since he allowed himself to feel those feelings, having locked that part of himself away after being so cruelly denied. It was an ancient wound, one long healed over, one in which he would not even scratch at by saying her name—Tarian's granddaughter.

She had returned the love and his passion, and even when her father forced her to marry another they still found solace in each other's arms and bodies. He had done everything for her, except the one thing she needed, for him to live in the day with her.

Notus had repudiated the existence of his son's love for Tarian's granddaughter until it was almost too late. When the Angel had stolen her away to his cave in Wales, intent on Choosing her, he did not count on her husband and his liege following, demanding her return.

It was too horrible to bear. He could not give up the meaning of his life. She would not go. She did not want to.

And then in came Notus, who talked of rationalities. Of what it would do to take her out of the sun, to take her from her family, to take her from her husband, to Choose her for his own passions and desires. Notus refused to understand.

He had wept and so had she. They had wanted to be together, they loved each other and then Notus told him to listen, to truly listen to her heart, to her body. And he did. He heard her beating heart pounding in vibrant emotion and then the smaller, faster one and he knew. Notus was right. He could not take her from the light when she carried the unborn child to her husband.

Crushed and sobbing, he gave her over to Notus who took her love, passions and caring for his son from her memories and her life, and reinstated her as wife to her husband before bloodshed could occur.

He had locked away his heart that night. The pain had been too terrible to bear. He could *never* allow himself to go through that again. The pain of love was a wound even iron dimmed in comparison, and now Fernando was saying he was in love with Jeanie?

He stared at the cobbles as they passed underfoot. What he did know was that he felt strongly for Jeanie and it terrified him. He could face an army, iron weapons abound, and feel totally at ease and calm, but it was one beautiful fiery young woman that made him flee in confusion and terror. Yet he wanted, no needed, her safe and happy no matter the cost. Was he in love with Jeanie?

Oh Gods, I hope not, he prayed, and shuddered at the possibility. *I can't go through it again.*

They continued to walk in silence, neither of them had anything to say to each other, and if one did it was highly unlikely that the other would listen, or hear, for that matter.

Homeless huddled together in dark shadows, hiding from unwanted prying eyes. To the eyes of an immortal they were grubby with dark sunken eyes and grim features. Some that they passed begged for anything, others hung their jaws in astonishment, while others whispered. To the ears of the Chosen the words were equal to their shocked expressions. Most recognized the Angel while a few wondered where the Good Father was and who was with the Angel. Fernando's face twisted with disgust at the comments not meant for his ears.

The Thames was nearby, and so was Southwark Bridge. They did not need to see the river. The increasing smell of bilge, sewage and waste was proof enough. He wrinkled his nose in disgust. The smell was common to most cities. Fernando, on the other hand, spat and pulled out a perfumed handkerchief, holding it to his face in a poor attempt to filter the smell. At least the wind was not blowing from the south.

The sight of a black clad figure up ahead, on the small street, made Fernando look up. It was a man, similarly cloaked yet obviously in an embrace with someone, or something.

A smile tugged at the Noble's lips in recognition. Lengthening his stride to keep pace with Fernando's hurried steps, the Angel broke the silence. "Who is it?"

Lips broadening into a grin, Fernando replied, "An old acquaintance of mine and a somewhat of an admirer of yours."

"What? An admirer?" It was preposterous.

"Rupert Randell," explained the Noble. "Made a little over two hundred years ago, was a solicitor who lost everything in the Great Fire and was helped by one Father Notus and his Angel."

He snapped his head around to stare at the man in a new light, disbelief reflected in his crimson eyes.

As if in response to his unspoken thoughts, Fernando explained, "I know his sire is neither you nor the monk, and no, he isn't mine. He's one of Barclay's. You may remember him, he was the last Master before Katherine took over."

He shook his head. He did not know Barclay, and never went to his court. Then again Barclay was one of the few Masters that respected the privacy and wishes of those around him.

"To hear it from Rupert," continued the Noble, "without your help he would have killed himself in desperation. *Oi*! Randell!"

The figure not more than fifteen paces away turned to greet the two, allowing the limp body of a homeless drunk to collapse in a heap. His dark eyes brightened with surprise at the sight of his friend and the Angel, and immediately vanished into a look of pain as he took a step that could not be completed.

A flash of realization passed between the Noble and the Angel and they both rushed to the fallen Chosen who lay face up, eyes unfocused and shivering violently. Concern filled the two as they watched helplessly the effects of what they knew to be the poison. There was nothing either of them could do except to make Rupert as comfortable as possible.

"De Sagres?" stammered Rupert, his body shaking so badly that his hand had to be caught by the Noble.

"I'm here," responded Fernando, his voice tight, without emotion.

"I-I'm so c-c-cold. What's ha-happening t-to me?" His body arched in a painful convulsion and he cried out.

Taking the opportunity to slip under Rupert's blonde head, his lap acted as a support for the dying Chosen and a length of white hair fell forward to brush the man's face.

The convulsion passed back into the bone racking shivers.

Fernando looked up at the Angel. It was obvious that he had no experience in dealing with this type of situation, and seemed ready to bolt. He looked to the Angel to take over.

He sighed at the realization that he would have to become the Angel again, but this time for a Chosen. It was a first and the realization twisted his gut that Katherine was right. "Shhh," he said calmly, "try not to worry. It will be over soon."

"I-I can't s-see," stammered Rupert. "Whose-whose th-there?"

"The Angel," he replied, gently. "Be calm, everything will be alright."

At the sound of the title Rupert's body somewhat relaxed for an instant before another scream rendering convulsion racked his body. "The-the Angel?" he managed a moment after the spasm receded once again. "Oh G-God, I'm d-dying." Another vicious betrayal of his body arched him, but this time for longer.

There was nothing either he or Fernando could say in response as the length and the violence of the convulsions continued to increase. With little time between death throws, he tried to sooth the man by telling him about all the good things he could expect. All Rupert could do was sob over and over that he did not want to die, until the last convulsion left him lifelessly limp with blood running from mouth, nose and ears. Shaken at the violence of the poison, he glanced at the Noble who extricated his crushed hand from Rupert's grasp.

"Is he dead?" inquired the Noble, obviously rattled, but more by the possibility that it could have been him.

"I don't know." He gazed down at the slack pale face. Checking for a pulse was useless, as was checking for breath. How did one check to see if a Chosen still lived? "Give me your knife."

Brows furrowed. "What for?" demanded the Noble, reaching for the hidden sheaths at the small of his back.

"We need to find out if he still lives." He took the dagger by the hilt. The pommel had a white swirled teardrop inlaid on it with a tiny black dot in the centre. It was a finely crafted instrument. It did not matter where he made the cut. The slice on Rupert's neck welled with blood but did not close. Wiping the blade on Rupert's cloak, he handed it back to Fernando, mindful of its razor sharp edges. "He is dead."

"*Merda!*" hissed Fernando. Sheathing the dagger, he stood in time to see two Bobbies running towards them, obviously drawn by Rupert's screams. They came to an abrupt halt as the Angel stood, gently laying Rupert's head down on the stone.

"Is there a problem officer?" inquired Fernando, innocently.

The shorter of the two nervously licked his lips. It was obvious that he was new to his line of work. The older, and more rotund Bobbie, hitched his thumbs in the pockets of his uniform jacket. There was a definite air of superiority exuding from this man that made Fernando scowl.

"We 'eard someone screamin' an' come t' check it out and we see two bodies on the ground and you two stand' o'er them. Would you like to be explainin' what the 'ell is goin' on or shall we go t' the precinct?" said the older officer and made a move to grab Fernando's arm.

The Noble knocked the rude hand away, his eyes narrowing at the presumption and locked onto the Bobbies' grey eyes. "No. I don't think so. There are no bodies here. My friend and I were just out for some night air. Do you understand?"

The older officer stood, his eyes wide and pupils dilated. "Yes, sir. Just out for some night air," he slowly replied.

The younger officer glanced nervously from his superior to the Noble and then back again. "Frank, what are you saying?"

Frank turned to face his partner, still under the spell. "Time t' go, John. Nothin' 'appenin' 'ere."

"But the bodies!" protested John.

"There ain't no bodies."

John grabbed his partner's shoulder in the hopes to shake some sense into him and was met with a blank stare. Swinging around to face the

Noble, he demanded, "What the bloody hell did you do to him?"

Pushing his hood back far enough to reveal crimson eyes, the Angel stepped forward to present the answer. "Nothing," he stated, fastening his eyes onto the Bobbie's. He could feel the man's frightened pulse and talked directly into his soul. "Nothing. Now let us be on our way and do not come back here."

It took a moment for the Push to come into effect. The officer's shock at the Angel's appearance was at first a barrier that quickly diminished with the force of will upon the other.

Slowly, John nodded and turned to his partner. "Let's go," he intoned. Frank nodded and they both walked away without any knowledge of the last ten minutes.

Once they were well past audible range the Angel let out the breath he had not realized he held.

"Well, that was a close call," remarked Fernando. "I guess we can count on them not coming back."

"Maybe not them, but someone else." He spun on his heel and sunk down next to the dead mortal. The stench of the man tickled his nose yet he rolled the grimy head to the side exposing the four puncture marks in a nice row along the jugular. They should have healed before the last moment when death took him, unless Rupert had fed on him until his death, in that case the puncture marks were clear signs of a Chosen's work. If Chosen were getting sloppy with their feeding, it was no wonder that mortals were writing about them and conspiring to kill them off.

A tiny trickle of congealing blood oozed from the wounds. Touching a finger to the red pearl, he brought the blood to his nose. A sniff revealed nothing so he touched the soiled finger to his tongue. At first there was nothing to mark the blood as different, but slowly the same sickly sweet taste, more intense than Peter's, exploded in his mouth forcing him to spit out the tainted blood. Standing, he nodded in response to Fernando's unasked question.

"*Santo Cristo Foda do Deus*!" Agitated, Fernando began to pace.

"I wish you would stop saying that." He returned to examine the mortal corpse for any clue as to how he was infected with the poison.

The Noble halted, his brown eyes blazing. "Why?" He was upset and now the Angel was reproaching his words!

"I know what it means." He pulled out a card from a moth eaten pocket. On it, in neat type written letters was the name and address of another soup kitchen in another part of the city. Turning it over, he found on the back, written in a flowing hand, the name *Corbie Vale*. Slipping it into his inner cloak pocket, he stood.

Fernando's eyes were angry slits. "I don't care if you or the whole bloody world has a problem with how I say things," expounded the Noble. "I will not change for you or for any other. Now, what the hell was that I saw you slip into your pocket?"

"A card," he replied, turning his attention to Rupert.

"And?"

He glanced up at the Noble once he discovered there was nothing on the corpse of the Chosen to offer any other clue. He stood, brushing his hands on his thighs. "I would strongly suggest that before you drain a mortal in your need to feed, you taste the blood first. It will not come right away, but if your victim is tainted you will taste a sickening sweet flavour, and it will be very likely that that person ate recently at a soup kitchen."

The angry creases in Fernando's face relaxed. "Sweet, eh?"

The Angel gave a quick nod. "What do you want to do with the bodies?" he asked.

The sudden change of subject brought Fernando's gaze to linger on the corpses for a brief moment before saying, "Leave them. Someone will find them soon enough."

He nodded. He did not like the idea of leaving the two bodies out like this. It seemed disrespectful to the dead, but they could not allow themselves to become more distracted than they were. Let someone else deal with the bodies, there was no place to hide them. They had more important things to worry about. Standing silently over the corpses, he mouthed a short prayer that he had heard Notus say many, many times through the ages and hoped that the intent, if not the words, would ease Rupert's and the homeless man's souls.

Ignoring the scrutinizing gaze of the Noble, he turned, determined to find out if Jeanie was indeed alive and if so, how did she fit into with the poisoning of the Chosen. It was extremely doubtful that she knew about the Chosen, and even more so regarding the poisoning, considering that if she were alive she would be a prisoner. But why? Why attack her? What caused her to be singled out, if indeed that was the case? The only reason he could fathom was her connection to him, and if all these theories were fact then he and Fernando were not only walking into a trap, they were being toyed with as well.

He regarded Southwark Bridge up ahead. Below the engineering masterpiece, the Thames undulated; a black eel, sleepy in the cool night. He did not want to even think of the water he would have to cross, or the effects the action would rend on him. Steeling himself from the unease of crossing the bridge, he focused upon the gas lamps illuminating Bankside.

The first few steps along the bridge were fine until they moved over the water. Then the familiar feelings of vertigo and nausea clutched at him, threatening to unbalance him. He could almost feel the bridge sway under his feet but knew that to be a falsehood. Swallowing down his gorge, he tried in vain to think of anything beside the unsteady movement far below his feet. The lines of lamps on the other against the city's backdrop were his anchor, as well as the droning of a voice he knew was Fernando. He prayed that Fernando was not expecting conversation.

"You aren't even listening to a word I said," blasted the Noble. He had no clue why the Angel had shut down, and for that matter, he did not care. He did care that he was being ignored yet again.

The words filtered through and the Angel kept his sight on the other side of the river, knowing that if he turned to face the Noble he would lose the tenuous hold he had over his unease.

The silence of the response and the fact that Fernando was unused to being ignored began to irritate the Noble. Used to hearing himself speak, he also expected to be heard. If he opened the conversation to include another he damned well expected that person's participation, but nothing came from the Angel.

Irritation built into anger, Fernando raised his voice. "Do you have nothing to add? Did you hear nothing I said, or was I just speaking to amuse myself." He stepped out in front of the Angel and halted. "*Caralho!* You're not listening to me even now!"

Focus on dry land shattered, the sudden rush of the depths of the river below washed over him and he placed a hand on the short protective wall in the hopes to hold his balance. He needed to get past the furious Noble and he took a tenuous step but was stopped once again.

"Get out of my way," he said thickly.

"Now why should I do that?" inquired Fernando, sarcastically. "You haven't heard a word I said. Why should I listen to you?"

Closing his eyes to help concentrate long enough to find the breath to answer, opened them and said in a rasping voice, "Please, Fernando, tell me once on the other side." This time he managed to push past.

Anger still unabated, and heightened by the brush off, Fernando stomped alongside the Angel's graceful strides. "I am not going to repeat myself. Do you have any idea how much you irritate me? *Seu Fodidinho!* And now you are obviously hiding something. What is it?"

"I've told you everything I know," he replied. Now if they could only get back onto solid earth he would not have to fear that the Noble would notice something wrong.

"Not bloody likely. You didn't tell me what was on that card you took from that transient."

Before he could respond four large men approached from the south side. Small clubs hefted in relaxed hands and one slapping his cupped palm invitingly. *Anywhere but here,* silently pleaded the Angel, his shoulders slumping under the cloak. Fernando seemed quite enthusiastic at the prospects of taking out his frustrations on someone, anyone, and placed his hands in easy reach of his blades.

"Oy, guv'nor, spare some for th' missus and me, wot?" asked the one in the lead.

A smile lighted the Noble's features as he responded, "My good sir, you would do better if you said please."

The man's brows shot up in surprise, obviously unused to receiving this type of response. Quickly recomposing himself to the jeers of his mates, he held up his club menacingly. "Th' only please me an' me mates need are these 'ere clubs. Now give us yer money."

Fernando's smile turned malicious. "Shall we give these gentlemen what they desire," he stated, glancing up at the Angel.

The ruffians chuckled at the prospect of new wealth received through violence.

Managing to hide the growing unease and nausea, he nodded. He disliked what he was about to do but there was no other choice. Who knew what they would do to another target if he and Fernando did not deal with them now. Pulling off his hood, he watched as the four tried to back away, fear filling their features, only to find the Noble suddenly blocking off their retreat.

Having moved passed the thugs too quickly for them to see, Fernando stood relaxed, a dagger in each hand. "I believe this is what you truly want," he grinned, a sadistic smile plainly revealing the sharp pointed teeth of the Chosen. At last the Noble was going to have some fun. With a quick flick of his wrists the blades flew, embedding themselves in the shoulders of two of the ruffians. Screams escaped their mouths, shocked by the pain but more by the cruel turn of fate that now placed them on the defensive.

Taking the release of the daggers as cue, the Angel reached out and with the training of centuries past and years to hone his abilities, quickly and effectively punched the leader in the face so that he fell backwards, unconscious and with a broken, bleeding nose. The last unhurt man, too terrified to scream, attempted to bolt but the Angel was there. Grabbing the ruffian by the neck, he turned the face away and sank his teeth into the unwashed neck.

Blood exploded into his mouth and it took all his effort not to swallow at first, tasting for the taint. All he found was the intoxicating sweetness of fear and sucked on the wound, filling himself of the life sustaining nourishment, hoping that his nausea would not rise. It did not take long to still the man's futile attempts to get free and just before death could claim the man, he released him to collapse onto the cobbles.

In shock of the sight of one of their own so brutally murdered, the two with the daggers in their shoulders found they could not scream for the hands that covered their mouths. Leaning between the two, Fernando still smiling wickedly, whispered, "Careful what you wish for, you might just get it. What? You don't like Yin and Yang? That is a shame. After all the trouble you went through to get them from me. Tch tch tch. That is too bad. I guess I can have them back."

He spun the two wounded men around like drunken tops and removed Yin from the larger man's shoulder. Free of its impalement the blood flowed fiercely down the man's chest, staining the already filthy shirt and coat. Yin did not remain bloodied for long as Fernando cautiously licked the blade clean to the horror of the men. Finding the blood untainted, the Noble raised a brow as if judging the quality of a fine wine and sunk his teeth into the man's neck.

Once drained, Fernando turned his attention to the last man standing and smiled. Red blood stained his teeth. "I take it that you now wish to keep Yang?"

Terrorized, the ruffian could only nod mutely, holding his wounded shoulder as his legs gave out.

Fernando sadly shook his head at the unfortunate reply. "I'm terribly sorry, but they are a matched set. Killed a slant eyes for them. So you see, I must have it back. Sentimental reasons of course."

Grabbing back Yang, he quickly dispatched the screaming man, and looked up at the Angel leaning against the bridge support with eyes closed, and then to the unconscious form of the leader.

"Is he tainted?" asked the Noble, bending over the only survivor, forgetting all about the two whom he just killed.

"I don't know," whispered the Angel. He kept his eyes closed in an attempt to keep his unease and nausea at bay. A light breeze pulled at his long white hair, causing the strands to fly in his face and he pulled up his hood.

"What do you mean?" demanded Fernando. "You took out one of them and you won't do the same to this one. I don't understand you. You feed off the one, yet not the other? By God, I took them both and now I won't need to feed for a week or more. This happenstance was fortuitous and you look like you've just fed off your brother."

Opening his eyes, he gazed at the unconscious body. "Then you take him." He could not handle any more. Maybe if they were not on this blasted bridge he would not have a problem, but right now even one was too much.

Face screwed up in disbelief, Fernando shook his head, knelt and finished off the last one. Wiping his mouth with a handkerchief, he stood, dismay still played on his features.

Lifting the corpse, the Noble said, "Are you going to help me, or what?"

Shoulders slumped, he sighed and easily picked up another of the bodies. It was an easy task throwing the corpses over the guard to land with a distant splash. No one would find them and if they did it would not be for quite some time. He knew he should feel some sort of remorse, he usually did, but his need to quit the bridge was pervasive in his being.

The sight of the black water below swallowing the last two bodies, forced him to back away from the edge, fighting to push down his rising nausea. "Can we go now?" he asked, wishing that the bridge would stop spinning.

"Sure," replied Fernando, mystified by the Angel's strange behaviour.

They quickly crossed the bridge in silence and without any further hindrance. Fernando occasionally glanced at his partner's intense features focused on nothing. Something had disturbed the pale man, and to Fernando's mind it was doubtful that the Angel would be this affected by the scene with the ruffians. No, there was something more, something that Fernando was missing.

Pursing his lips once they were off the bridge and seeing the Angel relax, he ventured, "You don't supposed that those men on the bridge were some sort of diversion." He knew the answer but he still wanted to hear the Angel's reply.

Finally back on solid land, he felt the shift and the evaporation of the nausea and vertigo. "I doubt it. If they were, they probably would have been tainted. No, they were just looking for trouble on their own."

"And found it they did," chuckled the Noble, dryly. "You're probably right. I wanted to confirm my own thoughts on the event. Now where is the soup kitchen that fair maid told us of?"

There did not seem to be much around. A few people dressed in average attire walked the street. Occasionally a carriage would roll by, drawn by tired horses. Not a block away, on the east side of the street, a large low square building, obviously converted from a warehouse, stood with its window's alight and its double doors thrown open.

Two men stood on either side of the old wide wooden staircase, batons hanging by leather strings from well-muscled wrists. These men were large and definitely not unintelligent. No one ventured in, but grubby people stumbled out in little clusters happily talking with one another or beaming in delight. The sign above the double doors, roughly painted in bright red, declared *London Free Kitchen*.

The name rang a bell and the Angel pulled out the business card. On it, it too, said *London Free Kitchen. How many were there?* He mused.

"I believe this is the place." He handed the card to the Noble. "I retrieved this from the old man that happened to be Rupert's last meal."

Fernando raised a questioning brow and flipped the card over. "Corbie Vale?"

He hitched a shoulder and took back the card. "Whoever Corbie Vale is we can count on him to be part of all this."

"True, if indeed they are the culprits."

"I imagine we shall soon find out." He walked towards the two men standing guard once all the riff-raff had left.

"What do you think you're doing?" hissed the Noble.

"I am going to find out if Jeanie is in there and hopefully end this nightmare." He turned to face the shorter man. "Do you have a problem with this?"

"Of course not! The idea is sound but the method ...there is no method!"

"Then what do you propose?" Fernando was correct. They needed some type of plan. Barging in probably would not be a good idea, but the idea of finding Jeanie alive was clouding his judgement and that was dangerous.

"Bluff it," stated Fernando, holding out his hand, palm up. A half smile pulled at his lips.

Reluctantly handing over the business card, he was unsure of the Noble's intent. With a nod of appreciation, Fernando turned and approached one of the men standing guard, a friendly smile on his face.

He was stopped from going up the stairs by a large outstretched arm, the baton now in a meaty grasp. The brute wore no expression and did not seem at all affected by Fernando's charming smile. The other guard turned. "I'm sorry, sir, but the establishment is closed for the evening. If you wish, you may come back tomorrow. The *London Free Kitchen* opens at half past four."

"You misinterpret my intentions, my good sir." Fernando inclined his head and held out the card. "As you can see, my friend over there and I have an appointment with Corbie Vale."

The man took the card and in the dull light emanating from the kitchen, read the card, mouthing the words. "This is one of our cards," he finally said, looking up. He did not hand it back, but slipped it into his pants pocket. "Unfortunately, Mr. Vale isn't here. He doesn't usually work at this kitchen."

"That is quite unfortunate," frowned Fernando. "He definitely told us to meet him here. Maybe we are a little early. We can wait for him inside." He made a move to ascend the stairs and found a hand on his chest preventing any forward movement.

"I'm sorry, sir, but I can't allow that." He kept his hand on the Noble. "I strongly suggest that you come back tomorrow or go to the other kitchen."

Fernando stared at the hand on his chest and slowly raised his eyes, his smile replaced with the onset of rage. "And I strongly suggest, sir, that you remove your meat hook from my person, *now.*"

The man's eyes widened in shock and dismay at the uncharacteristic response before his jaw tightened and his dark eyes narrowed menacingly.

"Gladly," he replied, and to drive his point home he gave the Noble a shove.

Stumbling backwards, Fernando had expected something like this and once he regained his footing he let Yin and Yang fly. Yang found his home in the throat of the brute that had begun his advance on the Noble. The large, silent man fell to his knees, blood streaming out of the fatal wound, and then collapsed onto the pavement, all the while trying to clutch at the dagger until he lay still. Yin found her home through the eyeball of the rude man, embedding deep into the brain. The man had no time to react to the intruding weapon before he too fell limply to the ground.

Admiring his handiwork, Fernando wiped his hands clean against each other and went to lean over the brute. An easy tug freed the bloody blade and he wiped it clean on the brown coat. He was not about to take any chance with the blood. Standing, he walked the two steps to the insolent man and realized he was doing all the dirty work.

"Am I going to get some help here?" asked Fernando, and bent, dislodging Yin from the socket of the dead man.

The Angel had watched the whole scene with a dour expression that grew at the violent deaths of the two men who had done nothing to warrant such an attack. Killing out in the open was dangerous and these two stacked the numbers to eight bodies in less than an hour. They were lucky that no one had witnessed any of the murders and he shuddered at the thought.

The homeless man had been killed by Rupert, taking the young Chosen with him, and the four on the Bridge were brigands deserving of no less, but these two on the stairs, they had done nothing except irritate Fernando by denying him entrance. The thought that Fernando could relish in cold-blooded murder appalled him.

Coming up behind the Noble, he asked, "What do you want to do with them? I do not think the police would like finding six bodies in the Thames."

Fernando pursed his lips in thought and then glanced up at his partner, a mischievous glint lighting his eyes. "Since this is a soup kitchen, there probably is a garbage bin in the back. We can dump them there." He reached down, grabbed the man's cold, limp hand, and hoisted him over his shoulder. "Don't you love the irony of it?" he chuckled, disappearing around the back of the building.

A sigh of resignation at the bad joke escaped his pale lips and he hoisted the brute and followed.

A dark lane followed the length of the back of the building, black in the absence of any gaslight or internal illumination. A few people huddled in their sleep for warmth under ratty blankets and refuse and he found Fernando dumping the body in a pile of garbage against the wall. Despite the bloodied face, the body appeared quite normal amongst the living ones. He bent and dropped his burden beside the other corpse in a way that made them appear to be passed out drunks.

He did not straighten right away. A dull light emanating from a window near to the base of the building caught his attention. Moving closer for a better look through the filthy glass and iron bars he saw, sitting on straw, Jeanie hunched over, shoulders shaking. He did not realize he had said her name until the Noble crouched beside him.

"Well I'll be damned," muttered Fernando. "That pretty little nothing was right. She is alive." He stood and slapped the Angel on the back. "Come on, you've got a fair maid to rescue."

Giving the Noble a sidelong glance, he stood but not without one last look at Jeanie.

I'll get you out, he promised and turned to Fernando. He was surprised at the slap on his back. It seemed almost friendly.

Rounding the corner of the Kitchen, they were going for the simplest way in, a frontal assault.

Taking the stairs two at a time they arrived before the open doors. Inside the brightly lit room could be seen rows of wooden trestle tables and old worn benches. Upon stepping in, it was evident the place was empty of patrons and staff. Along the west wall was the serving counter closed down for the night and at the north end of the dining room, on a raised dais was a speaker's pedestal. It looked what it appeared to be — a soup kitchen, but why would a soup kitchen have a gaol? And why was it imprisoning Jeanie? Nowhere could they find the entrance to the basement.

The answer arrived through the swinging door to the kitchen. The short skinny man wore a soiled wet apron and carried a tray of washed wooden plates. He dropped the pile with a crash at the sight of the Noble and the Angel staring at him.

"You. You're not supposed to be here," stated the man, ignoring the wooden heap that he would have to rewash. "We closed an hour ago."

"We're not here for a meal." Fernando took a step towards the little man. "We're looking for a friend. You may have seen her. A young, pretty woman, thin yet not skinny, about so high with green eyes and fiery long hair that falls in curls."

"Nope, haven't seen her." He bent to pick up the plates. "I'd remember her if I had."

"She speaks with a Scots accent," added the Angel, staying where he was, watching the man from the depths of his hood.

The man shook his head and stood, plates in hand. "Told you, I'd remember a girl like that." He piled the plates at the end of the serving counter and turned to go back into the kitchen.

"Then can you explain why she is locked in your cellar?" he took a step forward. He knew he was being lied to and it angered him. Why would they want to keep Jeanie?

The man halted, hand on the swinging door and did not turn around.

"Oh, nicely done," laughed Fernando, appreciating the subtle attack with the truth. He turned to face the kitchen help. "Well?"

The man got as far as pushing the door half open before both Chosen surrounded him. Fernando snatched the man's hand from the door the same instance the Angel wrapped his long white fingers around the man's sweaty neck.

He gave a slight squeeze, causing his prisoners eyes to bulge with the lack of oxygen. Relaxing his hand somewhat to allow the man to take a deep gasping breath, water wrinkled fingers clutched at his white hand in the futile attempt to escape.

"Where is the entrance to the cellar," he demanded. He ignored the Noble's vicious smile and bore his crimson gaze into the kitchen help's eyes. Chosen sensitive ears picked up every sound of the man's being as he quietly spoke into the man's soul. "How do I find Jeanie Stuart?"

His attempts to break free from the iron grasp vanished as a cloud descended. "Down the stairs from the kitchen," answered the little man, mechanically.

Satisfied with the answer, he let go of the throat and touched the man's forehead saying, "Sleep." Eyes rolled back and as if on cue the man slumped into his arms and he gently laid the man underneath the serving counter.

"Nice touch," remarked the Noble as the Angel stood. "I still don't understand why you didn't kill the insect."

"There has been too much killing," he replied, cautiously pushing the swinging door open.

"No such thing."

They stood on the threshold of a large kitchen stocked with skillets and huge pots that were arranged in an orderly manner along the counter. Above, on shelves lining the walls, a veritable storehouse of herbs and spices sat in containers of all shapes and sizes. In the centre of the counter a large sink filled with steamy soapy water and piles of food encrusted wooden trenchers sat waiting to be washed. It was highly doubtful that the job would get done this night. Along the far wall a large wood burning stove and ovens sparkled in the light, obviously cleaned earlier. There was no sign of the stairwell.

Opening the door farther was met by a solid thud. Fernando smiled up at his partner and they stepped into the kitchen, allowing the door to swing close behind them. Right beside the entrance stood a thick unadorned wooden door to the cellar. It opened without a sound. Cautiously, they stepped down the rickety stairs. Fernando's hands flexed and extended nervously, wishing Yin and Yang were in them. This was much too easy.

The cellar opened to a spacious room littered with scattered casks and barrels on the floor, and Jeanie huddled behind the barricade of iron bars.

At the sound of footpads descending, she looked up, her face drawn and her eyes red from crying. She could not believe who she saw, having resigned herself to the fact that the Angel would not care to find her. She sat there, in the straw, numb at the fantasy become reality.

His being leapt at the sight of the girl and only paused long enough for the Noble to pass the set of keys hanging on a hook at the bottom of the stairs. "Go rescue her and let's get the hell out of this place."

The keys felt cold against his hand but he paid it no mind. He covered the distance to the padlock on the bars far quicker than he should and he found that his hands shook as he tried the keys. It was the fourth one that turned the tumbler and snapped the lock open. Discarding the ring of keys and the padlock onto the floor, he pulled the iron barred door open and stepped inside, pushing back his hood.

Jeanie still remained on the floor, face full of shock. He was really here. Green eyes filled with tears and she threw herself on him, her arms wrapping around his slender waist as she buried her face in his chest weeping.

Unbalanced by her assault, he recovered himself long enough not to pull himself from her embrace. Reluctantly, his arms closed around her shuddering form and held her fast.

It felt odd, yet so right. He felt the warmth of her body encompass him and her heartbeat felt good against him. All that he wanted to do was keep her safe and happy. It terrified him even as he held her until the violence of her sobbing subsided.

"Are you alright?" he asked, gently lifting her by the chin with a finger to face him, but not breaking the embrace. She looked so lovely despite the effects of her crying. *I could drown in those eyes.* The realization stunned him to the quick.

Taking a couple of shuddering inhalations, Jeanie shyly turned her gaze from his burning crimson eyes to his chest and slightly drew back.

"Och, look what I've done," she sniffed. "I've gotten ye're shirt all wet." She laid a hand on his chest and drew it back when she realized what she had done.

A small smile lighted his features for a brief moment. It was so typical of Jeanie to worry over inconsequential things and yet so comforting.

"Are you alright?" he repeated, smile gone from his lips but not from his eyes.

Jeanie nodded and pulled back from the embrace, a frown bending her lips. "I thought ye'd never find me. I thought ye'd never look."

Surprise and hurt vied for dominance over her admission. "Of course I looked," he solicited. "How could I not?"

"But I thought–" Ashamed, she stared at the rush strewn floor as tears dripped down her face. Could she have been so wrong? She did not know what to think of the Angel any more. She just wanted to be in his embrace.

He laid his hands on her arms, causing Jeanie to look up at him. "I'm here now," he said.

"If the two of you are finished, I think you ought to take a look at this," called Fernando. He crouched by one of the barrels, his hand on a yellowed sheet of paper attached to it. To distance himself the embarrassing scene, the Noble had explored the contents of the room.

Moment dismissed by the taciturn declaration, the Angel lowered his eyes and his hands fell from Jeanie's shoulders, surprised that he was missing the momentary connection and turned around. "What is it?"

"While the two of you were playing damsel in distress rescued by her knight in shining armour, I decided to be more useful." Fernando stood studying the writing, paper now in hand. "This is the shipping order for these four barrels." He looked up long enough to point them out. "There are no names for the contents except this one is called *One*, this is *Two*, that *Three*, and the one over there is *Four*." He lifted the lid off of *One* and his brow lifted in surprise. Running his hand through the reddish brown powder, he grabbed a handful allowing the fine grains to slip between his fingers and fall back into the barrel. "What do you make of this?"

Intrigued at the discovery, he gave Jeanie an examining glance to see if she was all right and was returned by a sad frown before he walked to barrel *Three*. Lifting the lid revealed a greenish powder. The Chosen looked at each other before moving to the other unopened barrels that yielded two other types of powder. The smells of each were pleasant and unknown.

"They are just seasonings," he remarked, running his hand through *Two*.

"That's a lot of just four kinds of spice," responded the Noble. "They're not even named. Most of this will probably go bad before they can use it all."

Realization hit and he stated, "Not if these are the ones those two tried to force Tom and Alice to buy before torching the inn."

"What?" Shocked out of her reverie by the news, Jeanie took a step towards the two men, her eyes filled with concern.

"Yes," the Noble's head bobbed excitedly, ignoring the girl. "That would mean..." He grabbed a handful of spice from 'Four" and filled a pocket. "We need to take samples of these to make sure."

Before he could nod in agreement, Jeanie shouted, "What did ye say?" Her voice trembled as she fastened her pleading gaze on him.

Both the Angel and Fernando stared mutely for a moment, remembering Jeanie's presence. Fernando was the first to recover, going back to fill his pockets, mumbling in his native language, which, by the sounds of it were not complementary.

He shot the Noble a reproving glare and moved to the girl. "The *Rose and Thorn* burnt down earlier this evening. Arsoned by two men who tried to sell spices to Tom and Alice," he quietly explained.

"Oh, my dear God." Jeanie began to pace, trying not to cry again. She did not know if she had any tears left. Too much had happened too quickly and she was having difficulty making sense of things.

"Lily told me that you died in the fire." He tried to keep the hurt from his voice as he watched Jeanie pace.

"Then how did ye find me?" She halted and stared into sad ruby eyes.

"A woman told us you were carried away just before the fire," interrupted Fernando, now standing in the opened gaol with the other two.

Confusion filled her emerald eyes. "But that's no possible." Her gaze shifted between her two saviours. "I've been here all day."

It was their turn to be confounded. "But she said she saw you carried away this evening," he replied, pale brows furrowing.

"I dinna ken anythin' 'cept wakin' here just after noon."

The three of them stood silent for a moment before Fernando exploded. "*Carahlho!* What the bloody hell is going on?"

"The capture and disposal of the two of you."

They spun at the voice and found several men coming down the stairs with drawn sabres. A gasp escaped from Jeanie's trembling form as she found protection at the Angel's side. Fernando's face tightened in anger, more at himself for not having heard the approach of the men. His hands grasped the hilts of Yin and Yang. The Angel stared at the very deadly metal glinting in the dim light, his face drawn at the seriousness of the situation and the protection Jeanie expected from him. The man in front smiled, knowing he blocked the only exit. This fact was not lost on the three in the cage.

"I am quite surprised at how easily we managed. It took Sebastian over there quite a bit longer to get this far," said the sandy blonde leader, smile still intact.

Fernando glanced over at the three limbs he previously ignored, blanched and swore at the pile that could possibly pass for ash.

"Now, if you please, relinquish your weapons." Two men walked forward into the cage, sabres in hand, ready to take any arms presented.

"Not bloody likely," growled Fernando, throwing the daggers into the approaching men as the Angel pulled the door closed, forcing the dying men to stumble further into the cell.

He ordered Jeanie to get the lock that was lying in the rushes by the door. Holding the door took all his nerve as he saw the flash of metal descend towards his hands. He snatched them back in time as metal clanged against the metal of the lock as it snapped in place and the sabres impacted iron. Checking to see if he still had all his fingers, he sighed in relief and looked to Jeanie. Her face was full of worry and terror and there was nothing he could do. They were trapped.

"Get the key," shouted the sandy blonde headed man. It was obvious he was ill pleased at the apparent loss of control.

"I can't find 'em," replied another.

Realizing their dilemma, the Angel remembered where he had placed the keys. A quick search through the straw disclosed what the men were searching for. He held up the keys, jingling them a bit to get their captors attention. Fernando, having retrieved and pocketed Yin and Yang, now held both sabres in each hand, a murderous smile on his face.

The man in charge turned purple at the sight of the keys dangling from the hand of his would be prisoner. "Give those to me," he bellowed. "There is no way out, and I don't think you can wait until morning." His knowing laugh grated. "Definitely not. So in that case I'll leave some men here to stand guard. You four will stand watch." With a laugh he turned to go up the stairs, muttering something of how Mr. Vale would be pleased.

Relieved of their captor, he stared at each of the four men, his face tightened in anger at the sight of their fear of him, and turned to the Noble now standing at ease. "Let's get out of here." He did not care if the four heard him.

"And how, pray tell, do we do that?" mocked Fernando, relaxing on the hilt of one of the sabres pointed into the ground. "You have the key."

The Noble had a point, and going out the way they came seemed doubtful. It was likely there were now guards in place all over the kitchen if the sounds above were any indication. He scanned their cell and his gaze fell on the iron barred window. It was small, but not too small.

"We could do it," replied Fernando as if he heard the Angel's thoughts. "But what about them, and her?"

"Discretion." He would have to keep Jeanie occupied while the Noble worked his magic on the guards.

Taking the girl by the shoulder, he steered her towards the back corner opposite to the hanging corpse and put her in the corner, blocking her view. She hugged herself in an effort to warm her trembling form and did not look up. He could see that Jeanie was in shock from the events of the last twenty-four hours.

Removing the clasp from his cloak, he draped the too long material around her shivering shoulders and refastened the material. It was then that she looked up into his worried features. "Don't worry," he whispered, "we will be out of here soon." He so wanted to draw her close, yet was terrified at the thought.

"No," she shook her head, sending fiery wisps floating. "We're no' gettin' outta here."

Dropping down to one knee, he was able to gaze directly into her forest green eyes. Her trembling had eased a bit with the help of the cloak. "Do you trust me?"

She nodded weakly.

"Then trust me now when I say that I will do everything in my power to see you safe." He glanced away for a moment in astonishment of his own confession. Looking back at Jeanie he softly restated, "We will get out of here."

Full red lips parted in surprise at the fierceness of his words, Jeanie swallowed the dryness in her throat with a nod.

"Done," called the Noble.

He stood to face the four guards who now wore blank expressions. Whatever the Noble had done it was evident that their guards would be no trouble.

"Now what?"

"The bars on the window." He walked over to it, leaving Jeanie in the corner. "We remove them."

He wrapped his hand around the cold bar and gave an experimental tug. The masonry, old and crumbly, gave way enough to encourage another try. He knew he could easily pull them out by himself, but with Jeanie watching, he could not. He turned to face the Noble. "They are loose. The two of us can pull them out. The glass will be easier to deal with."

Fernando ogled in disbelief that the Angel would need help with such a simple task. Astounded at the preposterous notion, he sheathed the blades through his belt, shrugged and joined the Angel by the window. He gave his partner a long glare and placed his hands on the bar above his head. It came free with a tug and he tossed it to the ground, making metal ring on stone.

"What?" he demanded from the accusing crimson glare.

"Don't make it look so easy," hissed the Angel.

"Oh for the love of Christ," exasperated Fernando, but went along with the charade.

It went painstakingly slow trying to mimic the results of mortals but they managed to remove the iron bars one by one. The only mishap occurred when Fernando pulled the second to last bar too quickly from the bottom causing the jagged iron top edge to slide too fast out of place, cutting across the Angel's palm. The unexpected burning sensation caused him to jump back with a hiss. Sucking the wound until the pain somewhat receded he scrutinized it. The scratch was not serious and he shied away from Jeanie who wanted to examine his hand, saying that it was fine before rejoining in the effort to gain their freedom. Fernando's appraising gaze did not go unnoticed. It would be a disaster if either one got a glimpse of the bloody red scratch with the charred edges.

At last the final bar was removed and the glass broken as quietly and carefully as possible.

"You go first," he suggested to the Noble.

"Gladly," answered Fernando, pleased to quit from the dank surroundings and the Angel's strange behaviour. Hauling himself through the window took little effort, but he knew that the end of the escapade would ruin his clothing.

Alone in the cell, he turned to Jeanie and held out his uncut left hand. She took it. She was light in his arms as he assisted her through the window with less grace than the Noble for all the complications of skirts and cloak. Half way through the window she got caught on a shard of glass and he had to ease the material lest she be cut, at the same instance sounds of footsteps on the stairs made him rush.

With a final shove, Jeanie was through the window and he turned to face the woman from the alley ringed by men with drawn swords. In the limited light she seemed even more recognizable, but from where he could not recall. The expression on her face was one of surprise as he bowed his head and exited through the window.

Jeanie stood wrapped in his cloak while Fernando searched the area. Unable to take the time to find what the Noble lost, he grabbed Jeanie's arm. "Let's go, they've discovered us."

Fernando snapped his head around at the sound of pursuing feet and followed the Angel and the girl down the alley muttering angrily about running away from a good fight. He caught up as they came out onto a brightly lit street, the sound of pursuit in the distance, and looked to the Angel, amused to discover what was next.

Bereft of his cloak, he stood exposed to the street. The only sound ringing in his ears was Jeanie's haggard breath. He could not flag down a carriage, not like this.

"What—are—we—gonna—do—now?" panted Jeanie. She never thought anyone could run that fast and for the most part she had felt herself be dragged, feet hardly touching the ground. Her wrist hurt and the beginnings of a bruise began to develop. She was surprised to find the Angel's blood smeared on it and hastily she wiped it away.

"We need to find a cab." His eyes darted up and down the road, finally narrowing on a slowly approaching carriage in the distance. Slinking into the shadow of a nearby building, he hid himself from view. "When it comes, hail it."

"What the hell are you planning to do?" demanded Fernando.

He stepped back into the gaslight. "Do you think he will stop for one such as I? Hail him, distract him and then I will join you." He moved back into the comforting shadows.

There was nothing Fernando could do. The Angel was right. He would not stop if he were the driver.

As the carriage approached, Fernando hailed it, helped Jeanie into the comfortable confines and engaged the driver in conversation over fees and destination, allowing the Angel to sneak aboard. Once all three were inside and rolling, Fernando broke the silence. "They were gone."

Slouching down so his head would not hit the ceiling of the cab, his head rested against the wall, his long white hair disarrayed against the backing. He opened his eyes. "Who?"

"The men I killed who were on guard," replied the Noble, testily.

Jeanie mutely observed her two liberators, eyes widening through the conversation.

"They were probably discovered." He felt tired, his hand hurt and he wanted to get Jeanie to safety and that most likely meant a trip back over the Thames. He did not want this.

"Doubtful. By the looks of it, one got up and dragged the other away and both received killing blows."

"Are you sure?"

"I don't make mistakes about these things," responded Fernando, curtly.

The two Chosen stared at each other for a long moment as the carriage trundled along the cobblestone road.

XII

iolet Flowers stood enraged as she watched the Angel escape through the cell window. All around her the hired thugs gaped, open mouthed, swords held at relaxed angles. Realizing that no one had made a move to apprehend the escaping prisoners, Violet swung around screaming at the men to chase after them.

Shocked out of their reverie, the men hastened to the stairs, each clambering over the other lest they receive her wrath. The only men left standing were the four original guards, eyes staring into oblivion.

"They will not catch them, even with the girl."

Violet spun around. Her revealing blue dress with ivory lace scattered the dust on the floor. She found a trim dark haired man with fine features and dark, almost black eyes, advancing towards her. He was handsome despite his perpetual air of arrogance.

"Corbie Vale," she sneered. "Come to see the failure of your plan? I am sure Bastia will not be pleased when she hears of this fiasco."

Corbie stared at the soft white mounds exposed by Violets low cut dress, a smile played momentarily on his thin lips before meeting her frosty glare. He cupped his chin in appraisal. "No, I don't think she will like this at all, but no matter, there is always a second chance."

"She doesn't give second chances." Violet moved out of Corbie's stare to stand behind one of the automatons.

"You would know," muttered Corbie.

"And what is that supposed to mean?" she said hotly, peeking around the solid form, blue eyes blazing.

"Well, you did fail with Sebastian."

"That was an accident!"

Corbie made a disbelieving sound in his throat and rolled his eyes. "Please. I am not a fool. I was the one who had to clean up after you, and as you can see I made no mistakes."

"Then what about those two?" she sniffed. "The ones you let get away?"

Features darkening, he slinked up behind Violet and whispered into her pearl studded ear, "There would have been no mistakes had *someone* not led them here so early."

"Are you accusing me of sabotaging your schemes?" She remained where she was, feeling his words on her neck.

"Now why would I do that?" he said, sarcastically.

Spinning away, Violet gave a laugh. "Because you are vindictive, psychotic, a psychopath and a sociopath."

"All those, eh? One might think you were glorifying yourself," sneered Corbie. "At least you did not call me a liar. That title is reserved only for you."

"Bastard!"

"Bitch!" His hand slammed across her face, making her head snap sideways as she stumbled backward. "You ruined my plan to successfully capture and destroy those Chosen, for what? So that you can get your putrid hands on the one called the Angel? You disgust me. I think Bastia will be as repulsed by your secret agenda as I am!" He turned to go up the stairs.

Violet touched the cut inside her mouth with her tongue, the taste of her own blood fuelling her anger.

"I don't think so, darling," she sneered. He halted on the stair. "I've already been given the next attempt."

"Things change, Violet." Corbie continued up the steps. "I always make sure of that."

She was left alone in the cellar, except for the four oblivious guards, and the guttering candle snub. Once the light left she screamed out her rage.

XIII

The carriage came to a halt along a well-gardened strip of large homes. Sleeping inhabitants blackened most out, others had one or two lights on, either forgotten or in use by those who could not sleep. No other coaches roamed this remote suburban area near Hyde Park. Silence dominated the night, punctuated by the snorts and shuffling of the horses.

The Angel lifted his head from the cabin's wooden wall and opened his eyes. The scratch on his right hand was worse than he thought but he could not let on so he kept his fist in a tight ball. Willing the pain and heat away, he prayed he would not need stitches. The bridge crossing was even worse for it, and he had to feign sleep so as to escape any questing glares from Fernando. The carriage not only trundled along but also seemed to spin and swirl once they moved over the water beneath the bridge. Never before was he so gratified to be off of a bridge.

Fernando and Jeanie sat on the opposite leather bench. Fernando gathered himself to exit the close confines while Jeanie stared out the window still huddled in his cloak. She sighed sadly at the Angel and tried to force a smile. Despite the dark circles under her eyes she looked pretty.

She had not said a word since entering the cab and sometimes he had seen tears fill her eyes, only to be dashed away by her hand. He had freed her, she had been so happy to see him, now she would not even as much as look at him.

"Awright, folks," called the driver. "You're 'ere."

The Noble exited the cabin, landing on the fancy styled stone walk and helped Jeanie down, a slight scowl on his face, before turning to pay the driver.

This diversion allowed the Angel the opportunity to step out and stand behind the carriage. It was only when the driver chucked the reigns with a click and drove off did he step out to join the others on the walk.

"Where are we?" he asked, studying the fancy architecture of the surrounding homes.

"My place." Fernando pulled out a set of keys from a cloak pocket and turned to go up the walk of a very fine house. "I thought the farther away from those *cadroes* the better, and frankly your place is too small."

The Noble's home was a large three-story manse built in deep red brick with windows of large paned glass. Over the bay window of the main floor, leaded glass carved with a wildlife scene accentuated the grandness of the home. Drapes blocked access to view the interior.

"You can stay the day." Fernando slipped the key into the lock and gave it a turn. "There's safety in numbers."

The large dark oak door swung inwards revealing a beautiful interior of dark mahogany wainscoting that accentuated the patterned green velvet wallpaper. Off to the right, flanked by a banister of dark polished wood, a stairway with a glorious Persian runner led to the second story.

With a flick of the switch, the foyer lit up with gaslight, revealing the richness of the home. The Angel's eyes widened as Fernando moved into the parlour, lighting candles as he went. Jeanie gasped at the sight of expensive furniture arranged in a way so that all persons would face one another if seated. The polished hardwood floor reflected the candlelight to the vaulted ceiling plastered in a menagerie of swirls and designs, making the room appear brighter than the number of candles would suggest.

On the wall, opposite to the parlour entrance, a large fireplace, neatly stocked with wood and kindling awaited to be lit into life. Above the mantle, flanked by matching pillar candles, hung a large portrait of a young beautiful woman. Her delicate features intensified her large brown eyes and full red lips. There was an air of innocence around her despite the fanciful nature of her rich courtly gown from another era. Her brown tresses had been done in a most becoming, yet intricate network of pearls and combs.

Ducking under the lintel, the Angel entered the room, followed closely by Jeanie, not taking his eyes off the portrait.

"Ye hae a most beautiful home," whispered Jeanie as she stared, trying to take in the sheer richness of the place. Any doubt she had regarding Fernando's nobility vanished at the sight.

Finished lighting the last candle in the candelabra that sat on the baby grand, Fernando turned and blew out the taper. "Thank you. It has taken me many years to get it this comfortable." He gestured for Jeanie to sit on the cherry wood rimmed couch.

Noticing the Angel's rapt attention on the portrait, Fernando scowled. "Am I going to have to stand on ceremony, or will you sit?"

Breaking his gaze, he blinked not absolutely sure what the Noble had said. "Who is she?" he asked, seating himself beside Jeanie, who deepened her frown.

"She is the Lady Maria Isabel de Leiora, and she is very dead," explained Fernando with a finality that brooked no further comment. Seating himself on the opposite identical couch, he continued, "I brought you here because I figured we needed to have a little chat." He reclined against the back of the couch, placing his feet on the low table between them.

The Noble's condescending tone did not go unnoticed, and the Angel sat back. Whoever the Lady Maria Isabel de Leiora was would remain a mystery. He let his hands rest comfortably on his lap, ignoring the rising heat in his right. "What is it that you want to talk about?"

"A few things, in fact," remarked Fernando.

He waited patiently for the Noble to continue.

"First and foremost, no matter the reason we are not going to run off on a wild goose chase any longer. I will only follow facts. They are more reliable, though I have to admit this time it paid off." He began to empty his pockets of the different powders, careful not to mix them. Four neat piles of spices lined up on the table. Fernando continued, "Secondly, what are we going to do with her? I don't need a liability in this venture, and if she is going to become one, take heed, I will eliminate the liability before any harm comes to me."

Pale white features darkened at the veiled threat. "Pardon me?" he demanded, leaning forward.

"You heard." Fernando tried to match the Angel's glare but could not meet the smouldering ruby eyes.

"And so did I," interjected Jeanie, the shocks of the night's events threatened to repeat themselves.

Fernando raised a brow. "Ahh, so you've finally managed to find your tongue. I thought that it was lost forever. I so did miss it."

"Fernando," growled the Angel.

"Oh come now. If she's going to help us – if she still wishes it."

"I still wish," blurted Jeanie, not at all appreciating the treatment. "I can take care of myself."

"Like you did tonight?" pointed out Fernando. Jeanie closed her mouth without protest. "This one here," he pointed to the Angel, "may accept your help in this matter, but that does not mean I have to. I have seen how you listen to orders. Well, little miss, I do not and will not go through rescuing the damsel in distress again. Understand? That means you will not only listen, but you will do as I say, because if you do not you will never be able to listen to anything again." He ignored their glares, yet the Noble could see that the Angel recognized the sentiment in his words.

"Ye canna order me around," yelled Jeanie. "I did nothin' wrong. How dare ye–"

"Shut up, Jeanie," The Angel's voice was tired yet pointed enough to halt the girl in mid sentence.

Astonished, Jeanie could only blink. Never had he spoken to her in this manner.

In amusement, Fernando's eyes widened.

Taking a deep breath, he continued without meeting Jeanie's shocked green eyes. "Somehow they know your connection to me and this has placed you in great danger, for possibly only one purpose: to get to us. We cannot have you place yourself in situations that could get us all killed. You have no idea what you are dealing with."

"And ye do?" She shifted away from the Angel. She did not understand him. One moment he was kind and gentle to her and the next he was so cold and ruthless.

"To some extent, yes," he responded. Who wanted him, Fernando and the rest of the Chosen dead was a mystery slowly unravelling itself, but he knew them to be cunning and extremely dangerous.

"Then tell me," she implored.

"I cannot."

"Why?"

"I cannot." He paused a moment, the silence in the room overwhelming. "I have asked you to trust me, a task that is not easy, I know, but please try."

A frown formed on Jeanie's lips and her eyes fell to the intricate patterns of the rug. "Aye, I trust ye, but," she sighed, she wanted to do more than just trust him and he was making it oh so difficult at this moment. "I feel so useless, like a dog on a leash, ye ken?"

He nodded. He felt exactly the same.

Unexpectedly a loud rumble exploded in the room and Jeanie blushed. Fernando could only shake his head in exasperation. "There's food in the pantry." He jerked a thumb behind him. "Go help yourself. I'm sure some of Bridget's whores wouldn't mind sharing."

Standing up, Jeanie unwrapped herself from the Angel's cloak, folded it and gave it to him. "Thank ye," she said, blushing again as her stomach rumbled once more. Grabbing a solitary candlestick from the candelabra, Jeanie followed Fernando's directions to the pantry.

Alone in the parlour, his pale features hardened on the Noble.

"What?" cried Fernando.

"If you ever raise even a finger to harm Jeanie in any way I will see you dead." Crimson eyes flashed menacingly.

Surprisingly, Fernando chuckled before his face turned to stone. "Yes, I can see that you have it bad for that one, but let me point out one thing, you cannot be in all places at all times. If she does not follow orders, especially at a crucial moment, and the result is, how shall I say it, less than desirable, then she will wish that she had never been born. It is you who desires her presence, thus tying our hands to act in ways that are normal for us."

He looked away, knowing the truth of the Noble's words, but he would not allow Fernando to harm Jeanie. "If I have not said so before, I will say so now. I will take responsibility for any and all of Jeanie's actions, and I will take the consequences that come with them."

Tapping finger against his lips, Fernando quietly studied his partner. "Alright, then it's settled."

"What's settled?" Jeanie walked into the room, her arms laden with an open bottle of wine, a little black jar, a hunk of cheese and a package of crackers. Setting the groceries down on the table she produced three wine glasses from her large skirt pockets and sat down.

"That the Angel is going to take full responsibility for you." Fernando ignored her dumb expression, took his feet off the table and lifted the wine bottle. "You have expensive tastes, my dear. I usually reserve this vintage for special guests." He poured her a glass of the fine Beaujolais.

"It was all ye had." She nodded her thanks and took a sip. Putting the glass down, Jeanie looked at the Angel who stared out into the hall. "Ye dinna hae t' do that; take responsibility for me, ye ken."

He turned to face her. "It was the only way."

She let out a sigh and picked up the little black jar, trying to open it. "I've taken care of myself for as long as I remember. I can care for myself now."

Noting her frustration over the little jar, he took it from her grasp and opened it. The angry expression on her face stopped him short from returning the jar. Snatching it back, Jeanie curtly offered her thanks and gazed into the contents, frowning. A dunk of her finger revealed tiny black pearls stuck together that shimmered wetly in the candlelight. "Wha—what is this?" She wiped her finger on the jars edge, removing the little globs, and tried to read the foreign language on the label.

"It is Russian caviar," answered Fernando, dryly.

"I thought it was jam." Her mystified expression deepened into a frown and she glanced up at the Noble. "What's caviar?"

Fernando blanched noticeably at the revelation. Pursing his lips into a tight line, he replied, "Fish eggs."

"Oh, that's disgustin'." She dropped the jar on the table, spilling some of the contents.

Picking up the jar, Fernando unceremoniously dolloped some of the caviar onto a cracker and shoved it towards Jeanie's face. "You touched it, you eat it," he stated matter-of-factly, holding his anger in check. "I paid a pretty penny for this and you will eat it."

Jeanie made a face at the little black eggs glooped together on the wafer and took it from the Noble. Her sense of hunger abated at the sight and she glanced to the Angel hoping he would rescue her from this trap, but he seemed more intent on the Noble.

Cautiously, she took a bite. The salty round hardness exploded in her mouth. The taste was neither pleasant nor unpleasant and she took another bite. She could feel dark eyes intent on her as she washed down the mouthful with the Beaujolais.

"Aren't ye gonna hae some?" She broke off a chunk of cheese and popped it into her mouth, relishing in the normalcy of the taste.

"No, that's alright," declined Fernando. "We've already eaten."

Cautiously, Jeanie spooned some more caviar onto another cracker and popped it into her mouth. This time it was not so bad. It just took a bit of getting used to.

Nodding towards the four piles, her mouth still full, she asked, "Why d'ye take these?" She swallowed. "It dinna look to me like ye do much cookin'."

"How very astute of you." Fernando fingered the fine powder of the first pile. "I do tend to eat out quite often." He flashed a full-toothed grin exposing his sharpened teeth and ignored the Angel's disapproving glare. "The food is for my guests. As to these, I brought them on a hunch. The ambiguity of the contents of the barrels and this little bottle," — he pulled out the phial — "and a certain reaction, in the midst of other deciding factors, leads me to theorize that this is what will aid us in our search." He placed the phial at the end of the row. "But do these equal that and if so, how?"

Licking her fingers clean of caviar and crumbs, Jeanie picked up the little bottle and read out the numbers. "D'ye ken the names of these?" she asked, indicating the piles of spices.

Fernando placed a finger to his lips. "There were no names given, even on the shipping order, only numbers. One, two, three and four," he answered, mildly amused at the girl's involvement. If she had any knowledge he would use her. Fernando was starting to see some benefit of keeping her around.

Her wine stained lips pouted in thought as she read the bottle again. Wiping out the lid of the caviar bottle with the hem of her skirt – she could not find anything else – she placed it lid side down on the table before the phial. "Which one is *one*?"

Interest aroused, Fernando pointed to the pile on his left. "I believe this is *one*, that is *two*, that *three* and this one is *four*. Why?"

Jeanie flashed a smile and measured *one* into the palm of her hand. Satisfied with the amount she dumped it into the lid, and began doing the same with the other powders.

Intrigued, the Angel brought his attention to the careful measuring and mixing of the herbs and watched as Jeanie dumped the last spice and stirred with her finger. The intensity of the smell exploded into the room, causing him to gag before his hands could cut the putrid smell from infecting his nostrils.

Through tearing eyes he witnessed Jeanie's gasp as the Noble snatched the lid, ran to the door, arm covering his face, to hurl the contents and lid into the street. The door slammed shut, Fernando clearly shaken.

Reluctantly, the Noble lowered his arm, sniffing the air. The Angel followed Fernando's example. The smell lingered, and to the bemusement of Jeanie, he covered his mouth and nose with his hand.

"This is wonderful, just wonderful," muttered the Noble as he went about the room flinging heavy drapes aside and opening windows in an attempt to air the place out. "It's going to take forever to get rid of the stench."

A slight breeze stirred his long white hair and through the hand covering his mouth, he spoke, "At least we now know what those herbs are."

"Yes, but is it the cause of the poisoning?" Fernando found his seat. Already the room smelled better.

"Poisoning?" exclaimed Jeanie, backing away from the powders. Her hand grabbed another cracker and dunked it into a surprisingly empty jar. The smell had made her ravenous and all that now remained were a few crackers.

Lowering his hand from his face, he tried to soothe her. "There is nothing for you to worry about. Even if it is, it will not harm you. At least I don't think so," he finished in a whisper. He exchanged her frightened and confused sight for the frown on the Noble's face.

"Well," huffed Fernando. "There's only one way to find out if this is the cause."

"How?" Crimson eyes narrowed suspiciously.

The answer was quick and forthcoming as Fernando whipped out Yin, grabbed Jeanie's wrist and cut. Her scream of shock turned into a cry of pain as the Noble held her, allowing red beads to drip from the shallow wound onto the table. Try as she might she was locked in strong hands.

At her cry and the realization of the Noble's movements, the Angel bolted to his feet. It was totally unexpected and he moved in a haze of shock, but fast enough to grab the thick wrist and strike Fernando across the face. The Noble released Jeanie's wrist as he bounced against the back of the couch.

The malicious smile gone, he rubbed the side of his stinging face and tested his jaw. Fernando had never been punched that hard before. "You weren't kidding." The Angel glared at him and he brought his attention to the pool of blood on the table.

Shooting the Noble one last glare, the Angel sat beside Jeanie who rocked her embraced arm in an attempt to will the pain away.

"Let me see it." He tried to make his voice gentle despite the anger that swelled within. It seemed to work; Jeanie sniffed, nodded, and extended her arm, allowing him to take it.

Her skin was soft and warm to his touch. The cut was not deep and seemed to be clotting. He ran a thumb over the wound, making her flinch, but it seemed better. The smell of her hot blood called to him and he met her intense green eyes. For a moment they locked and there was nothing but each other. Startled, he released her.

"It will heal," he remarked, and then turned his attention to the Noble.

"Is there some place where she can rest?" His anger barely in check, his inquiry more of an order.

Brown eyes narrowed, yet the curl of his lips did not depart. "Upstairs," answered Fernando with a jerk of his head. "Second door on your left."

Nervous of possible further attacks, Jeanie stood, holding her wounded wrist and glanced down at the Angel, worry filling her eyes.

"Go ahead," he nodded. "It will be alright."

Jeanie turned, picked up the flickering candle in a plain silver holder and went half way up the stairs where she halted. Allowing for one final glance down at him, she briefly smiled, and hurried up the final steps.

He watched Jeanie's flight and slumped his shoulders at the slam of the door. Running an uninjured hand through his hair, he brought his eyes to bear on the Noble. "You had better explain yourself." His tone was cold and threatening. "For if you do not I *will* carry out my promise."

"Yes, you do have it bad for that one," chuckled the Noble. He swirled a finger in the pool of blood and popped the red stained finger into his mouth, sucking it clean, all the while keeping an eye on the Angel. "Delicious don't you think"

"You are a *vampire*," he sneered. He meant it purely in a derogatory way and at the raised brow he knew Fernando had received it as such. "There is nothing left to you except your own cruelty." He rose to his feet. "You care for nothing and as such nothing cares for you. I pity you." He turned to go up the stairs.

"Where do you think you are going?" bellowed the Noble, rising. Pity was for weaklings and to have it thrust on him infuriated him.

He placed a foot on the first step and addressed Fernando. "I am going to remove Jeanie and myself from your presence. This partnership is at an end."

"Fine, but don't you want to find out if it is that powder?" His half smile returned as the Angel halted halfway up. Pulling out the purchase order, Fernando waved it enticingly. "Not to mention I am the one with the next lead. What do you have?"

Knowing that Fernando was right, he reluctantly descended and came to tower over the Noble, who sat and opened the little bottle. Instantly the room filled with the horrible stench.

"You may have the leads. I can find more on my own."

"With her helping you? I doubt it." Fernando tapped the mouth of the phial, distributing a small amount into the red pool. "You allow her presence to limit you because you will not tell her the truth of what you are." He mixed the blood and powder together with a finger.

"And what is that?" he inquired, coldly.

Fernando shot the Angel a sidelong glance. "A va—, a Chosen, of course." He sucked his finger clean and spat. "It's the powder."

The culprit of the poisoning revealed, the Angel stared at Jeanie's tainted blood for a moment before bringing his gaze back to the Noble. "It is forbidden to tell mortals of our existence unless they are about to be Chosen. She is *not* to be Chosen. Yet you still think I should tell her."

"If you don't, I will." Fernando's face was all seriousness.

"No."

"Then you limit us both."

"We are partners no longer."

A deep chuckle resounded through the room. "You don't see it, do you? We're stuck with each other if we want to survive, and I have a feeling that you have much more to lose than I. Therefore you can pity me all you want and we will remain partners."

Shoulders slumped in resignation; he landed heavily on the opposite couch. "I do not want you to tell her."

"You will?"

"No," he shook his head.

"God damn it, man," exploded Fernando. He thought he was getting through to his partner. "Damn your stubbornness!"

"We are limited by what we are. What difference does this make?"

"A big difference," ranted the Noble. "She is going to figure out that we don't eat, we don't drink and that we can't go out in the day. She *will* notice that we are different."

Propping elbows on his knees, he rested his head in his good hand. "Notus and I have kept it a secret for five years, but if she finds out then I will deal with it if the time comes."

"I don't think it's a matter of if. It's a matter of when. Whatever excuses you and your sire conjured up aren't going to be applicable to us working together."

Silence fell between the two. Fernando was probably right about Jeanie yet he was reluctant to do anything about it. He had no idea how she would react if she found out, but he believed it would be the end of her involvement. It would also mean an end to her life since Notus made it impossible for him to use the Push on her. The thought of taking her life to keep his secrets opened a pit in his stomach.

Gradually the light in the parlour began to take on the subtle changes that were the prelude to dawn. Lines around objects became more defined and the yellow glow from the numerous candles became more restricted.

Slapping his hands against his thighs, Fernando rose to his feet. "It looks as if you will have to stay the day," he remarked, making the rounds to close windows, draw drapes, and snuff wicks. "It is too bad that we cannot at least witness the birth of the day. If there is something I miss it is that."

Following the Noble's example, he stood, cloak in hand and went up the stairs, leaving Fernando to stare oddly at him as he entered the second room on the left.

The door clicked shut behind him and he approached the window, its curtains wide open, allowing the soft grey light of pre-dawn to spill into the large room. Savouring the last remnants of the night, he drew the drapes, leaving him in near darkness to study his surroundings.

The bedroom was larger than he expected, with a canopied bed taking up precedence along the northern wall. A wardrobe, a chaise and a few dressers were neatly arranged, allowing for space and aesthetics. On the top of one of the dressers a porcelain pitcher and basin stood ready for use.

A sigh filtered in the silence, reaching sensitive ears. He turned to find Jeanie asleep in the large bed and quietly walked up to her. He picked up her clothes from the floor and hung them on the footboard before coming to stand beside her sleeping form. The light from the candle on the bed stand lit up the fire of her hair. A menagerie of red, gold, russet, cinnamon and even crimson danced in response to the flickering flame.

Kneeling down, he stared at her relaxed face and noticed for the first time the slight sprinkling of freckles across the bridge of her small slightly upturned nose. Long thick red eyelashes danced over dreaming eyes and she let out a soft moan from her full lips. The cut on her forehead was healing well and he so wanted to smooth the frown from her face. Instead, nervously, he allowed himself to touch one of the many curls abound on the pillow. Its soft tress encircled his finger and he luxuriated in the touch. He knelt there silently intoxicated by the sight, sound and smell of Jeanie.

Abruptly the short vigil was broken as she rolled onto her side. Standing up, he pulled the thick coverlet over her pale shoulder, her shift having slipped down her arm. Backing away, not wanting to retreat from the view, a shudder ran up his spine. *My Gods, this* is *love.* The thought filled him with terror and something else – joy.

It could not be, he had steeled himself from this possibility for so long. To have it happen again, now, confounded and horrified him, yet he so wanted to drink it in and let it wash over him.

Retreating to the washbasin, he found it filled with fresh water and placing his folded cloak on the chaise he went and dunked his trembling hands in the cool water. The scratch on his right hand cooled significantly, but the redness remained. It felt worse than it appeared and he flexed and extended his fingers experimentally. Hopefully, it would be better come sunset.

After splashing water on his face, he kicked off his shoes and collapsed on the chaise. It would be a very uncomfortable day's sleep. Blanketing himself with the cloak, he shifted the throw pillows and lay on his side, feet sticking off the end of the chaise, knees hanging off the middle. From this angle he could keep watch over Jeanie and closed his eyes. Before long the fatigue of the night's adventures pulled him to sleep.

XIV

The road was muddy, pocked with puddles of unknown depths and contents, and grew larger in the addition of the heavy rain that fell in torrents. Every so often the guard would march by, seemingly oblivious to the rain yet obviously bogged down by the drudgery of labouring through the deep, sucking mud. Occasionally horse and rider would kick up and churn the sodden street, casting globules of brown muck onto those unfortunate not to have removed themselves from the downpour.

Bouncing lights in enclosed lanterns usually commanded this time of night. Now they remained stationary as members of the watch would step into a local tavern to wash away the cold dampness. A few brave souls dawdled along, cloaks and lanterns swinging in the wind, fulfilling their nightly duty.

1386 was turning out to be a miserable year.

For two hours past sunset the evening seemed more alive than usual. Coaches, elaborate in their workmanship and pulled by the finest breeds, forced the guard apart as they passed. Attendants in rain-slicked cloaks, heads down in dour misery of the weather, glanced at the occupants of obvious noble worth.

Lightly, he hopped back; mud caked on his boots, in an attempt to dodge a spray of mud kicked up by the speeding wheels of a coach. Fast as he was, the splatter dotted his wool cloak already heavy with rain. There was no use trying to clean off the muck so obviously infectious to clean garments. With a resolute sigh he plodded on.

Hunger satiated earlier with the help of a one handed beggar tired and sick of life, he now only wanted to get out of this all pervading rain and into some dry clothes. Water had seeped into his boots not a moment after exiting the small back room of the warehouse that served as their home. Now he walked in water. The mud had not decreased the intake as he had hoped. His cloak hung heavily from his shoulders and had long since ceased to be effective. Rivulets ran down his back, milk white hair plastered against his pale skin, and his leather breeches clung uncomfortably as he walked.

Pulling the hood farther over his forehead, he hoped in vain that it would keep the rain out of his eyes. It was a miserable night and so was he.

A turn off the road and down an alley led him straight home. Homeless dotted the side of the building in hopes of at least a dry place for the night. Most were solitary, huddled beneath eaves, but there was one small group. As he approached the door to his home a small child broke from the group and ran to him. Her fair hair stuck to her thin face and her bare feet kicked up mud that stuck to her threadbare robe.

"Wait," she called, finally catching up to him.

Deciding that it did not matter if he got any dirtier, he knelt down on one knee and immediately regretted it. On nights like these the ache in his leg would spontaneously appear. He had thought that nearly two hundred years was long enough to heal completely. Evidently he was wrong, and ignoring the shooting pain he quietly asked, "What is it, Sarah?"

"Ma's started coughin' 'gain." Worried blue eyes fell to the mud.

"Did she not take the medicine Father Notus gave her?"

She bobbed her head and gazed up into the darkness of his cowl. "It's not workin' nomore."

He noticed the dark circles of privation and worry. "Did you not ask Father Notus for more?"

"I tried, but he's not home."

He frowned and glanced at the door. Notus said he would not be going out and that he had work to do. It was probably that his Chooser was so engrossed as to have not heard the rapping on the door. There was not much that he could do to help Sarah and her mother and sadly wondered what would happen to Sarah and her brother when their mother finally succumbed to the ravages of the cough. He did not doubt that that time was not too far off.

Reaching into the drawstring purse hanging from his belt, he counted out several shillings and handed them to her. "Get yourself and your family out of the rain and into someplace warm. I will tell the Father about the medicine."

Sarah's eyes went round at the sum of money in her frail hands. With a jingle, her hands closed in tight fists to ensure the protection of the gift. Her eyes were still wide as she flung her arms around him, repeating her thanks over and over.

Thrown off balance, both mentally and physically at the unexpected assault, he could only gape at her blonde head nestled against his chest. Closing his mouth, he reluctantly returned the embrace. She was thin, too thin. Her shoulders felt insubstantial under his hand and she shivered in the cold rain. Her heat warmed him and the smell of her young blood intoxicated him. It would be so easy to release her of the pain of this life. He shuddered at the thought, at his own ruthlessness. He would not do such a thing. It would go against everything Notus ingrained upon him. She still had a life to live and to take from an innocent was abhorrent. The villains and those asking for release were his prey.

He removed her bony arms from around his waist and forced her back a step. Her eyes were bright with excitement and he felt himself return her smile.

"You had best get going before all the inns are filled," he ordered, the usual sternness replaced with something more accepting.

She nodded enthusiastically and turned to go but before she had taken a step Sarah swung about, lifting up on her toes, and kissed him square on the cheek. Flashing another radiant smile she ran back to her family shouting, "Thank you."

He blinked in astonishment, the touch of her lips still warm on his face, and painfully rose to his feet, mud sticking heavily to breeches. He hoped that she would be all right and be one of the few in her position to make it to adulthood. The reality was that she would be lucky to live until next winter.

The mud squelched beneath his boots as the rain ebbed its downpour. Placing his hand on the door, he turned for a final glance back at Sarah and her family's departure, and then pushed in, the hinges squeaking with dampness.

A few candles illuminated the small room. One on the rickety table in the centre at which Notus worked unaware of his sons appearance, and the other two hung on the back wall in sconces. Without the need to glance up, Notus dipped the quill into the black pool of ink.

"Don't just stand there, close the door before you get everything wet," remarked the monk, carefully scribbling in a thick leather bound book.

Wordlessly, he closed the door and threw the latch. Aware of the puddle he was causing on the floor he removed the cloak and hung it from a peg beside the door and then proceeded to remove his boots.

Finished with his line, Notus sanded the expensive vellum and then poured it off into the little dish beside the book. "What took you so long?"

Surprised at the annoyed tone, he dropped a boot beside the cloak. "Besides the usual and slugging through the rain and mud and being stopped by Sarah, not much," he replied, tersely. He let one boot drop next to the other. The dirt on the floor stuck to his damp feet and he ran a hand through his rain soaked hair.

Notus blinked, finally taking in the full sight of his son. "You're soaked," he exclaimed, and stood up to find an extra blanket folded neatly on a shelf. "Don't move. I don't want you getting water all over the place."

Taking the rough spun woollen blanket from his Chooser, he began to undress. "I did say it was raining outside." He placed his sodden shirt on another peg to drip dry and unlaced the fly of his breeches.

"So you did. So you did." Notus turned back to the table and the book, flipping through the pages of ornate illustration and masterful calligraphy. This was some of his best work ever. Closing the book, he placed it on a waterproofed hide. "What did Sarah want?" He wrapped the book and tied it tight with leather thongs.

"Her mother started coughing again." He used the blanket to towel himself dry now that his breeches hung on the last peg. "The medicine you gave her is not working."

"It isn't?" Notus stood perplexed and watched his son cover his head with the blanket, furiously trying to dry his white locks. The long thick scar on his son's left thigh gleamed silver in the limited light, bringing horrific memories back to the monk.

Allowing the blanket to slip down, he swept his tangled hair from his face. "Did you not hear her knock?"

Puzzled, Notus slowly shook his head. "No."

He wrapped the blanket around his shoulders and walked to his pallet on the left wall. "It's all right. I gave them a few shillings and sent them to an inn. What is this?"

Releasing the blanket, it fell to the floor and he lifted up a finely tailored black gipon with silver ornamental buttons and silver embroidery. Even the small buttons on the sleeves, from elbow to knuckles, were finely crafted silver. Under the gipon lay a dagged mantle, obviously meant to button on the left shoulder, hose, shoes and an elaborate silver girdle lay neatly arranged on the bed.

"It is your outfit for the evening," replied Notus with a smile.

Open-mouthed, he could only turn and stare at the monk, and realized that Notus was wearing his finest habit and new sandals.

"You had best get dressed." His Chooser picked up the black hose, holding them out to his son.

Declining to take the material, he stared suspiciously. "What for?"

"To go to the royal wedding feast, of course." Notus hitched a shoulder and placed the hose back on the pallet. "I told you about this months ago. The Abbot of Westminster commissioned a copy of the *Missale Romanum* to be given as a gift to King John."

"John is not king. He's been dead for nearly two hundred years," he stated slowly. He could not make any sense of what Notus was talking about.

Notus let out an exasperated huff. "Not John Lackland. John of Portugal." Still seeing the confusion on his son's face, Notus explained, "To seal the Treaty of Windsor, the Duke of Lancaster's daughter, Philipa, is marrying – or will marry – King John of Portugal, and we have been invited to the feast in her honour before she departs to Portugal so as to allow the Abbot of Westminster to present that" – he pointed to the wrapped book – "as a wedding gift. So get dressed. A carriage will be here soon."

It took a moment for the reality of the situation to sink in. Anger and anxiety vied for supremacy. "No," he stated.

"No?" replied Notus, blinking incredulously.

He dropped the gipon onto the bed, the silver buttons clicked together. "I am not going." Anger tightened his jaw. "I have had my fill of royalty, whether it is Chosen or mortal. I will not be an oddity of speculation to be placed on display. Not again. Not ever again."

He stared out the window of the carriage, his face seemingly stuck in a perpetual frown. To halt the monk from continuing his sermon of honour, duty, responsibility and how he should, at least by now, be able to deal with larger crowds of people, he finally acquiesced and hurriedly clad himself with Notus' help. The long, tightly buttoned sleeves were annoying and he wanted to give the designer a piece of his mind for fashioning the sleeves to end at his knuckles, leaving only his fingers exposed to the night. The heavy silver girdle resting on his hips made sitting uncomfortable. He hated the fashions of this age.

Already he regretted coming along. The driver and footman had stood agape when they saw him, and he expected, if not the same, still more of a reaction come the reception. His scowl deepened at the happy humming from across the bench. It was next to impossible to get Notus to move on an issue when he was involved in any aspect of his work. For the first time people were going to have a face to go along with the Angel.

The carriage came to a sudden lurching halt under an overhang that led to large double doors ajar enough to permit light and laughter to spill into the night. On either side of the doors torches burned, sometimes hissing in the dampness. Beyond the doors would be a hundred or more people. He gave his happy Chooser one last look.

"You look as if you are going to be executed. Cheer up," grinned Notus.

His scowl deepened.

The footman opened the door and helped the monk out. Doubtful that the evening would be anything less than a disaster, he shook his head and followed Notus. Together they stood on cobbles slick with mud and water, and beyond the overhang the downpour petered into a slight drizzle. He hoped that the rain would end before they left, which he prayed would be soon.

They walked up to the doors that seemed to have sprung open, as if on cue, by two young pages that appeared out of nowhere. Notus' thanks could not remove the terrified stares of the boys. Refusing to acknowledge them, he felt the movement of air as the doors quickly shut behind him and heard through the thick wood their shocked whispers. Dismissing the expected response with a shake of his head and a sigh, he focused on the alcove in which he and Notus now stood. A few other guests, escaping the heat of the hall, gaped openly. Only the occasional whisper or shocked expression floated to his sensitive ears. He noticed that the monk's smile had slipped.

They approached the double doors leading to the hall. Silence was behind, music and laughter was before, and he desperately fought the urge to flee. Two terrified pages stood ready to pull open the doors at the herald's command.

The herald stood at the centre, dressed spectacularly in a dark blue cote-hardie and a red and gold tabard denoting his position. His eyes were wide and could not bring himself to not stare at the unusually tall young man with the white hair and red irises.

Noting the rudeness of the herald and feeling the resolute sadness from his son, Notus cleared his throat.

"I am most terribly sorry, Father," recovered the surprised herald, finally bringing his attention to the monk. His eyes flickered onto the strange young man. "How shall I announce you and...and your companion?"

"You know, I had not thought of that." Notus pursed his lips and turned to his Chosen. "How about Father Notus and the Angel?" He faced the herald. "Yes, that will do just fine."

The Angel thought that the man's eyes could not go any wider and was proved wrong. White showed around the blue-grey eyes while the lips mouthed the title in obvious recognition. Tonight was going as well as expected. All he needed now was someone to try and kill him and everything would be complete.

"The door if you please," interjected Notus, his smile gone.

Blinking as if waking from a dream, the herald coughed. "Yes. Right. Of course," and straightened his stance. At a clap of his hands the pages snapped to their work. On heavy hinges the doors opened. The herald turned, addressing the hall in a voice practiced and solemn. "Your Royal Highnesses—Father Notus and the Angel."

The closest to the doors turned their heads to see who the new arrivals were and their inviting smiles instantly transformed into wide gaping stares punctuated with the occasional look of terror. One woman in a flowing saffron houppelande and a chaplet head-dress let out a strangled cry and promptly fainted into the surprised arms of her husband. Gradually, bit by bit, each searching for the reason of the increasing silence, the hall fell quiet.

He did not need to look up to see all their eyes upon him. He felt them. Their heat was overpowering and the smell of mortal blood mixed with smoke and alcohol was intoxicating. He wanted to devour them. He wanted to run. To stop his trembling, he balled his fists and glanced at his Chooser. Notus did not look at all pleased as he walked down the steps to stand before the brightly coloured crowd. Left alone before the doors with sole attention upon him, he quickly followed down the few steps, catching up with his Chooser.

Grabbing the monk's sleeve, he forced Notus to face him. *You knew, as well as I, that this would happen,* he sent. Panic filled eyes penetrated through his cold mask. *This is why I did not want to come. We never meant the Angel to be revealed, and now I am. Why?*

Sad soft brown eyes met his. "I am truly sorry, my son," apologized the monk, taking his son's hand between his own. *I often forget how different you are, different from mortals and different from the Chosen. I only see you. I do not see what others see, and I am only reminded at times like these, after I realized the folly of my persistent nature.* "But it's not only that. His Highness, King Richard, wants to meet the Angel."

"What?" His voice was strangled. He could not believe this. "Why?"

"I do not know, but he made it a royal command." Notus' eyes fell to their hands. "I know you would have definitely not come if you knew about this." *Sometimes we Chosen must follow the rules of mankind lest we are discovered.*

A slow simmering anger fuelled him. Following the rules of mortals always led him to be discovered and it had nothing to do with being Chosen. Notus was right, if he had known he would have left London, or at least tried to. He wanted nothing more to do with these types of people. Now he was here, in another Richard's home, with another Richard's guests and trying very hard not to shake like a leaf. *Never do this to me again,* he sent. *You know I will do anything for you, but never do this to me again.*

Nodding, Notus gazed up at his son. His brown eyes blurred with unshed tears. *I swear upon all that is holy, I will never do anything like this again.*

He let out the breath he was holding and bowed his head. "Thank you."

A knowing smile returned to his Choosers lips and Notus patted his hand. "Now that is taken care of—"

"—we will stay to see the night through–" he continued. The corner of his mouth lifted. Maybe the worst was over.

"—and make the best of it," finished Notus as he slipped his arm through his sons, slowly making their way through the crowd of guests.

Conversation had quickly picked up with his descent into the hall. Most discussion consisted of the new and hot topic for the night—the Angel. He tried to ignore it and focused on the colours of elaborate dress. Gowns of embroidered silk flashed in the light of flaming braziers. Veiled heads of younger women bent together to privately comment on the virtues of current available men. Large plumed hats and turbans with liripipe denoted the men in bright clothing as colourful as what the women wore. Music of harps, drums and flutes overlaid the buzz of conversation. Only the very brave ventured a comment or two towards Notus and the Angel. Others shied away, allowing the strange pair to pass more or less unhindered.

He observed it all, the glances, the gestures, the expressions, and tried to steel himself from it. By far the tallest man in the room it was easy for anyone to spot him, and one person in particular did. Making a bee line towards he and Notus, a man of average size and colouring, wearing religious vestments, ploughed through the crowd, followed by a young man with a lady, no more than a girl, on his arm.

"Father Paul, how good it is to see you again," declared the man, a smile on his face and he looked up at the Angel. "And you as well."

"It is always a pleasure, Abbot," bowed Notus as his son inclined his head. "I hope the evening has been pleasurable despite the rain."

"Oh quite." The Abbot of Westminster flashed a brilliant smile that quickly faded. "I wish you would reconsider and come stay at the abbey. Then you would not have to travel so far to the Library. Not to mention many of us would love to have a man of such talent teach the novices your fine craft with quill and brush."

"I thank you again for the kind offer," replied Notus, "but I like being close to those who need me most and I don't think the Angel would find the restrictions accommodating."

"Ah well, one has to try." The smile returned and he opened up the space to allow the finely dressed couple to step closer. "Father Notus and the Angel, may I introduce Lord Henry of Bolingbroke, Earl of Derby and of Hereford, and his wife, Lady Mary."

"A pleasure, my Lord." Notus withdrew his arm from his son's and held out his hand.

The young earl brought his attention from the one the Abbot called the Angel and took the monk's hand. "And mine as well, Father. The good Abbot here has told me much of your kind works."

"You are the one the people call the Angel." Lady Bolingbroke's voice was high and clear with youth, yet hesitant as if she was not yet used to her station. Her husband eyed her suspiciously.

She was pretty. Long brown locks were hidden under a veil yet the plaits before her ears were left free. Her hazel eyes blinked nervously.

Unable to find his voice, he was relieved with Notus' response. "Yes, he is, my Lady." The monk flashed a smile that was gratefully returned.

"My cousin speaks oft of the Angel," replied the Lady, more confidently. "And how no one has ever laid eyes upon him. I must assume, sir, that it is a great honour to have you here."

He stared at her outstretched hand not knowing what to do or say. The thin blue veins of her translucent wrist held a sweet treasure that he would never allow himself to discover. The Earl and the Abbot stared curiously at his distress.

Take her hand in yours, say thank you, and kiss it, sent Notus, coming to his rescue.

Her pale hand was warm to the touch and her blood drew him even further. Straightening, he did not return the smile. A crowd of young eligible women watched in breathless anticipation, their eyes focused on him. Their whispers in the midst of the party were easily heard and he turned to stare in amazement when he heard one wondering to one another what it would feel like to be kissed by the Angel. The girl, having noticed his gaze, squeaked in surprise and instantly hid in the midst of her friends giggles.

"Your cousin, my Lady?" asked Notus, bringing his Chosen's attention back.

"My cousin, Father," replied the young Earl, "is King Richard the Second."

He glanced over his shoulder to where two men sat in high backed chairs, one young and handsome, the other older and darker in complexion. On either side sat two young ladies. The two men were caught up in conversation and the girl on the older man's right smiled at the Earl who nodded his head in response.

Notus' eyes widened at the revelation and then shook himself as he suddenly remembered the book in his embrace.

"I almost forgot," the monk held the leather bound package out to the Abbot. "I finished this tonight."

The Abbot's eyes brightened as he took it, unwrapping the package and opening a page at random. He gasped at the sight and stood transfixed as he slowly leafed through the pages. Curious, the Earl and his wife peeked at the book and their eyes widened.

"This is more beautiful than I ever expected," exclaimed the Abbot, breathlessly. Notus' smile widened. "Such artistry cannot go unacknowledged. It would be a sin!" The Abbot carefully closed the book to the regret of the onlookers, wrapped it up and handed it back to Notus. "You must present this gift with me."

"What?" Notus stood flabbergasted, the book in hand. "I cannot. It is yours to give."

"Nonsense," replied the Abbot, firmly, and grabbed Notus' free arm, leading him through the crowd before the monk could utter another word of protest.

A smile lit his ruby eyes yet did not touch the rest of his face as he watched his Chooser dragged away. Somehow it seemed justified to allow the Abbot to manhandle Notus so. There was no danger from the exuberant mortal and it was doubtful that the Abbot was in danger from the stunned Chosen he dragged. Without Notus, he glanced down at the young couple. The Earl seemed more interested in the on goings of a small group of men in lavish dress, while his wife stared up at him, a soft smile on her face.

Returning his attention to his wife, the Earl of Derby and Hereford patted her hand and unhooked her from his arm, saying, "Excuse me, my Lady, but I need to talk to Thomas." He scowled momentarily at his wife's frown and addressed the Angel awkwardly. "I…if you would be so kind as to stay with my wife, I would deem it a great favour." He turned and moved off into the crowd, leaving no room for protestation.

He watched as the Earl was consumed by the wave of people. The smile from his eyes now gone, he glanced down at Lady Mary who seemed unsurprised at this turn of events.

"I beg your pardon, sir," she attempted. "My Lord has a tendency to be focused only on fighting." She stared sadly in the direction that her husband had gone. She could not see, for all the people in her path that his height allowed, Lord Bollingbroke being slapped on the back from his friends and laughing along with them.

She attempted another smile and held out her hand. At his frown, Lady Bollingbroke cocked her head to the side. "Is there a problem?"

There was a problem. Her husband left her in the custody of someone who craved to drain her of her life, but instead he took her hand, wrapped it around his arm, and was rewarded by a true smile. Her touch and proximity made him nervous. It was not just the lust for her blood as she led him through the crowd along the path the Abbot had trailed Notus along.

"You do not talk much, do you?" she asked demurely, nodding her head in acknowledgement at a guest. "I take it that you would like to be anywhere but here."

Her astute observation surprised him and he stiffened under her light touch.

"I suppose I can understand that. Tonight you are the talk of the party. Tomorrow you will be the talk of the city."

He hesitated in mid-step, unsure of how to take the observation.

"I do not mean to pain you, but you are a rare person. Mysterious." She halted, bringing them to a stop and turned to face him. "I can see, as can any other person here, that your secrets are a temptation to discover and the one who discovers them will be the most sought after person, besides yourself, of course."

"Why are you telling me this?" He already knew what Lady Bolingbroke had said. He had experienced this in the past but not on such a grand scale. So many people who feared and despised him were also inexplicably drawn to him.

Surprised that he actually said something, it took her a moment to formulate an answer. "Because I would not wish to see the Angel entangled in this royal game." She threaded her arm through his and led the way.

He gazed down on her and was surprised at the affection he suddenly felt for her. Never before had he been treated in such an accepting manner from a complete stranger. It made the night seem worthwhile.

They halted before a large open space before the enthroned monarchs and in which stood the Abbot and Notus. King Richard was leaning to see the open book in his guest's lap oblivious to all else. He stood silently at the edge of the crowd, watching, Lady Bolingbroke's arm resting on his.

"This is most extraordinary," exclaimed the English Crown. "I have never witnessed finer."

"Nor have I," replied the Ambassador of Portugal, his accent thick yet unmuddied. He handed the *Missale Romanum* to a short, stocky man with dark features, in a lavish green and blue houppelande and a gold circlet holding back his silver streaked hair. The man opened the book, allowing a woman in equally elaborate dress to see the work of art. She was short, with her dark hair in an ornamental fillet. Her gasp of surprise was accompanied by the man's huge smile through thick neatly trimmed beard. A little girl jumped to try and get a better look.

"This truly is a magnificent gift. Thank you," beamed the Ambassador in delight. His brown eyes went wide and jaw slacked. His body trembled while his breath came in quick gasps. King Richard, wondering at his guest's plight, looked up and directly at the Angel.

Suddenly uncomfortable with the royal attention, he tried to take a step back but Lady Bolingbroke held him fast. He watched as the royal eyes filled with fear and then childlike curiosity.

Notus glanced nervously between his Chosen and the King and wondered what would happen next. It seemed that a hush had fallen upon the guests as they too waited apprehensively.

Time halted for what seemed like hours, only to be abruptly broken by the crash of the double doors flung open. He turned with the rest of the crowd to find an average sized young man swaying in a state of disarray. Soaked head to toe, and toe it was for he wore only one shoe, his ripped green doublet sported stains of unknown origins and his white hose were splattered with mud. The young man opened his mouth to say something and then shut it as if thinking better of it. When he opened his mouth again a deep resinous belch cut through the silence.

"Christ that was good." His accent, slurred as it was, was the same as King Richard's royal guests. Sniffing loudly, the drunken young man half staggered, half fell down the handful of steps, causing a few of the less sober guests to snicker at the plight of the youth as he haphazardly made his stumbling way through the crowd. Those he passed, especially the women, emitted short exclamations as his hands touched inappropriate places.

The Angel watched this spectacle, wondering why no one dealt with this impudent party crasher, and turned back to the monarchs. Richard and his Queen stared in dumbfounded surprise while the Ambassador seemed ready to order an execution.

What caught the Angel's attention was the man holding Notus' gift turned a lovely shade of dark purple and how the woman beside the Noble now clutched her rosary, fervently praying. The little girl between them was unsuccessfully trying not to break into fits of giggling.

It did not take long before the drunken young man broke from the crowd to stand, teetering on rubbery legs, before the monarchs. Unsuccessfully attempting a deep bow, he caught himself to the laughter of some guests. Straightening, he smiled wickedly at his soon to be queen and blew her a kiss.

Phillipa stared in horror.

"*Fernando,*" bellowed the infuriated man behind the royal couple.

Fernando appeared shocked, gazing through glassy eyes. A few unsure steps brought him in front of the royals, a smile warping his handsome face. He said something in a language the Angel did not understand that was met with gasps of horror to those who understood. Richard glanced around for a translation from the English man standing behind him. Utter rage swept over his features.

"I beg pardon," slurred the young man, cutting off Richard's chance to call the guards and attempted another bow. This one seemed more balanced and when he lifted his head the Angel noticed that the drunkard had turned slightly green.

"I-I being sick," stammered Fernando.

The Angel was beside the young man in an instant, forcing the mortal to his knees before he could vomit on the royals. He held the man's feverish neck, disgusted as a night's worth of drinking splashed to the stone floor. Murmurs of revulsion reverberated through the hall as well as orders to get the mess cleaned up. Not surprisingly, the body beneath his hand went limp and he had to catch Fernando by the collar to halt him from falling into the mess. The drunkard dangled in his grasp.

"Where do you want him?" he asked the Crown.

King Richard stared in fury at the hanging bundle. "So it seems that the Angel is not predisposed to help only the poor."

He stiffened at the acknowledgement.

"Take him to his quarters," ordered the Ambassador.

He glanced at the man at the end of his fist and wondered who the hell this idiot was so as not to warrant being tossed directly into the dungeon. He gave a little shake and was rewarded with a moan. When he looked up he found the woman behind the throne standing before him clutching her rosary. She seemed very tiny, as if she consciously tried to contract herself into something unnoticeable. She reminded him of a mouse in the den of lions.

"Please, you come." Her Portuguese accent was very thick and it was obvious that her English was hampered by the fear she felt.

He nodded in reply, sympathetic to her plight, and glanced over to his Chooser. *I will be back momentarily.*

Notus nodded, *I will see what I can do here.*

Hoisting the dead weight easily over his shoulder, he stood and followed the Lady out of the crowd into a hallway lit with interspersed flaming braziers. The little girl, obviously the Lady's daughter, followed gleefully, and by her tones he knew her to be berating and poking fun at the unconscious young man. The mother reabsorbed herself into her prayers, the rosary clicking as she walked, ignoring the little girl.

They walked along the poorly lit corridors, shoes and gown making soft scraping sounds against stone. Occasionally they passed guards who stood in place and servants who scurried out of the way. Deeper they went and soon he had lost his bearings. He would need someone to show him the way back. Up a flight of uneven stone steps and a turn brought them to a heavy wooden door that opened on well oiled hinges.

The room was large and obviously part of a suite. Candles illuminated the rich room, bouncing yellow light off the elaborate tapestries used for decoration and insulation against the cold outside. Across from the big bed, neatly dressed with a large coverlet and down feathered pillows, a large gloaming hearth flickered and danced. Finding no more appropriate a place to dump the body, he let the unconscious man collapse on the mattress, and turned to leave only to find the Lady before him.

"Please, you check?" she nervously asked, swatting the little girl's hand away from tugging on her gown. It was plain that the girl could not care less for the state of the young man and desperately wanted to go back to the party.

He nodded and sat on the side of the bed in an attempt to alleviate the Lady's worries and to get out as quickly as possible and without hassle. He guessed Fernando to be in his early to mid-twenties, but it was hard to tell for sure because the alcohol made his rumpled features appear drawn and older.

Dark, almost black hair lay strewn across a face slightly darkened with stubble, and he stank with ale and vomit that almost cut out the strong hot smell of blood coursing through his body. The vessel in Fernando's neck throbbed invitingly. If they were alone, without either the Lady or her daughter, he would not have stopped himself. He would not have killed the mortal, only added to the disagreeable state the young man would find himself come morning. It would be a fitting punishment.

Jostled by his movements to stand, the young mortal opened his dark brown eyes and let out an earth-shattering scream before passing back into oblivion.

Burning red eyes, the Devil's eyes, infected every alcoholic nightmare, so when the bucket of water was emptied onto his prone form Fernando was at first relieved and then cursed. Lightning bolts lacerated the insides of his eyelids and every beat of his heart pounded painfully through his head. He hoped that he was not dead because if he were then he would be in Hell and the thought of spending eternity in this state was too horrible to bear.

"My Lord, your Lord father demands your presence immediately," came a voice from the darkness.

Fernando recognized Pedro's voice but could not respond. Sometime during the night his tongue had grown thick and impotent.

"My Lord, are you awake?"

It took an immense effort to moisten his parched mouth enough to croak out a monosyllabic reply.

"Please, my Lord, you must rise. Your Lord father expects you promptly and if you are late it will not bode well for you." Worry mixed with panic tinged the servant's normally non-emotive tones.

Cracking open an encrusted eye, Fernando was met with the bright light of an early afternoon and Pedro's hovering form. "Go away," he hoarsely ordered and closed his eye. He did not care about Pedro and the thought of his Lord father made him ill.

"I am sorry, my Lord, but I cannot do that."

"Yes, you can. Now, go away!" His head threatened to split at his own raised voice, and he groaned in self-induced agony. "Tell the Fidalgo de Sagres I will attend him once I've recovered."

"I am sorry, my Lord, but I cannot do that," reiterated Pedro, firmly.

"Stop repeating yourself." Fernando tried to roll over onto his side but thought could not translate into action. Giving up, he sprawled on his back. "I'll see him when I'm good and ready."

"You will see me *now*," boomed a deep resonate voice.

Fernando's eyes flew open and he froze. His heart throbbed in his hung over sensitive ears. Few things could induce fear in the young noble. In fact he could only recall being afraid twice in his life, and neither of them were when he went to war. The first was when he was six. He had heard his mother screaming in childbed and how her earth-wrenching cries were cut short by death. Not even his newly born baby brother escaped death's clutches. The second time was when he stole his Lord father's sword to fight a duel, at the age of eleven. His father was so furious that Fernando could not sit for a week. He suddenly felt eleven again and resented it enough to push the feeling away.

With Pedro's assistance, Fernando managed to sit up and swing his baggy hosen legs over the edge of the bed. Across the room, standing behind a chair, stood Fernando's father, the Fidalgo Manuel de Sagres, in the splendour of rich dress marred by a face purpled with fury. Fernando sighed, ran a shaky hand through his dark thick locks, and waited. He figured that soon enough his father would start into his usual lecture.

An oppressive silence filled the room, making the servant fidget. If the circumstances were not so severe Fernando would have snickered at Pedro's discomfort. Instead he had to endure the pain of the door crashing closed as Pedro fled at the order from the Fidalgo and the realization that now father and son were alone together. Not as stocky as his father, Fernando believed he could take him in a fair fight. After all, he had youth on his side. He waited patiently as the Fidalgo casually sat down.

"Are you proud of yourself?" Some of the darker purple tones faded into lighter shades of red, yet the anger in the Noble's voice was barely constrained.

Fernando blinked in uncertainty. This was not expected. A lecture, a sermon, perhaps, but not this.

Without waiting for a verbal reply the Fidalgo de Sagres continued,

"Are you proud of how you embarrassed your cousin and his new wife? Not to mention humiliating yourself, your House and me in front of the English crown!" His voice rose to thunderous new levels, making Fernando involuntarily wince in pain. "Answer me, boy."

Oh how Fernando despised being called that. Grinding his teeth in anger and loathing, he managed a strained reply. "If I have offended, I most humbly and respectfully apologize."

The Fidalgo de Sagres leaned back in his seat, studying his dishevelled son over steepled fingers. "At one time I truly believed you to be sincere and prayed that you would change to become a man that would follow well in my path. I see now that I was wrong." Fernando blanched at the admission. "Your behaviour last night was the final abomination to this House. I will tolerate this no longer."

Fernando's father stood and slowly walked to the door. "From this moment on you no longer are you my son. All your lands and titles are stripped from you. The heir to the Fidalgo de Sagres will become part of your sister's dowry. Your betrothed, Maria Isabel, will go to his Highness' brother, Antonio. Take what money and clothes you can scrounge and leave. If you manage to find your way back to Portugal you will find no home." The Fidalgo de Sagres turned to leave.

Fernando sat stunned as his world was ripped from him, but with the mention of his beloved Isabel, rage boiled within.

"Wait!" Any pain he felt from last night's revels was inconsequential to what was happening now. At least his father had halted and turned to face him. "You can't do this to me!"

"I can and just did," replied his father in all seriousness.

"I've apologized." Fernando was not one to beg, but it was difficult not to keep the supplicating tones from his voice.

Manuel de Sagres cocked his head and seemed to view his son for the first time. Whatever it was he saw filled his dark eyes with sadness for the briefest of moments. "Apologized for what?"

It took Fernando a moment to answer. "For my behaviour last night." He was not sure what his father was talking about any more.

"You think it is just that," Manuel shook his head, "but it is more than that, much more. Do you even remember what you did last night?"

Unable to meet the eyes so much like his own, Fernando mutely shook his head. Everything was blank, from the time he left the whorehouse to the horrifying vision of the devil.

"I will not repeat it, ever, and will only say that if the Angel had not been there, it would have been worse. Now, I will leave you and pray that your mother—"

"Maria Terese is not my mother," came the usual retort that Fernando instantly regretted.

"—will bless me with a son in the fall since now both my boys are dead."

ANGEL OF DEATH

The door closed without a sound, leaving Fernando to stare at the carved oak. He sat for a long time, unable to move. If he did, he would find out that it was not a dream and he so wanted to wake. The thoughts of his lands and titles never meant much except the power to rule. Even his inheritance, now stricken from him, had always seemed unreal because his father was Fidalgo and Fernando always believed the man to outlive him, just out of spite.

Fernando could live without the deprecating games of Court, but what he could not fathom was a life without Maria Isabel de Leiora. Arranged marriages were commonplace, and yet when he first met his betrothed a friendship bloomed into a love so strong that they both counted the days to her sixteenth birthday so they could wed. It was a quarter of a year before what would have been his wedding. Now she was gone. All of it was gone. Fury filled him and his fist flew against the poster, sending a jarring stab of pain.

Cupping his bruised fist in the other, Fernando stood, swearing, and collected what he could. No matter the state of his disgrace he would leave with honour. After shaving, he dressed in his finest doublet of dark blue and clean hose and secured his heavy purse to his belt and his sword at his side.

Yes, I will leave, he thought as he left his room for the halls, walking with head held high. He would have revenge for this injustice.

He did not receive any hindrances in leaving the dark confines of the castle. Servants and gentry alike stared in surprise. They knew what he had done. Now if only he knew. It was doubtful he would find out now.

The bright sunlight stung his eyes as he headed out into the city to find the best way to forget. He passed carters and ware-mongers, chandlers and farmers selling late produce, potters and peddlers, until he found what he was looking for – the tavern. This was one of the establishments he could remember. A place to forget.

The door abruptly opened, allowing two off duty guards, in shimmering mail and red, to exit, stinking of stale ale. Neither gave the young noble a glance. Fernando was invisible to their drunken perceptions. He held the weather beaten door open and then entered the dimly lit establishment. Dust motes flickered in the thin rays of sunlight entering from thin windows near the rafters. The smell of the poor mingled with roasting food and ale overpowered Fernando's senses, yet strangely enough it felt comfortingly familiar.

Busy for this time of day, Fernando managed to squeeze his way past a serving girl with dirty blonde hair and a smudged face, to a lonely table in a darkened corner of the smoke filled room. Dumping his bundle on the chair, he sat in the other with his back to the wall so that he could not be taken unawares. Without a need to ask, a large mug of ale appeared before him. Normally, Fernando would have at least bantered with the wench, but not today. This afternoon he stared into the dark pool and mumbled something about getting something to eat. He did not even watch as the wench disappeared into the back.

He needed a plan. Maybe if he stayed away for a day or so his father will have forgotten, or at least forgiven. Fernando snorted at that preposterous thought. The chances that the all-powerful Fidalgo de Sagres would pardon him were as likely as Fernando's chances of getting into heaven. No, he needed to start thinking about his future. Money would not be much of a problem, at least for a while. He absently fingered the heavy purse filled with gold sovereigns. He thought of going back to Portugal and seize Sagres for his own before his father could get home. He fantasized the whole process, not tasting the food before him. It would take more money than his paltry bundle could manage.

Fernando sat the afternoon away, sipping mugs of ale that did not seem to erase his memory. Did he want to stay in England? The thought had crossed his mind. It was a more stable country than his own, but what could he do? Whatever it was it had to be something where he was in charge. That was certain. Taking orders was never a strong point for Fernando. Always in command of something, he was raised to rule. He sighed and finished the last of his fourth mug. He still had no plan.

The light had grown dim with sunset and Fernando only realized how long he had actually sat when another serving girl placed a lamp on his table. The patronage had changed to more boisterous men and women, who, by obvious appearance, were working girls. It was time to leave and find an inn to spend the night, and think.

Fumbling with the knot of his purse, Fernando shrugged off the prospect of paying too much. At this point he could not care and he pulled out a sovereign. It gleamed bright yellow in the lamplight. He knew it would draw unnecessary attention and it did. Several men, mercenaries by their hardened appearance, seated at a nearby table had grown quiet at the sight, but what caught the young noble's attention was the petite young lady of obvious profession.

Her skin was as pale as any noble Lady's and her blonde hair sparkled in a living version of the gold he held in his hand. The mysterious and hypnotic air about her only amplified her beauty. Her movement towards him was fluid and graceful in a way that reminded Fernando of a cat stalking its prey.

He did not return her smile as she pulled out an empty chair and sat opposite. He eyed her suspiciously, yet refused to acknowledge her powerful presence in any other way. Her smile faded and Fernando recognized her from the whorehouse of last night.

"I did not expect to see you so soon." Her voice was rich, seductive and distinctly French.

Fernando scowled, rolling the sovereign across his knuckles and noted that the whore had no interest in the large sum of money rolling deftly back and forth on his hand. He did not reply. Instead he chose to wait. She was beautiful in an exotic way, especially as a frown descended upon her features and she opened her mouth to speak.

A mace crashed down between them, shocking the whore from speech. Fernando gazed up at the weapon's owner, irritation in his eyes. The mercenary grinned wickedly, exposing rotting teeth. He wore a patch over his left eye and his bald head exhibited the signs of a poor shaving job. Fernando did not like the way he stared at the sovereign and nor did he like the odds if there was going to be a fight. The five men behind the veteran appeared equally dangerous.

Catching the coin in the palm of his hand, Fernando returned the glare. "Can I help you?" he asked coldly.

The whore appeared unafraid. In fact she seemed extremely interested, a peculiar half smile touching her lips.

"Aye, ye can," growled One-eye. "Give me and me mate yer money and the whore," he added as an afterthought, "and we'll let ye live."

Ignoring the fowl breath, Fernando laid the gold sovereign in the middle of the table, next to the mace, without breaking eye contact. He did notice, though, that the girl actually looked disappointed. He did not know what she wanted, but if it was bloodshed she would not have to wait long. Absently, he lowered his right hand to the hilt of his sword. He was going to enjoy the next few moments.

Fernando shook his head. "No, I don't think so."

The ring of naked steel reverberated in the sudden silence as Fernando's finely crafted *Toledo* sword viciously arched up and then down, severing One-eye's mace hand from the rest of his body. Too stunned at the surprising speed of the attack, One-eye stumbled back into his mates, clutching the bleeding stump and screamed his shocked pain. Fernando stood, his sword ready to defend, his eyes reflecting an inner fire. He had thoroughly enjoyed himself.

"Next time you decide to rob someone you should make absolutely sure that your victim is not armed," sneered Fernando, grabbing his bundle of clothing. It was then that he noticed the whore gazing hungrily at the dark red droplets glimmering on his sword.

The surprise of her strange attention was all that was necessary for the would-be thieves to become murderous villains. Swords rang out and it was all that Fernando could do not to fall as the men came after him. Tables crashed out of the way and fearful patrons fled while others cheered the unpaid for entertainment.

Down went one man and Fernando took up the fallen sword. With a blade in each hand the odds had turned favourable for the young noble despite the fact that there were still four of them. Years of training came out in his fluid dance, blocking and cutting. He knew that a malevolent grin curled his lips and he only halted his defence when there was no thief standing.

Breathing heavily the scent of death, Fernando dropped the thief's blade and bent to clean his sword on one of the bodies. Cheering and the clink of coppers being handed back and forth told Fernando that he had put on a good show. Not to disappoint his audience, he sheathed his sword and bowed. Cheers rose up, threatening to thunder down the roof. Grabbing his bundle from where he had tossed it, he escaped into the cool clear night to find the whore before him.

Befuddled at how she managed to appear in front, Fernando glanced back at the tavern and then to the girl who only a moment ago stood in the tavern. He opened his mouth, ready to ask how she had done that, but instead shook his head and pushed past her. Tonight he did not want what she was offering.

Fernando let out a sigh when he realized that she was walking discreetly beside him. Could she not take a hint? Spinning around to confront her and order her away, he found that she had suddenly disappeared. Confusion descended upon the Noble as he searched right and left and found no sign of her. This was becoming unnerving.

Unexpectedly, he felt a firm tapping on his shoulder and he whirled around to find her standing serenely not a foot away. This was too much. He knew he did not have that much to drink. "How the hell?" The words tumbled out of his mouth.

A smile tugged her lips. "You do enjoy killing, *non*? And you do it well."

What was this? Fernando had never met a woman like her. He decided to play along. "I enjoy what I do, and I do very well, and if you don't leave me alone I'll enjoy doing you."

At first she seemed surprised by his answer before breaking into peals of laughter. Several people glanced nervously at the two. Unnerved at the uncharacteristic response, Fernando took a step backwards.

"You may try, *monsieur,* but you will find it *impossible.*" Suddenly her features became threatening.

Fernando felt the mouse in the game and it ignited his anger. "What do you want?"

"What I want is you," she stated matter-of-factly.

It was Fernando's turn to laugh. "I have met many a woman who wanted such, yet none so brazen as to come right out and say it. Unfortunately, you are out of luck for I am in a rare mood not to wish for such lovely company for the night. Now if you will excuse me." He tried to move past her and stopped as her hand grasped around his bicep in an iron grip. He glared down at the whore, anger growing and vying with pleasant amazement.

She met his glare. "You misunderstand, *monsieur.* I have a proposition for you."

"And that is?" He tried to pry her fingers from his arm but could not budge the delicate digits.

"What I offer is not meant to be heard by mere mortals." She dragged him off, ignoring his protests, only to let go when they entered a poor hovel not far away.

"*Sue foda duma puta, eu vou te-matar por isto!*" shouted Fernando, rubbing his bruised arm.

"*Assis-toi!*" Her command rang hypnotically and she instantly realized why he did not comply. In a softer tone she said, "Sit."

Strangely unable to resist, Fernando sat down on the cot, mesmerized.

"Ah, now you will listen, *n'est-ce-pas?*" She began to pace, her cool veneer slipping into obvious nervousness, all the while keeping an eye on the Noble.

"You have something I want and in exchange I will give you what you want." Disregarding his confusion, she continued, "I noticed that you have a lot of money, money that I need to get myself out of this stink hole and into a place where I can run my own business. Normally, I would have just killed you and taken your money, but I see that, even though you are mortal, you have a blood lust that makes me offer you this. In exchange for your money—think of it as an investment in which you may be a silent partner—I will give you immortality."

Clearly this woman was crazy. "And if I refuse?" he asked, playing along with her madness. Investing in a whorehouse would bring new purpose into his life and generate revenue, not to mention the women, but what she offered in exchange was ludicrous.

She turned to face him. "You die."

Fernando blinked at the blatant answer. For one so small she had a lot of strength. Hoping to end the insanity, he calmly stated, "Then I guess my answer is yes."

Her smile lit up her face and she slowly approached, sitting on the cot beside him. "You made a wise decision."

Her kisses were soft. Maybe he could use some company, and he kissed back. The only type of immortality he knew was begetting a child and at this point he could not care less. Her soft lips caressed his cheek, moving to his ear where she gently sucked, sending shocks of pleasure through his body. She worked down to his neck, kissing, licking and sucking. He moaned in delicious contentment, running one hand to cup a breast while the other held the embrace. *Yes, this could do nicely.* Her lips felt cool against his hot flesh and then he felt searing white pain as she bit deep, furiously sucking his blood into her being.

Fernando awoke to find that he sat in a large bed. Everything seemed alien until he realized that he was in his home near Hyde Park. Running his hand through his hair, he remembered the date and that the Angel and the housekeeper were his guests. He had no understanding why he had dreamt of that time so long ago. Fernando was used to not remembering his dreams, but this was so accurate, so disturbing, bringing back with it all the emotions of that time.

Getting out of bed, he knew that the sun was still up but he could not go back to sleep. Maybe the Angel would wake in a little while so that they could get an early start as soon as the sun set.

He stood in front of the mirror, gazing at his reflection and gasped in shock. Spinning around to face the door, he realized that the red eyes of the devil so long ago had belonged to the Angel. The Angel was at that disastrous wedding feast. It was the Angel who his father had mentioned. It was the Angel who knew of the disgraceful behaviour that Fernando could not remember.

Oh dear God, he knows.

XV

The dark haired man stood at the top of the stairs, glaring down at the richly carpeted steps that would take him to Bastia. He despised the notion of standing before her, explaining how he had captured and then lost the Chosen he was charged to dispose of. Never mind that it was Violet's obsession with the Angel that ruined his plans. He knew that Bastia would punish him. Violet was his underling, as he was Bastia's.

His shoes barely made a dent in the plush carpeting as he took to the stairs, his back rigid, head held high. He would tell her and accept what would come, but he would have his revenge on Violet, if he were allowed.

The carpet runner ended where a marble tiled floor began. Red and black veins ran through the white stone lending an air of an ostentatious hecatomb and he smiled. His shoes staccato filled and echoed along the hallway that led him to his Lady. He knew she would be there. She was always there at this time of day and most times she was happy to see him and hear his reports on the systematic genocide of the Chosen. Tonight she would be displeased.

Laying a broad hand on the fine-grained door, he knocked and turned the knob, entering into her sanctuary. Candles brilliantly lit the room. He knew how many there were, he counted them himself when he restocked them every night – one hundred and forty-six. He would light each one before she woke, and by the time she retired only one would remain lit to light his Lady back to her bed. Now there were less than a third aflame, but their light did not diminish the richness of the room.

Gold and red themed the chamber as he stepped onto lush red carpeting that stretched from one end to the other. A candelabrum hung from a vaulted ceiling, gently cradling the guttering remains of the beeswax candles. In the hearth, a fire glowed brightly, its smoke staining the white mantle. Along the walls, sconces, some still alive with light, many others dead in darkness ran the room, leaving only enough space for astounding masterpieces of artwork framed in lavish gold. She would not be here, but in the room off to the right.

He went to the door, making a mental note of how many candles he would have to order for the next week's supply, and listened to the splashing of water mixed with musical humming. With a nock, he entered into his Lady's bathroom tiled with the same white, black and red, from the hall. In the centre of the room stood a black claw footed tub filled with steaming water, bubbles and his Lady.

She turned at his entrance, a magnificent smile stretching her heart shaped face. Dark eyes met his and he could do nothing but return her infectious grin. Her long wavy hair was pulled straight with the weight of the water while the bubbles covered modestly. Languidly, she lifted a supple leg out of the water and ran her hands down the length from ankle to knee, luxuriating in the feel of the water washing off her soft skin. Her smile broadened.

"It is good to see you, my little bird," she chimed, lowering the leg to cause the bubbles to stir. "What is your report for today?"

"My Lady," he began and then caught himself. Now was the moment and he was loath to turn her good humour into naught. "The plan went well—"

"Then the Angel is dead?" She perked up, sitting straight in the tub, causing the water to splash onto the tiled floor. The tops of her breasts floated high in the soapy bubbles.

He shook his head. "No, my Lady, it appears that the Angel and de Sagres have teamed up."

"That is unfortunate news, very unfortunate." She stared into the water, her arms rested on the sides, lazily swirling the bubbles with her fingers. "But you say the plan went well, but the Angel is not dead. Explain yourself."

"Violet sent them too early. I wasn't given enough time," he stated emotionlessly.

Anger swelled her features. "She did what?"

"She sent them to the kitchen a day early."

Dark eyes grew black. "Did she say why?"

"No, my Lady, she didn't have to. She has been obsessed with the Angel for years. Something must have happened. She wants to possess the Angel for her own amusement." He could not hide the disgust from his voice.

"I had thought Sebastian would have been enough to satiate her."

"She moved too fast with him. I was going to give her de Sagres to play with, but it seems her heart is set on the Angel."

The Lady in the water angrily pouted. "And you say that the Angel and de Sagres are working together."

"Yes, my Lady." He stood still waiting for her inevitable reaction. When it did not come, a frown pulled at his face. "My Lady?"

"Let her have the Angel, and de Sagres too." Her dark piercing eyes bore into him and he recognized the inner spark of her unique genius.

"I don't understand, my Lady. By giving Violet such responsibility, considering her new found obsession, it may end with our discovery."

She shook her head, her long hair stirring the water causing bubbles to burst, exposing more of the Lady's nudity. "I doubt it. One thing I can count on with Violet is her hunger to get what she wants and I would be a fool not to use that to our advantage."

"She told me you gave her the next assignment." Anger broiled within him. Something had changed for the Lady to elevate Violet, especially without telling him.

"Yes, my little bird," she cooed, "She is going to lead them on a merry chase off of this God forsaken island, and you are going to help her."

Stunned surprise turned immediately to exploding anger. "I will not."

"You will!" Her hand came crashing down into the water, causing bubbles to fly out of the tub to mingle with the sparkling colours of the marble tiled floor. "Once the Chosen are on the Continent, and distracted, you will be able to proceed to the next step – the continued genocide of the Chosen by completing the distribution network for my lovely spice."

The light of her logic touched the dark haired man, and he smiled. His Lady was right, as she always was, and this meant that they would be able to accelerate the process here and abroad. More eateries would be forced into using their herbal mixture and as word spread out more and more families would be fighting to buy the concoction to put in their own bland tasting food. More than three quarters of the population, rich and poor, would be poison to the Chosen of the British Islands. If Violet could keep the Chosen distracted, then the timetable would be cut in half, bringing the termination of all Chosen much closer to fruition.

"Are the letters written?" asked the Lady, leaning back against the side of the tub, relaxing at the plans coming to fruition.

"Yes, my Lady. I finished them tonight." He stood watching her face relax into a smile.

"Wonderful, then this is what I want you to do," she purred, reaching her arms upwards to stretch out the tension in her shoulders. "I want the herbs loaded and shipped tomorrow night with the appropriate letters going to our compatriots on the Continent. Spain, Portugal and Italy are quite eager to get started since they've seen our wonderful results here and in Germany, the Netherlands and Belgium. I've had missives from Austria and surprisingly, Russia, and now France wishes to join us since we have perfected the herbal mixture. I want Violet in charge of France."

"What?" he spluttered, disbelieving his ears. How could the Lady do such a thing? Violet has done nothing but get in their way with her insatiable hunger for playing with the Chosen.

"I want Violet out of my sight," explained the Lady. "She can prove herself by going to France and setting things in motion there, while making sure that de Sagres and the Angel follow. She has been a hindrance here. If she can prove herself there, then maybe I will reward her once the Chosen are exterminated. As for you, my little bird, you are my eyes and ears. You are to oversee the operations here and keep an eye on Violet, but more importantly I need you to make contact with the others in the eastern countries and follow up with the ones we have yet to hear from."

The dark haired man smiled, his own position elevated. He did not mind the extra responsibilities, but relished in how he could effectively step up the one sided genocidal war against the Chosen.

"I will write the letters, my Lady, and send them the packages to experiment with," he bowed his head, a smile on his face.

"And that's not all, my little bird," she fixed on him her darkly hooded glare. "You are to go with Violet. Make sure she understands with whom she is dealing and teach her to hold the reigns properly. If my little flower does not bear fruit by harvest time, then it will be time to prune her."

His smile brightened. Violet would have to fall back into line. Oh how she would hate it, but she would.

"Oh, and my little bird," his Lady's voice grew menacing. "If she fails, and France falls a step behind the rest, feel free to pluck her petals one by one. I'm sure you would enjoy that."

"Yes, my Lady, I most certainly would."

XVI

ifting from the binding threads of sleep and the bizarre dream of the past, the Angel woke but kept his eyes closed, sensing that the sun was still up. It was quiet in the room. The only sound was Jeanie's steady breathing and the external noises of the day penetrating into the room. It was Jeanie's presence, her sweet hot scent and the gentle soughing of her breath that filled him. He was content and did not wish to break the sense of unwarranted peace that filled him.

Relaxing as much as the cramped space on the chaise would allow, the memory of the dream drifted back. It was not surprising that he should finally remember Fernando from so long ago. What was surprising was how it all came back to him, and in such incredible detail. The revelation did not change his opinion of the Noble, but rather it enhanced it and explained many issues, even Fernando's enjoyment of tormenting and prodding into his life. He could sympathise with Fernando, but knew that such feelings would not be accepted by one such as he and he buried the feeling. After all, Fernando brought it down upon himself.

Only one thought lingered, *Did Fernando remember?* He doubted it, but somehow the possibility agitated him. Unable to fall back asleep he opened his eyes and all thoughts of his host fled.

Standing unaware by the heavy green velvet drapes, Jeanie peered outside through a thin gap between the fabrics that also allowed a strip of deadly late afternoon sunlight to cross the bed. Her long elegant fingers absently caressed the velvet, running up and down, changing the subtle patterns of the weave.

She was breathtaking standing only in her cotton shift, her hair aflame where the sunlight dared to touch. The light behind cast her firm young body in silhouette and he found he could not take his eyes off her long shapely legs, smooth flat abdomen, full rounded hips and large round breasts that slowly rose and fell with each breath. He had seen many a woman clad in less, but this time it was different, her whole being captivated and enthralled him. He wanted to watch, protect, devour and flee from her. Jeanie was, by far, the loveliest woman he had ever known.

Entranced, he watched with heightened senses as she pivoted on one perfect bare foot, her hand tightening on the drape. Her intention realized too late, he threw his arms to his face as intense white light splashed across the room, its deadly beam coming oh so dangerously close.

A cry of pain came unbidden and he shouted, "Close it! For the love of Christ, close them!"

The sound of the Angel's cry startled Jeanie. She had believed him asleep and she spun to see him with his arms shielding his face. It took a moment for his words to register and hastily she drew the drapes, plunging them into near darkness.

She had not heard him enter last night and had been surprised to find him curled on the too short chaise. She had thought to wake him, but as she drew close she could not bear to disturb him. He had looked so peaceful. The constant worry etched into his features had melted away leaving Jeanie wondering how someone so beautiful could be so sad. Now she all but ran to his side, knelt and placed her hands on his trembling arms.

"They're closed. Put yer arms down." Her voice was soothing yet tinged with concern. She could not understand the Angel's vehement reaction.

Feeling her featherlike touch on his arms, he reluctantly lowered them, blinking rapidly as he opened his eyes only to see nothing except blackness ringed in white. His eyes burned and he felt tears on his cheeks. Even squinting did not help the large dark patches to diminish.

"Dear Gods," he whispered and sat up with the help of gentle unseen hands that came to rest on his own.

He knew that Jeanie was before him, yet try as he might he could not see her for the darkness moved to everything he looked at.

"What is it?" implored Jeanie. Something was dreadfully wrong. The tears on his face frightened her and he squinted at her without seeing.

Shaking his hands free from her grasp, he rubbed his eyes and was rewarded with a lessening of the black spots. He pressed the heels of his palms to his eyes. The pressure helped to alleviate the stinging.

"Did Notus never tell you why we keep such strange hours?" he admonished, instantly regretting his harsh tones.

"Aye, he did explain why you sleep all day and wake only for the night." She felt horrible, like a child who forgot a simple rule, but the Good Father's reason never fully explained why the Angel chose the same way of life.

"Tell me. What did he say?" The pain and the panic of losing his sight diminished with the slow shrinkage of the darkness.

Jeanie gazed into pain filled crimson eyes and fear swept over her.

"My God, what've I done?" she uttered weakly. "Ye canna see me."

Squinting, he barely made out a dark shape before him and took Jeanie's hands roughly in his own, making her gasp in pain. Relaxing his accidental grip, he demanded. "Tell me."

"He only told me that ye do as he does because it suits you so that the two of you can bide together." His whole reaction terrified her.

The standard reason, proven effective over the centuries, had now lost its potency. Never before had either Chosen or Chooser ever imagined a reason to elaborate further and now he found himself explaining without thinking. "Look at me, Jeanie." He grasped her shoulders and gazed at the dark area that was her head. The large blackness had broken into smaller spots when he blinked. "I have not been able to go out in the day ever since I was a boy." He knew his tone was harsh and accusatory, but he could not stop. "The last time was before I was ten. I can never go out in the day. It will kill me."

Silence crashed between them. Only Jeanie's muffled sobs filled the void and with it came the realization of what he had done to her, blaming her for a life in darkness and for nearly blinding him. Releasing his vice grip, Jeanie collapsed with her head in his lap. He did not need to see that she would have massive bruises where his fingers had dug into her flesh.

"Oh Gods," he floundered. Remorse filled him even more with the returning of his vision. Bright flashes and streaks mottled the red curls that covered Jeanie's tear streaked face. Already he could see the blood marking her white skin with angry red spots. He placed a tentative hand on her head and bushed the silky locks from her face. "Jeanie, I'm…I'm so sorry."

Jeanie continued to weep.

At a complete loss, he could only allow his returning vision to take in her beauty as he gently stroked her head in an attempt to quiet her and to smooth out his own guilt. He did not know how long they stayed like that, Jeanie on his lap while he pet her. Part of him wanted it to go on forever; to touch her without her pulling away in revulsion or fear; to feel the silky smoothness of her hair and breathe in her clean scent of lavender and rose. Gradually, she came to a hiccoughing halt and he pulled his hand away as she lifted her head. Her emerald eyes were puffy and red yet still riveting.

She sadly regarded him, evoking new worries. "Jeanie, are you all right?" he ventured, cautiously.

Jeanie pursed her lips and gazed down, nodding.

"I'm so sorry, Jeanie," he apologized. "I did not mean to hurt you. I seem to be doing that a lot, lately. You did not deserve what I said."

"Aye, I did." Her voice was gravely from crying. "Ye had every right. I shouldna opened the drapes, knowin' better as I do. Can ye   forgive me?"

Dumbfounded that she would be asking for his forgiveness, he stared at her. "Of course, but I had no right to hurt you."

Jeanie followed his gaze to her bruising shoulders and shrugged. "Dinna fash yerself with that. My da used t' do a lot worse t' me." She watched his face blanch at the revelation and allowed herself the luxury of a small smile. Bridging his knees with her arms, she rested her chin on them and gazed up into his eyes. For the first time the stoic mask was removed, revealing the sensitive and caring man she had expected was there but never thought to uncover.

"Then why?" He shook his head. White hair brushed against her face.

"Why what?" She shifted her head to rest more comfortably on one arm.

"Why were you crying, if not because I hurt you?" It felt strangely wonderful to have her so close, touching him.

Jeanie pulled her eyes from his. "I think at first it was because ye did hold me so hard, but then I found I couldna stop. I was cryin' because of all that's happened, and then I kenned I cried because ye were holdin' me and for the first time ye called me by my name."

Disbelief made way for realization, and a groan escaped his lip. For four years he had always managed not to call her by name, believing that by doing so he could distance himself from her and his growing feelings. It worked, perhaps a little too well. And now he realized the distance was an illusion, blown apart by saying her name to her face.

He gazed at her resting her head on his knee and terror filled him. He wanted her so badly at that moment that it hurt. The emotions confused him. She was not running from him and to his memory she never did. He was the one who always ran. First he did so out of the belief to that to do so would make her more comfortable without having someone so strange about while doing her work, but he knew that was a lie. The truth that he kept from himself was that he never wanted to be hurt again and would not allow the possibility. Now Jeanie was here and though every instinct was to flee and to hide his heart, yet he could not. Hesitantly, he touched a stray copper curl veiling her cheek and brushed it off her soft face.

She closed her eyes at the touch of his cool fingers and recalled a saying that brought a smile to her face. *Cold hands; warm heart.* The Angel was proving to have a very warm heart indeed. She turned her face into his caress and opened her eyes, the blackened scab on the palm of his hand startled her and she pulled back, grasping his hand.

"Yer hurt!"

For one fleeting moment Jeanie's words did not register and he thought she was going to bolt, instead he watched her examine his hand. Though the cut was healing well, it was still ugly.

"I kenned ye had hurt yerself," repeated Jeanie, "but nae so bad. I'll go ask Fernando for some bandages." She stood and turned towards the door.

Tell Fernando! The thought brought him to his senses and he stood, spinning Jeanie around to face him. "No." If Fernando even suspected he was different it could mean the end of him, but how was he to tell Jeanie that? He looked into her startled green eyes. "Fernando must not know about it, ever," panic welled into his voice. "Promise me, Jeanie. Please."

"But yer cut should be tended to." She could not understand his angst.

"I'll heal, only never tell Fernando, please."

She nodded, promising without understanding the sudden fear in his eyes.

The tension suddenly left his body and the breath he held came out in a huff. He still held Jeanie and the sudden need for her overwhelmed him, driving away any and all fears he had only moments ago. Running his uninjured hand down the side of her face to cup her chin, he lifted her beautiful face to his. Spring eyes caught his and he could hear the quickening of her breath. The heat of her lips on his startled and exhilarated him and her mouth opened in response. Tentatively, they explored each other. Her hot blood scent drew him into a concupiscence he had allowed himself to experience so long ago that it was all but forgotten.

Breaking the kiss with a shudder, he took a step back. *Too close.*

Jeanie's face was flush, her eyes fluttered open to see the Angel staring at her with fear and revulsion.

"What is it?" she implored. She had dreamed so long for this moment and now she was unprepared for his unexpected reaction.

He swallowed audibly and in a voice husky with desire, said, "You had best get dressed." He turned towards the door and stopped when he felt her hand upon his back.

"What is it that yer afraid of?" Her voice was soft despite her worry.

"Jeanie, please," he pleaded, not turning around to face her. He knew that if he did, he would loose all constraint.

She could not let it go. She had come too far to do that. "Yer afraid of me?"

"No, I'm afraid of myself," he stated before fleeing the room, leaving Jeanie to stare in amazement at the door.

The door clicked shut behind him and he collapsed against the hard wood, his head resting against the lintel and his hands pressing against his eyes. Jeanie's intoxicating taste and scent filled his mind with thoughts he could not bear. Pulling his hands from his face, he gazed at his shaking fingers and immediately crossed his arms against his chest in an attempt to still his trembling. He never imagined that anyone could have such a profound effect on him. He had witnessed spells Chosen wove to capture mortals under the precepts of love, but he had never done so himself, and now he felt as entangled as a fly in a web.

Gods, I could have killed her. The realization terrified him. She could not find out the truth of his nature, and yet she had learned enough that could very well cause his downfall. Only once before had the blood been so irresistible – Tarian. The thought of the long dead girl and his encounter with her set him trembling anew. She had wanted him, not because she loved him, but because she believed he was something he was not.

Even with Tarian's granddaughter, his first and only love, he had never felt so scared. With Jeanie it was different, and plainly so. She had never shirked from him and this fact ignited a much deeper desire. *She can never discover the truth.* The thought of seeing revulsion and horror in her eyes if she found out would be too much for him to bear. He could not have Jeanie view him as others have.

Still hugging himself, he absently followed the hall runner down the stairs. So absorbed in his own thoughts he did not see Fernando rise from the couch in the parlour and nearly jumped out of his skin when the Noble demanded something from him. He stared at Fernando, his mind a swirl with thoughts of Jeanie and the image of the Noble five hundred years past superimposed on a Fernando of the present wearing a dark blue three piece suit and his hair pulled back in a tail.

"I demand to know what happened," barked de Sagres, oblivious to the Angel's obvious distress.

He stood silent, trying to comprehend the meaning and shook his head. "I did not tell her." He settled himself on the opposite couch, leaving his host standing.

"Not that." Fernando cut the air with a sweep of his hand and glared at his guest. "1386. London. The celebration for the English King's cousin," he stated shortly.

"What?" Crimson eyes stared up in confusion.

Fernando leaned over, levelling his eyes with the Angel's "I want to know what happened. You were there. I remember."

Had reality shifted? He could not get a grasp of the situation and he blinked blankly up at the Noble. Slowly, the dream came back and with it the understanding of what was asked of him. "You do not know?"

Straightening in indignation, Fernando glared down his nose at the Angel. "No, I do not. I was quite drunk if you would be so kind as to remember. After all it was the *Angel* who put me to bed," sneered the Noble.

The Angel stared in silence. Flashes of memory and the dream came to mind, allowing him time to compose himself from all the shocks he had received so early this evening.

"What do you want to know?" he asked, cautiously.

Fernando sat stiffly. "I want to know two things. First, what did I do and say before you put me to bed, and secondly, why the hell have you pretended not to know me. Is it to have some way to control me by bribing me with the information of my exile?"

It was suddenly obvious that he had some knowledge that Fernando lacked, giving him an imagined upper hand over the Noble, but at the mention of the exile, his white brows furrowed.

"I did not know you were exiled," he replied, sympathetically. "I did not remember you until this evening, and even if I had remembered earlier I would never have held that against you. What occurred happened life times ago and I am no man's judge."

Suspicion flared in brown eyes and instantly faded. Fernando was learning enough about the Angel to know that, strange as it may seem, he did not lie.

"You didn't answer my first question," de Sagres stated tersely.

He could see through the tension held in the Noble's body to see the fear the presence of the truth caused him. Lowering his gaze to the table between them, he searched for the words. "You came into the hall in a terrible state of disarray and thoroughly drunk," he began in soft tones. "You made your way through the crowd to stand before the throne, attempted a bow and said something before you nearly vomited on King Richard and the Ambassador for Portugal."

"What did I say?" asked Fernando, his eyes taking on the glint of a man faced with a horrifying truth.

"I don't know." He shook his head.

"You must remember what I said," pressed Fernando. "The memory of a Chosen…"

"I know, but that was five hundred years ago."

"Try."

He pursed his lips. Fernando's need was so much like his own; to find the truth of himself. He thought back to that night and closed his eyes.

"Esta e a puta Ingleza que vai polluir a sange Real!" he said, unsure if he remembered correctly until he opened his eyes.

Fernando had taken on the look of a man surprised at being mortally wounded.

The Angel was not about to inquire what it meant, he knew. Instead he asked, "Does that sound right?"

After a long silent moment, Fernando slowly nodded. "Now I understand," he said calmly and stood up.

He watched de Sagres move about the parlour, oblivious to all except his own thoughts. Without warning, a low growl of rage boiled up in the Noble until he exploded, smashing an end table into splinters.

"Raio esta parte da minha vida!" he roared. And as suddenly as the explosion occurred Fernando calmed down to a smouldering fury. "I guess I should be grateful that I was allowed my life," he chuckled, darkly.

He said nothing, calmly watching the Noble, wondering what was next in store.

Soft footfalls on the stairs caught both Chosen's attention and they turned in time to see Jeanie descend the remaining stairs carrying the Angel's cloak and shoes into the parlour.

"Ye left these in the room," she explained, laying the items down beside him, without looking at him.

"You look ravishing, my dear," stated the Noble. His rage set aside and sat down on the opposite couch to watch a blush darken her face.

The Angel silently agreed. He did not know where she had found the forest green dress with white embroidery and lace that accentuated every gracious curve and made her eyes shine like emeralds, but the sight of her in it ignited his desire for her anew and he painfully squashed it.

"It was the least fancy I found in the closet," apologized Jeanie. "I dinna want t' wear filthy clothes. If ye think yer lady will mind I can go and change." She turned to go back up the stairs.

"No, that's alright. Bridget won't mind, even if she notices it missing," explained Fernando. "If you're hungry, go help yourself in the pantry."

Jeanie gave her thanks and disappeared into the back with a quick glance at the Angel.

"You didn't tell her, yet you slept with her?" stated Fernando, after Jeanie was out of earshot. "You do like courting disaster."

He drew his gaze from the dark hall to the Noble's smiling face. "I did not sleep with her," he explained. The doubtful look on his hosts face forced him to continue. "She slept in the bed, and I on the chaise. I would never sleep with her." By God he wanted to. To have her be so wholly his, but it could not happen — ever. The kiss was dangerous enough.

"For some strange reason, I don't believe you," stated Fernando, "and frankly I've decided I don't care. What I do care about is that you keep your trap shut in regards to that night so long ago. I do not want that to become public knowledge, understand?"

"I do not know why you are so worried. I have no interest in any entanglements with you except in so far as we conclude this mystery."

"Fine." Fernando did not sound convinced. "Then onto my second point. Now that the sun's gone down we can go to the harbour and find out who is ordering these herbs. Once we have that then we can tell Katherine and go our separate ways. Agreed?"

"What about the Kitchen?" he replied, slipping on his shoes. "We were carefully led into a trap there so that they could dispose of us as they had Sebastian."

Fernando sat quietly. He had not thought about that. A grimace tugged at his face. "They know what we are."

The Angel nodded. He did not like the thought at all and worse yet was that their captors were mortals. "If we go back to the Kitchen we are dealing with just one of many in London, let alone Britain. We don't know how big this really is."

"I don't think Katherine knows." Fernando drummed his fingers on his thighs. "I think we're in trouble."

Silence crashed down between the two Chosen. The only sounds came from Jeanie's puttering in the kitchen.

He stared at the table between he and Fernando. They were indeed in trouble. They could go back to the kitchen, but what would that yield? Lackies doing the grunt work while those who issued the orders ran the show. It was them they had to stop and the only way was to follow the paper trail of the herbs. Once they found out who was trying to kill the Chosen, they could hopefully put a stop to it. Since the poisoners were mortals then it could very well be the spark of a long feared war between mortals and Chosen, and that could not be tolerated. The only disturbing thought was the young lady in the alley who had sent them there was at the kitchen as he escaped. If only he could remember who she was, maybe that would help, but memory of the Chosen or no, he could not place her face.

"We need to follow the herbs," he stated, resolutely. They had no other recourse.

Fernando huffed and nodded in agreement. "To the docks, then." He stood, walking to the front door.

He stood as Jeanie entered, daintily sucking sweet marmalade from her fingers.

She stopped inside of the door, noticing that the Angel was about to swing his cloak onto his broad shoulders.

"Are we goin' now?" she asked.

Unable to handle the Angel's apparent turn around, Jeanie had decided to eat in the kitchen. Looking at him now that she had seen him without his cool exterior mask, Jeanie realized the truth of his words. *Why is he so afraid?*

"Yes." Fernando turned around. "I suppose that even after what I did this morning you are still planning on joining us?"

"Aye," she replied, coolly. She did not like Fernando, especially after his assault on her. Her wrist still burned, but it appeared that if she wanted to help the Good Father and the Angel she would have to put up with the Noble.

"For better and for worse?" pressed de Sagres.

"Aye." *I doubt it could get any worse,* she silently added.

"Then let's get going." Fernando moved to the entrance of his home, retrieving his dark cloak and setting the lengthy fabric onto his shoulders. He picked up a long woman's coat and threw it at her. "Don't want to chill the blood, do you?"

Jeanie glanced from the Angel to Fernando and then back to the Angel, who quickly glanced away, as she slipped the coat on. Had things between them suddenly returned to the way they had been for the last four years? She had a horrible sense that not only had they, but somehow the distance between them seemed far greater.

She followed them out of the largest home she had ever been in and stood silently while Fernando hailed a cab. The sun having set only a short time ago left the sky inky blue with a smattering of stars. The Angel was firmly shut away under the cover of his hood. He did not say a word even as he helped her into the horse drawn carriage, his hand so cold against hers. She sat beside him and in the background of her thoughts she heard Fernando issue orders to take them to the docks before he too entered the cab.

ANGEL OF DEATH

They traveled in silence, each consumed in their own thoughts. He stared out of the carriage window, fully aware of the Noble's gaze and the warm, inviting presence of Jeanie beside him. It did not take a genius to see that he was hurting her, and he foolishly rationalized that it was better to cause her pain now before he did something worse.

What he found was that he was hurting himself as well. The ache went deep and knew that if he could reach out, even to give Jeanie some sense of reassurance, it would be well worth it and the knot in his gut would untie. If only Notus were around so that he could ask him for some advice. He discarded that notion immediately. Notus had never condoned fraternization of that type between mortal and Chosen. The Angel's affair with Tarian's granddaughter proved it. And Notus' vocal disapproval of his Chosen being used and using mortal women to bury his feelings of loss and depression over Tarian's granddaughter emphasised the point quite clearly. Notus would probably be the last being on earth to give him the advice he craved.

With Tarian, the solution was simple and clear cut. He could not stay. With Tarian's granddaughter, she was married to another and carrying her husband's unborn child. He could not take that away from her no matter how much they wanted to be together. The times were different and so was he. Fourteen hundred years changed a person in such minute ways that even he could not figure them all out.

An absurd thought appeared in his mind, *ask Fernando*. Sure, reveal something so significant to the most insensitive individual he had ever encountered, mortal or Chosen. He might as well tell the Noble about his reaction to iron and crossing water and therefore instantly sign his death warrant. No, he would have to follow his instincts concerning Jeanie. *Jeanie.* The thought of her plunged him into remorse and sent new fears through his mind.

Buildings and crowds of people quickly passed. Men in dark coats and bowlers, and women in dresses from the plain to the extravagant all blurred against the bright gas lit streets and pubs. The world had changed in remarkable ways and seemed to be shrinking and expanding. In the past the Chosen were easily hidden from mortal kind and moved around with comparative ease. With new inventions and creativity, the sights of mortal men were beginning to find their deepest secrets and bring them to light. It seemed that the Chosen had been brought to this light and were now being systematically eradicated, a thought that disturbed him greatly.

The blur of streetlights settled into a singular yellow glow and he realized that they had stopped. Buildings full of people taking their evening meals with friends could not stifle the yelling that was coming from the front, and he turned around to find he was alone with Jeanie. The question of the Noble's disappearance faded before the words reached his lips. One of the people yelling outside was Fernando. The shouting ceased and the

Noble re-entered, nearly shattering the door with slamming force.

"God damn it!" fumed de Sagres, settling back onto the bench. He encased himself in his cloak.

"What is it?" asked Jeanie. She had looked out the opposite window throughout the ride, afraid to look at the Angel and see the distance between them. She could feel his presence beside her as she kept her attention on the Noble.

"Those blasted automobiles shouldn't be allowed on the roads!"

"What happened? Why are we not moving?" inquired the Angel.

"Well, I'm glad that you finally woke up," snapped the Noble. "One of those goddamned machines came careening into the intersection where it slammed into a carriage, flipping it over and killing one of the horses, and maiming two others. They'll probably have to be put down as well."

"What happened to the driver?" asked Jeanie, her eyes shimmering with horror and worry.

"Which one?" rounded Fernando. "The carriage driver and his occupants are fine, but I wouldn't say the same for the automobile driver. Daddy's little rich boy made a wonderful stain on the road and his whore is being removed from the wreckage. Poor li'l thing lost her head." He smiled exposing his pointed teeth. "We'll be here until the mess is cleaned up."

"When will that be?" asked the Angel. He wanted to get to the docks as soon as possible. Since the would-be captors knew of their escape and they may very well be on their trail, or worse, covering up one.

"What do I look like, your answer man? Half an hour, an hour, who the bloody hell knows." Fernando settled back in the seat, brown eyes smouldering.

"We could walk," he ventured.

"And do you think your pretty little housekeeper would be able to keep up? I think not."

He turned to face out the window. Fernando was right, Jeanie's presence was hindering their ability to act in ways that were normal to them, slowing them down, but he had made a promise, one he was starting to regret for more than one reason. He felt her shift on the seat, taking her farther away from him.

The idea of being in such close quarters with the Noble suffocated him and his only escape was to watch the people as they swarmed around the accident sight, ignoring the cold and the drizzle, curiosity seeking morbid entertainment.

Some things do not change, he sighed.

A darting between clusters of onlookers caught his attention and focused it. Threading around couples and individuals, a boy of about nine, dressed in dirty, rumpled clothing and wearing a bowler hat too large for his size, appeared to be searching for someone or something. Those who bothered to notice the lad were repelled by his obvious foreignness and shooed him away. He knew it was he who Yi Li searched for. Turning to face Jeanie, oblivious of the situation, he realized he needed her help. The Angel could not become the centre of the mob's attention and Fernando surely would not do this for him.

"Jeanie," he spoke quietly and watched her startle and turn to face him, green eyes wide in expectation. It was invitation enough. "There is a Chinese boy over there, beside the blonde woman in the blue dress, grey coat and silver wrap. Do you see him?"

Jeanie followed the direction the Angel pointed and could barely make out the woman. It was clear that she had hoped for something more when he said her name and frowned when he tried to point the lady out. As for the boy, all she could see was a short, small shadow near the woman, and she nodded.

"What is this?" interrupted Fernando.

Ignoring the Noble, he continued. "Go to him and bid him to come here. The boy's name is Yi Li. If he refuses or puts up a fuss tell him you are sent by me—the Angel. Do you understand?"

"Aye, but why?"

"Please, Jeanie," he interrupted with a sigh, "just do as I ask."

She closed her mouth and looked ready to give him an earful. Instead she got up and left the carriage to walk towards the boy. He watched her from the window and felt Fernando beside him, also watching the girl.

"Are you planning to feed with her here, and on a child she caught for you?" queried the Noble. "I wouldn't have thought you the type."

Repressing a shudder of revulsion at such close proximity to the Noble, he replied tersely, "I am not."

Jeanie had just made contact with Yi Li, and as expected the boy initially put up resistance. Now he followed at her side, Jeanie's face a menagerie of anger, embarrassment and amusement.

"Then what's the boy for?" asked Fernando.

"We agreed last night that we should find out how the herbs work." He watched Jeanie come closer, walking in between people coming to see the gruesome show.

"Yes, but how does the boy fit in?" Fernando was now genuinely confused.

"His mother is a master herbalist, as is his grandfather," he answered and sat back from the window in time for Jeanie to open the coach door, allowing the boy to enter first.

The boy's face was smudged with grime and his wool clothing sported patches of dried mud. A bruise on his left cheek revealed itself when Yi Li tipped the brown hat back far enough to look at the cowled Angel and at the man who was not the Good Father. His smile of perfect white teeth slipped only momentarily before taking in the fact that he was in an expensive cab. He ignored the sound of the door closing behind and the jostle of the carriage as the lady sat beside the Angel.

His large slanting brown eyes came to rest on the Angel.

"You sent pretty lady to get me." The boy's accent was thick and smug for one so young. "You smarter than I thought."

"I am glad to hear that, Yi," replied the Angel, softly, the persona of the Angel enveloping him completely. "You were looking for me?"

Yi Li nodded, sending his hat down over his face. Jeanie stifled a laugh at the boy's predicament before he managed to push it back so that he could see again and lost his grin at the sight of Noble's scowling face.

"Why are we wasting our time with this urchin?" spat Fernando.

"You not so nice," rounded Yi Li. "Need to laugh more." He forced a staccato belly laugh. "You laugh like that, you won't be so constipated."

"Why you–" Fernando made to reach for the boy but found himself thrust onto the bench with a thud. He glared at the Angel. Was everyone under the protection of the blasted Angel?

"You were looking for me, Yi?" he repeated. Again the boy nodded, this time the smile was gone. "That is fortuitous. I need the services of your mother, or better yet, your grandfather."

A panicked glint alighted Yi Li's eyes. "That's why I look for you. I went to your home. Nobody there. I had to search and search."

He frowned beneath the hood. How could Yong Zheng Ru or Mei Li know his need? It may well be because it has been—what?—two nights since his last lesson with the old man, when he usually visited every evening, even if it was to talk for an hour. He sat quietly waiting for Yi Li to continue.

"Mama say you come quick," implored the boy.

"What is it?" Concern needled into him. It was not Mei Li's way to call for him.

"Grandfather needs the Angel." Tears welled into Yi Li's eyes, yet did not fall. "Grandfather in bad accident," he choked back a sob. "Got hit by a runaway horse."

The reality of the boy's words slowly sank in and to the shock of the others, he pounded on the roof shouting new orders for the driver to turn around and drive, as fast as the horses could pull, to another destination. The carriage gave a lurch and threw Yi Li next to a bewildered Noble. Jeanie grabbed hold of the handle hanging from the side lest she be thrown to the floor and stared at the Angel wondering what possessed him.

He ignored them, his crimson eyes echoed fear into the night beyond the carriage window.

The carriage came to an abrupt halt and gratefully the four piled out onto the sidewalk. Battered and dishevelled from the frantic ride, the Angel followed Yi Li through the unnamed blackened storefront without remembering to wait for the other two.

Through the small herb shop lined with walls stocked with hundreds of herbs and the back room they went. Only the sound of their hurried footfalls rang in the air until he threw open a door leading into a dimly lit stairwell that ascended over the shop. Voices and laughter echoed down the hall as well as a strange smell. He made one last check that his hood was in place and climbed the steep staircase, taking the steps three at a time. The sound of Jeanie's harried breath mingled with the voices of the people lounging on cushions in a smoke filled atmosphere as they reached the top.

"You brought us to an opium den?" exclaimed Fernando, disgusted at the sight of the pitiful mortals' futile attempts to escape reality.

Jeanie's gasp of surprise and the Noble's question went unanswered. Winding his way through the throng, he ignored all except that of the door at the back of the den. A few, not so deep in the effects of the drug startled at the sight of the Angel and the two strangers with him. These too did he ignore.

The door opened into a brightly lit room finely decorated with oriental art. The smell of perfumed joss sticks floated into the air from a little shrine in the corner. Fresh fruit and burning candles sat beside a tiny figurine indicated that the shrine was in active use.

"Please, come in," said the very beautiful Chinese woman. Dressed in blue silk, she sat before the shrine. Her thick black hair sharply contrasted her pale face and richly red painted lips. She stood with the grace to shame a Chosen and Yi Li went to stand by his mother's side.

The three did as she bade, the door closing behind.

"You come not alone," she stated, glancing from the Angel to the others and then back again. Her small, delicate hands were clasped in front.

It took a moment to figure whom Mei Li was talking about. "This is Fernando de Sagres and Jeanie Stuart."

"The Angel said that you are a master herbalist," interjected the Noble, already wanting to be on their way.

Mei Li raised a brow yet her face remained impassive. "Thank you for the compliment. Xiao Gui has always been kind to us."

A snort escaped the Noble's lips. The name Mei gave the Angel was one he was sure the Angel did not call himself. Fernando withdrew the tiny bottle, holding it out for Yi Li's mother. "Do you think you could find out what this is and how it works?"

Mei Li took a step and the phial disappeared into her tiny grasp. "I will try. Is this why you come? Did Yi Li not tell you?"

"Yi said that your father needed the Angel," replied the Angel. "And that your father has been injured."

Mei Li nodded, a frown matching the sadness in her liquid brown eyes. "Yesterday father went out for morning walk. Crossing the road, runaway horse knocked father down, trampling him. Doctor could do nothing. He say father is dying. Father knows. He's in much pain. We send Yi Li to find you." She bowed her head, turned around and opened the door next to the shrine before she left through another door with her son in tow.

Dim yellow light illuminated the sparse room. A dresser stood against one crumbling plastered wall. A pitcher and basin of chipped porcelain sat on top. The only other large piece of furniture was a bed with its cracked and peeling wooden headboard against the back wall. Immaculate white linen sheets covered the form of an ancient man. His white-filmed eyes stared into the room.

For a moment he believed Yong Zheng dead until he heard his laboured breathing. He took a step into the dimly lit room and remembered who was with him. "Jeanie you have to stay here," he said, turning to face Notus' lovely housekeeper.

Drawing her attention from the sickly old man, Jeanie stared into the darkness of his hood. "Why? I can help." She did not know how, but she wanted to be with him and be there for him.

He shook his head. "Not this time."

"But ye take Fernando, ye can take me."

"I'm not taking either of you. Not for this." He closed the door on the two of them, both agape at being left out for different reasons.

Fernando fumed at having the door closed on him. He wanted to see the Angel at work and he was not going to be stopped now, and if he played his cards right, so would the girl. Testing the door handle, he opened the door enough for him to spy. A smile played along his lips as Jeanie knelt to join him in his espionage. *Well, if he will not tell her...It will be interesting to see how she handles the truth.*

The Angel stepped towards the bed. Pushing back his hood, he knelt beside his teacher, and gazed into Yong Zheng Ru's milky eyes, praying that he would not have to do what he could already tell was necessary.

"I have come, Yong Zheng," he said in perfect Cantonese. No matter how many times he had done this throughout the centuries it still pained him to see friends in need of deaths release. He had tried not to feel, or like so many of the Chosen, to relish in the deception and final kill, but it never worked. Now, with Yong Zheng, the grief of the losses welled within, threatening to break.

"Ahh," sighed the old man, lifting his gnarled hand to be caught in the cool grip of the Angel's. Cool familiar fingers brushed away wispy strands of grey hair from his forehead. "I knew you would come, Xiao Gui." Yong Zheng halted, searching for breath. "I knew you were in danger, from within and without."

"What are you saying?" he frowned. He could smell death consuming his friend.

"I taught you, Xiao Gui, the forms handed down to me and you have taught me the practices of the ancients, for this I am grateful, but they come soon." He paused, his rasping voice threatening to break. "They came in the past. You forgot. They are coming again. They tell me to tell you."

Dumbfounded, he could only ask, "Who?"

ANGEL OF DEATH

Yong Zheng shook his head, instigating a coughing fit. Gently lifting the old man to a sitting position helped ease the violence of the fit and exposed the swollen purpled chest and abdomen where the scent of blood was the strongest. He did not need Notus' medical knowledge to know that Yong Zheng was bleeding into his belly. He covered the old man and settled him against the headboard.

After a few harried moments Yong Zheng Ru spoke. "I know that you need chi of others to live, Xiao Gui."

He swallowed, knowing without a doubt that his mentor in the newer martial arts knew his secret and waited.

"I cannot use it any longer. You need it more than I, Xiao Gui. I give it freely."

This was what he dreaded. With Yong Zheng Ru's strange talk he thought he would not be called to do the deed, but now he found he could not.

"I can't," he whispered, clutching Yong Zheng's warm hand.

"You must." Another fit took him and he continued once it was past. "They say you need it."

"Please," he pleaded. He did not want to do this. For the first time he did not want a mortals blood. He wanted Yong Zheng to live, to keep exchanging knowledge and stories.

The old man turned his sightless eyes onto the Angel who had become more a son than a student. "I am dying," he explained softly. "Don't let my chi go to waste, Xiao Gui."

He nodded, his eyes brimming with tears and was shocked to feel a hand on his face. Looking at the old man, his eyes met ones that had once seen.

"Let me see you one last time," whispered Yong Zheng Ru.

Slowly, gently, the old dry hands explored his face, this time, for the first and last time, he described what he looked like to his teacher and friend, all the while tears streamed down his pale face. He did not understand what was happening; all he knew was that Yong Zheng did not pull away in horror. When the old man finally withdrew his hands, he recognized the Cantonese word for beautiful.

The old man, fatigued by his explorations, his breath laboured, leaned his head against the board and the Angel knew it was time. Easing himself to sit on the edge of the bed facing Yong Zheng, he whispered, "Good-bye, dear friend."

With the hope it would not be too painful he leaned over and sank his teeth into Yong Zheng's neck. The taste of his tears mingled with that of his friend's blood. At first he let the old man's heart carry the blood to his mouth, but it did not take long for it to fail. There was no joy in the task and he despised his need for human blood even more. When he finally released his teacher, he wished only to leave the room.

Laying the body onto the bed, he wiped the tears from his face with the

Karen Dales

back of his hand and turned to leave. He found Fernando standing in the doorway. The Noble grinned and pulled the door fully open, revealing a terrified Jeanie quickly gaining her feet.

The world bottomed out, sending his mind lurching. All he could think of, over and over, was that she knows. *She knows!*

This was not what he wanted. Now he witnessed the undisguised horror of him in her face and before any could utter a word he pushed past them and fled into the night, his heart shattering.

It had gone so much better than Fernando had dared hope as he watched the Angel race into the night leaving Jeanie with him. Still smiling, he turned to the girl. "So now you know what you have involved yourself with."

"What are ye?" Jeanie took a fearful step backwards.

"What do you think we are?" he asked nonchalantly, circling the terrified girl.

"Devils," she whispered in horror.

Fernando chuckled in amusement. "No, not devils, something better. Vampires, my dear. Vampires. You are helping vampires."

"No," she shook her head. "They dinna exist." She tried to deny it but the image of the Angel draining the blood of that poor old man would not release its grip. Tears welled in her eyes.

"We do and now you have a choice to make." He so enjoyed the undisguised terror in her face. "Either you choose to continue helping us, knowing what we are, or I kill you. I might warn you, though, that I haven't fed tonight."

Jeanie's eyes went round in fright and she fled the opium den, the sound of Fernando's laughter fading behind her.

He could not help himself. It had been so long since he had so much fun. It would be interesting to see what would happen next. Fernando halted his booming laughter as the beautiful Chinese woman came back into the room. She looked so lovely in her navy blue silk dress.

"Where is the Angel and the lady?" she asked, glancing around the room.

"Gone," stated the Noble matter-of-factly. "What did you find out about the herbs?" *My God, it's been a long time since I've had Oriental.*

"It rare medicine." She handed the phial back. "Swallowed, it locks chi in blood and body. Given when chi is floating to prolong life for the dying."

"Locks the chi in the blood, eh?" repeated Fernando, staring at the little bottle with renewed respect. Making it vanish into a vest pocket, he took her hand and kissed it, sensing the blood beneath the skin. "Thank you." His eyes made contact with hers and a moment later she lay deeply unconscious on the floor.

Patting a kerchief at the corners of his mouth, Fernando stepped lightly over her body. Already the puncture marks on her neck were fading. He left the building without a thought or care except to get to the docks before dawn.

XVII

He sat on the floor in front of the couch, knees raised and arms creating a bridge for him to rest his chin as he stared into the cold dead fireplace. A delicate breeze drifted down the flue, minutely shifting ash, creating patterns only the imagination could define. A chunk of a half burnt log stood monolith to the desolation, mocking the totality of the dead fire's destructive capabilities.

It was so tempting to use that lone piece of wood to create a new fire that would turn it to cinders. Instead he grabbed the handle of the iron poker and stabbed the log. A charred piece snapped off, landing in the ashes, setting free several flakes before they too settled down. It was enough of an encouragement. Hardening his grip, he smashed the poker down on the wood, sending a flurry of grey flying.

Again and again he slammed the iron rod into the charred mass, beating it until nothing remained except shredded kindling. Ash filled the fireplace. A storm that refused to follow the laws of gravity, until slowly, almost imperceptibly, the ash began to settle. A few of the multitude landed in perfect balance on the iron poker. The fury of the storm abated, he was left with nothing but the purity of his own self loathing. All that was left to do was watch in awe of the beauty the flakes created. Greys, whites, silvers, and blacks flickered as they landed, creating new patterns until all was as still as before.

Withdrawing the ash-covered poker, he glanced closely at the flakes. It was hard to conceive that such beauty could be created from such destruction. Unbalanced at the movement, a few of the ashes floated free, descending onto his lap. The ash's beauty faded against the blackness of the fabric, leaving ugliness in its wake. Disgust registered for no reason and in a fury he flung the poker away, sending the ash flying.

It was too much. It was all too much. He cradled his face in his hands, his hair sweeping forward, shrouding him. All that remained was emptiness and for the first time in his existence he felt the oppression of silence. Not even the word of another rang in his mind. Without Notus he was lost. And now...he had seen similar expressions of horror on many people through the ages.

He had learned long ago to bury the emotions the stares evoked, but this time it was different. Every time he tried to push the feelings away they just bubbled back to the surface. He had never wanted to have Jeanie look at him that way. Never. Now it was too late. He hung his head and stared at the flecks of ash on his pants wishing the pain would go away.

The sound of the front door opening brought his attention to the source. Still seated before the dormant hearth, he twisted around and gazed over the back of the couch, his arms resting on the cushions for support. Time stood still. He could not believe what he was seeing. Not daring to utter a word, lest the situation evaporate as fantasy, he could only stare, slack-jawed in fearful apprehension.

Jeanie stood, her arms hugging herself, face streaked with tears. She looked around the dark room. She did not know why she had come back here. After fleeing the horrific revelations at the opium den, she had walked aimlessly through the dampened streets. The image of the man she loved feeding off the living blood of another wrenched her insides, as did Fernando's proclamation that vampires did exist and that they were such creatures in the world. Her eyes witnessed the truth, her mind denied what she saw, and her heart was crushed by it.

On she had wandered not realizing that she was closing on the only home she had felt truly welcomed and loved since her mother died. It was the Angel's expression of desolation at seeing her fixated in horror that sped her through the streets.

She knew everything now, or so she thought, and could finally understand why he was afraid of himself with her, why he pulled back at every instance, why he did not want her involved. It was because he was a vampire and he cared about her. But did she still love him? Her confusion over the truth of his nature and the stories of vampires she had read in novels and the penny presses made her head swim.

Jeanie did not realize where she was until she stood in front of the door to his home. Testing the handle, she had turned it and entered, her heart pounding in fear.

At first she had not see him in the darkness illuminated by the solitary candle on the tea table, and then he stood up from behind the couch, despair etched on his fine pale features. She took an involuntary step backwards and caught herself. Her racing heart slowed with the realization that he had not come near her. In fact he would not even look at her. Despite the terror she felt, her need to hear the truth from the lips she had tasted from won out.

"Is it true?" she whispered into the darkness. "Is what I saw and what Fernando told me true? That ye are a–" She could barely bring herself to say the word, "a vampire?"

He could not believe his eyes. She was here, standing in front of the threshold. Every fibre in his being told him that it could not be true, that it was impossible, but there she stood, fear and sadness commingling on a face that should never know those feelings. Part of him wanted to rush over to her, to comfort her, but at her retreating step he knew she saw him as a monster. And then she spoke the question that confirmed his worse fears.

Unable to stand any longer, the weight of his anguish pulled him to sit down on the couch, his back to Jeanie. He could not bear to see the horror in her summer green eyes. Instead he stared at the shattered, splintered piece of wood in the fireplace.

Surprisingly, the squeak of the floorboards came closer until he could feel her warm presence behind him, her dim shadow darkening the hearth.

She did not know what possessed her to come so close to the man she thought she knew. She found it hard to see him as a monster from a fairy tale, but it made so much sense. She had never seen him eat. He slept all day. And his reaction to the sunlight! Not to mention why would the Good Father have a vampire around? *Unless…Oh dear God! I'm the housekeeper for vampires! But they canna be, could they?*

She caught her breath in shock. It was not possible. The Good Father was so kind, so generous. He made the most delicious meals for her, and then she realized he never partook of them himself. It was impossible to think he would live with a vampire, let alone be one.

And the Angel, his explanations seemed reasonable and she trusted, even loved him, but the vision of him over the old Chinese man and Fernando's admission plagued her. She needed the Angel—no, she needed Gwyn – to tell her the truth.

"Please, Gwyn," she implored. "Tell me."

The use of the name sent him reeling and he groaned, hiding his face in his hands supported by elbows resting on his knees. Only Notus used it, and only sparingly. Notus usually used it when he wanted to press a point, knowing where the name came from and why. He knew that Jeanie had heard it, but never before had she used it. To hear that name issued from her lips wrenched his heart.

"What do you want me to say?" he implored. He could not face her and see what the truth would do to her beautiful face.

"Anythin'. Everythin'. Tell me what I saw was a lie." She stood trembling, watching his hunched over form. Terrified, but drawn nonetheless, Jeanie moved around to the end of couch. He still would not look at her.

"I–" He shook his head, sending alabaster locks flowing. "I cannot."

"What?" she gasped. *He couldna possibly mean…*

There was nothing left between them but to tell her the truth before her imagination could make this nightmarish situation worse. He was stunned that she had come to him. He knew Jeanie to have remarkable courage, but doubted she could handle what was next. The truth would certainly send her fleeing. He sat up and dropped his hands limply into his lamp, gazing at the fireplace. He spoke so softly in an attempt to hide his own pain that she had to strain to listen.

"What you saw is true. Some of us call ourselves the Chosen, but a new word has come to be used to describe us…Vampire."

Terror stripped away Jeanie's ability to breathe, her eyes wide. Every instinct screamed that she should run away lest this horror story character come after her, but her legs refused to move until they gave way and she sat down on the couch as far away as possible. All she could do was stare at him. Even in the dark she could make out the soft lines of his face, so youthful as to be almost androgynous. She had believed him older than her, but now he appeared so much younger and so incredibly sad.

They sat in silence, Jeanie gazing at him as he stared at nothing. Slowly, the initial shock wore down enough for her to ask, "And…and the Good Father is a … vampire as well?"

He nodded. "He is the Chosen who Made me." He could not understand why she was still there and he turned his face to meet hers. Fear reflected in her emerald eyes, as well as something he had never seen before—curiosity.

"Oh my dear God," she gasped. She had been working for vampires! Then a new thought came unbidden to her lips. "Were ye and the Good Father usin' me so that one day…" She instantly regretted her words.

Revolted at the implication, he rose to his feet and glared down at her in disgust. Unable to form a reply to such a horrible notion, he just shook his head in disbelief. Of all the questions she could have asked, of all the generosity his Chooser had shown her, how could she even think such a question? Without another word he left her and strode angrily across the room to his bedroom, slamming the door behind him, causing the frame and door to crack.

Kicking off his shoes, he picked them up and threw them against the wall, causing the painted plaster to shatter at the impact. Sitting cross-legged on the bed, he rubbed his face with his hands, scrubbing away some of the anger. After all that he had done for her in the past couple of nights, after the promises he made, the audacity to even ask such a question wounded him and demeaned Notus.

ANGEL OF DEATH

A soft rapping on the door brought his attention and before he could order Jeanie to go away, she opened it enough to poke her head into the room.

Jeanie did not know what moved her to ask such a question, but seeing his reaction and the resonating sound of the door crashing closed, followed by two other loud thuds, made her realize how badly she hurt him. She never wanted that. She wanted him to be happy and be hers. That alone propelled her forward.

"I'm so sorry," she pleaded. She stepped into his bedroom, candle in hand, still nervous, but now more out of the fear of the secret she harboured within that drove her to seek him out. She knew his truth, and though it terrified her, Jeanie knew she had to tell him hers. "I—"

"Why are you still here?" He cut her off, turning to face his unwanted guest. She knew what he was. She knew what Notus was, and still she pursued him. What more could she possibly want?

The question caught Jeanie off guard and she blinked a few times before she could answer. "Because I need to know the truth."

"You have your truth," he stated, harshly. He gazed straight ahead at the dresser in an attempt to ignore the girl.

"Aye, I guess I do." She sullenly nodded her head. She felt that she should leave and go on with her life, but seeing him there, hurt and angry, Jeanie could not see him as the monster the stories portrayed. He was the same person, made vulnerable by the truth, and she spoke hers, fear evaporating as her voice grew stronger with conviction. "I ken the truth verra well. The Good Father is well named for all the kind works he has done. He saved me from a fate worse than death. He gave me a job, gave me a home, gave me a life without askin' for none in return. I've ne'er seen him harm another. He hasna an evil bone in his body, yet ye say he's a vampire, a thing of evil that feeds off blood to live, but he isna so. And… and ye are his Angel—the Angel who hides from men's eyes lest they see ye, yet ye always assist the Good Father in his good deeds. I've seen ye brave dangers for me, and I ken in my soul ye wouldn' hae done so if ye were such an evil creature. Ye are that, but no evil. I saw ye no wantin' to do what ye did to the old man, but ye did it because he wished it. I canna believe the man I love to be evil."

He gasped in astonishment as Jeanie spoke. It was inconceivable that she so easily accepted the truth, but what floored him were her final words.

"What?" he exclaimed, disbelieving his own ears.

Bravely taking the few steps to sit on the bed, Jeanie placed the candle on the bedside table and turned to face him, a shy smile on her full lips as if she were suddenly embarrassed by her proclamation.

"I love ye," she slowly stated, testing the words again in her speech. "I've loved ye since I first laid eyes on ye and I believe, no matter what ye are, that wilna change."

Disbelieving his own ears, he stood, desiring to get away from her but wanting to be so close. He could not stop his shaking or the surge of confusing emotions as Jeanie gazed up at him, worry washing over her perfect face as he paced.

"You can not mean that," he said, finally coming to a stop. "It's not possible."

"What? For me to love ye?" Jeanie rose, distinctly aware of the creature before her. Of all the reactions to her admission she could not have anticipated this one.

"Yes," he cried. He found it difficult to get enough breath to speak and he turned away. It hurt him too much to see her in the soft candlelight. He felt her warm hand tentatively settle on his arm.

"My God, yer tremblin'." She so wanted to take him into her arms and comfort him, even knowing the fearful truth that he could kill her with a kiss. "Why? Why canna ye believe it possible that I can love ye. I've known ye for four long years."

"But you don't know me," he stated, abruptly cutting her off and spun around to face the second woman in his life to cause him so much confusion, so much pain. "You just found out what I am—what Notus is. I have existed for nearly fourteen hundred years off the lives of countless thousands. Those I did not kill in the need for sustenance I killed in self preservation and my Chooser's preservation, and in some cases, to fund our travels."

His extreme age stunned her more than the rest of the revelation. When she found herself coherent enough, she warily asked, "But ye dinna have to kill all the time, d'ye?"

"No," he explained. "Thank the Gods we do not have to kill to get what we need." He sat down on the edge of the bed, suddenly exhausted. "Now you know why it is not possible."

"Because ye have killed," stated Jeanie, sombrely. Try as she might she could not see him as a cold bloodied killer. Fernando, yes, but not the Angel, and not the Good Father. They were too kind, too caring, too giving. Nothing in the way they ever treated her was anything but gracious and, from the Good Father, loving. Even with the old Chinese man it was clear to Jeanie that the Angel did not want to do what he had done. A killer would not act that way.

"Yes, that is one reason," he sighed.

"What is the other?" she asked suddenly curious.

He opened his mouth to say but instead closed it with a click. If she could say she loved him now that she knew he was Chosen, then he doubted that she would love him less for his appearance. The thought was strangely comforting.

"It doesn't bother you that I have killed people?" he asked.

Jeanie sighed. She had to admit that it did bother and terrify her. What he explained about himself seemed so incongruous with the man sitting on the bed. She did not know how to answer.

"What will happen to me now that I know?" she whispered.

Gazing into Jeanie's worried eyes, he knew that she had a right to be concerned, but he did note that she had not answered his question and that disturbed him. Most mortals that found out were killed out of hand unless their silence was guaranteed by the protection of a Chosen or the memory erased with the Push. In extremely rare occurrences they were Made because they were told about the Chosen to have the choice for an immortal life.

"I told you that you could trust me with your life, it is still true," he said softly. "I will never let you come to harm."

"Never?" she asked, incredulously, staring into his large, beautiful ruby eyes.

"Never," he repeated in earnest and stood, knowing what he must do to make Jeanie believe and trust him. "I promised you that before when I asked you to trust me, and I will swear to it too if I must."

Crossing to the back of the room, he took down his sword from the wall and went back to sit on his bed. With a hiss of metal against its sheath the blade lay naked across his lap. Jeanie stared in awe at the beauty of such a sword.

"Before I was Made and became Chosen," he explained, gazing at the ancient sword, "the only other living soul I knew – besides the woman who raised me – taught me how to be a warrior – to wield a sword. This was his sword, given to me by his daughter after he was killed in battle. It is as old as I, maybe older."

Carefully grasping the sharp blade where the dragons intertwined, he lifted it so that the sword was held point up between them. "Take hold of the hilt," he ordered. "With both hands."

She did as asked, her hands shaking. Jeanie had never held or seen such a fine weapon. They, again, were things made of stories. There was no weight to the blade, held firmly in his white grip.

His serious eyes caught hers across the steel of the blade. "I swear to you, Jeanie Stuart, upon this sword, and before what Gods men believe now, that I will never let you come to any harm. If I do, may this weapon be turned against me." Slipping the sword back into its sheath, he laid it at the foot of the bed.

Jeanie sat strangely quiet, unshed tears glimmering in her eyes. "No one has ever made me feel so safe, so cared for. No one has done what ye hae done for me. I dinna think it matters if yer a vampire and what that all means. What ye were before I knew is still the same as what I know now and it makes me love ye even more."

Silence crashed between the two of them as Jeanie's insistence sank in. Noticing that something was wrong by his baffled expression, Jeanie asked, "What's wrong?"

The question snapped him out of his reverie and he shook his head. "Haven't you been listening to me?" Incredulous, he stood, leaving her to sit on the bed and stare up at him. "I am not human!" He thumped himself hard on the chest with his hand. "I am Chosen – vampire, immortal, whatever! I have lived by draining the blood of mortals for about fourteen hundred years! I have killed for my blood lust. How can you say you love me when it cannot be possible?"

Jeanie bore his outrage in stoic silence before she pushed herself off the bed to stand facing up at him. She sucked her teeth until her lips smacked, and then she bore in.

"For someone as *old* as ye claim, ye're pretty *daft*." He gaped at her. "Aye, I've heard ye, an it seems ye dinna hear *me* verra well. I told ye I love ye. I dinna care *what* you are. I only care *who* ye are. Life is horror and death. I've seen my fair share of it before I ever came here. I've known men who've kilt for nothing more than spilt whiskey and a   misplaced word or two. Ye are no like them in the least. If ye were ye wouldna hae sworn that oath and ye wouldna be tryin' so hard to push me away. And as for it no bein' possible for me to love the likes of ye, ye are so verra wrong. I told ye before, and I'll tell ye again, I've loved ye since the first, when I was newly brought to this home, saved by the Good Father, and until now I was too afraid to tell ye."

It was still not possible, and he wished he could wake up. Jeanie's words struck him to the core, yet he continued to deny them. "But I'm not human," he weakly stated, mournfully shaking his head.

The sadness in his large ruby eyes extinguished her anger and she took a step towards him. "Ye are, in here." She laid her hand on his chest. "That's all that matters to me."

Cautiously, Jeanie entwined her arms around him, pressing her cheek against his chest, listening to his heartbeat and sighed when she felt his arms encircle her, returning the embrace.

Time seemed to stretch into eternity and she knew what she wanted next but was afraid to ask.

Tilting her face up to his, she haltingly ventured, "Will ye make love to me?"

She was so beautiful, more wondrous than Tarian's granddaughter. There was a strength in Jeanie he never imagined. He could see the love in her eyes and he woefully realized that he was rejecting it out of fear. He had faced so many unknowns before but this one terrified and thrilled him. Bending down, he succumbed to his own needs and tasted of her lips again, desperately wanting to take her and felt her desire blossom as she opened for him.

Realization of what he was doing slammed into him and he pulled away, shaking his head.

"I cannot," he stated sadly.

He could not attempt the risk, but mainly because of a somewhat embarrassing truth.

"Is it because ye are a vampire?" ventured Jeanie. The kiss of his soft lips against hers made her whole body tingle and she desired more. Hearing his refusal confused her. She thought she felt the same need in him as they had shared the embrace.

"Chosen," he automatically corrected.

"What?" Jeanie's face lit with confusion.

"Chosen. That is what we have always called ourselves."

"Oh," she said, sadly. "Ye canna because ye are Chosen?"

"No," he replied, suddenly becoming uncomfortable at where this was leading. "Do not take it the wrong way. I do want to. I have for so long. Ever since Notus made a place for you in our home."

"Then why?" She stared in genuine curiosity, warmed by his admission of his desire for her.

Releasing her, he sat back down on the bed. "The risk and– " He gazed sheepishly up at her. "It's been centuries since the last time."

Jeanie blinked. The risk, whatever that was, was something she was willing to take, but this admission astonished her. "You mean in all that time you haven't?"

He nodded feeling the sudden flush of heat into his face and was glad that the single candle would mask his embarrassment.

"But you have—"

"Yes."

A small smile of understanding lifted her lips and she stepped close enough to lean against his knees. She placed a hand on his face and watched him close his eyes and sigh. "My first time was the night the Good Father brought me here, when he rescued me while I was being raped." His eyes popped open in surprise. It was clear that he had not known. "So I guess we can both help each other." She leaned over and kissed his full soft cool lips.

When she finally came up for air, he let his hands remain on her arms.

"Chosen are unlike mortals," he stated, suddenly worried. "I could easily kill–"

His words were stifled when her fingers pressed to his lips. "Shhh. Ye swore an oath to keep me from harm. I trust ye with all my soul that ye will keep true to yer word."

Jeanie did not allow him another word of protest by replacing her fingers with her lips, and this time he permitted himself to enjoy the kiss as she straddled across his legs. The sensual taste of her drove him on and he hungrily worked passionately down her throat. Luscious cinnamon hair tickled his face as he felt her pulse begin to throb with more urgency beneath his lips. Oh how he wanted to pierce her soft pale skin to taste of the sweet nectar, instead he pulled himself away from her inviting neck with a groan.

It had been so incredibly long since his passions were returned without expectation of being used. It was made more intoxicating by the fact that she knew what he was and accepted it and him. He did not have to hide from her. For the first time he did not have to conceal the truth of his needs or his desires. In his wildest dreams he never imagined this to be possible and he kissed her urgently, feeling her mouth open to his, allowing them to explore and taste each other.

Cupping his face, it was now Jeanie's turn to slowly work down his throat, sucking and licking. Head back, he closed his eyes and let out a hiss of delight as she nibbled on his neck. Unable to bear the teasing of her dull mortal teeth, he gripped her shoulders and pushed her away before he lost what little control he maintained.

"What's wrong?" she implored, witnessing her lovers struggle.

"Don't...don't do that," he finally managed to gasp.

"Why?" Her face contorted in worry.

"Just trust me on that." Her concern did not disappear, forcing him to explain. "I have never...with my own kind...but I do know that the exchange of blood is the height of the experience. If you had continued teasing me like that I would not have teased you."

Realization widened her eyes. She would have to be more cautious if she was to come out alive, but he swore an oath and he was well worth the risk. A playful glint alighted her sparkling green eyes.

"Tease, eh?" she smiled. "So teasin's out. I think I can handle that."

She found his mouth again savouring his taste, feeling his hands expertly working the fastenings of her dress.

She tasted so good and he wanted more, urged on by the sudden rapidity of Jeanie's breathing and beating heart. She wanted him as desperately as he wanted her, and he relinquished the last vestiges of control. It had been so long since he felt such visceral desire, but coupled with the love she had declared and his own unspoken feelings, he allowed himself to give in. The wall that had stood for centuries crumbled as if made of dust, releasing him to finally believe he could be truly loved for who and what he was, something he was told could never happen.

As soon as the last fastening released, Jeanie pulled back with a gasp for breath, smiled and pulled the dress over her head without any care for the delicate fabric, and tossed it to the side, landing puddled on the floor. Standing in her shift, Jeanie looked magnificent, and his need for her jumped as he watched her remove her shoes and stockings.

Craving to drink in more of her succulent form, he let his hands roam down her warm back, dipping them under her shift, lifting to expose what he had only ever seen in silhouette. Jeanie assisted by raising the shift over her head, letting it fall next to the dress. He sat there, basking in the sight of her nude form.

Tentatively, he ran his hand down her bruised shoulder to cup a large luxuriant breast. Running his thumb across her rose coloured nipple, he felt it harden in response. Encouraged by Jeanie's catch of breath, he took her nipple in his mouth, licking and sucking at her erect nipple, feeling her heart beat faster beneath his lips until she gasped.

Releasing her breast, he trailed kisses up her neck, past the intoxicating vessel, to feast from her mouth again. He felt her hands fumbling with the buttons of his shirt and could sense her urgency matching his. Without a care to the expensively tailored clothing, he ripped it open. With her help, they push-pulled the fabric off his shoulders without releasing their kiss. It was only when he tried to get his hands free that he reluctantly broke off to quickly unclasp the cufflinks. Once free, his shirt landing next to her clothing on the floor, he grabbed her, pulling her close and kissed her again, impaling her mouth on his, driven by the touch of her skin to his.

She managed to whip off his belt. She wanted to see him, all of him. The sight of his pale naked chest drove her on in her night of discoveries, but was met with resistance when it came to taking off his trousers. Standing back, she watched as he hurriedly kicked them off and sent his socks flying.

Naked in the illumination of a single candle flame, they imbibed in each other. Her dilated eyes flashed with a mixture of trepidation and desire at the sight of his arousal.

Taking her hand in his, he led Jeanie to straddle him as he sat on the edge of the bed. He wanted her to feel secure in her ability to do what was right for her, yet he needed to be consumed by her. Gently, oh so carefully, she lowered herself onto his rigid member, her breath coming in fearful shudders until he filled her completely, forcing a gasp from her lips.

The scent of her blood and the feeling of her pulse surrounded him in a soft heat that went through him like a shock wave. His eyes held hers, wide with surprise and excitement, as she slowly began to ride.

It was exquisite and he found her mouth again, moving together, filling her completely until each thrust caused her to moan. Releasing her mouth, Jeanie clutched at him as he bent her backwards to find the second best jewel. Her shocked cry as he held her with one hand and sucked, flicking his tongue on her nipple, encouraged him to plunge faster, and was rewarded by her increasing gasps.

Jeanie could not believe that it could be like this. Her hopes and fantasies of being with the Angel did not compare to the reality of having him impaling her over and over. She wanted him to devour her, as she wanted to take him deeper into herself, knowing that he had gone as far as she could allow him. Each thrust was an exquisite mixture of pain and pleasure until she realized that the pain in her legs started to override her pleasure.

Leaning up, she whispered into his ear, "My legs."

They halted their motion and he glanced down at her kneeling legs. With a nod, he lifted her effortlessly as he stood, never disconnecting them, and turned to lay her down on the bed. Raised on his knees, her legs wrapped around his slim waist, he held her and began once more.

The gasps came unbidden to Jeanie's lips as he drove into her. Her eyes rolled back as she clutched the insubstantial bed covers. His body an alabaster god looming above hers. Long white hair swept over her body, setting her sensitive skin afire.

All around him was the scent of her blood throbbing through her body, driving him on as her cries grew louder until he felt her begin to tighten around him. He did not know how much longer he could hold back his release as he breathed in her erotic scent.

He found her mouth once again, but it was not enough. He followed the curve of her jaw down to the throbbing vessel in her neck. The scent and the pounding heat of her heart tightly enveloped him and he knew he could hold back no longer. With a groan of release he sank his teeth into her neck.

An explosion of blood filled his mouth as Jeanie screamed her convulsing climax. The eruption of the taste, co-mingled with his own desires, rocked him and he rode the waves of his own throbbing release as more of Jeanie's blood filled him. On they rode. Every convulsion brought more blood, fuelling his shuddering release.

Suddenly Jeanie sagged beneath him, exhausted by the throws of her body and he reluctantly pulled his mouth off of her delicious neck. The four puncture marks glared angrily at him and then began to fade. In a short while they would be nothing more than a dull ache.

Gazing into her smiling face, he tenderly kissed her and returned the smile.

"I think this is the first time I've ever seen ye smile," remarked Jeanie, running her fingers along his cheeks. The smile made him appear even more youthful. "Aye, I like it. Ye should do it more often."

A small laugh escaped his lips—another first—and he pulled out to lie down, bringing Jeanie with him.

"I love you, Jeanie Stuart," he exclaimed before he kissed her again.

The flickering luminescence from the single candle turned the underside of the wooden canopy into a landscape mottled with light and shadow. His attention was drawn from the soothing sight by the movement beside him, and he moved his left arm, making room for Jeanie to snuggle closer. Her fingertips lightly traced the strong lean muscles of his chest. Content and truly happy for the first time in a very long time, he sighed. Wrapping her silky arm over his chest, he hugged her.

"Are you alright?" he asked, wondering at the marks on her neck that he could not see from this angle.

"Mmmm hummm," she smiled lazily, lifting her face to see his. "Aye, I'm fine. No. Better." She broke apart from the embrace to smooth out the worry in his face with her hand.

Her fingers felt hot to the touch and he turned his head to kiss them. "No dizziness or nausea?"

Her smile widened, exposing perfect, white mortal teeth. "Aye, ye a doctor too?" Jeanie shook her head, sending tousled curls to fall in her face and on his shoulder. "As I said, I'm better than fine and I'm no about to get up from here t' find out."

"Good, because I wouldn't let you up," he smiled, kissing the crown of her head.

A frisky sparkle set Jeanie's eyes ablaze. "And how are ye?"

The expected question sent him into quiet contemplation. "I'm not sure," he honestly replied. Jeanie propped herself up to stare with concern and confusion. "I am happy. Do not get me wrong. I am happier than I have been in such a very long time, and in a way I feel as if I really do not deserve it because of the danger I am. I could have easily lost control and killed you. I am afraid that maybe the next time I might. Gods! It was so hard to stop." He looked her straight in the eye. "I want you, Jeanie. I have wanted this for such a long time – all my life it seems, and that is so very long. And now that I have finally – finally! – have it, I am suddenly afraid of having it. I also do not deserve this now, of all times, not while Notus is still in so much danger."

Laying her head upon his smooth muscled chest, Jeanie fell silent at the fierce truth. The risks and the horror of the past few nights seemed so much like a dream. Fantastical by the unreality of the situations, Jeanie only now could begin to fully comprehend what she had stubbornly agreed to do, and how the Angel had tried to keep her in that illusion for her own good. Now that she had most of the truth, she needed to know more as she began to work out the pieces, trying to fit them together.

"Ye said earlier that the Good Father is the one who Made ye," she murmured, "and that means he's a va—a Chosen too." She felt him nod as he played with her hair. "Then who were the ones who took him? Why?"

If she could know about him and still be able to love him, she deserved to be told the rest. So Jeanie listened in silence as he told her about the Court and the Mistress who held Notus, as a tortured hostage, until he could find out how the Chosen were being poisoned and put a stop to it.

Jeanie was shocked to hear that if he failed it would mean Notus' death as well, and she knew in her heart that must not be allowed to happen. She listened while he told her of the powder and its horrible effects, and that he and Fernando were following that line of logic in a hope that the powder would lead them to the source.

Surprised to hear him groan, Jeanie shot up. "What's wrong?"

"I should not be here," he confessed, sitting up. "I should be out there with Fernando. We were supposed to go to the docks. Fernando has the powder and the shipping information. If anything happens to him, and subsequently the powder and the information, I'm back to square one!"

He made a move to leave the bed but was halted by Jeanie's hand on his pale shoulder.

"Fernando will be fine. He's a bastard."

Shocked at her language and the hostile tone, he let Jeanie continue.

"Bastards always come out with clean noses, so dinna fash about him. Let him do the dirty work for a change. If he gets into a bit o' trouble it'll be because of his arrogant mouth."

"Why Jeanie, one would think you do not like the man." He smiled in silent agreement. Actually, he liked the idea of letting the Noble do the dirty work, and he allowed Jeanie to guide him back under the covers.

"I dinna." Her smile was gloriously mischievous. "After all there canna be too many ways to kill a Chosen if ye are still around after so many years. I can hardly imagine livin' to fifty!"

"How many ways do you think there are?" he asked in all curiosity.

"I guess the cross isna one since the Good Father wears one. But why the morbid question?"

"I don't know." He hitched a pale shoulder, sending white locks spilling. "Maybe because I have always been involved in death." He ran his index finger down her freckle-splashed nose.

She caught his hand and gazed at the ugly scab on his palm. "I would guess cuts from iron bars?"

He snatched his hand back, and after a quick glance at the wound he balled his right hand into a fist.

"If that's the case why did ye no want me t' go and get ye a proper dressin'?"

"Because nobody except Notus knows," he snapped.

Perplexed, Jeanie asked, "Knows that Chosen can—"

"No!"

Jeanie drew back at the vehemence in his voice.

The precipitance in her face sobered him. "I'm sorry, Jeanie." He shook and lowered his head. Long white hair fell to hide his face.

The fact that Jeanie had found out and even accepted the truth of his nature and quest was one thing, but he never even considered the notion of telling her about the differences between he and other Chosen. Those imperfections that have been incapacitating, even life threatening, of which only Notus had knowledge. Any defect, any sway from the norm, and that Chosen's sentence was death.

Over the long years there had been three that had been found, that he had heard of. One who could not even go out if the moon was full because of the increased amount of natural light, and two others, Chooser and Chosen, who had taken on lupine qualities. All had died in the proscribed way: dismemberment of limbs and then left for the sun to finish them off. It was bad enough that his colouring marked him different. If others found out the true extent of that difference his fate would be the same as those other three.

Jeanie moved closer, perplexed as to why he had suddenly shut down. Brushing the soft milky hair from his face, she lifted his chin and stared at the worry creasing his brow.

"Tis alright. I forgive ye," she soothed. "Ye dinna hae t' tell me if ye dinna wish."

The injury in her voice brought him to gaze into her summer eyes. The last time he had see such a vibrant green was that spring day so long ago and a new thought entered to mind. It was a decision he hoped never to make, nor ever to regret. "Jeanie, I have trusted you more in the last few hours than I have anyone else in my life, save Notus." His mouth suddenly dry, he swallowed back the trepidation hammering his heart. "Can I trust you now never to tell anyone, Chosen or mortal, except Notus, what I am about to tell you?"

Jeanie recognized the gravity of the situation and nodded. "Ye told me that I can trust ye with my life and I do. Ye can do the same with me. I give ye my word."

A sigh of relief escaped from him and the corners of his mouth tugged his lips into a shy smile. Taking her hand in his own, he guided her slender fingers to the long silver scar on his right arm. She gazed questioningly up at him. "Feel it," he instructed.

She did so, feeling the softer skin that ran from his shoulder to the inside of his elbow, as he explained.

"Shortly after I was Chosen, Notus took me to a friendly village that was attacked by brigands. It was the first time I had *ever* been around so many people. It was the first time I killed in the manner of the Chosen. I managed to kill the raiders, but not before I took that wound."

He guided her hand to the back of his neck, under the heavy long hair. "Do you feel that?" Jeanie nodded, feeling a thin raised line, running horizontal, in the middle of his neck. "This is from the axe that was held at the back of my neck while the Master of Britain decided if I was of the True Blood. Because of the difference of my appearance, they believed that I should be Destroyed. Luckily my arm had healed sufficiently to appear as if I had received the wound before my Choosing, and the oaf holding the axe never noticed what his blade was doing to me. If he had noticed, it would have marked me different from the rest of the Chosen and that axe would have gone through my neck rather than rested on it. It was Notus' pleading that this was how he found me that — well, the axe did not fall."

Jeanie let her hand be guided one final time to the hideous scar that traversed the length of his left thigh. Her face contorted in confusion and at first she did not want to touch it.

"I received this one," he stated soberly, "when I was sent on a fools errand by Richard Lionheart to kill Saladin several months before the carnage at Acre."

She pulled her hand away in surprise. "Ye knew King Richard?"

He smiled at her awe. "Yes, I did." He grew sombre as he continued. "He sent me, alone, to assassinate his enemy. I managed to get into the camp, but there were too many people guarding his tent, as if expecting the likes of one such as I. I was surrounded and barely fought my way out. It was only possible with Chosen strength, speed and agility. I managed to mount my horse before a lucky Saracen tossed his javelin. If I had not been wearing my armour it would have gone through my leg, killing my horse to leave me at the mercy of those people. I would have died. Instead, somehow I made it back to camp. I do not remember much of the following year. It took me ten years to recover from that wound and it changed me."

"What does that have t' do with your hand?"

"Everything." He bore into her eyes with his own. "Chosen instantly heal except for burns and dismemberment. I heal quickly from burns except for the burns caused by iron pierced into my flesh. And since my last encounter with iron I am unable to cross water without becoming ill."

Jeanie blinked in astonishment. Stories and fables from her past floated to mind. "Are ye now saying that ye are one o' the wee folk?" she chuckled.

Shocked by the question and hurt by Jeanie's frivolity at his confession, he harshly retorted, "The woman who raised me thought so, having found me as a changeling child. So strong in her conviction, she never named me."

The playful smile on Jeanie's face collapsed at this extremely profound admission. "But I hear the Good Father call ye Gwyn. I thought it was yer name."

He shrugged, uncomfortable with where this lead. "It is, I guess," he sighed. "The woman who helped care for me after the first wounding named me so after what all the villagers thought I was."

"And what's that?"

Embarrassment gripped him and he scowled. "They believed me to be the Welsh God Gwyn ap Nudd."

Jeanie's brows shot up. There was still so much more to him that she did not know. The lover's mood had evaporated in the seriousness of the conversation. Wishing for its return, she caressed his face along his cheekbone to his ear. "It doesna matter," she spoke lovingly. "I'll keep yer secret."

A wave of relief washed over him, causing him to slump in the sudden absence of tension. Pulling Jeanie close, he embraced her. Never before had he been so totally accepted and he felt her warm arms encircle him, tenderly stroking his back.

"What about your back?" He heard her say into his neck, her breath titillating.

"After the woman who took me in and raised me was killed and my home destroyed I found a cave to live in. Unfortunately it was already occupied. The hide made a nice bed, but it was nearly I who decorated his abode." He ran his hand through her cinnamon curls.

They sat quietly for a long time, holding and caressing each other, enjoying the silence and the feel of one another's bodies. A deep satisfied fatigue rolled over him, and he found it difficult to keep his eyes open. Head lolling to one side, his cheek came to rest on Jeanie's head. Suddenly, without reason, he jerked himself away. Jeanie beamed up at him, her smile radiant and secretly amused. He questioningly gazed back, curious.

"Did ye ken yer ears come to a slight tip like the wee folk?" She answered his unspoken question and slid away, her smile wide.

Stunned at the unexpected admission, his hands flew to his ears to feel what Jeanie was talking about and was rewarded with the sound of giggling. Gazing up, he noticed her sitting on the edge of the bed bent over in muffled laughter. She glanced back at the perplexity in his eyes and burst out into a new round. Gradually, it donned on him that it was his reaction to her teasing that created her outburst and he realized how ridiculous he had been. A smile pulled at his face.

"Why you…" He made a playful leap to grab her and missed.

With a short exclamation Jeanie shot off the bed, leaving him lying where she had been sitting only a moment ago. She turned and smiled playfully, bidding him to follow as she took a step around the poster.

If this was the game she wanted to play, he was more than willing to oblige. He had never missed a quarry and was not about to do so now. Sliding from the bed, he stood and took a step towards her.

A short half scream half laugh escaped from her and Jeanie ran to the other side of the bed to stop short, the smile gone. Her eyes widened in amazement. She had not seen him even twitch a muscle. Now he stood where she had been running.

"How?" she muttered, dumbstruck.

It was his turn to grin mischievously. "One of the disadvantages of loving a Chosen." He pulled her close and bent to press his lips against hers.

Wrapping her arms around his neck, Jeanie felt her feet leave the ground, as he stood straight, holding her tightly.

"Oh no, not again," she feinted.

He smiled, his crimson eyes alighting with passion. Laying her on the bed, he covered her body with his.

"Yes again," he whispered, huskily. "This time is for you."

His mouth found hers and in his mind he heard her say, *Oh yes!*

XⱰⅰⅰⅰ

The stench of brine mixed with bilge and rotting fish pleased Fernando that he did not need to drink water, especially from the Thames. Then again he also did not have to inhale the fumes. Tucking the perfumed cloth back into his pocket, he exhaled in a huff. The slightly warmed moisture hung in his face for a brief moment before evaporating in the breeze.

The quay was deserted, not at all surprising to the Noble, except for the ships from distant ports anchored at the piers. Fernando figured that those who served were either in town sleeping the night away in friendly beds, or those unlucky enough to be alone, in cold, unforgiving cots. Either was preferable since he really did not want a confrontation. It had been so long since he had Chinese that he did not want to spoil the exotic lingering taste with something so base. It would be like having watered down ale after a sip of vintage wine.

He chuckled at the comparison as he walked along the wooden planks, his dress shoes thunking loudly while looking for the harbourmasters building. He was definitely glad to be alone under the brightness of a clear night sky. Though he would have appreciated it had the Angel acted the full partner he claimed to be instead of letting Fernando do all the work.

Maybe the stunt of leaving the door ajar, allowing that red headed bitch to discover the truth, would be enough to get rid of her and possibly allow the Angel to finally get his perspective back regarding the situation. Then again, if Fernando discovered and stopped whoever was behind the poisoning on his own, he would be considered a hero.

A vision flashed to mind; Sebastian's severed arm overlaid the image of the pile of ash in the cell. Repressing an involuntary shudder, Fernando knew that if someone could easily kill his grandsire, a Chosen renowned for his ruthlessness and sadism, then it might be better to break with tradition and continue to work with another Chosen. There was power in numbers, a concept long lost amongst the solitary night creatures.

The large sign above the entrance to an old weather beaten building looked as dilapidated, if more so, than the structure. Red paint chips threatened to flake away in the slight breeze. Fernando wondered when the last time this place had seen a paintbrush. A crude kerosene lantern hung high above the left side of the door, casting a sickly yellow glow. If this was a regular practice it was astonishing that the building had survived so long as to become run down. Stepping up to the entrance, Fernando found the door locked, but with a gentle squeeze and a turn the door popped open.

Despite the outward appearance, the inside of the building was impeccable. Whoever was in charge definitely knew how to run an ordered office. Even the papers on the counter were neatly stacked in priority. It would be easy to find the information he required.

Closing the door, Fernando pulled out the copy of the purchase order from his inside jacket pocket and sat down at the harbourmasters desk. Flattening the crinkled paper, he read in the darkness,

> *"V. Corneilli & Sons*
> *Shipping & Receiving*
> *Calais, Madrid, London*

Quantity	Item	Cost
10	Oriental Herbs	L1050

> *Deliver to London Free Kitchens Inc., London, England."*

The stamp indicating which customs office spelled out the office he now sat in. The fact that the barrels had to go through customs, even though the shipper and receiver was the same, meant that the order had to have come from either Calais or Madrid. The only way to find out was to find the ship that brought the spices and that meant searching through the files.

Fernando's shoulders drooped at the prospect of the monstrous search through the filing cabinets, only to perk up at the sight that each drawer was labelled. Fernando was instantly grateful to the harbourmaster, and had the man walked in at that moment he would have offered to Choose him. Finding the file was easier than breaking into the building.

Leafing through the papers, he quickly found a copy of the one he had but attached to it was the ship's manifest with the name of the ship, its port of origin, Calais, and the date of the ship's arrival. Fernando quickly pocketed the papers and discovered at the back of the file, a set of similar papers were stamped with yesterday's date. The only difference was the name of the ship.

Fernando closed the file, placed it back in the cabinet, and looked at the blackboard where all the ships were listed at the different piers. Running his eyes down the list, he found the *Papillon.* It was anchored at the other end of the dock. Deciding to follow his hunch, Fernando left the building.

Crates and barrels stacked neatly on the quay made a perfect hiding spot. Of course, Fernando would not have needed it if there were no activity on the pier and on the *Papillon.* Crouched beside a crate, he watched as the same four men walked to the ship carrying barrels similar to those in the soup kitchen. The men worked silently as they strode to and fro along the gang-board, stocking the ship with the barrels from the dock. Soon Fernando would have to give up his hiding spot, lest he be discovered.

He was certain that these barrels contained the deadly herbs but he needed to know where they were from and where they were going. Fernando decided that when the workers returned to the hold of the ship he would check out the invoice attached to one of the barrels. He perked up as he watched the four men return up the gang-board and found it strange that the last one up, one he thought he recognized, a heavy set man, halted way to sniff the breeze a moment before continuing on.

Out of sight, this was Fernando's chance. Moving with preternatural speed, he stood over the spice barrels. The invoices were nearly identical to the ones he had safely in his inner breast pocket. The only difference was that this ship came from Calais, France and was now onto LaCoruna, Spain and other distant ports.

This was better than he had hoped. Now he had the next piece of the puzzle. Maybe if he was feeling magnanimous he would allow the Angel to come along if only to show him how this investigation is to be done right. A smile crossed his lips and then a crushing pain. Stars littered the blackness behind his eyelids.

Fernando fell unconscious onto the dock.

The heavyset man stood over the supine form of the Noble, bloodied crow-bar still poised to give another skull crushing blow. Reluctantly, he lowered the makeshift weapon as his companions approached to stand impassively around the body.

"I see you got him," commented the man across from the heavy set one.

"You did nail him good," added another, smaller than the two.

"How long will he be out?" asked the fourth.

"I don't know," replied the heavyset man. "I crushed his skull."

The others nodded thoughtfully.

The fourth man bent down to gaze on the near shattered face. "Isn't he one of the two sent out after us?"

"I believe he is," replied the second man. "She will be pleased to hear of this, but what should we do with him."

They all looked at the fifth, the one Fernando had not seen, the one who gave the orders. "Let's make her happier, shall we? Dawn's only a few hours away; throw him into the Thames and let the sun finish what Mr. Haskell started."

The other men nodded at the order and lifted Fernando by each appendage. On the count of three they heaved the limp body into the water.

A splash was their only reward.

The fifth man watched the body slowly float away. A sinister smile crept onto his thin lips. "That's one down, one to go."

Turning back to the men, Corbie Vale snapped, "Back to work! Those spices won't ship themselves!"

"Yes, Mr. Vale," they chorused.

XIX

The lone candle on the night stand guttered out, propelling the two lovers into utter darkness, which was perfectly well since Jeanie had long since fallen asleep, head pillowed on the crook of his shoulder. The absence of light did not hamper his ability to admire her beauty, though the light from the candle had lit her fiery hair aflame. Now he could be content with what the darkness supplied. Her pale skin glowed with a vitality that betrayed her youth and spoke well of her recuperative powers. He did not need to see the ugly bruising around the fading puncture marks on her neck. They would be mostly healed by tomorrow night. He would have to be careful lest he turn her neck into a well used pin cushion.

He had not meant to drink from her a second time, only to please her. He came so incredibly close to losing what little control he maintained and he silently thanked Notus for every bit of training he received. Never before had he felt such intense pleasure in the act. It did explain Bridget's chosen profession and why so many of the Chosen seduced their prey. It made the feeding so much more intoxicating, more satisfying. Feeding off fear had its own pleasurable taste, one that he appreciated and hungered for, but the taste of pleasure shared was candy, having its own dangerously addictive qualities. He could still taste Jeanie's excited blood and though his hunger for blood was well satiated there was still part of him that wanted to devour her, to make her completely his.

Brushing a long, thick lock of copper hair out of Jeanie's sleeping face, he held her close. He could not recall how long he desired this with Jeanie. Fantasy made it seem from the first time he had seen her in this very bed those short years ago. In actuality he had slowly grown accustomed to her presence until he could not wait to see her and before the awkwardness between them would drive him into the night.

He had loved her even then, and now he felt as if his chest would burst from undeserved joy. Jeanie not only loved him but also completely accepted him as no other ever had. This was beyond all hope, and yet it was real. Jeanie was really here, sleeping beside him with his marks on her neck and her blood coursing through his body. He wanted this night to last forever and dared not pinch himself to see if this were some lovesick dream. That would be too much to bear. No, this was definitely real and when tomorrow night came it would bring new wonders to behold.

Jeanie let out a soft contented sigh and snuggled closer, half her body laid over his, her hot breath tickling his chest. Fully embracing her, his hands touched her silky skin. It was easy not to notice the cool temperatures in the room, but for Jeanie's sake he tried to find the quilt shoved to the foot of the bed.

Unable to reach it without disturbing her he managed to disengage his right leg from the sheet and with his foot he felt the bunched up cover. Frowning at the awkwardness of the situation and realizing there was only one recourse to provide Jeanie with the warmth she needed without disturbing her, he grabbed the coverlet with his toes and pulled it steadily upwards, careful not to release it, until he could grab it with his hand. She stirred slightly as he covered her with the quilt.

This is what he wanted to do. He wanted to take care of her forever. For her to always be with him. He wondered if all people in love felt this way, and especially if Jeanie felt the same. But what was forever to her? She already said she could not imagine living to fifty. That was a sobering thought. Forever meant two very different things. One was her mortal lifetime, the other, his immortal life. If she hoped for marriage and children she would be torn to hear that he could not give her such a life.

Marriage between Chosen and mortal, though not unheard of, was extremely rare and equally dangerous. And what of Notus? What would he think about this when he learns of it? That was easy. Notus would be ill pleased, possibly angry to hear of the whole situation. Notus never condoned his affair with Tarian's granddaughter. The monk must have thought at some point in their long relationship something like this would happen and together they would work it out, but not tonight, maybe never.

He groaned and felt his chest tighten and his eyes burn. The thought of losing the two last dearest people in his world pained him more than any previous loss. Auntie and Geraint's deaths were not his fault, a realization that took many centuries to accept. Yong Zheng Ru's death, still fresh and surprisingly on an equal level, filled him with guilt.

He had killed so many countless others because they needed the Angel to take away their pain and rarely had he batted an eye, steeling away his emotions, distancing himself. A hunter killing prey that needed killing, culling the weak from the strong. It hurt him to take the children as their parents knew of no other way, but it was his life, and these people held very little meaning in it. He was their merciful Angel of Death and he tried to take comfort in their solace as he took their lives into his own and knew it for an illusion.

Blinking back tears, the standard rationalizations of what he had done to that wonderful old man, and suddenly to those numerous others, did not stop the pain and remorse he felt at the old man's loss. It was easier to explain away the guilt of killing ruffians and cut throats if they approached first or were hurting others. He even made peace with himself as he took their lives, a predator preying upon predator as if it somehow made things more equal. But there was no rationalization over what had become of Notus and what might become of them all if he lost this game.

Notus had never done anything to another Chosen to remotely deserve such adverse attention. The Mistress could have selected another than he or even asked! There was no need to hostage for his help. And if he lost Notus…it was a thought he could not bear to consider. Notus was his life. Without him he would be totally alone in the world. He had done that before and he knew that he could not bear such an existence again.

And what of Jeanie? He dared not contemplate it.

Tears rolled off his cheeks onto the pillow. He had not such an overwhelming sense of melancholy since Notus decided they would be returning to London. Maybe it was the city. He had experienced more death and destruction here than in any part of the world, it seemed. Whenever they returned something bad always happened.

The last time was the Great Fire and then the plague, before that was the Crusade and before that was his own induction into the Family. Granted, the time he first met Fernando was not all that bad, except if he counted meeting Fernando as bad. If they all managed to survive, he would take Jeanie and Notus away, never to return to this accursed place. Right now it was a monumental if.

The Gods definitely had a funny way of controlling people's lives.

Wiping the wetness away with the back of his hand he realized the pattern of Jeanie's breathing had changed.

"I'm sorry. I didn't mean to wake you." He tried to hide the pathos from his voice, attempting to regain control of his wild emotions.

Chin propped on her hands, Jeanie saw without seeing the anguish in his face. "'Tis fine. But what of you? What's the matter?" Worry filled her words. "Ye were so happy earlier."

He held her close in the dark, and gradually, after a considerable time, he won his internal fight. "What is to become of us?" he whispered into the darkness.

"I'm no sure what ye mean." She hunkered down under the covers, laying her head on his shoulder. If only she could light a candle to see what was truly going on. She had understood the question because it was the last thing on her mind before she had fallen asleep.

"I don't think I can bear the thought of loosing you. Not after this." The touch of her face against his hands and her lips against his own were wonderfully reassuring. "I have waited so incredibly long."

"I'm no goin' anywhere," she whispered in his ear. "This is where I wanna be."

"But–"

"Hush." Jeanie kissed him again.

After a long moment, she drew back, taking in a gulp of air. The answer, though sweet, did not satisfy the sense of security he so desperately needed to remove the fear entrapping his soul.

"Jeanie…oh Gods, I don't know how to say this."

"Just say it." She gazed at him, green eyes full of concern and care.

Her soothing words encouraged him to continue in a way that bespoke of the trust he could now place in her. Hesitantly at first, grateful for the cloaking darkness of the room, he whispered, "I…I'm afraid, Jeanie. For the first time in a very long time, I am filled with fear." Exhaling his apprehension in a puff, he silently waited for her to interject.

Instead Jeanie was strangely quiet, staring at him in blind seriousness and worry. He could almost hear her thoughts asking, *What are you so afraid of?*

"I don't know," he replied. "No, that's not true. I'm…I'm afraid…" he closed his eyes willing down the rising panic. "I'm afraid of losing you. I thought that I could handle having you along in this quest, but now…I can't bear the thought of you coming to harm *because* of me."

"What are ye sayin'?" Her voice was oddly calm.

He opened his eyes, almost unable to meet her gaze. "I know that I gave you my word that you could help, but that was before." His words tumbled out unevenly. "I know I also swore an oath to keep you from harm. But I can't have you in this when one step too slow could cost you your life. I'm neither strong enough nor powerful enough to fight off both our enemies and other Chosen who may have their own ideas about a mortal with a Chosen, especially one such as I. If that happened I…I would die."

"Nothin' is goin' t' happen t' me while I'm with ye." She embraced him, feeling his fear returned in her own heart. "Don't ye think I have the same feelin's? I do. I'm terrified. That cell sobered me well, as well as knowin' the truth of what ye are and what yer fightin' for. It explains so much of the danger I was in and the words I heard, especially comin' from Fernando. I ken he'd rather see me dead. I ken now what he meant the first time I met him." She felt him involuntarily cringe. "But I'm no goin' t' let it stop me from bein' with ye. If I must, I can take care of us both. I love ye. I'm no goin' anywhere. D'ye believe me?"

"Yes. Yes I do." The words exploded in a rush. He felt a little better, more positive and more than a little ashamed. He had not expected such strength in her. They would have the time together to figure out what the future truly held for them. Right now he was content to know that she would be with him. After all, if he broke his word it would mean that he was dead, and he was damned to let that happen.

"I love you, Jeanie Stuart." He smiled and kissed her gently, tasting the sweetness of her lips. Oh how he could drink from those lips, her kiss as potent to his soul as her blood to his body.

Jeanie smiled; relieved to hear the sadness lifted and returned the embrace. "I love ye, too."

Snuggling closer, wrapping her leg over his, a frown tugged at her delicately featured face. "What am I t'call ye? Ye dinna seem to like it when I call ye by the name the Good Father uses, and calling ye the Angel seems so...." She let the thought hang in the darkness.

The question surprised him, and he halted his tracing of lazy circles on her back. He had not thought about it. Notus used that name sparingly, usually to get his attention more than anything else. It had been a title, a description, in the past when people believed him to be the Welsh God of the Hunt. Everywhere they went in the world he was more titled than named. Even Yong Zheng had called him Xiao Gui, which was more of an affectionate descriptive than a name. To hear the name being used by Jeanie had struck him hard because she had never used it before and because he was now no longer the Angel to her, but something more.

"Do you remember when I told you that the woman who helped heal me after my first wounding gave me that name and that it was because they thought I was Gwyn ap Nudd?" he ventured cautiously.

He felt Jeanie's head nod against his chest, intrigued.

"That's not precisely true. Auntie didn't name me because she believed me Fay and that one day I'd discover my true name. It was the villagers who foolishly believed their God had returned when, on occasion, one of them would see me hunting the woods at night. Having no other name and being presumed to be this Fairy Lord, the name unfortunately stuck."

Jeanie lay quietly for a moment, his words sinking in until she asked, "If ye could choose a name for yerself, what would it be?"

The question was completely unexpected and caught him off guard. Even Notus had never been so presumptuous. Without thought the answer came unbidden to his lips, "Gwyn," and stared at the darkened canopy in stunned silence. It was the first time he thought of himself by this name. It had always been there, but never before had he claimed ownership of it.

"Gwyn," he heard her test the name on her lips. "What does it mean?"

"White," he said, flatly.

He had expected a response, but the reaction he received made him scowl. Jeanie's titillating laughter filled the dark room. Once she was calm again, he realized that tears of mirth dampened his chest.

"Oh that's just perfect," cried Jeanie as she lifted her head to face him.

"You think it's funny?"

Hearing the hurt in his voice, Jeanie shook her head, sending dishevelled hair flying. "No, but it make's so much sense." Before he could utter a word of protest Jeanie found his mouth with hers. Pulling back, she whispered, "I love ye, Gwyn."

He smiled, accepting the truth to her words.

They lay together drinking in the feel of each other as they languidly explored one another. Not for the sexual pleasure they had consumed earlier, but for the pure delight in being in each other's presence. Jeanie had long since dozed off, purring to his gentle tracing of circles and other patterns on her back as she sprawled beside him.

Suddenly a loud banging at the front door broke the fragile silence and tore apart the precious moment. Anger at the intrusion welled within only to be quickly placed under tight control.

Jeanie rolled onto her side, her voice sleepy. "Who could that be?"

He shook his head and closed his eyes. A few deep breaths extended his perceptions beyond the sturdy walls to discover the subtle shift in the air – the slow warming of predawn. Whoever was at the door had better have a damned good reason to be disturbing them at this dangerous hour.

"Stay here," he ordered, slipping back into his cool calm exterior as easily as he pulled on his trousers and shirt.

Closing the bedroom door behind before Jeanie could think of protesting, he walked to the front door, the hardwood floor cold against his bare feet. Something did not smell right. Literally. Again the knocking, this time more enthusiastic than before and a turn of the knob revealed a sight he never expected to see. Only his eyes expressed the shock he felt, his features otherwise back under tight reign.

"Are you going to let me in or are you going to wait to see the sun bake me dry?"

He could only blink in astonishment. Standing on his doorstep stood the Noble appearing not so noble. In fact he was downright atrocious. Looking past the fact that Fernando was drenched through and through with disgusting smelling water, he was also covered in filth and a massive bloodstain covered his neck, shoulders and a bit of his chest. By the sunken grey flesh on Fernando's face, he quickly gathered it was the Noble's blood.

For a moment he considered closing the door on the man, leaving him to the brightening sky, but stepped back, allowing Fernando to enter just before dawn break. Quickly, he shut the door, closing out the deadly rays. It looked like it was going to be another glorious day.

Fernando leaned heavily against the closed door with a groan. Filthy water dripped onto the floor, filling the silence. The very act of putting his hand to his face bespoke of great pain.

"Oh to be mortal so I could have a shot of laudanum. Several shots." He squinted up at the Angel. "Then I'd be dead."

"What happened?" Curiosity won out. Something serious must have happened to make Fernando come here knowing he would have to spend the day.

Fernando dismissed the question with a wag of his limp hand. "I'll tell you once the room stops spinning."

"Do you want to sit?" he offered. He had not forgotten what Fernando had done earlier, but centuries of helping Notus help those in need brought about a customary, if non-caring, response.

"No, ye don't. Ye stay right there!" Jeanie stood in the bedroom doorway dressed only in her shift, her arms crossed against her chest, face livid. At the sound of the dripping she glared at the puddle forming around the Noble's feet. There was no way in God's green earth that *Fernando* was going to ruin the floors she tried so hard to keep polished.

The Noble's lips quirked into a painful smirk, "I see that my practical joke backfired on me." He glanced up at his reluctant host. "And you reaped the benefits. Twice in one night, eh? She's stronger than she looks."

Noticing where his gaze landed, Jeanie slapped a hand against the remains of the marks on her neck. Eyes wide with embarrassment, her other hand tried in vain to cover herself before going back into the bedroom, slamming the door shut in her wake.

Fernando winced at the sudden noise, his face twisted with a grimace of pain as cold fury rained down on him from fiery eyes.

"I could demand you leave," stated the Angel icily, and immediately thought about doing it.

"You could," Fernando's insufferable grin was back, in defiance to the tense situation, "but you would never find out what I have."

The bedroom door opened and out stomped Jeanie in the borrowed, wrinkled green dress, fumbling with the top back clasps. She crossed the room in a huff and barged into Notus' room, slamming the door behind. It was clear that Jeanie had taken the remark hard and that this was part of her revenge. If so, it was working beautifully as Fernando groaned at the sound.

"And what is that?" asked the Angel, returning his attention to the Noble. He was not going to let Fernando see how interested he was.

Notus' door opened and Jeanie came out holding a bundle of brown woollen cloth that she promptly tossed to Fernando. "Here, see if ye laugh at this."

Fernando unravelled the material. "A cassock?" Was there amusement in the Angel's eyes? Fernando could not tell. "And you expect me to wear this?"

"Aye, I do." Jeanie was not as skilled as the Angel in hiding her emotions. It was clear that her rage was barely held in check. "That is if ye want t' get past the front door."

Flabbergasted, Fernando demanded, "Are you going to take this from her? A mortal? She sounds as if she runs this place."

"As Notus' housekeeper she does," he stated, coolly. He ignored Jeanie's triumphant grin lest it become infectious. "I suggest you do as she bids or you can leave. I am quite sure the sun would do quick work cleaning you up."

Fernando's lips thinned into a scowl. He was caught between a rock and a hard place, and was beginning to regret coming here at all.

"When you are done changing," continued the Angel, "you can have a bath–"

"—cold water," interjected Jeanie. "I'm no starting a fire or wasting precious wood for the likes of him."

"—then we can discuss what happened and what you found out." Turning around, he grabbed Jeanie by the arm and led her back into his room. Fernando's prolific and colourful cursing mingled with the sounds of him disrobing.

Behind the safety of his closed door, he put a hand across Jeanie's mouth, stifling her laughter.

"Well done," he whispered with a grin.

She smiled back, obviously pleased with herself.

"You could have at least let him change in the bathroom. But after what he did last night I don't blame you for wanting this."

"If it hadn't been for Fernando we wouldna be here together like this. I just thought he needed t' know what 'tis like t' be manipulated instead of being the manipulator."

"If that is the case," he stated in all seriousness, "then you are a far better teacher than I, but be careful, he is Chosen, and like most, are stuck in their pride. He looks upon you not as a person but as prey."

Smile gone, Jeanie nodded. She would have to be more cautious in dealing with Fernando.

The sound of profanity ceased and they went back into the other room. Jeanie let out a bark of laughter before catching herself. The Angel raised a pale brow.

"Ye have lovely ankles," grinned Jeanie.

The Noble scowled. The monks robe was obviously meant for a shorter man. "Where's the bathroom?"

"Right over there." The Angel pointed in the direction and watched Fernando unsteadily make his way.

"I'll be a moment getting' yer soap and towels." Jeanie turned to the Angel. "What d'ye want t'do about that?" She indicated the pile of filthy water logged clothing. "Burn it?"

"No!" came a shout from behind them. Fernando all but ran to the pile, lifted it up and revealed two identical sheathed blades. "Oh, I see. This is some big joke. Well, ha ha, you got me. Now if you wouldn't mind I'd like that bath right now." Taking the soaking bundle, he disappeared into the bathroom.

A half an hour later Fernando emerged from the bathtub, his hair finally clean and curling about his shoulders. Pulling on the cassock, he began the tedious job of washing his clothes. A messy job, usually left to lesser beings, but he had to do it if he wanted to wear something other than the smock. He seriously doubted that he could get that bitch to do the job.

Though the depletion of precious blood and the healing of his battered skull had taken its toll on the Noble, he decidedly felt much better and was looking forward to nightfall when he would be able to replenish his loss. He did not imagine that the Angel would appreciate it if he had a bit of a snack off the girl.

Definitely not. The thought of being tossed out into the day was a great deterrent. He would have to behave.

It had been a surprise to find the girl with the Angel, and more surprising at what had obviously transpired between the two. *That whore has guts. I'll give her that.* Not too many mortals could reconcile the fact that vampires were real, let alone actually know one. Maybe he underestimated the girl, or was it that he underestimated the Angel? There was something irritating about his partner, something not quite right.

He thought back to Bridget's reactions to the Angel's presence. For someone so reticent and cool, there was obviously something deeper going on within the Angel that he was not privy to, but somehow seemed to be unconsciously picked up by the women they encountered.

What had that crone said when she saw the Angel when her livelihood blazed? She said that he was beautiful. Fernando shook his head. That would not be the word he would use. Elegant, yes. Graceful, in a predatory way. Men were not beautiful. That term was reserved for women, and the Angel, he decided, was not handsome. Long white hair, disturbing red eyes, facial features so androgynous that on any other person, male or female would be deemed pretty, angelic – or demonic.

Damn! Fernando threw a rung dry sock back into the tub and glanced at the door. A chill ran up his spine. *What in hell are you?*

"Why don't ye go t'bed?" Jeanie sat beside him on the couch, watching as he tried to fight the weariness in his soul.

He felt the full weight of his fatigue as he swept his hair from his eyes as he sat. The candles on the mantle flared and flickered. "I cannot. Not

Karen Dales

now. I need to know what Fernando found out."

Jeanie sighed. "Can't ye wait 'till night?" She snuggled up against him. "Then ye'll be able t' think clearly."

"I'm fine." *Gods, she felt wonderful.* He recognised the doubt and worry in Jeanie's eyes. "Jeanie, I am all right. I do not make staying in bed most of the night a habit."

"True, but ye never had a reason before and ye dinna get much sleep if I recall." She grinned mischievously.

"How could I with all that ruckus going on?" he stated in all seriousness.

For a moment, Jeanie could only glare at him in astonishment then noticed the glint in his eyes and the slight grin, and let him have it. Grabbing a cushion, she whacked him hard on the chest. "Why ye—"

Grabbing the pillow before another blow fell, he tossed it across the room, ignoring Jeanie's cry of protest, and kissed her full on the mouth. So soft, so warm, he did not want to stop.

"If I ha' known how ye Scots lasses were, I wouldna hae waited so long t' find one," he purred, desire deepening his voice.

Jeanie froze and blinked a few times, absorbing not the words, but how he said them. It was a perfect mimic. "How?"

"Scotland is quite nice to winter in. Nice long nights," he grinned. "Needless to say I am now fully awake, thank you."

"My pleasure," beamed Jeanie.

"Mine, too." He pulled her back to his side. After a long moment he whispered, "I have never been as open as I have been with you."

"Not even with the Good Father?" inquired Jeanie, incredulously.

He shook his head, sending long pale hair into her face that she scooped and tucked behind his ear. "There have always been certain…topics that did not seem appropriate. He does not deal well with *things* he cannot fully understand. I am not sure I blame him. I do not deal well with it either." He gazed down on her, green eyes reflecting his own pain, and turned away. "I'm sorry."

"For what?"

"I did not mean to scare you." He closed his eyes, shielding his embarrassment. "I have never lost control like that before."

"'Tis alright," she whispered. "It made me love ye even more."

He opened his eyes and gazed upon her candlelit face. So perfect. So terrifying. So his.

Heavy water logged sleeves clung annoyingly to Fernando's forearms. He should not have attempted washing his garments while wearing the cassock as it was extremely unlikely that the Angel would lend him another of the priest's habits. He would just have to endure the discomfort.

How long does wool take to dry?

Pleased at the disaster he had made of the bathroom, Fernando left, leaving his clothes hanging and draped over any and every possible fixture to drip discordantly upon the tiled floor. It was a small measure of revenge, especially against Jeanie, who would probably have to deal with the mess.

That's for the cold water.

After all, she was the housekeeper.

Vacating the small bathroom, Fernando came upon an unexpected sight: the girl snuggled against the Angel on the couch with candles lit on the mantle and other flat surfaces. It was not so much the fact that they were together, but rather the compassion mirrored in an alabaster face, making the Angel appear almost...human. It was only in the context of the girl did the Angel let others catch a glimpse beneath his finely crafted mask. *Don't forget, with the priest as well.* Otherwise the Angel was impossible to read.

Damn. That knock on the head sure did something.

Clearing his throat, the Noble approached the two, reflecting on how quickly the Angel assumed his façade.

"Sorry to interrupt such a heart warming scene, but since my heart is not warm, I suggest we get down to business. I for one would like to get a good day's sleep." He pulled a chair out from under the writing desk, noticing the journals were still there, and sat down. How tempting it was to be so close to those secrets and not be able to read them. Returning his attention to the situation at hand, he asked, "By the way, where am I going to sleep?"

The girl looked up at the Angel, her annoyed expression did not get past the Noble and he looked at his host, trying to hide the sudden unease he felt from the sight of those blood red eyes.

"You have a choice," stated the Angel. "This couch or Notus' cot."

"No chance for a bed warmer?" Fernando was impressed by the venomous glare the girl shot him and smiled sweetly in return. "I didn't think so." He glanced back at the Angel. "I'll take the cot.

"Now that's decided," continued the Noble, "we'd better get started." He paused, waiting for an interjection, but received none. They watched him, waiting for him to volunteer the information and it suddenly irked him that while he was out risking his neck, or rather his head, they had played at being bedfellows. Not a very fair trade at that. But now he was here, the only safe place closest to the waterfront that provided the sanctuary against the sun, and he was going to take the Angel's threat seriously.

Pursing his lips and taking a deep breath, he began. The Angel and the girl sat patiently as he told them about what he discovered at the harbourmasters office and what he witnessed before being cudgelled.

"I think that our next logical move is to go to Calais," concluded Fernando. He did not go into how he, a Chosen, was snuck up upon. It was something he could not fathom. "There, I'm sure, we'll find out who the hell is commissioning the transportation of the spices, and once we do, we'll find the person or persons behind the whole damned bloody mess and stop it."

Did he see the Angel's pale lips tighten? He could not tell. The girl seemed worried. By what exactly, Fernando could not comprehend. Story done, he leaned back, waiting for some verbal response. Damn, his head hurt.

At length the Angel quietly said, "I think you are right. Going to Calais may provide the answers we need. If they do not then we will have to go back to the soup kitchens and start all over."

Fernando smiled. "Well, I'm glad we're in agreement on that."

"I have a question." The girl leaned forward, frowning. "How are we goin' to get there and when will we be leavin'?"

"That's two questions," sneered Fernando, annoyed at having her even contemplate participating in the conversation. "*You* are not coming. And *we*," he indicated to the Angel and himself, "will leave tonight. There is always some fool captain willing to make quick money."

Jeanie glanced up at the Angel, her eyes a mixture of anger and appeal. The look was quickly noted and then the Angel's gaze fell uncomfortably on Fernando.

"Jeanie is coming with us. I hope I do not have to remind you of our agreement over the issue."

The finality of the statement made Fernando's hackles rise. "No. You do not."

The Angel nodded, cold eyes fixed on him.

Unable to withstand the glare, Fernando looked away, fuming at such arrogance, such presumption, and the blatant need to be in control. It was humiliating, and in that instance he realized his hatred for the Angel. Before it was sheer annoyance and maybe a little intrigue at the notion of being partnered with the Angel, the most elusive and unknowable member of the Chosen. But now, after seeing the compassion directed at mortals—*at mortals!* Fernando shook his head. If the Angel had to make a choice between the girl's life and the Noble's, Fernando knew which choice the Angel would make, and that angered him even more. A Chosen's life was worth more than chattel.

Biting back all the comments he would love to make, he managed, "What can she do to help? I presume you told her everything."

The Angel nodded again. "She can move about during the day, doing what we need done in a way that hopefully our enemies will not discover. If you will help us." The last was directed at the girl, his tone softer but still brittle.

Taken aback by the return of the Angel, Jeanie mutely nodded.

"Aye, I'll help in any way ye need me," she replied. "What d'ye want me t'do?"

Standing, an act both graceful and predatory, the Angel walked to the writing desk, forcing the Noble to swivel in his seat. On the shelf with the books sat an intricately carved wooden box inlaid with mother-of-pearl.

Fernando whistled his astonishment at the sight of the contents and could not decide whether to label the Angel a fool or overly trusting.

In the box lay notes of large denominations. From the bundle held in the pale hand, his long slender fingers barely enclosing it, Fernando roughly estimated a worth well over five thousand pounds. He watched the Angel leaf through the collection of notes, pulling out smaller denominations until he had a second pile worth several hundred pounds. The rest he placed back in the box.

"What I need you to do," explained the Angel, turning to face the girl, "is to hire a coach for the day and go to the wharf. Find a captain willing to take us to Calais, no questions asked, two hours after sunset. Make sure that we are the only passengers, and more importantly, that we have separate private cabins."

Fernando did not like the fact that the girl's confused expression matched his own. What did it matter if they did not have a cabin? The trip should only take several hours, arriving at the port before dawn.

"Give the captain a deposit and tell him that he will receive half upon boarding and the rest upon docking. Agree to whatever price he says."

"Are you out of your mind?" interjected Fernando.

"Just do it," continued the Angel, ignoring the interruption.

Jeanie blinked in confusion, trying to take in the directions. "And then what?"

The Angel's expression softened, allowing the luxury of a small smile. "Go buy yourself some new clothes. You cannot wear that all the time. Buy something nice. Make a day of it. Maybe stop at Reverend Iefan's to let Tom and Alice know that you are all right."

He handed her the bundle and Fernando thought the girl's eyes would pop right out of their pretty little sockets. Obviously she had never seen, much less held, such an amount.

Standing up, Jeanie gazed long and hard up the Angel. "I—I canna."

"I thought you agreed to help?" He cocked his head to the side, his hair falling to drape his querulous expression from the Noble.

"I did. I still do. But tis too great a sum." She held out the bills.

Fernando groaned at the ridiculousness of the situation. If he had handed Bridget that much money it would have quickly disappeared into her bodice.

"Just take it. It's not like you'll have this chance again." Exasperation filled the Noble's voice. "Listen darling, if a man gives you money don't argue with him. Just take it."

God he was tired. Where was that cot?

Jeanie glanced back up at the Angel as he curled her hand around the bills, his strong slender fingers holding her hand. He nodded, his features softening momentarily just for her.

Walking the girl to the door, she seemed hesitant to leave, but a few soothing words, and his key ring, instilled her with the determination to do what was necessary so that she could return quickly. Fernando actually thought it was sweet that she wanted to give the Angel the change. He physically slapped his face, hard, causing the two to glance back at him. If he did not get to bed soon he would turn into a sentimental sap. A condition he would rather avoid, even if he had to kill himself. He was glad when she was finally gone.

"Notus' room is over there," indicated the Angel. "I am going to bed. I suggest you do the same." He stepped into his room, closing the door behind.

Left alone, Fernando stood and for the first time he let the fatigue and aches of his body show in his movements. Today he was going to sleep, no matter how much he wanted to read the journals, and was glad that he did not have to traverse any stairs.

Opening the door to the monk's room, he stopped in mid-stride. It was small. Smaller than he expected, and the cot was just that. In fact it almost seemed misplaced amid all the books lining the walls.

Many of the books were untitled, some had gold leaf lettering in different languages, and along one wall was a row of cubbyholes filled with scrolls. Curiosity winning out, he pulled one of the smaller scrolls out. By its feel the vellum was old and he was careful to open it. The writing and illumination was elaborate, the words in a language that looked like English but was impossible to read until he read why. At the bottom of the page, written so small and fine that he had to squint, was a date and an initial, "1087 N."

This work by Notus predated him by centuries! Rolling it up, he placed it back into its cubby hole, wondering what was in all these manuscripts.

Lying down on the cot, he found it a little lumpy, but it did not take Fernando long to find a comfortable position. Staring up at the dark ceiling, he shook his head, amazed at his current situation.

It cannot get any stranger than this, he thought before allowing sweet oblivion to overtake him.

X X

he door locked behind Jeanie with a click and a jingle of keys. Releasing a yawn, she dropped the key ring onto the tea table under the sunrise painting with a clatter of metal hitting wood and considered the boxes littering the floor around her feet. The coachman was serviceable in bringing in her shopping, but his placement of the boxes left much to be desired. Finding the matchbox on the table, Jeanie struck a match and lit the lone candle on the stand. Yellow light spilled into a room deeply shadowed in grey, the only natural light slipping around the door.

Behind the two bedroom doors slept two very different vampires. The thought ran a shudder up Jeanie's spine. It all still seemed so surreal. The idea of vampires existing and that she had made love to one, feeling his sharp teeth extract a pleasure filled pain, made her head spin. Or was that the blood loss. Jeanie put a hand to her head. She had always thought that the Angel was different, but now that she knew how different he truly was, she realized how little she truly knew of the man she loved.

It was a thought that carried her through the morning and into the early afternoon. She was in love with a vampire. No matter what he called himself, the Angel – Gwyn – was a vampire, and it explained so much and evoked more questions. The thought terrified her and thrilled her, and she touched the bruising on her neck. The puncture marks were already completely healed.

Jeanie had not been aware of how noticeable they were until she went over to Reverend Iefan's after stopping at a nearby café for a quick breakfast. She did not think that Gwyn would mind her using the money for that. It was still strange to be using that name for him after all these years of calling him the Angel.

Witnessing Alice and Tom's eyes light up with tears of happiness and surviving their bear hugs, Alice, the ever dotting mother of wayward daughters, had noticed the bruising and commented on what she rightfully believed were love marks. Reverend Iefan took that as a cue to leave the three of them alone. Jeanie blushed furiously, turning her face completely red before having Alice encapsulate her in another, even stronger, hug.

"He loves you," whispered Alice into her ear. "He's always loved you, sweetheart."

Stumbling at the sudden release, Jeanie had nodded. A smile finally lighting her face at the truth confirmed.

Left out of the loop, Tom had stood grinning madly until there was pause enough for him to take centre stage and begin his monologue about how the Angel's generosity was already in the works to rebuild the *Rose and Thorn*. Jeanie had listened to Tom as they sat in Reverend Iefan's parlour, drinking tea and nibbling pasties that Alice had made. Jeanie had to force herself not to eat so fast. Even after a filling breakfast she was still starved. Alice interjected only to bring her husband's enthusiasm down to earth and the reality that they could not spend all of the Angel's money.

Jeanie had left, elated that her surrogate parents were ecstatic that she had survived the fire and that they were rebuilding. The question of how much money the Angel had floated to mind. The fact that he could afford to rebuild the Inn astounded her. Then again she had seen the wad of notes in the box and his almost cavalier attitude about her spending his money had swirled her mind.

The Good Father lived so simply, yet the Angel had such expensive clothing. The dichotomy astounded her. The only blemish to the wonderful reunion had been finding out that her friend Violet had not survived the fire. Jeanie silently assumed their drinking had caused Violet to fall into a drunken stupor, which incapacitated her ability to wake in time to escape the blaze, for that alone Jeanie felt mournfully responsible for her friend's death.

From the rectory, Jeanie had taken the cab to the wharf. Her mind spun between the loss of her friend and the happiness of being loved, while trying to keep focused on what she still needed to do. After many queries, she found Captain Richardson of the *Sea Witch* and after much cajoling convinced him to sail to Calais that night with three passengers.

The fee he quoted had made her blanch and she was about to argue when she remembered to pay any price offered. Again the question of how much money the Angel actually had swam silently in her mind. She did have the wherewithal to ask why so much. The Captain stated gruffly that sailing the Channel at night, late in October was suicide, but for the right amount he would do almost anything. Jeanie could not suppress her shudder of disgust at his innuendo and left, giving the man half her of bundle of money as deposit. She wondered how Captain Richardson would laugh when he saw that it was the Angel he would be ferrying.

ANGEL OF DEATH

Duty done, Jeanie had left the docks to the finer shops of London to follow the Angel's final order. It was time for something fun and for the first time in her life she had more money than she knew what to do with. She knew Violet would have been proud of her.

Now the boxes lay strewn on the floor and Jeanie was exhausted. It was only half past two in the afternoon.

Stacking the boxes next to the table, Jeanie stretched her back; hands reaching to the ceiling before crumbling back down and noticed the single candle was the only one left in the room. If she was going to have any light in the room when they all woke later, it was either going to be gaslight or candle flame. The Angel seemed to prefer candles. With a sigh, Jeanie pulled the box from under the tea table and began the arduous process of cleaning candleholders of old wax and placing in new candles.

Bone weary and eyes watering as another yawn stretched her face, Jeanie stood in the middle of the room holding the lit candle, its wax dripping slowly down into the holder. She surveyed her work, eyeing each cleaned and restocked candlestick along the mantle, the end tables, the candelabra on the Good Father's desk and the tea table. When all the candles were lit, the flat would glow with a warm yellow light that even Jeanie could read by.

Job well done, she decided it was way past time for her to get some deserved sleep. Knowing that this time she would be welcome in his bed made her smile. No one had come out as she walked back and forth between the living room and the kitchen, shoes clicking against wood as she cleaned and set the new candles, but she did not want to risk waking the Angel as she entered the bedroom. He had been so tired earlier.

Jeanie placed the candle down on the tea table and unlaced her shoes. Releasing her sore, hot feet from the confines of the black leather, she sighed as she wiggled her toes in their wool stockings. The cool hardwood felt refreshing on her soles. Padding to the bedroom door, candle in hand, she halted with her hand on the knob. A thrill of nervous expectation filled her with the realization that she was welcome to enter and join her lover in bed. It was with that thought that she opened the door as quietly as she could and slipped into the dark room, closing the door behind with a click that made her jump. Turning around to see if the sound had awoken the Angel, her breath caught at the sight the single luminescence presented.

On the bed, lying face down, his head nestled onto a pillow, the Angel faced towards her. He slept naked except for the tangle of sheets around his long lean legs. His right arm hug limply over the side of the bed, his fingers curling as they brushed the rug under them. Long strands of alabaster hair splayed across his back and over his face to hang over the large bed. Jeanie had never seen him look so beautiful, so human, or so youthful.

The thought snapped her breath back into her body and she realized that even though she knew how old he was as a vampire, he had never told her how old he was when he was – what did he say it was called? – Chosen. His height always made her believe he was older, well into his twenties, but seeing him like this made her doubt her earlier estimations, reaffirming how little she knew about him even after all that he had told her.

Tentatively, she made her way across the room to gaze down on his sleeping form. The light from the candle caused him to squint in his sleep. He uttered a small discomfited sound before turning his face away to bury himself further into the pillow.

Realizing her error, Jeanie placed the candlestick next to the burned down one on the side table and stood back to undo the clasps of the green dress. Difficult as it was, she managed to get enough of them undone to shimmy out of the heavy fabric before taking off her stockings.

Standing only in her shift, shivering in the cool air of the room, Jeanie halted a moment at the sight of the silver lines on his pale back playing hide and seek with hair equally as fair. Curiosity piqued, having only ever seen the hints of the scars, Jeanie remembered what he had said about how he received them before he was Chosen.

Gently, she lowered herself to sit beside on the bed, her hip touching his side. A soft throat sound emanated from him and he turned his head back to face her, eyes closed in sleep. With trembling fingers, Jeanie slowly swept soft thick locks from his face, careful not to wake him, and pushed the heavy hair off his neck and back, exposing the wide parallel scars across each side of his back.

The silver lines stretched across strong lean muscle, making Jeanie wonder what sort of occupant could do this to a person. Hesitantly, she touched his back, tracing around the scarring, the skin soft to the touch. Whatever had done this to him had been huge. Cocking her head to the side, Jeanie could almost believe that wings had been torn off his back, adding to the mysterious air of the Angel.

"It was a bear."

Jeanie squeaked and jumped at the sound of his gravely sleep filled voice. She pulled her hand away. Heart hammering between her ears she saw a single eye open, the other still buried in the pillow.

Gathering himself, he lifted and turned onto his side, brushing his hair from his face as he stared sleepily at her. "It was a bear," he repeated, his voice more awake. "I believe that is what you wanted to know."

Green eyes wide, Jeanie could only stare in astonishment. He was lucky to have survived.

"I—I'm sorry. I dinna mean to wake ye," she said, recovering from her shock and feeling more than a little abashed.

Hiding a yawn with the back of his hand, he waved the apology away. "What time is it?"

"Just after three in the afternoon," she replied, surprised at how normal and human his reactions were. So unlike the fictions she read. But maybe that was because he was half asleep.

A disgusted groan escaped from his full lips and he rolled back onto his stomach, hugging the pillow and closing his eyes.

"Did you find a ship to take us to Calais?" he muttered.

She nodded and then realized he could not see her answer. "Aye. Captain Richardson of the *Sea Witch* will take us. He expects us at half past nine so we can sail with the tide. It's at pier seven."

"Good," he mumbled. "Did you find something nice to wear?" He popped an eye open with a smile.

Jeanie returned the grin. It was so like him to think of her in these small ways. "Aye. I hope ye dinna mind, but I bought some other things the fire took with it."

"What's money for if you can't spend it on the people you care about?" he said softly, the return of sleep filling his voice. "Now come to bed, I missed you."

Eyes blurring with tears at the sentiment, Jeanie reached down to the foot of the bed for the coverlet and pulled it up. Slipping out of her shift, Jeanie blew out the candle and carefully made her way around to the other side of the bed and climbed in. She felt a shift on the mattress as he turned over, his arm encircling her around the chest. Tucking them both under the quilt, Jeanie could tell he was already fast asleep, his mellifluous breath tickling her neck.

XXI

he wooden planks of the pier creaked and groaned under his feet as the black water beneath rode in and out. Steadying himself, he placed a hand on the metal rim of the wooden cask next to him. He did not know where he was or why he was here. All he knew was that the

sense of disconnection made his stomach roil and he tightened his grasp.

Before him, a tri-mast ship rose and dipped with the swells. Its tightly bound sails black against the star filled night. It had been a long time since he had seen stars that bright. No moon illuminated the velvet canopy overhead. It did not hinder his ability to watch, in nauseating awe, the majesty of the ship.

A bell sounded, resonating painfully in his head and he clutched his hands to his ears, instantly missing the solidity of the cask. The pier swelled under him causing him to stumble before catching himself again on the cask, its rim cool and comforting against his burning hand.

The sound dissipated into the night, leaving only the wash of water against wooden posts and shore to sing with the sounds of stressed old wood. He brought his attention back to the ship before him and was surprised to see countless butterflies creating a kaleidoscope of brilliant colours along the masts and deck. They fluttered and floated as blackened shapes silently moved down the gang-board.

He could not distinguish any features of the dark figures floating down towards him. Only a rush of panic and the fear of being caught brought him into a crouch beside the wooden cask. It was then he noticed the yellowed piece of paper attached to the wood. He tried to read the sprawling letters and found all he could see was an autumn field covered with a cloth of gold. It made no sense.

Looking up, all the rainbow butterflies took flight in a swarm as one by one the dark shadows trudged casks up the gang-board and onto the ship. The bell rang louder than before and a skull crushing pain shattered through his being.

He floated.

All the stars winked out of existence. Only pitch darkness encapsulated him, buoying him. Was he in the water? He did not remember.

He felt no cold, no heat and surprisingly no pain. Drifting with unseen currents, nothingness touched him, caressed him, and flicked its unseen tongue over him until he shuddered.

Until he remembered.

Fear sparked within, pounding and throbbing in his ears. The rushing of his blood through his veins was the only sound surging his fear into terror. Clambering to obtain a purchase in the void, he found he could not move. His heart hammered violently.

No! It was not possible.

The sound of a thousand flies buzzed around him, muffling out the silence. "Open your eyesssssssss."

He whimpered. This could not be happening.

"Open your eyessssssss."

The command pulled a response from his body that his mind tried to deny.

It hovered before him. Putrescence dripped from its form. Red glowing eyes stood stark against the whiteness of its being. Its mouth turned upwards in a grotesque mockery of a smile. Razor sharp teeth glinted in non-existent light.

A hand made of bone and dust and flakes of rot brushed against his face. He tried to flinch away, but the hand grasped him hard, pinioning him until all he could view were the angry red eyes. A shudder ran through his body.

"Itsssss been a longggg time." Its voice rustled through the darkness, slithering and licking across his body.

"Wha–what d—do you want?" he stammered, surprised at his own courage.

The smile widened, sending tremors through him. "Sssso brave. Time hasssss made you brave, but you ssssstill fear. Delicioussssss." Its black rotting tongue flicked in and out.

His breath came faster, threatening to cause him to pass out.

"You are mine. Do not forget." Anger mixed with something else, something he never heard before. Could it be fear?

"Never fear. Never that." Its eyes blazed and then dulled. What passed for its fingers dug deeper into his cheek. "You made your ccchoissssse. I will never let them have you."

Them? Confusion sprinkled into the mix of terror and pain. All he wanted to do was run. To fly. To flee.

"I will kill you before they can have you." Its rasping voice rose in rage.

Head impotently held back, he sobbed in the knowledge of what was to come. Searing pain electrified him as the demon's mouth ripped into the soft flesh of his neck.

Bolting up in the bed, heart painfully pounding in his ears, he looked down beside him to see if his cry woke Jeanie. A vague sense of relief flickered over him at her curled form. The coverlet was tucked over her shoulder, her eyes closed in sleep. She had not stirred at his brutal awakening and he turned his head away from the peaceful visage that mocked his torment.

Trembling, he opened his hand and stared at the healing cut. It should not have been enough, but the truth was undeniable.

They were back.

Dear Gods They were back.

Shoulders hunched and head lowered, he clenched his hand in a tight grip as a sob wracked his body.

Jeanie murmured in her sleep at the sound and rolled over onto her back, splashing russet and cinnamon curls onto the pillows. He could not allow her to wake. He could not let her see him this way. She would want to know and even Notus did not know about the white-faced demons that have haunted and pursued him since childhood. None of them could ever know.

Silently, he slipped his shivering form from the bed. He had to get out. Seeing Jeanie sleeping so peaceful made a mockery of the horror gripping him. He wanted to be able to stay with her, to curl up and find comfort at her side, but his neck throbbed in pain and the threat turned his joy to ashes.

Closing the door behind him with a soft click, he hugged himself in a vain attempt to get his trembling under control and walked to the fireplace. He had to get warm. He had to get clean. His mind still reeled that They were back and It had sunk Its putrid mouth onto him. The scent of diseased and decaying flesh clung to him, soiling him from the violation. A new round of tremors racked his body.

It had been so long since the last time he was in their clutches. Most of the months he spent with them he could not recall, but what he did remember sickened him. The idea that it was starting again stole all the heat and breath from his body in a wrenching sob. He knew he would never be able to endure such torture again and hearing that It would kill him sent ice-fire down his spine.

Kneeling before the fireplace, he built a fire as fast as his preternatural abilities would allow and felt a very small measure of relief as the flames roared into life, washing him in golden heat. It was something, but he needed more and he hoped that the hot water tank set on top of the bend in the flue would heat quickly.

He rose from the roaring hearth, his tremors slowly dissipated with the comforting heat and walked to the bathroom door. The sight he was met with slumped his shoulders and he groaned in tired frustration. He did not need this. Not now. Not when all he wanted to do was slip into a steaming bath and let the waters slough off the tensions and relax his mind.

Over taps, sink and bathtub lips, over toilet and towel rods, damp wrinkled clothing hung above small pools of grey water. Fernando's Thames dunked clothing littered the room having long since ceased their discordant dripping. Closing the door with a heavy sigh, he scooped up the near dry apparel and dropped them in a pile on the floor next to the door before turning the hot water tap of the bathtub onto full.

The thunder of water exploded from the faucet filling the small room. Near boiling temperatures sent steam billowing to the ceiling. The moist heat tantalized and teased him until he cautiously stepped into the tub. Scalding temperatures ran through his feet and up into his legs, forcing the chill of the dream into retreat.

He sat down in the rising water, sighing as the warmth invaded his body, driving out the tremors. The steam in the room clung to his exposed cool skin, beading in a mockery of sweat that ran down the sides of his face. He let a shuddering sigh release the physical tension as the waters slowly rose until it was time to halt the water's progress.

Reaching for the scrub brush and the cake of soap sitting on a ledge over the taps, he began to scrub away the repugnant scent he knew could not be there, but one he could still smell. The bristles made his skin tingle in the heat, but it did not seem enough to drive away the sensation of the demon touching him. He needed to get clean and he scrubbed harder.

The smell of soap did not seem to overpower the putridity of the dream-scent. Grabbing the little bucket from the floor, he doused himself with the hot water and began to lather his hair. Over and over he drenched himself, desperately trying to get clean until there was nothing left of the soap.

The bucket dropped to the tiled floor with a clatter and he gazed at his palms under the water. Drops from his face created ripples over his hands. It was not from the steam anymore. Balling up his fists, he scrubbed the tears from his face and let his hands fall back into the   water with a splash. Staring at the wall before him another sob escaped and he closed his eyes in a desperate attempt to regain control.

It was indisputable, They were back and this time the threat of It killing him was more promise. He was completely powerless to stop Them as he was so many centuries ago when they played Their torturous games with him before the monks healed him. He knew he could not go through that again. He was not strong enough. Threatened from within and without he knew his nights were numbered. What infuriated him was that in the midst of it all he had found some measure of happiness and acceptance in Jeanie after so many long centuries of being alone. That They would take him away from her terrified and broke his heart.

If only he knew why. Why did They always torment him? He never made a choice to be under Their power despite Them saying so. He never chose to be Chosen. He never chose to be Their unwilling victim in Their sadistic pursuits. And again the question it always came back to – *why me?*

Releasing a strained sigh, he knew the question would remain unanswered.

He knew what he needed to do to preserve his sanity. Taking another deep breath, he reached back to the training the monks had given him and sat in the cooling tub as he quieted his mind. Slowly in and out, he focused on his breathing. In and out. Letting the breath relax what muscles the hot water could not. In and out, reaching for a sense of peace. In, bringing in peace and relaxation. Out, releasing his fears and anxieties. Slowly, he breathed until there was nothing left but the sound of nothingness.

He did not know how long he sat there in the bath water until the gentle sound of tapping at the door lifted him from the peace of the meditation. Reluctantly, he re-entered into the world of sound and sight. The tapping grew louder, mingled with the slow steady drip from the tap. With a final clearing breath, his eyes fluttered open as the door opened and he sat straight, eyes wide, at the unexpected sight of Fernando in the doorframe.

"I knocked," stated the Noble, contritely. "You didn't answer so I thought it was fine to enter." His brown eyes roamed around the small room, landing on his host.

He dropped his long legs under the water as best as possible and sat with his back against the tub, his hands clenched and he glared at his houseguest. Fernando's sunken face was much better, but the grey countenance and dark circles under the eyes bespoke of his blood loss.

"What do you want?" demanded the Angel.

A groan escaped Fernando as he bent to retrieve his dilapidated suit. "I came for these. You don't expect me to wear this smock all night." The brown monk's robe showed signs of having been slept in, and Fernando's long curling hair desperately desired a comb. Instead he used his free hand and gave his host a measured glare.

Wearily, Fernando sat down on the lidded toilet, clothing in his arms. "I'm leaving." Ignoring the suspicious look on his partner's pale face, Fernando continued. "I have to change and get ready for our voyage, and if I stay here any longer, one of us will end up dead. Your red headed vixen smells too delectable for me to stay here and for us not to come to violence. I need to feed."

He nodded and brought his attention back to the fleeting bubbles on the water. In that moment his opinion softened slightly at Fernando's consideration. "Jeanie found a ship that will take us. Pier seven at half nine, that's where the *Sea Witch* will take us to Calais."

It was Fernando's turn to nod in appreciation for the information and settling his bare feet on the tile as if to stand, Fernando thought differently. Clutching his bundle of clothing, his eyes grew dark. "I've been thinking." Silence fell between them, filled only with the dripping of the faucet. "I didn't hear or even sense who or what hit me. That's not possible. If it were a vampire I would have sensed him and it couldn't have been a mortal, it happened too fast."

Fernando took a deep breath, held it for a moment as if expecting some sort of rebuff, and released it in a huff.

"What do you think it was?" the Angel whispered the question into the tension thick air, afraid of the answer.

"I don't know." Fernando stood in one fluid motion. "Damn."

The door closed with a thud, leaving him alone in the bathroom, the water suddenly turning cold.

Jeanie awoke in absolute darkness causing her to wonder if she was still asleep. Touching her face, she realized there was nothing to see, not even her hand and reached out to find she was alone in the big bed. The sheets in which he had laid were cold to the touch and she wondered when he had awoken and why he had not woken her.

Stretching as a yawn forced itself out, Jeanie shivered in the cold room desperately desiring to stay under the warm protective covers but knowing she could not. Flinging the quilt back, she instantly regretted the action and sat up. It would be difficult finding her shift on the floor where she left it and a shock of cold ran through her as she left the soft rug for the hardwood floor, feeling her way around the bed. If only the Angel had left a candle burning for her.

Shuffling her feet so as not to stub them on anything, she found something soft and cloth like kicked up onto her foot. Reaching down, she lifted the material up. With a quick feel for the placement of the holes Jeanie smiled and draped her shift over her body. Now she had to find the door and was rewarded with a stubbed toe and a bruised knuckle before harsh bright light flooded into the bedroom. Tears blinked from her eyes until they adjusted to the dim lighting of the living room. It was enough for her to see she had put her shift on backwards and with a groan of annoyance, she shuffled it around to wear it properly. It was the sight of the Angel sitting motionless on the sofa with his back to her that arrested her movement.

It appeared that he had not heard her but Jeanie doubted that and frowned that he had not turned at her entrance. It was as if the Angel was back and her Gwyn was no longer. Worry caused Jeanie to bite her lower lip. After all they had been together in the past twenty-four hours, fear percolated. She could not lose him now.

Floorboards creaked as she walked and Jeanie came to stand behind him, still seemingly unnoticed. She could smell the clean scent of soap on him as she bent over the top of the couch, wrapping her arms on his white linen clad shoulders. His damp hair rested on her cheek as he sighed and leaned into her embrace. It was enough to send her fears flying.

"Ye smell nice," she murmured into his ear, enjoying his strong form in her arms. When he did not respond, she asked, "Are ye all right?"

"I'm fine." His whisper faintly carried in the silence.

Jeanie frowned. The Angel was a horrible liar. Even the Good Father had made that comment on occasion and now she could see the truth for herself. Something was wrong and it scared her.

"What's the matter?" she asked.

He sat straight and almost pulled out of her embrace.

"Nothing," he reiterated, trying to keep his voice neutral. "I'm fine."

"Yer a terrible liar, ye ken?" Jeanie released her arms and stood straight. Shoulders slumped in defeat the Angel leaned back against the couch and without looking up at her continued to stare at the fire. "D'ye wish to tell me?" she offered.

He shook his head, long damp white locks swung heavily. "I can't."

"Why no'?" A frown pulled at her face. "After all that ye told me–"

"Jeanie, please." The supplicatory tone halted her in mid-thought. "I've told you a lot. Please. There are some things…" He sighed and she knew she had pushed him too far.

"Is there…did I do somethin'?" Whatever it was that was making him distant again tugged at her insecurities.

As if sensing her plight, he turned to stare up at her; his garnet eyes reflected her pain. "Gods no. You're the only thing that has gone right."

A smile drifted to her lips. It was more than she had expected to hear. The Angel turned back to face the fire, hiding the anguish lest it infect Jeanie. He let out a huff of released breath as she laid her soft warm hands on his shoulders.

"Is there anything I can do?" she gently offered. She hated seeing him like this; so sad and something else she could not put a finger on. Noting the taught muscles under her hands, Jeanie instinctively began to use her fingers to work out the knots in his shoulders and was rewarded with a groan of pleasure.

"Gods, Jeanie, whatever you're doing is perfect." He dropped his head forward, releasing the curtain of hair so she could work unhindered through his shirt on his wet shoulders.

Jeanie smiled, finally seeing some of the worry leave him as she massaged his strong supple muscles, trusting that he would tell her when he was ready. She had to accept that maybe he could not tell her everything after all that he had surprisingly confided in her. In the meantime she enjoyed making him happy and if she read him correctly, he was thoroughly appreciating her efforts by the soft sighs he emitted especially when she worked at a stubborn knot.

"Where on earth did you learn how to do this?" He sighed, luxuriating as she worked her strong fingers along his neck.

"I used to do this for my mam when she got sick." Jeanie rubbed the long muscles in his neck, her smile gone with the memories. "After she passed, I'd do this for my da after he came in from the fields. Usually if I did, he wouldna beat me when he got drunk."

Silence fell between them as tense muscles finally gave way to her ministrations.

"I'm sorry," he quietly offered as Jeanie lifted her hands with a sweeping gesture off his broad shoulders.

Surprised at the unexpected reaction to the massage, Jeanie blurted, "For what?"

"That you lost your mother and that your father beat you." He lifted his head and stretched his neck side to side and then turned again to look up at her. "Someone so special shouldn't have had to go through that."

Her mouth formed a silent O at his sentiment. Jeanie finally realized how much he truly cared for her and she smiled. "I ken my mama would hae liked ye."

Surprise flitted across his face before he turned to face forward, closing her off from his pain. Whatever it was that had him in its grips was fierce and Jeanie knew she had to be stronger. Walking around the couch, she sat down beside him and took his wounded hand in hers. He felt cool to the touch and his fingers gripped hers in response.

"Yer a verra special person," she whispered. "My mama always told me

I deserved to be loved by someone extraordinary. She was right." He looked down onto her and she met his sad eyes with a small grin. "Whatever it is we'll deal with it together, aye?"

A slight smile touched his pale lips and he nodded.

Jeanie savoured the smile but noted that it did nothing to diminish the sadness in his eyes.

Realizing that they were blissfully alone, Jeanie looked around and queried, "Where's Fernando?"

The wall suddenly loomed high between them again and she instantly regretted asking as he turned away to stare once more into the fire.

"He's left." His soft melodious voice barely carried above the crackling of the wood forcing Jeanie to strain to hear him even sitting at his side. "He thought it best, all things considering. He'll meet us at the pier."

At the mention of their impending travels Jeanie sat straight in remembrance. "What time is it?"

The Angel shrugged a shoulder. "Half seven?"

Jeanie's eyes went wide. That meant they only had two hours to get ready and down to the ship, and here she was sitting on the couch and the Angel seemed completely disinterested. "I hae t'get ready. We need to pack." She stood, a list running and organizing in her mind.

"I've already packed," he stated quietly without looking up.

Beside the front door a black leather suitcase sat propped up against the wall, the sheathed sword stood point down beside it. Jeanie's breath caught at the realization that he was bringing the sword. The implied expectation of violence sent a shiver down her spine. How long had he been awake? The tension in the room thickened and she knew she had to do something to alleviate it before something was said that was better left unsaid.

"D'ye think I hae time to wash up?"

He gazed up at her and nodded. "There should be enough hot water, but you'll need to get another slice of soap from the cupboard. I'm afraid I used it all." His eyes lowered, discomfited.

"That's alright." Jeanie smiled and silently wondered how he could have used up a new cake of soap in one sitting. "Afterwards I'll put on the new dress I bought and we can go out. Ye can take me for some dinner."

"You mean at a restaurant?" His crimson eyes shot up to gaze at her, his mouth slack in what she could only imagine as horror.

"I–I thought," she stammered, confused by his reaction. "I thought when ye told me to get something nice…"

"I want you to have something nice," he insisted, "but that – oh hell." Jeanie's eyes went wide. She had never heard him swear before and he dropped his head in his hands before he looked up at her again, chin resting in his hand. "I'm Chosen, Jeanie, I don't eat at restaurants." His eyes followed her hand as it fluttered to her healed neck. She felt the fool.

The silence was cut with a loud grumble and Jeanie blushed even harder. In one fluid motion, the Angel stood, towering over her, and

Karen Dales

brushed a stray lock from her face causing her to tremble. "If you want, I'll take you, but we sit away from the others. I–I don't want people staring."

The breath she did not realize she held rushed out in a huff and she grinned. Of course, it was not because he was a Chosen, though that was part of it, but it was due to his appearance. Very few knew what the Angel looked like and now he was going to come out into the open for her. With a jump, Jeanie smiled and flung her arms around him, feet leaving the ground. Her body instantly heated as his arms swept her into an embrace and his lips hungrily met her own, threatening to devour her.

Flushed with desire, she reluctantly pulled away from the kiss and regretted that they did not have more time. He lowered her to the floor, her body sliding against his until the contact was regretfully released.

"Thank ye. Ye wilna be sorry." Jeanie smiled as she turned to go to the bathroom. "It'll be just like courtin', but in reverse."

A deep-throated chuckle followed her as she entered the pristine bathroom, content that she finally made him happy.

XXII

ernando stood at the end of the flagstone walkway dressed in clean clothing and a new black wool cape. Somewhere at the bottom of the Thames his long cloak floated, keeping the fish warm. Resting on the flags by his feet, a snakeskin suitcase was packed near to bursting with what he knew he would need over on the continent and hoped it would be enough. With more than enough time, Fernando had gone home, relieved to be out of the Angel's abode, but not before feasting on three unsuspecting victims.

He felt a world better and he knew his colour had returned along with the shape of his skull. The whores he let live. One did not salt the earth when it can be harvested from again. It was the pickpocket that was now nothing more than worm fodder. But before he set sail he needed to speak to Bridget, to warn her, to prepare her for the worst, whatever that may be. Something was out to see to the extermination of the vampires, and whatever they were, they were neither mortal nor Chosen. The thought chilled him to the bone.

Gazing up at the large house at the end of the walk, he noticed that all the lights were on in Bridget's home. *They must have a full house tonight,* he smiled.

Having woken in that God-awful cot had made him wonder what sort of penance Notus was performing. He should have taken the sofa; at least he would have most likely had a more comfortable sleep. Either was less enjoyable than staying in Bridget's bed, or worse, his own. But it was the hot-blooded scent of that damnable mortal girl filling the flat that drove him to retrieve his clothing knowing full well that the Angel was in the room.

Had Fernando been in any state of normalcy he could have waited, but his own blood loss cried out for its replacement and he had a feeling that the Angel was more than a match. Seeing the Angel in the bath, the scar on his arm—and had he seen another on his leg?—Fernando knew that one did not get scars like that from anything but warfare. It substantiated Fernando's theory that the Angel had fought, and often, before he was Chosen. It also brought up the question as to whether or not the Angel had continued the practice. If so, then Fernando knew he was out classed and that thought did not bode well, especially after that morning's headache and swim.

He touched the back of his head and let it drop. It was healing well. The knot in his belly, relieved somewhat by his indulgent feeds, did not dissipate. Fear was something that Fernando was not accustomed to experiencing and he pushed it away as he picked up the suitcase.

The sounds of yelling reached his ears well before he placed one foot in front of the other. It was Bridget's voice and it was clear to   Fernando that she was either very angry, very afraid or both. But the question was why? Bridget was usually outwardly demure. He had seen her temper on occasion, usually directed at him, but always with good reason.

A crash shattered the night and Fernando knew he had to do something. When Bridget started throwing things no one was safe. Speeding to the door, he dropped his luggage and wrenched the door open, yanking it off one of the hinges. In the front room, Bridget stood panting in fury, stray blonde hairs floated in a halo around her normally impeccable coiffure.

"You see, I told you. He's still alive!" Her voice slid dangerously. Her blue eyes held onto the intruders in her home. Along the staircase, Bridget's ladies hung onto the rail. Some in anticipation for their madam's legendary temper, others quailed in terror of what was to come. The ones in the parlour hid behind furniture. Only those that were her Chosen ladies watched with expectant expressions.

So it was he who was the cause of this explosion. Turning to face the one whom Bridget directed her anger, Fernando's fury sparked.

"You snivelling sack of puke," he rounded on Valraven who stared in dumb shock at the living ghost standing in the doorway. The two others with him Fernando recognized from his audience with Katherine – Roberta and Benjamin, two of the Mistress' toadies. Vampires who should never have been sired, having not a brain cell between the two, yet desired to lick the boots of their Lady. It was Valraven he stormed towards as he entered the whorehouse.

"You're supposed to be dead," blurted Valraven, completely caught off guard.

"I am, am I?" Fernando's fist caught Katherine's lackey on the jaw, sending him flying into the cabinet with a satisfying crash that mingled with the screams of fear from the mortal whores. Splintered wood and shattered glass and china rained down on the fallen vampire. Roberta and Benjamin backed away, fearing they were next.

Struggling to his feet, Valraven checked his jaw. "You were seen floating in the Thames just before dawn." The explanation fell from his quickly healing jaw.

"The reports of my demise are greatly exaggerated." Fernando had enjoyed sending the greasy looking Chosen into the cabinet, but the obvious reason why they were here infuriated him. "Get the hell out of here, Valraven. Tell Katherine that the Angel and I are still on this and if I hear one iota that you have even dared to even breathe on Bridget or any of these lovely ladies here, I *will* hunt you down and use your putrid head for target practice. Do we have an understanding?"

Valraven stumbled towards his assistants, his face taught with barely contained rage and humiliation. "This isn't over de Sagres."

"No it isn't," hissed the Noble. "Now get out of here!" Fernando's voice shook the house, sending Katherine's followers into the night as fast as their supernatural abilities would allow. "And the rest of you," he boomed, swinging around to face the entranced audience, "get back to work!"

Squeals of surprise and the sound of bare feet on slated wooden stairs answered the order as the whores raced up the steps as fast as their legs could carry them. When the swirl of the silken rainbow disappeared to the upper levels, Fernando turned to see that Anna and Beth had come to Bridget's side. Bridget still fumed, but seemed to be calming as her fledglings spoke soothing words.

"Anna, Beth, you two, go." Fernando's voice lost some of its anger, but the threat of not following the order was implicit. He watched the two seek askance of Bridget who nodded and then vanished in preternatural speed as they found the door leading to the basement and their rooms.

Finally left alone, Bridget rounded on her fledgling. "Where the hell have you been?" Her blue eyes sparked dangerously.

"Floating in the fucking Thames, thank you for asking," snapped

Fernando. This was not how he had expected this parting to go. Oh sure there would be some harsh words and maybe some tears on Bridget's part, but Valraven had set a new tone that carried even after his departure. "And please don't thank me from stopping Valraven and his minions from hauling your ass before Katherine."

The wind deflated from Bridget's sails leaving her looking haggard. Collapsing into the burgundy velvet chair, she failed in her attempt to capture the escaped strands of hair, her hands visibly shaking.

"They said you were dead," muttered Bridget. "They wouldn't believe me."

"Of course not," spat Fernando. "You didn't believe it yourself."

Bridget's head shot up renewed anger flashing into her eyes. "And how could I know any different. You're always closed to me, Fernando."

"It's better that way," he said, tightly.

"Is that why you're here?" Bridget stood, rearing for another row. "To continue this centuries old argument?"

Fernando's jaw clenched. As soon as Bridget had taught him to close himself off from her mental probing, he had severed that contact with her, separating himself completely. It was something that infuriated Bridget and led to some of their most passionate fights and their most erotic love makings. "No. I'm here to tell you I'm leaving for France tonight."

"France?" As quickly as the anger flashed, confusion filled its void. "Whatever for?"

"The Angel and I have a lead." Fernando began to pace the room, uncomfortable about what he next had to tell her. "Someone neither mortal nor Chosen is behind this. We have a chance to find out who and possibly end the threat."

Bridget's mouth fell open, her jaw trembling as her eyes filled with tears. It was the same. The same as when Sebastian last came to her before he was killed. They had taken away her sire and now they were going to take away her beloved. "You can't go."

Fernando halted in his tracks and gazed upon Bridget's fearful expression. It was enough to finally remove the rest of his anger. Coming to stand before her, he took her elegant hands in his.

"Bridget, I have to go," he said, softly. "If the Angel and I don't stop this thing then we're all dead. It's plain that even the rumour of my demise brought Katherine's hounds sniffing at your heels. I won't let you be next."

He was answered by a nod of her head. "Judith's dead."

The news stunned him.

"How?" he inquired and knew the answer before it left Bridget's painted lips.

"It was as you said," she answered. "Judith had a client who was tainted. It happened after you and the Angel left. I hadn't the time to warn her." She looked up into Fernando's eyes. "Oh Fernando, it was horrible. She screamed and screamed. Anna and Beth are terrified to feed even with the warning you gave us."

"That's why I have to go. I have to end this." Fernando tucked a loose lock of wavy blonde hair behind her ear, his hand lingering a moment on her cheek.

Bridget nodded. A tear escaped and was brushed away by his strong hand. "How will I know whether or not you…"

Fernando rolled his eyes. It was the same circular argument, but this time Bridget had a point. If she could sense him, even across the Channel, then maybe Katherine would leave her alone. He hated the idea of opening himself up to anyone, even Bridget, but the risks were too high and he had to keep her safe.

"Okay," he sighed.

Blue eyes widened in shock. It was the answer she had hoped centuries for but always expected the usual answer. To hear Fernando acquiesce now stood testament to the seriousness of the situation.

"Are you sure?"

"No, but you're right." Fernando led Bridget to the sofa and sat down. "I'm going to agree to this for the duration of this contemptible quest. When our enemies are crushed it's back to the way it is now. Agreed?"

"You're word on it, Fernando?" she asked, sceptically.

Fernando nodded solemnly. "As the last heir to the Fidalgo de Sagres, you have my word on it."

Rewarded with the smile he loved to see, Bridget placed her hands on either side of his head and stared deep into his eyes. Uncomfortable with the intensity of the gaze he knew he had to match it. His eyes bore into hers. He did not want this to happen and resisted out of habit. The pressure grew causing his temples to throb in time with his quickening heart.

It was not a matter of being able to read her. He could do that if he wanted. He chose not to. It was the matter of letting Bridget in. For centuries the wall that he had built to keep her out had remained impregnable, now he had to let her in. That was something he did not know how to do. The pressure built and he groaned. He could see the strain on Bridget's face and then quite suddenly, as if an audible pop rang through the room, the pressure was gone.

Can you hear me?

Fernando inhaled a shuddering breath.

Yes, he replied. He hated this. He hated being so open.

I know, love. Bridget smiled warmly. She knew what caused him to shut himself off from her, from everyone.

"Stop Bridget." Fernando lowered his head, covering his eyes with his hand. *I can't go there again.* He felt her sweep his dark curls aside.

"Alright." She lifted his chin and took away his hand. "I have what I want. Maybe when this is all over you will realize that this is what you want too." She leaned forward and kissed him deeply.

The sense of her passion swept through him, threatening to overload him. Under it, buoying the physicality of her desire was what he knew was there for so long but was afraid to acknowledge, or even allow for its return.

Breaking the embrace, he leaned back. "I have to go now."

"I know," she said sadly. "Just promise me something else."

"What now, Bridget?" Exasperated and shaken, Fernando stood and walked to the skewed door hanging limply in the frame.

"Come back to me alive."

Fernando turned to face his sire. Concern fought with fear for prominence on her beautiful pale face, and in her heart. "I will," he nodded.

Picking up the suitcase sitting on the stoop, Fernando stepped into the night. Bridget's touch on his body, mind and soul still lingered.

XXiii

ide by side they walked down the street. The beautiful day had turned into a jewelled night that brought with it the cold kiss of winter to come. Jeanie's breath steadily puffed light clouds as her shoes clicked quickly along the cobbles.

He slowed the pace. They had plenty of time to reach the ship and it was too easy for him to forget that his strides, even at a mortal pace, could leave many a person running behind. Even Notus would complain on occasion.

Shifting his grips on the suitcases, he bumped his sword strapped to his hip under the cloak. They had not conversed much since they had left the restaurant. Then again he had hardly said a word over dinner, allowing Jeanie to divulge the secrets of her life in Scotland. It was nice hearing her stories as he twirled the wine glass half full of Merlot between his hands. Every so often he would fake a sip and place it back down. He could not understand what was so appealing of the dark red liquid. It would have been nicer had he been able to wear his cloak.

He was sure that Jeanie was aware of the stares he received even if she could not hear the comments that his sensitive ears picked up. He had wanted to look up and gaze into eyes the colour of new growth, but he dared not lest he see the looks on the other patrons.

Jeanie had talked and enjoyed and tried her best to make him feel as if they were the only two in the restaurant and he deeply appreciated her attempt, but it was when she clasped her hand over his and said that they could go if he wanted that he released the anxious breath he had been harbouring. Noticing her mostly eaten plate and her empty wine glass, he had matched her eyes and nodded. Fishing out what he figured was more than enough, he dropped the notes on the table and they left. He had never felt so grateful for the camouflage of his long black cloak.

The special something Jeanie had bought had stunned him when she had come out of the bathroom wearing the forest green dress he had dreamed her in. Even down to how she arranged her hair under the lace and green hat held with a long dangerous looking pin. She looked the Lady. No evidence of her housekeeper self remained. And then she did the unexpected – she smiled at his reaction. Every part of her glowed and it was all he could do to stop himself from devouring her right then and there. He had to satisfy himself with a deep lingering kiss that stole her breath away.

Noticing that Jeanie had fallen back, he halted at the turn that would take them to the harbour.

A frown pouted Jeanie's lips. "I'm sorry. I dinna realize that it would be that bad."

His thin sculpted brows drew together, not understanding what she was referring to.

"It's just that I guess I dinna see what the other's see," explained Jeanie, reading the question on his shadowed face. "I just see you."

Finally comprehending what Jeanie was alluding to, he sighed and placed the suitcases down. Relieved of his burden, he took the couple of strides to stand before her. Taking her green velvet gloved hands in his, Jeanie looked up. "You and a very small number," he said, the corner of his mouth lifting subtly in a sad smile.

"But how can ye stand it?" implored Jeanie. A tear escaped, leaving a glittering trail in its wake. "I couldna hear all that was whispered, but…"

"You knew," he finished with a sigh. He had heard every word, from the malicious and cruel to the curious and dubious.

Jeanie nodded.

He gazed over her head into the night unable to match her forlorn expression on his behalf. "I can't," he whispered. "I never have and, most probably, never will." He returned his view to her beatific face and hitched a shoulder. "Why do you think I wear this cloak? I learned long before I was Chosen how different my appearance is and the reactions it creates in others. It's safer this way. It's okay."

More tears spilled down Jeanie's freckled face and she threw herself onto him with a fierce hug.

"Oh Gwyn, I wilna let that happen again. Ye dinna hae t'come with me." Startled at the low rumble of a chuckle, Jeanie pulled back to stare up into his crimson eyes alight with amusement.

"Jeanie, you have to eat," he smiled, wiping away the tears from her face. "I'm not going to let you go and enjoy a nice dinner while I lurk outside. I've tolerated this and much worse over the centuries, I think I can endure the glares and comments if it means I spend time with you."

Sniffing away her tears, Jeanie's eyes grew serious. "But ye need to eat too, aye?"

The seriousness of her question made the air heavy between them and he nodded.

"I do, but not as often as when I was first Chosen. In any case, if I do have to feed, you'll be the first to know." He trailed his hand down the side of her face to her neck until his fingers thrilled at the rhythmic dance beneath them. Feeling her pulse shoot up, he saw in her eyes the same need that pulled at him and he bent down to find her mouth inviting him to discover more had they not been in the middle of the walkway.

"Great. I did not need to see this."

A deep accented voice broke the mood, tearing them apart from one another still unsatisfied. Turning, they witnessed Fernando striding towards them, his dark cape fluttering back from his broad shoulders.

"Then ye dinna hae t'look," snapped Jeanie, rounding on the Noble's intrusion.

Fernando came to an abrupt halt at the vehemence in her voice and raised his brows in annoyance before darkening with fury. "I thought you were going to keep her under control."

"I'm not her master," whispered the Angel, not hiding the acrimony in his inflections. "I believe I made that clear."

Clenching his jaw, Fernando glared at each before stepping forward to the turn that would take them down to the harbour and the ship.

"It's almost half past nine," growled the Noble. "If you want this partnership to end sooner rather than latter, we'd best get moving."

Shaking his head at the audacity of the Noble, the Angel picked up the two suitcases and followed with Jeanie beside him.

"I dinna like him," she hissed, staring at the fluttering cape before her.

"He can hear you, Jeanie." He did not bother to lower his voice.

"I dinna care." She looked up at her lover and then at the Noble, their footpads ringing in the clear night. "I dinna like how he treats me, or ye for that matter."

He let out a slow breath. "I don't like it either, but for now we have to put up with each other."

"Yes, we do." Fernando halted and spun around to face them. "And if you don't mind, if you have something to say to me, say it to my face rather than my back." Answered only by stone silence, he turned around and took the steps down to the harbour that he had left not twenty-four hours earlier.

Picking up the pace, they followed him down the stone steps.

"Arse," said Jeanie under her breath and then squeaked in surprise when the Noble was suddenly before her, his hand on her throat, squeezing.

"Let her go, Fernando." Menace filled the Angel's voice.

The Noble realized the metallic ring echoing in the night belonged to the sword under his chin ready to decapitate him with any wrong utterance. He felt the Angel's strong presence behind him and swallowed his shock. He had moved with vampiric speed, but even he had not seen the Angel move. Opening his hand, Fernando released Jeanie who stumbled and coughed before she caught herself.

Furious, the Angel removed the sword from the Noble's neck and sheathed it as fast as he had drawn it.

"Don't ever touch her, Fernando." The promise of what would happen did not need to be uttered and Fernando backed away under the red glare.

Turning his attention to Jeanie, the Angel's face was taught with cold fury. He did not like being placed in the position of referee.

"Jeanie, if you have something to say to Fernando, you say it to his face." Her shocked expression at him seemingly taking the Noble's side pushed him to add, "You'd expect the same courtesy from anyone.

"I'm not a peacemaker. That's Notus' talent. I am sick of this fighting. It's this attitude that will see us fail." Ignoring the two of them, he picked up the luggage and continued down to the water's edge hoping that Fernando and Jeanie would not kill each other.

"I'm no gonna apologize," he heard Jeanie say to Fernando. "And I'm no afraid of ye."

"And I am certainly not going to apologize to a mortal, one that should be very much afraid," pronounced Fernando.

Hearing no bloodshed or further name-calling, he was relieved to watch Fernando walk right by him onto the wooden planks over the languid waves. It seemed that the Noble knew which way to go.

Staring at the slowly rotting wood ahead of him, he swallowed. A knot in the pit of his stomach started to form, accentuated by the soughing of the surf. He had not put much speculation into what he was about to endure tonight. The whole concept made his blood run cold.

When he agreed to come back to England, Notus promised him they would stay for at least a century before he would have to endure another crossing. Now, having been on the island for only five years, he was going to undergo the torturous voyage again.

"I hate that man," he heard Jeanie proclaim. She stood at his side watching the fluttering cloak grow smaller.

Breaking his gaze from the boardwalk and what was underneath, he quietly said, "You and he have made it abundantly clear of your dislike of each other."

"Ye dinna like him either." Jeanie stepped onto the wooden planks and pivoted to gaze up at him.

He could not answer knowing that his next steps would take him over the water and bring that gut wrenching sense of vertigo he always experienced. Only this time it would get worse once aboard the *Sea Witch*.

Sensing his disquiet, Jeanie frowned. "What's wrong?" She did not believe it had anything to do with her statement.

He took a shuddering breath and released it.

"Do you remember what I said about me becoming sick when crossing water?" he whispered, praying that Fernando was far enough that he could not hear.

Jeanie nodded. Fear sparked in her eyes, reflecting his concerns.

"I'm going to be – how can I say this?" He let out another nervous breath. "You're going to have to deal with the Captain and make sure Fernando leaves us alone in the cabin." He set down the baggage and pulled out his wallet. Counting out what Captain Richardson was expecting for his payment, he handed the notes to Jeanie.

"What's this for?" Her eyes grew wide at the amount in her hand.

"To pay the Captain." He stared at the water dancing between the planks. "I'm afraid I'm not going to be good company until we land in Calais."

Blinking in confusion, Jeanie stuffed the notes into her coat pocket and waited for him to pick up the suitcases before she resumed her journey to the ship. With her back momentarily to him, Jeanie did not see the Angel stumble as he stepped onto the planks.

The *Sea Witch* bobbed on the surf as Jeanie and the Noble stared up at the Tern Schooner's three masts. The sails fluttered in the light breeze as the crew made ready to leave port. One future passenger stood behind the two, his hands clutching the handles of the suitcases in a grip threatening to crush the hard wood as he kept his eyes closed in every attempt not to see world spin around him. Every part of his being tensed in the attempt to keep his trembling at bay, he did not want to open his eyes and see the gangboard leading to the deck.

"Ahoy!" came the cry from the ship. "I see that you and your companions are ready to depart, Miss Stuart."

"Aye, Captain Richardson," called Jeanie. "May we come aboard?"

"Please. And I take it that you have my payment?"

"Aye, half now and half upon reaching port."

"The gangboard is yours."

Jeanie took the lead up the inclined ridged plank. Her shoes clicked as she steadied herself with the rope railing. It was her first time aboard such a vessel and despite the Angel's reaction to the adventure she could not keep her excitement in check.

Upon reaching the deck, Captain Richardson held out his hand and smiled. When she first met him, she thought him a letch. Now he seemed to carry himself with the decorum of a naval officer. His blonde waves cut close under his hat; his smile lit blue eyes in a rugged square face when her hand shook his. She figured him to be in age with her father.

Fernando's sudden presence onboard wiped the smile from the Captain's face. "Miss Stuart said she would be bringing others," his accented voice slid lower. "And you are?"

"I am Fernando de Sagres, the last heir to the Fidalgo de Sagres," stated the Noble matter-of-factly as he took in the appearance of the *Sea Witch* and it's Captain. "And I take it, sir, that you are the Captain of this ship."

"Yes, I am," replied Richardson. His tone quavered under the Noble's intense glare.

"I don't recognise the accent, sir."

Blue eyes narrowed. "American, sir."

An amused smile alighted Fernando's face. "A man from the colonies – interesting. I don't believe I've had the pleasure."

A murderous expression ran fleetingly across Captain Richardson's face before smoothing to a more cordial one. "The United States has been independent from England for a long time."

Fernando waved off the correction and walked away as if finding more interest in the grain of wood in the decking.

The Captain scowled and turned back to speak to the lady when he witnessed the tall, cloaked figure slowly making his way up onto the deck. Mouth slack as the last of the passengers finally boarded, Richardson found he could only stare and did not hear Miss Jeanie when she spoke.

Clearing his head with a quick shake, Richardson tore his gaze away from the grim figure before him to the beauteous one. "I'm sorry ma'am, what did you say?"

Jeanie frowned and held out the bills. "I believe this is the agreed upon amount?"

Captain Richardson flicked his gaze to the money and took it out of her hand, reality snapping back at the firmness of the paper. Licking his thumb he counted out the notes and smiled, pocketing the large amount. "Jones will show you to your cabins."

A lithe young man with new sprouts of dark brown facial hair dropped down to the deck from the rigging and took a lantern from the hook on the rail. "If you'll follow me, ma'am," he said trying his utmost to ignore the grim figure standing beside the pretty lady.

Jeanie could not see the Angel's face beneath the hood, but she knew he had fallen into one of his silences. He had said that he was going to be ill on the voyage, but so far she had not seen anything to indicate his unease in crossing water. Walking up to him, she gazed up and noticed his eyes tightly shut. A touch on his arm startled him, snapping his eyes open before he sighed heavily, shoulders slumping.

Turning to face the crew hand, Jeanie followed the young man down under the deck. Thankfully, Jones remained respectfully quiet as they walked the small halls below deck.

The height below decks caused the Angel to duck under the planks. It was hard to keep his balance as he felt the ship rise and fall under the simple swells. Leaning against the walls for support as his feet moved leadenly, he knew it was going to be worse once away from port and then the nightmare would begin. Thankfully, Fernando had chosen to stay above deck. He knew it would impossible to hide from the Noble his discomfort and weakness and was immensely grateful when the young seaman opened the door to their berth in the aft of the schooner.

Jones smiled at Jeanie, ignoring the tall figure with her. The room consisted of a bunk bed, a simple wooden table and two stools. A single porthole looked out onto the waters. For a ship this size, the aft berth was quite generous. It was clear that Captain Richardson was well versed in carrying passengers as well as cargo. Hanging the lantern on the hook above the table, Jones nodded his head and scurried out of the cabin.

With the sound of the door closing, the Angel dropped the suitcases and tore away the restrictive cloak pin. The heavy wool fell and he leaned forward, laying shaking hands on the table. Everything spun and the earth seemed very far below. He opened his eyes at the touch of Jeanie's warm hand on his arm and saw only deep concern.

"Get some sleep," he said, thickly. "I'll be fine."

Jeanie made a deep throat noise of disapproval. "I'll no sleep while yer like this. Ye need to get t'bed."

A smile quirked his lips, "The bed's too small. I'll take the floor." He tried to stand straight and found the ceiling much too low. A cry from above decks and a lurch sent him grasping the bolted down table. They were under way.

"Let go." He heard Jeanie whisper. "Yer crushing the wood."

He did not know if he could. He was afraid that if he let go the ship would start spinning around him even more. Gentle hands unclasped his sword belt and he felt the weight lifted off his hips. He dared not open his eyes to see where Jeanie placed it. Again her warm hands found his and coached them to release the table. It was enough for him to risk opening his eyes. The world spun, but not too fast before he found the aft wall and sank to the floor, hugging his raised knees as his head leaned against the wall.

Seeing him weakened and sick frightened Jeanie. He was always strong, even in his silence and now she did not know what to do. He had said he would be ill during the trip, but she could not fathom how that was possible being that he was a vampire. Removing her gloves, Jeanie pulled the hatpin out and placed it and the hat on the table, and turned to latch the door before kneeling at his side. He did not seem to notice her until she placed a hand on his forehead. It seemed the most logical thing to do when someone was ill. What surprised her was that he actually felt hot.

Languidly, he opened his eyes and smiled wryly at her. Jeanie looked so beautiful with her hair up, allowing for wayward strands to curl in floating ringlets around her ears. Even her eyes sparkled despite her concern. He felt the ship move up and then, as quickly, back down, bottoming out his senses and tearing a pained groan from his lips. Closing his eyes, he leaned his head against the wooden wall.

Removing her hand from his head, Jeanie worried her lower lip. She had nursed her dying mother when she was younger. Back then she had help. She had known what to do and what she could not do. But this was different. How does one help a sick vampire? Before she had known his true nature she had wanted to care for him. Now that the time had come, she was bereft of knowledge.

"What can I do?" she pleaded.

Without opening his eyes, he responded, his voice a bare whisper. "There's nothing you can do, Jeanie."

"There must be somethin'." She smoothed white stray hairs away and touched the side of his pale face. "Ye look like death."

His crimson eyes popped open and his face darkened at the comment.

Realizing what she had said, Jeanie pulled back her hand over her mouth in a silent "Oh."

Releasing a deep shuddering sigh, he closed his eyes again. He knew that Jeanie had not meant it the way he took the comment, and that she reacted to how he appeared.

"Go get some rest, Jeanie."

She shook her head. She was not about to leave his side and was about to tell him so again when the rattle of the door, followed by a knocking, shocked her attention away.

"Who is it?" she called.

"Who do you think? Now let me in! We've got to talk." Fernando's insistent voice rang through the wooden door.

Eyes going wide, Jeanie glanced to the Angel whose fear laded gaze outmatched hers. She had never seen such alarm in his features and she knew she needed to protect him from Fernando's prying nature. Rising to her feet, she smoothed down her dress in an attempt to compose herself by dismissing her own worry and evoking the loathing she felt for the Noble.

"Go away, Fernando," she ordered in a firm voice.

"I'll do not such thing," came the tempered reply. "The Angel and I have matters to discuss and I'll not let this door, nor you, stand in the way."

Jeanie glanced back at the Angel seated on the floor beside the bunk, under the porthole. Terror glittered his eyes and he shook his head before closing them again with a groan as the ship lifted up and then back down, even causing Jeanie to stumble. She had to do something and quickly. The latch would not hold for a normal person and would most definitely give in Fernando's hand.

An idea popped into her mind and she smiled at the door.

"I dinna think ye want to come in right about now," she called.

"And why's that, li'l miss?" Fernando hissed.

"Because if ye didn't like what ye saw above the harbour, I doubt ye'd like what ye'd see here." She lowered her voice to a whisper knowing the Noble would still hear her and added, "Stop that, luv, he's on the other side. Oh!"

A disgusted sound came from the hallway followed the sound of the Noble's shoes on wood.

"Don't they ever stop," was the last she heard before the steps took Fernando above deck.

Releasing her tension with an explosion of air, Jeanie wiped away the beads of nervous sweat from her forehead with her hands, smoothed her hair and then turned back to the Angel. Her skirts rustled as she lifted them and lowered to kneel beside him.

"He's gone," she whispered.

Unable to speak the extent of his gratitude for the sake of the increasing swells beneath the ship's hull, he only managed a slight nod. Even that motion sent his head spinning and he groaned. Everything felt hot and closed in and he knew that this was just the beginning. Once they left the Thames for the sea it would grow worse.

Having felt useful in dealing with Fernando, Jeanie stared at the Angel's tortured expression. He had suffered this crossing before, he must have, she reasoned, and he would have done so with the Good Father. It was a question, a glimmer of hope of how she could help, but she had to ask. "What does the Good Father do for ye in times like these?"

The question surprised him and he dared to pop open an eye. Jeanie's features spun around. "Why?" he swallowed.

"Just answer the question," she pushed.

"He'd try to get me to talk." He licked his lips and let his eyelid enclose him in darkness. "He thought it would distract me."

"And would it?" She felt a stirring of excitement at the idea that there was something she could do to help him and then it was swept away at the shake of his head. "What else would he do?"

Silence fell between them, making Jeanie wonder at first if he had fallen asleep, but the increasing rise and fall of the vessel only made his face screw up in discomfort. When the ship suddenly pitched upwards and then crashed down, causing her to catch herself with a grip on the sturdy table, she heard him groan as he toppled onto his side, hugging himself.

The swinging lantern sent flickering yellow light across the small cabin. Jeanie could see him shivering as he lay curled on his side. Panic swarmed up and gripped her in an attempt to cut off her airflow. Half crawling, half walking under the weight of her skirts, she managed to sit beside his head.

Turning, she rested his head in her lap, his long white hair splayed messily against the green of her dress. Smoothing the strands, she felt his forehead again and was stunned at the burning heat radiating off. A fever this severe would kill and she fearfully wondered if it would do so to him. The idea that the Angel would be taken from her after having waited so long to be with him filled Jeanie with dread. It was too much like the final days of her mother's disease. Knowing naught else to do, Jeanie softly began to sing the songs she sang to her mother, all the while petting his face and forehead as he trembled in the wake of the illness.

Fernando had watched the casting off with interest, ignoring the fact that the Angel and his mortal had gone below. Now the Noble was above decks again, retreating to the beauty of the night on water. It had been a very long time since he had left for England and this newer sleek sailing vessel caught a romantic string in his heart. He had always loved sailing. It was the only part of his initial trip here, when he was mortal, that he savoured. Only on that vessel more hands were necessary for its functioning. Fernando was amazed that only a crew of seven, including the captain, were needed for the schooner.

Leaning out over the rail, he watched the dark waters of the Thames speed past as the wind whipped up and clouds scurried across the sky, hearkening to an oncoming storm. A smile lit his lips at the ride he knew he was in for and turned to lean back against the wooden rail to stare at the tallest of the three masts. She was a magnificent lady.

The sails bloomed and shuddered in the wind. Rigging, taught between sheets and deck, hummed. Yes, the girl had done at least one thing right, and he was going to enjoy the trip as much as immortally possible. The only dampening to his mood was being driven away from talking with the Angel. Fernando was starting to regret his decision to introduce Jeanie to the world existing in the dark of night.

Pulling out Yang, he watched the light glimmer and dance upon the blade. A shipmate paused in his round, distracted by the nobleman and the knife. He quickly found his pace after a dark menacing glare from Fernando paled him. A quirk of a smile lifted the Chosen's lips as the young man scurried to his appointed task.

Left alone with his thoughts, Fernando twirled the blade, its sharp point digging into his left index finger. Again, the speculations about the Angel arose. Swearing as he sliced his finger, Fernando ignored the quickly healing cut. A single bead of blood dribbled down his finger only to splatter against the deck. He shook his hand.

What was it that made his mind constantly go back to the Angel? He shook his head. It was like he was drawn to him, almost like a moth to a cold flame. He had seen such a reaction in the girls at Bridget's house, and even he could not account his sire's reaction. What made Bridget so interested in the Angel?

Maybe because there is something more to him than he appears.

Fernando gave a yelp and turned around, almost dropping Yang into the river. It took him a moment to recognize that the voice had come from inside his head and it was distinctly Bridget's.

Embarrassed, he turned around to see if any of the mortals had seen his breach in façade. Finding that he was blissfully alone, he sheathed Yang.

Don't do that to me, he sent, angrily.

Sorry, love, came the reply. Fernando could sense Bridget standing before her dressing mirror, concern filling her heart. *It's just that when you thought of me, I heard you.*

Fernando grumbled and turned to face the receding waters, leaning on the rail. *So you decided to pop into my head and answer my questions?*

Don't be angry, love, soothed Bridget. *You initialized the contact. I just answered it.*

Damning himself for a fool, he realized that Bridget probably sensed that and he knew he was too much out of practice to keep much from her. Luckily, as the physical distance grew between them, their connection would become more tenuous.

He felt her frown. *If you didn't want to talk with me then I'll go.*

Fernando let out a sigh. He did not want Bridget angry with him. He did not want possibly their last conversation to be a fight, even at this distance, and he remembered what she said about the Angel. *What do you mean there's more to him than he appears?*

Can't you sense it?

A frown pulled his face and he realized that he could sense something different about the Angel, something that scared him.

He's not scary, replied Bridget.

Then what is he? snapped Fernando. He did not like Bridget knowing he was afraid, especially of another Chosen.

He's not like us, love. He's Chosen, but there is something more to him. A power that I doubt even he is aware of.

Then he shouldn't have been left alive. The thought came unbidden and he realized how horrific it was. The idea of the Angel becoming one of the Destroyed Ones seemed terribly wrong and he did not know why. He had witnessed the Angel move faster than a Chosen, but that could that be due to his extreme age.

It could, agreed Bridget. *Can Notus move that fast?*

If the Angel's sire, who was older, could move like that then he would not have been caught in the Mistress' web. Nothing about the Angel made sense.

Fernando, you are in a unique position.

I know, he frowned realizing that was what scared him. The Angel was so unlike any other vampire. It was as if the Angel was a light in the darkness and did not even know it.

Fernando, the distance is growing farther, I'm going to lose you soon. He could feel her urgency. *Learn what you can and come back to me, love.*

And, he felt her hesitate, as if suddenly afraid, *take care of the Angel.*

He stumbled as the connection faded, but he could still feel Bridget's presence across the miles. Fernando could not understand why Bridget would ask him to take care of the Angel. The Angel was more than capable, and then some, but a frown pulled at his lips. *A light in the darkness,* he shuddered not knowing where that thought came from or what it meant.

A speckling of raindrops struck the deck, giving prelude to the deluge to come. Glancing up at the sky, Fernando squinted into the wind battered rain and disappeared into the dry safety of his quarters below. The darkness was complete in his tiny cabin at the bow and for a flickering moment he wished there was a light.

XXIV

He did not know what to expect when he decided to come back to the walled garden within the castle, but he had only moments before he and Notus took their leave of the High Chief and his court. It would be tenuous at best.

He knew that the High Chief was angry with him, and by everyone's accounts, rightfully so. It was for his protection and for the peace of the realm that Notus was taking him back to Ynis Witrin. But he expected that it had to do more with Notus' need to delve back into monastic life so as to find absolution for what he had done.

Notus would be furious knowing that his son now stood in the archway connecting the inner sanctum of the fortress to the beautiful garden bristling with new green growth and blossoming flowers. It was the green of her eyes he needed to see one last time and he doubted that Notus would understand. Or maybe he did? He lowered his gaze from the brilliance of the near full moon and frowned. Coming back to the place where they had first met and began their clandestine affair over a year ago suddenly seemed ill devised.

The cool night air enveloped him as he stepped onto the soft grass and entered the garden. Would she be here? A part of him desperately desired to see her, to embrace her, to taste of her lips and body. Another part evoked the new stabbing pain that he knew Notus' spell had wrought. Divided, only she could answer his questions. Did she remember him? Did she still love him?

The nightingales' song stilled into silence as he turned down the path and saw her there under the apple tree, its white blossoms glowing in the moon's magical light. He halted, his breath caught at the sight of her chestnut coloured locks braided and beautifully arranged under a coif indicating her married status.

Swallowing hard, he realized that she had not noticed him. He could hear her soft whispers of love and encouragement to the unborn babe growing within her, its heartbeat strong and vital. For a desperate fleeting moment he wished the child to be his and knew it for a folly. Being Chosen meant never having children.

He stood in petrified silence, watching her until her gaze lifted and found him. It was more than he could bear seeing fear cross her face as she stood.

"I'm sorry," he stammered. "I didn't mean to scare you."

Sensing his remorse, she stood a little straighter but did not approach.

"Do I know you, sir? You seem familiar somehow. Have I seen you at my father's hall?" Her voice was clear and unafraid.

It was all the confirmation he needed. Notus' wiping of her memories was complete. Sorrow filled him and he shook his head, unable to look into her green eyes.

"Yet there is something." Her slippered feet padded along the gravel path towards him.

He had always admired her strength and now it offered him a glimmer of hope. Looking into her eyes, he saw hers grow round as she fully took in his appearance. All hope dashed to the ground, shattering to a thousand pieces as she hitched her skirt and fled. Knowing he had to stop her, he managed to catch her wrist, and turned her to face him.

"Please, sir," she pleaded, her hands held together between them by his. "I'm a married woman. My husband–"

It was too much to bear. He had to know. "Do you not remember me?" he pleaded.

Frantically, she shook her head, sending stray strands of hair floating. It was the terror in her eyes that finally made him release her and he watched in misery as she turned and ran from the garden. When she was gone, he collapsed to his knees on the gravel, tears streaming down his face.

*   *   *

It was not the knocking at the door by the shipmate telling them they were preparing to dock that woke Jeanie, nor was it the sounds of the moorings locking the ship into place. Jeanie had been up for some time, having slept sporadically through the night. The Angel's fever induced dreams had made his sleep fitful and there were many times when Jeanie did not understand his mutterings. Those that were clear were just as confusing and made her wonder how many languages he knew.

Rising from the mattress she had dragged to the floor, Jeanie squeezed out from between the Angel and the wall, allowing the blanket to fall, and felt around in the dark for the box of matches she had seen him pack in his suitcase. Victory achieved, she struck the match, squinting at its yellow brilliance and found the lantern. There was enough oil for the wick to catch, illuminating the cabin in a soft glow.

She pulled her dress on over her chemise and went back to the Angel's side. He had stayed in his torpid state for the duration of the trip and now they were finally in Calais she needed him to wake, if he could. Laying a hand on his face, Jeanie realized that he was not as hot as before. For some reason the fever was diminishing.

"Gwyn," she called softly, "we're in Calais. 'Tis time to disembark." Jeanie hoped he would feel better once back on land. His face screwed up as if in pain, yet his eyes would not open. Jeanie called to him again.

The explosion of movement caught her completely off guard, sending her sprawling backwards with a cry. A loud resounding crack rang through the berth followed by a groan and the sound of collapse. Turning over, skirts tangling around her legs, Jeanie lifted up to see the Angel crouched, holding the crown of his head in both hands. It was enough to get her moving. She stood up and all but ran in the confined space to fall to her knees before him, fearful that he had badly hurt himself. Quickly gazing up, she saw the damaged joist that he cracked his head upon.

"Let me take a look," she said. She reached to lower his hands and examine the wound and halted as she saw his eyes.

"Crei?" he pleaded; his eyes wild and haunted as he gazed into springtime eyes. He could not believe she was here, but why was she dressed that way and why did his head hurt? He groaned and pulled a hand away from his head to see blood on it. Nausea swept through him as the ground lifted up and then sank back down. It was enough of a movement to cause him to land on his backside. A vague awareness of where and when he was slowly trickled back.

The woman he thought he knew rose up on her knees and made him bend his head. There would be no evidence of the wound, having healed quickly, but the worry on her face made his head swim. Images of the past and the present slammed into him and he shook his head. He could not understand what she was saying at first and then he gasped. Her facial features shifted ever so slightly, but the eyes, they stayed the same, even to the colour and the shape. The curls decorating her pale neck faded from chestnut to a fiery copper.

"Jeanie?" he whispered, finally recognizing her. It was the epiphany of how closely Jeanie resembled her that set him trembling.

"I'm right here." Jeanie hunkered down, brushing his hair from his face and was shocked to see tears glittering his face. "What's wrong?"

Frowning, he rubbed his eyes with forefinger and thumb and found the wetness on his cheeks. Nausea surged up making the room spin and he closed his eyes. He did not know what to say to Jeanie. He was as confused as she.

Something was happening to him and he did not know what it was. The memories of the past, usually forgotten and ignored, were surging to the present, confounding and confusing him. It was not unusual to remember little things, but this was too much like reliving them, with the demons coming back and everything else going on, he began to wonder about his sanity.

A knock on the door saved him from answering. "Miss Stuart, the Captain says you can disembark anytime you wish, ma'am."

Jeanie twisted to face the door. "Thank ye. We'll be up shortly." Turning back to face him, she continued, apprehension filling her tones, "We're here, in Calais. D'ye think ye can leave the ship?"

He was not sure if he could stand, let alone walk up to the deck, but if it meant leaving for the stability of land, he would crawl if he had to. With Jeanie's help he rose and clung to the table, carefully avoiding the wood beams overhead. He let Jeanie get their things together while he stood clinging for stability. He felt her unsuccessful attempt to buckle on his sword belt. He took it out of her hands, offering her a tired smile and managed to strap it on before the spinning became too great. Stabilizing himself for a moment by griping onto the table for support, both he and Jeanie waited for the room to stop swirling before he took the heavy cloth from her arms and the clasp from her hand. With her help he managed to encase himself in the comforting darkness of his cloak and went to pick up the suitcases.

"I'll take them," offered Jeanie as she shrugged on her mantle. A smile softened her face.

Relief flooded his as he gazed upon the most beautiful woman he had ever known and wished that the trip could have been an enjoyable one for her. He did not remember all that she had done for him, but he knew that she did what she could to take care of him and for that he was immensely grateful.

Jeanie unlatched the door and before she could open it, he laid a hand on her shoulder. She turned to face him, worry still in her eyes. "Thank you, Jeanie. Thank you for everything."

A smile bloomed on her face and she fiercely hugged him. It was the only thing that kept him standing under the spinning nausea, and he hugged her back, inhaling the soft smell of soap from her hair.

"Can we go now?" she asked, pulling away.

"Oh Gods, yes, please," he sighed and picked up the luggage. Regardless of how he felt, he was not going to allow her to carry the heavy burdens and silenced her protestations with a glance.

Opening the door with an uneasy smile and a shake of her head, hat back in place, Jeanie led the way to the stairs leading to the deck. Stooped in the short hallway, he gratefully followed, eager to finally have the world stop spinning.

Fernando stood on deck at the top of the gangboard as they emerged. His tempestuous brown eyes bored into the Angel. Thankfully Jeanie either did not notice or she chose not to care. If only the ship would stop spinning and return his stomach back into place he would have been able to ignore the glare and the pulsations of finely controlled rage that flowed from the Noble.

He halted, forcing Jeanie to stop at his side. He should not be able to feel that. He should not be able to feel anything from any other Chosen except Notus. Dumb fear uncurled itself around his heart and he knew that Fernando saw it despite being cowled beneath his hood.

A smile lifted the corner of the Noble's lips. "Had a pleasant time?" he disparaged.

"Aye, thank ye," came Jeanie to the rescue. "We had a verra memorable time." She smiled and nodded her head, yet kept her eyes on the angry Noble.

Fernando sucked on his lips, displeased. "I took care of our good Captain."

"Ye dinna—" Jeanie's eyes widened in shock.

"Give me some credit." Fernando made a disgusted sound. "I paid the man, though I must say that what you agreed to pay him was robbery."

"Well, if ye wanted to pay less, ye could hae gone and found a ship yerself," quipped Jeanie. "Ah, but I forgot, ye canna during the day."

Fernando's face darkened and he took a step towards her.

"Stop it," ordered the Angel. He was so incredibly tired of their fighting. Had they not listened to him before the journey? He sadly shook his head, answering his own question. Needing nothing more than to get off the floating torture device, he pushed past the Noble, ignored Jeanie's gasp of surprise, and descended down the plank for the solidity of the quay. The moment his feet touched the firmness beneath him, the world gratefully ceased its turnings and the nausea miraculously vanished.

Being on solid ground never felt as good as when he left a ship. With closed eyes he took a deep clearing breath and opened them at the sound of Captain Richardson biding Miss Stuart a fond farewell. Jeanie's polite reply floated on the salt laden breeze and he turned to watch her carefully navigate the ridged planking with Fernando not far behind. A scowl that seemed permanently etched had returned to the Noble's features.

Suddenly, Jeanie's heel caught and she stumbled, pitching sideways over the water.

Time stopped and he heard the dull ringing thud of the suitcases as he dropped them to the concrete. Preternaturally, he leapt to the base of the gangboard in the effort of halting Jeanie's plunge into the icy dark waters. He stopped, heart pounding in his chest as he watched Fernando grab her by the back of her collar and haul her one handed onto the plank, unceremoniously landing her on her rear. Reaching out, he pulled Jeanie the rest of the way. Her feet never touched the ground until he planted her beside him. The elongated sounds of the lapping water resumed their normal cadence and he held her upper arms as she swayed, disoriented.

"Is she alright?" asked Fernando, stepping off the gangboard, his suit-case still in hand, to stand beside her.

It sounded almost as if the Noble actually cared, and he turned his attention back to Jeanie. "Are you okay?"

Jeanie blinked and looked around. "How did I get down?"

"You don't remember," he frowned.

"I recall catching my heel halfway down, and then I'm here." Confusion washed over her and she glanced from the Angel to the Noble and back again. "What happened?"

With a shake of his head, Fernando chuckled and walked off. "Welcome to your second experience, or would that be third, with the Chosen."

"What does he mean?" Jeanie pouted in bewilderment.

Picking up their suitcases, he waited for Jeanie to join him as he followed the Noble down the quay. "You slipped. Fernando caught you before you fell into the ocean and I took you down the rest of the way."

"But I would hae remembered that," implored Jeanie.

"Not necessarily." He stared ahead, wondering where the Noble was leading them.

Jeanie shook her head walking quickly to keep up despite the slight ache in her ankle. "That dinna make any sense."

"We're Chosen, Jeanie." He smiled down at her as realization took hold, widening her eyes and slacking her jaw.

"That mean's Fernando saved me." Awe mingled with disbelief filled her voice.

He nodded. Maybe this was the beginning of a truce between the three of them. It was a hopeful thought.

"And ye?" she probed, glancing up at his shadowed features. "Are ye fine now?"

"Never better," he smiled as he placed one foot in front of the other, appreciating the solidity beneath him. Jeanie's face brightened as she returned the grin and wished he had one hand free just to hold hers.

The ring of a ship's bell resounded mournfully in the darkness, calling to a brother that never replied. Rounding the corner, he witnessed Fernando standing stock still staring at a large tri-masted ship. A sudden sense of apprehension came over him, banishing his delectation as he came to a halt beside the other Chosen. Images of the dream before the demons had invaded flooded back and he realized he stood before the ship that had been littered with kaleidoscopic butterflies. His breath swept away with the breeze. It was real and it was here.

"The *Papillon.* It's here," whispered the Noble in consternation. He looked up at the Angel. "No more excuses, we have to talk and somewhere where we can't be overheard."

At the name of the ship, a shiver ran up his spine. The dream had been real. Meeting the Noble's concerned eyes, he nodded. Let Fernando take it as he may, he could not let the other Chosen know he had had a dream of this ship long before he had seen it. The question arose as to why. Why had he dreamt of it in the first place? He glanced back at the ship's dark decks knowing he would receive no answer.

An imperceptible shift in the quality of the night sent a familiar   tingle across his body. "We need to find a place to stay, now."

It was Fernando's turn to nod in silent agreement. It was clear that Fernando did not wish to tarry by the ship. "The Captain suggested a place not too far from here." With one final glance back at the ominous ship, Fernando shuddered and turned, striding down the quay.

Knowing that Jeanie would be hard pressed to keep the pace, he held back enough to keep her moving. Jeanie huffed in exertion, suppressing any ability to comment on what had occurred. He hoped she would understand that they had to be indoors before dawn broke. More importantly, they needed to get away from this ship and the possibility of running into any of its crew. The fact that the *Papillon* was in Calais, when, according to Fernando's recounts, it had been in London the night before, proved dangerous evidence that they were on the right track.

The bellhop placed the key into the door and turned the knob all the while carrying three pieces of luggage. Swinging the ornately decorated door inwards revealed the presidential suite with its large paned windows angling newborn sunlight into the room. Both he and Fernando instinctually stepped back from the opening to stand on either side of the doorway, facing the hall. The light spilling from the suite made the gold on the door across the hall glitter and sparkle. Squinting in the diluted light, he turned to face the Noble across the swatch of faded sunlight.

"I thought you asked for a north facing room," he hissed.

"I did," replied the Noble, blinking back pain induced tears. "At least I think I did. It's been a while since I spoke French."

He leaned his hooded head against the wall with a thud and closed his eyes. Fernando had insisted on paying for the hotel suite, afraid that had the

Angel been left to choose the room, they would all be in a closet somewhere. Annoyed at the inference, he had walked away, letting the Noble speak his antiquated French to the concierge. Standing now in the hallway to the sunlight littered room, he realized he should have stayed and done the talking.

"Is there something wrong with the room, *mademoiselle et monsieur?*" called the young man in the middle of the room.

Jeanie glanced at the two Chosen hiding behind the wall and realized the problem immediately. Stepping into the large brilliant room, she sought a way to cast the palatial suite into darkness and found it. On either side of the windows heavy yellow and green brocade drapes were arranged tastefully tied back with golden ropes ending in long flowing tassels.

She glanced back at the confounded bellhop. "Is there a way t' close the drapes?" she asked.

Brown brows drew together over young pockmarked skin, clearly unable to understand her thick Scot's accent. "Pardon?"

Releasing an infuriated huff at the language barrier, Jeanie raised her voice. "Anyone care t' translate?"

Fernando opened his mouth to give it a try and closed it at seeing the Angel shake his head.

"The lady asked if there was a way to close the drapes," the Angel explained smoothly in French, pitching his voice to carry into the room.

"You could have told me you spoke French." Fernando rolled his eyes in annoyance. "Hell, you speak it better than me."

"Your French is three centuries out of date," he explained. "Perfect for the sixteen and seventeen hundreds, but it's stilted by today's standards."

"And you would know, how?" sneered the Noble.

"Experience," his voice darkened.

"What did he say?" called Jeanie from the room, adding to the tension. "Who?"

He heard her huff in exasperation. "The bellhop. Weren't ye listenin'?"

From the hallway he asked the bellhop to repeat himself and explained. "He said that you untie the cords. Once both sets of drapes are released there is a chain right at the back. You pull it and it will draw the drapes together." He heard the bellhop speak again and then step around the room. "He's going to show you how."

Slowly, the dim light flooding into the hallway diminished. Glancing at the Noble who had stepped away from the doorframe, he followed suit and found the hotel suite to be blissfully blackened. The only light that filtered in came through the edges and that was manageable. It also allowed for more than enough detail of the gold and yellow wallpaper to jump out at them. The vaulted ceiling sported a magnificent crystal chandelier that used electricity to power its massive bulbs. A large fireplace along the left side lay dormant, but the wood neatly stacked beside and in the hearth promised wondrous warmth on a cold night. A hallway off to the left beside the fireplace led to one of the bedrooms and en suite baths, another hallway off the right of the parlour led to the master bedroom and accessories. It was indeed a magnificent suite and he wondered how much Fernando paid for the privilege of staying in such quarters.

The Noble seemed quite at ease in such luxuriant accommodations as he stripped off his cape with a flourish and hung it in the closet to the right of the door. "This will do nicely," he nodded, taking in the room as if appraising whether it was good enough for one such as he.

"Will that be all?" nervously ventured the bellhop, realizing the one who had spoken to him was the one who frightened him.

Not daring to disclose his features to the nervous young man, he nodded and replied, "Yes, thank you." He heard Fernando fall into one of the plush chairs with a sigh.

The bellhop glanced at the unusual guests and picking the least ominous, he walked over to Jeanie and gave her the two keys to the suite and all but ran to the door.

"Remember," called the Noble in his stilted French, halting the young man's progress, "we're not to be disturbed for any reason. If we need anything, we'll let you know."

"*Oui, monsieur*," squeaked the bellhop. Grabbing the door handle, he pulled it shut as he left the strange hotel guests in the most expensive room in all of Calais. He did not even wait for a tip.

Suitcases neatly lined against the wall next to the closet, the Angel unhooked his cloak and lifted it off his shoulders, following Fernando's actions by placing it in the closet. Taking Jeanie's coat from her, he did the same and watched her as she sat on the couch with a fatigued groan and began to untie her shoelaces. The silence between the three of them grew until he realized Fernando's steady glare on him.

"Och, that's much better," sighed Jeanie, rubbing her stocking feet. Without looking up at the Noble sitting across from her, she continued abashedly, "I wanna thank ye for catching me."

A dark brow lifted in mild surprise and then lowered as he nodded. Fernando had not expected the mortal girl to state her appreciation. Her acerbic attitudes towards him left Fernando wondering if she had any civility in her. Now it seemed Notus' housekeeper could show some level of decorum.

Not to be outdone he replied curtly, "You're welcome. It was just instinct. Mortal chivalries haven't been divested from me yet."

Jeanie's eyes narrowed. She had stated her thanks and the vampire's reaction needled her. It seemed that no matter what the Noble said, it was some sort of personal attack. Opening her mouth to reply, she jumped at the sound of leather encased wood and metal hitting the table between them.

Before them, the Angel's sheathed sword laid the length of the cherry wood table. She met Fernando's surprised brown eyes and they both looked up at the Angel standing tall above them, his eyes flashing in a mask of nonexpression before he turned to go down the hall.

"Where do you think you're going?" called the Noble, angrily as he leaned forward. "We need to talk."

"If the two of you are going to continue sniping at each other, I would prefer to be away from it," he replied turning in the hall to face them.

Jeanie's chagrined expression was not lost on him and in that instant he wanted to console her, but the pettiness between mortal and Chosen had to stop.

Fernando's eyes widened with the realization that the Angel was going to leave him alone with Jeanie.

"What? And ruin the fun we've been having?"

Fernando glanced back at the girl and smiled at his joke. It was not returned.

"Okay. Fine." He sat back, arms across his chest.

"Jeanie?" ventured the Angel, hoping that she would follow suit.

Glancing between the man she loved and the one she loathed, she smiled. If it were meant as a joke, which she seriously doubted, she would take it as a joke.

"But I dinna get t' make him angry yet," she grinned.

Fernando's eyes widened in shock and let out a bark of laughter.

A tenuous peace established between the Noble and Jeanie, the Angel walked back into the elegantly decorated parlour and sat down on the sofa beside Jeanie. If Fernando wanted to talk, he would listen.

Recognizing that he now had the floor, Fernando uncrossed his arms. He would not look into the Angel's eyes. It was easier to do so when the tall pale Chosen was cloaked. Having him so close and obviously choleric made Fernando edgy, especially after what Bridget had told him.

The shipping note slipped into his hand as he reached into his vest pocket and he carefully opened it and laid it on the table beside the sword. He had never seen the Angel carry one before and had thought he had seen its outline under the vampire's cloak, but having it prominently displayed slammed home verification of the Angel's warrior status. The hilt looked incredibly old and worn, but its workmanship was not lost on the Noble as he realized that there was about five feet of sheathed steel. He pondered how used the sword appeared.

Fernando shook that notion off and brought his attention back to the situation at hand. "This little piece of paper landed me with a headache the size of which I hadn't experienced since I was mortal," he stated, waiting for some sort of derogatory remark. When none was forthcoming, he continued. "Before I was knocked out I watched barrels of the spice being loaded onto the *Kaleidoscope*. That ship is here when its paperwork stated it's supposed to be going to La Coruna, Spain, which means we're on the right trail. The problem we have now is to find V. Corneilli & Sons, Shipping & Receiving's office and there is no address on this." He leaned back waiting for a reply. "We need to find out who is ordering these herbs.

We know it's coming from Calais and to find out who, we need to see the original shipping orders."

The prospect of searching through Calais to find V. Corneilli & Sons slumped the Angel's shoulders. Calais was a large city. It was not as populated as London, but it was a booming port and that meant spending precious time searching. With only the night, it could take even longer.

"I'll go," said Jeanie.

"What?" Jeanie's offer surprised the Angel and he turned to face her and met with a determined expression.

"I'll go find the office." Jeanie leaned over and picked up the paper before reaching for her shoes.

"You can't go," he stated in disbelief at the same time Fernando said, "Great." He glared at the Noble.

"She's perfect," replied Fernando, refusing to look at the fiery eyes. "After all you're the one who said having Jeanie along will allow us to get things done during the day."

He sat up straight as if slapped. He had said those words but he did not mean to place her in danger. Sending Jeanie to the shipping house was like sending a mouse covered in milk into a crate full of cats.

"Fernando's right," agreed Jeanie. "It'll save time and it'll allow me to get something t'eat." She slipped on one shoe, lacing them up.

Disbelieving that Jeanie and Fernando were actually agreeing on something, he found that he was on the other end and he did not know what to do.

Fernando turned to face Jeanie, a half smile of approval on his face. He had not expected her to volunteer her efforts. "Just go and find the office. Don't go in. Be discreet and come back. If you find it today we'll take care of things tonight." He stood up, stretched and walked down the hall to the bedroom.

Jeanie nodded and finished tying the bow on the other shoe. She was not looking forward to leaving at this moment, but she was famished and at least she would be able to help. Anything to get the Good Father back sooner rather than later was better than sitting around waiting. What she could not bear to see was the distress on the Angel's face.

"One more thing," came Fernando's voice as he re-entered the parlour once more. "Jeanie, if you wouldn't mind?" He held out his arm in an inviting way towards the bedroom.

Intrigued by the use of her name, Jeanie rose and strode down the hall with the Noble in her wake. The bedroom door stood ajar, morning sunlight spilling into the hall. A smile quirked her lips as she entered the grandiose bedroom brilliantly illuminated with warm radiance. It did not take her long to untie the drapes and draw them together. Fernando would also have the extra protection of the drapes hanging from the canopied bed and she wondered what the master bedroom looked like.

"Thank you," said Fernando, stiffly, as she exited.

"Consider us even," she smiled as she walked back into the parlour.

Fernando watched Jeanie's shapely form retreat. Sniffing in amusement, he shook his head, entered the room and closed the door, a kernel of respect for the mortal girl developing.

He sat on the couch, the knot of worry tying itself tighter in his gut, as he watched Jeanie emerge from the hallway leading to Fernando's room. Whispers of russet and copper hair snuck out of the bun she had twisted it into at the nape of her neck, framing her tired face in soft tones. He had to stop her from doing this foolish task. Jeanie's help in obtaining passage to Calais was one thing, but sending her to find the office was too dangerous. Oathbound or not, he could not allow her to fall into danger, not again. Rising from his seat, he followed her down the other hall to the master suite.

The door opened at her turn of the gold and crystal knob, spilling bright sunlight into the hall. He should have expected it, but his thoughts of sending Jeanie out in a foreign country to look for the den of their enemies distracted him. He gave a gasp as he leapt back out of the direct light, taking shelter towards the end of the hall.

"Are ye alright?" she called, turning around to face him. Genuine concern washed over her features. She wanted to see the master bedroom before she headed out for breakfast and to search for the office. Never having been in such a grand place, she wanted to check out every nook and cranny. She felt a little kid again off on an imaginary treasure hunt and this time she wanted to find the treasure for real.

Nodding, he watched through squinting watery eyes as she entered the room. After a moment or two, darkness prevailed and he followed.

The master bedroom was grand, much larger than the entirety of his flat. The king sized curtained canopy bed sat against the far wall, its drapery open on the side facing him. Across from the bed, against the opposite wall, a large fireplace with a mahogany mantle was set with wood, ready for a match to be lit. A writing desk large enough to make Notus shake with envy sat beside the entrance to another hallway that ran back the way they came but along the curtains blocking the sunlight.

Jeanie popped her head out from the hall, an ecstatic smile of wonder on her face.

"Ye should see the bathroom!" she exclaimed, coming to stand beside the Angel next to the bed. "It's huge! And there's a closet that's bigger than the Good Father's room."

Her smile was infectious and he placed his hands on her shoulders, fingers brushing against the loose strands of hair. Oh how he loved to feel the softness of her cinnamon curls. He could understand her excitement at being housed in such luxury, as it was his first time as well. Notus tended to travel much more modestly. They would be most comfortable in the suite, though it appeared the bed was smaller than the one custom built for him back home.

"Ye'll be fine while I'm gone?" she asked, reaching up to caress his face when she saw the slight smile fall to a frown.

Pulling away from her embrace, he stepped back towards the bed. A sly smile played on her face for a brief moment believing something more nefarious might occur before she left until she caught the worried look in his eyes.

"Jeanie, you can't go," he stated matter-of-factly. He did not mean to make his tones harsh, but what was done was done.

Incredulous green eyes widened and then narrowed. "What d'ye mean? Of course I'm goin'," she blurted. "That's why I'm here, aren't I? T'help."

"Of course you're here to help, Jeanie." He took a step towards her, but she pulled back. "But it's too dangerous."

"To find an office?" Jeanie could not believe what she was hearing. Her heart began to hammer in outrage. "Dinna ye trust me?"

"Of course I do," he said, his voice rising to match hers. "How can you ask that of me? I've trusted you more than *anyone* in my life. It's *them* I don't trust." He shook his head, exasperated.

"I'll be fine, Gwyn." Her voice took on a hard edge. "I've taken care of myself before, ye ken that."

"Like when you were captured?" He knew he should not have brought up the topic, but he had to hammer in the point. Going and finding a ship to sail is a world of difference than going to the lion's den to find out who the tamer is.

Jeanie's mouth opened and closed in outrage before she found her voice. She could not believe he was using that as an excuse. "How dare ye? That wasna my fault if I recall correctly. Yer the one who brought me home. Yer the one who told me t'get some sleep."

The pit of his stomach froze in realization that Jeanie believed it was his fault she had been captured and maybe she was right. Jaw tight, he swallowed. "Yes, and I'm the one who should have been there to protect you. But I wasn't. But now I can. You're not going."

Green eyes flashed in fury and she strode towards him and jabbed him in the chest with her forefinger. "I am and that's final." Turning, she stomped towards the door only to halt at finding him blocking her path. She had not seen him move. This time it did not surprise her. Crimson eyes glowed angrily.

"For Gods sake, Jeanie." He loomed over her. "You're in a different country with a different language and I can't be there to protect you. I can't trust that you'll come back safe."

"Och, that's it, isn't it?" She walked away towards the windows. "Even before I ken what ye were ye had me come along, but now ye think I canna do what is needed without ye protecting me?"

"Stop twisting my words, Jeanie. You know that's not what I'm saying." He stood beside the bed watching her beautiful face fill with anger.

"Then why am I here?" Her raised voice rang through the room. "Just to warm yer bed and take care of ye during the crossing?" She would not back down. This was of a deeper issue and she was going to root it out. "Yer problem is ye dinna trust no matter how much you say that ye do. Ye canna even trust that I'll come back. Hiding beneath yer cloak and the Good Father, yer more fearful of the world than anyone I've ever met. Sure ye may hae good reason, I heard what those people said about ye at the restaurant, and them no knowin' ye. But ye hide only allowin' none but the Good Father and me t'see ye—to ken who ye really are. And then no' fully. I'm sure that if it had been possible and Fernando hadn't shown me what he did ye'd still would hae hidden from me too."

The shots hit home and he took a step back as if slapped. Heart pounding, he shook his head.

She knew she should not have said anything about what had happened in the ship once she saw his face fall and his ruby eyes widen. "I trust ye. I just wish ye allowed yerself to trust as much as those that love ye, trust ye. Trust me with this. Ye canna do this. I'll come back. I promise." Pulling the drapes back flooded the room in sunlight. She had to make her second point and this was the only way.

Not fast enough to recognize her unbelievable intent he leapt back into the shaded darkness of the draped canopy bed. Eyes shut tight against the burning light; he felt his ankles begin to heat as the sunlight spilled under the drapes. Sitting heavily on the bed, he hugged his knees. He had not been this close to burning alive since he was wounded during the Crusades. This time the woman he loved caused it. Crushed that she could do such a thing to him; his breath caught as anger vied with the pain of such betrayal. A warm hand touched his face and he started. Drawing back from her touch, he opened his eyes, blinking in the brightness to behold her saddened, yet firm, expression.

She hated having to do this, knowing how much it would hurt him. Even with all his powers as a vampire he was so terribly limited by his inability to trust in himself, more so, without being able to go out during the day. That was why she was here. He needed to be reminded of it.

"Gwyn," she said softly gazing into his pain filled eyes as she touched his face. "This is why I'm here. Ye canna move around during the day—I can—and we need to get the Good Father back now, no' later. Trust me, please?"

Lowering his legs to a crossed position on the bed, he lifted her hand from his face and hid his eyes behind his cupped hands. His stomach clenched at the realization that she was right and no matter how timorous he felt at her solitary excursion he had to let her go. He felt her lips on his head.

"I love ye." She whispered, her head pressed against his. "I promise I'll be back well before night fall."

He looked up at her, their faces almost touching. Concerned green eyes gazed into his and she leaned in to kiss him. It was not what he wanted, but he would take what he could get and before he knew it Jeanie pulled away to gasp for breath. A small smile lifted her face.

Their hands lingered together as she stepped away until the sunlight captured her and forced him to drop his hand and his gaze. He heard her step across the Persian rug towards the door and knew if he did not say anything now he would regret it.

Daring to peer across the brightly lit room he called, "Jeanie, please be careful."

The dark fuzzy image that was Jeanie turned. "I will."

The sound of the door closing left him trapped on the island of darkness. He did not know if she had done that on purpose, but surmised that most likely she did so as to keep him from stopping her. Apprehension filled him and he knew he could not sleep yet. Horrific images of Jeanie being captured or worse flowed unwarranted. Unable to actively do anything about it, he pulled the heavy brocade drapery closed, cutting off as much of the sunlight as possible and damned himself for a fool. He should have asked her to close the window coverings. Now he was trapped on the island the canopied bed created.

With a resolute sigh he shifted over to the centre, sat, raked his hair back with his fingers and closed his eyes. He had no choice. He had to trust that Jeanie would be alright without him. He needed to believe that she would come back to him. She was strong, smart and beautiful, and he prayed that it would be enough. Unfortunately it did not halt the smouldering anger of being imprisoned on a dark island in the middle of a sunlit sea. The implication of her trust of him fuelled that hurt.

Taking several deep breaths, he relaxed enough to begin the meditative practices he so desperately needed. As he did so a thought blossomed in his mind, popping his eyes wide open. *Oh dear Gods, Fernando must have heard everything.*

The clean cool white linen sheets felt absolutely wonderful. This was a better room than he had expected and he loved the curtained canopy bed that now draped protectively around his supine form. Even the mattress supported him perfectly. Captain Richardson knew how to pick his hotels and Fernando promised that if ever he saw that American again he would thank him for the advice, and once all the craziness of the poisoning of the Chosen was over with he would have to bring Bridget here. Now that would be a nice well-deserved vacation.

A smile lifted his lips until he heard a commotion outside of his room. Closing his eyes, cutting off the view of the intricately carved wood canopy, Fernando concentrated on the noise. Surprise pulled his eyes open with the realization that it was the Angel in a heated argument with the girl.

The smile returned. It was the perfect opportunity to glean more hidden secrets, and the first he discovered was the Angel's name. No Chosen knew the Angel's name, and now he did. He closed his eyes in hungry anticipation to hear more confidential information.

He had never expected to hear such emotion from the Angel, or Gwyn, as Jeanie called him. The intensity of the lovers spat drew him and he listened in rapt attention until he heard one door close and then the front door slam with the tumble of the lock turning. Whatever Jeanie had done, she had won the fight with the Angel and walked out, presumably unscathed. The seed of respect he found he carried for the mortal girl took root. Not many mortals who argued with a vampire lived to see the next moment.

Shifting onto his side, Fernando smiled. He had learned more about the Angel than any other Chosen. Much of it still remained occluded in mystery. Why a Chosen would need to be taken care of during a Channel crossing made no sense to the Noble. It was the revelation of the name that could be used as currency with others of their kind.

What Fernando would keep to himself, for now, was the disclosure of the Angel's lack of trust towards, it seemed, everyone. The reasons, held in trust by Jeanie and the Angel's sire, were yet to be discovered. This was a mystery he would deliciously glean and then he would have more pull amongst the Chosen. Even if he could not discover who was poisoning them, the knowledge of the Angel's secrets would hopefully be enough to get Katherine to release his properties and holdings.

Yes, this would do just nicely, he thought, closing his eyes in the anticipation of some truly wonderful dreams.

XXV

The sun descended in a shocking blue sky, basking the city in unusual warmth for the end of October. Bird calls from lonely standing trees and high reaching eaves mingled with the bustle of the busy city. Men and women alike hawked their wares, pulling or pushing small carts along the cobbled road only to be forced out of the way by grand coaches hurrying to unknown destinations on large rimmed wheels. Patrons moved from storefront to storefront carrying parcels of newly imported delectables. Others hurried by foot to appointments. It was so much like London that Jeanie could not wipe the grin from her face, but the reason was the self-satisfaction that she had discovered the whereabouts of the office of V. Corneilli & Sons.

Despite the concerns the Angel and Fernando had about how long it would take, Jeanie had been pleasantly surprised to find the office was fairly easily. After leaving their hotel room she had found the concierge more than helpful. A few slowly spoken questions ended in her showing the grey haired gentleman the battered shipping note. Rising from his seat, he guided her to the restaurant and invited her to have breakfast while he personally looked into finding the address for *la mademoiselle*.

Feeling quite conspicuous eating alone at a table in the centre of the restaurant, Jeanie graciously accepted the meal that most individuals seemed to be oohing and ahhing over. Soon her moans joined in the chorus as she bit into the sausage. When the waiter brought her tea at the end of the meal she knew she had to find out what it was that she was eating. With gestures and stilted English he walked away nodding, leaving Jeanie with the distinct impression that he was placating her inability to speak the language.

It did not take long for Monsieur Legard to reappear, her shipping slip in hand. With a smile and a nod, he placed it on the table and she could see, written in a small precise hand, an address.

Beaming at the elderly concierge, Jeanie had tried her best to express her gratitude and was relieved when he returned her smile. Then he explained that the sausage she had thoroughly enjoyed was imported from Germany and their restaurant was the only one in Calais that had them. He was thrilled she had delighted in the breakfast.

Ear tips burning red, Jeanie had sipped the last of her tea as the waiter brought the bill. Not wishing to sign it to the room, she pulled out of her coat pocket the money that should have gone to Captain Richardson. Her eyes went wide at the amount and then looked at the bill. Biting her lip she realized she had to change the pound notes into francs and reluctantly signed the bill to the room with what she believed to be a sufficient tip. She hoped that Fernando would not begrudge her having a meal. If he did, then she knew the Angel would pay for her, again. It was a thought she did not relish despite her knowledge that he would not mind.

Leaving the hotel to the bright crisp early morning, Jeanie had delighted in having the doorman hail a cab for her. She was starting to feel high born with all the attention and assistance from the hotel staff. So used to being the menial help, having the tables turned so dramatically and unexpectedly made her head spin as the coach shuddered and bumped along the road.

The sound of the horse's hooves clicking against stone mingled with the city's awakening as its natives arose to greet the day. The rights of passage of their regular morning rituals brought them to the trials and tribulations of another day. Soon grandiose shop fronts and tenements gave way to the smell of salt and the decay of the sea front.

Gazing out the window, low squat buildings lined up beside one another. Simple painted signs marked some of them as offices and warehouses. Others sat darkly with windows painted black or boarded up. Coaches moved past, while men on bicycles rattled into the business area on their way to work. The crescendo of industry filled the air and it took a moment for Jeanie to realize that she was no longer moving.

Hand reaching to open the door, Jeanie sat back, shocked, when it opened of its own accord and a wooden step was placed down outside the lip of the door. Peering around, she saw the footman standing still and tall, his white gloved hand holding the door open. Gathering the skirt of her dress, she stepped down with the assistance of his steady hand. Heady with the royal treatment, Jeanie wondered if this was what Cinderella felt like and worried when would her coach turn back into a gourd and the horses into mice.

In English and with much gesticulation, Jeanie managed to convey to the driver that she wanted him to wait for her. Paper in hand, she timorously walked to the warehouse front, its sign proudly proclaiming in white-rimmed red lettering on a black background;

Karen Dales

V. Corneilli & Sons
Shipping & Receiving

She was in the right place. This was the source of the spice that was killing the vampires in London. This is where they had to go to find the information to get the Good Father back.

Standing before the office, she stared up at the striking sign. Fernando had told her to find the place and come right back. She had found it, but she wanted to do more despite the Angel's fears. Uncertainty filled her as she realized she did not know what to expect on the other side of the door, let alone what she would do if things turned for the worse. Placing her hand on the weathered brass doorknob, she gave it a turn. A gasp of surprise escaped her slightly parted lips as the black painted wooden door easily swung outwards, sending chimes ringing. Stepping into the dimly lit front room, the door closed behind her with a soft click.

The small front office was unoccupied, in the centre stood a large oak desk with piles of papers stacked neatly along one side while the rest was strewn with writing utensils and scattered note paper. Gloaming gaslight lit up the space with a slight orange glow exuded from sconces irregularly situated along sidewalls made up of large chalkboards. Schedules, shipments and the names of the conveyances from port to port and country to country stood out whitely against the black contrast. Along the back wall, filing cabinets stood row upon row only to be broken up by the single door, leading to the warehouse.

Suddenly the back door opened, admitting a middle-aged man in professional business attire of dark charcoal grey. His bald pate gleamed above the close cropped salt and pepper hair around his ears.

"*Est-ce que je peux vouz aider?*" he asked, staring at her from across the room.

Jeanie frowned, unable to understand the words but got the gist of the meaning. She had come this far and had no plan. Damning herself for a fool, she was about to turn and leave when a glimmer of an idea popped to mind. Pointing to herself, she said as clearly as her accent would allow, "English?"

Realization widened the man's steel grey eyes as he stepped towards the desk and sat down. The chair squeaked against the wooden floor. "*Oui, mademoiselle*, I speak English."

Left standing in the middle of the room, Jeanie felt at a disadvantage and hoped that her quickly spun excuse for being here would be convincing.

"Oh, thank heavens," she feigned, speaking slowly enough that hopefully he would understand. "My name is Jean Anne Stuart from the Aberdeen Stuarts. I have travelled from Scotland on behalf of my brother's hotel, to make contact in the hopes to set up importation of certain spices that seem to be receiving rave reviews in England."

She watched the man's grey brows draw together as he glowered. "What spices would that be?"

Uncomfortable by his piercing stare, Jeanie tried not to fidget as she pulled out the shipping order. "My brother was recently down in London visiting his holdings when he came across an establishment for dinner. After thoroughly enjoying himself on the best meal he'd ever had, the proprietor gave him this."

She passed the shipping note to the gentleman.

Taking the wrinkled paper in his well-manicured hand, he flattened it out on the desk before reading it.

Jeanie nervously watched as the man's jaw tightened and then relaxed as he let out his breath in a hiss.

"My brother and I are hoping to bring this spice to Aberdeen. He is so hoping to have his restaurant be the first to use these spices. We are hoping that your shipping firm would be able to direct us to the individual or the company to make such arrangements."

The chair made a grinding sound as the man pushed it back to stand, paper still in hand. "I'm sorry *mademoiselle*, you would have to speak to Mr. Corneilli for that information, and he is currently out of the country."

Shoulders slumped in disappointment, she frowned. "When do you expect him back?"

Turning towards the back door, he stated, "When Mr. Corneilli is finished with his business abroad." With that he disappeared into the back.

Left standing, abandoned, Jeanie stood with her mouth open at the sudden departure and the rudeness of the gentleman—if he could be called that. Releasing a huff of exasperation, she turned and exited the shipping office, pleased to quit the dark dreary place. It was when she climbed back into the carriage that she realized that he still had the shipping slip.

Turning unsteadily on the step to gaze back at the office, she thought to go back in to demand the paper. She dismissed it when she realized that she no longer needed it. She could bring the Angel and Fernando here, and would it not be a sight to see Mr. Pomp meet two vampires who will not take no for an answer.

The coach jerked into motion once she was settled and the door closed, carrying her away from the decaying fish smell and the monotony of the warehouses. Leaning back against the embroidered cushion, Jeanie smiled at her accomplishment and it was not even noon yet.

The coach dropped her off at the hotel where Monsieur Legard was more than happy to exchange some of her sterling notes to francs. Still excited from her encounter at the shipping house, Jeanie hoped that the Angel would not begrudge her for doing a little shopping before going back to their room.

The sun dipped down towards the west when Jeanie returned to the hotel, shopping bag in hand. Her exuberance in the beginning had faded over time with the encroaching fatigue from the lack of proper sleep. She had intended to return earlier to the hotel room and the Angel when guilt at what she had done to him worried itself into her consciousness.

It was the look on his face as he sat huddled, sunlight blazing all around the curtained bed, that forced a knot into her belly. She had never seen him like that. The only time he came close was when she had opened the curtains in Fernando's home, but she had not known what sunlight could do to him. Now she did and Jeanie could not believe what she had done and cursed herself, feeling deplorable.

She had demanded trust from him. Yelling at him that he did not trust her and then had the audacity to turn it around, throwing it back in his face after all that he had disclosed to her. All she wanted was to go out and help and she flooded sunlight into the room instead of talking with him. She had not trusted him enough to let her go and she hated herself for that.

How could she have done such a thing to the man she loved? The knot grew larger, fed by guilt and self-loathing. She needed to apologize and prayed that he would forgive her, but fear of his rejection slicked the knot in a thick coat of ice. Jeanie would understand it if he turned away from her, but it did not stop the trepidation she felt as the key turned in the door and she stepped into the suite. She could not lose him. Not now. Not ever. The lock clicked as the door closed behind.

Placing the bag down on a chair, Jeanie shrugged out of her coat and sat down to take off her shoes. She knew she was stalling, but her feet were killing her. Standing up, she took a deep steadying breath and walked in stocking feet to the room she hoped to share with the Angel.

Hand on the crystal doorknob, Jeanie swallowed hard as she opened the door with trembling hands. Sunlight flooded the room. Guilt redoubled as she rushed in a panic to close the curtains against the afternoon light, her heart racing in her ears. It was only when the room plunged into muted darkness that she released the breath she did not realize she held. Head lowered, she anxiously walked to the bed as if it were the executioner's block. Every instinct in her screamed to run away as her hand shook. Taking hold of the thick brocade drapery, she pulled it back, not knowing what to expect.

Her breath caught. Crimson eyes pierced hers as she took in the full view of him lying diagonally on the bed, propped up on his side to glare at her. His alabaster hair cascaded and disappeared against the crisp whiteness of the pillow. His clothes lay at the end of the bed and she knew he was nude beneath the sheet and blanket. A blush of heat rose to her face and was instantly squashed at the hurt and anger burning in his eyes. It was clear he was waiting for her to say something.

Jeanie opened her mouth and found the words had dried up at the intensity of his gaze. She had seen him angry before, but never before had his blood red glare shook her to the core. Closing her mouth, she swallowed in the hopes to find her voice.

"I'm—I'm so sorry," she stammered, pulling her gaze away from his to stare through watering eyes at the patterns of green and gold of the bed curtain playing around her fingers. It was too horrible to see such a look on his beautiful face and she knew he was the Angel again. The couch was starting to look comfortable and she went to close the drape. She would take back the present she had bought him.

She heard the soft rustling of the sheets as he moved in the bed and jumped at the touch of his hand covering hers, halting her motion.

"Jeanie, look at me," he ordered, his voice stern, yet soft.

She looked up at him, his face so close to hers that she could feel his breath. The coverings pooled around his waist and she felt a flush of heat at the sight of him. Broad shoulders tapered to a slender waste revealing a long supple strength. The scar on his arm added to the mystery and gave him an added sense of danger. He was so beautiful. She felt him squeeze her hand and she snapped her focus to his eyes. The anger was still there, but mixed with it was haggard sadness. Jeanie damned herself for having put that there.

"Don't ever do that to me again." His voice shook with emotion, drawing her closer. "I've trusted you with not only my life, but Notus' too. I've given you more than any other person in a thousand years. I don't want to regret placing that trust in you. I love you, Jeanie." The anger flooded out of his face, leaving only sadness that took Jeanie's breath away with a gasp.

The image of him wavered and Jeanie realized tears cascaded down her face. "I'm sorry," she repeated over and over until he held her tight against his firm body.

Her face against his smooth chest, Jeanie could smell cotton and something else that sent a wave of desire through her body. Lifting her head, his strong hands cupped her face, thumbs brushing away the tears and she sighed when his soft lips found hers. Tension leaked out as she felt his urgency to explore her, to consume her, heart pounding as her body flared in desire. Jeanie opened her mouth in invitation, giving in to her need and fulfilling his desire to devour her.

Feeling her arms go round him, she sent a shudder through him as her fingers lightly danced on the scars on his back, his hair entangling around her fingers. A low growl escaped from his throat and he renewed his urgency. She sighed, delighting in his exploration. Soft lips trailed urgent kisses across her jaw-line until he found the hollow beneath her ear and followed it along her neck. Jeanie gasped as she felt him tease the sensitive skin. Sharp teeth brushed delicately over the throbbing vessel, sending shockwaves of need through her body.

With a cry of self-denial, she felt him pull away. The promise of more suddenly cut short, leaving her panting and disappointed.

His pupils were wide with need and she could hear his rapid breathing as he tried to regain control.

"Oh Gods, Jeanie," he cried, closing his eyes. "You smell so good."

Jeanie smiled and remembered that the lady in the store had allowed her to try some of the expensive perfume that she had eventually bought. After that kiss, she had no doubt that she was forgiven.

"Thank the Gods you came back." He opened his eyes and settled back down to sit on the bed. "I was so worried." Jeanie had not even noticed he had risen up to his knees to kiss her. Now she did, taking in the full sight of him and her heart skipped before beating faster. She did not doubt that he heard it.

"I found the place," she whispered thickly, unable to take her eyes off of him.

Crimson eyes went wide at her admission. "You did?"

Jeanie nodded, a smile blossoming at his surprise. "'Twas easy. The man at the desk had their address."

Finely shaped white brows furrowed as he looked past her to the curtained windows. "Then what took you so long?"

"I'll show ye." Taking the invitation to get the present, Jeanie turned and all but ran back to the front room to grab the parcel, her feet barely touching the ground. His confused shout of her name followed.

The finely decorated paper bag felt light in her hand as she ran back into their bedroom and her smile brightened further at seeing him sitting on the edge of the bed with one pant leg pulled up over a pale foot, his long thick hair draping down one side of his face.

"Ye dinna hae t'get outta bed," she beamed and bounced onto the bed beside him.

Stupefied by her reappearance, he let the trousers drop and kicked it off as he scooted back in the bed to make room for her.

"I hope ye dinna mind," she said, pulling out the two small boxes from the bag. Her grin widened at his confusion. "I still had the money ye gave me, so after lunch I bought these."

Opening the first box, Jeanie lifted the small crystal bottle with a fluted neck. Inside amber liquid gleamed. Etched on the outside, a flourish script *'Vamp'* read clearly, white against the golden liquid. A single white brow rose at the name on the bottle. With a mischievous grin, Jeanie opened it, releasing the scent of roses and sandalwood mixed with something indefinable into the air.

Jeanie watched the Angel's eyes go round.

"What is that?" he gasped as he took hold of the tiny bottle. Breathing deeply, he closed his eyes with a shudder.

Enthused by his reaction and afraid that he would spill the expensive contents; Jeanie took back the bottle and stoppered it. "The lady at the perfume shop said that this was all the rage in Paris and let me try some. When I saw the name, I knew I had to buy it. I hope ye like it."

"Like it?" His eyes popped open in wonder and she could see barely controlled hunger and desire fill his eyes. "It makes me want to devour you.

Do you have any idea how hard it was for me to stop?"

"Then ye like it, eh?" she grinned.

"Gods yes." He leaned forward to kiss her, giving into his desire.

Slipping out of his reach with a smile, the larger box in her hand, Jeanie poised it before him. "I bought this for ye."

Taken aback at the unexpected reaction, the Angel stared at the red and black stripped box and took it from her. No titling marked its surface and she watched in growing pleasure as his long, elegant fingers pulled back the folds to reveal a large glass bottle with reddish brown liquid inside. Freeing the cork, cinnamon mixed with a dark earthy scent filled the room.

Jeanie watched him frown, perplexed at the lubricous liquid. It was clearly not cologne.

"What is this?" he asked, rubbing the oily substance between his fingers.

"Here, I'll show ye." Placing her perfume down on the night table, she released her hair from its bun, pleased at the wide-eyed expression on the Angel's face as her hair fell in waves, ringlets smoothed out.

This was what she was waiting for and she enjoyed the growing passion on his face as she rolled down her stockings and tossed them off. The clasps on her dress were harder to undo, but she managed until she was standing only in her shift.

"Give me that and lie down." She held out her hand with a mischievous smile.

He placed the bottle in her hand, his brows furrowing. "Why?"

"Ye said ye trust me," she beamed, "trust me now."

Curiosity won out and he lay down, his head on the pillow, never taking his eyes off her.

"Och, no that way, silly." Jeanie placed his present on the table beside her perfume and jumped onto the bed beside him. "On yer belly."

She watched his eyebrows shoot up in surprise before he languidly rolled over, sweeping his hair out his face to look up at her. "Now what?"

This was what she wanted once the nice sales lady showed her the oil. To see him laid out on the bed awaiting her touch caught her breath until she realized his feet were dangling off the end of the bed. Suppressing a giggle at the sight, Jeanie brought her attention to his quizzical gaze and smiled. Taking up the bottle, she poured a little into her cupped palm and placed the bottle back down. Cinnamon and dark loam scented the air as she rubbed the oil between her hands.

"Ye seemed to like it when I rubbed yer shoulders back home. I think ye'll like this."

Her hands heated at the oils touch and she laid her hands on his back.

With strong long strokes she distributed the oil across his back, stopping only to brush stray silky white hairs out of the way. She watched his pale complexion take on a more rosy tone as the tint of the oil slicked his skin, warming it beneath her hands. She heard and felt his shuddering sigh, and smiled as his eyes fluttered closed.

Jeanie's fingers slid over tense muscles, willing them to relax. Stubborn knots broke apart as she worked deeply between his shoulder blades, her thumbs and fingers gliding with the oil. She smiled when she heard him groan in a pleasure mixed with pain as her fingers found sensitive spots along the scapula.

She trailed her fingers carefully down and around the scars on his back and felt him tense at the touch. She whispered for him to relax. The word seemed to have a magical effect and she watched his shoulders lower as he exhaled. The skin of the scars felt feathery soft, hiding bunches of knots under and around them. Gently, so as not to cause him to tense up again, she spent time coaxing the muscles to release. Those she could not, she had to resign to a gradual loosening.

She loved the feel of him beneath her fingers as she trailed lower, relaxing the muscles as if by the magic touch of her hands. His skin was soft and smooth, flawless despite the scars. She could not deny her own growing response to him as she worked lower. Every part of him was a product of his life before he was Chosen.

One that must have been verra hard, she thought finding only long lean muscle.

Replenishing the oil, Jeanie worked on his legs, enjoying how her fingers trailed down the slight grooves that delineated the muscles. Taut muscles relaxed and Jeanie could feel the athletic strength hidden in them. When it came to working on his feet Jeanie had to move off the bed and smiled as another groan of pleasure came from the head of the bed.

Pleased, she finished and stood up to walk around to the side of the bed. Sitting down beside his prone form, she brushed some loose strands from his forehead. She watched his eyes slowly open, a sleepy relaxation glazing them, and he smiled.

"That was incredible," he sighed.

"I'm no finished yet," she grinned. "Roll over."

"I don't think I can," he said, his voice muffled as he buried his face in the pillow. Pale arms tightened around the pillow, hugging it so as to anchor him.

Jeanie chuckled. This had gone better than she had hoped. "If ye dinna turn over I wilna be able to finish."

With a groan of effort, he rolled onto his back, his eyes catching hers, returning her grin with lips closed. She loved the way he stretched, arms reaching for the ceiling before lowering them to lightly rest his hands against his trim muscular abdomen.

Picking up the bottle, Jeanie poured some more of the wonderful oil into her hand and smoothed it over his marred thigh, enjoying the sight of his naked trust. With a single passing she could feel that the muscles beneath the skin felt wrong, out of place. The scar was large and puckered. Where the scars on his back felt soft and thin, the one on his leg was rough and ugly. Finding a tight mass, she dug her in her thumbs in an attempt to work out the tension.

He yelped, his hand crashing against hers, causing her to jump. Jeanie lifted her head to see he was sitting up, his face close to hers, and her hands dropped to her sides.

His disconcerted expression was fixed on his leg before bringing his gaze to land on her. "That hurt," he whispered, shaking his head, sending white strands waving. "That shouldn't have hurt."

Jeanie's mouth opened in surprise. "I'm sorry. I dinna mean to."

Pinched facial features relaxed. "I know, Jeanie." He reached out to caress her face, still clearly concerned. "It's just that it's been centuries since I've felt even a twinge." His soft whisper carried a sense of seriousness she did not understand.

"I'll just continue elsewhere, then?" she seductively asked, needing to change the topic.

He met her eyes, nodded, and lay back down, a lazy grin lifting his lips as he watched her. Jeanie did not need to be a mind reader to sense what he was thinking. Massaging him had warmed not only her hands, but she was not finished yet. With a final dollop of oil in her left hand, Jeanie hiked up her shift with the other and straddled him. This was part of the massage she had a feeling he was going to enjoy the most.

With a shuddering sigh, he closed his eyes, and she felt him stir beneath her.

"I think I like your surprises," he mumbled.

Rubbing her hands together, she placed them on his chest and began the long strokes to distribute the oil. Her hands glided over the skin of his smooth chest and abdomen, delighting her as she felt the contours of each muscle before running her hands down his sides,   feeling the ribs beneath. She heard his breath catch as her hands gently grazed over his nipples, feeling them erect under her careful ministration.

Oh how she wanted to have her lips discover what her hands had found and she leaned over. Cinnamon waves cascaded over to caress his skin and she felt his breath catch as she placed her lips at the base of his collarbone, the shift in movement causing her to lie fully onto top of his firm body. She set her arms to his sides, supporting her weight as the cinnamon oil fired her lips.

Slowly, meticulously she worked lips and tongue across and down, feeling his breath come in halting gasps at each pull of his skin. She wanted to devour him, draw him into the centre of her being and keep him there. She moaned when her mouth found his, his fingers entangling themselves in her hair. This time she was the invader and she opened her mouth, finding him willing to allow for her exploration.

He tasted faintly of metal and though not entirely unpleasant, it was still a surprise. She pressed further, tongues caressing until she felt the needle sharpness of his teeth. The promise of what those teeth could do pulled her back and she lifted her face from his.

Crimson eyes wide and dilated, his breath heavy, the need for her naked on his face, Jeanie knew she wanted what he offered without hesitation. It was the promise of ecstasy that drove her as each kiss kindled a fire that shot to her groin, driving a moan from her lips. Her need for him consumed her and she sat up, impaling herself on his rigid member with a sigh until she could not take any more. The suddenness of her movement drove a cry from his lips, urging her on as she slowly rocked.

Eyes closed, head thrown back, shocks of pleasure trembled her body. Each thrust drove a cry from her as she tried to take him deeper with herself. She wanted all of him and he did not begrudge her desires.

A shift in position made her gasp and she found herself gazing up at him. Strong pale arms wrapped around her, guiding her movements. Bending his head, his lips a butterfly's touch against hers as his hair spilled to caress her face. Reaching up, she brushed his hair from their faces and trailed deep kisses along his jaw, tasting him with her tongue. There was no roughness, just soft smooth skin.

He cocked his head to the side, allowing Jeanie to work herself down as they moved together. She found the pulsing vessel in his neck and kissed, pulling at the skin, grazing it with her dull teeth. She knew what this would do to him and was rewarded with a growl. His thrust went deep, forcing a gasp to escape her lips.

His movements became more urgent within her and she moaned, her mouth against his neck. Jeanie wanted all of him. Each thrust causing her to tighten in the precursor of exquisite release. Teasing the sensitive spot on his neck, she suckled and then bit not caring that he had told her not to do this.

His deep shuddering cry brought her head up and she stared into his eyes, their bodies fully entwined. The ruby iris was nearly gone against the dark blood red of his pupils and she instantly knew she had pushed him too far. Fear percolated up. She wanted to move, but she could not tear her eyes away from his and realized his hand pinned her.

He moved beneath her, never taking his eyes off of her. Each thrust found their limit, igniting her in pleasure borne pain that threatened to steal her soul. Her breath came in gasps matched by his, and she felt her head tilted back. She could not move except for what he allowed and she wanted it all, everything that he could give her.

Needle sharp teeth grazed against her neck and then sank deep within in unison with his thrust, breaking skin. Her cry of release rocked her body, shuddering, feeling his orgasm deep within, matching her own. Each pull on her blood renewed the never-ending spasms and she held him tightly, never desiring to let go as she rode each intoxicating wave.

Suddenly, she was sent flying backwards to land bouncing against the bed. Shocked and confused, the moment completely shattered, Jeanie rolled over in a tangle of sheet and blankets and got to her knees, her shift twisted around her legs.

Pain and terror contorted his beautiful face. His body tensed and curled as he sat on the edge over the bed, a spasm of agony ripping through him.

Something was horribly wrong. Scrambling over the covers, Jeanie knelt beside him afraid to touch him as another paroxysm twisted him.

"Oh my God! Gwyn, what's wrong?" she yelled, panicked.

His eyes squeezed tight as his body seized again. Once past, he opened his eyes and she realized he could not catch his breath. His pleading gaze froze her to the core, ripping into her heart. She did not know what was wrong. She did not know what to do.

Another seizure racked his body and she watched in horror as his eyes rolled back and he fell limply to the floor. Her scream rang deafly in her ears as she rushed to his side, tears streaming down her face.

The bedroom door slammed open, its crystal handle shattering as it embedded in the wall behind. Fernando stood wearing only his black silk robe, its hem swung against his bare calves, one hand on the doorframe, the other on the remaining knob. Dark brown waves normally neat and tidy now gave evidence of disrupted sleep.

Jeanie jumped at the bang, her eyes wide at seeing the Noble's face twisted with concern and rising anger.

"What the hell happened?" roared Fernando, taking quick steps into the bedroom to kneel beside the prone Angel, his dark hand looking for a pulse and finding none.

Jeanie shuffled back on her knees, pushed out of the way. Fernando turned to glare at her after taking quick stock of the situation, his large brown eyes filled with menace.

"What did you do?" The threat in his tone was explicit through his clenched jaw.

She had not expected the Noble to come into the room. Now he was here, maybe, just maybe he could help. After all he was a vampire.

Hiccoughing back her sobs, Jeanie stammered, "I dinna ken." She shrunk into herself as the brown eyes bore into her, filling her with fear. "One moment—"

"I know that!" spat Fernando, sneering. "I can smell it." Jeanie paled. Ignoring her, Fernando pressed, lifting her up by her upper arms until they were standing. "Answer my question."

"I dinna ken," sobbed Jeanie. Her arms throbbed painfully, her hands pressing against soft silk. Fernando was supposed to know what to do.

His eyes drove into her and she felt the tension leak from her legs, leaving them rubbery and unable to withstand her weight. He caught her before she could fall. Heart hammering in her chest, Jeanie watched his gaze slide down to her neck. Fear redoubled and she futilely tried to break from his grasp. His hand gripped hard enough to make her gasp. She stumbled as one hand released her arm and brushed the mark on her neck.

The sensation sent her trembling. She could not pull her gaze from his.

Drawing his hand away from her neck, a glistening red bead quivered on his index finger. Jeanie watched in horror as he brought the taste of her blood to his lips. Never taking his eyes off of her, he licked the red jewel, testing its bouquet.

Brown eyes flashing darkly were the only precursor to the pain of being slammed up against the wall. Blackness popped in her vision as her head bounced against the paper covered plaster. No longer supported by Fernando's iron grip Jeanie slumped to the ground, her tears momentarily halted by the stunning action.

"You stupid little bitch," roared Fernando, bearing down on her. "You're contaminated. You poisoned him."

Realization widened Jeanie's eyes and dropped her jaw. This could not be happening. There was no way she could have eaten anything with the spice. It was in England. Not here. Not France. Wasn't it? She had not eaten anything with the spice mixture. It was being given out in soup kitchens and she did not eat there. Then she remembered the breakfast and she burst into tears. Those delicious sausages and the fact that the hotel knew the address of the shipping house, it was too late to put two and two together. She had poisoned the man she loved.

Scrabbling out from under Fernando's grasp, Jeanie made a mad dash across the floor. He could not be dead. She grasped his pale shoulder and gave it a rough shake, tears spilled down her face. "Please Gwyn, please, dinna be dead. Wake up, damn it."

She felt a presence next to her and she looked up to see through watery eyes, Fernando kneeling beside her, his jaw tight in restrained fury. "Is he?" She hated how small her voice seemed as she pleaded with the Noble.

"I can't tell." His voice slid through his sneer. "I'll get a knife. If he heals he's alive, if not..." He let the sentence hang as he stood.

Panic flared up. "No!" she exclaimed. Fernando could not use a knife on the Angel. If he were still alive it would burn him and that would give him away. She had promised to keep his secret. She released a heavy sigh as the Noble stood over her, his hatred burning.

"There must be another way," she implored.

Reluctantly, Fernando knelt back down. After shooting her another threatening glare he closed his eyes and took a deep breath. Jeanie had no clue what he was doing and flinched when his hand landed against the scarred back, his hand almost brown against the Angel's white skin.

"Back away," ordered Fernando, his eyes still closed. "I can't hear."

Clambering to her feet, Jeanie haltingly backed up until she felt the wall with a thump. She did not know what Fernando was doing, but if it meant that the Angel would live, she would do it.

An eternity pressed forward and she forgot to breathe. Jeanie watched in silence as the Noble knelt over the Angel with eyes closed, his face tight in concentration. Without warning Fernando opened his eyes, turned the

Angel over and scooped him up only to be placed onto the bed.

Jeanie sucked in a deep breath and took a cautious step forward. The Angel lay askew on the bed, his hair splayed over and around his face. Fernando turned to her, bearing down on her and she scampered back up against the wall, terror billowing up.

"You are a very lucky mortal." She could hear the contempt in his whisper. His breath feathered against her face. Jeanie could not tear her frightened gaze from his. "He's alive—barely. If he were dead, you would be too."

Finding a spark of courage, Jeanie needed to know. "Why d'ye care?"

He leaned forward, his face inches from hers. "He's Chosen. You're not." He stepped away from her and stopped as he reached the door. "Not to mention you foolishly nearly cost me a valuable partner. Next time you eat remember this: if he dies, the Good Father you care about dies too."

Jeanie watched in horrific realization as the Noble left the bedroom. Running to the bed, she collapsed to her knees and clutched the Angel's pale cold hand to her face as she wept.

XXVI

The bathwater luxuriated against her skin. Her dark brown hair hung in water-plastered ropes against her face as she stared up to the shadowed ceiling. Opalescent bubbles glittered in the candle light, making musical pops as the tension left their skin. Smiling, she closed her eyes enjoying the relaxation her nightly constitutional always brought her. The only thing that was missing was the songs of her little bird.

Languidly, she ran a petite hand down her face and neck to gently caress her breast. There would be no reaction. Her little bird was across the channel with Violet making sure that her flower blossomed with the responsibilities she bestowed.

She dropped her hand back into the water with a splash and opened her eyes. She had not imagined that she would miss Corbie, but now he had flown she could not wait for his return. The others were no match to his ability to run the operation. He was the perfect successor to the control of the British Isles when all was in place and the extermination of the Chosen complete. Then she would be able to make her journey home, leaving the cold dampness to warmer climates. There she would rule as a Goddess.

Gazing down at the dark waters, the bubbles all but gone, she called out to the woman waiting behind the door.

The dark stained wood door opened, revealing a young woman with mouse brown hair and small eyes.

"Lydia, if you would." She pointed to the blood red robe sitting folded on the vanity. It was hard to find good help.

With a bob of her head Lydia quickly traversed the red and black speckled tile. Snapping the robe open, she held it for her lady at the edge of the black enamelled tub.

Lifting out of the tepid water, she stepped out of the tub, allowing Lydia to gently wrap her as if she were a child. She did not like the fact that she had to look up at her body servant. She would have to have a little talk with her absent bird when he flew home.

Water dripped little puddles as she went to sit in front of her vanity. Silver combs and brushes lined perfectly against the red stained wood. Picking her favourite, she passed it to Lydia who carefully began to work out the tangles. Closing her eyes with enjoyment, she ignored the occasional tug. This was one thing that Lydia seemed to be able to do better than her little bird.

Opening her eyes, she considered her appearance in the mirror and smiled. She cocked her head to the side, studying Lydia's drawn grey face.

"Lydia, child, when was the last time you ate?" she asked. It was unusual for her to care about the well being of those beneath her. If Lydia were not seeing to her own needs, she would be unable to serve properly and that would mean termination. Something that she could ill afford to do until Corbie came back.

"A day or so, ma'am," replied Lydia, her voice quiet yet strong.

She frowned. "That's my Lady."

Grey eyes widened and then dropped to her task. "Yes, my Lady."

Dismissing Lydia's disconcertment with a wave of her hand, she continued. "Tomorrow night, before you come to me, make sure that you are fed. I will not have you falling apart because you did not eat. Is that understood, Lydia?"

Lydia dipped her head, a slight smile on her face. "Yes, my Lady."

"Good." She relaxed into Lydia's careful ministrations of her tresses. "Has there been any word from Mr. Vale?"

"No, my Lady." Lydia pulled at a stubborn tangle. "Nothing so far."

Her face twisted in disapproval. She had hoped some word would have traveled to her by now. This was taking far too long. Agitated by the news, she stood, surprising Lydia by taking the brush from her.

Making quick work, she walked out of the bathroom, Lydia trailing behind. A knock at the door halted her and she swung around as Lydia nearly walked into her.

"Don't just stand there," she barked. "Go see who it is."

Yes, she would definitely have to talk with Corbie about his choices for body servants.

Lydia quickly walked to the door, opening it slightly. Hushed tones were exchanged and then she closed the door, a manila envelope in her hand. With the same urgency, she swept over to her lady and handed the letter over.

She frowned at the lack of writing on the envelope. Turning it over, a large waxen red seal remained unbroken. Her eyes went wide at the impression. Slipping in a finger, she snapped the seal and pulled out the folded parchment. The thick vellum crinkled and her eyes went wide with the recognition at the flourished script. Snatching the paper to her breast, she harshly dismissed the body servant to the bedroom to make it ready. Once alone, she cautiously lifted the parchment and read:

My Dearest Bastia,

How long has it been since I have laid eyes upon you, O my daughter? I know I have been remiss in my care and treatment of you over these many years as I choose to carve a different path; one that has taken me across the globe in search of the answers you know the questions to, but enough of that.

I am not here to lament our disconnection but to speak of concerns rumours have brought to my sensitive ears.

Your war upon the Chosen must cease. I understand the reasons for this, my little cat, but there will be nothing to be gained in educating the Chosen to your existence. Their ignorance of you is your bliss. I wish you could see this for the truth, but alas, I know your heart.

It has also come to my attention that you have found the Angel and his Chooser. My congratulations. Long have I searched for them. Do not presume to drag them into your crusade. Leave them alone. Do not harm them, for the Angel, I pray, will have the answers I crave.

I am returning to London as quick as I may. I do not presume to usurp your position. That has never been my wish. I am coming to seek an end to my searching. If my seeking has availed me not due to the vengeance you are inflicting upon the Chosen, then take care. My wrath will be complete.

Leave the Angel and his Chooser alone*!*

Thanatos

Fear sparked anger bubbled up as she reread the letter. How dare he order her around? That time was long past. She scrunched the expensive paper into a tight ball, her knuckles whitening with tension. She would not give up the destruction of the Chosen because of him. She had set her own path and she would follow it through to the bitter end.

The image of Notus' mock crucifixion flashed a warning in her mind, coupled with Corbie's report of the Angel having followed Violet to the continent. A growing sense of self-preservation flooded her face. It was too late to leave the Angel and the Good Father alone, they were firmly ensconced in her machinations and if all went as plan they would be disposed of in a matter of a fortnight.

Damning Thanatos for his interference, she whirled around with a shriek, demolishing every breakable in her rage.

XXVII

ain.

It was the first sensation that returned to his rising consciousness. Each muscle, each tendon, was a pale reflection to the deep bone-burning ache that sent him gasping for relief. Even the act of breathing sent his head spinning with the rise and fall of his chest. Heart hammering in his ears, he dared not open his eyes. He did not know if he could. The only succour was the soft bedding and the goose down pillow, and even then he felt that he lay on stone.

His shallow breathing had loosened the tense band around his ribcage. He attempted a deep breath and felt it catch as the effervescent scent slammed into his body, pulling a groan through his rough, dry lips. A deep, gut-wrenching hunger shuddered through him, sending a stunning pain through his head.

Licking his lips in the attempt to moisten them, the fragrance escalated. He could almost taste the blood in the air. It drew him to take deeper inhalations in the attempt to feast upon the bouquet. The scent was not enough. He needed more. He needed to fill his mouth with the luxuriant taste, to feel its hot liquid burning his throat to ignite the centre of his being.

Hunting the source of his desires, his eyes fluttered open and instantly regretting the action. Bright candle flame glittered off the canopy like a million suns. He squinted into the reflected light and attempted to raise his hand to hide his face. The weight of his body made it near next to impossible.

A scuffle across the room poured the blood scent closer to him. It drove him to find its source so that he could drink from its magnificent font. With a groan of effort he shifted onto his side, waited for the room to cease spinning, and on shaking arms, lifted to sit. Muscles cried out in protest, making it clear that their choice would be to lie in the bed, but the intoxicating scent drove his hunger into action.

Looking through tousled locks he witnessed Jeanie's relieved approach with growing horror. It was her that he smelled, desiring to drain to her precious last drop. It was her that he wanted to rend apart with his teeth with animal ferocity. It was the woman he loved that forced his lips back over his sharp teeth, shuddering in the constrained attempt not to leap and devour her. Every fibre in his being called out to be satiated by her blood.

"Get out," he growled, trembling in anticipation and restraint.

Jeanie halted in her joyous approach, the blood draining from her pale, drawn face. Fear and anguish turned her eyes liquid and set her chin quivering.

He despised himself for the misery he evoked in her, but he had to save her from himself.

"Go!" he roared.

His heart broke as tears spilled down her beautiful face.

Turning on her heel, Jeanie fled the bedroom, her sobs filling the suite.

Wretched, he swung his legs over the side of the bed. Placing elbows on knees, he hunched over, head in his hands. Dishevelled locks cloaked his face. Daring to breathe deeply, he was rewarded with the retreat of Jeanie's scent, if not the sound of her sorrow. The terrible hunger still ached, demanding succour and he closed his eyes in an attempt to gain control.

The sound of a pop brought up his attention and he lifted his head. Fernando stood stoically before him, a green wine bottle in hand. A strange scent flitted up from the opened neck and he wrinkled his nose as his hunger flared to life. Taking the proffered bottle, he found his hands violently shook and was surprised when the Noble steadied his hands with his own. Together they lifted the bottle to his lips.

Inhuman blood ran thickly down his throat. The texture and temperature forcing a shudder while his body greedily grasped for more.

"Slowly," whispered Fernando, and he listened.

His mind reeled at why the Noble was helping him. Such compassion seemed incongruous to the Chosen's previous nature. The slaking of his thirst with the strange blood stilled the tremors enough for Fernando to release his hands. Gripping the bottle as if a lifeline, he pulled another room temperature draught into his greedy body.

Each mouthful sent shivers down his spine. Never before had blood tasted this divine. Lifting his lips from the kiss of the bottle, he held it slack in his hand.

"What is it?" he asked, lifting it once more to his lips.

"Pig," replied the Noble matter-of-factly.

He halted the progression of the bottle to his lips in surprise and then noted it was empty. Dropping his hand, he placed the bottle on the night table next to the candle.

"It wasn't hard to find a butcher who slaughtered his animals by bleeding them," stated Fernando, noting the Angel's inquisitive look.

From behind his back, Fernando offered a second green bottle filled to the neck. Gently easing out the cork with a second pop, he offered it.

This time his hands did not shake as he brought the contents to his lips.

"I figured that if you survived, you'd need to feed," continued the Noble. "Having a Chosen in the throes of the hunger would be detrimental."

He frowned at the half filled bottle in his hand. "What happened?"

"You don't remember?"

Fernando's incredulous tone lifted his gaze to meet brown eyes and he shook his head, frowning.

"It seems that your mortal lover unknowingly ate something with the herbal mixture and when you bit her she inadvertently poisoned you."

His eyes went wide and then guilt pounded into him. It was no wonder Jeanie was in the other room sobbing. She probably believed he was furious at her.

Closing his eyes with a groan, he rubbed his face with his free hand. "How long was I unconscious?"

"Three nights." He could feel Fernando's angry glare but refused to look up. "Three nights lost."

Shame and guilt poured into him. So much time lost to one day's momentary joy. The only recompense was that Jeanie knew where the office was and he frowned. Even while he fought the poison in his system Fernando and Jeanie should have gone there.

"Did Jeanie take you to the shipping house?" he asked.

"No," stated Fernando, tersely, obviously annoyed. "She said she wanted to wait until you recovered. She wouldn't even tell me where it was so I could go alone." He let out a huff. "Did you know she's immune to our Charms?"

He frowned. He had thought it was just he. Notus seemed to have no issue in mesmerizing Jeanie. His jaw tightened and he closed his eyes at how stupid he had been. Of course! Notus made sure she was insusceptible so as to protect her from other Chosen.

Dispirited, he nodded.

"Phag," spat the Noble, clearly disgusted. "That is not helpful."

"What time is it?" he asked, desiring to change the topic away from Jeanie for the moment.

"An hour before sunset or thereabouts."

He caught the Noble's eyes with his own. "We'll go tonight once the sun is down."

Fernando's eyes lowered suspiciously. "Do you think you're up for it?"

"It doesn't matter." He shook his head. "I need to feed, and I've wasted too much time lying in bed."

A hungry grin spread over the Noble's features. Turning, Fernando walked to the door.

"One other thing." He saw the Noble pause at the door. "Would you mind sending Jeanie in?"

Relief washed over Fernando's features. "Oh God, yes. Anything to get her to stop crying."

Surprised at the compliance and the help he had received, he stared at the floor in front of his bare feet.

"Thank you, Fernando," he said solemnly.

"You're welcome, Gwyn," replied the Noble.

The sound of the name spoken by Fernando's lips stunned him to the quick and his snapped his head up to find the Noble had left. Eyes wide with foreboding, he stared at the bottle in his hand. Finishing the tepid liquid in one final chug, he placed it next to the other empty one and wiped his mouth along his arm leaving a red streak against white.

The commotion arising from the other room caused him to lift his head. He could hear Jeanie's reticence to enter into their room, sobbing her denial that he would want to see her was incongruous to Fernando's demands. It took the Noble's bellowed order to send Jeanie scurrying to stand by the opened door.

Afraid to enter, she hugged the frame in an attempt to gain succour, her eyes red and swollen from crying. He could tell she wanted to come to him, but feared his reaction. Seeing all this on her usually soft features broke his heart and he went to stand so as to go to her but found the ache in his muscles, no matter how much decreased by the pig's blood, still hampered him.

It was his groan at the sensation of his feet painfully taking his weight that sent Jeanie flying into the room to land on the floor before him on her knees, shoulders hunched and shuddering with new wracks of sobs. Over the din, he could hear her mumbling over and over how sorry she was and that if he sent her away she would understand.

Heart wrenched at the dejection she poured forth, he painfully lowered to one knee before her. He could not stand being the source of her misery. Brushing back tangled curls, he lifted her sorrowful face by the chin. Red rimmed her vibrant green eyes and he shook his head. Jeanie should never have to suffer like this and he hated himself to be the cause. Wiping the tears from her face with his hand, he followed the softness of her cheek to the side of her head where he cradled her in his hand. Even through the salt scent the smell of her blood jumped his hunger, but this time it was much easier to restrain.

"I'm so sorry," spluttered Jeanie between sobs, new tears streaming down. "I dinna realize that…that…" She collapsed against him, his bare chest soaking in refreshed tears.

"Shush," he whispered over her cries. He held her to him, feeling her warmth, petting her hair in an attempt to calm her. He could feel his eyes welling with unshed tears, having hurt her so. "It's not your fault."

Jeanie pulled away just enough to look up at him, sniffing. "Then why did ye yell at me to leave if yer no mad at me?"

He brushed an errant lock from obscuring her face and tilted his head to hide his sudden sense of self-disgust. "I'm not mad at you. I had to save you." Her eyes questioned him, encouraging him to continue. "If you had stayed," he glanced down at the floor suddenly ashamed. "I would have killed you. I had to save you from myself."

"But why?" He could hear her plaintive tones.

"I have never felt such a driving hunger before," he tried to explain. "I was barely able to control it. Had you stayed any longer…" He shook his head.

He watched her eyes go round in understanding. "But I nearly killed ye."

"I don't have much of a memory of what happened. Fernando told me, albeit briefly, but I can't blame you, Jeanie. How were you to know that the herbal mixture was in the food you had eaten?"

It was Jeanie's turn to look away as if unable to relinquish her responsibility of his current state. He brought her head up to gaze into her eyes.

"I love you, Jeanie. Nothing ever can change that."

The fierceness of her embrace nearly toppled him over and he felt her mumble her love against his chest before pulling away.

"Do you think we can get off this floor?" he asked, managing a gentle smile and was rewarded with one in kind.

Groaning with the exertion to stand, he gratefully sat back down on the bed with a sigh, Jeanie beside him. "Yer still in pain?"

"I'll be fine once I properly feed," he explained with his eyes closed, willing his aching muscles to relax. "You'll be fine to take us to the shipping house tonight?"

"Aye," she nodded, sniffing back the remnants of her weeping. "But maybe we should wait 'till yer better?"

He shook his head. "I've wasted too much time. We'll go once the sun is down. Until then—" a smile lit his eyes "—I am sorely in need of a nice hot bath and if memory serves, the tub in the ensuite is more than large enough."

The red sadness swept away, leaving green eyes sparkling as she stood up. On stiff legs, he followed Jeanie into the bathroom, never relinquishing his grip on her hand.

XXVÍÍÍ

very jostle of the wheels against the cobbles sent stabs through his legs and up his spine to pound painfully in his head. He tried to relax against the leather padded backing of the coach, but it only increased the rattles and bobs. Eyes closed and jaw clenched, he prayed to whatever Old Gods remained that they would arrive soon at the office.

He could feel Jeanie's warmth sitting beside him, her bouquet perfuming the air, driving his hunger to be released from its taught leash. He had hoped the bath they had shared would have relinquished some of the ache the poison had left in his body, but it was blood he needed, not hot water.

Even Jeanie's gentle ministrations with the soapy water to ease the spasms did little to offer relief. What he needed was to feed and for the first time he was afraid to do so. Having seen his fear reflected in her eyes, he knew that she did not want to chance sending him back into that paroxysm of pain. They had touched each other, washing off days of pain, both physical and emotional, with chaste tentativeness.

"We're here," said Jeanie, her voice loud in the sudden silence.

Opening his eyes in relief, he saw the Noble in the seat across from him shift to leave the coach. Fernando's unexpected help was still mystifying, as was the Noble's grin when both he and Jeanie had exited the bedroom. There had definitely been satisfaction on the Noble's face, but there had also been something more sinister behind the smile. Despite the return to the cool façade of the Angel a sense of growing dread took hold, making him wonder how much besides the name, Fernando had heard.

Last out of the coach, he stood to his full height under his cloak, feeling the pops along his spine as they protested the stretch. The pressure of the sword belt ached across his hips as the ancient blade tipped his balance. He needed to feed, and soon. He could not continue feeling this way.

He caught Jeanie's concerned gaze and smiled briefly at her as the driver clicked his tongue, sending the coach rattling away. Bringing his attention to the white rimmed red lettering of the office sign, the whole building seemed to shimmer a sense of menace. This was the place they should have attended three nights ago and he hoped that the answers they sought were still there. He walked up to the black painted door.

"I doubt that you had noticed," said the Noble as he strode over to him. Dark eyes shifted to glance into the night as he hugged his cape closed. "But we've been tailed since leaving the hotel."

Turning to look in the direction Fernando had indicated, he could see a dark shape flit from one shadow to the next. The figure seemed to move too fast for a mortal and knew how use the darkness to make himself invisible. A sense of recognition flitted through his mind but he shrugged it off. If it was someone involved with the poisoning of the Chosen then he would be hunted down once they got their answers from behind this door.

"You're not remotely interested in finding out who that is?" asked Fernando, incredulous that the Angel seemed disinterested in their tail. Ever since he had indicated that he knew the Angel's name after providing the bottles of pig's blood, the Angel seemed confused, even concerned, in how to relate to Fernando. The discomfiture had continued, shutting the Angel down to nary a word spoken. The only indication of thought or feeling was the pained expression the Angel displayed on their journey and the smile he gave to the girl.

"They'll be time after," stated the Angel, noticing Fernando's growing anger. Glancing over to Jeanie, she huddled against the chill night air with her hands in her coat pockets. He knew she too was hungry; Jeanie had refused to stop for a quick bite. Not to make sure they got back on track with their investigation, but because she was afraid to eat anything with the spice. It was a fear he understood now all too well.

Turning the brass doorknob, the loud crunching click of the door lock being busted resonated into the quiet night, making Jeanie jump. It was the tinkling of the chimes as the door swung open that sent Fernando swearing under his breath.

"You could have mentioned those," hissed the Noble.

"I forgot," replied Jeanie, hotly. "In any case, what could ye hae done about it?"

Scowling, Fernando shook his head.

Ignoring them both, the Angel stepped into the small front office. A single oil lamp burned brightly on the desk sitting in the centre, illuminating stacked papers against the litter of individual sheets lining the wood. An elaborately decorated silver fountain pen lay on its side over top a single white sheet. It was clear that someone was staying late to finish some work.

Fernando entered, followed closely by Jeanie. The door closed with another jostling of chimes, sending Fernando's eyes rolling in exasperation. Jeanie flashed him an angry look to which the Angel sighed and shook his head. A sound from behind the inner office door caught his attention and he raised his hand to quiet any voice from his partners. They stood silently awaiting the entrance of the office worker.

"I thought I had locked that door," came the aggravated French from behind the door. The handle turned and the bald headed manager halted in mid-step to stare at the three intruders to his solitude. "We are closed for the day, come back tomorrow," he said, tersely.

Stepping forward, Fernando flourished a bow that seemed both insulting yet respectful. "I do apologize for our late arrival, but my colleagues and I have some questions about your business that must be answered. We cannot brook any more delays."

Closing the door behind him, the middle-aged man straightened his tie and buttoned his jacket. "I'm sorry, sir, but we are closed."

He walked around the desk, wary of the tall, cloaked figure on the other side and halted to stare at Jeanie. An angry frown pulled at his lips as he went to open the door to let his unwelcomed guests out. "Now if you please."

He stumbled back as the cloaked figure seemed to magically appear before him. Fear widened his grey eyes and he crossed himself.

Slipping back the hood with a pale hand, the Angel stared down at the little man, anger and hunger vying for supremacy. "You have information that we require."

The scent of the mortal's fear laced blood exploded into the room and he opened his mouth to savour it.

"Wha-what information do you need?" stammered the man. Beads of nervous sweat appeared on his forehead. He backed up until the sound of the thump proved he had gone as far back against the desk as possible.

Stepping into the mortal's line of sight, the Noble's smile widened. "You took a piece of paper from Miss Stuart three days ago. I'm sure you recall its contents." Fernando was rewarded with a quick nod. "Good. Then you can tell us who is issuing the orders for these barrels of herbs to be sent to England."

"I cannot tell you that, sir," stated the manager, finding strength in meeting normal looking brown eyes rather than the terrifying red of the tall creature blocking the exit.

"I don't think that you understand the predicament that you are in," advanced the Noble. "You have a choice in this matter. You can either tell us by your free will or we can take it from you." A silver flash emanated from Fernando's hand and a dagger hung casually.

The mortal began to tremble in fright, his eyes wide and fixated on the blade.

Having not understood a word transpired, Jeanie stepped forward, appalled at Fernando's threatening position.

"Stop it," she cried, "yer scarin' him."

"Of course I'm scaring him," snapped the Noble, refusing to take his hungry eyes off the middle-aged man. "How else am I going to get what we need?"

"Ye can ask him nicely." She met the man's pleading gaze.

"Did it work for you?"

Fernando's snide comment brought her back at how she was treated by this same self-styled gentleman only three days ago.

"No," she frowned.

"Shut up and let me do it my way." Victorious, he stepped forward revelling in the terror he was evoking in the man. "So what is it going to be?"

"I-I can't." The man shook his head. "If I tell you they'll kill me."

"Tch tch tch, and who is to say that I won't kill you if you don't tell me." Fernando spun the blade between his two hands, the point drilling into the tip of his index finger.

At the man's moan of despair, Fernando swooped over, blade pressed against the man's straining neck. A rivulet of blood seeped along the steel to drip liquid rubies onto his white collar.

Disgusted with Fernando's incessant need to torture his victims, the Angel stepped forward as his hunger broke its leash with the shedding of mortal blood.

Standing over the Noble, his whisper strained against his flooding desire. "He's mine."

"Gladly," smirked the Noble, removing the blade from the mortal's throat. Methodically he ran his finger along the side of the dagger, transferring the stain of blood. Breathing in its fear-tinged aroma he licked the jewels, cleaning his finger. Surprised to find the blood untainted, he smiled.

Taking note of the Noble's reaction to the blood, the Angel turned his attention to the man. The red beads welled alluringly along the cut. He could not wait much longer to satiate his hunger. It seemed to have a life of its own, pressing him into action. He knew Jeanie was there in the room watching, this time knowing what he was and what he needed. He could only hope she would forgive him for what he was about to do.

He locked onto grey eyes, driving his gaze into the man's. Catching the staggered rhythm of the mortal's breathing, he waited until the man's pupils dilated and his posture relaxed.

"You will tell us who is ordering the herbs that are poisoning the Chosen." He spoke in harmony with the manager's beating heart. "You will tell us where we can find this person. You will tell us the truth for any lie will cause you agony."

A whimper escaped the mortal's throat.

Surprised at the man's resistance, he felt his anger rise. His eyes bore into grey.

"Tell me," he pressed.

The man's opposition shattered.

"Madam Fleur de la Montagne," he sputtered under the effect of the Angel's powers. "She has a villa outside of Balinghem."

"I know the area," responded the Angel. He ignored Fernando's raised brow. "What is the name of the villa?"

The manager slowly shook his head without breaking eye contact, his breath coming more rapidly. "Please, please," his voice whined, "they'll kill me."

The Angel drove his gaze into mortal eyes, speaking to the man's soul. "Do you know what I am called?"

The mortal's head shook vigorously.

"I am called *l'Ange*."

The scent of hot urine filled the small office. It was clear that the manager had heard of him. Behind him he heard Fernando's offended expletive as he got wind of the released bladder. He did not want to see Jeanie's reaction. Returning his attention to the man, he could see tears streaming down the shaved face to drip into the puddle on the floor. It was only through his will that the mortal remained standing.

"*Le Jardin*," muttered the man. "The villa is called *Le Jardin*."

Satisfied with the answers the hunger finally broke free. Swooping down on the manager, he barely registered the scream as he sank his teeth through the slightly stubbled skin, piercing the jugular. The salt of sweat mingled momentarily with the rushing hot metallic taste that quickly filled his mouth. Spurred on by the lack of taint in the blood, he euphorically swallowed, basking in the adrenalin heightened flavour.

It felt so long since the last time he had allowed himself to feed unrestrained.

Holding the mortal in a fierce embrace, he pulled on the wound, seeking only to fill his mouth and his being with the living essence. Again and again he suckled, drawing out more of the life giving fluid, its thick sweetness filling his mouth, enlivening his centre. Time existed within the expanse of the slowing heart; each chamber struggled to fill and then to push. It was when it fluttered that told the Angel his meal would soon be over. Choosing to take his time to savour the richness of the blood, he allowed the failing heart to push its fluids into him until it faltered into a stumbling rhythm. He so wanted to drain the manager to the quick but knew the consequences if he did. Forcibly pulling himself out, he caught his breath in a great sigh.

It would not be long before the manager expired from extreme blood loss and he laid the man down, watching as the four puncture marks began to close. Grey eyes glazed over. The sound of the heart fluttered once, and then stopped. A release of breath escaped dead lips.

Stepping back from the corpse, he felt the usual shame mixed with the elation the blood gave him. Any remnant of pain in his body magically vanished with the fulfillment of his hunger. A figure off to his right caught his attention and he looked up to see the Noble, a knowing smile on his face, pointing to the corner of his own mouth. Frowning at first by the strange gesture, he quickly realized that Fernando was indicating something else. He touched his mouth and drew back the last remains of the manager's blood. Red tipped pale fingers. It was tempting to lick the delicious red liquid off his fingers but instead hastily he wiped them on his cloak.

"Do you know where *Le Jardin* is?" asked Fernando, breaking the silence, having more than enjoyed witnessing the Angel in action and could now guess with certainty which Angel the mortals believed him to be.

"I have a good idea," answered the Angel. He turned away from the Noble's disparaging smile and found Jeanie huddled in the corner. The sense of enjoyment from feeding fled, leaving a hollow satiation in its stead.

He took a step towards Jeanie in the hopes to comfort and halted as she retreated further into the corner. He did not know what to say to take away the memory of what she had witnessed. When he fed off of her it was not only about the blood. There was love and trust, given and received. He knew that this was the first time she had seen him truly feed in the manner the penny presses described. The shame intensified and he lowered his gaze to the wooden floor.

"Why? Why did ye have to kill him?" Jeanie's voice sounded small.

Taking a steadying breath he met Jeanie's imploring gaze, fully aware of Fernando's intense presence. "I am Chosen, Jeanie. I could have let him live, but at what cost to us?"

He watched her eyes go round. The manager would have most likely gone to those they were seeking. The manager was part of the conspiracy to kill the Chosen, though it was strange that he was not tainted. "I have never lied to you about what I am, what I have done."

Jeanie's breath came in quick gasps. "But when I saw you with the old man..."

Realization dawned on him and he groaned, finishing her thought. "And with you. But it is not always that way. This...this is usually the way.

Feeding off those mortals who delve in cruelty to others. This man was part of those killing off the Chosen. I could not let him live even if I wanted to."

Jeanie trembled, hating the fact that he was right. "What do we do now?"

"We rifle through this place to see if the information can be corroborated and then set this place alight," replied the Noble. Moving around the room, he began with the filing cabinets along the wall, throwing inconsequential papers onto the floor.

Knowing it was the only way to cover their tracks and to possibly sabotage any future shipments to Britain, the Angel turned from Jeanie to help the Noble in the search. Jeanie joined them, muttering in sad resignation.

It did not take long to find the file that held all the shipping orders from one "*Madam Fleur de la Montagne of Le Jardin, Balinghem.*"

What shocked and caused the Noble and the Angel to meet their eyes in fear were the numerous countries the spice was being sent to. The poisoning of the Chosen was not isolated to the British Isles. It was an all out attempt to exterminate the Chosen from every corner of the earth.

Closing the thick file, Fernando tucked it inside his vest for safe keeping and broke the side of the oil lamp reservoir against the corner of the desk. The Noble sprinkled the pungent liquid all over the floor, dousing the body as best he could with what he had left. Once done, using a soapstone paperweight, the Angel knocked the gas lamps from their copper hoses sending hissing vapours into the room.

"Everybody out," ordered the Angel.

Fernando dropped the lit lamp wick onto the body. The fire caught with a whoosh as he walked out the door, the chimes ringing pleasantly.

Grabbing Jeanie by the arm, the Angel pulled her out into the cool night air, raising his hood against possible prying eyes.

"Keep walking," he ordered, following the Noble as they left the block the warehouse resided on.

Jeanie did the best she could, but she was no match for their easy strides, and found herself huffing and puffing in the cold air. If it were not for the Angel's grip on her upper arm she would have stopped long ago.

The explosion behind them shook doors, shattered windows, and caused them to stumble in mid-stride. Turning around, all three watched as the yellow-orange glow of the conflagration lit up the sky. Knowing that there would be nothing left of the murder, the Angel viewed the destruction in resolute silence. The sound of the fire roared in his ears.

Glancing down at Jeanie's shaken form, he turned around, ready to vacate the premises before the fire drew curious onlookers. Fernando caught his eye, smiling like a satisfied cat as he patted his chest where the file was lodged, and nodded. It was high time to be leaving.

The quick clicks of their shoes accompanied the snapping of fire eaten wood as it sparked hoards of fireflies high into the night air. Turning down a street, they saw the first of many men and machines of the fire brigade race down the cobbles, horses foaming at the quick pace they were forced to pull their heavy loads.

The three sped up their pace but kept it to a mortal one that Jeanie could keep with. Each turn took them farther away from the destruction until they were able to slow down, the fire naught but a silent orange illumination against a black backdrop. Assuming they were heading back to the hotel, the Angel caught up with the Noble, placing Jeanie between them, her breath puffing white clouds.

A flicker of movement down an alleyway caught his attention. It seemed that their tail was back. Noticing Fernando's frown, he knew the Noble had seen it too.

"Do you not find it odd that the manager was untainted?" asked the Noble. His eyes glanced up and fell back down, fixated on the walkway ahead.

The Angel nodded. In a flash of insight he knew why. "They knew we were coming." Barely audible footpads scurried far behind them.

"The trap is preparing to be sprung." Fernando unsheathed his blades, concealing them under his cape.

"What trap? What are ye sayin'?" Jeanie's voice rose in anxiety.

"Madam Fleur de le Montagne seems to want us to find her," answered the Angel. Movement along the rooftop caught his attention and he rested his hand on the pommel of his sword.

"That doesn't make any sense," stated Jeanie, oblivious to the goings on around her. "She's the one tryin' t'kill the Chosen, why no poison one or even both of ye if she knows yer commin'?"

Fernando turned down into a dark cul-de-sac of dormant warehouses and came to a halt. "You are absolutely right, and the only way to find the answers is to spring the trap."

With a nod of agreement, the Angel saw that Jeanie stood confused at where they found themselves, and at the answer. She did not notice the silent figures standing in the darkened doorways and alleys, or the one perched on the rooftop of the warehouse in front of them.

A tense silence filled the night.

"I never expected to see you back so soon," called the dark figure on top of the building. His rich French voice filled the oppressive quiet.

"What do you want, Hugo?" replied the Angel, throwing back his hood to have an unrestricted view of his surroundings.

"You know this vampire?" Fernando shot a dark gaze at the Angel.

The Angel nodded, refusing to move his eyes off of Hugo. He heard Jeanie's gasp of surprise.

"Where is *Le Bon Père?*" said Hugo.

"In London," retorted the Angel. "Answer my question." He heard the shiftings of the Chosen around them coming closer and tightened his grip on his sword. Sensing Jeanie's distress, he drew her to his right side and brought her inside his cloak. Her eyes went wide as he drew the ancient sword, still concealing it under the panels of heavy black fabric.

"You are without the amnesty of *Le Bon Père's* presence, *L'Ange*," answered Hugo, menacingly. "You were told by *Le Maître* that if you set foot on French soil without being under *Le Bon Père's* protection you would be Destroyed."

"Now what could you have done to have gotten the Master of Paris into such a knot?" Fernando's whisper held a cocktail of amusement, fear, and simmering anger.

The Angel glanced sharply at the smirking Noble. "Since Aimeri became Master of the French Chosen, they've become quite irrational as to who is and who isn't pure Chosen."

Fernando's eyes widened, feeling that he was on the brink of another discovery of the elusive Angel. "What are you saying?"

"They don't like my looks," stated the Angel, matter-of-factly.

Ignoring the Noble's bark of laughter, the Angel brought his attention back to the Chosen on the roof, fully aware of the slow onset of the others around them. "Let Aimeri show himself."

"You know that is not possible," spat Hugo, "*Le Maître* is in Nice mourning his beloved Marie. While he decides whether or not to partake of the sun, I am in charge."

"*Merda*," swore the Noble, testing the grips on the daggers.

The Angel returned his attention back to Jeanie, knowing that no matter what happened in the next few moments he had to do everything in his power to protect her.

"Hold on," he whispered, wrapping his right arm around her chest. He felt her trembling arms encircle his waist. Her terrified eyes met his. "Whatever you do, do not let go."

"What are ye going t'do?" asked Jeanie. Her eyes wide in fright, she gripped his belt.

"I'm going to fight with one hand tied behind my back." He tried giving Jeanie a confident smile, but only the corner of his mouth lifted, belying his concern.

The sudden whoosh and subtle change in the air was the only warning of the attacking Chosen. With Jeanie tucked in one arm he spun with preternatural speed, brandished his weapon and cleanly cleaved through the waist of the male Chosen who flew at him. Blood dripped down the single, wide blood groove, stealing away its silver gleam. There was no time to think, only to react as others, having realized the Angel and his partner were armed, drew their own bladed weapons.

Fear lacerated through him as he realized how difficult it would be to overcome the odds while protecting Jeanie. Schooling his expression, he fixed his grip around Jeanie's waist and slipped into the centuries of training and practice.

The French Chosen did not attack one at a time, but rushed he and

Fernando. Back to back with the Noble he fought, easily deflecting knife and rapier attacks. None managed to touch him, but with his long reach and well-trained hand, he caused many to lose hold of their weapons.

A cry from his right drew his attention from the knife attack before him. Easily sidestepping the clumsy thrust, he brought his blade through the neck of the off balanced Chosen, decapitating in an easy fluid blow. Red rain sprayed. It did not slow him down as he used the momentum of the swing. Pivoting on one foot, he brought the ancient sword to shatter the rapier intended to stab him.

The Chosen holding the ruined blade stood dumbfounded before fear dissolved any gusto of the battle. The last thing he saw was the Angels furious red eyes before darkening cobbles stared back at him.

Out of the corner of his eye, the Angel saw that Fernando was more than capable with his two daggers. Defending against another foolhardy attack, he realized he had to end this before he decimated the French Chosen. Unhanding one female Chosen of her dirk, he ignored her screams and sought the one who could end this.

Finding Hugo watching from his vantage point on the roof, the Angel came to the only decision he could make.

He rushed to the building certain Fernando could hold his own, and shouted for Jeanie to hold on. He did not know if she heard him or not as there was no time. With the speed and strength of the Chosen he leapt, landing forcefully on the roof. He felt Jeanie's stumble and he held her tightly, barely giving her time to gasp for breath before he advanced on Hugo.

Witnessing *l'Ange* leap effortlessly to his position, Hugo unsheathed his broadsword. The clean blade rang clear, barely before meeting the long sword in a parry of crashing sparks and thunderous clang.

Moving easily on the flat roof, the Angel pressed his advantage. Height and centuries of training forced Hugo's adequate defence back as their blades met again and again in a shower of sparks.

"Do you yield," the Angel called out over the ringing metal.

"Never," seethed Hugo. He swung again, his sword stopped once again by *l'Ange's*. "I'll see you in hell first. The English Chosen will not win their war against the French."

Not understanding Hugo's reasons for the fight, he pressed on, forcing the French Chosen to meet each swing, each thrust, with less and less effective countermeasures.

Stepping forward, he swung, knowing Hugo would meet his sword with his. When the crash of metal against metal came, he spun, Jeanie gripped in one arm, his cloak flowing out around him in a grim parody of black wings, and stepped inside Hugo's range. His sword landed against his opponent's neck and halted, biting deep enough to let Hugo know that if he pressed the attack further, he would not only lose the battle, but his head as well.

Glaring down at the temporary leader of the French Chosen, he watched as Hugo's blood swelled into his sword's blood groove to mingle with those that he had already slain.

"Do you yield?" the Angel demanded once again, his voice filled with the promise of death.

Hugo stared up at him, hatred written cleanly in the ice blue of his eyes. Momentarily impressed at Hugo's bravado, the Angel released his arm from around Jeanie. Ignoring her stumble to the ground to land undignified with her legs a skewed under her and her head in her hands, he shifted Geraint's ancient blade, drawing the line in Hugo's flesh further across by gripping with both hands. The threat of the beheading became a promise and he stared into Hugo's startled eyes.

"I have no wish to become *Le Maître*," hissed the Angel between clenched teeth, "but know this, if you do not drop your weapon and call a halt to these hostilities, the last thing you will see is *me*."

The clatter of metal against the roof rang as Hugo raised his hands in placation.

Relaxing his stance, the Angel relinquished his sword from Hugo's neck. He stood back, sword poised in his hand, waiting to see if he would still have to follow through on his threat.

Hugo checked the quickly healing wound across his neck as he took in the full countenance of *l'Ange* and shuddered involuntarily. His blue eyes went round at seeing the mortal girl on the rooftop and realized where she had come from.

"You fought while holding onto that mortal?" asked Hugo, incredulously.

Not even offering a nod, the Angel's stared impassively at Hugo. "Imagine if I had fought free of the encumbrance." He watched the French Chosen pale. "Now order your Chosen to stand down or the next attack I present *will* have your head."

Face tightening in the anger of defeat, Hugo's voice resounded in the dark cul-de-sac of warehouses ordering his Chosen to abnegate the battle. Once the sounds of combat came to a clattering end, he brought his attention back to the Angel. "You may have won this round, *l'Ange,* but next time, whore on your arm or not, I will win."

Wiping off his blade on his cloak, the Angel sheathed the sword without taking his eyes off of Hugo. In an explosion of motion that not even the other Chosen could foresee, the Angel turned and back kicked Hugo in the centre of his chest.

The Chosen's breath erupted out as he was propelled up and then over the edge of the rooftop to disappear to the street below with a sickening crunch.

Not bothering to check where Hugo landed, the Angel turned towards Jeanie, worry rising at the sight of her shaken and dishevelled form. Kneeling on the gravel roof, he was almost afraid to touch her but made his blood splattered hand reach out to caress the fiery curls from her face. When she looked up at him he thought she was going to be ill. Sweat shined her pale face.

"Dear God," sighed Jeanie, catching her gorge and swallowing. "I knew ye could move fast, but—" She put a shaking had to her forehead. "Now I ken what an egg feels like when beaten."

The admission filled him with grief. All he wanted to do was protect her, not hurt her. His eyes fell to the stones between them.

Jeanie saw his splattered face fall. Despite the gruesome nature of the spots they almost seemed to belong on him. "Why did ye send him flyin' off the roof?"

"He called you a whore," he stated, raising his head to look in her impossibly green eyes. Watching as her face widened in surprise in a glint of fierce love, he stood, his hand outstretched.

She placed her hand in his and let him lift her gently to unsteady feet.

"Promise me one thing?" she asked, smiling.

"Anything." He returned her squeeze, but not her smile.

"Dinna protect me like that again," said Jeanie. "Yer lucky I dinna hae any dinner tonight or ye'd be wearing it now."

"You have my promise," he smiled. Despite having been tossed around, Jeanie's hair, loose and flying in every direction, made her even lovelier. He could imagine the sight the two of them made. Another shared bath was in the foreseeable future and this time maybe more could come from it, if they were both careful.

"How are we gonna t'get down?" Jeanie broke his reverie, staring at the edge of the rooftop, her face drawn in apprehension.

Frowning, he recognized her consternation. He knew she was not going to like the answer. "The same way we got up here—we jump."

"Oh no." Jeanie shook her head, backing away from the edge with hands raised against the possibility. Stumbling on the loose gravel, she spun around. "There's got to be stairs around here."

He knew he was going to have a battle if he left her to her own devices and he did not have the time, sure that Hugo was probably waking from his plummet with a headache about now. Not letting Jeanie have another word in the matter, he swept her off her feet, cradling her as he walked to the edge. He met her shocked expression with a leer. "You had better hold on."

"Gwyn, don't you –" Jeanie's protest was cut off with a high piercing scream as he stepped off.

Time halted as they fell to earth, his cloak billowed up, trailing behind. Jeanie nestled her face against his shoulder as her arms fiercely encircled him. The impact, when it came, shocked them both, but he managed to not stumble.

"Well, it's about time," admonished Fernando, his arms crossed over his chest. There was no sign of the oriental blades.

The scene of destruction tightened his jaw and his hands clutched protectively on Jeanie, not wanting to release her to witness the gruesome death and dismemberment of many of the French Chosen. He felt her head lift from his shoulder, testing to see if they were truly back on the ground. He could not stop her as she craned her neck, twisting herself from his hold, to stand on the cobbles.

Blanching at the sight, she spun back to him to bury her face in his chest. He felt her shudder and he embraced her, not caring what the other Chosen would think.

The remaining Chosen stared in fearful awe of the Angel standing in their midst after nearly decimating a quarter of their numbers. The woman he had dismembered held her disembodied hand in her remaining left, weeping about how she would never be able to play her harp again. Ignoring her cries, his eyes fell to the one who had attacked him first.

The young man, Chosen not far past his youth, lay in two halves. His torso separated from his lower extremities by several feet. Blood pooled around spilled viscera, steaming in the cool air. Still alive, the boy sobbed until he saw the Angel standing nearby.

"Please," implored the boy through hiccoughing sobs. "I can't live like this. I can't be half a man, half a vampire."

Knowing what he had to do, the Angel took Jeanie by the shoulders, forcing her to look up at him. "I don't want you to see this. Go to Fernando."

The cold hard determination in his face halted any protest Jeanie could have made. She did not want to leave his side, but it was obvious that he was fully the Angel again.

Abandoning Jeanie to make her decision, he stepped around her to stand over the youth and looked up when he heard Jeanie scurry to the Noble. He did not expect any warmth from the man, but was surprised to see Fernando stand protectively by her side and whisper something in her ear.

"*L'Ange*, please," cried the disembodied Chosen.

"Is this what you truly want," he asked the young man.

Tears glistened trails down the side of the French Chosen's face to pool in his ears as he nodded.

Turning away, the Angel looked over to Hugo who staggered over with squinting eyes and a hand on the back of his head. "He's yours, Hugo. You heard what he's asked of me."

"I have," replied Hugo, his voice tight with pain and annoyance.

"You'll accept what I do here tonight and not hold it against me or mine?" His question was more statement.

"Do I have a choice?" bristled Hugo.

He accepted Hugo's answer and turned back to the young man. Unsheathing his sword, it rang through the silence. He ignored the other Chosen around him who stared and muttered to one another as he placed the tip beside the young man's neck.

"I am not the Good Father. I cannot give you absolution." The young Chosen sobbed harder. "I am *L'Ange de la Mort* and I can give you release, but before I do I will give you two things." His eyes caught the Chosen's watery hazel eyes. "I forgive you for your ill fated attempt to kill me." Shame filled the young man's face. "Second, I will make sure that your dying wish is fulfilled."

A sob caught in the young man's throat. "I want my ashes taken to my mother."

Stunned at how truly young this Chosen was, the Angel let out a slow breath and swallowed. "Hugo, you heard?"

"Yes, *l'Ange*, I heard," came the reply. "It will be as Aimé asks."

A sigh of relief released from Aimé as the Angel gave a curt nod and he solidified his awkward position for the gruesome task. "Go with God."

Lifting the ancient blade across for the backhanded strike needed, he watched Aimé close his eyes. Silence reigned and he focused the power of his swing to cleanly decapitate. Through the force, the tip of his blade caught sparks against the cobble as Aimé's head was rended from shoulders and sent flying.

The hush was broken by the sound of the head clattering against stone.

Hardly any blood marked the gruesome task, having poured forth earlier.

Lifting his blade, he wiped it against the corpse and placed the sword in its sheath. Faces caught in grief, some in anger, watched him as he strode over to Jeanie, whose pale green face proved that she had watched the whole spectacle. Once close enough, she stepped into his embrace, shuddering. He gave Fernando a nod of thanks that was returned with one in kind and turned to leave. Their motion towards the exit caused the other Chosen to take up action to clean up the mess.

Halting not a dozen steps away, he ignored Fernando's questioning glare and turned to face the French Chosen.

"Hugo," he called out. "How did Marie die?"

"You should know," sneered the Chosen. "After all it is because of you English and your war against us."

Frustrated by the erroneous answer, he shook his head. "Tell me."

Hugo stepped over a corpse missing only her head and strode over, but kept his distance. His Chosen stood stock still in expectation of another break out of violence. "Aimeri took Marie out to the Cabaret for some entertainment and then for some refreshments. It happened after she consumed a young German visitor."

"So why do you think it's because of the British?" asked Fernando, his interest piqued.

Hugo's eyes narrowed, noting how this other Chosen distanced himself from his compatriots, but did not consider that this other's accent was tinted heavily by something else. "Because we have traced the source to the shipping company that you conveniently blew up to cover your tracks."

Astounded at the audacity of the claim, Fernando glanced up at his partner.

"Can you believe this guy?" he asked rhetorically in English before walking off.

"Fernando, wait," called the Angel and was surprised to see the Noble halt and turn around. "It was the spice."

"Like I couldn't figure that one out?" Fernando shook his head and walked back. "We should let these idiots get what's coming to them."

A part of him wanted the same thing as the Noble. He could not deny it after how Hugo and his troupe treated them, but he could not let it lie. He turned back to the French Chosen. "The Chosen in England have been sorely afflicted by the same situation. We're here in Calais because we have followed a similar lead." He knew Fernando was not going to appreciate what he was about to offer Hugo. "I'm willing to share the information we have—"

"What? Are you crazy?" exploded Fernando in English. "After what they tried to do to us?"

Ignoring the outburst, the Angel continued. "—if you are willing to allow us unmolested passage anywhere in France this takes us."

"Why should I allow this?" asked Hugo, interest piqued.

"Because if we're right, you don't have to do anything. If we're wrong we're most likely dead."

A hopeful smile lifted Hugo's thin lips. "Alright, tell me."

He ignored Fernando's roll of the eyes. "Not here. You and one other can come back with us to our hotel. I know you know where we are staying."

Hugo chuckled humourlessly. "We've known your movements on our land since the night after you arrived."

"I know," stated the Angel, meeting Hugo's eyes with abhorrence. Hugo took an involuntary step back before catching himself. "Will you come?"

"What's to say you won't kill me when we get there?" Hugo lifted his chin in defiance.

"I'll offer you the same that Aimeri offered me – amnesty."

Hugo visibly paled at the tightly controlled anger the Angel directed at him and bowed his head in the knowledge of what he had done, not only to the Chosen under his wing, but to *Le Maître's* reputation.

"I will come." With an order thrown over his shoulder to the remaining Chosen, Hugo faced his nemesis.

His arm wrapped around Jeanie, the Angel turned to walk out of the sprung trap. "Two other things," he said as he pulled up the hood of his cloak.

"What?" scowled Hugo.

"We speak in English as not all of us here speak French."

"I will not," balked Hugo. "You and your other Chosen speak it well enough. I will not debase myself for a mortal."

The Angel came to a halt, forcing the others to the same. Jeanie glanced questioningly up at him having understood none of the conversations except for Fernando's occasional outburst in English.

Riding the dangerous air from the Angel, Fernando stepped close to Hugo. "Firstly, my name, sirra, is the Noble Fernando de Sagres, the last heir to the Fidelgo de Sagres."

"What's the second," asked Hugo in English.

"You're paying for the cab," answered the Angel, dispassionately as he walked on, Jeanie's warmth beside him.

Fernando's howls of laughter lit up the night as the orange glow in the distance diminished.

XXIX

eanie sat on their bed, pulling the silver brush through her towel-dried locks. Normally, she luxuriated in the feeling of a relaxing bath, but this time all she had wanted to do was remove the dried blood. No matter how hard she scrubbed it did not clean away the memories of what she had witnessed. Now she sat, wearing only her shift, not knowing whether or not her shivering was because of the cool air on her freshly bathed skin or from residual shock.

Whichever was the case, Jeanie could not banish the gruesome scene of devastated life that the Angel and Fernando had wrought. Nor could she reconcile seeing the man she loved, who treated her so gently and so caringly, with the vampire who extinguished the warehouse manager's life. Neither could she settle her mind on how fast she had moved in the protective embrace as the Angel fought their would-be assassins.

The dichotomy of the man who deeply loved and cared for her, and the Angel he was, scared her. He had told her what to expect and in her arrogance she had assumed that she could handle the worst. She was wrong. Despite the alien nature of the Chosen and what she had previously seen and experienced with them, nothing had prepared her for tonight's horrors.

Water droplets glistened against the white bristles and trapped red hairs in the brush as she absentmindedly settled it on her lap. Another shudder ran through her at the remembrance of seeing that young man weeping, and then witnessing his beheading. She had jumped at the sight and sound of the Angel's sword sliding through flesh and bone, sparking across the stone below. If she could have shed tears for the young vampire she would have, but her shock at the sight made her grateful she had not eaten.

It was not until they were walking away from the warehouse district with the orchestrator of the ambush that she found out why the one called Hugo had done what he did. The carriage ride back to the hotel was tension filled. Hugo's ice blue eyes lingered on her with disdain and a sparkle of hungry lust. No matter how hard she tried to cleave to the Angel, she knew she was the lone deer in a cage of fierce predators.

It had been the longest ride she had ever experienced and she was more than grateful when they came to a halt outside the hotel. Never before had cobblestones felt so wonderful under her feet. Jeanie was even more relieved when the Angel told her she could go back to their room and that he and Fernando were going to have a talk with Hugo.

Turning from the three Chosen, Jeanie fled through the doors, down the hall, to will the elevator to rise faster than its worn mechanisms could function. She would have barred the door once she had opened it with a key in a trembling hand, but she knew either Fernando or the Angel would have no trouble against it.

Pulling the abandoned hair from the brush, Jeanie felt a tear trickle down her cheek. She had never imagined that her love would be so confused with terror.

The sound of the lock in the front door turning the tumblers shot Jeanie straight up. She had not expected them back so soon, but glancing over her shoulder to the clock sitting on the writing desk told her that dawn was not that far away. So much time had passed since she had closed the door behind her to seek the refuge of a hot bath.

A mumbling and the sound of a door closing shut precipitated footsteps leading away from her room. Releasing a tension filled sigh, Jeanie felt almost relieved that it was Fernando going to his room, but it begged the question as to where the Angel was. Shoulders slumping, she found that a part of her did not want to confront the Angel despite how much she longed to be held in his strong embrace.

She continued to sit motionless on the bed, waiting for the inevitable to come. The sound of the table clock ticking grew louder with each passing second. Fear welled and she hated the feeling. It almost came as a relief when she heard the front door open and admit the suite's final occupant. She heard him shuffle around the main room, opening and closing the closet before heading down to the room they shared.

When his tall, slender form appeared in the doorway, Jeanie's eyes went wide. In the substantial gaslight she could see the speckles of rust coloured dried blood on his beautiful face and hair, marring his perfect whiteness. Despite the lack of his long black cloak, he still stood as the Angel until understanding flared hurt in his crimson eyes.

Breaking eye contact, he sighed and walked into the room to deposit an armload of groceries onto the writing desk. Grapes, a couple of apples, a small wedge of yellow cheese, bread and a bottle of wine sat on a table meant for study.

"I thought you might be hungry," he murmured, not daring to glance in her direction.

Although she knew she should not have been surprised at his obvious thoughtfulness, Jeanie watched in dumb silence as he stepped down the hall that led to the bathroom. It was when the sound of rushing water flowing from the taps filtered to her ears that she realized she had not said anything, not even a thank you. Despite his deplorable appearance, Jeanie could not deny that he was still the same man she fell in love with. The only problem was reconciling that fact with the horror she had witnessed that night.

Taking a shuddering breath, Jeanie knew that he had been right; that she was acting in the way that he had always expected of her right from the first night they had spent together. She recalled her strength of determination in the face of her ignorance, but now she could not deny the truth of his actions, nor his words. It came down to the final question – could she fully accept him?

Tonight he had made her an accomplice not only to murder, but also to theft and arson. It seemed to Jeanie that he held no remorse in his actions and it was hard to imagine him to be so cold when he was so warm and considerate. He was the Angel and Gwyn, and it was Gwyn she had always loved. If she wanted that love to continue, Jeanie knew that she had to become strong and accept the Angel.

Determined to accept what she could not change and finding strength in what she could, Jeanie stood and walked over to the hallway to find Gwyn standing, dripping wet with a towel wrapped around his hips. The whiteness of the towel only accentuated the paleness of his lean trim figure. His eyes flickered momentarily on Jeanie before quickly taking in the untouched food and the uncovered windows. The first lightening of dawn's approach forced him to squint.

His long strides brought him to the cord where he hastily pulled, forcing the thick brocade drapes closed. The heavy fabric swished with the speed of its movement across the rail. Without a word, he walked over to the bed and sat down.

She knew it was now or never. "Gwyn, I—"

"I'm so—"

Their eyes caught each other and Jeanie's heart soared at the slight smile on his face with the realization that they had both spoken at the same time.

"Ye go first," she offered, sitting down on the bed opposite him.

Wet white strands swung clear beads of water onto the bed. "No. You go first."

Jeanie caught the serious tone that extinguished the ruby glitter of his eyes. Summoning up her waning resolve, she took a deep breath. "Ye were right." She waited for a response and receiving none Jeanie continued. "I said that I could handle the fact that ye were a vamp—Chosen—and all that entails, but I was wrong."

She watched as he broke eye contact to frown at the space between them.

"What are you saying, Jeanie?" he asked, his tone full of the expectation of pain.

Shifting closer, Jeanie ducked her head so that he would be forced to look at her. "I love ye. That isna gonna change." He lifted his head, his frown turning to one of confusion. "I also ken that ye are who ye are and that canna change either, tis I that has t' change. I've seen more than I care to admit, but I hae to accept it or I dinna think I can be with ye."

"Do you think you really can when even I cannot?" he implored. Pain coloured his visage.

"I dinna said that I like it," Jeanie shook her head. "And I must say I'm happy to hear that ye dinna like it either, but answer me one question."

"What?"

"Why did ye kill the warehouse manager when ye told me ye dinna hae t' kill to get what ye need?"

His eyes went wide at the unexpected query before the frown returned. His voice fell to a near whisper. "I didn't plan on it, but the poisoning had left me so starved that I couldn't control myself. I had never felt that before and it was *so* incredibly difficult to keep control when you always smell so intoxicating."

Surprise caught Jeanie and she smiled. It seemed that he always knew the right thing to say. She knew she had to be stronger than she had been before. Leaning over, she kissed him long and deep. Cool arms encircled her as he drew her into his embrace. The dampness of his strong body soaked through her shift.

Hungrily, she loosened his towel, all the while opening herself to his delectable kisses. She had not realized that he had gently laid her down until she felt him sheath himself in her, sending her body into throbbing need.

Their lovemaking was furious. Her need to have him fill her completely drove all other thoughts from her mind. It was when his sharpened teeth cautiously slipped through the sensitive skin of her neck, sending a shock of ecstasy running from throat to groin, that caused her to cry out as her body convulsed its release.

The rich scent of horse filled his nostrils. Standing beside the large black charger, his fingers absently scratched behind the velvety twitching ear. The sharp contrast between his colouring and the dark soft hairs stood out beneath the gaslight emitting from the tall posts besides the entrance to the hotel. It was only when his hand brushed over the white blaze on the horse's forehead did his fingers seemed to disappear. He tried to ignore the shaking of his hand.

The horse, enjoying the attention, pressed into the caress with a snicker of satisfaction while the two other horses snuffled in jealousy. It was the tall black that received the affection from the dark cloaked figure.

He had come down to the lobby well before sunset, staying to the shadows, enjoying the anonymity his cloak provided. Jeanie's acceptance of what happened and their fervent lovemaking provided a short-lived solace. Falling asleep, entangled in each other's arms and legs, should have been enough, and it was, until They came back into his dreams.

He shuddered in remembrance of Their claims upon him and a sob tore from his throat at the left over sensations of Their mouths ripping into him, feeding off his fear and his essence. It was happening again and there was nothing he could do to stop it. Only this time the white-faced demon was bent upon his torturous destruction rather than to give in to something else. Whatever it was that drove Its fear fed Its anger, and he was Its unwilling victim, unable to free himself except through wakefulness. The memories of their putrescence and their vile touch on his skin sent him trembling.

The horse turned her head and pressed against his chest as if to console. He brought his limp arms around the black's neck and laid his head against the horse. The blood scent exploded through him but he found he did not want to taste. He could not do that to the innocent beast. Just feeling the heat and presence of a living creature gave him some sense of stability.

Ignoring the stares of the people exiting and entering the building, he and the horse stood together, his hands absently petting and scratching.

"I'd wondered where'd ye gone." Jeanie's voice was tinged with concern as she and the Noble walked out of the hotel. Each held their suitcases ready for the next leg of their journey.

Straightening up, he walked to the side of his horse and checked that his bag was firmly attached to the saddle. He could not match Jeanie's eyes right now and Fernando's probing expression made him even more uncomfortable.

Taking in the sight of the three horses, Fernando frowned. "Horses? You hired horses?"

"How else do you expect to get to Balinghem?" he countered, refusing to look at the Noble.

Fernando walked to the dun gelding and studied it for a moment. "If we didn't have the girl we'd be able to get there in no time."

He closed his eyes and sighed. It was the same old argument.

Jeanie stared nervously up at the chestnut. Her saddle was markedly different from the other two. "Ye expect me t'ride that?"

"Well, if you don't want to come along..." Fernando let the sentence hang.

Jeanie turned to face the Noble, dropped her bag and placed her gloved hands on hips covered by her green coat. "I'm coming and ye canna stop me."

"Heaven forefend," feigned Fernando, his hand to his breast. "Who else will warm the Angel's bed?"

The slap resounded in the cold damp air. Fernando lifted his hand to the side of his mouth and brought away a finger coloured with blood. Raising a brow at the sight, he tested his jaw and smiled.

Jeanie's eyes went round at the Chosen's expression. She had not expected to hit him, but he had it coming for so long. Now her blood ran cold at the realization of whom she had slapped and noticed that Fernando stood between her and the Angel.

From beneath the darkness of his hood, the Angel watched the growing tension between the two, his own thoughts muddied by his daytime hauntings. Absently, his left hand fell onto the pommel of his sword.

Slowly turning on his heel, Fernando walked over to the saddle strap to fasten his bag. He would remember this insolence, despite the fact that had he said similar to Bridget or any of her girls they would have hauled off one as well. It was the ominous threat of the Angel and his near mythical use of his blade that halted the Noble in any retaliation. Last night's slaughter astounded him and added an extra notch to his fear of the Angel. It was a feeling Fernando attempted to squash with bravado.

Swinging up onto the saddle, Fernando enjoyed the greater height. It had been a very long time since he had horseflesh between his legs and, taking the reins, he hoped he remembered how to ride. "Are we going to stand here all night?"

Jeanie tried to hide her relief by picking up her bag. She had no idea how to ride a horse.

Taking a look into the deep brown eyes of the chestnut she murmured, "Nice horsey," and patted it on the nose.

It seemed friendly enough but her experiences with horses in the past had always been with her being in a cart or coach. Her nervousness increased by the Noble's annoyed grumble.

"Here, let me help you," offered the Angel. Taking Jeanie's bag, he watched her face blossom into a radiant smile before twisting into concern at what she saw on his face.

Before she could ask, he turned away and focused his attention on firmly securing her suitcase. He knew he took overly long but he found the time necessary to compose himself enough to face her. Turning back, her head cocked to the side in study, she emitted a high-pitched squeak as his hands went around her waist and lifted her lightly into the saddle.

"Hook your leg around this," he stated, helping Jeanie to position on the side-saddle. He did not look up until she had arranged her skirts to cover her legs and placed a warm hand on his face.

"Are ye alright?" she asked.

Removing her hand from his face, he collected the reigns and placed them in her hand. How could he tell her that he was not fine? He could not even tell Notus about the white-faced demons and what they have done to him through the ages. "You do know how to ride, right?"

Jeanie shook her head and frowned. The fact that he had not answered her question struck a chord. The last time she had seen him like this he had lied. Now he did not even attempt to explain.

"Oh for heaven's sake," swore Fernando, rolling his eyes skyward.

Ignoring the Noble, the Angel took the lead rope from Jeanie's hand and tied it to a loop on his saddle. With lithe grace, he mounted the black, settled his cloak around him and the horse, and chucked the reigns while gently squeezing the black's barrel.

Needing no more encouragement, the horse turned at the pull of her reigns and headed towards the road, Jeanie's horse following closely.

It had been quite a while since he last rode a horse and it was one of the few pleasures in his long life, always bringing with it a sense of peace. Riding seemed to be the only time he felt free of the encumbrances of his existence, but this time it would not be the case.

He heard Fernando's horse canter up beside him.

"Do you happen to know where we are going?" asked the Noble, enjoying the smooth muscles move between his legs.

"Yes," he answered. He stared straight ahead refusing to look at Fernando. With an added pressure to the horse's sides, he tried to break away from the Noble and failed.

Sensing the Angel's gloomy disposition and knowing he would not receive more of an answer, Fernando frowned and fell back until his horse was behind the chestnut. A silent chuckle escaped his lips at seeing the mortal girl jiggling along, miserably trying to hold on to her horse. It was going to be a long, quiet, journey in the dark. Glancing up at the sky, the wind beginning to stir around them, Fernando's smile slipped with a sigh. The night promised to be a cold and wet one as well.

The faint light reflecting off the fast moving clouds were the only indication that civilization still existed. Skeletal arms of sleeping trees reached out for the three as they followed the road away from Calais and into the barren lands between populaces. Their breath mingled with the soft mist undulating its growth along the road's surface, deadening the solitary sound of regular footsteps of horses' hooves on the hard packed road. The wind whipped up to suddenly die, only to be stirred again.

Tipping his hood lower over his face, he tried to ignore the memories and shuddered. He knew Jeanie watched him with worried interest, wishing for some word from him to alleviate her concern, but there was nothing he could say so he remained silently ensconced in his cloak, staring into the dark night ahead. A terrible sense of foreboding had filled him and if it were not for the gentle clop-clop of the horses he would almost believe he was entering into the world of the white faced demons.

He watched in growing dread as the mist grew thicker and higher around the horses' legs, slinking further up along tree trunks and obscuring bushes and the road ahead. Swirling motions caused by the wind never forced the fog to relinquish its hold, but seemed only to froth it further.

His breath steamed out of him and fluttered down to merge with the thickening atmosphere as it reached up, trying to grab each exhalation to feed its growing form. A chill settled around his legs as the fog smouldered higher, leeching precious heat stolen from mortal blood.

Normally, the cold would not be much of a bother, but the freezing mist sent a shiver up his spine and he pulled his cloak tighter around his body. Try as he may the fog seemed to draw out his precious heat from every part of his body. The renewed sensory memory of feasting mouths upon his body set his jaw and caused him to swallow hard in an attempt to abate his trembling.

Movement out of the corner of his eye caught his attention and he turned to peer into the darkness. The black whuffled her unease but continued on with her plodding pace. Ignoring the horse, he watched in chilling horror as a figure seen only in his nightmares momentarily pass before him.

Its great maw opened in a sharp-toothed grin. Its eyes burning red embers. Putrescence dripped from Its raggedly translucent form to merge with the swirling fog. Terror struck, he could only watch as other forms manifested. With the promise of a hunger yet to be satiated, their eyeless sockets peered at him through the mist.

Wrenching his gaze away, he stared at the obscured road ahead, his heart beating painfully in his ears. This can't be happening. He dropped the reigns and rubbed his face with hands as white as the creatures around him. *I must be going mad.*

"Not mad." Its deep voice hissed with the sound of a thousand deadfall leaves scrabbling the earth.

A tendril of wisping mist swirled up to his face. The touch was solid, a torturous promise that shocked an icy shiver down his back.

Please, no, he implored closing his eyes in denial of the manifested reality around him.

"You are mine," Its voice purred through the darkness. *"Never forget that you will die before I ever let them have you."*

The solid fog instantly evaporated as a mix of hard rain and sleet flooded from heavy silver touched clouds. Panicked, he took the opportunity to flee, kicking the horse into a reckless speed for the conditions.

He ignored Jeanie's cry and Fernando's cursing. The only thing that mattered was his need to get away from the white-faced demons that had invaded his waking world.

On the horse sped into the dark, his cloak flying behind him, snapping heavily with each movement, his face stinging and wet from the cold rain mixing with his tears. It was only when his horse slipped and stumbled before righting herself on the muddied road that he resigned and reigned in to a slower pace. Had he been able, he would have pressed on.

Ignoring Fernando's shouts, he stared through the curtain of near frozen water for any sign of his tormentors.

"What the hell is wrong with you?" demanded the Noble, his horse sideling up to the Angel's. Everything had seemed so peaceful, and then suddenly, as the rain poured down, the Angel bolted. Cold water showered over him, quickly drenching him. Fernando silently swore that whoever made him lose his cloak in the Thames would pay dearly for his misery. Catching the cape, he pulled it tight around his body.

Glancing at Fernando's seething features, the Angel was glad for the rain that washed away his tears. Realizing that he could give no answer, he turned back to focus on their journey, praying that his tormentors would not return.

A signpost stood in stark relief against the clouds as they came upon the crossroads. Tilting his sodden hood back to read the carved and painted lettering, he allowed the cold water to wash over him as he read. His shoulders slumped in the realization that they were a little more than halfway through their journey. Turning his horse to follow the road to Balinghem, his eyes widened in surprise as Fernando leaned over and grabbed his horse by the bridle.

"I asked you a question," seethed Fernando. His grip hardened around the wet leather, causing it to creak. The black tried to dance out of his grip.

"Let go of my horse." Anger surged, warming him. He knew it was not the Noble he was upset with, rather it was the white faced demons that he was powerless against, and Fernando had made himself into a handy target.

"I will not." Fernando eased his horse over to the Angel's in an attempt to straighten up in his saddle without losing his grip on the bridle. He would not look up at the Angel's reaper like features; Fernando had to retain some sense of his anger. Witnessing the Angel's eyes lit with fury was not something he wanted to see.

"Release my horse," demanded the Angel through clenched teeth. He pulled the reigns causing the black to try and wrench her head from the Noble's grasp but failed.

"You idiot," spat Fernando, ignoring the rain as it turned into stabbing ice needles. "I'll not have you cause my horse to pitch me into the mud. I don't know what the hell has gotten into you. You're the one who wanted to bring these damned beasts because you wanted your mortal paramour to come along."

Fernando eyes lifted to defiantly meet his own. They glared at each other through the hissing downpour. Finally, the Noble reluctantly removed his hand from the bridle once he realized no answer was forthcoming.

Chucking the reigns, the Angel forced his horse past Fernando's scowling form, his own restrained anger crying out for bloodshed. His left hand absentmindedly crossed over to rest on the hilt of the sword rocking on his hip. Never before had he desired to feel his blade cut through flesh and bone, to spray hot blood, to take a life. All he needed was one more excuse to let loose the rage and his slim control would be broken. Once past the Noble's hot glare, a part of him was disappointed that the Noble had backed off.

The sleet turned into rain and back again as he rode, soaking through his wool cloak until he could feel the cold water dripping down his back. His hand loosened its grip on the sword. The water washed away his burning anger, leaving a sullen desire to be out of the persistent downpour and the potential of further contact with the demons.

"Gwyn!"

The name shouted through the night snapped his attention backwards as he pulled his horse to a halt. Hearing the name on Fernando's lips unnerved him and he knew the Noble had used it explicitly to gain his attention. Schooling his features into cold anger, he watched Fernando thumb in Jeanie's direction.

"We need to find shelter now," shouted Fernando through the downpour. "I'd prefer to be out of this horrid weather and I don't believe your mortal housekeeper can keep to her saddle much longer."

His gaze followed the Noble's to find Jeanie swaying in her saddle, her curling hair plastered straight against her head and shoulders. She had said nothing throughout their tumultuous ride and witnessing her pale wan features he felt a hard knot of guilt rise in his gorge. In his self absorbed brooding he had completely forgotten that Jeanie rode with them in a deadly frigid rain.

Swinging down from his saddle, his shoes squelched in the ice-slicked mud as he strode over to her and placed a pale hand upon her freezing face. Fear for Jeanie's well-being caught his breath. Fernando was right; they had to find shelter and fast.

Green eyes flickered open and gazed unfocused upon him.

"I'm sorry," she mumbled through chattering teeth.

Shaking his head against the apology, he could not believe her audacity as she sat her horse completely rain drenched and frozen to the bone. He had to get her off the horse and warm her lest the cold send her to an early death.

"Can you unhook your leg?" he asked, his features filling with worry.

A vague expression clouded over Jeanie's sickly pale features and she frowned. "Eh?"

Grasping her clammy leg, he slipped Jeanie out of the saddle and carried her to his horse where he settled her astride and then swung up behind her. Deftly, he curtained his cloak around the both of them in the hopes that his meagre body heat, mingled with the horse's, would help Jeanie retain some of her own. Even soaking wet, his wool cloak should provide some insulation against the storming night.

With one arm around Jeanie, he picked up the reigns, forcing the black into motion. He heard her sigh and felt her body go slack against his. Jaw clenched in worry he searched the dark night for any sign of a place to sequester themselves from the rain. The road was familiar and he thought he saw what he hoped to find. Indicating to the horse to move faster, he found the turn off from the main roadway and down another that was hardly more than a cart track.

"Where are we going?" Fernando brought his horse up beside the Angel's, his eyes squinting against the watery onslaught. "This isn't the way to Balinghem."

"You wanted out of the rain." He searched through the darkness of the tree-canopied track. The mould scent of fallen leaves filled the air. "Jeanie needs to be indoors." He glanced over at the Noble's wary features and then to the track ahead. Again Fernando's strange compassion mixed with conceit confounded him.

Fernando frowned. "There's nothing down here. All there is are open fields past these damned trees."

"We're on the outskirts of St. Martin's Abbey."

"How the hell do you know that?" Fernando shot the Angel a look of surprise as he twisted in his saddle to see if they had passed some sort of sign that he missed.

Squinting through the rain, he saw what he was looking for – lights from the Abbey. "Notus and I stayed here for a year before we returned to England," he answered matter-of-factly. He kicked his horse into a trot; seeing the Abbey so close drove his worry.

Fernando followed suit, happy that he would soon be able to dry off even though it would cost them even more time from searching for the estate.

"What were the two of you doing here?" asked the Noble, recognizing an opportunity to uncover more secrets about his elusive partner.

The question surprised the Angel. Fernando had not tried to pry into his past for some time, but this query seemed to come from genuine curiosity.

"Notus did some restoration work on some of their older manuscripts and trained those interested in the art of scribing and illumination."

Strangely, talking about Notus seemed to ease his mood and he wondered if some semblance of a connection between he and his Chooser had re-established itself. He shook that notion off with a frown, knowing the distance between them was too great.

Amazed that a Chosen would desire to live for year amongst mortals, let alone work alongside and teach them, Fernando mutely shook his head before a confused frown took its place. "And what did you do there? You don't strike me as one to follow holy orders and practices."

"I hunted, read, or practiced," he answered laconically. The turn from talking about Notus to himself prickled and he hoped his terse reply would halt any further inquiry.

Fernando let his horse fall back a length, surprised at the Angel's response. Another question formed, ready to leave his lips, but something in the Angel's tone told him not to press the issue. He was getting further in his discoveries about the Angel and to be stymied yet again frustrated the Noble into calculating silence.

XXX

ounding the bend, the trees gave way to the stone wall surrounding the cluster of buildings that was St. Martin's Abbey. Yellow light flickered from ancient windows indicating that at least some of the inhabitants were still awake. Between the stone walls an arched opening revealed a muddied track leading into the monastery's grounds. Turning his horse, he ducked under the arch and followed the flickering lights to the Cathedral in the hopes that the doors would be unbarred.

Movement off to the left caught his attention. Squinting through the heavy rain he saw a young monk not much past his early twenties shuffling in his drenched black robe. Equally sodden logs of wood balanced precariously in his arms as the monk endeavoured to find his way back into the dry shelter of monastery. Hearing the horses approach, the monk turned his head and lost his balanced burden in a clatter of wood smacking against wet wood before landing with a splash. Eyes widening at the strangers approach, the monk ran for the side door that was left ajar. His thin voice rang through the downpour.

The Angel watched the fumbling display with a mixture of relief and annoyance. Swinging down from the horse, he scooped up Jeanie's unconscious form and carried her up the few steps to the Cathedral's doors barely aware that Fernando followed. Through the rain splattered night he could hear men's voices chattering nervously from behind the doors. With hands full, he gritted his teeth in frustration that the doors had not opened and gave the old wood a kick, leaving behind a streak of mud.

The doors boomed and shuddered against the hinges with the promise that with another such forceful pounding it would cave in. Glancing down at Jeanie's sickly pale face, her breath slow and shallow, he knew that if they did not open the door in the next moment he would force them down. Preparing his stance for another blow that would shatter the heavy doors from their frame, he relaxed his posture at the sound of the bar being lifted and the door opened. Without so much as a word of thanks he strode into Cathedral and demanded to see the Abbot from the cluster of monks surrounding the drenched young man he had seen in the courtyard.

An old monk with rheumy grey eyes stepped forward from the group. His age, if not his tenure in the monastery, lended to leadership. *"L'Ange,* is that you?"

Relief flooded through the Angel and he tossed his head back to throw off his hood. Long white locks of hair draped free to add to the sound of dripping.

"Yes, Brother Bartholomew," he replied. Ignoring the surprised gasps of the other monks, he gazed down at Jeanie's slack form in his arms not bothering to hide the worry from his face. "We need help."

Brother Bartholomew's gaze shot at the girl in the Angel's arms and began to shout orders to the other monks milling about. They bolted into action. The young wet monk sighed as he sullenly ambled out of the door and back into the rainy night.

"Come with me," ordered the old monk. Turning on his sandaled heel, Brother Bartholomew strode down the corridor, taking them out of the Cathedral and towards the guest rooms of the monastery.

Two monks walked at a casual pace ahead of them and turned at the sound of the ringing approach of booted footsteps against the stone floor. Their eyes went wide at the sight of the Angel carrying a young woman and another man striding behind.

Brother Bartholomew's features, set in stone, called out to the two. "Brother Marc, go and find the Abbot. Brother Claude, go and fetch Brother Absolon and tell him we have need of his medical knowledge. Don't stand there gaping, go!"

The two younger monks fled down the corridor and through a doorway.

"I'm not going to ask you what has brought you here on this horrible night," proffered the old monk as they made a turn down a darkened hallway. "I'll leave that to the Abbot. I'm sure he'll have the same questions I have." He halted at a door and finding it unlocked, Brother Bartholomew turned the handle and opened it.

The Angel would have smiled at the sight of the old room he had shared with Notus but relief filled him at seeing two young monks moving quickly to make the room hospitable. A third successfully started a fire in the hearth and began to set and light beeswax candles in the sconces. Finding the single bed made, he gently laid Jeanie down, her frozen soaked hair drenching the pillow beneath her. Already the warmth seemed to be doing its work until he noticed that her breathing and heartbeat were near non-existent. Panic flooded through him and he watched in dazed horror as Brother Absolon flew into the room.

"Oh, it's you," commented Absolon before turning to attend to his patient. "Get out and let me do my work."

He was about to demand to stay when he felt gentle hands on his arms guiding him out into the hall. It was only when the door had closed, cutting him off from Jeanie that he noticed the Abbot standing before him.

"Don't worry, my son, Brother Absolon may have a horrendous bedside manner, but his medical talents are God given." The Abbot eyes fell to the scowling Noble, frowned and then looked back up at the Angel. "Where's Father Paul, *l'Ange*?"

Emotionally exhausted, he leaned against the wall, his sword clattering against stone. Eyes closed and head leaning against the wall he was aware that he was leaving a puddle on the floor. What could he say to Notus' good friend? The truth was impossible. "He's in London."

"Then why aren't you there with him?" The Abbot's terse tone cut through him.

He opened his eyes to look down at the dark haired, plain looking monk in black robes and prayed his lie would be taken for the truth. "I'm on an errand for him."

"All three of you?" A thick brown brow rose in incredulity.

"Yes," responded the Noble.

Surprised at Fernando's rescuing of the situation, he glanced down at the other Chosen and was met with a smile that told him that this little favour would have to be returned.

Not noticing the truth of the exchange between the two guests, the Abbot turned his attention to the Angel's companion. "And you are?"

"I am Fernando de Sagres, the last heir to the Fidalgo de Sagres." Fernando made a swooping bow to the Abbot that was tinged with mockery.

The Abbot grimaced. "And the young woman?"

Fearful that the Noble would say something completely inappropriate, the Angel cut him off before Fernando could reply. "Jeanie Stuart; Father Paul's housekeeper."

"Father Paul sent his housekeeper?" asked the Abbot, aporetically.

Fernando glanced up at the Angel with a shrug that told him he was on his own to answer this one. With a sigh, the Angel met the Abbot's gaze.

Identifying the sad weariness in the Angel's disturbing crimson eyes, the Abbot visibly softened. "That's alright, my son. You will tell me the truth when you are ready. In the mean time I will have guest rooms made up for you and your companion." He turned to leave his two guests.

"Father Theodore," called the Angel. He stood up away from the wall and took a pace towards the Abbot. "I wish to stay in my old room."

The Abbot shook his head. "Miss Stuart is in there being tended to by Brother Absolom. In any case, unless the two of you are married, it would not be proper."

"Please Father." He hated pleading in front of Fernando and knew he would pay dearly, but he was loath to leave Jeanie's side. "Let it be like when I stayed here with Father Paul."

Face screwed up in consternation, the Abbot shook his head in disbelief. "A pallet on the floor by the door? Again?"

"Yes." He ignored Fernando's stare of wonderment.

"And what of your friend?"

"I'll have my own room, thank you," replied the Noble.

Father Theodore nodded. "Fine. I'll have the room next door made up for you and, *l'Ange*, a pallet will be brought for you."

"Thank you." He offered, recognizing the extreme generosity of the Abbot.

"Don't make me regret it, *l'Ange,*" called the Abbot as he went in search of some Brothers to set things up for his guests. "Make yourself at home. Don't brood outside the door. I'll come find you when Brother Absolom has word."

Around a turn, the Abbot disappeared from view, but his presence still filled the halls.

Shoulders slumping, he removed his cloak pin, allowing the waterlogged fabric to slump to the floor and removed his sword to stand it against the wall. He slid his back against the wall until he sat on the cold damp stones, his arms resting on his raised knees.

"He said not to brood outside the door," smirked the Noble.

A spark of annoyance filled him as he looked up at Fernando standing before him. Recognizing that if he stayed there the Noble would badger him, he stood and grabbed his sword. The cloak could stay there on the floor until he returned. The Abbot said he would find him when there was word on Jeanie's condition.

Taking long strides in the Abbot's path he heard Fernando call out as he retreated. "A pallet?"

"The beds are too short," he replied brusquely. Ignoring Fernando's laughter he turned the corner in the hopes to find some solitude.

He did not know how long he wandered the hallways of the monastery before the sounds of men in prayer tickled his hearing. Following the soothing sounds that were so similar yet so different than the ones from the East, he found himself standing in the vestibule to the Cathedral. The heavy doors to the outside were closed and barred against the storm and the puddles he had left in his wake had been thoroughly dried. In the Chancel a dozen monks sat in prayer singing Compline.

Something in the sound, if not the words, drew him to find a seat on the pew furthest away, hidden in shadow. Gently, so as not disturb the chanting with discordance, he laid his sheathed sword along the pew beside him.

Still wet from the journey, he leaned forward, placed his arms on the pew before him and laid his head. It was an awkward position in the cramped confines, but he could not make himself look up at all the brilliant light that sparkled off of votives and altar candles. It was not the brightness that bothered him, but rather what he felt he did not have the rights to.

Worry squeezed his eyes shut in a vain attempt to keep back the tears. He could not loose Jeanie. It was his self-indulgent thoughtlessness that caused her to be near death. Yet how could he not have reacted the way he did at seeing the manifestation of the demons? A shudder ran through him at the death sentence It had meted out. If only he knew why, maybe he could change it or at least run from it. If only he could run from his dreams.

Never before had they manifested so concretely and he wondered if either Jeanie or Fernando had seen them. That possibility frightened him even more. Whatever he was being led to, he had an ominous feeling that it was not just to find out who was poisoning the Chosen and to free his Chooser. Something darker was at work and he shuddered to think what that could mean.

A warm hand lightly rested on his damp shoulder, its heat penetrating the thin cotton of his shirt. Lifting his head, he sat back feeling cold wood and looked up to see Father Theodore's gentle face.

The Abbot relinquished his touch and sat down beside him, closed his eyes and bathed in the sounds of prayer.

Realizing that patience was in order the Angel sat in quiet expectation, waiting for the Abbot to speak.

"Your Miss Stuart is going to be fine."

Father Theodore's soft voice released the tension he held in an explosive sigh. He closed his eyes as the worry he had held tightly in check bubbled and broke. Swallowing hard, he looked at the Abbot beside him through shimmering eyes.

Father Theodore patted the Angel's leg and smiled. "Brother Absolom said that had you waited any longer Miss Stuart would have passed from this world from hypothermia. She owes her life to you."

Guilt screwed up his pale features and he turned his head away to stare into the darkness. Hearing confirmation that it was his actions that nearly caused Jeanie to die cut him to the quick. If Fernando had not brought Jeanie's condition to light they would still be on the road and she would have died. The thought that it was actually the Noble who saved Jeanie's life wrenched the guilt further.

"Miss Stuart is more than Father Paul's housekeeper, isn't she?" gently ventured the Abbot, seeing the Angel's reaction. In the year that the strange young man had stayed with the Brothers of St. Martin's never had Father Theodore seen such emotion on the normally aloof Angel.

Without glancing back at the Abbot he nodded.

The Abbot took a deep breath and let it out in a sigh as if coming to an important decision. "If it is something your kind does with mortals, then have Father Paul marry the two of you."

Shocked, the Angel turned to face the monk. "How?"

Unnerved by the garnet coloured eyes boring into him, the Abbot stared at the monks standing up and talking to each other before vacating the Cathedral. He nodded his acknowledgement of the monks as they past, offering "good mornings" and blessings to those who offered greeting. Once the last monk had left he returned his attention to his guest. "I'll not break the seal of the confessional, but I will say this: I know what you are." He turned to study the surprised pale face beside him. "I know that you will be respectful and leave my brothers alone as you and Father Paul did in your year here, but the other one, de Sagres, he is of your kind, isn't he?" The Angel mutely nodded. "Will he?"

He could not believe his ears. The Abbot knew and Notus had probably told him during confession. "I'll tell him that St. Martin's is under my protection."

Father Theodore raised a brow. "Will that be enough, l'Ange?"

"It should be, Father," he frowned. He hoped that Fernando would not jeopardise their stay by feasting on one or more of the monks, and that hospitality etiquette would be something that the Noble still held to.

Standing with groaning effort, the Abbot patted the Angel on the shoulder. "I pray so, my son. In the mean time go and get yourself dry. I know you cannot catch your death, but I don't appreciate you dripping all over God's floors."

He caught the glint in the monk's eyes as Father Theodore turned and left the Cathedral. A half smile flitted across his alabaster face and then fell. Gazing at his hands nestled on his soggy lap, he turned them over. Black against white, the scrape on his right hand was red and healing well. He clenched his hands into fists and closed his eyes.

Father Theodore's mentioning of marrying Jeanie had surprised him more than the realization that the Abbot knew he was Chosen. It was something he would have loved to propose had he been mortal, but it was not something he could offer her. He did not know if he could watch her grow old and then pass away, yet he knew that he could not live without her.

The only other option was to make her into one of the Chosen and he knew that Notus would never allow that. It was hard enough to hide his deficient blood from the rest of the Chosen. He could not pass it down to another and have their lives be risked. He could not allow the possibility of having the white-faced demons come to another — especially to one he loved.

His gaze lifted to the crucifix above the high altar. An image formed in his mind, Notus' battered and blood drained body over that of the gruesome sight of Jesus' torture. Dropping his gaze back to his clenched hands, he shuddered.

He felt assaulted from every direction, threatening to send him into madness. Only in Jeanie's arms had he found some semblance of peace since this whole travesty began. Eyes lifting, his gaze fell on the statue of the Blessed Virgin and the blazing votives at her feet.

A tickling of the past remembered pulled at him to peer closer at the loving compassionate features of her face, as it seemed to transform, its deep eyes meeting his gaze. Fear trickled up his spine in expectation of another visit from the white-faced demons.

No, not them, came a voice of infinite peace.

He could not believe what he was hearing. The many layered female voice seemed to ring throughout the Cathedral, but he knew that the words were only for him. Shaking his head in denial of the reality he was thrust into, he stood ready in attempt to flee from madness.

It's been too long.

The comforting voice magically sloughed off his fear and he peered closer at the icon of the Blessed Virgin. It appeared to change, transform, to take on the visage of not only one but of three women. He stood fast despite the racing of his heart.

Remember what you have been taught, to remember who you were supposed to be.

The mysterious words pulled at him and he stepped closer to the shrine. Staring up at the fluctuating visage, he let out a gasp as a wave of peace flowed through him.

Remember. Speak the long forgotten words.

Placing his sword at her feet, he knelt on the prieu dieu. He rested his elbows on the small desk and buried his head into his hands. He was not Catholic, no matter how hard Notus had tried before giving up centuries ago. Auntie's teachings were too strongly ensconced even after all these years. Yet, for the first time in his life he felt pulled to kneel before a shrine.

With eyes closed, ancient words from his childhood rose unbidden in his mind and he spoke the long dead language Auntie had taught him beneath the full moon.

The words formed easily on his pale lips. The prayer to the Goddess warmed his body and he joyfully felt his mind slip into a peaceful oblivion.

The Choice has been remade.

A fierce scream of wind raced through the Cathedral.

XXXI

he monks had more than satisfactorily set up the quaint, yet small, guestroom, having covered and stuffed the small window with blankets until not an inch of light would be seen come the morning. It was not long before the young monk who had seen them first in the courtyard, still drenched through and through, had slogged miserably with their luggage after stabling their horses. With a fire raging in the hearth, Fernando had managed to arrange his possessions on the meagre, simple wood furniture to steam in the heat or to drip dry.

Fernando closed the door behind him, leaving the blissful heat of his room to the cooler domains of the monastery's corridors. His fresh clothing clung damply on his body, a testament that even his expensive luggage could not keep out such a downpour, but at least it was better than walking the halls drenched.

The door to the other guestroom opened and Brother Absolom started at the sight of the Noble dressed in shirt and trousers standing before him. The monk queryingly glanced down each end of the hallway. "Where's the Angel?"

The question should not have surprised Fernando, but he found it odd that the Angel was not with Jeanie and shrugged. "You're guess is as good as mine, Father."

A bushy grey brow rose. "I'm not a priest, just a humble monk."

Rebuke accepted, Fernando flashed a grin and turned to go down the hall.

"Are you not going to inquire as to how the young lady is doing?" asked the monk.

Turning on his heel, Fernando halted. "I figured that had she died you would have told me and you wouldn't have asked where the Angel was as he would be with her. As it is, I'm sure she will be just fine."

Surprised at the young man's obvious disregard for his travelling companion's fate, Brother Absolom shook his head in disbelief, sending wispy grey hairs flying, and decided to take the opposite way down the hall.

Fernando chuckled as he walked down the darkened corridor. He had no doubt that the Scot's girl would be fine. She was too annoying to roll over and die, but he had to admire her determination and her ability to hold her own. Despite her naïveté, innocence and her utter lack of forethought that nearly killed the Angel, Fernando was starting to like her fire and loved to needle her just to see her rise to the bait. It was too easy.

A frown flitted across his face. It was too much like having an annoying younger sister.

Shaking off that notion, Fernando set back his shoulders, determined to make the best of the situation. If they could not get to Balinghem tonight to find the records of where *Le Jardin* was, then maybe someone here would be able to lead him to the answers.

Torchlight flickered in their sconces, creating yellow pools of light far enough apart from each other that they formed an archipelago in the darkness. His frown deepened as he realized that at this time of night most, if not all, of the Brothers would be abed and that he should have asked Brother Absolom when he had the chance.

Rounding a corner, he collided with the young monk who had brought in his bag.

Still soaked to the skin the monk ricocheted onto the floor with a wet smack. His fatigued glazed eyes blinked upwards to see the monastery's guest standing before him.

Fernando sighed in annoyance that his nearly dry clothing now clung soggily. He should have heard the mortal sloshing down the hall and damned himself for his sloppiness before he realized his luck.

"I'm sorry, sir," stammered the young monk. Wet black wool smacked against stone as he attempted to untangle himself and stand.

"My fault," offered the Noble, recognizing the truth of his words. He held out his hand and hoisted the monk to his feet.

Under the pungent scent of wet wool floated the promise of revitalizing blood. His eyes held the young man's, feeling the throbbing pulse in their united hands. It would be oh so easy to sup and wipe away the memory of it ever happening.

Shaking off the clasp, Fernando backed away, damning the protocols of etiquette that demanded that any Chosen housed or guesting under a mortal roof would be forbidden to partake of that mortal's blood.

"Are you alright, sir?" queried the monk, witnessing the Noble's sudden anger.

"Fine, just fine," scowled Fernando. "Maybe you can help me."

"I'll try," said the monk, diminutively.

Fernando peered closer at the young man. "You haven't been a monk long, have you?"

The monk lowered his eyes. "No. I took my vows last year."

That explains it, sighed Fernando.

"I'm looking for a villa—an estate—in these parts. It's called *Le Jardin*. Do you know it?"

The monk chewed on his lower lip. "I don't think so." He looked up with a hopeful expression. "But you can check the library."

Pleased for the lead, Fernando pressed, "And where can I find that?"

The young monk told him and without so much as a thank you Fernando turned around and headed back the way he had come.

The creek of hinges exploded into the deserted hall as Fernando pulled the ancient wooden door open. He hoped that this was the place, having found the maze of corridors confusing. A rush of cooler moist air pulled at his clothing, encouraging him to enter the extremely large room. Not one to ignore an invitation, Fernando stepped into the dark and closed the door with a boom that resonated off the ceiling high bookcases filled with tomes and scrolls.

Gazing around, he let out a whistle. Never before had he seen such wealth. He could see why Notus stayed here for a year. Manoeuvring around the desks set up for scribing and others for study, he came to stand before one of the bookcases and gazed up to its heights before bringing his eyes back down to rest on the ancient leather covered tomes before him. Gold flakes of remnant lettering were the only clues to what was held between the covers. Laying his hand on the cool leather, Fernando began to walk the length of the Library, his fingers bouncing from one book to the next and huffed in annoyance. It would take years to find the answer to where *Le Jardin* could be found.

Turning at the sound of the door opening, Fernando stood silently in the darkness as at first the flickering yellow flames of a trifurcated candelabrum entered, followed by the elderly monk who had first met them. Fernando smiled as he felt his luck increasing and he took a step towards Brother Bartholomew.

"Wha—? Who's there?" The monk squinted his rheumy eyes in an attempt to see past the pool of candlelight.

"Just one of your newly arrived guests, Brother." Fernando graciously smiled, stepping into the light.

The elderly monk's eyes widened in surprise and then squinted in suspicion. "Couldn't sleep, eh?" He moved past Fernando and set the candelabra on the closest desk and placed an old worn book beside it.

"I'm not one for sleeping at night," offered the Noble, coming to stand next to his quarry. He leaned against the desk almost sitting on it, causing it to creak as his weight shifted it minutely along the floor.

Brother Bartholomew harrumphed and studied the monastery's guest. "And I take it that you found yourself wandering our peaceful halls, finally ending up alone in the dark in the Scriptorium?"

"Actually, I was hoping to get in some research before bed." Fernando casually turned and ran a finger down the front cover of the book, enjoying the texture. The topic matter did not interest him, but rather the monetary value of such a text. "I have to admit that I was surprised to find another so disinclined to sleep."

"I'm old, but not a fool." Brother Bartholomew picked up the book as if the Noble's touch was befouling its sacredness, and hugged it to his chest. "I also find that my needs for sleep have diminished greatly in my advanced years. The solitude of quiet study, alone with God, at night is something I have come to appreciate."

Fernando inclined his head and picked up the candelabra. Following the monk to the other side of the Library, Brother Bartholomew expertly placed the book into the toothless gap awaiting it amongst its brethren.

"Now what is it that you are researching?" The monk turned around to face the Noble. "Bear in mind that I do find it quite odd that you were without light."

Smiling at his good fortune, Fernando pretended to study the book spines. "I was looking for a candle or a lamp," he lied.

"Ah well," accepted Brother Bartholomew. "And your research?"

"I'm looking for an estate in these parts named *Le Jardin*." He turned to study the old monk. "Have you heard of it?"

The monk stuck out his lower lip in thought as he ran his mottled pale hand through the remnants of his white hair. "I don't believe I do."

A frown pulled down Fernando's face and he sighed, his luck running out.

"Just because I haven't heard of the place doesn't mean we can't find it?" offered the monk with a smile. "Come with me."

Fernando followed the brother towards the far back wall where a wide simple oak cabinet ran almost its length and ran almost a yard deep.

"It's been a long time since I've had the pleasure of a good archive search, especially of the secular books."

With a groan and the creaking of bone against bone, Brother Bartholomew crouched down, slid the cabinet door wide and began to shuffle through the large books laying flat one on top of the other. "Bring the light down here, my son, my eyes are not what they used to be."

Kneeling down on one leg, Fernando held the light for the monk who muttered and groaned as he shifted books that were at least a yard in height. The Noble ignored the hot candle drippings falling on his wrist and intently watched as the man who was well past his prime slide out a book that was half as wide as it was tall. Its thickness bespoke of many pages.

"You're a young man – take this and place it on the table behind you."

Fernando did as he was bid, finding the weight to be unremarkable for his strength. The book slid home on the table with a thunk that rang through the room and he placed the candelabra beside it. He heard the door to the cabinet slide shut and Brother Bartholomew recommence his groans as he regained a more vertical stance.

Glancing at the title, Fernando wished he had bothered to learn how to read French. "What is it?"

"It's a topographical survey of France," huffed the elderly monk as he came to stand beside the Noble. "Collected within the last century, I believe. If your estate is at least fifty years old, it will be in here."

Elated at the prospects of finding *Le Jardin*, Fernando hoisted the cover exposing large sheets of paper covered in very tiny writing and many, many wiggly lines.

"How is it that a monastery would have such a find? One would think it would be at some governmental establishment."

Brother Bartholomew passed a page to be flipped to the young man, enjoying the mystery and the company it brought. "I believe it was stored in Calais' ministry office and once a newer survey was published, this one, as well as the others, came here. One should never throw away a book, no matter how old or irrelevant it may seem. Someone will always come along proving its applicability."

Fernando matched the monk's sparkling smile. He had no doubt that he was going to find the next step in his journey all with the help of this amiable elderly man. Yet it seemed strange that Brother Bartholomew had been so displeased at seeing the Angel again. It begged the opportunity to find out more about his elusive partner.

"If you don't mind me asking," he ventured, helping to flip another of the large pages filled with statistics. "You didn't seem all that surprised to see the Angel."

The monk halted his procession of another page and gazed askance at the guest. Pursing his lips together, he let the page down and turned to face the Noble. "One does not forget a nearly seven foot tall albino."

"That's true," remarked Fernando. "But you also did not seem all that pleased to remake his acquaintance."

Turning back to study the small script, Brother Bartholomew turned another page, his tense silence filling the room. "I neither like nor dislike the Angel. It is not for me to judge, but rather His. But the Angel's presence in our monastery, though quiet and seemingly unobtrusive, brought speculations and disharmony amongst the brothers."

Sensing that he was on the break of some new revelation, Fernando stepped closer to the elderly monk, took the page and flipped it. "How so?"

"You're travelling with him, so you must have some inkling as to what I mean."

Knowing all too well what the monk hinted at, Fernando nodded. Even as a Chosen, the Angel seemed to elicit a sense of unease in those around him.

"He told me he spent a year here in the company of Father Paul. The Angel doesn't strike me as a devout Catholic."

Brother Bartholomew placed his hand flat on the page and turned to face the Noble. "Are you researching where this estate is or the Angel? Gossip is the devil's work and I will not be drawn into such idleness."

"Please forgive me, Brother." Fernando bowed his head in the hopes to appease the man. He did not want to force the information from him with his preternatural abilities, but he would if he had to. "It is that I need more information of the man that I am accompanying. If we were to find ourselves in some trouble I would need to know if I could count on him."

"And you don't believe you can?"

Fernando's brows rose in surprise at the shocked expression on the elderly monk's face. "I'm not sure. He told me that he spent his time here hunting, reading and practicing."

"Hunting – I don't know about," answered the Brother. "There's not much around here to hunt. As for reading, yes, he did do a lot of that. He would read in here only when Father Paul taught his classes or worked, bringing books back to the room they shared when Father Paul was elsewhere. As for practicing, that he did—a lot." He let out a huff.

Sensing he was on the brink of some sort of discovery, Fernando pressed, speaking gently in time with the old man's heart. "Practiced what?"

Brother Bartholomew's shoulders slumped. "What did he not practice? Shortly upon their arrival the Angel would go out onto the cloister garth after Vespers—sundown—and practice what Father Paul called, his forms. There he moved like a dancer but with all the insinuation that any motion could bring death. When he practiced with his sword, it became extremely obvious which Angel he could be if roused."

"And this is why you aren't pleased at seeing him again?" Fernando's eyes lighted at the knowledge.

"Yes," said the Brother. "To the novices he became what they had hoped they could have become. We lost quiet a number of them because of the Angel."

"He didn't kill them, did he?" ask Fernando unable to hide his shock.

"Heaven forefend! They just left with visions of heroics dazzling their young minds. Others were left questioning their faith. It was what happened when we had other guests one weekend that shattered our peace." Brother Bartholomew turned back to flipping the large pages a little more rapidly than before.

Not willing to leave this without some sort of conclusion Fernando gently Pushed, "What happened?"

"A young man of obvious means stopped for a couple of nights with his pregnant wife and their servants. She wished to be blessed and he humoured her." Brother Bartholomew's fingers began to tremble, rattling the large sheets as he turned them. "The man having heard the gossip of some of the less disciplined monks went to see the Angel at practice. The next evening he challenged the Angel to a duel."

"He what?" Fernando could not believe his luck or his ears. He licked lips in anticipation.

"The Angel at first ignored the gentleman, but the man forcefully insisted. Turning to face the young husband, his expression cold and emotionless, the Angel accepted. The man had his servant bring out a pair of duelling foils. It was over before it began. They saluted each other and then the Angel dropped his sword to the ground, side stepped the thrust, grabbed the man's hand and twisted. The sound of bone snapping surprised everyone, but even more so, the young husband who fell to his knees in pain. It was then that the Angel bent down and whispered something in the man's ear that set the man running, yelling orders that they were leaving right then and there. After that incident the Angel's practice time changed to after Matins."

"And you saw this?"

Brother Bartholomew hung his head and nodded. "I was looking for one of the novices and found him watching the Angel. I admit I became enamoured as well and witnessed the whole proceedings."

Pleased by the greater information Fernando smiled and took the next page as it was passed to him. "Is that it?"

The monk leaned closer to the page that laid out the specifics of the Monastery and its surrounding properties. Off the north-eastern boarder, lands belonging to *Le Jardin des Dieux* with the estate in its centre, were clearly marked.

"I believe it is," answered the Brother, relieved at the change of topic.

"Do you think I can get a rough copy?"

"That I definitely can do, my son," smiled Brother Bartholomew.

Quick paced steps echoed down the hall. In his hand Fernando held the folded map carefully crafted by Brother Bartholomew. It was not the discovery of *Le Jardin* that lightened his steps, but rather hearing more about the Angel. Having witnessed the Angel's graceful defence with sword in one hand and Jeanie in the other, Fernando had been awed, something that rarely happened to the Noble. Hearing that the Angel regularly practiced these forms, with and without bladed weapon, confirmed yet again the incongruities of the man he travelled with.

Notus' account of the Angel's mistaken Choosing in his journal, coupled with the Angel carelessly admitting he became a warrior after receiving his scars made no sense. How does a young man holed up in a cave become a warrior of such skill and expertise? If indeed the Angel became a warrior after being Chosen, then the only conclusion to be drawn was that the Angel received his scarring wounds afterwards as well. That could not be possible unless there was something impure about the Angel that could brand him to be a Destroyed One.

Fernando frowned. It always seemed to come back to that possibility and he did not like it for some strange reason. Despite the Angel being, well, the Angel, Fernando did not wish that extermination upon him. The closer he came to breaking the barrier to the Angel's secrets, the less thrilled he became with the responsibilities and the possibilities those answers brought. He would trade them of course, without hesitation, if it meant his life or the Angel's.

Absentmindedly, he crunched the paper in frustration and then swore at his abuse of the map. Opening up the paper, Fernando halted and smoothed it out as best he could. Thankfully, the markings made by grease pencil had not smudged too badly. He folded it carefully and renewed his search for the Angel.

Fernando's first inclination was to go to the cloister garth just in case the Angel was picking up his old practices again despite the horrendous weather. Not finding the Angel there, Fernando managed to trace back to the guest quarters. First, he knocked on the Angel's door and hearing nothing but Jeanie deep in sleep, Fernando gently opened it to confirm what his ears reported. The Angel was not in his room. Since only Brother Bartholomew peopled the Library when he left, Fernando had no clue as to where else he could look for his elusive partner.

Wandering the halls in his search, Fernando halted when he found himself standing in the vestibule of the church. Drawn by the flickering candlelight which seemed to warm the chill of the sanctuary, he took a step through the doorway and into the nave.

It was a large church for such a monastery, simple in its design, lending to it an aesthetic beauty. Scowling at the sight of the dead man on a cross, Fernando was about to turn to leave when he caught sight of his partner kneeling before the shrine to the Holy Mother.

"Now that is a sight I thought never to see." Fernando walked over to where the Angel knelt at the prieu dieu, his dishevelled hair masking his pale face.

Fernando watched, as the Angel seemed to wake, rolling his broad shoulders and lifting his head. A long fingered hand reached out to grasp the sheathed sword resting by the feet of the Virgin, sending the Noble's heart beating faster in anticipation of a clearly mismatched fight. The Angel knelt back and then stood, sweeping his long tresses away from his face with his free hand. Swallowing hard, Fernando lifted his head defiantly, matching the Angel's hard gaze.

"What do you want, Fernando?" The Angel's voice was thick with an accent the Noble had never noticed before.

"I've been looking all over for you." Fernando turned to follow the Angel out of the Church and into the corridors that would lead them to their rooms.

"You found me. What is it?"

Fernando sped up his stride to keep pace with the Angel's. "I found the location of *Le Jardin*."

The Angel came to an abrupt halt and turned to stare down at the Noble. Not to be discomposed, Fernando opened up the map and held it out for the Angel to study. A smile blossomed on Fernando's dark lips at the shock on his partner's face.

"Where did you get this?" asked the Angel, handing back the parchment.

"Brother Bartholomew was most helpful."

Crimson eyes flashed dangerously. "What did you do to him?"

Very aware of the slip, Fernando placed a hand over his heart feigning injury. "Why, nothing. I would never be so uncouth as to break our etiquette rules. He was most pleased to help me look through the records in their Library."

Frowning slightly, the Angel resumed his journey to the room he shared with Jeanie, Fernando at his side. "What do you have in mind?"

"We go after sunset to check out this Garden of the Gods," replied Fernando.

The Angel curtly nodded. "And if we find Madam Fleur de la Montagne?"

"Simple," stated the Noble as they rounded the corner. "We kill her and put an end to the poisoning of the Chosen."

The Angel came to a halt before his door. A flicker of worry came and went before he placed a hand on the knob. "Fine. Sunset it is."

Fernando stood at the door to his guestroom and faced his partner. "You'd better be quiet. Jeanie's asleep."

"How do you know?"

"I popped my head in when I was looking for you." Fernando smiled at the startled expression and opened his door. "She's going to be fine."

Closing the door behind, Fernando entered his room leaving the Angel standing in the hall. It was one thing to figure out the Angel. It was another to keep the Angel from figuring him out, he hoped.

XXXII

t was not the sound of the door closing quietly with a click, nor the shuffling of sandaled feet as they padded across the stone floor, and neither was it the sound of a tray clinking into place on the lone table in the room that finally pulled Jeanie's sleep fogged mind to consciousness. It was the scent of fresh baked bread and chicken that flared her nostrils and sent her stomach gurgling in anticipation. Stretching her arms above her head, her back arched as she groaned with relief. Jeanie dropped her arms and snapped her eyes open.

Despite the glorious warmth the bed supplied, Jeanie had no recollection of where she was or how she arrived. Quickly sitting up, she met the surprised gasp of the young tonsured monk with one of her own as she scrabbled to lift the bed sheets to her chin.

"Where am I?" she asked. The room was small with a roaring fireplace, a small oak dresser, a desk with single chair, and one single night table, and of course the single bed she laid in. On the wall above the headboard a crucifix dangled against the stone.

The young monk cleared his throat, turning his eyes from her and back to setting the desk to a dining table. "You're in the Monastery of St. Martin's."

"How...how did I get here?" Jeanie frowned. The last thing she remembered was the strange fog lifting as the freezing rain pelted down. She shuddered at the memory, glad that the rain had come to banish the gruesome figures swirling in the mist.

"The Angel brought you here." The young monk turned to exit the room. "You were half frozen and near death. Brother Absolom has given orders for plain and simple foods until you recover."

So many questions swirled in Jeanie's mind. Placing a hand to her forehead in an attempt to halt the spinning, one question floated to the surface, breaking away from the others in evidence to its importance. "Where's the Angel?"

The monk glanced down at the floor next to her bed and quickly left the room.

Jeanie peered over and smiled. His tousled white locks whispered across his face and the arm flung over his head as he lay on his back. White against white, his other hand splayed against his chest as it slowly rose and descended in deep sleep. A thin linen sheet covered by a simple woven brown wool blanket tucked around his lower body. It had been so long since she had seen him so peaceful.

Carefully, so not as to wake him, Jeanie pushed down her covers and swung her bare legs over the other side of the bed. It was then that she realized she was naked. Blushing furiously at what she must have displayed to the monk, Jeanie glanced around and found her shift hanging over the footboard.

Once dressed, she followed the delicious scent of hot food and found a bowl of chicken broth steaming in unison with the small loaf of bread. A growl responded and without further ado, Jeanie sat down and ate, dunking in ripped pieces of fluffy bread into the soup and puffing over the spoon.

The questions she had left unspoken arose, slowing her consumption of breakfast. One answer was self-evident. The Angel slept on the floor because the bed was too small for two, let alone someone of his height. It warmed her immensely that he did manage to sleep beside her. The other points that filled her mind remained unanswered and would have to wait until the Angel awoke.

Jeanie glanced to the small draped window near her bed and frowned at the diffuse light filtering in at the edges. She had no sense of what time it could be. Only the light indicated that it was day. How many more hours would it be before the Angel awoke remained as mysterious as to how long she had slept.

A whimper sounded from across the room snapping Jeanie's attention from the broth sodden bread in her fingers to the figure sleeping next to her bed.

It came again, followed by a sob.

Placing down the wooden spoon with a clatter, Jeanie rushed over to his side chewing on the last morsel. Worry and dread filled her.

White brows drawn together over closed eyes, scrunched in pain. Jeanie anxiously watched glittering tears gather at the distant corners and then trail down. Incomprehensible words mumbled from his pale lips. It was clear to Jeanie that the Angel was in the throes of a nightmare he could not wake from.

Swallowing down her own concern and the bread, she brushed his silken strands away from his face. She wanted to wake him, to free him of whatever past memories grasped at him, and find comfort with her.

Placing her hand on his shoulder, she gave him a little shake in the hopes that would break him from his slumber. Instead, he thrashed in his sleep and cried out. His fear and torment tore at her heart. She had to wake him. With more force, she shook him and called his name.

Crimson eyes snapped open. He gasped for breath, sat up, and scrabbled away until he hit the wall.

He could still feel Them, grasping at him with putrescent skeletal hands, their execrable mouths clambering to gain purchase on his body. Shuddering, he knew the threat was now a promise made and he did not know why. Nausea threatened to overpower him but he managed to swallow it down. He felt sullied and marked. Leaning his head against the cool stone, he closed his eyes as he failed to get his breathing under control. It was now a matter of time before They reaped their reward from his flesh, bone and soul, and a terrible premonition filled him.

Light headed, he knew that had he not awoken he would be forever with the white-faced demons. He trembled at the thought.

"Gwyn, are you alright?"

Jeanie's distressed tones added to his turbulent mind and found he could not answer as he hugged himself in a vain attempt to get his shaking under control.

A hot touch alighted on his shoulder, catching him unawares. Instinctively, he pushed the offending touch away. It was too cloying, too demanding of his flesh, too reminiscent of cold dead hands clambering to use and abuse him. It was too real of the reminder of a promise yet unfulfilled.

It was only when he heard Jeanie's gasp of shock and a thump as she tottered over onto her rump from the force of his action, that he realized she was not part of the dream. Opening his eyes, he saw her beside him, green eyes staring up at him with surprised hurt that swept his breath away, leaving guilt to enter into the mix of obstreperous emotions.

He could not let her know about the dreams that were not dreams. Not even Notus knew about them. He swallowed down a dry gullet. "Just a nightmare."

Jeanie stared at him, disbelieving the lie because of the truth it hid. She had never seen anyone react like that from a nightmare and massaged the feeling back into her hand from his blow. "That weren't no ordinary nightmare."

Abashed, he lowered his eyes, the dream and its effects diminishing but not forgotten. "I'm sorry." He took a deep shaking breath, let it out slowly and felt control returning.

Jeanie moved closer and tentatively placed her hand on his forearm that hugged his chest. This time he did not shove her away, but rather glanced up at her. Jeanie could feel him trembling beneath her fingers.

"Do ye wish t' tell me about it?" she offered, her voice soft and soothing.

He shook his head, sending his long hair brushing over his arms and her hand. He could not tell her. He could not tell a soul.

Made uncomfortable by her probing concern and her proximity, he stood, grabbing his trousers and quickly slipped them on.

A glance at the curtained window and the tingling along his skin told him it was still day, but any thought of sleep became its own dream.

Frowning, he realized that once the sun was down he and Fernando would be visiting *Le Jardin*. The sense of foreboding that had slowly relinquished its hold upon awakening slammed back into his gut, causing him to gasp.

"What is it?" Jeanie stood up and went to his side. His erratic behaviour since he awoke confused and confounded her. She had never seen him so out of sorts. It begged the question as to what had happened to him since they arrived at the Abbey.

A chill ran up his spine.

"You can't come," he whispered, refusing to look at her. He knew in some deep recess that tonight would change everything and he was impotent to stop it. The only thing he could do was to keep his oath to keep Jeanie safe.

"What are ye talkin' about?" Confused, Jeanie tried to catch his distraught blood red eyes, but he only turned away from her.

He took a deep steadying breath and closed his eyes. To keep his oath he would have to break a promise. "Fernando found the whereabouts of *Le Jardin*. He and I are going there tonight."

Jeanie could not believe what she was hearing. Events and facts seemed to be moving at lightning speed. One minute he was in the deep throws of a night terror and the next one he was informing her that they were further along in their quest than when they left Calais. Her mind reeling from the information, Jeanie did not know whether to be disconcerted or happy. "When do we leave?"

"You're not coming." He turned and found Jeanie's shocked expression questioning him.

"What d'ye mean?" She shook her head in disbelief. He had promised her that she would go with him. The idea of being left behind rankled.

Shoulders slumping at the spark that flickered in her emerald eyes, he sat heavily on the bed and gazed at his hands on his lap. The cut that had appeared to be healing was now ringed in red. Closing his hands into fists he gazed into Jeanie's eyes, hating what he had to do.

"I need you to stay here. I need to know that you are safe."

"But I'm safe when I'm with you," bemoaned Jeanie.

Unable to bear Jeanie's stupefied expression, he flickered his gaze to the curtained window and then at his torturous bed and the promises that were made there. When he met Jeanie's eyes again he knew that who she saw was the Angel returned.

"I need you here, where it is safe," he reiterated. "If Fernando or I don't make it back by dawn, you are to take the money I have in my suitcase and return to England. If Fernando is with you, go and try and free Notus with what you've learned. If you go alone, take what money is left and go back home to Scotland."

Jeanie could not believe what she was hearing and shook her head in denial. "Ye sound as if yer never comin' back."

It was the flicker of admission in his ruby eyes that caught her breath and irked her. She could not let him go without her. "I'm goin' with ye," she stated plainly, her anger rising.

He had a feeling that this would happen, as it seemed to happen over and over throughout this horrid quest. This time he could not allow Jeanie to dissuade him. "Not this time," he said, slowly rising to his feet to stare down at her, the full countenance of the Angel upon him.

"How dare ye? Ye said–"

"I know what I said and I know what I promised." He countered her growing fury with cold control. Jeanie no longer rattled him. "I also know the Oath I swore on my sword."

Jeanie's head snapped back as if slapped.

Pressing his advantage, he stepped into the gap. Wide green eyes met his. "If I have to, I will tie you to this chair."

"Ye wouldna dare," hissed Jeanie.

He hated seeing such emotion on her beautiful face, but he had no choice and matched it with the full force of the Angel. "Try me."

Jeanie's choler fled at the presence of the Angel and for the first time fear of him grasped her innards, making her legs weak. Taking a step backwards, she turned and fled the small room they shared, sobbing as she slammed the door behind her.

The loud crash of the door making contact with the frame resonated through the room and shook his bones, leaving him weak and despondent. It was done and he hated how it had gone. He wanted to tell her how much he loved her and what that meant to him, but the chance was irrevocably gone.

Turning to his suitcase that sat on the floor against the wall, he knelt, opening the latches and lifted. Everything he needed was here except for the sword that lay on the floor beside the case.

Black leather boots, soft and supple in his hands were but a pale imitation of Jeanie's touch. Slumping in self-defeated victory, he prayed that Jeanie would understand and forgive him if he survived.

xxxiii

Ilently, he slipped behind the sculpted coniferous hedge. Shadows engulfed him as a treacherous gibbous moon threw off her cloudy veils to the impassioned breath of the western wind. Crouched down, his hands sunk into the cold loam purchasing his balance. The only evidence of his presence was the slight wisp of breath that the wind whipped away.

A rustle of fabric and a scuttle of jostled deadfall behind and off to the right sagged his shoulders as he shook his head at the Noble's noisy approach. He was starting to wonder if he should have left both Jeanie and Fernando behind and gone alone. Unfortunately, he could not tie Fernando to a chair.

The Noble hunkered down beside the Angel and noted the disgruntled expression. The Angel had seemed out of sorts since they had met up outside their rooms after sundown, and Fernando did not need to be a genius to figure out why. The lack of Jeanie's presence and the slamming that had awoken him was enough to tell him what he needed to know. It was the Angel's raiment that was a surprise.

Crouched beside his partner the Noble noted the soft matte black boots, the fine knit black turtle-neck sweater tucked into black cotton trousers, and how the worn black leather straps crossed in the middle of the Angel's chest while securely holding the sword on his back. Even the Angel's long white hair was given to contrast with the black suede headband holding stray white strands while the rest was interwoven in a single long braid.

"You've done this before," stated Fernando in a quiet voice.

The question caught the Angel off guard and he pulled his gaze from the large villa to land briefly on the Noble who was ill attired for what they were about to do. It was clear to him that whatever knowledge Fernando may have had early on in his immortal life was no longer remembered after centuries of relative civilian comfort. Returning to his study of the sparsely illuminated building, he gave a curt nod.

Fernando followed the crimson gaze to the large estate, wondering what the Angel searched for. He was not surprised at the answer, but it begged another question. "You do this sort of thing a lot?"

He closed his eyes and huffed out his exasperation. Maybe there could have been a way to keep Fernando at the monastery. The image of a raging Fernando bound and gagged momentarily flitted a slight smile to his lips. There was only one way to get Fernando off his back, just for this evening.

"I will answer you, but only on one condition." His voice slid into the night, mingling as if one of the natural nocturnal sounds.

It was not what Fernando expected for an answer. "What condition?" he drawled, squinting in suspicion.

His hard eyes fell onto the Noble. "It is clear that you have never done this before. I will answer your question if you will follow my orders. If not, then turn around and go back to the monastery. I will take care of this myself, unhindered."

Rage broiled up in the Noble. He began to splutter indignantly when a white hand covered his mouth, stilling his immanent outburst. Fernando could feel the Angel behind him, tense and focused, and wondered at the swift, silent movement that took him by surprise.

A whisper of warm air tickled his ear and he realized that the Angel spoke so softly that he had to strain to listen."For the last seven hundred years Notus has never once needed to earn a single penny. Do you understand my meaning?"

He hated being pressed against the Noble, breathing in his dark scent, but it was only when he felt realization sink in that he released his hold to gaze into shocked brown eyes.

"Shit," swore Fernando. It explained so much. Irritation tickled the surface. Finally comprehending how truly dangerous his partner was needled him as pride and ego fell a notch. No longer could Fernando say he was the most knowledgeable in the killing arts.

Oh he had bested his skills with dagger, sword and western fighting forms with other Chosen who kept up their mortal practices, but it was plainly obvious that the Angel was his superior in this, and it rankled.

"Good," stated the Angel matter-of-factly. He turned to peer over the hedge at the seventeenth century three-story manse.

Made of grey stone, each large block was carefully crafted. Around the arched front double oaken doors, sculpted stone flowers created a trellis of petrified foliage. Over the vaulted entrance, a magnificent stone canopy hung upon Roman columns, promising refuge on the rainiest of days for carriages and visitors alike. On the southern facing wall to the left, from his vantage point, defoliated ivy climbed, promising the greening of life back into stone which tentatively reached out to begin the process along the front facing. At regular intervals, precisely spaced on either side of the door, eight large arched windows faced towards them. It was the large plate glass windows on the second floor's south side that piqued his interest.

Flickering lights emanated from several windows on the main floor. Only two illuminated the second floor's north wing. The third level was completely dark.

The distant sound of horses' hooves crunched the loose gravel of the road, leather and wood creaked, and iron shod wheels shushed over stone alerted him of a new presence to the seemingly unpopulated estate. Signalling Fernando to hunker down, they carefully spread the branches to watch the canvas covered wagon, driven by two men and pulled by four horses, as it passed through the iron barred gates. Only the soft sounds of sleepy draught horses pulling their heavy load flitted to the Chosen's ears.

A chuck of the reigns and the horses headed south of the great fountain in the centre of the circular drive. The cement goddess with stone flowers in her hair, cradling a large jug, stood bereft of water. Only brown and golden leaves filled the basin.

With a whuffle and a snort the horses came to a halt, giving leave for the two drivers to effortlessly leap off the cart and land heavily onto the drive.

"Oy," called out the tall heavyset man who had held the reigns.

The shorter, yet broader man, stood languidly with his arm supported on the side of the bench. "D'ye think they heard?"

The tall man turned to his partner with a feral grin. "They had better or they won't see dawn."

"Lucky them," chuckled the broad man. He turned to the sound of two pairs of feet running along the path that led off the drive to the south of the property.

Noting the distraction, the Angel sought to gain a closer approach. With a tap on the Noble's shoulder he silently left the shelter of the shrub's shadow. It was easy to keep to the shadows, but the time it took required patience. Each movement was timed with the wind whisking new veils around the moon, only to be blown away no matter how hard the lady tried to cling.

Methodically crossing open spaces with preternatural speed and uncanny silence, he found the vantage point he had hoped to reach undetected. In the darkness beneath a bush creatively styled to look like a nesting swan, he lay on the cold ground, the damp grass soaking his sweater. Near him, the gravel track to the stables led to the two men and the wagon.

"Well it's 'bout time the two of you showed up," declared the driver in obvious irritation.

The Angel shot a glance over his shoulder to where Fernando waited beside a hedge and raised a hand indicating for him to stay where he was until the two pairs of legs ran past. He ignored the scowl and turned back to the action around the cart.

Two younger men, barely out of their teens, arrived and skidded to a halt, kicking up stones. One bent over, huffing in an attempt to regain his breath. The other, hands on his hips and taking huge gulps of air managed to gasp, "I'm sorry, sir. We weren't expecting you back tonight. The Mistress told us it would be tomorrow evening."

"Well, things change," snapped the passenger, annoyed by the impertinence of one beneath him.

"I want these barrels taken inside." The driver thumbed in the direction of the hidden contents of the wagon.

The two younger men's eyes went round as their jaws dropped. "But where, sir? The Mistress didn't say anything about you bringing it here."

The driver, his ire up, took a threatening step towards the two who cowered and trembled.

"If the two of you wish to see the dawn," snarled the driver, "you will take it down to the basement."

With the four men distracted, the Angel waved the Noble over, hoping that the raised voices would mask any sound Fernando made.

Sliding onto his belly beside the Angel, the Noble firmly regretted the attire he had chosen. A fine Italian suit and the cape were proving more of a hindrance, and not to mention, Fernando fully doubted seeing this suit clean ever again. He was about to say something when the Angel shot him a cold glare.

Jaw clenched in anger, Fernando turned to watch the interplay between the carters and the haulers and nearly jumped out of his skin when the Angel's breathy voice tickled his ear.

"Did you bring your knives?" whispered the Angel. He knew they had to find out for certain if what he suspected was true, and that meant looking in those barrels before they were taken away.

"Always," replied Fernando, wondering what the Angel had in mind.

"Do you think you can take out the two that just arrived, without them, or you, making a sound?"

Fernando's eyebrows shot up. "You mean kill them?" Maybe taking directions from the Angel would not be too hard to swallow.

The Angel nodded as he calculated the best way to take down the other two if Fernando managed to do what was expected of him. Killing the driver would be easy. It was his passenger, on the far side of the wagon that he would have to stop from running to the villa and that meant he would have to go down first. Rolling slightly onto his side, the Angel slipped his fingers between the wide leather baldric and his chest and pulled out three *shuriken*, their points glistening.

Eyes wide at the deadly metal disks, Fernando glanced at the Angel's cold eyes and shuddered inwardly.

In another time, in another place, the Angel would have enjoyed finally seeing fear on the Noble's face and knowing he was the cause. Now he had only the present and his immediate future required dispatching these four unsuspecting individuals. He could easily do it without Fernando's help, but the chance of one setting off an alert would be greater.

Sliding the *shuriken* over each other, careful not to slice himself with the sharpened poisoned tips, he nodded his head, indicating to Fernando to take out his blades.

Reaching to the hidden sheaths at the small of his back under his suit jacket, Fernando pulled out Yin and Yang and tested their balance as his elbows dug into the soft lawn. Over the silver and gold of the pommels, Fernando watched the younger men walk towards the back of the cart. It was now or never. Once they were in the confines of the canvas it would be near next to impossible to take them down silently. Timing was everything.

With a quick glance at each other, both the Angel and the Noble exploded into action. Bolting up from under the swan, Fernando let fly the two daggers with supernatural speed as the Angel snapped the *shuriken* into the air.

Time halted in the blur of preternatural movement. The slight breeze fell into nothingness, allowing for the moon to finally be modestly dressed in wisps of veils without fear of having them ripped away. The steaming breaths of the horses smoked long and thickly like coal fired chimneys. Four men stood statuesque, movement frozen, unable to perceive or comprehend what flew at them.

Three darkly glittering shapes spun in slow motion, a mockery of the speed in which they cut the air. With deadly accuracy, the bladed disks caught the passenger unawares.

The first killed instantly as it deeply embedded itself through the frontal lobe, snapping the head back in a jerk. The other two, landed at precisely the same moment, lodging them in the exposed throat in a grim representation of a grin, cutting off any potential cry.

Without glancing over to see Fernando's blades successfully finding their own killing marks, the Angel followed the flight of the *shuriken*. It took less than a blink of an eye to grab the driver around the head, one arm around the throat and the other cradling the head. The only sound in the night came from the crunch as vertebrae spun and snapped before he dropped the surprised corpse to the gravel.

In what took less than a second, four men lay dead on the ground, blood trickling from wounds.

Time sped up and the wind tore away the gossamer veils the moon feebly clung to. The horses puffed and stomped at the strangers' sudden appearance, their breath stolen by the breeze.

Gripping a limp hand, the Angel dragged the corpse of the driver to land beneath the shadow of the swan before turning to retrieve the other.

"It's too bad we couldn't kill them as Chosen," stated Fernando as he retrieved his blades before depositing his two bodies to join with the first.

"This is thirsty work."

Surprised at the statement, the Angel hesitated over the dead passenger's body for a moment before bending and removing the *shuriken*. With a quick wipe on the body, he gingerly replaced the disks and hoisted the corpse over his shoulder. Though the blood always tantalized him, he never let himself kill in such a manner when working. It was a distraction that could prove deadly and so he squashed it, preferring to use the methods and skills he learned over the centuries, unless absolutely necessary.

Four corpses lay like elongated dark eggs under a nesting skinned mother swan. Fernando smiled at the handiwork before turning to join the Angel at the back of the wagon.

"Age before beauty," he offered, gesturing towards the inner darkness of the canopy.

"You go. I'll cover you," replied the Angel, stepping to the side and into the wagon's shadow.

Grabbing the wooden edge of the wagon, Fernando effortlessly hoisted himself up and over into the darkness. There was little room to move or to stand and he understood the Angel's preference in him making the assay. Nearly stumbling on top of a barrel in the effort to remain erect, he took out Yang and jimmied the top open. He did not need to open any of the others. They were the spices.

Jaw set, Fernando turned and jumped down, the gravel hissing under his feet. It seemed that despite burning down the warehouse, the poisonous herbs were still making the rounds. Fernando wondered how effective it would be to assassinate the lady of the manor.

"It's the herbs."

Suspicion confirmed, the Angel stepped out of the dark cover of the wagon, his senses stretched for any possibility of discovery. It was strange that no one had noticed the sudden disappearance of the four men. The only sound that reached his sensitive ears was the Noble's expensive black leather shoes on the gravel and what the wind vibrated through bush and hedge.

He did not like the fact that everything appeared dead quiet, as if waiting for some hammer to fall to shatter the still night. Turning to face the villa, he crouched in the wagon's shadow and studied the light emanating from the large picture windows. Nebulous shapes passed across the yellow gloaming. The diffuse quality of the light meant only one thing: candlelight was used conservatively. The shadows proved someone was home, but was it whom they hunted for?

The limited perceived activity on the ground floor was enough of a deterrent. They would have to find a more covert means of entrance. It was only a matter of time before someone would realize that a wagon with harnessed horses stood in the drive with no one around.

He let out an irritated huff. If he had more time to study the villa and the occupants within he would have come up with a feasible plan. He did not like making it up as he went. It grated against every grain of training he received.

A shift in the translucent drapery brought a darkened form into sharper focus. Someone had noticed the deserted wagon. Grabbing Fernando by the top of his vest, he yanked the surprised Noble down into a crouch and lifted his hand, forestalling an indignant outburst.

Without taking his eyes off the occupied window, he pointed and was gratified to hear Fernando's jaw clicking shut. They needed to leave the front of the estate now.

Grasping the Noble by the wrist, he turned and brought a single finger over his pale lips. Without receiving a word of protest, he turned away from the wagon and sped into the night without a sound. He could not say the same for Fernando.

Keeping solely to the darkness, despite the flirting moon, he made his way around the estate to view the back. Gardens dried up and covered foretold the existence of a summer paradise in hibernation. Resting conifers outlined a grand concrete patio decorated with stone benches. A murky man made pond the size of a swimming pool and statuary standing alone or in small clumps would make the groundskeepers of Versailles jealous. It was the negritude of the trees that he appreciated the most as he set to study the back half of the villa. He ignored Fernando's breathless swearing as the Noble came to squat next to him, brushing pine needles from his suit jacket.

"Well?" complained Fernando. He was starting to wonder if agreeing to follow the Angel in this was a good idea.

The windows on the first level were dimly lit, paralleling the gloaming of the front. Dim figures moved back and forth. On the second floor, lights shone from two unclothed windows while the others remained dark. What was surprising was the plate glass walls from the front south side seemed to continue around the south facing to open up to the west. Whatever the room held would be exposed from sun up to sundown. Again the third story was dark.

Studying the top floor, the Angel knew this was where they would gain entry. The question was how. Each window held iron bars at the base, making admittance noisy and difficult. Eyes grazing over to the north, he caught what he first dismissed, a set of French doors stood darkly recessed behind a small balcony of waist high, stone topped, balustrade. It would have to do.

Without forewarning the Angel left the succour of the trees. He ran and then leapt, catching himself on the balustrade. It was higher than he had anticipated, but managed to swing over the wide stone rail to land effortlessly.

There was very little space as clearly the balcony was made for one. Turning to gaze down, he watched Fernando's blur of preternatural motion and caught the Noble by the arm when he missed the height, dark fingers grazing the stone between the pillars.

The Angel helped Fernando up and over.

Ignoring the Noble's soft cursing and preening, the Angel turned and peered through the small square window on the door.

"You could have warned me that you were going to do that," grumbled the Noble. It was not the Angel's saving catch that he took issue with, but rather the whole leap without warning. Fernando could not recall the last time he had done something like that, ever.

Darkness and the dim outline of abandoned furniture filtered to the Angel's sensitive eyes as he placed a hand on the doorknob. With a gentle turn, he felt the simple mechanism grate, and with a soft crunching sound and a click, the door opened.

It was not the pain in the neck that woke him, but rather the weight that pressed down upon him. When he opened his eyes, he discovered he could not see what lay on top of him. The only sight offered was the grass that tickled his nose. With painful effort he forced the muscles in his neck to pull and release in tandem until the shuddering force of the crack and pop settled his head properly upon his shoulders. It was then he realized he was under a pile of cooling flesh.

It was not panic that took him, but rather the unsettling memory of his first night climbing out of a paupers grave, smelling and dusted with lye, and with a terrible hunger. With a heave, he pushed the dead weights off, watching in fascination as two flopped bonelessly to the grass. The figure of his partner, shifted and groaned, lifting his pale hand to his forehead and then throat before fluttering his eyes open.

Almost too quickly they helped each other to their feet and glanced down in wry wonder at the corpses that would never get up.

"Well, I guess they didn't live to see the dawn," chuckled the one who had sat shotgun, and then coughed.

"Nope," tested the driver as he rubbed his neck.

"Who do you think nailed us, Bob?"

Bob glanced around into the darkness and frowned before a fiendish smile split his face. "Who else but the Angel?"

The passenger's face paled. "D'ye think it was him?"

Noticing his partner's apprehension, Bob turned on him. "Get a grip, Greg. Who else d'ya think would come here? Sheesh." Bob rolled his eyes, appreciating the absence of pain. "She wants him here. Granted he's a bit early, but I don't think she'll mind that."

Greg took a breath and let it out in a huff. "Fine, but you heard what Mr. Vale said when we met him on the road back."

Almost envying the corpses, Bob glanced back to the house. They were here. Mr. Vale was on his way to Spain or some such country to continue the supply chain. They bore the message to Mr. Vale of the warehouse's destruction and almost believed themselves slaughtered by the raging expression on their master's face. Now they had another message to give to her. He had no doubt she would kill the messenger, but now, maybe, just maybe, he would not have to give it to her just yet. The fact that the Angel was on the grounds and had taken down the four of them with no sound and no warning thrilled Bob. Yes, she would be more than pleased to hear that the Angel had discovered her whereabouts.

Smiling in self-satisfaction, Bob lifted a dark bushy brow. "C'mon, Greg. The night is still young and we have a message to bring to the Mistress."

Greg's eyes widened and then caught on to his partner's meaning. Falling into step beside Bob, they headed towards the front door, eager to give their news.

It was a mausoleum set for a princess. A large white four poster bed with swooping flourishes detailed in gold embossing made the headboard a visage of protective angel wings over a dusty grey mattress that had not had the company of a warm body in years, if not centuries. The large armoire, dressing table and wardrobe were similarly fashioned in a gaudy combination of fuzzy grey-coated white and dulled gold. The washing stand of white flaking wood still held its white and gold enamelled pitcher and basin. Everything, including the plush rug was covered in a heavy coating of grey dust that had not been disturbed in years. Even the air itself cloyed at their lungs, threatening to suffocate them had they not been immune to such threats.

Removing a handkerchief from his vest pocket, Fernando held it to his face and ran his finger along the dresser before shaking off the accumulated dust.

"Don't they have servants?" he grimaced. He hated how each step burst a plume of ancient detritus into the air and onto his increasingly ravaged suit.

The brass and crystal door handle to the rest of the house was unlocked, but the Angel kept the door closed. Glancing back at his journey across the abandoned room, he could see his and Fernando's footprints as clearly as if they had stepped through freshly fallen snow. Pursing his lips at the sight, a flicker of worry was instantly overridden by the knowledge that no person had been up here in years and therefore it was highly unlikely that anyone would discover their presence.

It was the proceeding journey down into the unknown architecture that concerned him. Not knowing the floor plans, let alone how many people occupied each level and room, left him wary about taking the next step, if only he knew for certain where he could find Madam Fleur de la Montagne.

Closing his eyes, he cocked his head to the side, straining to listen for any living soul outside the door or even down the halls. The only sounds that flitted to his preternatural hearing were distant and of several people on the lower levels. It was now or never, and releasing a quiet huff of held breath, he carefully opened the door, mindful of the possibility that it would treacherously give their position away.

The hall was dark, faintly illuminated by the flickering yellow glow ascending the stairs, casting dark and elongated shadows. It appeared that the whole third level of the manse had been abandoned at the same time as the grand bedroom. The hall runner was thick with dust, dulling the red and masking any finer details. Waving Fernando to follow him, he raised a pale finger to his lips to silence the Noble from uttering another derogatory remark.

Fernando clicked his jaw shut at the cold commanding glare. He was finding it difficult to keep silent and let the Angel lead the way down the hall. What surprised Fernando was the complete absence of sound his partner made. There was no shadow of doubt in Fernando's mind that the Angel had skills and abilities that confounded most Chosen.

They stood at the top of the stairs, close to the side most cloaked in darkness. The easy part was over. Now they were to descend into light and possible discovery before completing what they had come to do.

"You follow my lead," whispered the Angel as he started down the steps. Oh how he wished that someone would blow out the lights. He would have to do it as he went along.

Keeping his back to the yellow painted wall, he knew exposure was imminent once the banister on the other side opened to the second floor. Slipping his fingers between his chest and the straps, he came away with four *shuriken* and held them casually. Anyone seeing them would die instantly.

With senses strained to the maximum, he descended sideways, mindful not to knock any of the paintings above the dark stained wainscoting. One step, and then two. No sound emanated from the second story. Only the candles aflame in the brass sconces indicated that there could be a presence. After a brief moment's consideration he ruled out extinguishing the flames, realising that if he did, it would indicate to those below that something was amiss. He would have to move fast to take down any potential threat of discovery if necessary.

With the Noble further up the stairs, he continued downwards and then halted when the runner covered step creaked under his weight. He crouched, straining to hear if his presence was detected and so he could manage a preliminary view of what was beyond the banister. Thankfully, nothing presented itself. The noises from below continued, yet it seemed that a few more voices had added to the mix.

Almost at the second floor landing he froze. Voices were coming closer to the top of the first flight of stairs. Quickly taking account of the doors closest to their position, he swept across the hallway, placing his back against a doorjamb. Before the Noble could follow, he held up a pale hand and waved him back against the stairs.

The voices approached. They needed to hide. Placing his ear against the door and his hand on the knob, he turned it once no sound issued forth.

Gratefully, the door opened inwards on well-oiled hinges to a dark broom closet. It would be a tight fit. Holding the door slightly ajar, he peered out, and watched the shadows of the individuals ascend at the other end of the hall. Fernando would have to move fast and he waved the Noble over. It was snugger than either would have liked. Fernando grimaced at having his face nearly pressed against the Angel's chest.

"As I have explained, sir," came a nervous nasal voice from the other end of the hall, "Madam Fleur is still dressing and doesn't wish to be disturbed."

"I understand that, Gustav," replied a gruff familiar voice, "but this is important and I cannot give you the message."

"She will be greatly displeased, sir." Fear emanated from Gustav's voice.

"That's for me to worry about," snapped the man.

"But...but, I wish to see the dawn, sir." Fear turned to terror.

"It's over rated. Now tell Madam that I am here and have a message from Mr. Vale for her."

The gulp was auditory in the broom closet without the aid of Chosen hearing.

"Yes, sir."

A knock reverberated down the hall and a door opened with a whisper.

"Gustav, Madam wishes not to be disturbed," came a young female voice. "You know that — Oh! It's you!"

The sound of the door swinging open to bounce off the wall reached their ears as well as the surprised squeak before the door slammed shut.

"What do you think is going on?" The Noble's susurrant voice stirred the air.

He shook his head and closed his eyes in concentration. Nothing but soft incoherent mutterings alighted his sensitive hearing. The house had been well made for the rooms to be all but sound proof.

Long minutes passed pressed in the closet before his crimson eyes snapped open at the sound of the distant door opening and a new, yet familiar, voice added to the mix.

"Robert, darling," drawled a seductive feminine voice. "Would you please go ahead and make the necessary preparations."

"Yes, ma'am." Heavy footfalls fell further down the hall.

"Oh, and Robert."

"Yes, ma'am?" He halted at the other end of the corridor.

"Thank you for bringing these matters to my attention. You will be greatly rewarded. Please inform Gregory of that fact as well. In the meantime, feel free to take Marie Terese."

A female gasp of terror mixed with Robert's happy reply. A scuffle and then a sobbing plea filled the air. "Please Madam! I want you! Please! You promised me!"

"Serve me better and then maybe next time," came the haughty reply.

A squeal and then the footfalls resumed to descend out of hearing.

"Gustav?" The squeak and the soft sound the two remaining, moved towards the stairs. "Please prepare my entertainment room, and lay out my writing desk. Mr. Vale wishes me to reply and so I will." The menacing smile was evident in her tone.

"As you desire, ma'am," replied Gustav with a hint of awe as they descended down the stair.

Silence followed, punctuated only by the occasional voice floating up from the first floor. Bequeathed the second story, the Angel turned the handle and opened the door a crack to see if they were truly alone. No sound of life, or any person appeared to be awaiting them, and he cautiously opened the door and stepped out, slipping the *shuriken* back into their hiding place.

Fernando followed, relieved to be free of the small confining space, smoothing down the front of his suit with both hands.

"What now?" he whispered, his brown brows pulling together.

It was clear that the Madam was the lady they sought and most likely the head of the conspiracy to eradicate the Chosen. Frowning, the Angel cautiously walked the length of the hall to the door of the Madam's room and entered. Here was an opportunity to learn something about their adversary. If they were lucky, she would return alone to the room, but after her statement about going somewhere else, it was highly unlikely they would be able to ambush her here.

Stepping in close behind the Angel, Fernando quietly shut the door and turned. The room was grander than the one they had initially breached.

A large oak bed, stained a rich dark brown, pressed against one wall. The gold coverlets and pillows were pristine with nary a wrinkle, appearing as if no one ever slept in the grand bed. The wardrobe, dressers and wash-stand were of the same dark wood. Silver candelabras decorated the flat surfaces, some still flickering brightly with lit beeswax candles. The dressing table and the small padded chair were the only real evidence that someone used this room on a regular basis. Silver backed brushes and combs were littered among jewellery and cosmetic jars and brushes. The truly strange aspect from the seemingly normal appearing room was the heavy red velvet drapes covering the windows.

Across the red and gold Persian rug, the Angel nudged one of the drapes away from the window in the hopes to peek if the bodies had been discovered. What he found was a boarded up window. Surprised, he moved to the next one farthest away from the bed and found a board covering only half of the window, leaving the bottom half to a black painted glass.

Allowing the drape to fall back into place, he turned to the Noble, loath to inform him of what they must do if they were to be successful and be back at the monastery before dawn. Slaughtering every last mortal in the home just to take down Madam Fleur de la Montagne and thus end the threat against the Chosen was a necessary evil. He had done such actions in the past as a matter of course and employment, but to see the Noble's face alight with sadistic pleasure decreased his ability to emotionally detach himself from the task at hand.

"Just remember, kill with your blades and do not feed on them," concluded the Angel, quietly. "We can guarantee they are tainted."

"That's obvious," snorted Fernando. Reaching to the sheaths hidden at the small of his back, he pulled out Yin and Yang and held them loosely. With a lopsided malicious grin, he followed the Angel out of the room.

The slither of steel against wood whispered as the Angel unsheathed his weapon. Grasping the worn hilt in his left, the blade flashed close to his face in expectation of discovery.

Quietly, they followed the distant voices down stairs that widened out to a grand foyer of white, red and black tiles arranged in large geometric designs. The sconces above the dark stained wainscoting glittered brightly between paintings framed in elaborate gold.

Alighting from the last step, he felt the wrongness of the situation tighten his shoulders. He rolled them, releasing most of the tension, but not the concern. Suddenly, the distant voices cut out and left them in silence. It took all his effort to squash the rising dread at the realization they had most likely walked into a trap. Straining to hear, the sound of anticipatory heart beats and breathing confirmed the fact and he knew they were surrounded. The only recourse was to gain the high ground and he turned to ascend the stairs, halting at the sound of approach.

Over half a dozen men appeared, armed with rapiers and knives, to stand threateningly at the top of the stairs. Finding the route cut off, the Angel turned to find more men with naked steel filing in from the front door at the same time that others moved in from the south and north wings of the main floor.

Fernando's exclamatory oath caused several of the men to chuckle in anticipation.

"I do hope that you have a plan to get us out of this," sneered the Noble, his back pressed against the Angel's, Yin and Yang poised for defence. It had seemed such a simple plan at first: gain entry, find Fleur, kill her, go home. Though he had no doubt he would survive this battle, Fernando disliked the notion that the tables had turned and the playing field was now controlled by outside sources.

Disinclined to reply, the Angel watched as a slight figure appeared at the top of the stairs. Her thick black hair fell in luxuriant waves over slim shoulders. The claret coloured gown lit up and intensified her piercing blue eyes. Surprise caught him off guard for a fraction of the moment. It was the same woman who had led them into the trap at the soup kitchen. Anger flashed through him at the realization that he and Fernando had been carefully controlled and manipulated with every step by this woman.

"Ah, how wonderful to finally have you in my home." Her voice purred in pleasure as she descended down a step. "I want the Angel alive," she ordered, coldly. "Kill the other one."

"Yes ma'am," came the enthusiastic reply of the man to her left.

Shock showed on both the Chosen's face, eliciting a pleasurable smirk from the man. Descending down the stairs, sword in hand, was the driver that the Angel had killed.

"Surprised?" Holding the high ground three steps up, Bob levelled the blade in preparation for an offensive strike. "Good."

The stance on the stairs and the grip on the blade spoke volumes of the dead man's lack of knowledge, but the Angel never relinquished his cold gaze on those dreary green eyes.

"You are not Chosen." It was a statement rather than a question. The Angel shifted his position, feeling Fernando do the same at his back.

"You're quite correct, my dear," replied Violet Flowers. She descended one more step, caressing her flowing locks. "We're oh so much better."

Robert's blade came down in a blur of deadly speed, surpassing that of mere mortals, and crashed against the Angel's broadsword in a shower of sparks. Momentarily caught off guard by the swiftness of the attack, the Angel moved, accelerating to flowing preternatural speed.

Light and sound protracted as his body set into the movements of centuries of practice. Flowing only slightly slower than himself, he caught Fernando peripherally, sweeping and slashing at those who pressed their attack. Some of the men seemed to stand still in the face of severed life. Those he recognized as mortals were easy to cut down. It was those who moved in equal measure to the Noble that were the real threat.

Feinting a downward slice, he shifted the long blade to deliver a horizontal cut across Robert's exposed abdomen. Blood spewed forth, adding to the increasingly slippery and treacherous footing of downed mortals, and then dried up as the wound closed, sealing itself as if it had never been.

Wide eyed at the sight, he felt the burning sting of metal against his rib cage as someone else's blade got through his momentarily downed defences. Forced back to the task at hand, he knew he was fighting for his life against the unknown.

Without any further thought, he abandoned all rationality to the muscle and sensory memory of centuries of battle. He and Fernando would escape or they would die having taken as many of their enemy with them as they could.

XXXÍU

houlders hunched to her ears and arms across her chest, Jeanie struggled to keep the cool night air from swiping her precious body heat despite the effectiveness of her green wool coat. A blast of wind whipped her hair around her face, taunting her until she pulled her hand from her underarm and brushed the offending locks from her eyes.

The sun had set some time ago, taking with it the Angel and Fernando. She knew she was defying him in following, but she had to help, no matter the cost, even if it meant that he would stop loving her. Her feet tread loudly along the empty gravel road that would take her to the entrance of the villa, a lonesome sound against the creak and groan of trees and shrubs bending to the power of the playful wind.

In near hysterics, Jeanie had fled into the halls of the monastery dressed only in her shift. She could not believe what he had threatened, what promise he had broken, and her heart ached in loss at the sight of the Angel replacing the man she loved—the man she had believed loved her.

Tears streamed down her face, blinding her to the astonished expressions of the monks she ran past. Her bare feet slapped against the cold solidness beneath. Jeanie's only desire was to find a way out, to run away from the pain and heart break, and was stopped by falling unknowingly into a monks soothing embrace.

With soft words of consolation he steered her towards an office, his arm comforting around her shoulders. Once the oak door closed, he dismissed the shocked clerk with a wave of his hand and deposited Jeanie in the chair before the large desk.

Still weeping, Jeanie accepted the clean rag without looking up, blew her nose and wiped her face. She regained what little composure she could muster, clutching and twisting the rag. She did not know who the man was, but was grateful for his compassionate silence.

The chair behind the desk grated against stone and she heard him settle into it.

"I am Father Theodore, the Abbot of St. Martin's," he stated, kindly. "If there is anything I or the other Brothers can help with, Miss Stuart, please let me know."

"But I'm no Catholic," replied Jeanie, glumly.

Father Theodore let out an amused huff. "Yet you serve Father Paul and are here with the Angel."

Jeanie's eyes went round and she wondered at how much the Abbot truly knew.

She heard him lean forward, placing his forearms on his desk. "I am known for having two very good ears and a quiet tongue, if that will be of any help."

The complete sincerity of the offer swept Jeanie's breath away and before she knew what she was doing tears fell from her eyes as she related what had transpired between she and the Angel. When she had finished she, sat glumly, tears spent.

Father Theodore stood with a sigh, went to his sideboard and poured an amber coloured drink into a small glass. Returning to his desk, he sat on the corner nearest to the young woman and offered the strong drink into her shaking hands.

"The Angel loves you. Do you believe that?" stated the Abbot.

Jeanie sipped at the brandy, felt its warmth radiate from her belly outward, and nodded, watching the brown liquid slosh in the glass.

"Then you must trust his reasons for wanting you here," offered Father Theodore.

"I do," said Jeanie, weakly, and looked up from her drink. "It's just that I'm afraid."

"Of what?"

New tears surfaced to trickle down her face. "That I'll never see him again. That he thinks I dinna love him."

Realization dawned on the Abbot's face and he stood, walked to an inner door, opened, and called to the clerk in the other office. "Do you know where the Angel and Mister de Sagres went, Brother Amadieu?"

"I'm sorry, Father," replied the monk, "I do not."

"I do." Jeanie's small voice flitted across the room.

The Abbot turned back to his guest, eyebrows raised.

"*Le Jardin*," answered Jeanie, meekly.

"Brother Amadieu, would you please find Brother Bartholomew," requested the Abbot, frowning as he closed the door.

It had not taken long for Brother Bartholomew to arrive, repeat yet again what had transpired in the Scriptorium last night, and provide Jeanie the information she needed. Once the old monk had left, the Abbot regained his seat behind the desk and gazed thoughtfully at her.

"I cannot presume to tell you what you should do, Miss Stuart," he said, "but I must council you to decide carefully what is the correct course of action. It is clear that the Angel wishes you to be safe for he loves you dearly. You must decide whether or not your love for him will include trust.

"I will have Brother Amadieu escort you back to your room."

Jeanie had walked in silence beside the clerk very much aware she was underdressed, and appreciated the averted gazes from those they past.

Within the corridors no sound issued, save for the shuffling of feet, they moved from one section of the abbey to the other. Jeanie's mind raced, filled with conflicting thoughts and emotions.

Having Father Theodore sit silently, without judgement, as she expressed her anguish and anger alleviated much of the weight that compressed her heart. She could think clearly about the situation for the first time since she woke. Decision made to keep her promise to do whatever she could to help free Father Notus, Jeanie closed the door with a muffled thanks to Brother Amadieu and turned to get dressed. The Angel be damned if he was going to stop her from doing her part, and since he was not there to tie her up she was free to follow.

Righteous anger had fuelled her quick steps as she left the property of the Abbey, Brother Bartholomew's directions still firmly stuck in her mind. It was the cold, the dark, and the realization that she had no plan to speak of that wore down the burning fire of her resolve to cooling embers.

Le Jardin appeared grandly as she stepped into the break of the eight foot high stone wall that outlined the front of the property. The driveway was long and unencumbered by large trees or bushes that could conceal any of the magnificence of the mansion. The foliage that presented itself seemed only to enhance the regal nature of the place.

Halting at the sight, Jeanie thought, for the first time, of turning back. With no plan, the only recourse was to walk up and knock on the door, and that reeked of stupidity. What was she to do? Ask if the Angel and the Nobel were there as if she were a child going to a friends house to play? Frustrated and angry at herself, Jeanie knew she should have listened to the Angel and stayed at the Abbey. It was her hurt pride that had whitewashed her ability to think clearly and made her act rashly, as it usually did.

This time she caught herself before she could do anything utterly stupid. She would trust in the Angel and believe he would return. Shaking her head, Jeanie turned on her heel to begin the trek back down the road and to the Abbey. She would wait for the Angel. When he returned victorious, she would apologise for doubting and mistrusting him.

Focused and determined, Jeanie did not see the rough hand until it was clamped over her mouth and a strong arm lifted her around the waist until her feet dangled.

Screaming, Jeanie kicked and tried to thrash, memories of her first night in London flashing to mind.

ANGEL OF DEATH

"The Mistress will be well pleased." The deep male voice whispered with the promise of violence if unheeded. His fetid breath tickled her ear, sending shivers down her neck as she felt herself being carried to the villa.

The intoxicating thrill of capturing the Angel dulled as Violet observed the one sided battle turn against her favour. Impotent rage grated her teeth while her eyes grew wide, unable to turn away from the exotic dance of the Angel that felled more and more of her servants. She had never seen the like and her desire to possess him grew with each new fountain of blood.

She had been delighted to see the shocked expression shattering his usual cool countenance when he realized that Robert was not mortal and that the Angel was surrounded with those of her kind and their servants. The unknown was always an initiator of fear and she needed the Angel to fear. It was the first path to possession and oh how she desired that. To have a Chosen completely hers, especially the Angel, Violet shuddered in anticipation and licked her painted lips.

A growl rose unbidden deep in her throat, irritated that Robert had been so stupid as to allow the Angel to decapitate him. The stunned expression on the Angel's face turned to realization and then deadly determination when Robert did not rise. Fury sparked when the Angel shouted to de Sagres to acquire a sword and follow his lead.

The mortals had all fallen and Violet was intelligent enough to know that she and her kind were next.

Nicolas fell, the shocked expression on his face forever frozen on his rolling disembodied head.

Violet retreated up a step, eyes glued to the battle between Gilles and the Angel. A wordless exclamation of triumph exploded from her tense body as Gilles blade sliced across the Angel's right breast. A blackened red line appeared on white flesh suddenly exposed and the Angel grunted in pain. A momentary shock of pleasure ran through Violet only to be squashed as Gilles head came within feet of Nicolas'.

De Sagres dispatched Leroi and Violet took another retreating step. Only a half dozen of her kind kept the Angel and de Sagres busy, meaning she only had moments before she would have to flee.

A muffled sound entered the fray from the front door and Violet smiled, victory singing through her blood.

"If you do not wish to be the cause of Miss Stuart's death," shouted Violet, smiling. "You would be smart to surrender now."

The shocked green gaze from her friend titillated Violet. Gregory had saved them all and though a reward was due to him, Violet would not let him have the girl. Jeanie was hers and Violet wished that it were she who held Jeanie in such an embrace.

Eyes locked on her friend, Violet could not appreciate the stunned expression wash over the Angel as he lowered his weapon. It was when it clattered to the red soaked floor that she turned her attention back upon her catch.

"I will not," shouted de Sagres. He raised his borrowed blade to resume his attack on Dartagnan and was halted by the Angel's white hand around his wrist.

"Please," pleaded the Angel when Jeanie's muffled scream rang through the room.

Violet stood taller, a smug expression on her face. She had won and she would have her way no matter what Corbie told her.

"Gregory, be a dear," she drawled, "take Miss Stuart to my parlour and don't hurt her." Violet's eyes darkened. "She's mine."

"Yes, ma'am," replied Greg, enthusiastically. Without effort he hoisted Jeanie up the stairs, ignoring her sobs.

Feeling secure, Violet descended down several steps but maintained her distance and her elevated status. The last of her boys ringed the two Chosen with raised blades. "Dartagnan, would you be so kind as to escort de Sagres to the Solar?"

"Over my dead body," growled Fernando, his blood splattered chest heaving.

"Soon enough." Violet waved her hand and a shot rang out. Fernando's body collapsed to the floor, his head wound adding to the red pool beside him.

The Angel stood stock still, his hands tightly clenched. Blood splatter accentuated his pale fury; white wisps of escaped hair clutched his face.

"What do you plan to do to Jeanie?" he demanded.

"Anything I want," purred Violet.

Another shot rang out and the Angel collapsed to the floor beside the Noble.

"Gustav, please take the Angel to my entertainment room and have him properly prepared," ordered Violet. A shiver of anticipation of her heart's desire ran through her and she turned to go upstairs.

She halted at the sight of a dishevelled Marie Therese with smoking duelling pistols. "Well done, Marie Therese," beamed Violet. A smile blossomed on Marie Therese's pallid face. "For this I will reward you whatever you desire."

"I wish only to serve you forever, Mistress," replied Marie Therese.

Violet nodded and ascended the steps. "Prepare yourself, child. You will not live to see the dawn."

"Oh thank you, Mistress," grovelled Marie Therese, clutching the hem of Violet's gown, tears streaming down her face.

Walking past her body servant, Violet beamed. She would rebuild, but first she desired to see her friend.

*　　　　　*　　　　　*

He was on fire. Every nerve and fibre of his being flamed, licking ribbons of agony from his wrists into a starburst of flares to his fingertips, down his arms, into his shoulders, across his chest and finally, up to throb in time with the pulsating pain that was his head.

Fragments of reality began to coalesce in time with the steady beat. First came the awareness of his body and he groaned as the pulsations increased, sending waves of nausea that threatened to overwhelm him. He could feel the minute intricacies as muscle, skin and bone knit together remaking his damaged temporal lobe. If he had not felt so horrible, he would have been jubilant that it had been lead shot in the pistols.

Gradually, the migraine eased to a dull headache and he groaned as lightning shot up his arms. Raising his chin from his chest, he could almost feel his brain shift back into proper position, but the effort left him drained. Head lolling back, he realized he was erect and opened his eyes.

Blurred black and white images washed over his vision, wavering until he could see the shadowed stone ceiling over his head. It was then that he realized it must be a stone floor that grated into his bare knees and the tops of his feet. He was kneeling with legs apart and had no recollection of arriving in this awkward position.

Uncomfortable, he tried to pull his legs together to purchase a greater balance only to feel the shooting pains in his arms and chest. His legs were pinned. It was then that he realized it was the cold touch of metal from behind his knees and over his ankles that held him firmly in place.

If that were the case, then what was holding him upright?

Turning his head, the answer chilled him and forced him to try and yank his arms down from the iron manacles that grated into his flesh.

Excruciating pain caused him to cry out and cease his movements. Kneeling, with his arms outstretched, he could feel the poisonous metal rip into tendons and bone. He could see black tendrils as the iron seeped into his veins, creeping up into his hands and descending down his arms, threatening to send him into oblivion.

Panicked, his mouth suddenly dry, he swallowed. It was what They promised and he felt his heart beat faster in time with his increased breath. He was trapped, held prisoner, and the need to purchase his freedom panicked him.

He closed his eyes and took a shuddering breath. Unable to make his fingers grasp firmly around the iron chain, he knew he had no choice and with a groan he pulled down in the hopes to snap the chains. Instead intense fire flared down his arms, into his chest and threatened to engulf him. His heart sped up as his breath left him trembling.

Relinquishing his attempt, he could only hang there, panting as the pain re-established itself.

Eyes squeezed shut, he could feel cool tears drip down the outer corners of his eyes. The fever associated with iron poisoning grew with prolonged contact and he knew that it was a matter of time before They came for him to exact their punishment. If he could remain conscious, then hopefully they would be held at bay until he was free.

For what seemed an indeterminable time, he waited until the pulsating fires diminished enough to be somewhat bearable and for rational thought to be attempted. He was caught, manipulated by this mysterious woman who had claimed Jeanie as a friend in that alley so long ago.

They had used Jeanie to capture him.

Concern for her snagged his breath. He could not let himself imagine that the Lady of *Le Jardin* would kill Jeanie. She had said to her servant not to harm her. It was a faint hope, but it was all he had. How they found her, let alone managed to capture her, sent a chill up his spine to clash with the inferno the iron was making of him.

Closing his eyes, his body shuddered uncontrollably. He hoped that those at the monastery would be all right and they would forgive him.

Fernando, he had no doubt, was as good as dead. Once word reached Katherine, so too would Notus be Destroyed. The Noble had been right. Jeanie had been the liability that had cost them everything, but he still loved her. More tears flowed knowing that it was his lack of will that had brought her into harm's way. He had broken his oath to her and betrayed Notus' love, and because of that they would most likely soon be dead.

Opening his eyes, he lifted his head. If he could have slouched his shoulders in despair he would have. There before him, standing against the stone wall, leaned his bloody sword with its dark sheath lying on the floor. On the wall, a series of hooks displayed all manner of torture devices. His eyes took in the sharp surgical implements; their gruesome configurations denoted that they had very little medical application except for the sole purpose of pain induction. Each and every one of them, he could see, was made of steel, but it was what hung on the end that riveted his attention and set him trembling anew.

Fastened to a steel rod, nine chains of small iron links hung. On each tail wire barbs stuck out like thorns arrayed on a rosebush, but it was the ends of the links that widened his eyes in horror. Large iron weights, sharply edged, acted as the plumbs. Even in the complete darkness of the dungeon he could see the small flakes of caked on blood and flesh. Nausea threatened to overpower him and he knew that the Lady of the Garden of the Gods did not need to be here to begin his torture. It had already begun. Closing his eyes, he managed a shuddering breath, anything to remove the sight of what was to come.

Voices penetrated the darkness, drawing closer, accompanied by footsteps. Hanging impotently, he knew that the Lady, joined by a male, descended down the stone steps. Her commanding voice issued orders and the heavier foot falls increased in speed and in volume, bringing with it the flickering orange glow of torchlight.

Eyes still shut, he tried to relax in an attempt to feign unconsciousness in the hopes that she would leave disappointed. He knew it was the cowards' way out, but he needed time to think. Already he could feel the greedy coils of the white faced demons attempting to clutch at him, ready to catch him in their putrescent embrace should he succumb to the poison seeping into his being.

The slip of wood into its bracket preceded softer foot falls, heralding the Mistress of *Le Jardin's* arrival. "Alright Gustav, what is it that you wanted me to see."

Her annoyed tone echoed off the walls, making him wonder how big the room truly was.

"This, Mistress," replied Gustav, excitedly.

Dread solidified in his stomach. He heard Gustav's approach, followed by his Mistress'. It took all his mental reserves not to panic and just allow himself to continue to hang there.

"What's this?" she questioned, curiosity piqued.

"When I personally prepared the Angel, as you requested, my Lady, I noticed this reaction to the iron manacles. Even the wounds he took above are not healed. They appear burnt," replied Gustav. "As you can see, my Lady, the Angel is truly unlike any other Chosen, if indeed his is Chosen."

"Of course he's Chosen," she snapped. "He's not mortal and he's not one of us. What else could he be?"

"I do not know, my lady," came the cowed reply.

The Lady emitted a deep-throated sound of disaffection. "Leave me."

"Yes, my Lady."

The scurry of retreating steps left him with the knowledge that he was alone with his captor.

"You can give up the pretence of being unconscious," commanded the Mistress of *Le Jardin*. "It may have fooled my mortal servant, but I am above such childish deceptions."

Opening his eyes to slits, he saw her standing in height with him, wearing a rust coloured silk shirt beneath a red leather corset tightly laced so as to accentuate her sensuous figure. A fine woollen skirt of the same colour as her shirt hung down to the floor in thick pleats. Raven black tresses escaped from its elaborate up-do to dangle and swirl about her ears and neck, but it was her eyes that captured his attention.

Angry at the cruel delight he saw, his jaw clenched. "What have you done with Jeanie?"

Momentary surprise flashed from vivid blue eyes. "She's fine, for the time being." The Lady lackadaisically stepped around him, surveying her catch, each footfall rang through the dungeon.

"I would have thought you would have asked a more poignant question," she purred, coming up behind him, her breath tickling his neck.

He forced down a shudder at her closeness. His only hope was that she told the truth. His eyes widened as he felt her cool hands travel down along his sides to finally embrace him around his hips, the full length of her body pressed him from behind.

"Do you not wish to know why you will be kept alive while the Chosen de Sagres will die with the dawn?" she whispered, trailing her fingers up his abdomen.

Turning his head away from her lips, he let his gaze land on the far wall and swallowed. The information was double sided. At least Fernando was still alive, and with that there was hope, but for him, there was none and so he kept silent.

Her hands fell away and he felt her step back. "When I ask you a question, you will answer it," she erupted.

A cry of pain shocked through him as the Mistress yanked his braided hair, snapping his head back. His arms strained against the shackles.

The poisoning effect set him trembling. On weakened legs he managed to right himself so that the shackles eased their bite.

"Interesting," she drawled. She continued her circumambulation, coming to stand before him, hands on her slim hips, sadistic delight illuminating her smile. "You are unlike any other Chosen I've ever had."

The Lady walked over to the devices hanging from the wall and he heard the scrape of metal against stone. He only had eyes for the serrated scalpel in her delicate hand and involuntarily recoiled. Increased agony shot down his arms, pulling from him a groan.

The smile on his torturers face grew at his distress. "Do you know why you and none of your predecessors were unable, even with your preternatural strength, to free yourselves from these bonds?"

The knowledge that there had been others added not only to his nausea, but to his rising panic. Unwilling to give in, he clenched his jaw, forbearing any possible response. It should not have been a surprise when she guided the blade into the sword wound, searing muscle, as she sliced deeper into his chest. The sudden flashing anger should have been enough.

Agonizing pain filled him and caused him to cry out.

The scent of his burning flesh nauseated him.

It was when she hit bone that he nearly lost the fight against unconsciousness and what that would bring.

Cool relief followed in its wake as the blade was removed and her finger traced along the wound, worming her finger in deeper.

Panting, he opened his eyes and stared at her shimmering form as he fought to get the pain and trembling under control. Hate wound round his belly. The desire to pummel the smug expression from her face surged.

"You *will* answer my questions," demanded the Mistress, haughtily. "I am more than pleased to correct your rudeness as I see fit." Her finger hit bone, long fingernails scraping painfully.

"I don't know," he gasped, his voice rough. If she would tell him, then maybe he would be able to figure a way out.

"Now that wasn't so difficult." She smiled beatifically at his compliance and removed her hand from the wound, wiping the bloodstain onto his chest.

She leaned forward, rubbed her cheek against his and whispered, "Because the manacles have a post that is hammered through the wrist. The damage done makes it near next to impossible to grasp anything. You can't imagine how many Chosen pulled so hard their hands popped off."

He felt his gorge rise as she moved away, tittering. It explained so much of why the reaction to the iron was moving faster than expected. The iron was bleeding into him because it was through him. He swallowed and gasped. There was no way out.

"Why?" he rasped. "Why are you doing this?"

Astounded, her fine black eyebrows rose, she cocked her head to the side. "To you personally or you in the plural sense of the Chosen?"

"Both." He closed his eyes momentarily, feeling the draw of oblivion and shook his head in an attempt to clear the fever from his mind. Pain borne fatigue owned his soul.

The sound of her skirts rustled towards him and he felt her body press against his. It took all his reserves not to flinch away or attempt to pull his arms down as she laid one arm on his shoulder to wrap languidly around the back of his neck while her other hand skilfully descended along his body, altering her motion once she found what she was seeking.

"The answers are quite simple," she sighed into his ear as her hand expertly worked below. "Do you know how many nights I heard Jeanie speak about you? About her desires for you? The erotic speculations? About your unmatched beauty? Do you not think it would captivate any woman's imaginings to possess the Angel, to discover these delicious secrets?"

Eyes shut tight, he tried to drive his mind away from what she sent through him.

"I've had many men and women, mortal and Chosen, through the years." She licked a path along his jugular, sending a shiver up his spine. "But to possess the Angel, to own him body and soul, to have him completely mine to do as I please, is a delectation undreamed of."

He could not believe what he was hearing and steeled himself from what her expert hand elicited until he felt her fingers grip his braid, viciously yanking his back head. Agony ripped past and convulsed against the sensations she was sending through him, pain mingled with visceral desire, and he groaned.

"You would be wise to do as I wish," hissed the Mistress, fury captivating and twisting her features. "It's your choice whether Jeanie lives to see the dawn."

Comprehension of what she demanded from him drew a sob from his raw throat. He did not need the white-faced demons to bring his fears to reality they were already here.

With only one path leading to hope for Jeanie, he relinquished any possibilities for himself.

The clutch on his braid released, sending him rocking on the chains until she stopped him with her body.

"You see how easy capitulation is?" The smile was back in her voice.

Despair welled, pulling tears from his eyes, and he tried to ignore Violet's lapping at their tracks. Resuming her position against him, she laid her hands on his body. A moan of pleasure vibrated against his neck as her mouth found his throbbing jugular. He gasped at the raw sensation. His eyes snapped open before scrunching shut in the attempt to shut the feeling off. She manipulated his flesh while shame burned brighter than the fever.

"You Chosen are so pompous in your belief that you are the ones chosen by your God," she hummed in his ear, between kisses. Her cool lips pulled at his flesh. "That you are the only ones who feast on mortal flesh."

Panting to push down the conflicting physical responses to her and the iron, he found it difficult to focus on her words. He felt the shift of her skirts, the press of her body tight against him, and loathed his traitorous flesh.

"So ignorant. So foolish. So easy to destroy."

Teeth scratched against his neck at the same time the shock of cold flesh enveloped him.

"All the stories, all the legends," Violet grasped his braid, pulling his head back as she rode him. "They weren't about you."

Gasping, he watched in growing horror as the sadistic smile in violet eyes grew.

"You usurped our name. You usurped our position. You pretend you are greater when you are lesser. Humanity is the taint of the Chosen because you never are born Chosen. Thankfully, we Vampires are born of the grave, leaving humanity behind." Anger flashed, icing her eyes to a chilling blue. Her dull canine teeth elongated to sharp needle like points. "The Chosen die in their ignorance. Vampires rule, sending the strongest of the Chosen on tasks that can only fail so that we can exterminate the rest."

Pain and pleasure rocked through his tortured body as she bit deep into his neck. He could feel her teeth penetrating him as cold lips began their deadly suckle. With each drawing, he felt his body weaken as his blood flooded out of his body to fill hers in time with his body's throbbing release.

The Chosen were not Vampires.

Vampires were real.

Vampires were the ones succeeding in the genocide of the Chosen.

He damned himself and the Chosen for their presumption.

Oh, how wrong they all were.

He wept.

XXXV

eanie's mouth felt full of cotton. Smacking her lips, she tried to bring much needed moisture and found none. Head pounding, she carefully opened her eyes and wish she had not. The dim candlelight was enough to make her groan as she lifted weighted arms to cover her face. A rumble from her stomach added to the distress. Jeanie was hungry, but more than that she was incredibly thirsty.

Arms flopping impotently to the sides of her head, she made another attempt to open her eyes. Slowly, she was able to take in the swirling patterns of the stucco ceiling. Violet's bed was comforting to her weary body, but this did not look like Violet's room at the Rose and Thorn.

Memory crashed into Jeanie, causing her to gasp. The cold hand clamped over her mouth as an unknown assailant carried her bodily. The Angel's destruction gored the front entrance of the mansion and his beautiful crimson eyes reflecting despair in defeat. Violet standing triumphant on the stairs as Jeanie was whisked past. The sounds of two shots and then being thrust into the grand room she now found herself in.

Jeanie had first railed against the locked door, crying out to be released. Self-hatred boiled up at the comprehension that it was she that had brought about the Angel's capture. The idea that he would be killed because of her stubborn selfishness made her slam against the door, pounding it until the wood split her knuckles and fingers.

It was a shock when the door clicked and opened, revealing her friend in glamorous attire. Violet entered the boudoir and closed the door behind, all the while watching Jeanie's blood well in the scrapes. It was all the more horrific what Violet did next.

Grasping Jeanie's hands in a vice like grip, Violet purring like a mother cat, licked the wounds clean.

Jeanie tried to pull away, but could not. This was her friend. The one who always laughed at the penny presses that Jeanie brought back, especially ones about vampires; the one who had been so supportive of trying to find a way for Jeanie to be with the Angel; the one who lived down the hall; the one Alice always had misgivings about; the one Tom steered clear of; the one who was behind the poisoning of the Chosen.

It all seemed surreal; this creature standing before her, with her blood staining Violet's lips.

"Exquisite," sighed Violet, running her tongue over lips. "Had I known how delicious you would taste, I would have made you mine years ago."

Jeanie's eyes widened and she stepped backwards until she ran into the dressing table, her body trembling. "What are ye?"

A secretive smile pulled at the corners of Violets lips, her blue eyes sparkling. "My dear friend – do you realize you are the only one I call friend? No? No matter." Black waves swelled and then settled on Violet's shoulders as she shook her head. "I am that which all mortals fear. I am a Vampire."

Jeanie could not believe what she was hearing. "Ye're...ye're poisoning yer own kin?"

Violet was upon her faster than she could imagine. Their faces only inches apart, so close that Jeanie could smell her fetid breath and trembled at the fury in Violet's face.

"You mistake me for a Chosen?" roared Violet.

Pain smacked against Jeanie's back and head and she found herself being lifted off the floor, Violet's petite hands bruising her upper arms.

"The Chosen are nothing," raged Violet. "It will be the Vampires who will rule."

Shocked and dazed, Jeanie fought to free herself only to give up at the sight of Violet's smile. Normal appearing teeth gave way to the gruesome reality of the sketches found in her novels. Violet's teeth grew into two long points and before Jeanie could react, sharp pain rendered her motionless as her once-friend bit deep into her neck.

No sensations of pleasure. Only horror and pain as Jeanie tried to make non-functioning limbs fight against what Violet drew out of her until the blackness overwhelmed her.

Supine on the silk, the scent of cooked meat and fresh bread drifted to Jeanie's nose and she inhaled deeply, sending her stomach into a frenzy of rumbling. Blissful saliva flooded her mouth and she sat up, swinging legs over the side to dangle bonelessly. An upsurge of nausea and stabbing lights made her groan as she sat, gripping the edge of the gold coverlet in suddenly clammy hands. A few deep breaths steadied the spinning room and reduced the sledgehammer battering her brain to a dull throb. Turning her head in the direction of the delicious fragrance, Jeanie caught her breath as renewed pain flared in her neck where Violet had bitten her.

Clamping a hand over the wound, the pressure dulled the sharp pain. Jeanie carefully stood and stumbled towards the dressing table. Hand trembling, she pulled out the red and gold embroidered cushioned chair and sat down with a sigh.

In the mirror before her, Jeanie barely recognized herself. Dark circles bruised her eyes and tainted the corners of her mouth, starkly contrasting her wan face. Even her lips had taken on a tinge of blue. Swallowing down the fear reflected in her green eyes, Jeanie cautiously lifted her hand away from the wound on her neck and gasped. Two scabbed over holes were surrounded by blackened flesh.

Tears welled and dripped down. A part of Jeanie's mind was amazed she had enough moisture for that. Tilting her head, she brushed errant locks from the bite mark. They were so unlike what she had experienced with the Angel. This was neither soft nor pleasurable.

Tentatively, she touched her fingertips to the holes and moaned.

Lowering her eyes from the mirror, she dropped her hand to the red stained surface of the table and the silver tray that contained a plate of rare steak, new potatoes and greens. A small loaf sent wisps of steam into the air, while condensation dripped down the silver pitcher filled with ice water.

Despair flooded through Jeanie, forcing the tears to flow faster. Everything had gone so horribly wrong and her fears for the Angel clenched her belly into knots. Jeanie knew she could not live without him and she picked up the knife left for her to cut the meat. Its silver gleamed in the candlelight. It would be so easy to plunge its serrated edge into her abdomen, but she remembered what he had asked of her to do if he never returned and she dropped the knife with a clatter against the table.

She had to find a way out of here and escape back to London with what she had learned. Maybe it would be enough to purchase Notus' freedom and then they would be able to grieve together, but to do that she needed sustenance.

Picking up fork and knife in tremulous hands, Jeanie cut through the juicy red meat, its appearance sending a flood into her mouth in expectation. She had no doubt that everything was spiced with the poisonous herbs, but she had to eat. The first bloody mouthful vanquished any rational thought as Jeanie rapaciously tore into her meal, washing large chunks down with gulps of water.

Bit by bite, Jeanie felt her strength returning, yet the pervading fatigue still ached her joints and muscles. Sopping up the red juices left from the nearly raw meat, Jeanie settled back against the rod iron backing of the seat and sighed. She hated the fact that it had been the most delicious meal she had ever had.

Strength returning, Jeanie stood and walked to the draped windows.

Sweeping the red velvet curtains proved her entrapment. Shoulders slouched in defeat. Jeanie went to the other window covering and pushed them out of the way.

A glimmer of hope flushed through her and she knelt down to peer through the small space left at the base of the window that allowed the night to creep in through a badly painted job.

It would be a tight fit once she figured out how to break the glass. The only hesitation was that the ground was far below. A sigh shuddered through her and she knew what she had to do, there was no choice except for what she would use to break the window. She could not remain here.

Groaning as she stood from her crouched position, Jeanie paced the room, discovering what item would be best to shatter the glass when she heard voices outside her door.

Frozen with renewed fear, Jeanie placed the tall silver trifurcated candlestick back down on the night table. It was when she heard Violet's voice that all thought fled her mind and she felt herself being drawn to the door. A sudden desire to hear her friend speak again welled within as she touched the dark oak.

A tremor passed through her with Violet's soft tones.

Stunned at the sudden craving to do the Mistress' desires, Jeanie's eyes widened and dropped her hand from the wound on her neck.

Her breath came in short gasps and Jeanie tried to school her feelings. She knew something was wrong and shook her head. Thinking was becoming hard to accomplish. All she could do was to stand there, pressed against the door, listening intently.

"Here is the letter, Gustav. Please make sure that Mr. Vale receives it before he sails tonight."

A rustle of paper, and then silence.

"Yes, my lady. What should I inform my Lord in regards to the Chosen?"

Violets laugh weakened Jeanie's legs, sending her sliding down the door. "Tell Mr. Vale that de Sagres has been dispatched with the dawn. As for the Angel," stated Violet, possessively, "he is mine and he will continue to be mine until I bore of him."

Jeanie's eyes popped open at the sudden realization that he was still alive and pressed her ear against the wood.

"Of course, my lady," replied Gustav. "Do you desire to keep the Angel in the entertainment room? Or shall I make alternative arrangements?"

"The entertainment room is fine, Gustav," smiled Violet as she walked down the hall.

"Master Vale will not like that, my lady," replied Gustav.

"I know that," snapped Violet. "France is mine. She said so. While Mr. Vale is here, he is under my authority."

"Yes, my lady," cowed the servant.

"Good," said Violet, brusquely. "I want that letter sent so that Mr. Vale has it upon awakening at sunset. A copy is to be sent by telegraph to my Lady. Return with Mr. Vale's reply."

Jeanie pressed harder against the wood as their voices faded.

"Prepare my crypt, Gustav. The sun is near to rising."

Gustav's reply descended down the stairs and out of Jeanie's hearing.

Pushing herself away from the door, Jeanie stood, elated with the knowledge that the Angel was still alive. The news changed everything. If she could get out and find some help she could come back and rescue him. It would be difficult. Her reaction to Violet's presence unnerved her, but Violet would be asleep with the dawn and Jeanie was relieved that the Vampire would not be sleeping here.

Strengthened with renewed purpose, Jeanie picked up the candlestick and went to the window. It was now or never. Crouching down, with the drapery cloaking her presence, Jeanie waited for the first hints of dawn and the realization that with it, Fernando de Sagres would be dead. Closing her eyes, she was surprised to feel sadness at the Chosen's passing.

The night turned to a dull grey and then to the return of colour. The sun still had not peeked over the horizon but there was enough light for Jeanie to see how far up she truly was. It did not matter, she had to make the attempt. Turning her face away, she smashed the glass with the candlestick.

Shards flew across her hand, lacerating it. Ignoring the stinging pain, Jeanie smashed again and again until the opening was large enough to squeeze through.

Dropping the bloodied candlestick onto the floor beside her, Jeanie took a deep breath, prayed that the rest of the window would not slide down on top of her, and pushed her head through.

The descent was precarious, but she found what she had not expected to find, a trellis buried beneath rose stalks. Ducking her head back in, Jeanie knew going out head first would not give her the purchase needed to climb down and she turned around. Carefully, she stuck her legs out and hissed as her stockings caught on the glass shards, ripping the fabric and scraping her skin. Disregarding the pain, Jeanie pushed herself backwards, her skirts snagging. She knew she must look ridiculous but she pressed on until she balanced precariously on her stomach. Floundering with legs dangling and feet slipping, Jeanie managed to find purchase on the trellis, and with a sigh began the descent.

It was slow going, her hands and knees punctured over and over by vicious thorns. Jeanie sighed in relief when she finally came to stand amongst a monstrous garden. Shadowed from the first rays of dawn, she watched the colours return. She knew she was at the back of the villa and to find her way to the monastery she would have to go around to the front.

Sucking at one of the scrapes in her hand, Jeanie stepped out of the sleeping garden only to jump back with a squeak at the sound of shattering glass.

Gingerly, she peered up at the window that had not fallen and wondered what had made the sound. A streak of movement flashed in the corner of her eye and she turned towards it in expectation of being caught.

Trails of smoke leading directly to a smaller building on the south end of the property confounded her. Heart hammering in her chest, Jeanie followed in desperate hope, constantly alert for any pursuers.

The seam between the two wall length mirrors was firm and unyielding to Fernando's prying fingers. Since awaking, he cursed his throbbing head and surveyed the room. There was no furniture to cast shadows, no candles to create light, only the ambient illumination from the external world showed the bleak future of what would happen come the rising of the sun.

Turning his back on the glass, Fernando leaned heavily against it with a hiss. All three external walls were glass, and though the floor was of white marble streaked with black, the walls and ceilings were solidly mirrored. Once the sun rose there would be absolutely no place where the sun would not shine.

If he could find the hidden door, Fernando might have a chance of escape. Returning to his search, he began to feel the first changes that would herald the sun's rebirth and moved his hands along the seams in desperate hope to find the one that would lead to darkness.

Completing the circuit around the room, anger swelled at his failure, sending his fist to shatter the mirror in front of him. The tinkling sound as glass hit marble did not relieve his anger, nor did the wainscoting directly behind the shattered mirror.

Fear born hate seethed within him and he stomped over to the southern facing window trying in vain to ignore the rising prickling feeling along his skin. He was in time to watch a rider remove his mount from the stables and gallop out to the road.

There was no comfort in the knowledge that he had been right about the mortal girl. Jeanie had proved to be the liability Fernando had expected her to be, but he did not know whom he should be angrier with, she or the Angel. Instead, he chose both equally.

Gazing over the southern yard, he could see the stables and their blissful darkness within. It would not be long before the sun kissed the sky and set his flesh aflame. Jaw clenched, Fernando knew there was only one option left and threw a punch to break the glass. He was rewarded with a spider web of cracks. Somehow the glass was reinforced.

Swallowing down his rising panic, Fernando tried again, stumbling when his fist got stuck in the hole he had made. Thick glass sliced into his skin as he freed his hand, to heal instantaneously.

Fernando peered through the hole and tested the glass with a finger. He had never seen such glass before and then he realized why the two inch thick window portrayed the world differently than it should. Expelling a shaking huff, he glanced to the east, through the leaded pane, to the rays sneaking into the sky. If he did not act soon, he would add to the streaks of black on the marble tile.

Stepping as far back as possible from the hole he had made, his back touching mirror, Fernando took a deep shaking breath and did something he had not done since he was a child, he crossed himself. If God was listening then maybe there was hope, but Fernando doubted it in any case.

A roar rumbled deep in his throat and he pushed off from the mirror, accelerating with preternatural speed to the hole in the window. Sunlight flooded into the room the instant his shoulder made contact with the glass. A rain of shards sliced into him, his blood igniting as his skin smouldered, and then he was falling.

Blinded, burning agony ripped through Fernando, his body combusting as the full power of the sun poured over him. The impact onto the dewy grass expelled all his breath, leaving him unable to scream. Skin charring, eyes blinded, Fernando stumbled as fast as his roasting muscles could carry him towards the scent of horse and the promise of bloody healing.

It was a blessed relief when darkness embraced him, extinguishing the flames as he stumbled into the stables. Only the burning pain and the violent hunger filled his being.

Reduced to a mindless hungering beast, Fernando blindly grasped the mane of the horse in the closest stall. He acknowledged the bite of the terrified beast with a grunt, his sole attention on the blood scent.

Trapped in its cubicle, the horse reared. Fernando stepped close, ignoring the stabbing hooves, yanked the horse's head down and found the fount. A victorious growl shook him as he sunk his teeth into the struggling beast. Life giving blood exploded into his mouth, filling him faster than he could manage. Drops of blood welled in the corners of his mouth to drip down his chin and onto his bloodstained shirt.

A shudder stabbed through him as he suckled the wound, holding the horse still in an iron embrace, driving his teeth deeper when he felt the flow begin to slow. He felt the horse stumble to its knees and still Fernando held on, nursing the rejuvenating fluid until the heart began the stutter. The horse whinnied in terror and then convulsed, its body going slack.

Fernando lifted his head from the velvet neck with a gasp and closed his eyes. Energy pulsated through him, heralding the beginnings of his body's reparations. Eyes opening, he found he still could not see. There was only one thing he could do. Standing up, his joints creaking, Fernando laughed and turned to go down the stable intent on feasting on each of the panicked beasts.

A new scent caught his attention halting him, its bouquet far superior to that of the horses. Following instinct and his olfactory senses, Fernando lunged at the intruder.

*   *   *

Jeanie screamed as the crisped and blackened figure, smelling of charred meat in tattered bloodied clothing, threw itself at her. Pink teeth in a fearsome growl missed her neck as she jumped sideways to escape the deadly jaws. Landing in a pile of hay, it took only a moment to realize what stood before her, stalking her with a feral grin.

"Fernando," she cried as he grasped at her, trying not to gag at the scent. His burnt body fell on top of hers. "It's me!" Impacting on the threshed flooring, all air left her lungs in a whoosh.

Shocked at hearing the familiar voice, renewed hatred bubbled to the surface and broke, masking the agony of his tortured flesh. She was the one who allowed this travesty to occur. She was the mortal who should have been killed long ago. She was the one who did not deserve the protection of a Chosen.

Bearing down, frustration snapped at him as he felt Jeanie squirm out of his mouth's reach.

Realizing that what was left of the Noble mindlessly hungered for her blood, Jeanie knew that if bitten again she would die. She did not have much in reserve to keep him at bay, but she had to do something to survive this attack. She remembered her meal laced with the deadly herbs.

"I'm tainted," she yelled. "Fernando, no!"

Jeanie's words slapped him back to cogency and Fernando ceased his attack. With teeth clenched, he hoisted himself off the girl, every muscle protesting a meal denied. He had so wanted to rip her throat out with his teeth, to feast on her hot blood as it poured into him, to savour the taste of his revenge. Instead, he stood trembling and gazed down at the black blob lying in the hay that was the Angel's love.

"You fucking bitch," he hissed, his jaw burning with the movement. Pain enervated through him and he stumbled backwards until the wall propped him up. "I should kill you for what you've done."

Blackened patches of skin sloughed down his face to land in the straw, leaving glistening red skin and blood filled blisters in its wake. Jeanie could only watch, numb to the horror except for the rising nausea. Fernando's words echoed in her head, springing forth tears and she knew the truth of them.

"He's still alive," she muttered, unable to glance up at Fernando's slowly healing form.

"What?" Surprise flushed through the Noble only to be quickly quenched. "How do you know this?"

"I overheard Violet." Slowly she regained her feet, but still could not bring herself to look at Fernando.

"Ah yes. You're friend from the Inn," sneered the Noble.

Jeanie stared dumbfounded at Fernando.

"You think I didn't know." Fernando took a shaking step towards her. Charred muscle rustled like dry leaves. "She sent us to find you at the soup kitchen. She was all worried about you. Little did I know you were just part of the plan to entrap us and destroy us."

Eyes wide, Jeanie could only shake her head in defiance. What if the Angel believed the same? Swallowing her fear, she found something else in its place—anger. Furious at the betrayal by her false friend and her complete naiveté and she lashed out

"Ye stupid git," she yelled. "D'ye think I'd bed the Angel just to see him kilt? What a sorry existence ye've had. I was snatched while out for a walk. Violet was my friend. I trusted her and she turned out to be a monster!"

The horses whinnied and pounded against their boards as Jeanie's voice faded from the stables. Silence fell between the two as Jeanie attempted to get her anger under control.

"When I heard ye'd been kilt I actually was sorry," she whispered, brushing away her tears. "When I realized ye were still alive I was happy. Now ye just disgust me."

The bold truth of the girl's words rocked Fernando to the core. It was not what he expected from her or from anyone for that matter. His own anger diminished with the realization that she was just as much a victim of Violet's, if not more so. For the first time in a very long time, Fernando felt compassion and shame. He glanced up to see her figure turn towards the open stable doors.

"Where do you think you're going?" he demanded, his eyes squinted with the light silhouetting her form.

"Back to the monastery." Jeanie stepped out into the sun, watching the villa for any signs that her escape had been detected. She felt safe in the warming rays, knowing she was beyond Fernando's grasp. She would never allow herself to be a pawn of his or anyone else's again.

The thought of being trapped in the stable, awaiting discovery, filled the Noble with panic. He knew full well he did not have the strength to fight against whatever numbers the Mistress of Le Jardin threw at him, no matter how many horses he consumed. He had escaped the Sun Room, but had not planned on how to leave the property now the sun was fully up.

"Wait," he called out. The idea he was dependent upon this mortal girl for his escape galled him.

Jeanie turned at the call and took in the ragged and wounded form of the once Noble Fernando de Sagres standing well within the shadows of the structure.

They stared at each other, waiting for the other to speak.

Fernando broke first. "You said the Angel was still alive."

"Aye, I did." Jeanie stepped closer, still standing outside.

"And you're just planning on leaving?"

She did not know if Fernando could shock her further until now. "Ye just dinna get it, d'ye?"

Fernando bristled and attempted to straighten his burnt back.

"I'm goin' back to the monastery to get help to free the Angel."

Jeanie's eyes flashed threateningly and then she smiled. Help was standing right in front of her *if* she could find a way to make him do it.

Fernando barked a laugh. "You think that a handful of musty old monks can free the Angel? You don't even know what you are fighting against."

"Oh but I do, Fernando." Jeanie stepped into the darkness and realized he could hardly see her when his eyes did not focus properly. She found the card and held it close.

"What?" He could not believe what he heard and stepped back from the girl. The bloodscent sent tremors through him and he knew he had to feed again, and soon. "You're lying."

"I am not," she affirmed.

Surprised at her conviction, Fernando glared. "Then tell me."

She wanted to whoop and holler at catching the Noble in his manipulative trap. He seemed in such poor form that she was almost sorry to take advantage of him, but it was the only way. "I'll tell ye *after* ye help me free the Angel."

Clicking his jaw shut, Fernando shook his head. "I can live without that knowledge."

Jeanie blinked in disbelief. She had not counted on him calling her bluff. Chewing on her bottom lip, she found what she needed to up the ante. "I'll get ye to the monastery too."

"And how do you propose to do that?" he scoffed. "A nice stroll in the sun would limit my usefulness in obtaining the Angel."

"There's a covered wagon beside the stable. I used to drive carts with my da. I ken how to hitch them too. Add a couple of horse blankets and ye'll be fine."

Slowly, Fernando nodded, agreeing to the terms. It was his only way. "If you get me back to the monastery and allow me time to heal, we'll go back to get your precious Angel. Then you'll tell me who or what is behind the poisoning of the Chosen."

"Deal." stated Jeanie, sticking out her hand and instantly regretted the action. Crisped flesh slid in her touch, creating cracks that oozed red and yellow gore. It took all her resolve not to vomit.

Fernando took her hand in his scorched and blackened one. "Deal." He let her pull away faster than he would have liked, but still he admired her fortitude even as she wiped his burnt and suppurating flesh from her hand onto her skirt. "One other thing."

"What?" snapped Jeanie, halting in her progress of cleaning her hand. She checked between her fingers and grimaced.

"Pick your two horses for the job," smiled the Noble, his face ghastly as more skin sloughed off. "The others are mine."

Jeanie sighed at the necessity of what was to become of the poor beasts and nodded.

XXXVI

I t is the attachments in one's life that suffering is created. The pain our bodies create is just one such visceral attachment. Detachment from one's expectations of sensation will cause pain to cease, allowing one to transcend physical perceived reality."

"What about pleasure?"

"So to with all forms of attachment, whether it be of the physical, mental, emotional or spiritual. Through detachment comes transcendence."

The words of his first Master rang through his mind as if he and the monk were sitting in his dimly lit cell. Of course that was impossible. Master Tsang was over seven hundred years dead. Yet the substance of the words rang true more so now as he hung from the iron shackles.

He could no longer feel his hands. The last time he ventured a glance, they were blackened and swollen, the iron band cutting and smouldering into his inflamed wrists. The smell of his burning flesh mingled with the soot the grease torch released.

Mouth parched, he tried to swallow and felt his dry lips crack. He was on fire from the iron borne infection and he knew that what he heard was not what she had said.

Time had lost meaning in the torture the Lady of *Le Jardin* exacted upon him, yet some part of him knew that what seemed to be nights of torture were only several hours.

He vaguely recalled her storming down the stone steps and taking up the serrated knife. It was difficult to recall when there was a time when that bloodied blade was not part of her hand, and somewhere in his fevered mind he believed that the knife was her hand.

With meticulous care and a surgeon's skill, she carved into his body, following previously treaded paths. First came the chest wound. Sizzling meat and blood wafted up causing him to retch and incurring her wrath when he refused to answer her questions. Then she traced the ancient scar on his arm, opening it up in a slow mockery of the single slash that had first rended his flesh and exposed his deadly differences.

He had turned his head away from the flicking of her cold tongue to lap at any blood that oozed from the burnt flesh, ashamed that the coldness gave some relief. Still he refused to reply.

With each passing of the blade as it dug deeper, the questions repeated, slicing muscle fibre from muscle fibre in a cautery that added to his agony until the words became a mantra, whispered into the flesh as she consumed him.

"Where is she? Where did she go? What is she going to do? If you tell me I will stop."

He refused to believe her even though his body cried out for him to relinquish the knowledge so as to be freed from the torture.

Through the Lady's fury and constant repetition he knew that somehow Jeanie had escaped, eluding recapture. He silently repeated each question, clinging to them in the hope they provided as his body was riddled in unrelenting agony. His voice broken from screaming, a part of him was grateful that he could barely utter a word otherwise he would have answered the Mistress long ago. Anything to make her stop, to ease the pain if only for a little before she would find another reason to pick up the knife and begin her work anew.

Another presence entered the chamber, cutting off the litany, bringing a momentary respite from her slicing attention. He released a sob at the sudden relief before a frustrated scream shattered the silence that turned his gut into a knot, sending shudders along his body.

A new mantra began as she stabbed into the scar on his leg, carving the old wound open in one easy stroke. The jarring of blade against bone sent him swinging on the chains.

Through his cries, he heard the words repeated again and again as she worked the knife. "Where is de Sagres? Where are they hiding?"

Gasping, his eyes closed, he could feel the cold touch of the white-faced demons beckoning him into their embrace. Their torture would be a release from the suffering he endured and he opened his eyes.

The Lady's contorted face looked up to meet him. The inferno that raged through him blurred his vision. She could do anything to his body, but he would escape, he realized, and she would never find him. No one would ever find him again. Not Jeanie. Not Notus. Not Fernando. They would be free while he fled into the awaiting arms of the demons. It was his choice. He accepted it.

"Why are you smiling?" snapped *Le Jardin's* ruler. She lifted the gore-besmeared blade to his face and held it there.

"You've lost," he rasped, not knowing nor caring where the words came from. They stole his breath away and he closed his eyes, the tug from the demons more insistent. It would be his choice that he would endure. The known tortures of the demons were preferable to the unknown devices she had yet to put into action.

He groaned as he felt his head snap back.

"What are you talking about? I never lose." The Mistress' fetid breath raised his gorge.

His breath came in quick gasps as she sawed her way along the knotted scar on his leg, each pass sending spasms through his body as she repeated her newest questions. Over and over the new mantra sounded in an effort to force the answers from his torn and burnt flesh. It was when he realized that the questions had stopped, halting the blade's motion, that he opened his eyes.

The Lady of *Le Jardin* stood at the implements hanging on the wall. Carefully, she placed the bloodied blade on the small table against the stone and picked up something else.

His eyes widened as his breath and heart raced at the sight. Cold terror impaled him and he found he could not relinquish the gaze until she was beyond his sight. Again he felt his head snap back, the cold metallic touch of the scourge's rod pressed upwards under his chin.

"I have had my fun," she hissed, "but it is starting to grow dull. I had believed that the Angel would be more fun than this. Answer me."

An explosion of air ripped through his lips. "They know." His raw throat barely allowed the whisper. "Jeanie and Fernando know about the Vampires poisoning the Chosen and you will never find them."

He felt her tense with the understanding of the truth and he closed his eyes. "You may possess my body, but my soul belongs to Jeanie."

Another scream of rage shook the room and he felt her sudden release that sent him swinging.

He knew it should not have been a surprise what happened next, but the intense agony of feeling the barbed iron lashes rip and flay him, lifting and separating, searing skin and muscle, pulled him closer into the embrace of the demons.

A second followed by a third lashing, as the Mistress raved.

In her fury she cursed her failure with the Angel and screamed her defiance against whose orders she had broken. She had failed her Mistress, the Lady Bastia, Mistress of Britain, Mother of All.

The sound of tearing and the smell of burning seemed remote as the inferno that became his back radiated through his body, numbing his mind.

Four.

Five.

Six.

The metallic taste of blood filled his mouth and he wondered whose it was.

He lost count after eleven. His body was numb as he swayed on the chains. He wondered if he could die from this torture and decided he did not care.

Let go.

A woman's voice, multilayered in its harmony, rang through his mind above the sound of the decimation of his body and he whimpered.

It's time to let go.

Closing his eyes, he could see them. The white-faced demons were close, Their hungry expressions inviting.

You made a choice. Come.

Darkness descended between he and the demons. White putrescent faces twisted in impotent rage before they were obliterated by nothingness.

With a sigh, he fell into the Void.

Jeanie stood outside Fernando's door, hand poised to strike the wood and halted. It was a day and a night since they arrived back at St. Martin's amid a flurry of questions from the monks that received them. The worse was trying to explain *l'Ange's* whereabouts and their damaged presentation. She had even heard Fernando thank God that there was a cloud obscuring the brilliant fall sun when he exited the covered wagon, his body layered with blankets, to enter the dark stone walls of the monastery.

Upon witnessing the burnt ruin of Fernando's face, an elderly monk sent several others scurrying. The Noble had barked a laugh, which turned to a grimace of pain, before letting the old man guide him to his room. Jeanie had been surprised to witness the healing changes on Fernando's face and hands, but they were far from healed. She wondered how many more horses it would take. Guided by another monk, Jeanie followed him to the room she shared with the Angel and was told to wait. Father Theodore would wish to speak with her.

The inviting bed pulled at Jeanie. Succumbing, she lay down. It did not take long to fall into a dream-plagued sleep that left her more exhausted than before. In every nightmare Violet's youthful body, her soft lips and sharp teeth penetrated her mind leaving her desiring the Vampires touch. Each time she woke, her body shivered in anticipation while her mind reeled against what her body desired.

Shaking off the reminiscence, Jeanie knocked on the door. They had waited too long already and she was anxious to get back to *Le Jardin*. The problem was that she felt pulled to see Violet, to feel her betrayer's touch, to hear the Mistress' voice. It was growing hard to keep her focus on rescuing the Angel.

"Come in," came the brusque response.

Jeanie turned the handle and pushed. She had not seen the Noble since returning and stood in shocked silence.

Fernando fastened the top two buttons of his blue pyjamas and turned. "Didn't your mother teach you that it's impolite to stare?" He turned back to the small mirror hanging on the wall above the washbasin, patting his dark hair into place.

Shutting her mouth, Jeanie stepped into the room and closed the door. She could not believe the change that had come over him. No longer burnt, Fernando's skin took on a deep bronze colouring, as if darkly tanned. There were still a few patches that appeared red while others seemed to be peeling.

"There's a chair over there if you wish to sit down." Fernando absently waved to the seat next to the dormant hearth and turned. "I presume that you have come to discuss the other half of our bargain."

The hard wood seat forced Jeanie to sit straight. "Aye."

Fernando harrumphed and walked over to the single bed, casually sitting down with one leg bent before him while the other dangled to the floor. His dark brown eyes locked onto her form. "And I presume that you have a plan?"

Jeanie opened her mouth to snap a retort and then shut it. Taking a deep breath, she let it out in a huff. She doubted that Fernando would agree with what she had in mind, but he had promised.

"Aye, I do." Jeanie crossed her arms over her chest. "I was hopin' t'go back today."

"Fine," replied the Noble. "Now if you don't mind, I've fed on nearly every cow from here to Bellingham — not a pleasant task to say the least — and I am tired." Fernando stood and gracefully walked to the door. "I'll meet you at sunset."

"No," barked Jeanie as she stood.

Fernando turned to face her, eyebrows raised. "Pardon? Are you releasing me from our agreement? If you are, I am quite amenable to that."

"I'm no doin' that either." Jeanie paced a few steps and then halted. She had made him agree to go and rescue the Angel, but could she make him agree to the next? "We need to go now, during the day."

Fernando's bark of laughter rang off the stone. "Oh, this is rich."

With preternatural speed he had Jeanie up against the far wall, his hands resting flat against the stone beside her head, his body pressed against hers.

"What makes you think I'll agree to step outside during the day again? I may be a lot of things, but I am not suicidal, nor am I self sacrificing."

The scent of Fernando's breath mingled with the sudden bump of her head against the wall, made Jeanie wish she had not eaten. Lifting her gaze to meet his, she could still smell the lingering scent of burnt flesh.

"Because if we dinna go now and wait for night we'll both be kilt."

"You're saying a lot of things, li'l miss," scoffed the Noble. "But you're not telling me anything that I want to know."

"Our agreement was that I'd tell ye after we got the Angel back."

"It was, but you didn't say that you wanted to go back during the day." Fernando tilted his head, his gaze resting on her pale neck peeking out through the green scarf.

Jeanie's hand absently rose to touch the puncture wounds from Violet's bite, her breath coming faster at the sensation.

"Well, that's interesting," stated the Noble, "and I thought you were just hot for the Angel."

Jerking her hand back down, her fingers curled into a fist. Oh how she wanted to strike him but knew it would be an act of futility and most likely would break their agreement. "I'll tell ye now who are killing the Chosen if ye agree to come with me now."

Fernando pushed off from the wall, giving them space. "I doubt there is anything you can tell me that is worth the price of me going out in the sun again. The Angel's most likely dead in any case."

Locking her jaw, Jeanie felt the surge of anger and forced it down. It was not the time, nor the place, yet. She did not know how she knew, but there was no doubt in her mind that the Angel still lived. Lifting her balled fist up to her neck wrap, she carefully untied the knot and pulled the fabric away.

"The one's killin' the Chosen are Vampires."

The simplicity of the statement riveted Fernando's gaze back onto her neck. The fact that he did not laughingly dismiss her notions chilled her and suddenly he was upon her, lifting her chin to study the two dark marks on her neck.

"You're lying," hissed the Noble, spittle hitting her face. "The Chosen *are* Vampires."

Despite the firm, immobilizing grip, Jeanie managed to minutely shake her head. "That's what they want ye to think," she gasped. "All the stories, they weren't about the Chosen. They are about the Vampires. Vampires who canna bide the day and must sleep in coffins. Vampires who afear sanctified objects. Vampires who die with a stake to their hearts. Vampires whose mark is two wounds instead of four. Vampire marks that dinna heal quickly, but linger like this."

Glaring at the unhealed puncture wounds, Fernando ran a dark finger across them, barely catching Jeanie as her legs caved out from under her. Steadying the girl on her feet, he watched as Jeanie's eyes contracted and her heartbeat slowed.

Once she was stable he released her, confusion darting his eyes back and forth before realizing the truth to her words. A Chosen's bite would have healed. A Chosen's bite would have been four. Any mark left would not have caused such a reaction in a mortal if touched.

"Fuck."

"So d'ye believe me?" Fully recovered, Jeanie took a tentative step forward.

Fernando screwed up his face and shook his head in a futile attempt to shake off the truth.

"It's not possible. It's ridiculous, yet it makes sense. It was so difficult to kill them."

He turned his back and walked over to the desk, laying his hands flat on the worn wood. "We assumed mortals, but the stories about Vampires were just that - stories. Many of us thought the fictions were based upon some mortals meeting us but not really knowing." He lifted his head. "But how could they exist?"

"How is it that the Chosen exist?" answered Jeanie. The Noble's obvious disturbance at the truth sent shivers up her spine.

Stepping away from the desk, Fernando cocked his head and regarded Jeanie before finding his suitcase. "Touché. If this is truly the case then I need to get back to London. This is not what we first thought it to be. Shit. Genocide of the Chosen by Vampires."

"London?" barked Jeanie. She knew she should not be surprised at him going back on their deal, but she would not give up on the Angel. Walking over to the bed where Fernando placed his open bag, she slammed it shut, nearly missing his fingers. "Ye promised me."

Irritation flashed across brown eyes as Fernando stepped back. "This information goes beyond our arrangement."

Jeanie opened her mouth, an impotent reply remained wordless on her lips as her fist struck the Noble's jaw. For a brief moment she was shocked at her action and the blood that welled from his split lip before fear curdled her stomach at seeing the cut heal to nothingness.

Surprise flashed across Fernando's features as he tested his jaw. "I could easily kill you for that."

"I ken." Jeanie clenched her teeth. "So are ye gonna honour our agreement or are ye gonna prove that ye have as much honour as a Vampire—which is to say none."

Fernando's head jerked back. Releasing a huff, he flung open his suitcase.

"You're going to wish you were never born after we get the Angel back," he growled, pulling out rumpled black pants. "Now get the hell out of here. I'll meet you at the entrance and you had better make sure you have that damned covered wagon and enough blankets. I'm not in the practice of risking my neck."

Stunned at the Noble's compliance, a smile slowly lifted her lips as she made for the door. "Ye'll be happy t'hear that it's raining out."

The door closed behind her. A string of expletives that would make her father blush muted behind the old wood. Grinning at her success, she hurried down the corridor that would take her to the stables and the covered wagon.

XXXVII

Miserable, Fernando sat cross-legged, blankets solidly covered him as each bump and shift of the cart stabbed healing muscles. Gritting his teeth, Fernando could do nothing to release the anger and frustration he felt at allowing himself to be wrangled into such an undignified position *twice!* The first was, albeit, necessary to save his life, but to agree a second time was degrading. He hated how Jeanie had wound him into her machinations to free the Angel, but he could not dispute what she had shown him. Not only of what was murdering the Chosen, but the necessity of honour when those who would see his kind wiped from the earth, held none.

For centuries, he and other Chosen had, at first, laughingly accepted "Vampire" as a description of who and what they were despite the complete fabrication of what the mortals believed them to be. Foolishly, the Chosen assumed the mortals were fictionalizing them and used the name to fashion themselves a new vision based upon the horrific images the stories lent. It seemed to give permission to act in ways that were, well, more to the liking of those Chosen who revelled in moral depravity. After all, was it not expected of Vampires to act monstrously?

A jarring bump threatened to topple the Noble over. If it had not been for the blankets stabilizing him, he would have. Instead, he hissed through his teeth and placed a hand along the wooden slats in an effort to keep his purchase. The rain beat down upon the canvas, drumming pools where the fabric sagged until even the tight weave was no match for the persistent fluid. Drips splattered down onto the blankets, adding their incessant metronome to the discord.

Releasing a huff, Fernando still found it difficult to grasp the reality that

Vampires existed and they were the ones killing the Chosen. The evidence on Jeanie's neck corroborated by her story was indisputable. Added to the fact that the men he had stabbed and sliced who did not fall had moved nearly as fast. Shivers ran up Fernando's spine.

If he could not tell the difference between a mortal and a Vampire, then what chance did the rest of the Chosen?

Or worse yet, he thought. *What if we can't distinguish between a Vampire and a Chosen because we're all calling ourselves Vampires?*

Mouth suddenly dry, Fernando licked his lips and swallowed. Fear coiled around his belly. It could only mean that those he knew for absolute certain to be Chosen could be trusted, and that was a dwindling number.

Fernando's first instinct was to run back to London to tell Mistress Katherine what he had discovered and let the Court deal with the repercussions. But how do you fight this? Worse yet, would Katherine believe him even if he brought Jeanie along? The coil drew tighter and he knew she would not. The only one who could possibly add to the veracity to these claims would be the Angel. If Katherine would not believe the Angel then many others would, thereby placing pressure upon her to act accordingly.

Fernando frowned. Yes, many would believe the Angel over him because despite everything else about the man, the Angel was honourable. A flush of embarrassment rushed through the Noble. Fernando would do the honourable thing. After all, he was the one who instigated the partnership and he had absolutely no doubt that had the situation been reversed the Angel would now be sitting in this Godforsaken cart on the way to rescue him. The realization made him even more uncomfortable than the ride.

The cart came to a stop with a creak and a shudder. The discrepancy between the sound of falling rain on either side of the wagon and none on the covering canvass proclaimed they were sheltered. Lifting off the blankets, Fernando took a cautious peek and found himself in muted darkness. Dull grey light sifted in through the back exit. Though the sun was still up, it was clear that the bulging clouds masked most of the suns deadly rays.

Unexpectedly, Jeanie's head popped into view as she pulled on the latches, opening the end so that Fernando could easily slide out.

"C'mon." Her breath puffed before her soggy face. Dark red ropes of hair plastered her face and shoulders. "We canna stay here all day."

With the snap of metal and wood, he was able to get out. Feet landing with a squish, he felt the cold mud seep around his booted ankles and gazed up. Above him, dark grey stone protected him not only from the rain, but also from direct light. A shiver shot through him with the realization he was out in the day with no recourse but to trust this mortal girl to get him back to safety, along with the Angel, if they found him. Skin prickling, Fernando absently scratched his arm.

Glancing at the girl, Fernando noticed that she was soaked through and through. Her normally healthy looking appearance was fraught with blue tinges around her mouth, including her lips, and dark bruising around her eyes. It did not take a genius to realize that Jeanie was unwell and pushing herself past the limits her body could well afford.

"So what's your plan now?" demanded Fernando, his voice gruff.

Jeanie glanced at the front door. "We go in."

"Through the front door? That's insane."

Jeanie turned to face him. Her normally vibrant green eyes, dulled to ocean depths. "Violet will be in her crypt—or so I overheard. Ye and the Angel killed almost every mortal she has, and any Vampires left will be dead to the world, too. I assume ye can handle any mortals we will find still awake, let alone alive."

Pursing his lips in annoyance, Fernando bit back an argumentative reply. Instead he asked, "And what if the Vampires wake? I'm not in the best of shape to fight them one handed while I attempt to protect you."

A sarcastic smile lifted the edges of Jeanie's lips. "Ye, protect me? I wouldna believe it even if I were t'see it. In any case, Vampires canna wake during the day."

"And how do you know this?"

"The stories."

Fernando straightened and watched her go to the front door. It was bold and downright foolish, but he had to admire her audacity and hoped that she was right.

The door opened on heavy creaking hinges. To all appearances the entrance was a mausoleum. No sound came from any part of the mansion and they both stood in quiet awe at the lack of evidence of the battle that had ensued only two nights ago.

Stepping in, Fernando closed the door and winced at the resounding bang. They both halted in anxious expectation until they could not hear sounds of approach.

"So where did you say Violet has the Angel," whispered Fernando, eyes not relinquishing his surroundings.

"Her entertainment room." Jeanie frowned.

He could see and sense the returning of warmth in Jeanie's face as the blue edges gave way to a healthier pink. "And where's that?"

Jeanie's frown deepened. "I dinna ken."

"Well, that doesn't do us any good," huffed Fernando. "You can't expect us to go from room to room looking for him. We'll be caught for sure."

The front door slammed opened admitting a dark blonde man of middle years, dusting off droplets of rain from his hat onto his coat. "Whoever left that blasted wagon there will not live to see the dawn." Muttering angrily, he did not notice the two intruders until he lifted his gaze.

Turning to face the man from the night of the attack, Fernando smiled. "Tried it. Didn't work."

The mortal's head snapped up eyes wide and jaw slack.

Not one to pass up an opportunity, let alone a chance for revenge, Fernando grasped the man by the throat and slammed him into the doorframe. Blue eyes rolled before fixating on him in a squeak of suffocation.

"Dinna kill him," shouted Jeanie, coming to stand next to the Noble. "Yet."

Surprised by the girl's coldness, Fernando smiled. "I never thought you'd come around."

Cold hatred filled Jeanie's eyes.

Fuzzy warmth filled Fernando and he turned to face the man squirming and gasping in his grasp.

"You! You're supposed to be dead," rasped the man between laboured breaths.

Fernando enjoyed watching the bulging eyes, wondering when or if they would finally pop their sockets. "The rumours of my demise are greatly exaggerated. Wait. This is getting repetitive." He squeezed a little tighter.

"Ease up, Fernando." Jeanie laid a hand on his arm and fixed her gaze on their prisoner. "We need him able to talk."

Pleading blue eyes flashed to Jeanie as he tried to speak.

Fernando let go with a resolute sigh. He was so enjoying the slow demise he was offering. It was scarce punishment for the pain and indignities he suffered. "Fine. You'd better talk."

The man's eyes flickered from the Noble to Jeanie. "Oh thank you for coming back. I knew you couldn't to stay away once my Lady kissed you."

Jeanie's hand snapped up, covering the puncture wounds, her eyes wide. "That's no' why I'm here."

Fernando caught the tremor of her voice.

"What's the problem?" he asked, eyes narrowing.

"Nothing," retorted the girl, shaking her head. "Violet be damned. She'll no hae me."

Realizing that he had no understanding of what Jeanie was talking about, Fernando turned back to their unwelcome guest. Eyes boring into the man's he quickly caught the beat of his heart and the rhythm of his breath and Pushed hard. "I'm going to give you one chance and one chance only. Tell me where the entertainment room is."

The man stumbled as if struck and Fernando caught the man by the arm to keep him upright. Without breaking eye contact, the Noble smiled as he felt all resistance in the man fade and dullness descended over his eyes.

"Down the hall, through the doors off to the right. A set of stairs will go down to the north cellar," came the monotone reply.

"I think we got what we needed from him." Fernando turned to face Jeanie. Her face hardened once more and she nodded.

Fernando turned to face the hypnotized man and regarded him with a head cocked to the side, wondering in what manner he was going to kill this pitiful excuse for a mortal. Sudden inspiration flashed to mind. "Do you wish to do it or shall I?"

Obviously pushing the girl too much, Fernando watch Jeanie turn her back and walk away.

Bringing his attention back to the man, his smile broadened. "Die," he Pushed.

A shuddering sigh escaped from pale lips as the man's blue eyes rolled up before his body slumped to the floor. Wet clothing smacked the tiles as the scent of bladder and bowels released.

Fernando's smile grew. He always wanted to try that, never knowing if it would work. Too much of a hand's on type of person, he enjoyed seeing the blood and feeling it course through him. This time he knew the mortal was worth none of his efforts. The blood was tainted and forfeit. Turning from the corpse, he followed Jeanie down the hall towards the stairs that would take them to Violet's entertainment room and, hopefully, the Angel.

In the flickering glow from the single guttering torch Fernando stood at the bottom of the cold stone steps unable to catch his breath at the revelation before him. It was not what he expected. Then again, he did not know what to expect. Stunned, Fernando was deaf to the sounds Jeanie made as she wiped her mouth, tears spilling down her face. All he had eyes for was the Angel dangling from shackles and the splattering of blood that slicked the floor.

It was the gaping wounds on the Angel's chest and thigh that first caught Fernando's attention. Black rimmed red meat glistened, flashing the white of exposed bone. Swallowing down a surge of nausea, Fernando noticed the scent of burnt flesh and grimaced. Eyes coming to rest on the shackles that held the Angel, the Noble realized he could not distinguish between the black of the iron and the black of the swollen flesh of arms and hands that once were bone white. Even the redness of the seared meat on the Angel's upper arm was incongruous to the paleness of the Angel.

He's dead.

The thought came unbidden and he shook his head trying to deny the reality before him. Had the Angel been alive there would have been some healing, some evidence of life, but Fernando could see none. The Vampires had done away with another of the Chosen, yet it was not that which ignited the anger within the Noble. He was not sure he liked the reason behind the anger. One thing was certain, he would do everything to make the Vampires pay.

Jaw clenched, Fernando pulled his gaze away to find Jeanie standing at the other end of one of the chains, scrabbling at a way to release the mechanism that held the Angel limply in place.

"What are you doing?" Fernando strode over to her and grabbed her arm. With a jerk she brought her gaze away from the Angel to land on him.

"He's dead. We need to go. Katherine needs to hear of what we know."

Jeanie shook her head and shrugged out of the grip, tears no longer falling. "No. I canna leave him. He isna dead." Turning back to the lever, she tried to give it another pull.

"You stupid girl." Fernando turned to walk back up the stairs. It was fine with him if she wanted to stay and get caught. He would figure some way to drive the cart back to the monastery. "If the Angel were still alive he would have healed from his wounds."

"He's alive." Jeanie huffed. The lever would not budge. She would have to find another way to release the Angel and went to stand before her lover, lower lip quivering.

The Angel's face was unmarred and slack. Strands of white hair stuck to his face while the long braid hung dishevelled before his chest, dotted with dried blood. Reaching up, Jeanie laid a tremulous hand on his face.

"I'll free ye," she whispered.

A soft groan responded, snapping Fernando's eyes wide. Somehow the Angel was alive!

Impossible to believe, Fernando found himself at Jeanie's side. Too incredible to believe, he searched the Angel's face and found nothing. Shoulders slumping, mouth pursed in exasperation, Fernando shook his head, annoyed that he was taken by such a simple release of gases as the Angel's corpse began its return to the earth.

Resigned, Fernando resumed his egress. "He's already free."

They could not bring back a corpse, no matter how attached the girl was. What would they do with it anyway? Fernando shook his head and was shocked when Jeanie grabbed his hand, pulling him around to face the devastation in her eyes.

"Ye were able to ken he was alive before," said Jeanie meekly, her eyes falling from contact. "Ye can do it again."

Yanking his hand from her grasp, Fernando opened his mouth to berate her but held his tongue. The faint spark of hope filling her misery grated his teeth. "That was different."

"It's not." She pulled him closer to the Angel's dangling corpse.

Releasing a huff, Fernando closed his eyes and quickly counted to ten. It was enough time to recognize that to fight the task would only ensure they would remain longer and get caught again, something he was not going to allow happen. If acquiescing got them out faster, then he would do it.

"Fine." He shook off the warmth of her touch and gazed at the Angel.

Scowling, he placed his hands on the corpse's shoulders and nearly jumped out of his skin at the heat blazing off of the black tendrilled flesh. Eyes widening, Fernando could only hear the racing of his heart as he watched the Angel's face screw up in pain. A corpse did not radiate heat. Hell, Chosen did not radiate heat. Under the realization that the Angel was indeed alive came the thrill that Fernando was finally going to find out the truth about his partner.

"Find the keys for the manacles," Fernando shouted as he reached up along blackened arms to search for the keyhole.

"I canna find them," replied Jeanie, her voice frantic as she searched the table and the wall of gruesome implements. Metal clinked against the stone floor as gored utensils dislodged from their hooks.

Gritting his teeth, Fernando shook his head. He did not want to try what he needed to do. Managing the best grasp on the Angel's burning arm he gave a gentle tug. It was the strangled gasp from his unconscious partner that made Fernando release his grip. The shackles would not release their prisoner. That in itself was odd. It was clear the Angel was the strongest of the Chosen he had ever met, so it stood no reason that even he could not have broken free. Frowning, Fernando reached up, his fingers pushing between swollen black skin and the hard metal. He would try and pull the locked manacles apart.

Fingers grasping the thick metal, Fernando took a deep breath and held it as he pulled on the shackles, willing them to come apart. Painstakingly, he felt the hinge open and was rewarded with the sound of the locking mechanism cracking and breaking. His hands flew apart with an exultation of breath that left the Noble stunned. In his hands, two pieces of iron gleamed wetly, but it was the stake projecting to join through the centre that turned his stomach. Fernando flung the offending ruins to the floor. The sound echoed off the walls.

Returning his attention to his tortured partner, Fernando blanched to see the Angel dangle precariously from one ruined wrist. "Jeanie, hold him while I free his other arm."

Snapping from her stupor, Jeanie raced over to gather the Angel's weight around her shoulders. Her face pressed against his unwounded breast, she was rewarded with the sound of his faint heartbeat. Fear and hope twisted her tear stained face, and she nodded her readiness.

Fernando grasped the other shackle as best he could and pulled, this time noticing the sizzling wet sound as the iron bar relinquished its purchase. The manacle broke apart, freeing the Angel.

Unable to withstand the Angel's full weight suddenly upon her, Jeanie held him as best she could as he slipped to the stone floor. Shock sent her hands to her cover her mouth.

Realizing that something was wrong, Fernando let the metal clatter to the ground and glanced over. Mouth slack at the sight of the Angel's ruined back he found he could not look away. In his long life Fernando had seen slaves whipped, seamen, soldiers and convicts flogged, some to death, but never before had he seen such damage done. Lines of blackened and burnt flesh outlined charred and torn muscle where skin had been thoroughly flayed away. There was no part of the length of the Angel's back that had any white skin remaining. The Angel was a mess of scorched flagellation marks and cauterized red glistening muscle.

With effort, Fernando pulled his gaze away, searching for what could do such a thing and found, several feet behind the Angel, the steel scourge. Picking it up, the Noble nearly dropped it for all the gore still remaining on the iron barbs. Despite all the Angel had suffered, thought Fernando, he should have been able to heal from this. It did not make any sense. He looked over to see Jeanie kneeling, gently turning the Angel onto his side to place his head in her lap.

Fernando's hand tightened on the discipline. The realization that she knew the Angel's secret infuriated him and before he knew it, Fernando yanked the girl up from her position of comfort.

"He should be dead, but he isn't. He's alive, but he's not healing." He gave Jeanie a shake and lifted the deadly scourge to dangle gruesomely before her eyes. She blanched as Fernando's fury pressed forward. "As Chosen he should have healed, but he hasn't. If I whip you with this, your flesh would tear, it wouldn't burn."

Jeanie yelped and tried to pull from his grasp, weeping in her failure to flee.

Disgusted by the girl's reaction, as if he would do such a thing, Fernando tossed her to the floor.

"If it had been me or any other Chosen tortured here," he hissed, "no physical mark would remain if left alive."

He knelt down and grasped her chin, forcing her tear filled eyes to lock onto his. "He's been carefully hiding something from me since the beginning. Hell, he's always hid from the Chosen. You know what it is. If you want my help you'd better tell me, now."

Jeanie fell sideways at the sudden release as the Noble stood, catching herself with outstretched arms.

"I promised," she gasped.

Squaring his shoulders, Fernando glared down his nose at her and waited.

It did not take long for Jeanie to realize what she had to do to save her lover.

"He said that his life would be forfeit if ever found out," stammered Jeanie.

Eyes flashing at the closeness to the secret, Fernando could taste victory within his reach. "His life is forfeit if you don't tell me."

Watery green eyes gazed up imploringly. It was clear that she did not want to break her promise, but to regain the Noble's help she had to do as he wished.

"It's the iron," she sighed resolutely, closing her eyes in pain. "It burns him when cut."

Victory turned Fernando sour with the realization that the Angel's secret marked him to become a Destroyed One, and the responsibility of that disclosure now rested upon him. It was his worst expectation, one he found he did not relish. "How is that possible?"

"Please help me take him back to the monastery," she implored, rising to her feet. "I've told you what you wanted to know."

Fernando snorted. Now he knew and the responsibility that came with the secret surprisingly sent a deadened weight into his gut. Kneeling down, he gathered the Angel's dead weight over his shoulder and stood. The smell and touch of cooked flesh assaulted his senses and he walked to the stairs. Maybe if he were lucky the Angel would die of his wounds, letting Fernando off the hook for what was expected of any Chosen. He wondered if the Angel could die at all.

Silently, they ascended the stairs, Fernando's mind racing with the discoveries over the last twenty-four hours, the evidence held securely over his shoulder.

XXXViii

 eanie sat hunched over on the rickety wooden seat, slick leather reigns looped through her fingers. Bitter rain pelted down from an ironclad sky as the wind scourged her exposed face and hands, flaying her body of precious heat. The horse blanket Fernando insisted she wrap herself in was soaked through, but wool, even wet, provided enough warmth to keep from shivering.

Supported between her thighs, the Angel's sheathed sword leaned so that its hilt rested over her shoulder. She did not know what possessed her to pick up the blade, except that she knew how important it was to him. It was the only rational thought that popped into her mind as she dumbly watched Fernando carry the Angel from the torture chamber.

Not knowing what to expect upon finding the entertainment room, Jeanie realized that what she found sent her into a numb panic that filled her head with white noise and confusion. Witnessing him prisoner, suspended and trapped, his body a testament to Violet's sadism and desire to possess him, ground out any rationality except one — to free the Angel.

Jeanie understood she was freeing him from one horrific demise to be placed upon the executioners block the Chosen kept for those they deemed impure. She trembled at the thought of the power Fernando now held over the Angel, and subsequently Notus. If she had to, she would sneak into his room during the day and kill him herself, or at least die in the attempt. It would be one way to ensure that she would be with the man she loved. But first things first, she had to get him back to the Monastery in the hopes that something could be done to heal him.

Chucking the reigns, Jeanie clicked her tongue against her teeth, she urged the two miserable draft horses to hurry along the muddy track. Despite nearing noon, light could be seen from the large stained glass that adorned the west facing of the church. It was a beacon of hope and Jeanie wept at the sight.

The wagon slipped sideways on the churned mud as the horses turned through the gateway. Jeanie's hand clutched the wooden bench in an attempt not the slide off and sighed once the wagon righted itself. Through the thick canvas she heard Fernando swear with the sudden lurch. Ignoring him, she sought the lonely door down from the cathedral's massive entrance.

Jeanie coaxed the horses to turn the wagon until they were facing away from the old wooden door and pulled hard on the reigns. The horses halted, their white and chestnut legs covered in grey-brown muck, and lowered their heads in exhaustion. Unfortunately their work was not yet complete. Pulling high and back on the reigns, Jeanie clucked again and the horses took a halting step backwards, clearly not liking the reversed movement.

She could feel the horse's reluctance and Jeanie pulled harder, swearing under her breath as she willed the damned beasts to push the cart back towards the door. A defiant whinny and toss of a head forced Jeanie to yank even harder, forcing them backwards until she felt the wood of the cart hit the stone of the wall. She let the horses relax, which allowed the wagon to roll a little forward. Holding the horses, she found the break with her foot and pushed as hard as she could until the satisfying clunk told her that unless the horses bolted, they would not be going anywhere.

Releasing the reigns, Jeanie jumped down, holding the sword tight to her chest. The mud squished around her ankles as she sloshed towards the door. She could hear Fernando rustling inside the wagon as she banged her cold, white fist against the wood.

Nothing.

Rising panic forced her to hit the door harder. She could almost imagine the sound reverberating down the corridors. When no response came she raised her hand yet again and halted, almost hitting the young monk who had yanked open the door.

"Oh, thank God," she sighed at the same time the monk said, "I'm sorry miss, Sext will be starting in just a moment."

Ignoring the monk, Jeanie pushed past and let the sodden blanket slip to the floor. "Where's Father Theodore?"

The monk's eyes widened at the sight of the soaked girl embracing a large sword. His mouth opened and closed, fish-like.

It was clear Jeanie was not going to get any answers from the stunned monk and she turned towards the church where she could hear people settling in for service. The sense of urgency she felt upon the road crescendoed and broke. She needed help.

Leaving a stomping trail of mud, Jeanie entered the cathedral with the monk following behind. Had it been another occasion, she would have stared in wonder at the magnificence of God's house, as it was her eyes darted back and forth until she found the one she was looking for. Wet skirts clinging to her legs, she bolted forward, down the isle before the monk behind her could stop her.

"Father Theodore!" she cried as she halted before the elaborate wooden chancel.

A hundred or more pairs of eyes turned to stare down at her and she inwardly cringed but she could not let them intimidate her. Straightening, she found the eyes of the man she was looking for. Father Theodore stood before the Altar, prepared to start services, his face stern yet curious as to why anyone would interrupt their proceedings.

The silence in the cathedral was palpable. Shaking, the words exploded from her. "The Angel, he's hurt."

It was enough to shatter the Abbot's composure. "What?" He took several steps towards her, ignoring the murmurs in the choir.

Finding courage in his attentiveness, Jeanie hugged the sword tighter. "The Angel, he's hurt bad."

The words sunk into the Abbot as his eyes momentarily widened before he spun around to the monks awaiting his direction. "Brother Bartholomew will take over services for Sext. Brother Absolon, come with me."

Opening a gate that Jeanie had not noticed, Father Theodore stepped away from his flock and joined her at the crossing. Brother Absolon rose with a groan from his seat in the choir and made his way down to meet them.

"Brother Yannick, come with us," ordered the Abbot.

The monk behind Jeanie bowed his head.

Not waiting for Jeanie to lead the way, Father Theodore strode down the aisle, the two monks in tow. "What happened?"

"He-he was..." Jeanie gulped, unable to say the word.

The Abbot shook his head, his lips pursed. "Where is he?"

"In the wagon." Jeanie halted by the open door, forcing the other two to stop and turn to watch Fernando jump out and into the safety of the church.

Releasing a growl of annoyance, Fernando shook his head. "It took you bloody well long enough."

"Mr. de Sagres, if you please, where is the Angel?" The Abbot's sharp tone brought the Noble's head around. The wrong person had taken offence.

"He's in the wagon." Fernando thumbed towards the open door. "And I'm done for today. Tonight, whether he lives or dies, we're going to have a talk, li'l miss." His brown eyes bore into Jeanie and she took a step back, bumping into Brother Absolon. With a huff, Fernando turned and fled down the hall, his steps echoing off the stone walls.

When silence reigned, Father Theodore turned towards the wagon, and with an effort belying his age, jumped up to the wagon bed. "Brother Yannick, please fetch me a light."

The younger monk turned his head and found none that would be safe to carry into the confines of the wagon.

Seeing the monk's confusion, the Abbot rolled his eyes. "Go to the chapel and get a votive."

"But my lord Abbot—"

"But nothing. Light it with a quick prayer for the Angel and then bring it here," ordered Father Theodore.

Lifting the front of his robes, Brother Yannick ran down the corridor to where beautiful choral music floated. A moment of silence except for the sweet sound of prayer mingled with the staccato rain beat and then Brother Yannick came racing down the hall carefully holding the flickering flame. Taking the proffered candle, Father Theodore muttered his thanks and turned into the dark of the wagon.

The sound of rustling was followed by a sharp intake of breath. Father Theodore came to the doorway, still standing in the wagon, his face pale and filled with worry. "Brother Absolon, in here, now!"

The perpetual scowl on the healer's face twisted into concern at his Abbot's reaction. With Father Theodore's and Brother Yannick's help he ungracefully managed to join the Abbot in the wagon.

Seconds passed like hours as Jeanie watched, powerless to help, wondering what these two men would do. She jumped when Father Theodore leapt out of the wagon, leaving the candle and Brother Absolon behind.

Without taking any notice of her, Father Theodore rounded on Brother Yannick. "Go get a stretcher from the hospital," barked the Abbot.

"B—but, my lord Abbot," stammered the man. "I can't carry it by myself."

Not to be dissuaded, Father Theodore expanded on his commands. Brother Yannick was to go and disrupt Sext services and get Brother Jean Marc—Brother Absolon's apprentice—and return with the stretcher. Brother Amadieu was also to be called from prayer to go to the Angel's room and set the pallet with room to work, while the novice who cleans the hospital was to bring to the Angel's room Brother Absolon's surgery.

Once the orders were issued, Brother Yannick turned and fled back down the hall to set into motion the Abbot's commands.

Jeanie watched the proceedings in silence, hopeful that something could be done, and did not notice Father Theodore's attention fall onto her.

"Walk with me," he ordered, slipping his arm around her damp shoulders.

Jeanie craned her neck to see monks running this way and that and tried to break away to stay by the wagon, anything to stay close to the Angel, until, at the Abbot's firm insistence, she walked away.

"You don't have anything to worry about." The Abbot's tones softened. "Your arrival to St. Martin's elicited a similar response, so they should be well drilled by now." He turned down a hall towards the locutorium. With most of the monks and novices at Sext, the corridors were empty except for a couple of young novices scrubbing the floors.

It was a nice chamber. Benches lined the walls encircling a moderate sized dark oak table that had seen better days. Its surface indented and marked with years, if not decades, of use. The chairs were of padded blue and yellow velvet, faded and worn thin in spots, a testament that they too were as ancient as the table. On the far wall a cold fireplace sat bare.

Father Theodore motioned Jeanie to sit and she did so, only relinquishing her embrace on the sword once she sat down. Reverently, she placed it on the table before her. The steel rings clattered against the wood.

It was a long time before either of them spoke. Each stared at the ancient sword.

"I will have someone come and bring you some food, dry clothing and to light a fire," sighed the Abbot, breaking the silence. "Another room will be set up for you—"

"No." Jeanie kept her eyes on the sword, her hand absentmindedly caressing the worn black leather grip of the hilt.

"It would be better if—"

"No," she interrupted the Abbot yet again, this time meeting his eyes. "I'm the best one to care for him. I'll stay with him."

Father Theodore's eyes widened and then softened. "My dear," he came around the table and sat down beside her. "I know what the Angel is. He's in good hands. I will make sure that he has what he needs to recover."

Jeanie shook her head. Whether or not Father Theodore truly knew was a moot issue, the point was she needed to be there to care for him.

"Do you wish to tell me about it?" offered the Abbot, his voice tender.

Jeanie shook her head. How could she convey to this man of God the horrific act that had occurred to the man she loved, all because she let her stubbornness rule her. She felt, rather than witnessed, the Abbot lean back against his chair.

"Alright. I'll come again when I have news about the Angel." The chair scraped the floor as Father Theodore stood. The sound of his soft footsteps stopped at the door. "One thing. I was under the impression that the Chosen can heal immediately from their wounds. The Angel is Chosen, is he not?"

The question snapped Jeanie's head up, terror written across her features. Her mouth suddenly dried up and she found she could not reply.

Father Theodore broke eye contact and glanced at the floor before him in contemplation. With a resolute sigh, he turned and walked out.

Jeanie could not leave it like that and raced over to the door before it could close, surprising the Abbot.

"Father," she shouted and then lowered her voice to a whisper. "He is Chosen, but…"

"What is it, my dear?" The Abbot took her elbow and guided her back into the privacy of the locutorium.

Not knowing how else to say it, the words rushed out in a jumble. She explained that iron burns the Angel and why she thought it was so and what that could mean if word got out. Father Theodore's brows rose in response to her rising anxiety until he had to guide her back to the chair, forcing her to take deep calming breaths.

"Your secret is safe with me, my dear," he said as he prepared to leave again. "Lately, I have become quite adept at keeping secrets."

The door closed behind him, leaving Jeanie to the solitude of the room. Sword before her, she let out a sob. What she had told the Abbot was only a dry run of what Fernando expected from her come nightfall. Clutching the sword into an embrace, she shuddered to think how the secret was soon to become a death sentence.

True to his word, food, clothing and a roaring fire accompanied Jeanie's solitude. When the novices came in, under the supervision of a Brother, Jeanie's attention refused to waver from the black clad sword before her. Respecting her desire for quiet contemplation, the residents of St. Martin's left as quickly as they could. It was the sound of her stomach rumbling loudly to the scent of warm bread and cheeses that finally drew her attention away from the sword. Mechanically, she ate, and then changed out of her wet clothing. She could not remember the last time she had slept and despite the warmth of the room and the fullness of her belly she refused to give in. Clutching the Angel's sword, Jeanie left the room.

The corridors were filled with flowing robes as monks briskly walked from one place to the next. Many moved in clusters, making it difficult to discretely pass them by. It did not take Jeanie long to realize she was lost. A friendly monk, recognizing her plight, was happy to assist her in the right direction, and before she knew it she stood at the door to the room she shared with the Angel.

Nervous, Jeanie's hand shook as it alighted onto the simple brass knob. The Angel was in there, but she did not know what to expect. It took several calming breaths before she could turn the knob. A shriek escaped her, as the door was wrenched open. Brother Absolon's stood on the other side, his face wide with surprise. It was clear neither of them had expected the other.

Once hearts and breathing calmed down to near normal levels, Brother Absolon stepped back to let her in before closing the door.

"You should have knocked," stated the monk, gruffly.

"I'm sorry," stammered Jeanie, her heart gradually returning to its regular cadence.

Her focus shifted from the elderly healer to scan the room. Everything seemed to be in place. The only difference was that the Angel lay on two pallets, one on top of the other, before a small warming hearth. Lying on his left side, Jeanie could see the horrific wounds on his back. She took a step towards him. It was enough of a movement to send her flying to his side, the sword clattering to the stone floor beside her.

Jeanie brushed his long white hair from the side of his face. He was still unconscious, his expression almost serene. Gradually, she took in the sight of him. Clean white bandages wrapped his whole right arm, from shoulder to fingers that were grey and no longer black. His left arm was bandaged from elbow to fingers, and rested up by his face. A padded bandage carefully covered his right breast and another was wrapped securely around the length of his left thigh. Pillows supported him so that he leaned forward, making it difficult to roll backwards.

Silent tears dripped down her face.

"I've done all that I could." Brother Absolon's voice held no warmth, only cool professionalism. "Father Theodore told me not to use steel needles to suture *after* I had started. Needless to say, since I don't have anything but, I had to make do. You're Angel is a very interesting individual — medically speaking."

Jeanie swivelled on her knees and gazed up at the monk who was in deep contemplation. "Will he be alright?"

Broken from his meanderings, Brother Absolon blinked, turned and sat down on the simple wooden chair. "Before I came to the Order I was a physician in the army. I have seen much in my long career, but nothing to the extremes I have tended to today. By all accounts the Angel should have died from such wounds. Instead, there he lies, slowly on the mend." The monk leaned back, making the chair creak under his weight. "I suppose that you want to know what I managed to do?"

Jeanie nodded, silent in her expectation.

Brother Absolon steepled his index fingers in clasped hands and brought them to his thin lips. "It's ever the way." Dropping his hands back into his lap, the monk sat straighter in the chair, a professional air enveloped him. "The wounds on his arm, leg and pectoral were easily stitched after I overcame my surprise at the burning the needle caused. His back, well, there is not much I can do. In time it will heal, but the damage is done. It was the injury to the wrists that caused the most difficulty. I have never seen living bone burnt before. The damage is extensive and I have done what I could with my crude implements to repair the delicate tissues. Splints have been placed within the wrappings to minimize movement, but it is my professional opinion that the Angel will have lost the use of his hands."

She could not believe what she was hearing. The cold, detached way the monk reported his care made the whole proceedings a dream. Shaking her head in disbelief, Jeanie stood to face the dispassionate man.

"Get out," her voice sounded rough to her ears.

"Beg your pardon?" A bushy grey brow rose. It was clear he had never been talked to like this before.

"I said get out." Jeanie's voice grew louder, her arm thrust out to point at the door.

Brother Absolon slowly stood, his face flushed with indignant rage. "I would remind you, my dear, that—"

Regaining some of her control, Jeanie gritted her teeth. "I thank ye for yer help, but ye're wrong. The Angel will make a full recovery."

"I am a physician with—"

"Ye are a monk, and he is the Angel," glowered Jeanie.

Apoplectic, Brother Absolon stood and briskly walked out of the room, slamming the door in his wake.

With the last of the echo dissipating in the room, Jeanie let out a huff that made her head swim. Fatigue crashed through her and she went to sit down on the bed. The nausea receded as the vertigo dissipated and she lay down. Jeanie hoped that the Angel would not begrudge her a short rest before she went to care for him, at least until the room ceased spinning. Heavy eyelids closed of their own volition and before she could stop herself, Jeanie fell asleep.

XXXIX

arkness surrounded and comforted him as he drifted in the void he had once feared. Nothing but the gentle current gave indication that he moved, but he did not care. He was away from the pain, embraced by the blackness that swept all his senses away.

If he was dead, he did not know it and nor did he care. He exalted in the *feeling of nothingness. The beautiful lack of emotion.*

Nothing could touch him and he could touch nothing. He floated in the depths of unconsciousness and revelled in its comfort.

Time refused to exist.

Space, an illusion in as far as he could see, was nothing.

He floated, giving himself up to whatever and wherever he may be. Not even the white-faced demons dared to disrupt the rapture of detachment.

Mind numb, body senseless, he drifted upon the vague currents for untold ages and smiled.

A tug.

A pull.

A shift of the current.

An infinitesimal change of direction.

An unwelcome pressure evoking a growing sense of disquiet which was quickly dismissed.

He refused to open his eyes. He no longer cared.

If they were back, so be it. No more would he fear them. No more could they cause him pain. No more would he flee.

In the rising current, he waited serenely for their return, willing to offer them anything they might wish.

The current's pull became stronger and with it came tongues of heat that licked over his body. Still he refused to open his eyes. Throwing open his arms, he tossed his head back in expectation that the searing would eradicate his body to leave nothing of substance.

He sighed. He gasped. He did not open his eyes.

Jeanie woke with a start and gazed about the room wondering where she was. It was not the first time she felt this way upon awakening here, but after a moment the disorientation dissipated and she stretched. Rubbing her eyes, Jeanie grimaced. She had not meant to fall into such a deep asleep and wondered what time it was. A glance out the small draped window deepened her frown. The sun had already set, or it was in the process since the storm seemed to be petering off. Rising to her feet, she quietly walked over to the Angel and knelt beside him.

Tenderly, she laid a hand on his forehead and shook her head at the heat under her palm. Still caught in a fever, Jeanie wondered if he would wake but thought it better he slept. She did not know what to do for him, but she knew from taking care of her mother, that unless the fever broke on its own, there was not much that could be done except to make the patient more comfortable.

A gentle knock on the door jammed her heart into her throat as she spun around to watch it open.

ANGEL OF DEATH

Her pulse pounding in her ears settled at the sight of Father Theodore entering the room, followed by a novice who carried a tray of steaming food. With a sigh of relief, Jeanie rose to her feet and smiled.

"How is he?" asked the Abbot.

Jeanie noticed his right hand hidden beneath his scapular, and turned back to the unconscious Angel. "I dinna ken."

The novice placed the tray on the table and with a nod of thanks from the monk, left the Abbot and his guests alone. Once the door was closed, Father Theodore pulled out a bottle from his robes and placed it down beside the tray. "A pig was slaughtered for tomorrow's meal and I managed to have the brother in charge procure me this. I hope it will be alright."

Jeanie walked over to the table, lifted up the bottle and gave it a sniff. Blood, obviously fresh by its warmth, wafted from the glass. "Thank ye, Father. I hope it'll do."

Walking over to the Angel, Father Theodore crouched down and laid a hand on the bare shoulder, closed his eyes and muttered a prayer before standing up and making the sign of the cross.

"Compline services will be starting in about a half hour. I know you have made it clear you aren't Catholic and that you wish to stay with the Angel, my dear, but you are most welcome to take part," invited the Abbot. "I can have a novice watch him for you, and if needed he can come and get you."

Eyes glittering with gratitude, Jeanie gazed at the stone floor. "I'll...I'll think on it, aye?"

"As you wish," replied Father Theodore as he headed to the door.

Warmth stole through his body. Not a burning, soul consuming inferno, but rather a gentle all pervading heat that tenderly embraced, kissing his skin.

All motion had ceased and a new sensation tingled awareness throughout his body. Soft coolness tickled along the edges of his arms, torso, and legs. Beneath that was a sense of firmness.

He no longer floated. The rational knowledge that he now lay prone did not give him impetus to open his eyes.

The perfume of lush greenery wafted and he sighed. Behind the green came the sweet aphrodisiac of what could only be flowers and he breathed deeper.

It was the scent of peace. The fragrance of home. He wanted to bury himself in it and never leave.

A trickling of water. The buzzing of insects. The titter of birds. Soft sounds awoke his ears. He smiled and nestled into the softness beneath. It was the music of life. A composition of ordered chaos that bespoke of innocent times. A time when he was a child and the whole world consisted only of he and Auntie.

Auntie.

It had been eons since he had thought about her. Centuries since he last mused upon his life before being Chosen. Decades upon decades that layered the ancient past into oblivion. A knot formed in his stomach and he opened his eyes.

Emerald grass waved before his eyes, dancing in the brightness of mid-day. Panic!

Pushing himself upright, he looked around. A glade of immense beauty encircled him. He sought a way to hide from the light until he realized his skin did not burn and the brightness did not hurt his eyes. Stunned into immobility, he could only stare open mouthed at the kaleidoscopic flowers and trees. Never before had he witnessed such awesome beauty.

Vibrant purples, reds, oranges, yellows, greens and even blues bespoke of a painter's brush held by the hand of nature.

Slowly, he turned around. Each bud, each stem, each leaf and flower and fruit evoked wonder until he beheld the bubbling spring.

Tinkling music was the sound of water against the large rounded rocks that encircled the small well. The clear water churned gently in its natural cauldron. The scent drew him and he took a step.

Self awareness slammed into him and he gazed down upon himself. Clad only a deerskin kilt, his body held no mark, no scar, no evidence of the trials of suffering he had endured. His pale skin did not even redden under the warming light. He did not know where he was and nor did he care. Whatever the place, to him it was a dream come true, a paradise of all that had been denied to him.

Lowering his hands, he smiled.

The gurgling of the pool flickered louder, as if to regain his attention. Answering its insistence, he walked the steps towards water. He luxuriated in the soft springiness of the grass beneath his bare feet. He savoured the scents of flowers as he gently pushed them aside to kneel before the well. He sighed at the calm the burbling brought him.

His heart skipped a beat at the sight of a large silver chalice sitting on a rock, a finely wrought chain attached to its stem. The light shifted and glinted off the silver, casting a white aura around it.

Curiosity flowed through him and he picked up the squat chalice with the wide base in both hands. On it, just under the lip, were characters he had never seen before but somehow he could read.

"I am She who gives the gift of joy unto the heart of mankind.
I am She that gives knowledge of the spirit eternal.
I give peace and freedom and reunion.
My name is Mystery."

Without a second thought he dunked the chalice into the water, brought it to his lips and drank.

The bouquet was of flowers. The taste was of the iron of earth, the metal of blood. The feeling was cool and refreshing. Energy flooded through him. He gasped.

> *"Blessed be he who has been brought in these ways.*
> *Blessed be he who kneels at the Altar.*
> *Blessed be he who drinks from the womb of creation.*
> *Blessed be he who speaks truth."*

A chorus of female voices spun him around on his knees still holding the chalice to see three tall, slender women walk towards him from a path he had not noticed earlier. He had seen these wondrous women before. He watched, awestruck as they approached. Each movement identically made together.

For all of their similarities, of height, slenderness, and incredible beauty, the differences were remarkable. Identical in the gossamer style of their robes, the colours mated with the differences.

On the left stood a woman with long white hair that brushed the back of her knees. Her skin was pale as milk. It was her eyes that took him aback. Her irises were white while the pupils were cream.

In the middle stood a woman with long flowing vibrant red hair the same length as the woman of white. Her skin was ruddy, as if she had spent too long in the sun. She had the same eyes as he.

On the right stood the remaining woman of long raven black hair, as long as her sisters. Her skin was black and her eyes were the opposite of the woman of white. Pupils and irises a black void.

In unison they gave him a small smile and approached until he was forced to look up at them. Together they reached down, their long delicate hands lifting the chalice he had not realized he proffered. A hand of the White Lady and a hand of the Black Lady brushed against his as all three took the goblet, sending a shock of energy that made him gasp.

Awestruck, he watched as the Red Lady let the White Lady sip first then she and then the Black Lady drank in turn. Holding the chalice together, the three lowered it to him. Still on his knees, he accepted it, refusing to relinquish his gaze upon the Ladies.

"Drink to the bitter dregs," they chorused. "For the cup holds the wine of life and only through it may your answers be received."

Confused, he gazed into the remaining water within the chalice. No longer did the water appear crystal clear. Swirls of white, red and black churned within. Sudden fear welled within him and the impulse to toss chalice and water away caught in his throat. Somehow sensing his disquiet he felt three gentle hands alight onto his head and a wash of calm flowed through him. Without looking up, he bent his head and drank from the chalice. The flavour was clear and clean until he reached the last three gulps. Tilting his head back, he found it difficult to drink to the final drop.

The hands released him and took the chalice. Its chain snapped.

Slowly the Ladies, with right hands holding the stem, turned in a graceful dance. Thrice did they circumambulate, coming to a halt next to the pool where they ceremoniously lowered it onto a stone.

"Blessed be he who is Chosen," they chorused. "Blessed be he who is the One."

Together, they bade him to rise.

He stood only a head taller than they and he took a confused step back, cautious not to trip into the spring.

They smiled up at him. "Speak the words."

"Wh—where am I?" His voice was rough with disuse.

Frowns pulled down their full-lipped mouths. "Too late?" they chorused, as if speaking to themselves.

"Possible," said the White Lady.

"The prayer was heard," replied the Red.

"Choice was remade," stated the Black.

"Time's irrelevant," they chorused. They turned their attention back to him. "Speak the words."

Confused he shook his head. "What words?"

"Fear holds. Fear binds," they chorused.

"Fear of pain," said the White Lady.

"Fear of living," remarked the Red.

"Fear of Them." The Black Lady turned and pointed to the sky which had suddenly turned to night as if someone had blown out the sun.

A sudden chill enveloped him and he crossed his arms over his naked chest. A cool wind grasped at the Ladies diaphanous robes, causing them to flutter and snap. He watched in horror as a swirling of white descended from the dark.

Translucent figures spun around a single spot on the grass not far from where the three Ladies stood. With the Ladies between he and the white faced demons he watched as the central figure solidified. He gasped.

A chuckle made of dry leaves and cracking branches filled the glade. "Did you believe you could essssssssscape?" The White Faced Demon stepped out from the swirling to stand before the Ladies.

He wanted to run. He wanted to flee. He had believed it did not matter if It came. He had lied.

"Hold!" commanded the Three, and he felt himself rooted to his spot.

The White Faced demon cocked its putrescent head to the side in contemplation before lifting it again. "He is mine. He chose."

"He was a child," chorused the three angrily. "He has re-chosen."

"It doessssssss not matter." It tried to flow around the Ladies, only to find Its efforts blocked. Its face twisted in frustration. "We will not let thissssssssss come to passssssssss."

"You made your choice on the Time of Crossing," snapped the Three.

"Yesssss," It hissed. "We want exisssssssssstence. We want life."

"You made your choice," countered the Three.

AПGEL OF DEATH

"Give usssss our Bridge."

"No."

"Give him to Ussssss!"

The three Ladies turned to face him, sadness filling their eyes. "Your fear has chosen. Your fear has ruled. Attachment has brought suffering. To live you have been born. To be born you had to die. It is the Circle. But it is the Mystery that holds it all. Please, speak the words."

Their sorrow pulled at him and he knew that if he could not find what he was looking for within him, they would have no ability to save him. He lowered his head. He did not know.

A hand reached out and touched his face. The Red Lady smiled sadly as she lowered her hand over his heart. Jeanie sitting in a pew at St. Martin's, her head bowed in prayer, her face wet with tears, flooded his vision and his breath caught.

"You know," whispered the Red Lady, a sad smile on her lovely face.

Lifting his head, he gazed at the White Faced Demon and then back at the Ladies. Determination replaced fear. The words came unbidden, as if someone else spoke them. "Love is all. Love supported by Will."

He did not need to see the Ladies smile. It was the look of horror on the White Faced Demon that proved the truth. Without hate for the pitiful creature, without anger for all Its trespasses against him, without fear of what It could still do to him, a warming sense filled him. The Ladies stepped away from him as he approached the Demon.

"No more," he stated. "You fed off of me to feel life. No more. I take back all that you took from me."

The Demon tried to flee, but he grabbed its strangely solid substance and pulled it struggling into an embrace. "I forgive you," he whispered as he sank his teeth into the putrid neck, tears streaming down his face.

Emotional exhaustion enveloped Jeanie as she sat in the pew at the back of the church. She had decided at the last moment to take up Father Theodore's advice, especially since he had sent the promised novice anyway. It had been awkward watching him nervously watching her and the Angel. Without a word, Jeanie had left just in time to hear the beginning of services.

She had never sat through a Catholic mass before and found it quite lovely with the beauty of the voices in canticle. It was as if she were hearing angels singing. It did not take long before the prayers melted out the tension that had supported her for so long and she found herself silently weeping.

Through her water filled vision and her soft hiccoughing, a sense of peace washed through her when her eyes alighted upon the shrine to the Virgin Mother. The statue seemed alive with all the flickering lights of the votives at her feet. Jeanie caught her breath at one point when she foolishly envisioned that the statue turned its head to look at her with a sad smile.

Shaking off the vision, Jeanie relaxed into the seat and stared at the brilliance of the magical ceremony.

She did not know how long the service was to last. Time seemed to have stopped until she felt a presence sit down beside her.

"It is lovely," remarked Fernando. "Luckily, I was first born and therefore not promised to the Church."

Jeanie's heart sped up. She knew why the Noble was there. It was time to keep her end of the bargain, but to do so would betray the man she loved. Was it not already too late?

She raised a hand to scratch the sudden tingling of Violet's mark and at the touch her body shivered. A sudden sense of foreboding gripped her innards and she turned to face the cathedral's doors.

Perturbed, Fernando turned towards her, his face twisted with anger. "Is this just another evasion from the little talk we agreed upon?"

Jeanie shook her head, her heart pounding loudly in her ears. She could almost hear Violet talking to her. *Open the doors*, it called. It made no sense, but the pull was alarming and she rose to do the voice's bidding. With Fernando following at her heels she strode over to the heavy double doors and threw them wide open.

The rainstorm continued to rage, but beyond the low wall to the grounds Jeanie could see mounted horses coming up the path. Amongst them, wrapped in a magnificent white fur coat, its hood drawn tight around her face, sat Violet in side saddle. The dozen others fanned out as she approached, the glint of steel in their hands.

"Shit," swore Fernando. "Close the doors, Jeanie. Close them now!"

The White Faced Demon was gone.

The others were not. They swirled around him. Reaching to touch but pulling back at the last moment.

"It is done," the Three Ladies chorused, a smile on their faces.

Confused, he tried to step out from the swirling beings but found they would not let him go. "What is done?"

They walked towards him and the swirling beings relinquished their attachment. "What was to be," they chorused.

"But what is that?" He extinguished to sudden surge of anger. He knew that becoming short with these fantastical women would result in not finding the answers he so longed to be fulfilled.

"A first step," replied the White Lady.

"A belated awakening," responded the Red Lady.

"An initiation of potential," stated the Black Lady.

"Your seeking has availed you naught," they chorused. "Seek within yourself. Accept the Truth that was, is and ever shall be. Blessed Be he who is the Bridge of Life and Death."

The answers confounded him. It was not what he expected and he frowned.

 Sensing his disquiet, the White Lady placed her hand upon his left cheek, the Red Lady placed hers on the centre of his chest and the Black Lady placed her hand on his right cheek. "All answers are found within. The truth will set you free."

 Suddenly, all three turned their heads away from him in unison as if seeing something he could not. When they turned back to him concern was written over their delicate features. "Now you must return. The Testing has come. We will not leave you."

 "I don't understand." A sudden vertigo filled him and he closed his eyes.

Excruciating pain fired his brain and he snapped his eyes open. Every part of his body was on fire, dazing his mind. A sense of urgency filled him, forcing him to stand. It was as if he were a marionette, having little control over his body.

 Lightning shot up his left leg but it did not give way as he looked around the room. In a chair, leaning against the wall next to the hearth, a novice sat in slumber, chin resting on his chest above folded arms. He was back in the monastery, but he had no recollection of how he got here.

 The sense of exigency grew and he turned towards the door. There was something he needed to do, but he did not know what. Every muscle in his back and leg protested the movement as he hobbled towards the door. Stretching out his hand to turn the knob, he winced at the movement and noticed the thick bandages. He could not seem to make his fingers work.

 Hurry or what you hold precious will be lost. The chorused voices of the Ladies filled his mind.

 Panic filled him and with great effort, using both hands, he managed to open the door. Swaying with fatigue and burning heat, he exited into the corridor. He did not know which way to go, but let the pull guide him. With each step, with each movement, he lost the sense of awareness as the pain and fever grew. It seemed that even the walls of the monastery shimmered in and out of existence.

 The hall was longer than ever. It was increasingly difficult to keep his eyes open and it was harder to draw breath until he was sliding against the wall, another door before him.

 Here, came the voices.

 Whimpering at the thought of opening the door, he gritted his teeth and almost passed out as his bandaged hands twisted excruciatingly with the doorknob.

 A blast of freezing cold and rain set him shivering. A part of him stood incredulous that they wanted him to go out in this. The other half watched in horror at the sight of Jeanie fighting against Fernando as the Noble tried to pull her back through the Cathedral doors. Both were soaked to the skin.

Jeanie fought like a *bean sidhe* as she tried to break loose. She seemed to want to run towards the woman on the horse.

Time halted. The rain froze motionless in the air. Terror welled within at the sight of his torturer.

"Let her go, Chosen," shouted the Mistress of *Le Jardin*. "She is now mine. You can see how she desires to serve me." Her cold malicious laughter filled the night.

"Over my dead body," replied the Noble, hoisting a screaming Jeanie up by the waist, her legs kicking impotently into the air.

"So you care for this mortal?" The Lady's horse stamped the wet earth.

"No," stated the Noble, "but a chance to deny you is worth the shot."

Violet tilted her head back and laughed into the rain. "How droll. How noble." Her face twisted into a sneer. "How much like a Chosen and as such you have a choice. Give me Jeanie and the Angel and I will allow these so called men of God to live. If not, my men will slaughter them all."

Jeanie's frustrated cries escalated as Fernando stepped back towards the Cathedral doors.

Call them. Call them now, rang the Ladies voices in his fevered brain. *They are yours to command. Let them taste life in death.*

Confused, he shook his head not understanding what they wanted of him. Whatever verbal exchange was going on between Fernando and his torturer was lost to the voices in his head.

Call those who you feared. You know the words.

Head swimming, his vision fixated upon the Vampire and her company. His only desire was to see them eradicated from the earth and the words flowed. The ancient rune of summoning he was taught by Auntie came unbidden from his lips.

Jeanie thrashed wildly in Fernando's slick grip as he backed towards the open church doors. Soaked through, the rain and the girl's movements made it difficult not to crush her ribs into powder while he tried not to slip on the muddied ground. Cursing under his breath, Fernando wanted Jeanie to shut up so that he could think of what to do. His dark hair plastered to his face, he spat out soggy red ropes that slapped every time Jeanie swung her head in the hopes to unbalance him. It was bizarre how Jeanie wanted to run to the Lady's side. It was as if her mind was not her own. Fernando would have released the girl if he had not realized how much the Lady wanted her, anything to infuriate that bitch Vampire.

Managing the few steps, he realized that the monks from the service were behind him, watching with wide horror filled eyes as the marauders brandished their glistening blades. Placing Jeanie back down on the stone, the wind still whipping her manic hair, he barely managed to grasp her wrist in her attempt to flee to the Mistress' side. Swinging Jeanie around, the flat of his hand met the side of her face with a resounding slap. He did not hit her with his full strength, but the satisfying violence was enough to snap her head to the side, green eyes wide in shock. Hopefully it was enough to break whatever spell she was under.

"Look over there!" shouted a monk behind him.

Following the pointed arm, Fernando joined the others to see the Angel standing at the other door as if in a trance. His nude pale body seemed to glimmer in the darkness and Fernando could see the Angel's lips moving.

All of a sudden the rain and the wind ceased and a deathly silence filled the void. Fernando heard the woman's laugh turn into alarm as her horse, as well as the others, grew skittish.

The monks behind the Noble all sucked an audible intake of breath and held it, watching as a pearlescent swirling mist rose up from the muddy ground. Their heart rates jumped in fright, caught in the expectant horror of what was coming.

Fernando too held his breath and watched.

The mist thickened into a dense fog, its undulations churning, cutting off the vision of the would-be invaders. Strangely enough none of the tendrils elected to sift into the Church. Even the monastery's stone steps seemed immune from the mist.

Slowly, shapes coalesced within the fog and Fernando took an involuntary step back. A monk behind him grunted as the Noble accidentally stepped on him, but none dared take their eyes off the unfolding scene.

Grotesque human-like forms swirled, their faces white and their eyes black in their ghostly apparition. Several of the monks whimpered. Others began praying, the clicking of beads through nervous fingers accompanied the mumbled words. Several others fled when one of the white-faced ghosts turned and smiled maliciously at them before turning its attention away. Fernando found Jeanie clutched to him, his arm holding her protectively as they watched in stupefied terror.

Suddenly there was a rushing sound, as if a great wind threatened to blow the church and the monastery to rubble, and then came the cries. Screaming horses, shouting men, Violet wailing. The cacophony of agony continued on and on until suddenly, the deafening silence returned.

Panicked breathing and racing hearts were the only sound as they witnessed the fog lowering, the ghosts gone, to settle at waist height. The churning surface revealed the Vampire and her entourage, including the horses, were nowhere to be seen. There was no sound of fleeing into the night. It was as if one moment they were there and then in the next all evidence of their existence had been eradicated.

The bubbling surface shimmered and Fernando's eyes widened as three tall figures appeared as if made of mist. He could tell they were female, but what was truly remarkable was their colouring—white, red and black. They advanced through the vapour, heading towards the Angel who had sunk to his knees.

Behind the Noble, he heard the monks fall to their knees, some of them

Karen Dales

prostrating themselves, weeping as they began the old liturgy, "Hail Mary, full of Grace..."

Jeanie buried her face in Fernando's chest, sobbing and calling out over and over, "Mama, mama ..."

Stunned, Fernando watched the Triple Lady bend over the Angel, each whispering something before placing a kiss on the Angel's head.

Eyes rolling up, the Angel groaned and toppled over unconscious. The three women shimmered and then were no more, taking the mist with them.

xL

he grass was soft and damp as he sat cross-legged. Before him the spring burbled its glittering waters. The silver chalice, its chain broken, slowly rolled between his two hands.

He watched in fascination the shimmering colours of the water's surface as the light reflected its lazy movement. It was beautiful to watch, but what he truly wanted was to taste it, to drink to its completion and then dip it full into the spring.

He lifted the cool metal to his lips, his breath panting in expectation, and closed his eyes in rapture as the cold water slipped past his parted lips and into his mouth. Flowers, sunshine and beauty tantalized his taste buds as his body warmed the water, releasing the bouquet. He inhaled through his nose and sighed, allowing the waters to slide into his body. A shudder of pure energy filled him and he sipped again and again. Each time life's pulsating energy filled him to near bursting, drawing him to take deeper draughts.

Once the chalice was drained, he placed it down onto the rocks. He would drink again soon. For now, he watched the white demons swirl and swim lazily around him. They were his and he was theirs. No longer could he fear them. No longer could they rule him. Extending a pale hand towards them, they brushed across his fingertips, drawing out the energy he offered them.

It did not take long before he felt the pull of the chalice once more. Lowering his hand, he turned his attention to the silver cup, grasped it gently by its stem and then dipped it deep into the radiant pool of water.

Diamonds dripped from the chalice as he pulled it out. Water clung and absorbed into his hand and forearm, sending a blissful shock as if he touched something alive. This time he did not savour each sip, he devoured it, gulping down the taste of blood, air and fire.

"I don't know how he managed to make it to the door let alone down the hall," *came a voice filled with awe and fear. It trickled into the summer glen. It piqued his curiosity. Lowering the empty chalice to the stone beside the pool, he stood and cocked his head in an effort to listen better.*

"I've cleaned him up as best I could, Father."

"I know, my son." *The man's voice was so incredibly weary that he wanted to reach out and console the man. Instead he stepped away from the well and closer to the void that solidified, blocking off a path away from the sacred grove.*

"What is the Angel, Father? I have never witnessed his like before."

He heard the tired sigh. "I believe you have answered your question within your question."

He stood next to the void. The white-faced demons swirled around him expectantly. He thought he recognized the tired man's voice. The one the other called "Father". He shook his head. He did not know who they were talking about.

"Will the Angel survive, Father?"

"I don't know." *A shift in attention.* "Brother Absolon?"

A new voice entered into the conversation. "I do not know, Father. I have encountered many people in my long career, but none as unique as the Angel. The burns on his body were not made by fire, but by iron. His back has been flayed raw and cauterized, as were the knife wounds. I have dressed the wounds as best I could but it is the infection in his blood that is something I cannot treat. His fever is likely to kill him if it is not lowered. Its rising higher than any man could suffer. I'm going to start with cold compresses, with your blessing, Father."

Realization dawned upon him. They were talking about him, but it made no sense. He was right here. He was healthy. There was not a mark on his body. He wanted to shout out to them that he was fine.

"Yes, go ahead. With God's blessing."

A shudder of energy flowed through him and he raised his hand to pound against the blackness to let them know where he was.

His hand fell into the void.

*　　　*　　　*

The touch of the cold compress against his forehead was ice-fire through his body. Pain erupted. Contractions split and damaged muscle. A scream of pure agony tore from his dry lips as he convulsed. Every part of his body was on fire.

"Grab him," shouted Father Theodore at the same time Brother Absolon issued, "Make sure he doesn't turn onto his back, for God's sake."

Frozen hands grabbed at him, trying to still the violent shudders, but it sent him back into that dark cold room and he sobbed. "No. No. Please no." He heard his pleading as if someone else made them. "Please stop. Stop. No." They were the words he had used in that dungeon that was her entertainment room when the pain became too great. The lashes fell, the blade seared, his blood burned, he wanted to die.

A hand lovingly touched his face and he screamed, sending him tumbling into her embrace. His back arched in agony in an effort to get away, but he could not. He was trapped. He could not bear her touch, not that, never that again. He whimpered, repeating over and over for her to stop, to please stop.

After forever the seizure released its hold, leaving a wake of desolation through his agony.

"What did they do to him?" a voice whispered into the encroaching darkness.

Father Theodore's worried voice answered closely to his ear. "What does the Devil ever do to an Angel if he manages to catch one?"

The answer tightened his throat, forcing a shuddering sob before he gratefully slipped back into the sweet darkness. The white-faced demons buffeted him, enclosing around him in the Void.

Voices spoke in a darkness-tinged red with pain. The language seemed familiar but he could not make out the meanings. Fire burned along his body cancelling out any desire to follow the heated discussion. He did not dare to open his eyes. He did not know if he could. He did not care. Darkness enfolded him into its embrace.

Where were They? He frowned.

Where was the light? Where was the Grove? Where were the Ladies?

The absence of voices momentarily masked the sound of footsteps towards him. Head swimming, he felt a cold hand touch his forehead and he groaned, his back spasmed at the touch. Pain raced up his neck and threatened to crush his skull while at the same time it ran across his hips and down his legs. He clutched his arms to his chest, his hands locking into tight fists as if to fight the pain, all the while lightning flashed through his closed eyes. Every part of his body was held in a paroxysm of agony that tore breath from his tattered body. The crushing sensation around his ribs made it impossible to inhale and he whimpered, feeling hot tears in the corners of his eyes. It was the lash again and again and again and all he wanted to do was curl up and die but his body refused to relinquish its harsh grip.

"Shhh," whispered the voice.

It was real. It did not sound like the Vampiress' sultry tones. She was real, but who was she? He tried to move out of the strictures of pain and gasped.

A freezing hand on his shoulder sent his body shivering and he sobbed. The touch was ice against his burning flesh. He wanted it gone. Its coldness as painful as the heat his body generated.

"Dinna move." Recognition dawned. It was Jeanie. She was with him, but where were they?

An intoxicating scent reached his senses. The cold rim of a spoon touched his lips and he felt thick fluid spill into his mouth. It took all his strength to swallow.

One. Two. Three more and he was exhausted. The seizure left him suddenly limp and panting. He felt cold lips on his temple before the darkness claimed him once again. Jeanie's whispered words of love followed closely.

He needed to move. His body felt cramped and battered. Sure that was what was causing the pain, he licked his parched lips, refusing to open his eyes. He lay on his side, the mattress pressing uncomfortably into his hip and shoulder. For a moment he had no idea how to gain a sitting position, his head spun just at the thought.

Slowly, he managed to get his elbow under him. It was enough of a movement that forced his body forward, causing his right arm to reach over to stop him from rolling onto his stomach. The shock of pain jammed through his wrist and set off an explosion in his upper arm and across his chest and back, threatening another seizure. Gasping, he waited fearfully, with eyes closed, for it to subside. It did so but the smouldering in his arm and wrist was enough to let him know that at any movement the fires would start up again to threaten another fit that would send him back to oblivion.

Strong freezing hands rested on his burning shoulders sending his teeth chattering and his body shivering. He wanted the touch to stop but could not utter a word for the clicking of his teeth. With help, he painstakingly managed a sitting position. Each movement sent lightning up and down his back. Several times he momentarily blacked out until he realized it was best if he kept his eyes closed. The arms of the stranger did not let him fall but gently carried him until he was able to sit.

Gasping, he hung his head and held his bandaged arms crossed on his chest in an effort to will the pain away. The throbbing of his arms and back pulsated out of sync with that of his leg and he sat there with eyes closed hoping he would not pass out again. The precursor to another paroxysm terrified him so he stayed still.

Innumerable minutes passed, but he did not care. Gradually, he opened his eyes. Staring at his bandaged arms, he winced as he brought them away from his chest. In the white bandages around his forearms long pieces of flat wood were ensconced from knuckles down to his elbows. His right upper arm was expertly wrapped, tying in the bandage over his chest. Any movement of his right arm sent flashes of pain up into the side of his head, making him nauseous, but it was his back that he knew was the worst. He did not need a mirror to see that. Every motion painted a picture of his torture, forcing him to relive every excruciating laceration. He felt his chest constrict and his eyes well.

Swallowing down the emotion, he carefully brushed away the linen sheet covering his thigh and frowned at the large bandages surrounding his upper leg. The tightness encircling him renewed. It had taken him so long to recover from the original wound. He did not know how long it would take now. Eyes suddenly burning, he closed them to the tears that would have eventually come.

Sitting there, the fire in the fireplace all but dead, he trembled in the memory of everything she had said and done to him, spilling her secrets as easily as she spilled his blood, ripped his flesh and stole his hope. She strove to break him, to make him completely hers, and she had nearly done so. All he had had to do to make the pain stop was to plead and grovel his loving adoration for her. To tell her what she wanted. That he would forever be hers. It was always there, at the tip of his tongue. The shame and the humiliation always bit back the words, leaving trails of tears down his face for her to rail against.

Yet here he was, still alive while she, he was almost certain, was dead. It did not erase what she had done to him and even had she never scarred his body, he knew the effects of her torture seared his soul, separating and isolating him from all others with expert precision.

He knew the Vampire's secret and how it was set to destroy the Chosen. It was the only glimmer of hope but it was enough to make him open his eyes and lift his head.

The world suddenly spun and slid sideways. His stomach bottomed out and his breath caught painfully at the sight of Fernando sitting smugly in the chair across from him. A wave of conflicting emotions rolled into him making him gasp. Panic set in. He wanted to flee, but it was impossible. He was as firmly trapped as if he still dangled from those accursed chains. This time it was not the metal scourge that he feared; it was the lash of Fernando's tongue. His breath came in short gasps.

"I think it is high time for the Angel to explain what the hell he is and why he's been masquerading as a Chosen," stated the Noble. He leaned back, glowering down over his crossed arms.

Fernando's words splashed cold shock over him and dried his suddenly slack mouth. He could not withstand the Noble's fierce glare and broke eye contact to stare at the grey stone between them. Trembling, all he could think to reply sat dumbly on his lips. He could not bear to be put through questions that he himself could not answer. Whatever the Mistress of *Le Jardin* had broken in him, Fernando sought to shatter the rest to pieces and he was powerless to stop it.

Closing his eyes he knew that though he was Chosen he could no longer deny the radical differences. What was he then? — A question that haunted him from the moment of his birth. The Ladies called him Chosen, but They called him the One. They declared him to be the Bridge of Life and Death, but what did that mean? He could not tell Fernando this. He could not tell anyone.

The door to the room opened. He did not need to turn to see Jeanie enter. The tension suddenly tightened and he heard Fernando's chair creak as the Noble shifted forward.

"Leave him alone," commanded Jeanie, flying to his side. Relief washed over him and he closed his eyes, releasing the tension he did not realize he held.

"I will not." Fernando stood to glare down at them. "You have evaded me at every turn. The Angel is awake. I will have my answers or I will have no choice but to go to Hugo and tell him what I have witnessed."

Panic sent his heart hammering anew. He knew exactly what it meant and knew that Hugo would have nothing but glee to declare him to be Destroyed, even to have a hand in dismembering him before the sun could rise to finish him off.

Jeanie stood. "Ye dinna have to do anything." Fear tinged defiance shook her voice.

"You're right," sneered the Noble, "I don't, but I'm not about to place my neck in the sun without a good reason. Any of the Chosen would have healed from these wounds in a matter of a day, and none of the Chosen can do what he did a fortnight ago. Even the snivelling monks here believe him to be a true Angel. They're calling it the miracle of St. Martin's. He's awake. It's his decision."

What was this? Confusion swam and he shook his head to clear it, and instantly regretted it with the spinning of the room and the promise of a seizure the motion caused down his back. Panting back the pain, he managed to push the promise into a threat.

Did he hear correctly? Was the Noble Fernando de Sagres, last heir of the Fidalgo de Sagres, offering his silence for the price of his deadly secrets? It seemed incongruous to the Chosen he has gotten to know. No matter, there was no choice.

"It's alright Jeanie," he whispered, his throat raw. Refusing to look up he did not need to see Fernando's smug expression nor Jeanie's shocked face. Victory, pleasure and a hint of fear flowed over him and he knew they were not his feelings, but whose? Notus was too far away, was he not?

He felt Jeanie settle down beside him, her breath tickling his shoulder. "Ye dinna hae t'do this."

"Yes, he does," stated Fernando as he sat back onto the wooden chair. "By all the evidence, as a Chosen, he should be Destroyed."

Jeanie gasped.

Centuries of keeping his differences secret from other Chosen finally came to an end. It was his and Notus' worst nightmare, and it had finally come. Thankfully, Notus was not here to witness. It would have broken his heart. Instead it set Jeanie trembling with the realization of what was in store and to feel her fearful presence beside him broke his heart.

"What do you want to know?" he whispered in defeat. Broken, he closed his eyes, waiting for the inquisition to begin. His back twitched painfully as if expectant for the lash, and he grimaced.

"Everything," declared the Noble, basking in his victory.

He took a deep breath and caught it as the expansion of his ribs sent a shock of pain up his back. Slowly releasing it, he bowed his head, allowing the veil of his long hair to obscure his face. He did not know where to begin. He did not know what to say.

Witnessing the Angel defeated so thoroughly, Jeanie rose up on her knees. "Ye can see he's no up for this."

"I wouldn't have had to do this if you would have made yourself available to answer my questions as you had promised," said the Noble, contemptuously. He returned his attention back to the Angel, a conceited smile curling his lips. "Explain to me how a Chosen, if that's what you are, can be so injured by plain iron weapons and who where those three women that came out of that demon filled fog after that bitch vampire and her lackeys suddenly disappeared."

He snapped his head up, his eyes wide in fright. He could not believe what he was hearing. Fernando saw the three Ladies and the white faced demons in the mist?

"What?" he breathed, unable to say anything else. No one in his whole life had ever seen them, only he.

Fernando sniffed disparagingly. "We all saw you muttering at the door as the storm abated and the fog rose bringing with it the most grotesque apparitions anyone has seen. When they left three women materialized. Jeanie claims to have seen her mother and the monks are all a-buzz about having seen the Virgin Mary bless you."

It could not be true. They could not be real. They were part of his dreams, a part of his nightmares. They were his secret shame that he withheld from everyone in his long life. No one ever knew. Not Auntie. Not Geraint. Definitely not Notus. To hear now that they were indeed real made all his experiences solid and indisputable. It gave too much evidence to the potential truth he had been denying about himself since the day he was brought in as a changeling by Auntie. His panicked breathing escalated and he shook his head in denial, staring into Fernando's burning brown eyes. He wished he could pass out.

"Are you Chosen?" asked Fernando, abruptly.

"Yes." The word hissed out automatically and he broke the probing eye contact again, suddenly doubting the truth of his own conviction. Jeanie's hand reached over his lap and clasped his bandaged hand, giving it a tiny, yet painful, squeeze. He knew it was for support and love, but it still hurt. He could not face her, but accepted this little bit of offered strength. "You read Notus' journal." His whisper was barely audible.

"As much as I could before you snatched it from me, yes." Fernando's eyes narrowed. "Are you saying that you inherited these attributes from your Chooser?"

"No!" The word exploded unexpectedly and he gazed at the Noble sitting imperiously over him. If Fernando believed that Notus was the source then he too would be Destroyed. He could not allow that to happen. "Notus only knows about the—" he took a shuddering breath "—the affect iron has on me. He does not know about the other. No one's known. That... that's new."

Fernando's eyes widened in surprise and the Angel felt a wall of fear hit him as he heard Jeanie's quick intake of breath.

"So what are you saying?" pressed the Noble. "That you've suddenly been able to conjure demons to do your bidding and spirits to—" Fernando closed his mouth unable to find the words.

"I—I guess so," he mumbled. Frowning, he remembered what They told him after the demons had dispatched the vampires. *Blessed Be he who is the Bridge between Life and Death. Blessed Be he who has returned once more. Blessed Be he who is the Light in the Darkness. They are now yours to command, use them wisely.*

Silence crashed down between them as Fernando sat to contemplate the revelation. The Angel waited, his head bowed and eyes closed once more. He had given the Noble ample ammunition. He hoped at least Notus would be kept safe.

When Fernando broke the silence some of the harsh accusatory tones were diminished. "How is it that a Chosen can do these things and be so affected by iron? If this weren't so serious I would almost expect I was part of one of the fairy tales Bridget loves to read about."

"And what if it were?" ventured Jeanie, cautiously. "I mean a fairy tale?"

Disbelieving what Jeanie had said, he turned his face to see the determination written in her bruised pale face. Pulling his hand from her grasp, he wished he could have hid his face in his hands, but the bandages did not allow for that. Instead, he groaned and stared into the almost dead fire.

"What are you talking about?" said the Noble, gruffly, taking in the Angel's irritation.

Jeanie glanced at the man she loved and then back, knowing that the ambiguity of what he was before he was Chosen was a touchy topic, one that was the hardest to believe because he himself could not. Jeanie spoke slowly, deliberately choosing her words. "What if before the Angel was

Chosen he wasna human? That would mean that once Chosen he'd be different, aye? Then that would have t'be considered, wouldna it?"

"That's preposterous!" shouted Fernando. "You're stretching my ability to—" He halted in mid-sentence; the appearance of the Angel closing his eyes and minutely shaking his head in defeat caught him off guard.

Feeling Fernando's glare, he turned to face Jeanie not masking his hurt. "How? How could you?" Tears burned in the corner of his eyes.

She placed her hand on his face so much alike to how the Ladies did that it made him gasp. "Because I love ye and I dinna want to see ye Destroyed. I dinna save ye from Violet—" she gave a little shudder— "just so that Fernando could hae ye put down."

"What are you two talking about?" interrupted the Noble, his ire and curiosity piqued.

"Tell him," implored Jeanie, green eyes glimmering. "If it'll save ye, tell him. Please."

He opened his mouth to protest. Anguish solidified in his chest and he lowered his gaze. He wanted to refuse, but so much had been revealed, what was it to reveal this?

Slowly, in hushed tones, he did something he had never done before, not even to Notus, he spoke the story of before he was Chosen. He spoke of his life with Auntie and how and why she had taken him in and kept him from all others. For the first time he told, in detail, what had happened to him in his sacred grove when he was but a child and how the white-faced demons first visited him. He detailed the changes he had succumbed to after the attack and visitation. Speaking of Geraint caught his voice, and remembering that it was himself that caused Auntie's violent death brought long held back tears to glimmer in his eyes and track down his face. He talked about his lonely life in the cave and what the local villagers believed him to be, but it was his detailed description of how he became Chosen and that the demons had appeared to him at that time that brought a gasp from the Noble.

"Notus has never known," he quietly concluded, unable to meet the incredulous looks on both mortal and Chosen, "about them—about me." Shame heated his face and he stared at his bandaged hands. "To him I was —am—someone lost who needed to be cared for, protected, and out of guilt for his broken vow and what he believes it has done to me." He took a deep shuddering breath and continued. "Notus—Paul—continued what Auntie had hoped Geraint should have done had he lived, and wove a web of mystery around me that spoke more to the truth than he knew so as to keep others away from me, to stop the questing of my nature and isolate me in an effort to protect me. I accepted this for the same reasons that I accepted and was finally made to understand why Auntie kept me apart.

"I was nameless until after I was Chosen. Paul took the name Geraint's daughter gave me and then discarded it, denying what it meant when he found out, probably out of fear and re-created it in the Angel instead centuries later."

"And what name was that?" Fernando's voice was barely audible for the awe it held.

"Gwyn," he replied automatically. "It was believed I was Gwyn ap Nudd returned. The Lord of the Dead and the Otherworld. King of the Fay. Leader of the Wild Hunt. Reaper of men."

Silence thundered through the room until the scrape of the chair indicated that Fernando had stood. The Noble walked to the door, and halted. "I'm making arrangements for us to return to London." He spoke matter-of-factly without turning around and proceeded to turn the doorknob.

Caught in surprise by this declaration, he lifted his head to see the Noble standing there, ready to walk out. "Fernando," he called, thinking quickly. "The Chosen need to know about the Vampires."

"I know," said Fernando, wearily without turning around.

"Wh—when we get back, call a council."

Fernando nodded and walked out.

Returning his attention back to Jeanie, he saw tears shimmering on her face. A swelling of fatigue overtook him and he slumped. The fever that had broken when he awoke was back and he could feel every throbbing wound.

"You came back for me," he stated.

"Aye," nodded Jeanie. "Fernando and I brought ye out."

"Why?" He believed he knew the answer, but he had to hear it from her lips.

Jeanie sighed. "Because I love ye and ye would hae done the same for me—had done the same. I couldna live with the ken that it was because of me that ye died."

Tears pooled in his eyes and he stared at his wrists. Fearful but needing to know, he asked, "How bad, Jeanie?"

She shifted her position and placed her forehead against his, telling him what Brother Absolon had said about the loss of ability with his hands and what else he had done to repair some of the damage caused by the torture. When she was done, he had no doubt that to stand before other Chosen like this would be a death sentence and there was no hope he would ever completely heal from this.

Shaking with exhaustion and fever, and emotionally drained, he lay down on his left side and fell asleep to the sound of Jeanie singing an old Gallic lullaby while she stroked his head.

Fernando leaned heavily against his closed door and scrubbed his face in an attempt to alleviate the shock of the full disclosure. It was as he had hoped and feared. He now held the key to whether the Angel lived or died, but the revelations that came with it stunned him. The questions they brought paralysed him with childhood fears of pagan spirits riding out of the night, lights leading innocent and guilty a-like to their deaths, and demons and angels fighting over the souls of men.

Pushing off the door, he began to pace around the small room.

He had discovered more than any other living being about the Angel. What was worse was that the Angel had not asked him what he would do with the information. It was as if the Angel had resigned himself to be Destroyed. To witness the complete defeat of the Angel was not what he wanted, and nor was it truly expected. There was such vulnerability in the Angel. The torture had seen to the destruction of the Angel and what Fernando now saw of the man who was Chosen, yet not. This humbled him and bound him further to a partner that he had sought out. The cloak of the Angel was in tatters leaving the real person raw and bleeding underneath.

The room suddenly seemed too small to continue pacing and he dropped onto the bed. What was he to do with the information? Once back in London Bridget would instantly know that something was wrong and he knew he was incapable of warding off her probing now that he had agreed to open himself to her. His knowledge would put her in danger as well unless he chose to keep the secret and could convince Bridget of the same.

The quandary seemed suddenly lifted at the realization that the Angel most likely would insist on joining in at the council and to do so would invite his Destruction. Katherine would make sure of that. She had always seen the Angel as a threat to her position. To see him so damaged and weakened would thrill her to no end. The Angel would be killed and Notus would be forced to watch, and Fernando reluctantly admitted that he did not want such a fate to occur.

The visualization of such an outcome shook the Noble, as did the understanding that Katherine would most likely believe that he knew about the Angel's differences and hid them from her. Her paranoia was well known and feared. Standing up, Fernando went to the door and left his room to start the necessary arrangements to get them back to London.

Not knowing what to do with the truth about the Angel clouded his mind and fogged his emotions, leaving him angry with himself for becoming so entranced with discovering the truth about the Angel. It had not turned out the way he had expected.

xlí

he breeze pulled at his hair, whipping it around his shoulders and face. Each time the strands slapped his back he stiffened. Standing on the wharf, supporting himself on his good leg in an effort to alleviate the burning aches, he carefully crossed his arms over his chest and winced. He could feel Jeanie's warmth beside him and knew that she wanted to help him but an arm around his waist would most likely make him buckle.

It had been humiliating enough allowing her to help him dress, padding the waist of his trousers so that the fabric would not rub. He could hardly stand the touch of the light cotton shirt and refused the jacket and cloak. He did not care that he was dressed out of season and would draw attention. The slightest touch across his back was a slash of fiery pain reminiscent of the lashes of the metal tailed scourge, threatening another immobilizing spasm.

If dressing for travel had been torture enough, riding horseback was worse. Each sway, each pounding step, drove red-fogged pain through his mind. Several times they had to stop as another fit took hold. Brother Absolon and Father Theodore both had beseeched them to wait until he was better healed, but there was no choice. Too much time had passed and they needed to get back to London, especially with what Violet had revealed to him. He had been barely conscious when they rode their horses into Calais. It had been Fernando's suggestion that they tie him to the horse that kept him from falling into the mud-strewn road.

The revelation that the Mistress of *Le Jardin* had been Jean's best friend at the Inn still rocked him. It also explained why she had always seemed so familiar. Whenever he had seen her, Violet had made him uncomfortable with her stares. It was hard to imagine that it was she who had smoothly manipulated Jeanie and him. Then another thought gripped him, Violet wished to possess him even from the first time he walked into *The Rose and Thorn* with Jeanie. He shuddered and tried to hold himself together.

The ship bobbed up and down, making his head spin and he closed his eyes. He did not want to contemplate the journey across the Channel. He had not told Fernando about that added difference and he doubted Jeanie had either. Between the gusts he could make out the Noble talking with the First Mate, finalizing the orders and expectations. It would not be long before he would hobble painfully up the gangplank. The thought sent him trembling.

"Are ye alright?" asked Jeanie. Worry tinged her voice and she came closer, holding his sword along her front. "Ye dinna hae t'do this now. We can wait 'til ye recover some. Brother Absolon said ye shouldna' be walking 'round."

He opened his eyes and frowned at her bruised face, realizing that none of them had come away without injury. The purple tinged green and yellow marked the healing that was already making promise of the return of Jeanie's beauty, yet now there was a strength in her eyes he had not ever seen before, tempered with horrific experience and violence. He had never wanted to see that in the springtime of her eyes.

"Too much time has passed," he whispered. "There is no choice."

Jeanie nodded and returned to stand next to him on the pier.

Closing his eyes once more, he breathed deep the moist salt scent the breeze carried and halted in mid-intake. A presence crept up on him, several in fact. Waves of curiosity and fear predominated and he knew they were Chosen.

The French, having been informed about the Vampires in a letter Fernando had sent to Hugo, now watched from darkened abodes to witness the Angel and his entourage leave their soil. Another presence over powered the others, the loathing an emotional spear directed at the Angel, and the Angel knew it was Hugo. The power of the emotion nearly staggered him, but he managed to hold his ground and he knew, somehow, that there was a new Master of Paris and Hugo had gained it.

It was not a surprise that some new ability came with his wounding, something always seemed to be given in exchange for his suffering, most often it would distinguish him farther apart from others. There was no exception this time. The conscious awareness of it came slowly with Fernando's presence. He had at first been able to sense Fernando's position within St. Martin's, and then, when that awareness settled, he became the unwilling observer of Fernando's emotional state. It did not make sense and there seemed to be no way to block it. One thing was certain was that the Noble did not sense the same from him.

Irritation mixed with concern stepped towards him. It was Fernando; the Noble's talks with the First Mate complete. Forcing a deep breath, he tried to push back the mixture of emotions from all directions and opened his eyes. The feelings still buzzed at the edge of his awareness. Fernando's tired brown eyes seemed larger in the bronze colouring the sun had bequeathed him.

"Let's go," stated the Noble, gruffly turning away, yelling at one of the crew to be careful with their belongings.

Jeanie lightly touched his arm. "I'll take care of ye."

"I know," he whispered, attempting to make the best show of not being injured. He grit his teeth as his left foot touched down, sending excruciating shocks up his whole body, and slowly made his way towards the ship. He knew he was limping badly and he felt a stitch in his leg give way under the tight bandages. A hot liquid sensation spread out on his black trousers to drip down his leg.

It was difficult to manage across the gangboard. The sudden vertigo gripped him as soon as he was past the dock and over the water and worsened as he staggered onto the deck. Miraculously, he remained standing. He closed his eyes in hope that the sensation would abate, but the world started to swirl and detach. Faster and more furiously it tilted and spun until he could not catch his breath. The deck seemed to heave under his feet and then bottom out. The fever that had been simmering all evening spiked red hot and blackness swam over his vision as a woman screamed a name.

His whole body ached and throbbed. Those were the first sensations that came to mind even before he opened his eyes. The second was that he lay face down on something soft and comfortable. He wanted to go back to the sacred grove, to drink more from the font of the well and watch the white faced demons swirl, but he had come back to the tattered remains of his body.

Curious, he opened his eyes and let the vision of dark red silk register as well as the appearance of his left forearm bereft of bandages. Blackened flesh encircled his wrist as he attempted to twist it for a better look, but it was the sight of the stitches in the centre of his wrist that caught his breath. He knew that the back of his wrist faired no better and he tried to flex his fingers. Pain shot up as his digits failed to fully complete the move. Closing his eyes, he sighed, his head throbbing with the effort.

He did not know where he was, but the bed—if that was what he was on—was comfortable. It did not rise and fall and all sense of vertigo had been dispelled. Wherever he was, he was no longer at sea and was grateful for this, but it still did not answer his question.

Taking another deep breath, he became aware of a multitude of feelings emanating from around him and knew without a doubt that other Chosen were close, but what he picked up made no sense, making the headache thunder. Joy, anger, annoyance, boredom, worry, hunger and sexual rapture confused him. He knew they came from at least five Chosen somewhere nearby, but he did not know where. He needed it to stop.

A sudden gripping captured the breath at the revelation that he must be awaiting the verdict of his destruction from the Mistress of London. Fernando must have made the only decision he could and went to her to divulge the secrets of the Angel. He shuddered at the thought of what was coming, but regardless of the fact that he now knew her secret, it was all the more reason to Destroy him and Notus.

Pulling his arms down to his sides to push himself up, he knew he had to find Jeanie, to tell her to flee, but a shock of pain up his back forced a grunt and held him fast to the bed. He could feel the oncoming of the seizure snaking up his spine with every movement.

"Stay still," ordered a woman. "The more you move about the harder it is to make sure your wounds are properly redressed."

He turned his head to face the other direction, trying to catch a glimpse of the woman whose weight settled down beside him, and instantly regretted the action. He could feel her cool reticence flow over him at the same instant a shock of cold flared up his back. Gasping he closed his eyes against the pain. She put something on his back, and every time the cold liquid touched he felt its stinging lash.

Anger, worry and dejection flowed from the woman and he sucked in a breath with the realization that she was Chosen and that she was witness to his differences. Trembling at her touch, he wondered what it was she placed upon his body. Was it something that would help the sun to immolate him? But did she not say she was redressing his wounds? Moving his arms up to his sides again, he tried to push himself up only to feel a strong hand push him back down.

"I told you not to move." The woman sighed and resumed her painful ministrations. "This was never how I wanted to get the Angel into my bed."

The admission froze him in place, bringing with it a flash of memory of Violet's possession that sent him shuddering. His hands made to grasp the pillow under his head, but were held in place by the pain stabbing through his back.

He was back there, immobilized and the seizure that had been held at bay for so long suddenly let loose. With the constriction of damaged muscles, he gritted his teeth and closed his eyes at the explosion of pain all along his body. His body shook with the force that belied the damage and he tried in vain not to cry out.

"Oh dear." Concern and shock poured from the woman. "I-I'm sorry. I didn't realize. I wasn't told."

He felt her stand and move away as he shut his eyes to the memories. The sharp metal cutting flesh. The touch of her lips and tongue against the wounds. A hand brushed his hair from his face evoking the torture and he whimpered. Images both visceral and mental played through him of Violet's physical desire to capture him. He did not know if he begged aloud for her to stop through his chattering teeth. Without opening his eyes he could feel the Chosen's presence before him and heard the rustling of her skirts as she knelt beside his head.

"Don't fight it," she whispered. "Let it out or it will consume you and taint the rest of your nights."

He shook his head and wanted to voice his denial of everything that was ever done to him because of his differences. His breath came in great heaving sobs. Tears ran down his face to drip into the silk covered pillow. He never wanted this life. He never chose it. All his life the choices were taken away from him because his differences set him apart. Shame sent him shivering into fatigue as the seizure abated.

He heard her shift again and felt a wash of empathy from her. "Trust me. I know."

A cool hand graced his brow and then a soft cloth wiped away his tears before he heard her stand and walk away, allowing him time to regain his tattered emotions and for his body to relinquish its agonizing hold.

"Damn that man," she hissed.

Wondering whom she was damning, he opened his eyes once his trembling had abated. Exhausted, he could see through blurry eyes, the female Chosen standing with her back to him before the roaring fireplace. Despite her sincerity in caring for him, he did not doubt that she held watch over him until such time his sentence would be carried out. After witnessing his display of weakness he had no doubt it would be soon. If that were the case then he would meet his fate upright and not lying in a sick bed. Gathering his arms to his side once more, knowing that it could send him into another fit, he gave a push. He regretted the tugging and splitting of his healing wounds the movement caused.

Painstakingly, he managed to sit with his legs over the edge of the bed, panting with the effort. His head spun and he put out a hand to halt the motion, but it just added to the nausea. He closed his eyes, waited for the vertigo to cease and opened them once more. The crimson silk sheets swirled about him accentuating the paleness of his skin. He hated feeling so helpless and tried to grasp the top sheet so as to give him some modesty, but the material slipped through his feeble fingers. A frustrated huff turned the woman around, her blue eyes wide. He had thought he had recognized the voice, but now he knew who she was. Fernando's Chooser stood with arms crossed as they stared at each other.

Clothed in a simple gown of deep blue, Bridget's hair was modestly arranged allowing for locks of sun gold to curl and drape down her neck in an attempt to make her appear older. Worn blue eyes betrayed her worry and her fatigue. He knew he was at a great disadvantage but she seemed not to take note. Instead, she took a steady breath and straightened, her visage transforming into a strong formidable lady. What surprised him was that she met his gaze and refused to be daunted. The force of her anger hit him and he gasped, breaking off eye contact to stare at the plush burgundy rug.

"Tell me something." Bridget's voice filled the room. "Why did you have to bring Fernando into your secret?"

Shocked at the implication, he returned his gaze to the Noble's Chooser as she stood glowering over him. He opened his mouth to respond but could not find the words. He had not wanted Fernando to know. No other Chosen was to ever find out. He could not believe she was blaming him for being tortured and Fernando's choice to rescue him. Stripped of every secret, his body a testament to his utter defeat to the truth of what he was, he lowered his head in humiliation.

"Do you realize that if Katherine finds out we're all dead?" Bridget swung around and started placing small bottles back into a wooden case, the glass clinking. "Damn Fernando for bringing you here." She swung around to glare at him again and then suddenly the fire of her anger was doused. "And damn me for a fool, too."

Unable to meet Bridget's gaze, he closed his eyes. Her emotions were erratic, confusing and made his head spin. They did not make any sense to what she was saying. She did not feel as though it was his fault but rather Fernando's. That and the background emotions from the other Chosen in her home forced him put his face in his hands, wincing at the pressure. He had to do something about all the noise. He could not keep feeling all the emotions of the Chosen around him.

A wash of strong concern flowed and wrapped him as he felt Bridget's hand alight on his battered shoulder.

"I'm sorry," he muttered, not knowing what else to say.

"No. It's not your fault," replied Bridget. She knelt and took his hands in hers. Carefully, so as not to exacerbate his wounds, she began dressing them in white gauze bandages, inserting the flat wooden boards to immobilize his wrists. "Fernando told me everything when he brought you in. How could he not? You were unconscious and he was very put out. I wouldn't let him go without receiving an explanation. I believe Jeanie would have told me, but, well, I couldn't count on a mortal's retelling. Fernando released the information through our bond, which I now believe, was in everyone's best interest."

She took his arm and he glanced at the stitching job overlaying the old scar as she began to bandage it up as well.

"Why?" he asked, hating how small his voice sounded. "Why are you doing this?"

Halting in her work, the roll of gauze in her hand, Bridget glanced up into the Angel's face and realized the full extent of his meaning. With a sigh she continued to redress his wounds. When complete she stood to retrieve more bandaging from her box and halted in mid-action.

Placing the roll down, she turned back to face him. "Do you know what the Angel is?"

The question stunned him. For all the world he could not find an answer to her question and he frowned.

"Shall I tell you?" Bridget stepped forward, forcing him to lift his head to meet her eyes. "The Angel is Chosen, but he is so much more than that. He is a myth that forces others to re-evaluate what it means to be Chosen. He forces us to question our own natures and why we are Chosen. The Angel, despite not being human, has more humanity within him than those who have Chosen to give it up. He knows what is most precious because he never had it. The Chosen have much to learn from the Angel because we have given up something that he still grasps at."

The words bowled him over and set him trembling.

"But, I'm not," he whispered, staring at his bandaged wrists..

Bridget smiled and nodded. "You are. What Fernando relayed to me was just the final piece of the puzzle. Did you not realize why Fernando wanted to work with you on this supposed mystery? To find out if you were indeed born Chosen as all the rumour and conjecture has been going on about for centuries? To find out what was so different yet so alluring to even the Chosen?"

"It was to find out my secrets that no one ever knew." He closed his eyes. "The ones that set me apart to be Destroyed."

"That part, I believe, was never his intention. He was quiet upset about the responsibility it left him." Bridget's voice was comforting, eliciting a trust he did not understand.

He nodded, confused. Fernando knew everything and he had shared it with Bridget. How many others knew?

"He's not going to tell Katherine or anyone else for that matter, and neither will I." Bridget stood to retrieve her gauze roll.

Hearing that his secrets were now shared and not exposed widened his eyes. It made no sense. Fernando had always tried to pry and wheedle his way into his life, and now that his secrets were laid bare, the Noble was not going to exploit them? It seemed so incongruous to the man he had gotten to know over the last few weeks. He watched Bridget bandage his left thigh, the thick blackened gash under the stitches pulled at the twisted scar beneath and he shook his head in disbelief, sending his hair to brush against her hands. "Why?"

Bridget stopped. "Tell me, you haven't spent much time with our kind, have you? Have you ever seen the Chosen work together for anything good and right? Are there any true friendships between Chosen anymore except perhaps between Chooser and Chosen? Of course we have our Mistresses and Masters, but that is more for show and control of who is and isn't allowed to live in our lands. They have always been there to allocate and give permission, or not, to protect our hunting grounds. But they do not form a true community. Community is an inherent human quality that is created through bonds of friendship and need—the desire to serve something larger than oneself. By the nature of being Chosen we have no community, no friendships with each other except to exploit, as I take advantage of the Chosen who work with me.

"From what I understand, it hasn't always been this way, but only the Elders, the ones so old that they cannot be found by us any more, remember this time. The Good Father is one of them. You are lucky to have him as your Chooser. The Chosen are lucky that he hasn't disappeared taking you with him.

"If the Chosen were to lose you, the Chosen lose their connection with the past and thus their humanity. You have come to represent something that is truly noble about being Chosen, something truly human, but most of all, despite what Fernando may say, for the first time in his life as Chosen, he has a friend. We have a friend."

He could not believe what he was hearing. Fernando — a friend? He thought of all that the Noble had done for him and he for the Noble. If that was the case it was indeed a bizarre friendship, but he had no other comparison except for his relationship with Notus. Everyone else, except for a select few who were teachers or mentors, he kept at a distance, out of fear of being rejected as different, even when they declared that it did not matter. Some accepted and were friendly because of what they believed him to be out of fear or the need to define him as different because of his appearance. No one managed to penetrate his walls isolating him, except Notus, and even then, not fully. Not until Jeanie had accepted him so completely, so readily, that he knew what he had been missing in his long life. Now Fernando knew and accepted, counting him as a friend, bringing Bridget with him and with it the threat that if his secret were discovered Fernando and Bridget would stand with him to be Destroyed. Tightness constricted his chest and throat as he bowed his head, humbled beyond words. He closed his eyes against the welling of tears, afraid that the moment would pass taking with it the dream he thought this was.

A sudden wave of maliciousness crashed down. Hatred and jealousy flew in all directions slicing into his head with pounding force. He closed his eyes with a groan. Somewhere in the house above two of Bridget's Chosen were in the thick of a fight. He did not need to hear the words, the waves of anger and potential violence was enough. Over laid with the fight, several other emotions filtered through. Surprise, elation and enjoyment mixed with annoyance. It was enough to make his head throb painfully and threaten another seizure. All he wanted was to have them stop and this new ability to disappear.

"Are you alright?" He felt a wash of concern as Bridget alighted a hand onto his face.

He did not know what to say, yet feared to shake his head. The emotions crescendoed and he screwed up his face at the intensity and the pain.

"Two Chosen. Fighting upstairs," he gasped.

"What?" Bridget's hand released him and he felt her go still, searching for her Chosen to find out what was going on.

The impact from Bridget's fury made him groan. It was too much.

Shuddering with the bombardment of emotions from more than half a dozen Chosen, he clutched at his head.

Stop it, he shouted as he rocked back and forth on the bed, disregarding the effect the movement caused on his tattered body.

Still the argument raged.

Stop it.

He could not bear the intensity. His head felt as if it were being cleaved in two.

Stop it!

Everything stopped. No emotions flitted towards him. The crushing headache subsided into a low throb. He heard Bridget stumble backwards, catching herself on the bedside table and he looked up knowing that somehow he had made it all stop, but for how long he did not know.

"What? How?" stammered Bridget, her eyes wide. "How did you know Anna and Beth were arguing? And what was that?"

"I don't know," he sighed, the exhaustion he had been feeling expanded and all he wanted to do was sleep. He tried to pinch the headache away but his fingers would not work to compress the bridge of his nose. Bridget took a tentative step towards him. This time he could not feel her emotions and was surprisingly disconcerted.

"You can feel other Chosen's emotions, can't you?" Bridget's voice was soft with a mix of awe and fear.

Closing his eyes, he nodded in defeat. She knew everything else, why not this?

"And you can project your own onto us?"

He glanced up at her wide blue eyes. "I—I don't know."

Bridget edged closer, suddenly wary of what she had in her room. "I was talking with Anna and Beth, angry at their usual argument over who got a particular client when all of a sudden I felt as if someone pushed us apart. That was you, wasn't it?"

His face screwed up. He did not know what was happening to him. More and more he was removed from what it was to be Chosen. Words failed him but he knew that Bridget spoke the truth and he nodded.

"Can you hear them—us—as well?" asked Bridget, tentatively.

"No," he whispered.

"And you've always been able to do this?" Bridget's voice grew stronger, more confident and full of awe.

"No," he sighed. "It started after."

Silence crashed down after he heard her say, "Oh."

This new development was clearly too much for Bridget. His obvious differences from other Chosen had become even more pronounced and he realized that he probably had sealed his doom to be Destroyed. He doubted that Bridget would accept this as well as the other differences.

Bridget came before him and knelt down to look at him, as if sensing his disquiet and shook her head. Self-loathing broiled up at the pity on her face and he tried to look away but her hand caught his cheek forcing him to keep eye contact.

"Tell me the truth. Fernando believes you were never human. Jeanie says you are Fay. There are rumours to that effect. What do you say?" Her voice was rock steady as her blue eyes bore into his.

All breath left him in a huff. It was the same thing over and over and over again. "I don't know." His voice strained even to his ears.

Bridget's hand fell from his face as she stood up, a sad smile on her face. "I was once human, but for a long time I lost my humanity until Fernando brought you into our lives. Even Fernando wasn't immune. He is not the same as he once was. There is more to him, me, us, now. I don't believe he expected this, but there you have it." She turned to click her wooden box closed and held it against her chest. "I guess he and I have a lot to learn from our friend."

She turned towards the door, a hand falling onto the crystal knob. "I'll send Jeanie down. She's been sick with worry since they brought you here." Bridget turned around, her visage suddenly serious. "I've never seen such devotion and love from a mortal towards a Chosen in my lifetime that was not Pushed into them. Jeanie has a fiery spark that makes her fiercely loyal to those she cares about. If you love her as much as she loves you, Choose her. The Chosen may have a lot to learn from her as well."

Without waiting for a response, Bridget opened the door and left him alone in her room. He sat stunned by the admission and the suggestion. It was not that he had not contemplated it before, but to have it endorsed by another Chosen seemed surreal. Before their excursion to France he dared not to even consider the possibility for fear of driving Jeanie away. Now, after everything she had done for him, protecting his secrets from Fernando and saving him from Violet, all in the name of her love for him, he knew he could not live without her. Yet, he found he was fearful to ask. If she said yes, it would drive Notus out of his life. If she said no—he did not want to contemplate that. All he knew was that he could not continue in this broken body without her. He could not live past her death and he could not allow Notus to wipe away her feelings towards him as he did to Tarian's grand-daughter so long ago. It would be a torture beyond what Violet had done.

He glanced up at the sound of Jeanie entering the room, halting just before the door. The bruise on her face had faded to yellow, but the redness that rimmed her eyes foretold of a mixture of fatigue and worry. It was the dark circles around her eyes that stabbed at his heart and he knew she was afraid to come closer. Painfully, he lifted his left arm in an effort to beckon her over and immediately winced at the half made action. It was enough of an offering that Jeanie immediately flew towards him, halting before she could embrace him, her hands outstretched as if she did not know what to do with them.

It was not what he wanted. He needed to feel the reality of her. Without a care for the potential of another seizure he awkwardly pulled her closer with his good arm, ignoring the pulling of the stitches in his wrist or the twinges up and down his back and chest.

She came willingly, yet tentatively, afraid her touch would cause him pain, but he did not care.

Breathing in her soft clean scent, he could smell lavender and rose as he leaned his head against her breast and sighed. Whatever tension Jeanie held, melted away as she stepped closer into the embrace and her hands came up to stroke his head. All he wanted was to feel her warmth and sigh into her chest, luxuriating in the sound of her steady heartbeat.

After an eternity, Jeanie gently pulled away yet kept touching him, his face, his hair, his shoulders, ever so careful not to come into contact with his wounds. He basked in her attention and her touch, yet did not attempt to do the same. He knew he could not without eliciting more pain.

"Are you alright," they asked at the same instant.

It seemed so natural to speak their shared thoughts at the same time that he smiled softly when Jeanie chuckled.

"I'm alright," offered Jeanie, knowing he would want to hear about her first. "Bridget and the others hae been verra kind t'me, lettin' me stay here." A blush rose to her cheeks and flushed down to the top of her chest. Lowering her eyes, her lips twitched in an effort to hide a smile.

"What is it?" Genuine concern warmed him, but was dampened by the strange reaction.

She bowed her head as if ashamed and huffed out a nervous breath. "It seems I've become a bit of a celebrity here."

He could tell she was reluctant to explain and a frown knitted his fine white brows together. "Celebrity?"

"Aye," said Jeanie, demurely. Her blush grew darker. "It seems that being the paramour of the Angel has its own, um, complications, aye?"

He blinked dumbly at her until the comprehension of what she was referring to widened his eyes and slackened his jaw. He wanted to be angry at Bridget's whores but realized he could not find the energy. He remembered how they had reacted when he first arrived with Fernando in what seemed years ago. The Chosen ladies had seemed greatly interested in him and after what Bridget spoke in passing only moments ago, he sighed. It was the same thing over again. It was the same reasons why Violet had wanted him and abused him. His stomach turned and he frowned.

"Don't fash yerself about it," rushed Jeanie, witnessing the realization dawn upon him and then turn sour. "I used to be able to turn Violet's attention away from ye when—" She halted, stunned at the reaction of what she had stated.

The use of Violet's name stole the breath from his body. He had known Jeanie had talked to the Vampire about him and had done so for years. Violet had made it perfectly clear what they had discussed and how it had enamoured the Vampire to possess him, body and soul. Shaking his head, he tried to deny how such speculation had led him to such abuse, and it was starting again. Jeanie could try and divert their queries about him, but it would only heighten their desire to learn more. It was that potential that sent shivers up his spine.

Witnessing the panic in his wide crimson eyes, Jeanie realized her mistake too late. "Oh Gwyn, I'm so sorry." She fell to her knees before him. "It's all my fault. If I hadn't ever talked with Violet—" He winced at the name. "—about ye she wouldna hae wanted ye."

Shame filled him and he squinted his stinging eyes closed, pushing down the panic. "No, Jeanie. She still would have done what she did." He opened his eyes and gazed into her watery green depths. "She was a Vampire set out to destroy every Chosen. The Angel would have still been her target regardless of what you may or may not have told her. The Angel...I-I've always been set apart. To many—Chosen, mortal or Vampire—it is enough to create a desire of possession. A person can believe they have the right to possess, or destroy, another if that other is different."

He took a shuddering breath at the sudden realization his own words brought him. "I have always been dehumanized by those around me and by those who believe they love me."

Jeanie's soft warm hand reached up to caress his face. "Never. Never by me, my love."

The desire to cover her hand with his was overpowering, but to lift his arm to do so would invite agony. Instead, he basked in this simple touch of affection and knew the depth of Jeanie's love for him. He wondered if it would be enough.

"I know, *cariad*," he whispered the lie as he turned his face into her hand to kiss her palm.

He knew what had initially drawn Jeanie to him. It was the same as Violet, Fernando and all the others, the mysterious Angel, and he did not know who that was anymore. One thing he clung to was Jeanie's love and his for her. It was the only genuinely real thing because he was no longer the Angel to her and he knew he could not lose that. The thought of having been so desperately alone for most of his life and having to go back to that desolate life stilled his breath. He knew what he needed to do and damned the consequences. Bridget's words carried a weight that brought fear to tickle his awareness and he lifted his gaze to Jeanie.

"What is it?" asked Jeanie, her voice catching at the sudden mixture of sadness and fear in his eyes.

He took a deep shuddering breath. "You know I love you." She nodded. He could see the worry pinch her cinnamon brows and hated what he realized they needed to discuss. "I cannot give you a life where we will grow old together, where I can give you children and we can live a life that every mortal dreams of. It is not something I can give. I do not think it is something I was ever meant to have no matter how much I may dream of it." His voice caught in a tight sob. "I do not have the strength to watch you grow old and die."

Stricken by his words, Jeanie drew back. These were things she knew, but never gave any thought of for fear of what it would mean. Now that he had spoken them Jeanie realized what she had hoped for with the Angel had been dashed to scattered fragments when she discovered his true nature. Dreams of living a life together, growing old together, possibly having children together, they were only ever an illusion. She had not the time to properly understand what it would do to her desires to be with the Angel. Now he spoke them and she held her breath, waiting for the hammer to fall, suddenly afraid that despite their love he was going to end it.

Sensing her fear, he sighed as his surged upwards to meet it. When next he spoke he knew he leapt into the unknown more terrified than when succumbing to the Void and the demons that dwelled within. "I can only give you what I am—Chosen."

Realization dawned on Jeanie's face until she gasped.

xlii

It took a fine finesse of coercion, trickery and blatant manipulation to force Katherine into calling the Chosen to court without her or her lackeys discovering that I or the Angel are in town, let alone alive." Fernando slouched in the single plush green chair that sat beside the roaring fireplace in Bridget's room. He was dressed in his finest, a stylishly cut tux with an ebony walking stick with a round silver grip and footing that sat across his knees.

"But tonight?" countered Bridget. She sat at her dressing mirror pinning her golden tresses into an elegant fashion. Her royal blue gown trimmed with ivory lace accentuated her slim corseted waist and exposed the top of her chest quite magnificently. "You've hardly given us any time to prepare."

From the bed, the Angel sat and watched the dynamics between the Noble and his Chooser, his head swimming with the emotions washing over him that were incongruous to what they were saying to one another. It was as if what they spoke to each other was a way to get a reaction that would ensure a fight, but their emotions were desirous for one another. It was like watching an old married couple nitpick at one another just to prove there was still love. A gentle scrape of the bristles of the brush against his bare back snapped his spine straight and caught his breath.

"Sorry," stated Jeanie as she pulled the brush through the ends of his hair. She was already dressed in the green dress she had worn when they had crossed to France. This time her hair splayed loose around her shoulders, curling down her back.

Bridget and Fernando turned their attention at the indrawn breath. Concern and discomfort flowed from their relaxed postures.

"You could have tried to give the Angel more time to recover," accused Bridget, turning to glare at her Chosen.

The Noble shot a non-committal apology at the Angel and turned his attention back to Bridget's primping. "What did you expect me to do? Do you know how hard it was to track down Maurice? The old sod was so terrified about being dragged before Katherine and told that now that the Angel and I were dead, that it was his responsibility to continue in the search. If I hadn't found him when I did, Maurice would have been on the next ship to the Americas."

The Angel listened intently to Fernando's tale while trying not to wince every time Jeanie pulled the brush through his tangled hair. He would have preferred to do it himself, with his fingers, but that seemed impossible now. He hated how he now relied upon others to help him even with the simplest of tasks. Jeanie relished in the caring of him and he felt even more embarrassed that Bridget and Fernando were in the room to witness his frailties.

Since having napped after his long discussion with Jeanie, his awareness of the other Chosen had come back. At first it overwhelmed him, causing a pounding headache. Jeanie had been concerned, rolling onto her side beside him, as he tried to catch his breath. He could not answer her. Gaining a sitting position had nearly caused him to tremble as if another fit would take him. It was when he tried to only focus upon his breathing that he found that the emotions of the other Chosen seemed to distance themselves. As he moved deeper into the meditation he found he was able to turn it into an annoying buzzing sensation. Now that both Fernando and Bridget were in the room with him, he could feel every emotion they haphazardly threw out. It was distracting from the conversation.

"So you threatened and cajoled the man," stated Bridget, flatly. Finished with her hair she opened up a box of cosmetics and brushes and began to expertly apply them.

"I did not." Fernando feigned hurt, placing a bronze hand over his heart. "I would never do that to another Chosen."

The Angel watched Bridget snort in disgust and shake her head. He knew, as well as Bridget, how Fernando would use whatever tactic necessary to get what he wanted, for the most part. He could feel the Noble's satisfaction and a hint of childish glee at such behaviour. "Yes, you would," he whispered. He felt Jeanie's careful strokes halt and Fernando's displeasure. "You did with me," he said before he knew what he was saying.

"And look where it has all got us," accused Bridget, turning around. "Oh don't look at me like that Fernando." Before the Noble could counter with a harsh word or two, Bridget raised her voice, cutting him off to sit and glower. "What did you do to make Maurice contact Katherine for another court?"

"Us?"

"Stop sulking," demanded Bridget as she turned back to her mirror, "and tell us what you mean."

Fernando picked the walking stick up off his knees and weighted the finely tooled wood in his hands. "I told Maurice that he would have the answers to Katherine's demands and the evidence would be myself and the Angel."

Bridget placed her lipstick brush down very precisely onto the table, straightened her back and turned around. The Angel did not need his new awareness to sense how angry she was. The room was thick with her disapproval and his head pounded anew.

"Did you not stop and think, Fernando?" she demanded.

The Angel winced at the sudden wave of raw emotion.

"The Angel is no state to stand before Katherine and the rest of the Chosen. You're condemning him to be Destroyed. He hasn't had enough time to recover."

Another wave from the other side of the room swelled and crashed into the Angel. "He's had almost three fucking weeks. Katherine believes we are dead. Hell, Maurice nearly died of freight, if that's at all possible, when I showed up at his home. He thought I was a ghost! The meeting is set for tonight. What was I supposed to tell him? Wait until the Angel is healed? That would be just brilliant."

The fury that Chosen and Chooser sent outwards pounded into his head and he groaned, thankful that Jeanie had halted her brushing. He tried to focus on his breathing, but the pounding was too intense and every breath made him nauseous.

"The two of ye stop it right now," shouted Jeanie from behind him. She had watched the whole tirade in shock, and worse yet, how it affected the Angel. "What is it with ye Chosen that ye act like children? One would think that after living as long as ye have ye'd have grown up a tad."

The Angel would have turned and kissed her right then and there had it been physically possible to do so. Instead he felt a surge of pride for Jeanie, as the anger the two other Chosen held suddenly collapsed into surprise, taking with it the pounding headache.

Bridget's eyes went round before her whole face lit up in a smile. "You are quite right, my dear." She turned to face her Chosen. Fernando glowered at the mortal. "Has she always been like this?"

"Yes. Unfortunately," replied the Noble, gruffly, his arms crossed over his chest and the stick across the arms of the chair.

"How delightful that someone, especially a mortal, can put you in your place."

"Both of your places," quietly remarked the Angel and quickly regretted his words.

It was not like him to speak out of turn like this and he stared down at his bandaged wrists. Initially there had been some concern about what would happen if someone saw them beneath the cuffs of his shirt. It could draw undue attention. Instead he would wear an out of date shirt with frills on the cuffs that would cover most of his hands. He was just waiting for Anna and Beth to quickly make the shirt and wondered how Bridget had found two seamstresses willing to become Chosen prostitutes. At least the two were not brought into his deadly secret.

"Yes, well," dismissed Bridget and turned the conversation back onto track. "So what are the arrangements that you made with Maurice?"

Fernando sat straighter and glared at each one in turn before continuing, lingering longer on Jeanie than the Angel liked. "He's going to meet us outside of the building at a quarter to and then go in by himself. His audience is on the hour. He's going to tell Katherine he's made the discoveries that she wanted him to and then we're to enter."

"That sounds all well and good, Fernando," chastised Bridget. "But what are you planning on telling the Mistress of London?"

"What about me?" Jeanie piped in as she began to cinch off the Angel's hair into a tail with a black leather thong. She enjoyed working her fingers through his soft straight hair

"You aren't coming inside." Fernando scowled. "You can come with us, but you're not entering that building. I believe we already agreed upon that."

Jeanie let out a huff of resignation. She knew after the last time she followed them what her actions had caused. Little did either Fernando or the Angel know that she had left the monastery to pursue them and thus caused them the harm that befell them. Guilt and shame would forever plague her soul every time she saw the marks left on her lover's body. She would be content that this time she would go with them, even if not into the building itself. She would wait outside, under the light post, where she had first met the Noble and had began such a perilous quest to release the Good Father. Jeanie brought her focus back to brushing the long tail of white hair.

Fernando smiled victoriously, pleased that the mortal girl finally learned to listen to her betters. It had been the Angel's suggestion that she come along, but not go in. It seemed the most reasonable solution to the hellcat's desire to follow them everywhere. He returned his attention back to Bridget, noticing how much the lady she appeared in her blue dress, make-up and stylized hair. If the Angel and Jeanie had not been in the room, Bridget's clothing would not have remained on her for long.

"I hadn't gotten to that part yet," sighed the Noble. "We do have to tell her about the spices, how they are being transported and that England isn't the only country being affected, but we also have to tell them about the existence of Vampires."

"That's the hardest one that even I find difficult to believe." Bridget rose gracefully and glided to the door to her bedroom, opened it, muttered a thank you and closed it, holding the finished shirt for the Angel. "If you hadn't agreed to open our bond again, Fernando, allowing us to share as a Chooser and Chosen should, I wouldn't believe your story, even with Miss Stuart as proof." She offered the white material to the girl before returning to her seat by the dressing mirror. "The whole concept that there are other immortals out there that drink blood, yet are well defined in mortal literature as Vampires is unbelievable. The Chosen had always believed themselves to be named so by mortals, only that their facts were mostly skewed. How are you going to make Katherine believe that there are Vampires, and that they are not just Chosen choosing to use that mortal term? Neither you nor the Angel can link to her and pass on your memories as you did with me."

Silence plunged into the room, leaving only the sound of the licking flames in the hearth and Jeanie's steady brushing of the Angel's hair to fill the void.

Closing his eyes against the luxuriant feeling of having his hair brushed, the Angel knew the answer. Jeanie's knowledge from reading the penny presses and Violet's admissions during his torture gave him the ammunition he needed to gain Notus back and set the Chosen into a war of survival. He sighed heavily and spoke quietly. "Katherine does not matter. It is the Chosen that matter and we need to have as many of them there as possible."

"What, to see you limp down the carpet?" sniped Fernando, sitting up straight.

He met the Noble's brown eyes. "If they must, yes." He heard Jeanie's gasp and watched Bridget turn to face him as if recognizing that he was actually in the room with them. "But I hope that is not what they will be focused upon."

"What do you have in mind?" Bridget stood up and went to stand next to Fernando, her small dainty hand coming to rest protectively on the Noble's shoulder.

Waving Jeanie's brushing away, he welcomed her help in clothing himself in the long elegant shirt. He winced as he twisted his back and pulled the stitching in his chest until the light cotton rested on his body, hiding the blackened wounds.

He pushed down his embarrassment as he watched Jeanie carefully clothe him. When his wounds were all concealed under the uncomfortable fabrics he attempted to stand beside the bed. His thigh pulsated with the promise of increased pain if used and his back twitched as if readying for a spasm, but he managed to stay standing.

Breathing back the pain, he met Fernando's glare and then Bridget's eyes, slowly pulling the full countenance of the Angel over him like comfortable armour. He watched Chooser and Chosen as their eyes went round at the transformation.

He stood, wounded and damaged, and wondered how long he could affect this glamour when it was the Angel that brought such destruction to his life. He made his face a mask of non-emotion despite the desire to grimace with the realization that the Angel was always an affectation to keep people away from him. It had horribly backfired and now he stood, feeling a fake behind the mask, and wondered who he truly was.

After a lengthy period of time, the Angel whispered darkly, "We declare war."

Bridget and Jeanie's gasp met with Fernando's beam of approval.

He wanted to lean against the light post outside the deserted theatre that served as the court for the Chosen of London, and thus all of Britain. Instead he remained erect beside it. The circle of gas light cascaded about him, Jeanie and the two other Chosen. They had arrived early. The cab they took had made good progress across the sleepy city. It had been a dreadful ride; one he knew would have been enjoyable had he not been jostled into pain at every bump or sway. It was as if the driver purposely rode over every pothole the road manifested just for this trip. The Angel suspected it was punishment for going uncloaked and therefore terrifying the old man with his appearance.

It was Bridget's first experience travelling with the Angel but her remonstration of the driver to accept his riders despite their appearances shocked him. No one in his long life had ever stepped up for him in this way and it made him re-evaluate Bridget's offer of friendship as possibly being sincere. It was a strange feeling because with her fury at the driver came a strong protective and caring feeling towards him.

Jeanie came over to stand beside him and slipped her warm hand into his. Her strong fingers curled up to grasp his and he wished he could return the gesture, but his own fingers could only twitch painfully at the attempt.

Fernando and Bridget stood quietly. The Noble tapped his walking stick against the top of his black leather shoe while Bridget leaned her head against his shoulder as if to rest a moment. The Angel watched the two Chosen so at ease and comfortable with one another and felt a pang of jealousy.

It felt oddly comforting to finally be fully accepted for who and what he was, yet it did not override the years of isolation and loneliness placed upon him by others throughout his very long life. A large part of him could not trust Bridget and Fernando's offers of friendship despite how he found himself desiring to be finally included. It itched his skin as if waiting the sun to appear, proving the rule of his life: that due to his differences he would always be feared and thus threatened.

Yet the sun did not appear. Jeanie still stood by him. And Fernando and Bridget were keeping his secrets. All this wiggled a wedge of doubt into the reasons Notus kept him apart from all others, mortals and Chosen alike, except for when it served Notus' desires. His breath puffed a white cloud before his face to finally dissipate into the frosty night air and he frowned.

The sense of nervous anticipation pulsating between the two other Chosen shifted its tone as they turned to face him. A question cocked Bridget's golden head at the same time Fernando stared haughtily.

"When was the last time you fed?" queried Bridget, her blue eyes penetrating him.

The question, coming out of the blue, stunned him and he blinked. White brows knitting together, he frowned trying to recall and then it came to him. It was the night they went to the warehouse that they arsoned. His mind tumbled at the realization that it had been nearly a month, the longest he had ever gone without needing sustenance. What was even more shocking was that he was not even hungry now. He quietly mentioned this, his words barely audible in the still night.

"That's no' true," interjected Jeanie, glancing up at him. "I fed ye as best I could while ye were unconscious at the monastery."

His frown deepened and he shook his head. He did not remember.

"I saw what you fed the Angel and a couple of spoonfuls once or twice a night is hardly enough to stave off starvation," stated the Noble, plainly. His walking stick dug into the crack between the cobbles as if trying to dig up the truth.

It was evidence of more changes, but the Angel tried not to think about what this one might mean. The silence that filled the night was broken by the steady pace of a man walking down the road towards them.

Saved by the distraction, he watched the Chosen he assumed was Maurice slowly progress. Skittering fear and awe flowed from the newcomer. This time the Angel did not lower his eyes from the other. Maurice glanced quickly away, his fear pulsating. It was clear that Maurice was terrified, not only of what he was about to do, but with whom he was meeting. The Angel sighed with the realization that some things never change.

Fernando stepped forward, his hand extended in greeting. "Thank you, Maurice, for meeting us tonight." Their hands clasped momentarily; bronze flesh against pale.

Maurice was the first to pull out of the embrace. "If I hadn't done what you asked, I would be on a nice long cruise to the Americas eating rats and wondering what Indians would taste like." His awkward smile showed his discomfort despite his poor attempt at a joke. Maurice gazed up at the Angel. "So that's him, eh?"

It was the same thing over again. He was not seen as a person, but an object of speculation. He found anger instead of the usual resolute sadness. His jaw clenched tight and his gaze bore into Maurice's grey green eyes until the Chosen became uncomfortable and shifted his attention to the girl at the Angel's side.

"A mortal?" Maurice turned his flabbergasted attention onto the Noble. "You brought a mortal? Do you know what Katherine will do if she finds out that a mortal knows where our meeting place lies? Are you crazy?"

"Calm down, Maurice," placated Bridget, her hands raised up in supplication.

"Calm down. Calm down!" Maurice's panicked voice rose. "You're telling me to calm down!"

"Shush," extended Bridget. She glanced over to Fernando, completely at a loss of what to do.

"The hell I won't," shouted Maurice, ignoring the two door guards at the theatre turn their attention towards them. "I should have taken that ship to the Americas! She's killing Vampires who won't do what she wants them to do!"

The sound of a gloved hand slapping flesh punctuated the night. Bridget shook her hand and glared at Maurice. "Shut up. Get in there and do what Fernando told you to do."

Snapped out of his panic, his eyes wide with shock, Maurice held a hand to his stinging cheek. A sneer of anger transformed his pudgy face. Before he could even issue a threat in return Fernando stepped closer, his hands gripped tightly at either end of his walking stick.

Realizing that there in to Katherine's court was about to bail, the Angel hardened his voice. He did not want to step closer as he knew Maurice would notice his obvious limp.

"Stop this." His voice rolled into the night with an implied threat. He felt Jeanie's hand tighten on his and he directed his attention to Maurice. How he hated the look the other Chosen gave him, but he pressed forward. "You say Katherine's killing Va-Vampires," he suppressed a shudder at saying the word and hoped Maurice and the other did not notice. "We're here to inform the Chosen what is going on so that her killings will cease."

Maurice snorted a laugh. "What? You're vying to become Master? After all these centuries?"

The statement stunned him. He knew what they needed to do, but never considered the implications. Both Fernando and Bridget turned to stare at him as if having never expected this possibility. He could feel their dread at what the keeping of his secret could cost them if he became Master and he shook his head. "No. The Angel—I—am unsuitable for such a task."

Relief washed over him from his friends. It seemed that even in their acceptance of his secrecy there was still one aspect that would place them at odds with their friendship and that was if he was placed in a position of authority over them in the hierarchy of the Chosen. It was clear that even to Fernando and Bridget he would never be deemed equal due to his differences.

The surprise that flitted from Maurice was even more unnerving. Eyeing him suspiciously, Maurice shook his head in disbelief and turned his attention back to Fernando. "I'll go, but you and the Angel better show up before Katherine decides to do away with me too."

Maurice turned on his heel and walked up the theatre's steps and into its dark confines.

With Maurice's presence gone, the Angel breathed out in a huff and slumped his aching shoulders. The ever pressing emotions of the other Chosen was wearing on him and he wondered if he could manage the influx he was due to receive upon joining Maurice in front of Katherine.

"Are ye sure ye hae t'do this?" Jeanie's soft voice flitted in the breeze as she gazed up at him. "Maurice said Katherine's killing Vampires. Maybe she's found out the truth about them."

He slid his gaze from her pale drawn face to the moistened cobbles and shook his head. He could feel curiosity and compassion from Bridget mixing with Fernando's annoyance as they stared at him in expectation. "That's not possible."

"It could be," extemporized Bridget. "If that's the case then you don't have to go in."

Bridget's concern flowed over him, surprising him. Except for Notus, he had never met another Chosen who seemed so genuinely concerned about him, and he gazed upon Bridget in a new light. He wondered why she ever Chose Fernando in the first place.

He pulled his attention back to her words, recognizing that he was responding not to what she was saying but to what she was feeling. It was becoming distracting again and he wished he could learn to shut off this new found ability. "I have to go in to bring Notus out."

"Fernando and I can do that," offered Bridget.

If Bridget's concerned had surprised him, her offer stunned him. "I-I can't let you do that."

"Why no?" Jeanie's pleading eyes bore into his.

"Because he's the one who Katherine is truly scared of," stated Fernando, tapping the cobble by the side of his foot. "I was there when you walked down the aisle that first time we met at the theatre. I saw her face before she gained control of herself. I wouldn't be surprised if the Angel here is the only one Katherine *is* afraid of and fear can be a great motivator."

Biting his tongue, the Angel knew that was not the real reason he needed to go and save Notus. It was because he knew her secret. The idea of sharing this information with the others was necessary. He did not want to, because with it came the memories of how he gleaned this knowledge. His fear of those memories pushed back any fleeting impulse to divulge the secret. He would act on it, but that was because he was dealing with it now and not remembering the how.

Fernando turned to face the theatre. "I think it's about time."

Bridget fidgeted the fox fur wrap snugly around her shoulders and slipped her arm through the Noble's. "Shall we?" her voice hinting at the nervousness they all shared.

The Angel nodded and took a faltering step before Jeanie's clasp brought him to a halt. Turning around, his breath caught. Despite the fall of the lamplight and all the tribulations she had suffered for him, she was still beautiful in her worry. "I'll be back soon. I promise." He tried to put confidence in his tones. What came out gave voice to her concerns.

"I'm afraid for ye." Jeanie's breath caught. "It feels as though I'll ne'er see ye again." Tears threatened to break from her liquid green eyes. "I could easily go in and bring ye out from Violet's a hundred fold, but somehow this is different. I dinna ken what I would do if ye dinna come back to me."

He took his hand from hers and lifted his impotent hand to brush against her soft face, wishing he could do more. "I am coming back, Jeanie. I was stupid to stay away from you as long as I did. I will never make that mistake again. You are my heart, *cariad*."

He could not hold himself back any longer. Her warm lips were soft and yielding against his and he lingered, savouring her taste.

Too soon he stood straight, the bending had sent a shock of pain up his back and he gazed down at the only woman he had truly given himself completely to. "Stay here. I will be back with Notus and then the three of us can talk."

Jeanie nodded, her lips slightly parted. "I love ye, Gwyn."

His lips twitched into a soft smile, imbibing in her visual presence before turning his back.

Painfully, he followed the Noble and his Chooser to the base of the steps to the theatre. Once there, he realized that they had witnessed the whole exchange.

"Aww, wasn't that just sweet," simpered Fernando.

"Shut up, Fernando." Bridget whacked the Noble across the head.

"Ow. What did you do that for?" Fernando massaged the back of his head.

"If I have to tell you…" Bridget let out a huff and rolled her eyes to the dark clouded heavens. "Men," she groaned, detaching herself from her Chosen and alighted up the steps.

Fernando shot the Angel a dark look as if it were his fault and shook his head. "Katherine can't be worse than Bridget," mumbled the Noble as he followed up and into the building.

Worse, thought the Angel as he stood at the base of the stairs. Turning to glance once more at Jeanie, he was returned with a apprehensive smile.

He wanted to return a more genuine one, but found he could not muster even the semblance of a smile. Lowering his eyes, he hobbled up the stairs, taking them one at a time.

xliii

He stood by the entrance to the inner sanctum, listening to the heated conversation between the Mistress of London and Maurice. Maurice seemed to lose heart with every verbal stab of the Mistress' tongue. The humiliation and fear that rolled off Maurice made the Angel feel almost sorry for the cowardly Chosen. It was the feelings of embarrassment, annoyance and plain disgust from all the other Chosen in the hall that kept the Angel from emotionally siding against Maurice. He scowled at the thought that other Chosen's emotional states were affecting his, distracting him yet again from what he needed to do—to listen.

Fernando and Bridget stood off to one side of the doors in expectation for the indication that they should enter. Their own disgruntled natures mingled with the rest of the Chosen as they too listened in, waiting for the cue to throw open the doors and walk down the aisle. The tense minutes crept by, Katherine's voice rose in annoyance as Maurice's became mousy. It was shameful to hear a Chosen acting in such a manner.

"Fine," the Mistress all but yelled. "You say you have evidence to present as to who is killing off the Chosen after I only sent you out three nights ago, then present it. I seriously doubt that what you have to show us will yield anything. After all, those who I have sent out have not yet returned, and there have been many."

This was what they were waiting for, but Katherine's words made the Angel wonder how many other Chosen she had sent out to be tortured and killed. He felt a hand on his arm and he gazed down at Bridget. Fernando nodded. It was time.

Allowing the Noble to open the double oak doors, the Angel stepped out of the way, wincing with the movement, to stand on Fernando's left while Bridget stood on her Chosen's right. Slowly, they walked down the red-carpeted isle that led to the Mistress sitting in her ornate throne on the stage. The stunned expression on her pale heart shaped face gradually metamorphosed into one of fear born fury.

It was clear that she had not expected the Angel or the Noble to appear before her ever again and she closed her mouth with an audible click. Maurice's glib smile was triumphant. He nodded a bow towards the newcomers and backed up towards the sides of the auditorium to join the other Chosen. Some now stood in shock, their seats forgotten, while others sat transfixed upon the show that was about to present itself.

A cocktail of emotions exploded into the room nearly causing the Angel to stumble. It was so incredibly hard to keep their feelings down to a dull roar. The sound of his pounding headache was enough of a barrier to push the feelings back so he could catch himself before his leg could give out.

It was painful to be around so many Chosen, but one thing was certain the Vampires outnumbered the Chosen present. It was the only logical assumption he could come up with for those 'Chosen' he could not feel. In fact, they appeared to be illusionary because he could not sense their emotional presence. His jaw tightened in an effort to control his own rising panic. The odds of them surviving this confrontation were against them.

They made it to the front and the Angel was grateful for Bridget and Fernando's slow pace. It made his efforts to hide his limp easier. It was further evidence that they were going to keep his secret.

Coming full circle to stand before Katherine, he stood with a Chosen he could now contemplate as a friend. Notus' limp form still hanging on the t-bar behind her, the Angel shifted his stance to a less painful one. He met Katherine's eyes before she darted them around the room as if seeking someone. Not finding who she was looking for, her gaze landed not on him, but rather, the Noble. It was to him that she addressed herself.

"I find this quite a surprise, de Sagres." Her purr trembled. Catching herself, she cleared her throat and continued. "Maurice did not say anything about you and I was under the impression that you and the Angel had fled to the continent."

Fernando bristled, but it was Bridget who replied. "The Noble Fernando de Sagres, last Heir to the Fidalgo de Sagres and the Angel did not flee, my Lady, but left to follow a lead. As you can see they have come back."

The Mistress sniffed a suppressed laugh, her graceful hand waved dismissingly. "Oh Bridget, you have always been good with words. It is such a shame that you are a whore. You could have made a delicious lawyer."

A trickle of laughter sped between the walls only to be quickly quenched.

"I think I shall take that as a compliment, my Lady," replied Bridget with a graceful incline of her head, her blue eyes never leaving the Mistress.

Lazily, as if to cover up her discomfort, Katherine leaned back in her throne and crossed her supple legs. The black of her hair seemed to disappear against the dark of the wood. "So tell me what you have found out. I will then decide if it is enough to give you what I promised."

"And do you recall what you promised?" demanded Fernando. He ground his walking stick into the plush carpeting.

Katherine laughed haughtily. "I am the Mistress of London. I rule the Vampires of the British Isles. I know what I promise and I know what I will deliver. Present your findings."

Repressing the disgust at her words, the Angel took a quiet breath in and let it out in an effort to stave off his own growing anxiety of what he was about to do. It was his turn and even Bridget and Fernando's expectation of what was to be disclosed swelled the wave of the Chosens anticipation. Turning his back on Katherine, he addressed those attending the gathering. He knew without looking, which ones were Chosen and it was to these he let his gaze fall. He had never stood before the Chosen and spoken so openly. It went against centuries of experience and his nature to keep isolated. He steeled his voice and pitched it to carry.

"The Noble Fernando de Sagres and I have followed the signs left by our predecessors of this fools quest. It has taken us to the bowels of a free kitchen here in London—"

"Don't address them," yelled Katherine, clearly unnerved by the Angel's dismissal of her. "Address me. I am Mistress."

The Angel halted his testimony to glance momentarily back at Katherine. His hard, threatening gaze silenced her as she sat back. Was she trembling?

He returned his attention back to those that mattered. "What we found there shocked us. Four herbs, mixed together, create a spice that is being placed into mortals' food. The spice itself is disgusting to our sense of smell, but titillates those of mortals. It accentuates the flavours of their food while at the same time it locks their energies into their blood and body. To us, it is like drinking from the dead."

Gasps of horror flitted through the room, mingled with a flurry of questions. The bombardment of their fear and their need to know swept away their words as he closed his eyes against the impact of their emotions. Gradually it subsided enough to let one Chosen speak up.

"Who is doing this to us?" asked a dirty blonde haired woman, her hazel eyes filled with wonder and fear.

"You get ahead of the story, Georgina," replied the Noble. "Let the Angel finish."

"Your pardon, sir." Georgina bowed her head solemnly.

Clear to continue, the Angel took his cue from Fernando's nod of encouragement. It was still strange to see that on the Noble, but then again it was he, not Fernando who was sticking his neck out at this moment.

"Taking the shipping information from the barrelled herbs, Fernando was the one who discovered where they were coming from and who was sending them."

The Mistress gasped. "That shouldn't have been possible."

Her barely whispered words tickled the Angel's ears and he chose to ignore the strange statement. "We went to Calais, found the shipping house and managed to glean the information of who was actually in charge of the whole operation." The nervous whispers, especially from the Vampires grew, forcing him to pitch his voice louder. "We went to *Le Jardin*, a mansion near Balinghem, and discovered the persons responsible." The cacophony of emotion and words threatened to knock him to his knees. Closing his eyes, he took a deep breath and felt Bridget's soothing hand on his arm. He opened his eyes to see panic and chaos threatening to break loose. Carefully, his chose his next words. "They did not live to see the dawn."

"How dare you," spluttered Katherine, her beautiful face twisted in rage.

"Who was it?" called out one Chosen.

"Tell us," demanded another.

"Shut up! Shut up!" bellowed a Vampire. "He's telling lies."

"The Angel does not lie," roared Fernando.

A quivering silence slammed into the room. The threat of violence was close.

He scanned the room. No one was seated now, not even Katherine. It was time to disclose the truth and let loose a war that was in the making for a long time.

"Those whose purpose is to eradicate the Chosen are Vampires."

Shocked laughter mixed with disgust murmured off the stone walls. It was Katherine's mirth that rang the loudest. "Vampires? Vampires you say? We're all Vampires here."

It was the opening he expected. Swivelling on his good leg, he positioned himself to face Katherine. "No, we are not. The Chosen have been led to believe we are Vampires by Vampires in an effort to lead us into complacency. It is easy to affect genocide on a race of beings when they are unaware of an enemy who are set out to destroy them from the inside out. Subvert them, confound them, warp them with your cruel definitions and then destroy them. Take out the strongest one by one in a way that conceals the greater purpose: to destroy the Chosen so that the Vampires will rule, as they have ruled over the Chosen with our permission."

"That's...that's preposterous," came Katherine's weak reply.

"Is it, Bastia?" hissed the Angel and enjoyed watching her eyes widen.

"What did you call me?" Katherine could not hide her shock.

"Bastia. It is your real name. Your little Flower told me much before she died." He did not lie, but rather grossly truncated the truth to let the Vampiress believe the opposite had actually occurred.

"Holy shit," exclaimed Fernando. Comprehension blossomed on his face. The Angel had carefully edited the words, but the Noble knew enough of what happened to fill in the spaces. Violet had divulged everything to the Angel in the belief he would never be released from his torture. Fernando wondered what else the Angel had suffered at her hands to glean this information.

Bridget's widened eyes flitted between her Chosen and the Angel, wishing for someone to fill her in.

The Angel refused to look at his friends. The wash of stunned sympathy from the Noble took him off guard. He directed his words to the Chosen in the theatre without releasing his gaze off of Bastia, the Vampire who styled herself Mistress of the Chosen of London. "Katherine is an alias, isn't it, Bastia? A Vampire, you forcibly took over the Mastership of Britain from a good Chosen who was tired of being Master. It was the first step in your plan for genocide."

"B-but the Chosen are Vampires," stammered Maurice.

"Never say that," snarled the Angel. He was shocked at his own vehemence and endeavoured to soften his tones. Even though his answer was to Maurice, his words were for Bastia/Katherine. "The Chosen are not the same as Vampires. We are as different from them as humans are to apes."

It was the final straw snapping Bastia's resolve into blind fury. Screaming her rage at being discovered and thwarted, she all but flew herself at the Angel—the one who should have died in Violet's clutches regardless of what Thanatos wanted. With nothing left but to deal with the exposure, she would be the one to finish what Violet had failed to do. Her actions sprung her Vampires into open battle against the stunned Chosen. No longer behind the veil of deception, the Vampires were now at open war with the Chosen and she would be victorious.

It was the last thing he expected as violence slammed into him the same instant that Bastia flew at him. He had a moment to register the pure hatred maligning her beauty before she was on him, falling upon him with a force that was too much for his slowly healing leg. Collapsing under her slight weight lights popped in his vision as he landed agonizingly on his back. He could hear her screams of frustration swirling in the midst of the battle beyond.

It was a surprise when the long dagger flourished in her hand. Panic riveted him. He did not know how much more the effects of an iron weapon would create in him this time, but the idea of discovering it the hard way made him bring up his arm in an attempt to block the descending blade over and over as he strove with this other arm to find something to end this fight. Each time he felt his flesh part to the cauterizing blade, the greater the difficulty it was to keep the black spots from joining in his vision.

The more he deflected her feeble attempts the greater her fury. He needed to get her off of him. He needed to get off his back, but his body did not seem to respond. Centuries of training and practice fell to nothing as he felt his back begin to tighten in prelude to another seizure. He knew if that happened she would kill him.

The sound of Bastia's throne shattering beside them was barely enough time for him to cover his face from the flying bits of wood. It was a moment's reprieve as Bastia had done the same, but she quickly brought her attention back to the task of destroying the Angel. His forearm cut into ribbons, his left hand found what he hoped would work, if the stories about Vampires were true.

Fear and the desperate need to end this fight made his fingers work. Grasping the shattered leg of what was once a beautiful piece of woodworking, he lifted it, turned the pointed end towards Bastia and drove it deep into her heart as she raised her arm in attempt to decapitate him.

Shock was the first expression that widened her eyes as she gazed down at the long piece of oak sticking into her chest. The knife dropped to the ground beside him an instant before her body slid from his, convulsing in its death throes. It was what Jeanie had told him about Vampires. It was enough to kill the Mistress of London.

Groaning in agony, he managed to push her off and roll over onto his knees. He tried to support himself on his hands but they were now useless, so he rested on his aching and burning forearms as he tried to catch his breath. The sounds of battle seemed distant but he could feel the Chosen's rising concerns that the Vampires were winning.

Crawling a little ways away from Bastia's decaying body, he rested his forehead against the plush carpeting in the hopes that the room would cease to spin. There was no choice if the Chosen were to win. He worded the ancient spell of summoning.

The mist rose steadily from the ground, unnoticed by those who still fought. When it was of a height with him he could see the thickening of the vapours until one of the demons flowed towards him.

What is your bidding, Sire? Its words throbbed through his head. Its desires were as obvious as its gruesomeness.

Without a thought the words came to him in the ancient language Auntie taught him when he was a boy. It was the same language They and the Ladies used. "Take the Vampires. Do not touch or harm the Chosen."

As you so order, Sire, so shall it be done. It flowed back into the rising fog.

Surprise and panic gave way as Chosen and Vampire realized what was ascending from the floor. Fernando swore, immediately recognizing the threat, and grabbed Bridget, hugging her in an effort to seem small against the rising demons. Soon the whole theatre swirled with the thick white mist and what it held in its vapours.

Mayhem commenced.

Screams and shrieks of terror seemed far off through the mists. Those Vampires who managed to move seemed to stomp heavily in an effort to flee only to have their cries and footpads cut off. The sounds continued on for an insufferable amount of time as the swirling mists and its denizens continued to follow the orders of the Angel. When the last cry was uttered, the mists dissipated.

Breathing heavily as if he had run for miles as a mortal, the Angel watched the dark spots in his field of vision connect until all was blackness.

"Get up." The words and the sense of urgency pounded between his ears, yanking him from the grove and the delicious spring water it held.

"Dammit Gwyn, get up!"

The use of the name shocked him awake with a gasp and he realized he lay face down on the red carpet. He was so incredibly tired that all he wanted to do was lie there, close his eyes and slip back to the sacred grove.

"Come on. Get up."

Rough hands grabbed at him, hauling him bodily to his feet. Swaying, he blinked down at Fernando's dishevelled form. It was obvious that the Noble had taken a few cuts from some of the rips and slashes in his once expensive tuxedo. Bridget was beside him. Her long golden hair no longer sported the perfect style but rather gave testimony to the brawling and cat fighting she had done. Gone was her fox fur wrap and one of the shoulders of her dress was ripped. Beside the damage done to their clothing they appeared perfectly healthy. He doubted the same could be said for himself.

"We managed to get Notus down, but he's not waking," said Bridget. Her eyes flickered over to where the old Chosen lay on the stage, surrounded by a handful of Chosen in equal physical disarray.

His heart lurched at the sight and he carefully hobbled to the stairs leading up to his Chooser. He accepted Bridget's strong support as he winced with every step despite the fact that the surviving Chosen stared openly at him. It was clear that the questions of what the Angel truly was would spin around, spawning dangerous speculation. He wondered how many saw the blackened and bleeding knife wounds along his forearm.

Once on the stage, he was better able to survey the damage to the Chosen and the Vampires. Only a few decapitated bodies lay on the floor. They belonged to the Chosen. Nothing remained of the Vampires taken by the mists.

In the middle of the red carpet the Vampire Mistress of the London lay sprawled and shrivelled with a large piece of wood sticking up out of her chest. He scowled at the corpse and shook his head at the incalculable damage she and her kind had wrought upon the Chosen. Turning his face from the scene, he brought his attention to Notus' unconscious form.

Sallow skin hung loosely from Notus' slack face, making his salt and pepper hair even more stark. It was apparent to all that he had been nearly drained, but it did not explain his torpid state. Standing over his Chooser's supine form, the Angel's breath caught and he gritted back tears. He knew what needed to be done but he did not know how much he could give.

He had never fed Notus since the night of his making. It had always been the other way around, Notus offering himself for his Chosen to nurse at his wrist when the iron wounds made it impossible for the Angel to hunt. Now he had to return the intimacy but he did not know if he could. Not when the memory of Violet's teeth penetrating his flesh was so new.

"So it's true," stated a Chosen, matter-of-factly. The man swept back unruly blonde locks as he stood by Bastia's dried up corpse, gazing in disgust. "Vampires are real and they've—she—duped us into believing it was just a word attributed to the Chosen. What idiots we are!"

"We've grown too complacent, Jonathan," replied Georgina, pulling at the rip in her bodice to cover her naked breast. "We've let ourselves accept whatever has been thrown to us, especially those things that stroked our sense of self importance. Katherine did that and we allowed it."

"Yes, we did," added Maurice who had leapt down from the stage to scowl at the body. He turned to face the Angel. "And now that the Angel killed Katherine are we allowing yet another pretender to rule over us as Master?"

Many of the Chosen gasped at the statement. To the Angel, he had prayed it would never come to this and his mouth turned to dust as he tried to swallow. Here he stood, albeit supported, before the remaining Chosen of the council for the British Chosen. It was a position he never wanted to find himself in, in any court.

Wild speculation and accusations flew not only at him but also at each other. The Chosen debated what had actually transpired in the last half hour and what was the Angel's significance in it. Bridget and Fernando watched dumbfounded at the vehemence in many of the Chosen. It had been the Angel that had saved them from the Vampires. Could they not see that? But they did not.

The volley of words rose until a dark haired Chosen yelled, "I still smell blood."

Several nervously chuckled at the statement. "Of course you do, Maurice," placated Jonathan. He pulled his ripped suit jacket to settle properly across his shoulders. At the sound of the tear increasing he shrugged it off and threw it to the ground. "This place is littered with Chosen and Vampire blood."

"That's not what I meant," sneered Maurice. "I still smell blood, it's burnt, and it's coming from the Angel."

Wary curiosity, fear and anger swarmed the Angel, but it was the concern from Bridget and Fernando's audacity that floored him. He could not deny the blood dripping from the slices into his forearm. He could not deny the cautery the iron blade had done. His shirt was ripped for all to see the wounds that marked him different. Bridget's arm steadied him as the realization struck.

"We've all wondered who and what the Angel is." Maurice struck a pose as if he were a politician in the House of Commons giving a speech to the Throne. "According to our ancient laws handed down to us by the Elders and their Elders, the Angel is now Master. We have a right to know if he truly is Chosen."

The one-two punch stole the Angel's breath and all he wanted to do was sit down, tend to Notus and leave. He was too ensnared in his own sloppy machinations to retreat. He opened his mouth to reply, but surprisingly Fernando stepped forward.

"The Angel is Chosen," stated the Noble, briskly, his ire up. He quickly glanced at the Angel and then addressed Maurice and the others. "I have spent more time with the Angel than any other person here save his Chooser. In that time I learned much about the Angel."

The Angel winced at what he knew was coming. Fernando was going to divulge everything. He knew he should never have trusted the Noble.

"Shhhh," whispered Bridget, a slight smile on her smudged lips. "It's going to be alright."

Fernando turned to glare at his Chooser and the Angel, "Do you mind?" He returned his attention to the Chosen. "What I have learned is that the Angel is what he is—The Angel."

"That doesn't explain that demon filled fog," snapped Maurice. "Where did that come from? Why did it only go after the Vampires? Who controlled it?"

"You're right, it doesn't explain it," stated Fernando matter-of-factly. "But a Chosen has a right to privacy or do you want to explain why you fuck little boys in your basement."

Maurice's face paled and then reddened with indignant rage. Turning on his heel, he strode out of the theatre, the door ringing closed with his wake.

"Shouldn't someone stop him?" suggested a pretty blonde Chosen.

"Why?" offered Fernando. "Maurice is a coward. He shouldn't ever have been given the Choice. He'll be on the first ship to the Americas in an effort to get as far away from the truth as possible."

"So the Angel is now Master," queried Georgina, her eyes narrowing to find a reason why he should not be Master.

This was not what he wanted and he shook his head in denial. He had told Bridget and Fernando that he would not take up the mantle. It was not for him.

"It seems so," scowled the Noble as he backed up from the edge of the stage. He had done as much as he was willing to do to for the Angel. Regardless of what others may think of him, Fernando kept his word.

It did not feel right, but an idea blossomed to mind. If they believed him to be the new Master then they would accept his first and only decree as Master of London. It was the only way out of the tangle he found himself.

"No," he whispered, shifting his position to face the Noble. "I was never raised to rule anything or anybody." Silence fell upon the auditorium as every Chosen turned to face him. Expectant curiosity flowed. Even Bridget, who still supported him, gazed up at him surprised at his response. He caught Fernando's shocked eyes with his own. "It should be someone who was raised to rule others. One who was trained from birth even though denied it into adulthood." He winced as he placed his hand on the Noble's shoulder. "Fernando, last Fidalgo de Sagres, and Lady Bridget of Brittany–" Bridget gasped. He inclined his head to whisper; "I recognized your accent when you spoke French." He continued his address to the Chosen. "—You are now Master and Mistress of London, monarchs of the Chosen of Britain."

A silent concussion rocked the room, causing the glass around the gas lamps and the sconces to twitch. Several Chosen stumbled before catching themselves to stare wide eyed while others fell to the floor with the impact. When all had resumed their upright positions a wash of relief and happy acceptance flowed from them. Several even smiled while others nodded appreciatively. What they all could not account for was the strange occurrences attributed to the Angel, but the general sentiment was that they were happy he was not Master.

Tentatively, Jonathan cleared his voice. "There is still the matter of the Angel, my Lord and Lady. The Chosen have experienced too many odd happenings, from the demon filled mists to finally this strange explosion we all felt at the Angel's proclamation. You infer that the Angel is Chosen yet there he stands, requiring support, with wounds on his arm that will not close."

The Angel stared at the new Master of London, knowing he had put his life in the Noble's hands. Would Fernando honour his promise even now?

The sudden flush of power Fernando had received with the Angel's pronouncement made him smile and he glanced at Bridget before meeting the worried crimson eyes. Cocking his head, appreciating the irony of the circumstances, the Noble turned to face the other Chosen.

The Angel had given him something he had refused to ever dream about, always believing himself a disinherited foreigner. Even after stripping the Angel of his secrets the Angel gave without asking for anything in return. Fernando now understood the difference between the Angel and his Chooser and the rest of the Chosen. Bridget was right. Given the powers the Angel possessed, Fernando needed to make sure the Angel would stand with he and Bridget and never against them. There was no doubt in the Noble's mind that the Angel would make a formidable enemy.

He Sent his idea to Bridget and she affirmed the decision with a grin. He knew what the first order of their new reign needed to be and addressed the Chosen. "The Angel and his Chooser are under the protection of the Master and Mistress of London. Any who gainsay it may quit these lands immediately or have their lives forfeited."

The Master of London's declaration floored the Angel. It was not what he was expecting. The Noble was actually keeping his promise and then some. For the first time in his very long life he was safe from prosecution and the threat of Destruction was nullified, as long as their friendship, continued. It was such an alien state of mind that all he could do was stare dumbfounded.

It was Bridget's next words that stripped him from his stupefaction. "You are given permission to Choose whom you love, regardless of who may try and say otherwise. Now, heal your Chooser and go home. You have sacrificed much for the Chosen, not only here in Britain, but in the rest of the world. We will see to it that the word goes out."

With the new Mistress of London's help, the Angel sat down beside Notus' unconscious form. Painfully, he managed to support Notus' head in his lap and pushed up the tattered remains of his left sleeve with feeble fingers, exposing the blackened manacle wounds and the fresh gashes in his forearm. He could not use his wrist. It would have to be the inside of his elbow. Lowering his arm, he pressed his feverish skin against Notus' cold blue tinged lips.

"Drink," he whispered unable to keep the urgency from his voice. "Drink Notus. It's me. Your son."

The corpse like mouth opened and he felt stinging as needle sharp teeth pierced his flesh. He wanted to immediately pull away as he felt the power of Notus' suckle on his arm, imbibing with each pounding of his heart.

Images flashed to mind. He could see Notus' fight against those Vampires that had brought him here against his will. He could feel the monk's stunned defeat. Blurred images and sensations flowed into him of Notus' exsanguinations by the Vampires and then the binding of him to the t-bar.

The visions of Notus' torture evoked his own by Violet, sending him reeling. He yanked his arm away, feeling Notus' teeth rip his flesh into a gaping wound that quickly closed, and he scrabbled away, ignoring the pain that shocked up his arms, leg and back with the movement. It was only a couple of feet away from his Chooser that he halted, eyes closed and gasping, his whole body shaking from the memory.

Bridget's quiet voice stirred out of his panic as she knelt beside him. "It's okay. Everything is all right. You're here, not there. You need to get control. You're projecting your emotions and it's scaring everybody."

He managed to return to the here and now, but it was Notus' voice that widened his eyes.

Stretching with a yawn, Notus stood with the help of the Master of London. "What an odd dream." The monk turned to face the Chosen around him, his face going slack with the memory of where and why he was there. "Oh." Slowly his eyes comprehended what he saw decaying on the carpet and then widened in apprehension.

"Where's my son!" he demanded.

"Here, Notus," answered Bridget from the Angel's side. "He's here."

Notus whirled around to see his boy on the stage floor next to the woman who had spoken. Panic set into him but was quickly quenched at the smile on her face and his son's look of utter relief. The monk took a couple of tottering steps towards them.

It was so good to see his Chooser awake and moving. He wanted to smile and get up, and was about to when Notus knelt down. The sallowness was replaced by a faint pinkish glow, but he could still see that the monk needed more.

"You look a little worse for wear, my son," smiled Notus, his brown eyes twinkling.

Usually such a statement would have caused him great consternation, but he had learned some things from being with Jeanie and Fernando. "I could say the same for you, old man."

He met his Chooser's stunned expression with a slight smile and was rewarded with a boisterous laugh before being caught up in a fierce bear hug. Enduring the crushing pain, he closed his eyes, breathing deep of his Choosers scent and he knew that everything was going to be all right. He hugged Notus back, enjoying their first embrace, ever.

Pulling away, Notus brushed back tears with his hands. "I was so worried about you."

The statement shocked a laugh out of him. "You worried about me?"

Notus had the wherewithal to look abashed. "Well, after I closed you off..."

"I understand," he replied, realizing that he truly did. He would have done the same if Notus had been around the time of his experiences with Violet. Reaching up, he touched Notus' face and gazed deep into brown eyes. The monk's eyes widened momentarily and then he sighed. *I truly do.*

Notus nodded with a knowing smile and rose to his feet. *Let's go home, my son. I'm famished. Then you can tell me everything.*

With Bridget's help the Angel managed to rise to his feet.

"Go," she gently ordered. "Fernando and I can manage."

Glancing at the Noble's perturbed expression, he turned back to the new Mistress. "Thank you," he whispered solemnly. "Thank you for everything."

"Didn't you hear your new Mistress of London?" barked the Noble. The gruffness belied the slight playful tone underneath if one had spent a month with the man. "Go home."

His lips quirking with a slight smile, the Angel bowed his head to his friend. "Yes, sir."

Limping down the stairs and up the centre isle with Notus' confusion washing over him, the Angel happily ignored the stunned expressions of the Chosen as he passed.

xlív

The cobbles clicked under her shoes as Jeanie paced back and forth beneath the light post. At first she went around in circles about the tall iron spire, but with the speed of her apprehension she found she became dizzy no matter which way she circled. Giving up, Jeanie decided to pace a straight line. Walk five steps, then turn. Walk five steps back; turn again, over and over until she lost count. The only comfort was the rhythm her steps created.

To say that she was nervous was an understatement. She understood the reasoning behind the Angel's desire to keep her out of the theatre. Jeanie did not have to be told the hard way. She learned her lessons, unfortunately, at the expense of the man she loved. It had been a surprise that he had even offered that she come and wait. She was not about to ask, but could tell he almost expected another confrontation about where she was allowed to go. It was a harsh realization that the Angel expected another fight on that issue. It seemed to be the only thing they ever fought about and it made her sad that they would ever raise their voices at each other. Quietly, she accepted his offer and did not demand more.

Click. Click. Click. Click. Click. Swivel.

Now she waited outside the same building, underneath the same light post as she did over a month ago, marvelling at all that she had learned and experienced in that time. It all seemed so surreal. The Angel was hers so totally that the offer he made still spun her mind. The fact that he, Fernando and others were immortal blood drinkers called the Chosen was incredible. What was even more frightening was that not only did the Chosen exist, but Vampires were real too, the evidence of both on her body.

Jeanie dropped the hand that had absently risen to brush against the scars of the bite marks that Violet had given her. It was another indication of the differences between the two sets of immortals. With the Angel, the marks were gone within hours and any bruising left behind was gone within the day. Not so with the Vampire's marks. They were slow to heal like any other wound.

What was completely unsettling was when the wound was touched, it sent shivers of desire for a Vampire to feed off of her. She never had that with the Angel and nor did she tell him what the effects where when he noticed the scars the first time.

Click. Click. Click. Click. Click. Swivel.

It had been hard enough seeing the devastation Violet had inflicted upon him. He would always bear the scars once he healed, but she wondered about the wounds that were not visible. Jeanie had witnessed the Angel in the throes of a nightmare before, yet it was nothing to what she had seen him go through afterwards. She could not count how many times she had awoken to hear him cry out, pleading for Violet to stop, his body shuddering as the memories convulsed through him. The only thing she could do was cradle his head and sing the Gaelic lullabies her mother had sung to her. Most often it had been enough. Other times she had to cry out for help to keep the seizure from causing the Angel more harm. What surprised her the most was Fernando's help when there was no other around, especially after the Angel's secrets were laid bare.

Click. Click. Click. Click. Click. Swivel. Stop.

Jeanie had expected the Noble to become more abusive towards the Angel, instead Fernando distanced himself and when they did come in contact he was often disgruntled or distracted. Gone was the superiority. Fernando was a man who was straining under the burden of his newfound knowledge. Jeanie just wished she knew what Fernando's decision would be.

Click. Click. Click. Click. Click. Swivel.

Jeanie returned to her pacing, desperately hoping that Fernando and Bridget would keep the Angel's secrets so that he could come back to her.

Before long, the constant pacing and worrying created scenarios in her mind, raising her anxiety and the rhythm of her pacing. She did not know how long she did this. She ignored passers-by who openly gawked at her distracted state and did not notice when the street became quiet except for her drumming feet.

Click. Click. Click. Click. Click. Swivel.

She continued, wondering what was happening inside and why it was taking so long until she saw a man she thought she recognized exit through what appeared to be a side entrance. He hesitated briefly before approaching her.

*　　　*　　　*

ANGEL OF DEATH

Corbie Vale had returned to London earlier than he expected. Business concluded successfully in Spain, he had returned to Calais to see what had become of the Angel and de Sagres under Violet's plans. He never could understand Violet's obsession with the Angel when he could barely stand in the Chosen's strange presence. There was something inherently wrong about the Angel that made Corbie's back crawl. Yet after the arson, Corbie had only wanted to see the Angel's head on a platter. Thankfully, many of the barrels of poison were already on his merchant ships.

Landing back in Calais, he had sent a letter to Violet that came back unopened, sparking Corbie's ire. His Little Flower was always petulant and wilful, irritatingly so, that there were many times that he wanted to pluck her petals to prove a point. That was what he had intended when he hired a horse and driver to take him to *Le Jardin*. What he found stunned him.

The place had been abandoned save only a starving new Vampiress. When confronted, the woman told the story of how the Mistress left with her remaining Vampires to retrieve her prized possessions and never came back.

Corbie had killed the weakling Vampire in disgust and waited at *Le Jardin* for several nights. When he could only conclude that Violet either left or was defeated by the escaped Chosen, Corbie hastened back to Bastia. She needed to know the failure of the Little Flower and what that could bode for their plans.

His hand on the backstage door, Corbie opened it and took the six steps up into the darkened theatre. He let the voices guide him to a concealed place behind stage right. Standing with his back to the curtain, he listened.

Bastia's voice was raised in annoyance as she lorded over the solitary Chosen. It was when she abruptly quieted at the sound of the audience doors opening that Corbie dared a glance. Incredulous to who walked down the carpet, Corbie could only dumbly watch the events unfold. Anger simmered at the growing realization that everything they had worked for was coming undone and all their plans were laid bare to the vile Chosen.

The Angel was alive and so was the Noble, but their scars from their run in with Violet showed plainly on both. How a Chosen could survive direct contact with the sun widened Corbie's eyes. A Vampire would completely and totally incinerate almost instantly.

Corbie watched in growing horror as the house of cards he and Bastia created began to teeter and start its accelerating collapse. What was the worst was now the Chosen of London knew about the existence of Vampires and that they had been thoroughly duped.

Bastia's disclosure as a Vampire was even more of a shock. The Angel and de Sagres had discovered everything!

Rage shook Corbie. Centuries of careful planning and preparation came to naught. Hiding in plain sight of the Chosen, Vampires had achieved many of their desired ends with these infernal pretenders. It was the Vampires who were supreme and their machinations to terminate the

Chosen in a nice quiet way had nearly been complete in Britain. Now it was over. The violence that erupted in the theatre was testimony to the blood baths that would now occur where Vampires lived in the same areas as the Chosen. There was no way that Corbie could think of containing this breach.

It was the sight of the fog rising out of nowhere that swept Corbie's fury into terror. It was when the Vampire saw the forms within fog that he turned, fleeing down the steps towards the stage exit.

Slamming the door closed behind, Corbie leaned against the black painted wood in an effort to regain what logic was left to him. He hated the cowardly way he fled as he saw the mists swirl around Bastia's corpse.

The Angel had won and it infuriated Corbie. Firing his own hatred of the creature, he knew that he had to recoup his losses and find a way to continue the destruction of the Chosen. Most of all, he desperately wanted the Angel to pay.

Pushing off the door, he saw someone standing beneath the light post. Corbie smiled wickedly at the plan suddenly evolving in his mind as he walked towards the girl.

The sight of the man Jeanie had seen when she had been held prisoner at the Kitchen dried her mouth to ashes. She did not need to ask him what he was, the scar on her neck, and strangely the small one on her wrist, tingled. Every instinct in her cried to run but she was riveted to the spot, her green eyes wide with the pounding of her heart between her ears.

"It's been a while, has it not?" purred Corbie, completely enjoying the girl's fear.

She was the Angel's paramour, if Violet had been correct. The girl was also the only mortal that Violet wanted to possess for herself, believing this tart to be a friend.

Vampires had no friends, even amongst their own kind. There were those they used and those they discarded. Corbie was sure that Violet's sentimentality about Jeanie had been the stake in his Little Flower's heart.

Jeanie tried to take a step backwards but found she could not move. This time there were no bars between them and she gasped as his hand snaked out, lightning fast, to grab her around the wrist. His pale fingers tickled the scar on her wrist, causing her breath to catch.

She did not know what was wrong with her. She should run, but she could not. A desire to bend to this Vampire's will surged past her fears.

Corbie's smile widened as the Vampire Effect took hold on the girl, but it did not include his eyes.

"We've not been formally introduced, Miss Stewart. I am Corbie Vale, Lord of Valraven and as you have already surmised, I am a Vampire."

He lifted her wrist to his mouth and rubbed it against his lips, teasing himself with the scent of her blood so easily accessible beneath her pale flesh.

"I gave you this when you fought so valiantly to save the Chosen Notus. I hid it of course, cutting the flesh after I had drunk your sweet nectar."

Ecstasy shot from Jeanie's wrist to her groin, making her legs weak. Her mind tried to make her body flee, but her flesh responded traitorously to the Vampire's touch. She did not want him, but her body's desires were not to be denied.

He pressed close, forcing her arm behind her back while his other hand whipped around to grasp her by the back of her neck, his fingers gently playing Violet's mark.

It was too much. Her mind stopped fighting and her legs gave way, all she wanted to do was to serve the master of her body.

Corbie grinned, exposing his extending incisors. It was said that revenge is a dish best served cold; tonight it would be as cold as the grave.

Jeanie could not have pushed the Vampire away even if she had wanted to.

Corbie held her and her body convulsed as he bit deep into her neck.

It took him a moment to take in what his eyes beheld as he stood outside the doors to the theatre. Notus stood beside him and wondered what had happened to their joyful reunion. His Chooser's query echoed mutely in his mind. It made no sense as to why Jeanie laid sprawled beneath the lamp-post, the yellow light a circle around her limp form. That was not how he had left her there. She had been full of life and promise, and was hopeful and expectant for his return. They had so much more to discuss. The taste of her lips last kiss on his burned.

His breath caught as comprehension slammed into his gut nearly bowling him over.

"Oh no." He whispered his denial despite the truth laid before him. "Oh Gods, please no."

"What is it?"

He ignored Notus' panicked query and descended down the steps towards Jeanie's supine form as fast as his preternatural abilities would allow, all pains forgotten except the new one blossoming in his chest. Collapsing to a halt beside her, he could only shake his head in denial of what he saw through his tears, his hands raised, afraid that touching her would instil reality.

Fiery cinnamon curls splayed about her head like a blossoming rose, but it was her deathly pallor and the silence of her heartbeat that told him the truth. It was not supposed to be like this. She had been safe. She had not followed him in. He had promised her, given her his Oath, his love, but it had not been enough.

A cry of utter despair tore through him as he picked up Jeanie's lifeless body and hugged her lolling head to his chest as he sat on the cobbles. The green spark of summer was gone from her eyes and he closed them with a trembling hand. This was not how they had planned. They were supposed to go back to their home together with Notus.

He sobbed over her, his tears dripping onto her cooling body.

"Oh my dear God." Notus' stood behind his weeping Chosen, shocked at seeing his housekeeper dead in the boy's arms and crossed himself. The words spilled out before he could recapture them. "What have you done?"

The implication of Notus' question snapped his head up to gaze at his Chooser and he knew the answer. He had done nothing. That was his crime. He had failed to protect the woman he had given himself so completely to. He could only shake his head and bring himself back to stare at Jeanie's flaccid face knowing he would never see her smile, never hear her voice nor feel her joined to him ever again. It was a loss he never expected to experience and he did not want to let her go even in death.

Brushing errant locks from her face, he saw the two puncture marks marring her perfect neck and he knew without a doubt that it was a Vampire that had killed her. A new groan escaped him. Whatever pains his body had suffered were nothing compared to this. Vampires had taken Jeanie from him. He had been so stupid believing she was safe outside. She should have come in with him. They knew what Jeanie was to him and one of them had killed her.

"My boy," said Notus, incredulously. "What is Jeanie doing here? Did you bring her into this?"

Burying his face into her hair, he could not bear the accusatory tones from his Chooser.

"She wanted to help," he said meekly, not looking up. He cradled Jeanie, rocking them both.

A wash of Notus' shock rolled over him and he bowed beneath it. He felt his Chooser kneel beside him. "Let go of her, my boy. She's gone. Let me take care of her."

He shook his head, denying the truth. Another sob tore through him and he felt strong hands on his arms pulling him away. He knew what Notus was doing. He had seen the Good Father do the same for countless others who had refused to give up their beloved dead.

"No," he bellowed, clinging harder to Jeanie's corpse. He could not let her go.

The hands fell again, more insistent than before. With it came determination and a hint of anger. *She's gone, my boy. Go home and let me take care of her. We'll talk after.*

In too much pain to resist, both physically and emotionally, he watched Notus take Jeanie's body from him as if it were happening in a dream. Jeanie's limp form dangled in his Choosers arms, appearing as though she was a sleeping child.

It was not a bed Notus would carry her to, but to a coffin in the morgue Notus dealt with for the others he cared for in this manner. To see the monk dealing with Jeanie in this same manner fractured his heart and he gasped.

Tears blurred the last visage of Jeanie's beautiful form as his Chooser disappeared into the night, leaving him so desperately alone.

xlv

Notus sat at his desk, quill in one hand, his face buried in the other, as black ink dropped its load onto the once clean piece of paper. It was the fourth such attempt to collect his thoughts and write them down. Each time amounted to another sheet crumpled into a tight ball with nothing more than a word or two followed by drips of ink. He was starting to consider breaking out the fancy fountain pen the boy had given him as a Christmas present three years ago, but doubted that would fix the problem.

Three nights since his release from Katherine's clutches had yielded nothing but silence and a growing apprehension that something was terribly wrong. He had been so incredibly glad to see the boy after being released from the t-bar that his hunger had been a second priority.

He dropped the quill onto the paper and rested his head in both hands.

Forty days had passed strung up and drained on that damned mockery of a cross. Forty nights of terror, not knowing if he would be allowed to live to see the next night. Nine hundred and sixty hours of separation between him and his Chosen, never knowing what would become of the boy.

It was not the torture of being hung up on the bar, but the fear of what would become of his son, that had first encapsulated every thought until he was forced to realize there was absolutely nothing he could do about it. He took the only way out; he went within, into deep contemplative prayer and meditation where nothing could touch him. He never knew if they drank from him after that first instance. If they had, he had no recollection of it.

Scrubbing his face with his hands, Notus sat up and pushed the paper away, uncaring that the ink on the nib would dry it to uselessness.

So much of what had happened still remained a mystery, even to the issue of Jeanie's involvement and her death. What struck Notus even more was the boy's reaction over the girl's corpse. He had never seen the boy react like that.

The chair squealed against the wood floor as he pushed away from the desk and stood up. He had too much nervous energy to sit and write, but he did not know what to do. Picking up the balled papers off the floor, he tossed them into the waste bin beside the desk and began to pace.

Notus could not believe Jeanie was dead. It made absolutely no sense to him as to how that could be possible. She had been the housekeeper. What was she doing there outside the theatre? The boy said she wanted to help, but that made no sense either.

The monk grimaced at the last time he saw her as he laid her down on the table of the funeral home he dealt with when those he helped to pass needed a proper burial. Notus would never let anyone be buried without some shred of dignity, even if they never had it in their life. In Jeanie's case, he owed it to her and left her there with the funeral director in his dressing gown, with instructions to provide the very best for her. The middle-aged man had nodded solemnly and accepted the I.O.U. on good faith.

Collapsing onto the couch, Notus realized he missed Jeanie's fiery nature and willingness to do what was asked of her. He had all but expected her to come over the first evening after his release. She had been such a good girl that it was like having a daughter in the home, one that was always willing to test out his culinary concoctions to see if they tasted palatable. Sometimes she would bring a recipe from Alice and they would have fun figuring it out together. It was almost as if she had more in common with him than the boy.

Notus groaned and leaned forward, bracing his elbows on his knees so that he could bury his face once more in his hands.

The boy.

He had not seen the lad since he had left him sitting under the lamp post. He knew the boy was home, he could feel his presence behind the closed door to his room, but whenever Notus attempted to communicate he was met with a solid wall. The times he tried to knock on the cracked door he felt such an over powering feeling to leave that Notus let his hand drop before his knuckles could rap twice. He did not remember seeing the door with a crack in it before.

Worry over the boy grew as the nights passed without nary a word or thought shared between them. Notus knew now that he should not have accused the boy of Jeanie's death, but having just been released to find his son in such a state and then the girl being murdered…it was too much to take in so soon. If only the lad would talk to him, to tell him what had happened in all the weeks he had been hung up on the t-bar. Maybe then he could make some sense of everything and find some meaning in the girl's death. There had been meaning in her life, there had to be such in her death.

Three nights and the boy had not come out, had not made contact in any way. There had been periods when the boy had shut himself off, probably unconsciously, in a effort to hide his strong emotions when they surfaced. It was one of the things that Notus had learned to accept rather than change in the boy. To let him have time alone when he needed it, whether he stated it or not, but somehow this was different. He had never seen such a strong display from his son as he did three nights ago. No, that was not correct, only once before, life times ago, with another girl.

"Ah, no," gasped the monk. Comprehension pounded him backwards against the couch. Could it be possible? He shook his head. The boy was always evading Jeanie whenever she came over for her chores and would leave as soon as it was polite or reasonable to do so. Confusion washed over the monk as he sat there with no other logical explanation.

A knock on the front door snapped his attention from his meanderings. The rapping came again.

Standing, Notus hesitantly walked to the door, listening for any possible malfeasance to occur again and realized how shaken his experience with the Mistress of London had left him. No physical mark remained on him, but he had discounted the emotional damage that had been done through his capture and suspension. Laying a hand on the door, he listened intently for any possible threat and jumped back when the knock came again.

"Come on," came the male voice.

"Shush, Fernando," replied a woman's voice Notus recognized. "Maybe they've gone out."

Fernando snorted. "Sure, then why can I hear breathing coming from the other side of this damned door?"

In the realization that the two on his doorstep were the Chosen from the theatre, Notus' eyes widened. Turning the lock, he opened the door and stood back.

Before him, a dark man wore a brown suit that seemed to accentuate the sun kissed colour of his skin. His almost black hair was slicked back into a tail and in his gloved hand was a simple yet stylish ebony walking stick. The woman, by contrast, wore her golden hair in a tight bun held by a navy blue hair net and a little chapeau studded with aquamarines within its net that matched the blueness of her eyes, while the modest dress and long coat matched the hat. Both appeared to be ready for an expensive evening on the town.

"Can I help you?" offered Notus, hesitantly.

The man Notus supposed was Fernando stepped past him and into the foyer followed by the woman, her hands in a mink muff.

"I thought that Jeanie would have been the one to answer the door," commented Fernando, glancing around the empty apartment.

The girl's name shocked Notus and he stood straighter. Closing the door to the outside world, he trapped himself with these two strangers. He watched the man take off his black leather gloves as he walked into the living room. The woman stayed where she was.

"Jeanie is your housekeeper, is she not?" Fernando turned to face Notus, an expression of pompous expectation tilting his head.

"Was," bristled Notus, instantly not liking this man.

It was the woman's delight that surprised him the most. "Oh that's wonderful! Then the Angel and she—" The lady cut off at the horrified expression on the monk's face. "What is it?"

"Jeanie's dead." He did not mean to have the words come out so abruptly and nor did he expect the impact of the hard truth to sting his eyes. Notus turned away, ignoring the others as he crossed the room to his desk, taking up the dried quill and cloth in a futile attempt to clean the nib.

He was surprised to hear the woman's gasp in concert with the man spluttering, "What?"

The click of the woman's shoes told Notus that she had moved further into his home. He ceased the rubbing motion along the quill tip and noticed that he had snapped the tip clean off the fine writing utensil. Frowning, he placed it and the cloth down on the desk.

"I guess we should have figured that something was wrong when the Angel did not send Jeanie for this," remarked the woman to Fernando. Pulling her hands out of the muff, she placed the furry tube under one arm, while she opened her coat and pulled out the Angel's sheathed sword. "Jeanie always made sure this came with him, even if he could not hold it."

The woman's words made no sense to Notus and he took the ancient blade from her dainty hand. He would not draw it. It was the boy's, given to him by his sister, previously owned by his father—a truth he would never relinquish.

He stood the sword beside his desk and lifted his gaze to the two Chosen. "What do you mean? Who are you?" He knew he sounded rude. It was completely unlike him. It was yet another indication that his trials in the Mistress' court had profoundly affected him.

Surprise lit up the woman's heart shape face, widening her blue eyes. "Oh dear, we have been rude, Fernando." She shot the man a remonstrative glare before returning her attention to their host. "Please let me introduce ourselves to you—although I'm sure the Angel has mentioned us—I'm Bridget and this is Fernando."

"And we're now the new Master and Mistress of London, thanks to the Angel," added Fernando, seating himself on the couch.

Notus' eyes went round at the announcement, even more confused and worried. What would the new Master and Mistress of London want with him or his son? Suspicious of the blasé nature Fernando held in the monk's home, Notus stepped away from his two supposed guests.

Noticing the monk's unease, Bridget tilted her head in concern. "Did the Angel not tell you about us? About what happened?"

Notus warily shook his head. "We have not yet had a chance to talk." It was not a lie, but came close enough to one by the omissions in the statement.

It was the Master of London's turn to appear flabbergasted before he shook his head in wry amusement. "That's so bloody like him."

The statement dropped Notus' jaw. It was clear that these two knew his son well, but how? Confusion from the missing fourty days swirled and he sat down in the chair that now served at his desk.

"Maybe you would be so kind as to enlighten me, sir," said Notus, slowly. "Perhaps it would clarify many questions I have about what happened during my detainment."

Fernando leaned back and glanced at Bridget. Notus was well versed enough to be aware that these two were communicating silently as only Chooser and Chosen could do. The only question was which one was the Chooser and which the Chosen.

Finally Fernando let out a sigh through his nostrils and nodded. "Alright. Though both Bridget and I think you should hear it from the Angel. Ah, the joys of being the one in charge. Where is the Angel, by the way?"

"In his room," stated the monk.

"For all this time?" asked the Mistress.

Notus glanced down at the strips of wood that made up the floor and nodded. He could sense the tension arising from another conversation between Chosen and Chooser.

Finally Bridget spoke up. "Do you mind if I go in to talk with him?"

"It's not me who will determine this, my Lady, but rather him." Notus hitched a shoulder. "You are welcome to try. His room—"

"Yes, I know," cut off Bridget as she turned towards the broken door. This time Notus hid his surprise that she knew where it was, but could not hold it when she opened the door and went in.

"Bridget and I agreed that I'll tell you what I know," said Fernando, snapping the monk's attention around, "since she is of the belief that if I don't then you'll remain in the dark and that will not be beneficial to either you or the Angel."

"I appreciate that, sir."

"First thing that you can do is cut the 'sir' crap and call me Fernando. Gwyn does."

The use of the name for his son proved beyond a doubt that this Chosen knew the boy well. He nodded solemnly.

"Good." Fernando offered a quick smile and embarked upon his tale.

He sat and stared over his arms, the lower part of his face buried in the pillow that was hugged to his chest by his bent legs. Jeanie's scent lingered over top of the clean linen of the white pillow-casing. It was the last vestiges of what remained of her and he refused to let go for fear that the brief time spent with her would become a myth within his memories. He could not allow that. She had been too precious to him, too important, too loved.

He let out a shuddering breath and closed his eyes, wondering if it were possible to run out of tears. Jeanie's death was still too raw and the memories of her flaccid body in his arms too painful. Violet could have scourged him to death and it would have paled against the torment he now felt at Jeanie's loss.

Swallowing down his pain, he buried his face in the edge of the pillow, drinking in what remained of their infinitesimal time together and damned himself for allowing fear to block him from acting upon his love for Jeanie sooner. There had not been enough time for love when there should have been. It burned his heart and tore at his guts.

The hours after Notus had taken Jeanie away had been excruciating. Too many times he contemplated watching the sunrise for the first time since he was a child. It would have put an end to his agony and guilt, but he knew that Jeanie would not have wanted that. She had sacrificed too much to ensure that he survived. To throw that gift away would dishonour her memory.

Her memory. His memory of her. That was all that he had left. That last kiss, last touch, and last fleeting smile hiding her worry. It was burned into him, a constant reminder that he had utterly failed her.

He wrapped his arms around his legs, bringing his legs tighter to his chest, squishing the pillow, and ignored the twinges his visceral wounds set off. Their pains were nothing and he sat on his bed, his back against the headboard that served as an island to the wreckage of his life.

If he dared to open his eyes to the darkness he would see the destruction his guilt and mourning had created once he came home. The pent up rage at his failure and the fury of his loss had sent him dashing nearly every piece of furniture into kindling. The nicely tailored clothing was now littered amongst the wreckage. It was only when he approached the bed did some sense come to him and he had collapsed, sobbing into the twisted sheets that had been left unmade when he and Jeanie rose to leave for France. Her scent lingered, stealing his anger and replaced it with grief.

He did not know how long he had laid there weeping. At some point Notus had come home but he dared not to go to his Chooser and nor did he want the monk to come to him. He was too raw and Notus' admonishment over Jeanie had been a deterrent for any contact. He could not bear any more accusations than he himself could supply.

Whenever he felt the monk's concern, he shut if out. Whenever he heard his Chooser approach his door, he silently screamed for Notus to leave him alone until the monk's presence retreated. He knew Notus was anxious, but could not care and he buried himself in Jeanie's pillow in an effort to escape into his memories.

It was the sweet touch filled memories he desired to flee into. Instead, when he found himself dozing, images of Jeanie underneath him or on top of him would turn into a nightmare where she turned into a blood drained corpse, where it had been he, and not a Vampire, who had bled her dry. When these images swarmed his mind, he would bolt awake, gasping, to renew his weeping. Now he just sat there, staring blankly into the dark, inhaling Jeanie's sweetness and refused to sleep.

Beyond his bedroom door he sensed, rather than heard, Fernando and Bridget's presence outside the flat and then listened as they entered. He tried to close off the conversation between the new Mistress and Master with his Chooser, but hearing their stunned expressions upon finding about Jeanie only tightened the band around his heart.

He had expected Fernando to shout gleefully and was surprised at the Noble's dumbfounded feelings. It was Bridget's gasp of shock coupled with sadness and worry that pulled a small whimper from him. They had known what Jeanie was to him. Even Fernando had grudgingly begun to respect Jeanie after she had saved the Noble from Violet and the Vampires. Now they were here in his home, talking to Notus and he still wanted to be left alone with his memories of Jeanie.

It should not have come as a surprise when he felt Bridget's questing emotions, as if she were testing whether or not she should approach him. There was a moment's pause when he could feel Fernando's frustration at Bridget, but it dissipated into acquiescence. He knew he could try and stop her from entering his room, but he also knew that if he did, it would get her back up and Bridget would barge into his room in a huff of indignation. Strangely enough, a large part of him wanted her to come in.

Clutching his legs to his chest, he waited for Bridget to enter.

The door creaked open allowing for a slight draft to stir the darkness and mix it with the diffuse light from the main room. The clicks of Bridget's shoes followed by a click from the door told him that she had entered and shut it behind her. Despite having allowed her in, he recoiled at her presence and hunkered further into the pillow at his knees.

He attempted to shut out Bridget's shock at the devastation but found he could not. Another quickstep into his room and Bridget found a used candle lying beside the shattered ceramic holder and a box of matches. It did not take long for the Mistress of London to shed light upon the ruins, setting the nub with its flickering wick down on a piece of broken wood. He felt the bed dip under her weight, but dared not open his eyes to see the pity on her face.

"Oh Gwyn," sighed Bridget. "I am so sorry."

He clutched the pillow tighter to his body, squeezing his eyes in an effort to push back the tears. He felt her cool hand alight on his burning arm. The pain of the knife wounds on his forearm exploded at the touch, forcing a hiss.

He felt Bridget stand and move closer until her cool hand rested on his forehead.

"You're burning up." Bridget dropped her hand. "If Fernando hadn't shared with me his knowledge I would never have believed it possible."

Bridget sat down beside him on the bed, her hip touching his stocking feet. Maybe he was ill again. It seemed likely considering the damage Katherine's blade had done.

"Let me take a look at this."

He felt Bridget's hand take his in an effort to straighten his arm so as to examine the wounds, but he snapped his arm back.

"No," he whispered, hoarsely. He did not want to relinquish his grip on the pillow.

The cool hand found its way back on his. "Then at least let me look at it this way, alright?"

He knew Bridget was pushing out of deep concern for him and he nodded. She was right that it needed tending, but he did not care. It was not that wound he nursed.

Gently, Bridget rolled back the sliced shirt, exposing the blackened and glistening wounds gaping wide enough that she could observe the whiteness of bone beneath the deeper of the gashes.

"The wounds need stitching," stated Bridget. "I can do this for you, but I'm not very good at it. Maybe I can ask the Good Father."

The mention of his Chooser snapped his head up and opened his eyes.

"No." He could not let Notus see him like this. The monk would be horrified and guilt ridden, and then when he calmed down enough Notus would return to being accusatory for Jeanie's death. "Notus can never know."

Bridget calmly cocked her head in disbelief. "Know that you were hurt in the attempt to free him? I believe Notus would want to know the sacrifices you have made for him."

Her words stole his breath away and stung his eyes. Lowering his gaze, he pressed his face against the pillow and inhaled. The sacrifices were made for Jeanie and were all for naught.

"I know you are hurting," whispered Bridget. "I don't need to feel it to see it written on your face and on your body. But to push the man who has cared for you all these centuries away, at this time, when he, too, is mourning Jeanie's death, will do nothing but create an irreparable rift between the two of you. I will not believe it for one minute that you went through everything that you did to get your Chooser back only to push him away when you need each other the most.

"Let me go and get him. Fernando is telling him everything so you don't have to," continued Bridget, disappointment colouring her nurturing tones. "I know it is really not his prerogative and that you should be the one telling the Good Father, but if you can't or won't, then Notus has the right to hear it from someone. What do you want to do?"

They sat there in silence and he knew that Bridget was right, but he could not bring himself to say so. Even Fernando's accounting would not give credence to his own isolated mourning because Fernando did not know either. The only one who could possibly guess was sitting beside him.

After an indeterminable period of time he felt Bridget's weight leave the bed. "If you cannot choose, then I will." She walked to the door, her steps clicking loudly.

"I cannot believe you to be Chosen if you cannot choose," she said harshly.

Stunned at the multilevel implications, he dropped his legs, allowing the pillow to fall. Painfully, he turned his stiffened body so that his legs dangled over the side.

"Wait. Please, Bridget. Wait."

She turned, her hand on the knob. Raising her blonde brows, the rest of her face did not relinquish its stony expression.

He lowered his gaze to the broken pieces of wood and clothing littered on the floor and felt ashamed. He made his decision.

Gradually, he told of how he and Notus had found Jeanie laying beneath the lamppost after leaving the theatre. Through his tears he spoke of how he had held her lifeless form and found the vampire marks upon her neck, proving his failure to keep her safe. In a breaking voice he told of Notus' accusation and that it had been his fault she was now dead. Weeping, he told of his last visage of Jeanie being carried away by his Chooser as Bridget's strong arms closed around him.

"I did what you suggested," he cried against her shoulder. Bridget's gentle stroking of the back of his head halted. "She said yes. We wanted to wait until after Notus came home. She wanted his blessing. I know as I always have known, he would never have given it." It was the final truth lay bare and it shattered him. Clutching at Bridget, he held on as he sobbed.

It was always going to be either Jeanie or Notus. Fate had decreed which would be taken away, but Jeanie's loss left him unable to reconnect with Notus, thus leaving him with no one.

When he finally regained control of himself, Bridget relinquished their embrace and gazed into his teary eyes.

"You should have told Notus all this, not me." She wiped his tears from his cheeks with her thumbs, while ignoring her own.

He closed his eyes and shook his head. "He wouldn't understand."

"I think you underestimate the capacity of the love he has for you."

Eyes opening, he stared into Bridget's sky blue eyes, his heart aching at the compassion he found there. How Fernando ever managed to deserve such a Chooser was beyond his comprehension and now knew how lucky the Noble truly was. He nodded.

"Let me go and get him," offered Bridget, breaking from their embrace. "You two need to talk."

He watched her take two steps before he made his decision. "Bridget?"

"Yes."

"Before I talk with Notus, could you...?" He glanced down at the wounds on his arm.

Bridget smiled and nodded. "Just tell me where I can find a needle and thread."

He told her and watched as she exited, nervousness vying for prominence over the despondency he had felt for the last few days.

Notus sat quietly in his chair, listening to the unbelievable tale the Master of London spun. At first the whole notion of the boy teaming up with this incorrigible young Chosen in effort to free him seemed completely incongruous to what he knew the boy. The lad would have gone on his own, as he always had, to discover what he needed to, but to realize that the boy had agreed upon a partnership with this Chosen made him wonder how much, or how little, he truly knew of the young man he had spent nearly a millennium and a half with.

The story grew even more unbelievable with Fernando's inclusion of Jeanie into the mix and how the Angel had insisted upon it. The Master spoke of the phial found and Tom and Alice's establishment burnt, which brought a gasp from Notus. Fernando was quick to add that the Angel had sent Alice and her family into safe keeping, which the Master still thought was strange. Notus was happy enough to hear that his boy had done the right thing by these kind and generous people, and nodded as Fernando continued with the discovery of Jeanie's capture in the free kitchen and the trap. Notus could tell the young man was omitting some items but let the matter slide until Fernando told of Yong Zheng Ru's death and Jeanie's discovery of the Chosen.

"Jeanie found out?" sputtered the monk.

Fernando inclined his head. "Naturally, I couldn't allow her to continue with us, restraining us from acting in ways that are normal for us just because she was mortal. In the end, I did a favour to both the Angel and Jeanie."

"How so?" stammered Notus, incredulously. Jeanie was never meant to know about the Chosen. It would have been disastrous for her. It had been disastrous for her.

Brown eyes boring into the monks, Fernando's jaw tightened momentarily. "Very simply put, if Jeanie hadn't accepted the truth, she would have been released from the mad quest. Instead she proved her bravery in more than one way."

Notus shook his head. "I don't understand."

"Of course you wouldn't," sniffed the Master. "You're a monk. The Angel is not. When I arrived with more information before sunrise that same night, the Angel and Jeanie had firmly solidified their relationship. What is the saying you priestly sorts have? 'The truth shall set you free?' It did that for the two of them."

It suddenly made perfect sense as to his boy's reaction to Jeanie's corpse. If they had fallen in love... He took a deep breath in and let it out slowly. The evasions, the questing looks, the tensions that made his son flee into the night, it was perfectly understandable and Notus damned himself a fool for not having noticed it before. The boy had been in love with Jeanie from the beginning and she had returned it, but neither had acted upon it because the Angel would never let anyone get that close to him ever again since that time so long ago.

Jeanie had been a formidable young woman. Realizing their secrets, she would press forward. The lad, starved for love and affection, would have readily accepted it from her because he too desired it. Notus remembered how the boy was after Tarian's granddaughter was taken from him, but Jeanie's death was worse. Notus buried his face in his hands and groaned.

Fernando halted his retelling until the monk regained his composure and then continued with the adventures to Calais, including the Angel's accidental poisoning which brought a gasp from the monk.

Notus sat stunned, barely comprehending that his son voluntarily made another crossing of the Channel and survived the poisoning. The Master's description of how they had found the information at the warehouse and that the Angel had fed in front of the girl before they fired the building, sent his mind swimming. He barely took note when Fernando glossed over the encounter with some of the French Chosen before they left for Balinghem.

It was when Fernando spoke of their holing up at St. Martin's that Notus' mind focused once more upon the story. Irritation surfaced momentarily before being squashed at the thought that his son would have let Jeanie become so ill on the road. It was clear as the tale progressed that it was out of the Angel's deep love for the girl that he did not press on to Balinghem, which proved to be beneficial for the quest as well as Jeanie's well being. It was nice to hear that Father Theodore was still Abbot and that Absolon still the doctor.

The moment of happiness dissipated as the Master began his descriptive narrative of the Angel and his assault upon *Le Jardin*. Sitting in rapt attention Notus listened about the Mistress of *Le Jardin* being Jeanie's friend from the Inn and the battle that ensued.

Shock rolled over him as Fernando described how there were those amongst their attackers who were not Chosen but were not mortals as well and how, through Jeanie's capture—something that Fernando still could not figure out how that came about—both he and the Angel were also captured.

A growing sense of dread filled Notus as Fernando glossed over his own escape from *Le Jardin's* Sun Room and Jeanie's assistance to get him back to St. Martin's. It explained the young man's golden brown skin. The Master was indeed lucky to be alive, but what about the boy?

Fernando approached this topic cautiously. He spoke of Jeanie's insistence to free the Angel and used her knowledge of who was exacting the genocide of the Chosen against Fernando to do what she needed, to free the Angel. It was further proof that Jeanie was indeed a remarkable young woman in snagging a Chosen to do what she needed.

Fernando spoke of the Vampires.

Notus was shocked at the revelation, but yet at the same time it made perfect sense. How such creatures were able to hide in plain sight of the Chosen mystified him, but that was not what he wanted to know at this moment and Fernando knew this.

The description of Fernando and Jeanie finding the Angel in Violet's entertainment room filled Notus' mind with images of torture and abuse. Tears welled up in his eyes as Fernando explained that it was Jeanie's insistence that the Angel was still alive that forced Fernando to act.

"I didn't believe her," explained the Master. "The Angel was all cut up and burnt. By all rights he should have been dead, but he wasn't."

Notus closed his eyes and held his breath. He knew what was coming. Centuries of hiding his boy's differences were now coming to light. It was his worst nightmare coming true.

"Jeanie told me about the Angel's reaction to iron," stated Fernando matter-of-factly. "Later, when we got him back to the monastery and the Angel had recovered enough, we had a long talk."

Notus let out a shaking sigh. "You're here to pronounce him to be Destroyed."

"Heaven's no!" Fernando sounded upset at the notion.

It was not the answer Notus had expected and he felt his eyes bulge in disbelief. "What?"

Fernando placed his walking stick across his lap and rubbed his hands. "I know that the Angel was accidentally Chosen and there is a great question as to what he was before he was Chosen. Until that mystery is solved I will live by the adage, 'Keep your friends close and your enemies closer.'"

"So you deem my son to be an enemy?"

"I cannot discount the eventual possibility," remarked the Master. "No ruler, mortal or Chosen, can have the luxury of knowing his friend's mind, but the Angel's abilities and potential usefulness outweighs any differences. He proved it just three nights ago, again."

"I'm sorry. I do not understand."

Fernando cocked his head and peered at Notus, his finger tapping his lower lip. "When we talked at St. Martin's he spoke of changes that occurred to him after severe exposure to iron. What he experienced at *Le Jardin* could be classified as that. Somehow your Chosen can now not only sense all other Chosen's emotions, but he can also summon a deadly mist. It was that which removed the Vampires that attempted to attack St. Martin's and did the same three nights ago at the theatre. Whatever the Angel is, such abilities could be useful in this war against the Vampires. I was taught that when one was in war one used whatever tools one had at hand to ensure a win. This means that I, and Bridget, will not allow the Angel to be Destroyed."

"So long as he serves your needs," stated Notus, clearly understanding the implications of the Master of London. It was something he never believed could be possible, but now that it was laid before him, the monk was not sure if it was just a way to blackmail the boy.

"Partially," stated the Master, inclining his head. "Despite his differences, what we have gone through together in finding out the truth about the Vampires and their efforts to eradicate all Chosen, has made us unlikely friends, strange as that may sound."

Notus leaned back in his chair, astounded.

Unexpectedly the door to the Angel's room opened and Bridget exited. Notus watched as the Mistress of London walked towards them, asked where the bathroom was and headed off in the direction Fernando gave her. It was clear that it was not Fernando's first visit to their home.

When Bridget came out with his medical box, Notus stood up. It was the box that held the items necessary for his son if he was wounded by iron. He was about to say something, but Bridget quickly walked past him and went back into the Angel's room.

Worried curiosity got the better of him and Notus turned to Fernando who now stood. "If you'll excuse me." He did not wait for the Master's reply.

Hastening to the boy's room, he hesitated before opening the door. Though there were no welcoming feelings directed at him, Notus was also aware that there was nothing pushing him away from entering. The door squeaked on its hinges and revealed a sight that compounded the shocks into stunned inaction.

What once had held ornate, yet simple furniture, now appeared to have had a bomb go off in the middle of it. Only the bed remained unscathed and he knew that it had been the boy's temper that had destroyed everything. Lifting his gaze from the shattered remains, he watched Bridget help the boy out of the ripped shirt.

His son's sole focus was on the removal of his clothing that he remained unaware of his Chooser standing in the doorway. Notus' eyes widened and his jaw slackened at the sight of the blackened wounds on the boy's chest and arms. He could even see black ribbons beginning at the top of the lad's pale shoulders and realized he did not want to see the ruin of his boy's back.

His gasp of alarm brought both his son and the Mistress to look at him. It was the dejection and the sight that the boy had been crying that lowered Notus' hand from his mouth. What Fernando had described was nothing to what the monk could see on his son's face and body. Without a moment's hesitation, Notus put aside his own hurts and went to his son's side.

"Oh my dear boy," offered the monk, stepping into the place where Bridget had been just a moment ago. "Fernando told me what happened."

The boy glanced at Bridget as if he did not know what to do and then dropped his gaze to his lap, his arms hugging his bare chest. Bridget pursed her lips, shook her head and left.

Alone, Notus gazed at his son. Though the lad had saved him from Katherine, the damages both internally and externally to his son by the Vampires were more than he could ever fathom. All he could do was fix what hurts he had unknowingly placed on the boy.

Notus placed a tremulous hand on the boy's face and was rewarded with direct eye contact. *I'm so sorry that I accused you of bringing Jeanie to harm.*

The boy's breath caught and his crimson eyes shimmered before glancing away.

Notus could feel his son's guilt and misery and knew that there was nothing he could do to take it away. He only had brought back his son to himself.

The monk's eyes welled and broke. *I loved her, too.*

Their eyes met an instant before they embraced.

Bridget quietly closed the door behind her and turned to face her Chosen, tears glimmering down her cheeks. She knew it was from the Angel's projection coupled with her own regrets for the remarkable Chosen. She saw Fernando's eyes well before he crashed his walking stick against his leg in an attempt to regain composure and wondered when the Angel would learn to master his new found abilities.

"Do you think they'll be alright," asked Fernando once control over his own emotions had been established.

Bridget shrugged, wiping her tears with her fingers. "I don't know, but at least it's a start."

Fernando walked over to her and led Bridget to the door. It was time to leave, but he knew they would be back. "Do you think the Angel will be ready soon?"

Threading her arm in Fernando's, Bridget let her Chosen open the door. "We can only hope so. Any responses yet from our telegrams?"

"Yes." Fernando shut the door behind them as they walked into the cold night. "Already skirmishes are breaking out. Hugo and several other Masters and Mistresses are concerned. They are asking for a Grand Council."

Bridget came to an abrupt halt and spun Fernando to face her. "They're asking for what?"

Fernando waited a moment for the merry couple to pass them before pulling Bridget back into their evening walk. "A Grand Council. I know. I haven't heard of the like before, but word about the Vampires has gone out and they want to hear what the Angel has to say. I think we over did it in our original telegram."

"We just told them the truth," said Bridget, aghast.

"I know," muttered Fernando. "But panic is setting in and I agree with them that there has to be some consistency in dealing with the vermin. They started this war. We're going to finish it. Now the issue is how and the only way I can think of is the Angel."

Bridget nodded solemnly and resisted the temptation to glance back the way they had come. "He's going to rule us all, isn't he?"

Fernando staggered to a stop. Gazing at the city, a shudder ran up his spine as he remembered the blast of energy they had all felt at the Angel's proclamation of the new Mistress and Master.

The Angel, even having not fed properly in nearly a month, was more powerful than Fernando could imagine. He pursed his lips and pulled Bridget tighter to him as they set off to his home.

I'm afraid he might already.

epilogue

orbie Vale sat perched upon the granite tombstone and watched the dark patch of earth before him. He had done this for the last two nights now and wondered if he had done too much. Of course, the revenge would not be as sweet, but it would do just as well. But this, this would be grand if his plans came to fruition.

He could still not believe the utter ruination of all that he and Bastia had worked towards. All those years of working their way into the ranks of the Chosen so that when Bastia took over as Mistress it was a seamless, if yet bumpy, transition into becoming Katherine, Mistress of London. She had believed it best that she take the role so that he could do what he did best; connive and manipulate behind the scenes to create what they so desired, the destruction of the atrocious Chosen with their high morals and righteousness. No others would dare to bring the Chosen down, but Lord Valraven and Bastia had no qualms to make an attempt.

It was going perfectly. Bastia was in power, bringing about subtle changes to the Chosen's notions of what it meant to be Chosen, only agreeing upon certain nefarious individuals to be made Chosen while Corbie increased their ranks by creating his own coterie of Vampires, who then, with his permission, created their own.

It was too bad that Corbie and Violet were the only two of Bastia's coterie left, but it had its own benefits. Now Corbie was Master of a strong line of Vampires beholden only to him. Of course he was upset at first by Bastia's untimely death, but it did also release him to act completely autonomously from any other Vampire. As far as he knew he was now the oldest Vampire and he planned on using it.

Did he see the earth shift? He peered closer, tapping his upper lip in expectation. A birth of a new Vampire was a remarkable thing and this one was going to be special. If everything went accordingly then his vendetta against the Angel would begin.

Oh how he despised that creature. He hated the Angel with every ounce of his being. Bastia had been in awe of the Angel, but she had been also fearful. It made perfect sense why she chose him for the quest and why she led him to Violet in France. What Corbie could not understand was why, at the last moment, she sent notification that the Angel was not to be harmed. Granted, it came too late. Corbie doubted that Bastia ever knew that.

Yes. The earth did shift! Little brown lumps teetered before falling to the side. Revenge was at hand. It was a small measure to what was unleashed three nights ago. Vampires in the city were nervous and Corbie had received word that those in other countries were now under scrutiny by the Chosen. Some managed to flee while others were killed. Many others remained hidden awaiting instructions.

The war he and Bastia had hoped to win through cunning was coming to the forefront and he was ill equipped to handle this. It was not Corbie's way. Subterfuge was his speciality, but he would manage.

The earth tumbled as if pressed from beneath and he leaned forward expectantly. *Come, my flower. Grow.*

"Mr. Vale, should I bring the boy, now?" asked the man standing behind Corbie.

Corbie nodded without turning to face the head of his coterie. "Yes, Brian. Bring the urchin. I don't want my new flower to wither before the moonlight touches her."

"Yes, sir." Brian walked a few yards away and lifted a boy of about six off the ground. His dark head lolling, the boy was unconscious. With a little shake the boy's blue eyes rolled in an attempt to awaken. His dirty clothes were torn and badly mended in places. Corbie knew the child would not be missed.

Brian came to stand beside his Master, holding the child at arm's length. It was clear he had done this before.

The land shifted again, this time exposing pale white worms working their way skyward. Corbie pushed down his excitement to watch the birthing.

Slowly, hands emerged, flailing in their effort to free themselves and found purchase against the ground. A sudden tremulous heave and the body of a young woman in nothing but a white shift lay on the ground. Her cinnamon curls were littered with brown dirt that rained down as she staggered to her bare feet. Startling green eyes shifted from each of them to settle upon the boy's dangling form.

Corbie smiled to see her lick her lips. "Feed, my beautiful flower."

The young woman pounced upon the boy who had just awoken.

A shrill scream cut through the cemetery, widening Corbie's grin.

"Rose. Your name is Rose."

about the author

Karen Dales is the Award Winning Author of the widely acclaimed *The Chosen Chronicles,* having won Siren Books' Award for Best Horror and Best Overall 2010. *The Chosen Chronicles* include *Changeling, Angel of Death* and *Shadow of Death.*

She is currently at work on the next book in *The Chosen Chronicles - Thanatos* as well as a historical fiction novel.

Born in Toronto, Ontario, Canada, she shares her life with her two cats, one son and husband.

Visit her website at www.karendales.com

www.ingramcontent.com/pod-product-compliance
Lightning Source LLC
Chambersburg PA
CBHW071341020726
47502CB00001B/194